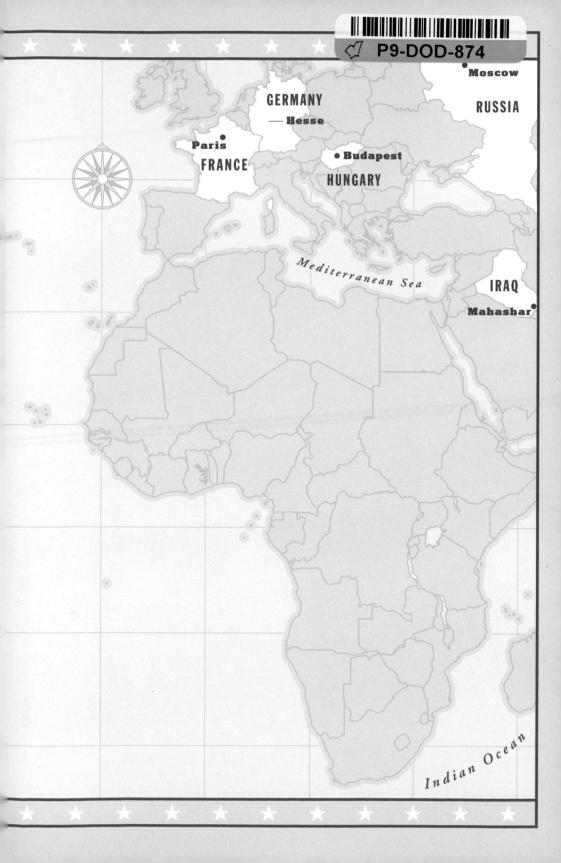

THE
HUNTERS

ALSO BY W.E.B. GRIFFIN

THE
HUNTERS

W.E.B. GRIFFIN

G. P. PUTNAM'S SONS
NEW YORK

G. P. PUTNAM'S SONS
Publishers Since 1838
Published by the Penguin Group
Penguin Group (USA) Inc., 375 Hudson Street, New York, New York 10014, USA • Penguin Group
(Canada), 90 Eglinton Avenue East, Suite 700, Toronto, Ontario M4P 2Y3, Canada (a division
of Pearson Penguin Canada Inc.) • Penguin Books Ltd, 80 Strand, London WC2R 0RL, England •
Penguin Ireland, 25 St Stephen's Green, Dublin 2, Ireland (a division of Penguin Books Ltd) •
Penguin Group (Australia), 250 Camberwell Road, Camberwell, Victoria 3124, Australia (a division of
Pearson Australia Group Pty Ltd) • Penguin Books India Pvt Ltd, 11 Community Centre, Panchsheel
Park, New Delhi–110 017, India • Penguin Group (NZ), Cnr Airborne and Rosedale Roads, Albany,
Auckland 1310, New Zealand (a division of Pearson New Zealand Ltd) • Penguin Books (South Africa)
(Pty) Ltd, 24 Sturdee Avenue, Rosebank, Johannesburg 2196, South Africa

Penguin Books Ltd, Registered Offices: 80 Strand, London WC2R 0RL, England

ISBN-13: 978-0-399-15379-2
ISBN-10: 0-399-15379-9

Printed in the United States of America
1 3 5 7 9 10 8 6 4 2

This is a work of fiction. Names, characters, places, and incidents either are the product of the author's imagination or are used fictitiously, and any resemblance to actual persons, living or dead, businesses, companies, events, or locales is entirely coincidental.

While the author has made every effort to provide accurate telephone numbers and Internet addresses at the time of publication, neither the publisher nor the author assumes any responsibility for errors, or for changes that occur after publication. Further, the publisher does not have any control over and does not assume any responsibility for author or third-party websites or their content.

26 July 1777

The necessity of procuring good intelligence is apparent and need not be further urged.

George Washington
General and Commander in Chief
The Continental Army

FOR THE LATE

WILLIAM E. COLBY
An OSS Jedburgh first lieutenant
who became director of the Central Intelligence Agency

AARON BANK
An OSS Jedburgh first lieutenant
who became a colonel and the father of Special Forces

WILLIAM R. CORSON
A legendary Marine intelligence officer
whom the KGB hated more than any other U.S. intelligence officer—
and not only because he wrote the definitive work on them

★

FOR THE LIVING

BILLY WAUGH
A legendary Special Forces command sergeant major
who retired and then went on to hunt down the infamous Carlos the Jackal.
Billy could have terminated Osama bin Laden in the early 1990s
but could not get permission to do so. After fifty years in
the business, Billy is still going after the bad guys

RENÉ J. DÉFOURNEAUX
A U.S. Army OSS second lieutenant attached to the British SOE
who jumped into Occupied France alone and later
became a legendary U.S. Army counterintelligence officer

JOHNNY REITZEL
An Army special operations officer
who could have terminated the head terrorist of the seized cruise ship
Achille Lauro but could not get permission to do so

RALPH PETERS
An Army intelligence officer
who has written the best analysis of our war against terrorists
and of our enemy that I have ever seen

★

AND FOR THE NEW BREED

MARC L
A senior intelligence officer despite his youth
who reminds me of Bill Colby more and more each day

FRANK L
A legendary Defense Intelligence Agency officer
who retired and now follows in Billy Waugh's footsteps

OUR NATION OWES ALL OF THESE PATRIOTS
A DEBT BEYOND REPAYMENT

I

[ONE]
Danubius Hotel Gellért
Szent Gellért tér 1
Budapest, Hungary
0035 1 August 2005

When he heard the ping of the bell announcing the arrival of an elevator in the lobby of the Gellért, Sándor Tor, who was the director of security for the *Budapester Neue Tages Zeitung,* raised his eyes from a copy of the newspaper—so fresh from the presses that his fingers were stained with ink—to see who would be getting off.

He was not at all surprised to see that it was Eric Kocian, managing director and editor in chief of the newspaper. The first stop of the first *Tages Zeitung* delivery truck to leave the plant was the Gellért.

The old man must have been looking out his window again, Tor thought, *waiting to see the truck arrive.*

Tor was a burly fifty-two-year-old with a full head of curly black hair and a full mustache. He wore a dark blue single-breasted suit carefully tailored to conceal the Swiss SIGARMS P228 9mm semiautomatic pistol he carried in a high-ride hip holster.

He looked like a successful businessman with a very good tailor, but he paled beside Eric Kocian, who stepped off the elevator into the Gellért lobby wearing an off-white linen suit with a white shirt, a white tie held to the collar with a discreet gold pin, soft white leather slip-on shoes, a white panama hat—the wide brim rakishly up on the right and down on the left—and carrying a sturdy knurled cane with a brass handle in the shape of a well-bosomed female.

Kocian was accompanied by a large dog. The dog was shaped like a boxer, but he was at least a time and a half—perhaps twice—as large as a big boxer, and his coat was grayish black and tightly curled.

Kocian walked to a table in the center of the lobby where a stack of the *Tages Zeitung* had been placed, picked up a copy carefully—so as not to soil his well-manicured fingers—and examined the front page.

Then he folded the newspaper and extended it to the dog.

"You hold it awhile, Max," he said. "Your tongue is already black."

Then he turned and, resting both hands on the cane, carefully surveyed the lobby.

He found what he was looking for—Sándor Tor—sitting in an armchair in a dark corner of the lobby. Kocian pointed his cane at arm's length at Tor, not unlike a cavalry officer leading a charge, and walked quickly toward him. The dog, newspaper in his mouth, never left Kocian's side.

Six feet from Tor, Kocian stopped and, without lowering the cane, said, "Sándor, I distinctly remember telling you that I would not require your services anymore today and to go home."

A lesser man would have been cowed. Sándor Tor did not. As a young man, he had done a hitch in the French Foreign Legion and subsequently had never been cowed by anyone or anything.

He pushed himself far enough out of the armchair to reach the dog's head, scratched his ears, and said, "How goes it, Max?" Then he looked up at Kocian and said, "You have been known to change your mind, Úr Kocian."

"This is not one of those rare occasions," Kocian said. He let that sink in and then added: "But since you are already here, you might as well take us— on your way home—to the Franz Joséf Bridge."

With that, Kocian turned on his heel and walked quickly to the entrance. Max trotted to keep up with him.

Tor got out of his chair as quickly as he could and started after him.

My God, he's eighty-two!

As he walked, Tor took a cellular telephone from his shirt pocket, pushed an autodial button, and held the telephone to his ear.

"He's on the way to the car," he said without preliminary greeting. "He wants me to drop him at the Szabadság híd. Pick him up on the other side."

The Szabadság híd, the Freedom Bridge, across the Danube River was a re-creation of the original 1899 bridge that had been destroyed—as had all the other bridges over the Danube—in the bitter fighting of World War II. It had been named after Franz Joséf, then king and emperor of the Austro-Hungarian Empire. It was the first to be rebuilt, as close to the original as possible, and, when completed in 1946, had been renamed the Freedom Bridge.

Eric Kocian simply refused to accept the name change.

"If the communists were happy with that Freedom name, there's obviously something wrong with it," he had said more than once. "Franz Joséf may have been a sonofabitch, but, compared to the communists, he was a saint."

———————

There was a silver Mercedes-Benz S500 sitting just outside the door of the Gellért.

For a moment, Sándor Tor was afraid that the old man had grown impatient and decided to walk. Then there came a long blast on the horn.

Tor quickly trotted around the front of the car and got behind the wheel. Kocian was in the front passenger's seat. Max, still with the newspaper in his mouth, was sitting up in the backseat.

"Where the hell have you been?" Kocian demanded.

"I had to take a leak."

"You should have taken care of that earlier," Kocian said.

It wasn't far at all from the door of the Gellért to the bridge, but if Kocian had elected to walk he would have had to cross the road paralleling the Danube, down which traffic often flew.

The old man wasn't concerned for himself, Tor knew, but for the dog. One of Max's predecessors—there had been several, all the same breed, Bouvier des Flandres, all named Max—had been run over and killed on that highway.

It was a standard joke around the Gellért and the *Budapester Tages Zeitung* that the only thing the old man loved was his goddamned dog and that the only living thing that could possibly love the old man was his goddamned dog.

Sándor Tor knew better. Once, Tor had heard a pressman parrot the joke and had grabbed him by the neck, forced his head close to the gears of the running press, and promised the next time he heard him running his mouth he'd feed him to the press.

"Turn on the flashers when you stop," Kocian ordered as the Mercedes approached the bridge, "and I'll open the doors for Max and myself, thank you very much."

"Yes, Úr Kocian."

"And don't hang around to see if Max and I can make it across the bridge without your assistance. Go home."

"Yes, Úr Kocian."

"And in the morning, be on time for once."

"I will try, Úr Kocian."

"Good night, Sándor. Sleep well."
"Thank you, Úr Kocian."

Tor watched in the right side rearview mirror as Kocian and the dog started across the bridge. Tor already had his cellular in his hand. He pressed the au-todial button again.

Across the river, Ervin Rákosi's cellular vibrated in his pocket, causing the wireless speaker bud in his ear to ring. He pushed one of the phone's buttons—it did not matter which since he had programmed the device to answer calls whenever any part of the keypad was depressed—and heard Tor's voice come through the earbud:

"They're on the bridge."
"Got him, Sándor."
"He'll be watching me, so I'll have to go up the Vámház körút as far as Pipa before I can turn."
"I told you I have him, Sándor."
"Just do what I tell you to do. I'll pick him up when he passes Sóház."
"Any idea where he's going?"
"Absolutely none."

It was Eric Kocian's custom to take Max for a walk before retiring, which usually meant they left the Gellért around half past eleven. Almost always, they walked across the bridge, and, almost always, they stopped in a café, bar, or restaurant for a little sustenance. Lately, they'd been going to the Képíró, a nar-row restaurant/bar which offered good jazz, Jack Daniel's Black Label bourbon, and a menu pleasing to Max, who was fond of hard sausage.

But that was no guarantee they'd be going there tonight, and if Sándor Tor had asked the old man where he was going the old man would either have told him it was none of his goddamned business or lied.

In fact, it was Sándor Tor's business to know where the old man was and where he was going, and to keep him from harm. His orders to protect Eric Kocian—"Cost be damned, and, for God's sake, don't let the old man know he's being protected"—had come from Generaldirektor Otto Görner of Gossinger Beteiligungsgesellschaft, G.m.b.H., the German holding company that owned, among a good deal else, half a dozen newspapers, including the *Budapester Neue Tages Zeitung.*

When he came off the bridge, Tor saw Ervin Rákosi's dark green Chrysler Grand Caravan at the first intersection in a position from which Rákosi could see just about all of the bridge. He continued up the Vámház körút for two blocks and then made a right turn onto Pipa. He circled the block, on toward Sóház U, pulled to the curb behind a panel truck half a block from Vámház körút, and turned off the headlights.

Tor's cellular buzzed.

"He's almost at Sóház U," Rákosi reported.

"I'm fifty meters from the intersection," Tor's voice said in Rákosi's earbud.

Thirty seconds later, Eric Kocian and Max appeared, walking briskly up the steep incline.

One of these days, Tor thought, *he's going to do that and have a heart attack.*

Tor reported: "He just went past. Follow him and see where he goes."

Thirty seconds after that, the Chrysler came slowly up Vámház körút.

Sixty seconds after that, Rákosi reported, "He's turned onto Királyi Pál. It looks as if he is going to the Képíró."

"Don't follow him. Drive around the block and then down Képíró U."

Tor backed away from the panel truck and then drove onto Vámház körút and turned right. When he drove past Királyi Pál, he saw Eric Kocian turning onto Képíró.

A moment later, Rákosi reported: "He went in."

"Okay," Tor ordered, "you find someplace to park where you can catch him when he comes out. I'll park, and see if I can look into the restaurant."

"Got it," Rákosi said.

Tor found the darkened doorway—he had used it before—from which he could see into the Képíró restaurant.

Kocian was sitting at a small table between the bar and the door. A jazz quartet was set up between his table and the bar. There was a bottle of whiskey on the table and a bottle of soda water, and, as Tor watched, a waiter delivered a plate of food.

Sausage for the both of them, Tor knew. Kielbasa for the old man and some kind of hard sausage for Max. Kocian cut a slice of the kielbasa for himself and put it in his mouth. Max laid a paw on the old man's leg. Kocian sawed at the hard sausage until there was a thumb-sized piece on his fork. He extended the fork to Max, who delicately pulled off the treat. Kocian patted the dog's head.

A procession of people—including three hookers, one at a time—entering and leaving the restaurant paused by Kocian's chair and shook his hand or allowed him to kiss theirs. The more courageous of them patted Max's head. Kocian always rose to his feet to accept the greetings of the hookers, but as long as Tor had been guarding him he had never taken one back to the Gellért with him.

In Vienna, he had an "old friend" who was sometimes in his apartment—most often, coming out of it—when Tor went to get him in the mornings. She was a buxom redhead in her late fifties. Kocian never talked about her and Tor never asked.

The band took a break and the bandleader came over to Kocian's table, patted Max, and had a drink of Kocian's Jack Daniel's. When the break was over, the bandleader returned to his piano and Kocian resumed cutting the sausages—a piece for him and a piece for Max—as he listened to the music, often tapping his fingers on the table.

Tor knew that the old man usually stayed just over an hour and had gone into the restaurant a few minutes before one o'clock. So, glancing at his watch and seeing that it was ten minutes to two, he had just decided it was about time for the old man to leave when he saw him gesturing for the check.

Tor took out his cellular, pressed the autodial key, and said, "He's just called for the check."

"Let's hope he goes home," Rákosi replied.

"Amen," Tor said. "You get in a position to watch him on the bridge. I'll stay here and let you know which way he's headed."

"Done," Rákosi said.

Eric Kocian and Max came out of the Képíró five minutes later and headed down the street toward Királyi Pál, strongly suggesting he was headed for home.

Tor watched him until he turned onto Királyi Pál, called Rákosi to report Kocian's location, and then trotted to where he had parked the silver Mercedes.

He had just gotten into the car when Rákosi reported that the old man was about to get on the bridge.

He had driven no more than four minutes toward Vámház körút when his phone vibrated.

"Trouble," Rákosi reported.

"On the way."

Tor accelerated rapidly down the Vámház körút and was almost at the bridge when he saw that something was going on just about in the center of the bridge.

Max and the old man had a man down on the sidewalk and the man was beating at the animal's head with a pistol.

Rákosi's Chrysler Grand Caravan was almost on them.

And then a car—a black or dark blue Mercedes that had been coming toward Sándor Tor—stopped and a man jumped out and, holding a pistol with two hands, fired at the old man and the dog.

Rákosi made a screaming U-turn, jumped out, and started firing at the Mercedes as it began to speed away.

"I'll get the old man," Sándor Tor said into his cellular. "You get the bastards in the Mercedes. Ram them if you have to."

Rákosi didn't reply, but Tor saw him jump back into the Chrysler.

Tor pulled his Mercedes to the curb.

The old man was sitting down as if he had been knocked backward. Tor saw blood staining the shoulder of his white suit.

The man on the ground was still fighting Max, whose massive jaws were locked on his arm.

Tor jumped out of the Mercedes, taking his pistol from its holster as he moved.

He took aim at the man Max had down, then changed his mind. He went to the man and swung the pistol hard against the back of his head.

The man went limp.

Tor looked down the bridge and saw that both the attackers' Mercedes and Rákosi's Chrysler had disappeared.

He punched another autodial button on his cellular, a number he wasn't supposed to have.

"Inspector Lázár," he announced. "Supervisor needs assistance. Shots fired on the Szabadság híd. One citizen down. Require ambulance."

So far as Tor knew, there was no Inspector Lázár on the Budapest police force. But that would get an immediate response, he knew. Before he had gone to work for the *Tages Zeitung*, he had been Inspector Sándor Tor.

He went to the old man. The dog was whimpering. There was a bloody wound on his skull.

Christ, I only hit that bastard once and he was out. I saw him beating on Max's head and Max never let loose.

That dog's not whimpering because he's in pain. He's whimpering because he knows something is wrong with the old man.

"An ambulance is on the way, Úr Kocian," Tor said.

"Sándor, I need a great favor."

"Anything, Úr Kocian. I should not have let this happen."

"What you should have done is gone home when I told you."

"Do you want to lie down until the ambulance gets here?"

"Of course not. The first thing I want you to do is call Dr. Kincs, Max's veterinarian, and tell him you're bringing Max in for emergency treatment."

"Of course. Just as soon as I get you to the hospital—"

"The Telki Private Hospital. Don't let them take me to the goddamned Szent János Kórház. They'd never let Max stay with me there."

"All gunshot victims are taken to Szent János Kórház," Tor said.

"And you can't fix that?"

"No, I can't."

"Jesus Christ, what are we paying you for?" the old man demanded and then ordered: "Help me to my feet."

"I don't think that's a good idea, Úr Kocian."

"I didn't ask for an opinion, goddamn you, Sándor! Do what you're told! Get me the hell out of here before the police show up."

The old man winced with pain as he tried to get to his feet.

A police car—a Volkswagen Jetta—came onto the bridge. It pulled up beside the silver Mercedes and a sergeant and the driver got out.

"What's happened?" the sergeant demanded.

"That man and two others tried to rob Úr Kocian," Tor said.

"Who are you?"

"Sándor Tor, director of security of the *Tages Zeitung*," Sándor said as he reached down and pulled Eric Kocian erect.

"What are you doing?" the sergeant said.

"I'm taking Úr Kocian to the hospital."

"An ambulance is on the way."

"I can't wait. Take that slime to the station and I'll come there," Tor said.

He half carried the old man to the Mercedes, hoping the sergeant was not going to give him trouble.

"I'll meet you at the Szent János Kórház," the sergeant said.

"Fine," Tor said.

I'll worry about that later.

The old man crawled into the backseat. Max got in and jumped on the seat and started to lick his face.

Sándor closed the door and then got behind the wheel.

"Take Max to Dr. Kincs first," the old man ordered.

"You're going to the hospital first. I'll take care of Max."

"Not one goddamned word of this is to get to Otto Görner, you understand?"

At that moment, Tor had just finished deciding that he would call Görner the moment the doctors started to work on the old man at the Telki Private Hospital.

"I'm not sure I can do that, Úr Kocian. He'll have to know sometime."

"I'll call him as I soon as I can. I'll tell him I fell down the stairs. Fell over Max and then down the stairs. He'll believe that."

"Why can't I tell him?"

"Because he would immediately get in the way of me getting the bastards who did this to me."

"You know who they are?"

"I've got a pretty good goddamned idea. They know I've been nosing around. They want to know how much I know about the oil-for-food outrage. Why do you think they tried to kidnap me?"

"Kidnap you?"

"The sonofabitch who came after me on the bridge had a hypodermic needle."

"A hypodermic needle?" Tor parroted.

"It's in my jacket pocket," the old man said. "When we get to the hospital, take it and find out what it is."

"They were going to drug you?"

"They only started shooting after Max and I grabbed the bastard on the bridge. Jesus Christ, Sándor, do you need a map? They were going to take me someplace to see what I know and where my evidence is. When they had that, *then* they were going to put me in the Danube."

"Where is your evidence?"

"In my apartment."

"Where in your apartment?"

"If I told you, then you'd know," the old man said. "Someplace safe."

"You don't want to tell me?"

"No. Can't you drive any faster? I'm getting a little woozy."

A moment later, Sándor looked in the backseat.

The old man was unconscious. Max was standing over him, gently licking his face as if trying to wake him.

Sándor turned and looked forward again, and thought, *Please, God, don't let him die!*

He pushed another autodial button on the cellular, praying it was the right one.

"Telki Private Hospital."

"I'm bringing an injured man to the emergency room. Be waiting for me," Tor ordered.

Five minutes later, he pulled the Mercedes up at the emergency entrance of the Telki Private Hospital. A gurney, a doctor, and a nurse were outside the door.

Tor helped the doctor get the old man on the gurney.

"He's been shot," the doctor announced.

"I know," Tor said.

The doctor gave him a strange look, then started to push the gurney into the hospital.

Tor put his arm around the dog.

"You can't go, Max," he said.

Max strained to follow the gurney but allowed Tor to restrain him.

Tor looked at his watch. It was two twenty-five.

[TWO]
Estancia Shangri-La
Tacuarembó Province
República Oriental del Uruguay
2225 31 July 2005

At almost precisely that moment in real time—by the clock, it is four hours later in Budapest than it is in Uruguay—a U.S. Army Special Forces medic, Sergeant Robert Kensington, who had been kneeling over a stocky blond man in his forties and examining his wound, stood up and announced: "You're going to be all right, Colonel. There's some muscle damage that's going to take some time to heal, and you're going to hurt like hell for a long time every time you move— for that matter, breathe. I can take the bullet out now, if you'd like."

"I think I'll wait until I get to a hospital," Colonel Alfredo Munz said.

Until very recently, Munz had been the director of SIDE, the Argentine organization that combines the functions of the American FBI and CIA.

There were three other men in the room, the study of the sprawling "big house" of Estancia Shangri-La. One of them—a somewhat squat, completely bald very black man of forty-six—was lying in a pool of his own blood near Colonel Munz, dead of 9mm bullet wounds to the mouth and forehead. He had been Dr. Jean-Paul Lorimer, an American who had been a United Nations diplomat stationed in Paris and who had taken some pains to establish a second identity for himself in Uruguay as Jean-Paul Bertrand, a Lebanese national and dealer in antiquities.

Eighteen days earlier, on July thirteenth, Dr. Jean-Paul Lorimer had gone missing in Paris. A week later, his sister, who was married to J. Winslow Masterson, the chief of mission of the U.S. embassy in Buenos Aires, Argentina, had been kidnapped from the parking lot of a restaurant in San Isidro, an upscale Buenos Aires suburb.

The President of the United States, suspecting the kidnapping had something to do with international terrorism and wanting to know what was going on without that information having to be slowly filtered through State Department and intelligence channels, had sent to Buenos Aires a personal agent—an Army officer serving as executive assistant to the secretary of Homeland Security.

Major C. G. Castillo had arrived in Buenos Aires on July twenty-second. The next morning, El Coronel Alfredo Munz of SIDE informed the American ambassador that Mrs. Masterson had been found in a taxi on the riverfront, drugged and sitting beside the body of her husband, who had been shot before her eyes.

The President had been enraged. He telephoned Ambassador Juan Manuel Silvio to personally tell him that he was placing Major Castillo in charge of both the investigation of the kidnapping and murder and of the protection of Mrs. Masterson and her children until they were safely returned to the United States.

When the Air Force Globemaster III carrying Masterson's family and remains—and the remains of a Marine Guard sergeant, who had been murdered when driving a female Secret Service agent away from the Masterson residence—touched down at Keesler Air Force Base in Mississippi on July twenty-fifth, Air Force One and the President of the United States were waiting for it.

The President sent for Major Castillo. Just before he got off the Globemaster to go aboard Air Force One, Mrs. Masterson told Major Castillo that her kidnappers wanted to know where her brother was hiding and that they would kill her children if she didn't tell them. They had murdered her husband to make the point the threat was serious. Mrs. Masterson told Castillo that she had absolutely no idea where Jean-Paul Lorimer was or why the kidnappers were after him.

When Castillo reported to the President aboard Air Force One, the President showed him the document he and Secretary of State Natalie Cohen had just made law:

```
TOP SECRET—PRESIDENTIAL


THE WHITE HOUSE, WASHINGTON, D.C.


DUPLICATION FORBIDDEN
```

COPY 2 OF 3 (SECRETARY COHEN)

JULY 25, 2005.

PRESIDENTIAL FINDING.

IT HAS BEEN FOUND THAT THE ASSASSINATION OF J. WINSLOW
MASTERSON, CHIEF OF MISSION OF THE UNITED STATES
EMBASSY IN BUENOS AIRES, ARGENTINA; THE ABDUCTION OF
MR. MASTERSON'S WIFE, MRS. ELIZABETH LORIMER MASTERSON;
THE ASSASSINATION OF SERGEANT ROGER MARKHAM, USMC; AND
THE ATTEMPTED ASSASSINATION OF SECRET SERVICE SPECIAL
AGENT ELIZABETH T. SCHNEIDER INDICATES BEYOND ANY
REASONABLE DOUBT THE EXISTENCE OF A CONTINUING PLOT OR
PLOTS BY TERRORISTS, OR TERRORIST ORGANIZATIONS, TO
CAUSE SERIOUS DAMAGE TO THE INTERESTS OF THE UNITED
STATES, ITS DIPLOMATIC OFFICERS, AND ITS CITIZENS, AND
THAT THIS SITUATION CANNOT BE TOLERATED.

IT IS FURTHER FOUND THAT THE EFFORTS AND ACTIONS TAKEN
AND TO BE TAKEN BY THE SEVERAL BRANCHES OF THE UNITED
STATES GOVERNMENT TO DETECT AND APPREHEND THOSE
INDIVIDUALS WHO COMMITTED THE TERRORIST ACTS PREVIOUSLY
DESCRIBED, AND TO PREVENT SIMILAR SUCH ACTS IN THE
FUTURE, ARE BEING AND WILL BE HAMPERED AND RENDERED
LESS EFFECTIVE BY STRICT ADHERENCE TO APPLICABLE LAWS
AND REGULATIONS.

IT IS THEREFORE FOUND THAT CLANDESTINE AND COVERT
ACTION UNDER THE SOLE SUPERVISION OF THE PRESIDENT
IS NECESSARY.

IT IS DIRECTED AND ORDERED THAT THERE IMMEDIATELY BE
ESTABLISHED A CLANDESTINE AND COVERT ORGANIZATION WITH
THE MISSION OF DETERMINING THE IDENTITY OF THE
TERRORISTS INVOLVED IN THE ASSASSINATIONS, ABDUCTION,
AND ATTEMPTED ASSASSINATION PREVIOUSLY DESCRIBED AND TO

RENDER THEM HARMLESS. AND TO PERFORM SUCH OTHER COVERT AND CLANDESTINE ACTIVITIES AS THE PRESIDENT MAY ELECT TO ASSIGN.

FOR PURPOSES OF CONCEALMENT, THE AFOREMENTIONED CLANDESTINE AND COVERT ORGANIZATION WILL BE KNOWN AS THE OFFICE OF ORGANIZATIONAL ANALYSIS, WITHIN THE DEPARTMENT OF HOMELAND SECURITY. FUNDING WILL INITIALLY BE FROM DISCRETIONAL FUNDS OF THE OFFICE OF THE PRESIDENT. THE MANNING OF THE ORGANIZATION WILL BE DECIDED BY THE PRESIDENT, ACTING ON THE ADVICE OF THE CHIEF, OFFICE OF ORGANIZATIONAL ANALYSIS.

MAJOR CARLOS G. CASTILLO, SPECIAL FORCES, U.S. ARMY, IS HEREWITH APPOINTED CHIEF, OFFICE OF ORGANIZATIONAL ANALYSIS, WITH IMMEDIATE EFFECT.

SIGNED:

PRESIDENT OF THE UNITED STATES OF AMERICA

WITNESS:

Natalie G. Cohen

SECRETARY OF STATE

TOP SECRET—PRESIDENTIAL

No one anywhere had any idea why anyone was so determined to find Jean-Paul Lorimer and was perfectly willing to commit murder to do so. But it was obvious to Major Castillo that the best—indeed, the only—course of action was to find Jean-Paul Lorimer and the place to do that was in Paris.

A CIA agent in Paris seemed to have some answers. He told Castillo he suspected that Lorimer was involved in the Iraqi oil-for-food scandal, which had just come to light. The CIA agent said he thought Lorimer had been the man who distributed the money involved. He also said he thought he knew where Jean-Paul Lorimer was: cut in small pieces in the river Seine.

Castillo had gone next to Otto Görner, the managing director of Gossinger Beteiligungsgesellschaft, G.m.b.H., in Fulda, Germany. He had a close relationship with both the holding company—which owned, among a good deal else, all the *Tages Zeitung* newspapers—and with Görner himself.

Görner told him that he agreed with the CIA agent, that Lorimer had some connection with the oil-for-food scandal, which he had also been looking into. He also pointed him to Budapest, where the editor in chief of the *Budapester Tages Zeitung*, Eric Kocian, had a list of names of people he strongly suspected were involved.

Kocian had never heard of Lorimer, but said there obviously had to be a "bag man," and it could easily be a UN diplomat who could travel around Europe and the Near East without drawing attention to himself. If Lorimer was that man, those deeply involved in the scandal would want him dead and would be willing to kill to see him eliminated.

Kocian also said his information suggested that much of the oil-for-food money was going to South America. On condition that Castillo would not reveal either his name or the names on his list to any U.S. government agency, Kocian gave him a list of names of people who he thought—or knew—were involved and who were in South America, mainly in Argentina and Uruguay.

Castillo had gone back to South America, where he found that Lorimer's name had not come up to any of the U.S. intelligence agencies operating there or to SIDE. But he had also learned that Uruguay was known as the "money-laundering capital of the Southern Cone." So he went there.

The FBI agents in Montevideo, euphemistically called "legal attachés" of the embassy, had never heard of Lorimer either, but one of them, Special Agent David W. Yung, Jr., did say that he recognized a squat, bald, very black man in one of Castillo's photos as being the Lebanese antiquities dealer Jean-Paul Bertrand, who owned an estancia called Shangri-La and was known to be there.

Yung was quickly informed that that in fact was a picture of Jean-Paul Lorimer.

The thing to do with Lorimer, Castillo then had decided, was to repatriate the missing diplomat—by force, if necessary—and he set up an operation to do that. He had just identified himself to Lorimer in Lorimer's office at the estancia when the barrel of a Madsen submachine gun smashed the office window and sprayed the room, killing Lorimer and wounding *El Coronel* Munz.

They had been attacked by six men, who were all killed in the next few minutes. None of them carried identification of any kind.

The third man in Jean-Paul Lorimer's office was dressed—as Sergeant Kensington was—in the black coveralls and other accoutrements worn by Delta Force operators when engaged in clandestine and covert operations. He was cradling in his arms a black bolt-action 7.62×55 sniper's rifle, modified from a Remington Model 700. Had he not pushed his balaclava mask off his face, Corporal Lester Bradley, USMC, who was nineteen, would have looked far more like what comes to mind when the phrase Delta Force operator is heard.

With the mask off, it had just occurred to the fourth man in the room, *he looks like a kid who has borrowed his big brother's uniform to wear to the high school Halloween party.*

He was immediately sorry for the thought.

The little sonofabitch can really shoot, as he just proved by saving my life.

The fourth man was Major (Promotable) Carlos G. Castillo, Special Forces, U.S. Army. He was thirty-six, a shade over six feet tall, and weighed one hundred ninety pounds. He had blue eyes and light brown hair. He was in a well-tailored dark blue suit.

He turned to Munz, who was looking a little pale from his wound.

"Your call, Alfredo," Castillo said. "If Kensington says he can get the bullet out, he can. How are you going to explain the wound?"

"No offense," Munz replied, "but that looks to me like a job for a surgeon."

"Kensington has removed more bullets and other projectiles than most surgeons," Castillo said. "Before he decided he'd rather shoot people than treat them for social disease, he was an A-Team medic. Which meant . . . what's that line, Kensington?"

"That I was 'Qualified to perform any medical procedure other than opening the cranial cavity,' " Kensington quoted. "I can numb that, give you a happy pill, clean it up, and get the bullet out. It would be better for you than waiting—the sooner you clean up a wound like that, the better—and that'd keep you from answering questions at a hospital. But what are you going to tell your wife?"

"Lie, Alfredo," Castillo said. "Tell her you were shot by a jealous husband."

"What she's going to think is, I was cleaning my pistol and it went off, and I'm embarrassed," Munz said. "But I'd rather deal with that than answer official questions. How long will I be out?"

"You won't be out long, but you'll be in la-la land for a couple of hours."

Munz considered that for a moment, then said: "Okay, do it."

"Well, let's get you to your feet and onto something flat where there's some light," Kensington said. He looked at Castillo and the two of them got Munz to his feet.

"There's a big table in the dining room that ought to work," Kensington said. "It looks like everybody got here just in time for dinner. There's a plate of good-looking roast beef on it. And a bottle of wine."

"Okay on the beef," Castillo said. "Nix on the wine. We have to figure out what to do next and get out of here."

"Major, who the fuck are these bad guys?" Kensington asked.

"I really don't know. Yung is searching the bodies to see what he can find out. I don't even know what happened."

"Well, they're pros, whoever they are. Maybe Russians? Kranz was no amateur and they got him. With a fucking garrote. That means they had to (a) spot him and (b) sneak up on him. A lot of people have tried that on Seymour and never got away with it."

"Spetsnaz?" Castillo said. "If this was anywhere in Europe, I'd say maybe, even probably. But here? I just don't know. We'll take the garrote and whatever else Yung comes up with and see if we can learn something."

When they got to the dining room, Kensington held up Munz while Castillo moved to a sideboard the Chateaubriand, a sauce pitcher, a bread tray, and a bottle of Uruguayan Merlot. Then he sat him down on the table.

"You going to need me—or Bradley—here?" Castillo asked.

"No, sir."

"Come on, Bradley. We'll find something to wrap Sergeant Kranz in."

"Yes, sir."

Sergeant First Class Seymour Kranz, a Delta Force communicator, who at five feet four and one hundred thirty pounds hadn't been much over the height and weight minimums for the Army, was lying facedown where he had died.

A light-skinned African American wearing black Delta Force coveralls sat beside him, holding a Car-4 version of the M-16 rifle between his knees. Despite the uniform, Jack Britton was not a soldier but a special agent of the United States Secret Service.

"Anything, Jack?" Castillo asked.

Britton shook his head.

"It's like a tomb out there," he said. And then, "Is that what they call an unfortunate choice of words?"

He scrambled to his feet.

"Let's get Seymour on the chopper," Castillo said, as he squatted beside the corpse.

The garrote which had taken Sergeant Kranz's life was still around his neck. Castillo tried to loosen it. It took some effort, but finally he got it off and then examined it carefully.

It was very much like the nylon, self-locking wire-and-cable binding devices enthusiastically adopted by the police as "plastic handcuffs." But this device was blued stainless steel and it had handles. Once it was looped over a victim's head and then tightened around the neck, there was no way the victim could get it off.

Castillo put the garrote in his suit jacket pocket.

"Okay, spread the sheets on the ground," Castillo ordered. "You have the tape, right?"

"Yes, sir," Corporal Bradley responded.

He laid the sheets, stripped from Jean-Paul Lorimer's bed, on the ground. Castillo and Britton rolled Sergeant Kranz onto them. One of his eyes was open. Castillo gently closed it.

"Sorry, Seymour," he said.

They rolled Kranz in the sheets and then trussed the package with black duct tape.

Then he squatted beside the body.

"Help me get him on my shoulder," Castillo ordered.

"I'll help you carry him," Britton said.

"You and Bradley get him on my shoulder," Castillo repeated. "I'll carry him. He was my friend."

"Yes, sir."

Castillo grunted with the exertion of rising to his feet with Kranz on his shoulder, and, for a moment, he was afraid he was losing his balance and bitterly said, "Oh, shit!"

Bradley put his hands on Castillo's hips and steadied him.

Castillo nodded his thanks and then started walking heavily toward where the helicopter was hidden, carrying the body of SFC Seymour Kranz over his shoulder.

[THREE]
Aeropuerto Internacional Jorge Newbery
Buenos Aires, Argentina
2345 31 July 2005

When the Bell Ranger helicopter called Jorge Newbery Ground Control, announced that he was at twenty-five hundred feet over the Unicenter Shopping Mall on the Route Panamericana on a VFR local flight from Pilar and wanted permission to land as near as possible to the JetAire hangar, Ground Control immediately cleared the pilot to make a direct approach.

"You're number one to land. There is no traffic in the area. Report when you are at five hundred feet over the threshold. Visibility unlimited. Winds are negligible."

There is not much commercial late-night activity at Jorge Newbery, which is commonly thought of as Buenos Aires's downtown airport. The airport is separated by only a highway from the river Plate and is no more than—traffic permitting—a ten-minute drive from downtown Buenos Aires. Very late at night, the tarmac in front of the terminal is crowded with the Boeing 737s of Aerolineas Argentina, Austral, Pluna, and the other airlines which will, starting very early in the morning, take off for cities in Argentina, Uruguay, and Brazil.

The informality of the radio exchange between the Bell Ranger and Newbery Ground Control would have driven an American FAA examiner to distraction, but in practical terms there was nothing wrong with it.

Ground Control had not bothered to identify the runway by number. There is only one, about seven thousand feet long. And since he had given the helicopter pilot permission to make a direct approach, and the winds were negligible, there wasn't much chance the pilot would misunderstand where he was supposed to go.

"Newbery, Ranger Zero-Seven at five hundred over the threshold."

"Zero-Seven, you are cleared to make a low-level transit of the field to the right, repeat right of the runway for landing at the JetAire hangar."

"Mucho gracias."

"Report when you land."

"Will do."

As the Bell Ranger came down the field, over the grass to the right of the runway, the doors of the JetAire hangar began to slide open.

A sleek, small, glistening white jet airplane—a Bombardier/Learjet 45XR with American markings—sat, nose out, behind one of the doors. It was connected to ground power and there were lights visible in both the cockpit and cabin.

Four men pushing a trundle bed, which would attach to the skids of the helicopter—the Ranger does not have wheels—and permit it to be rolled into the hangar, came out and waited for the helicopter to land.

"Newbery, Ranger Zero-Seven on the ground. *Mucho gracias.*"

"You're welcome. Have a nice time."

"I'll try."

The Ground Control operator had assumed—not without reason—that the Bell Ranger was owned by a wealthy estanciero who had flown into the city for a night on the town. That happened three or more times every night. Sometimes the tarmac in front of JetAire was as crowded with private airplanes and helicopters as the terminal tarmac was with airliners.

As soon as the Ranger had been trundled into the hangar, the doors began to slide closed again.

Three men came down the Lear's stair door and approached the helicopter as the pilot pushed the cockpit door open.

The larger of them was Fernando Lopez, Castillo's cousin. He was a dark-skinned man in his midthirties, six feet two inches tall and weighing well over two hundred pounds.

Lopez saw something he didn't like on Castillo's face. "You okay, Gringo?"

Castillo nodded.

"Solez?" Fernando Lopez asked.

Ricardo Solez was a special agent of the Drug Enforcement Administration assigned to the U.S. embassy in Buenos Aires. He had been drafted from the DEA by Castillo for the Estancia Shangri-La operation.

"He's driving the Yukon back here," Castillo said. "He's all right."

"I thought the kid was going to do that," Lopez said.

"Bradley's in there," Castillo said, indicating the helicopter.

"How did it go, Charley?" Colonel Jacob Torine, USAF, a tall, slim redhead in a sports coat, asked.

"Not well," Castillo replied. "Lorimer is dead. And Kranz bought the farm."

"Oh, shit! What happened?"

"And Munz took a hit," Castillo went on. He looked at the third man, who was slim, in his early forties, with shortly cropped thinning hair and wearing a light brown single-breasted suit.

"Well, hello, Howard," he said, not kindly. "Your boss send you to see how badly I bent his chopper?"

Howard Kennedy had spent most of his adult life as an FBI agent. Two years before, he had abruptly abandoned his prestigious duties in the FBI's Ethical Standards—read Internal Affairs—Division to go to work for Aleksandr Pevsner, a Russian national, who, it was alleged in warrants issued for his arrest by nearly a dozen countries, had committed an array of crimes ranging from being an international dealer in arms and drugs all the way down to murder.

"I came because he thought I might be useful," Howard Kennedy said.

"What happened, Charley?" Colonel Torine asked again.

"There were some other people at the estancia. Six of them . . ."

"Who?" Kennedy said.

". . . all dressed in black and armed with Madsens," Castillo finished.

"Who were they?" Kennedy pursued.

"I wish to hell I knew," Castillo said, and turned to Torine. "How soon can we go wheels up?"

"All I have to do is file the flight plan. It shouldn't take long this time of night."

"Howard, can you take care of Colonel Munz?" Castillo asked.

"Does he need a hospital?"

"The bullet's out, and he's been given antibiotics. Unless he develops an infection, no."

"Who took the bullet out?" Kennedy asked.

Castillo ignored the question.

"Take him home, Howard. Right now, he's still in la-la land, but that should wear off in no more than an hour. Then he'll start to hurt."

"Can he walk?"

Castillo nodded.

"I don't like this," Kennedy said.

"Howard, didn't your mother ever tell you when you go somewhere uninvited, you're likely to find something at the party you won't like?"

"I have no idea what you're talking about. And if I wasn't here, what would you have done with Munz?"

"He gave me a number to call if something went wrong," Castillo said. "I just want you to remember I didn't have any idea you would be here."

"Okay. So what?"

"Special Agent David W. Yung, Jr., of the FBI is in the chopper."

"Oh, Jesus Christ!"

"I'm going to tell him that who was here when we got here is classified 'Top Secret Presidential.' I have no reason to believe that he will breach security regulations."

"Then you are naïve."

"Well, what do you want to do?" Castillo asked.

Kennedy looked at him for a moment, then walked quickly to the fuselage door and opened it.

"Well, how are you, David?" he said. "Long time no see."

He put out his hand.

"I thought that was you, Howard," Yung said.

"Glad to see me?"

" 'Surprised' is the word that comes to mind."

"I'm on the pariah list, but I don't have leprosy," Kennedy said, nodding at his still-extended hand. "We go way back, David."

Yung looked at Kennedy's extended hand.

"Yeah, we do," he said and took it. "And I just realized I'm glad to see you."

"That you saw him, Yung, is classified Top Secret Presidential," Castillo said.

"That's good," Yung said. "That saves me from having to decide what to do now that I have seen him."

"Do you mind if I interpret that to mean you wouldn't have reported me even without Charley's invoking the criminal code vis-à-vis unauthorized disclosure of classified information?"

"To tell you the truth, Howard, I don't know what I would have done," Yung said.

"Okay, Howard, get Colonel Munz out of here," Castillo said.

"He's unconscious," Yung said.

"Probably asleep," Castillo said. "Shake him and find out."

El Coronel Alfredo Munz woke instantly when Yung touched his shoulder.

"Aha!" he said, cheerfully. "We have arrived. I must have dozed off." He spotted Kennedy. *"¡Hola, Howard!"* he cried. "I didn't know that you were going to be here."

"Alfredo, can you walk?" Castillo asked.

"Certainly I can walk," Munz said and tried to get out of his seat.

"That'll be easier if you take the seat belt off," Castillo said, then added: "Unfasten it for him, Yung."

Yung did so. Munz got out of his seat and went through the door. He started to walk across the hangar floor, then felt a little woozy and staggered. He put his good arm out like the wing of an airplane, cried, "Wheee," and started trotting in curves around the hangar.

Kennedy went quickly to him and steadied him.

"What we are going to tell my wife is that I shot myself when I was cleaning my pistol," Munz confided to Kennedy. "And you are my witness. My wife says you have an honest face."

Kennedy maneuvered Munz over to Castillo.

"Howard'll take care of you now, Alfredo," Castillo said. "Thanks for everything."

"It was my great pleasure," Munz said and bowed.

"I suppose we'll be in touch, won't we, Charley?" Kennedy asked.

Castillo nodded. "Tell your boss thanks, Howard."

"I'll do that," Kennedy said and then started guiding Munz toward the rear of the hangar.

Castillo walked around the Ranger and opened the copilot's door.

"Bradley, load the stuff—everything in the chopper that belongs to us—into the Lear and make sure there's a seat where we can put Sergeant Kranz."

"Yes, sir," Corporal Lester Bradley said.

"I'll give you a hand with the body," Yung said.

"Just put him over my shoulder," Castillo said. "I'll carry him."

Five minutes later, Jorge Newbery Ground Control cleared Lear Five-Oh-Seven-Five to the threshold of runway thirty-one.

[FOUR]
Office of the Commander in Chief
United States Central Command
MacDill Air Force Base
Tampa, Florida
1235 1 August 2005

There were several reasons that Command Sergeant Major Wesley Suggins was rarely in the commander in chief's conference room when the twelve chairs around the long table were occupied by what he privately thought of as "the heavy brass."

Or even when only three or four of them were occupied by what he privately thought of as "the light brass."

He defined the heavy brass as general or flag officers whose personal flags carried three or more stars. It also included a few heavy civilians. The liaison officer between the Office of the Director of National Intelligence and Cent-

Com was one of these. He was a member of what was known as the Executive Civil Service and held the grade therein of GS-18, which carried with it the assimilated grade within the military establishment of lieutenant general. The State Department, Central Intelligence Agency, and Federal Bureau of Investigation liaison officers each carried the Executive Civil Service grade of GS-16, which carried with it the assimilated grade of major general.

The light brass was brigadier generals, rear admirals (lower half), and GS-15 civilians and below.

The primary reason Command Sergeant Major Suggins almost never took a seat at the conference table was not, as most of the light and heavy brass believed, because he was an enlisted man and would be out of place in their exalted senior company.

The primary reason was that General Allan Naylor, the CentCom commander in chief, had decided that Command Sergeant Major Suggins had more important things to do than sit at the table for long periods with his mouth shut.

This was not to say General Naylor did not want Command Sergeant Major Suggins to know what transpired at the frequent conferences; quite the contrary. It was General Naylor's habit after most conferences—there were at least four every day, including the twice-daily intelligence briefings—to motion Suggins into his office and solicit both his opinions of what had been discussed and his recommendations as to how an action decided upon could best be implemented.

That Command Sergeant Major Suggins was not physically present in the conference room did not mean he hadn't heard what was being discussed. The room was equipped with a wide array of electronic devices, including a battery of microphones placed around it so that even the sound of a dropped pencil would be detected.

Sometimes the conferences were recorded. At all times, what the microphones heard was relayed to a single-earphone headset Suggins put on the moment the door to the conference room closed, the red light above the door began to flash, and the CONFERENCE IN PROGRESS DO NOT ENTER sign lit up.

It was commonly believed by those seeing Suggins wearing his headset that he was taking the opportunity, while a conference was in progress, to listen to the Dixieland recordings of Bob French's Original Tuxedo Jazz Band, to which he was known to be quite addicted. Suggins did nothing to correct this erroneous belief.

About the most important thing Suggins did while not sitting at the conference table with his mouth shut was field General Naylor's telephone calls. There were usually many, and almost all of them from people really important—

or who believed they were really important—and who all believed they had the right to speak with General Naylor immediately.

Some of them Suggins deftly diverted with white lies: The general was jogging or indisposed, or speaking with the president or the secretary of Homeland Security or the secretary of defense, and he would have the general return the call the moment he was free.

There were some callers, of course, that Suggins did not try to divert. These included, for example, the president of the United States; the secretaries of defense, state, and Homeland Security; the director of National Intelligence; and Mrs. Elaine Naylor.

When one of these luminaries called, Suggins would turn to a laptop computer on the credenza behind his desk and quickly type, for example, if the caller were the secretary of Homeland Security, the Honorable Matthew Hall:

```
HALL?
```

The message would instantly appear on the screen of what was nearly universally—and not very fondly—known as the general's IBB, meaning "Infernal Black Box."

The IBB was in fact a laptop computer identical to Suggins's. General Naylor always had it on the conference in front of him, situated so that the screen would be visible to no one else.

The system was effective. Whoever had the floor in the conference room would not have to stop in midsentence as Naylor's telephone rang or Command Sergeant Major Suggins came through the door.

Naylor could read the message and quickly type his reply:

```
CAN I CALL IN FIVE MINS?
```

Or:

```
PUT HIM THROUGH
```

Or:

```
CAN YOU TAKE A MESSAGE?
```

Etcetera.

The regularly scheduled afternoon intelligence briefing had been in session for about five minutes when one of the telephones on Command Sergeant Major Suggins's desk rang.

"Office of the Sink. Suggins."

C in c was often pronounced "sink." And "Command Sergeant Major Suggins speaking, sir" wasted time.

"Jack Iverson, Wes," the caller announced. "I've got an interesting in-flight advisory for your boss."

Chief Master Sergeant Jack Iverson, USAF, was the senior noncommissioned officer of what was informally known as "the Air Force side of MacDill." MacDill was an Air Force base. The United States Central Command was a "tenant" of MacDill Air Force Base.

"Shoot," Suggins replied as he spun in his chair to the laptop on the credenza. His fingers flew on the keys as Iverson relayed the in-flight advisory message:

```
FOR CINC CENTCOM
CHARLEY URGENTLY REPEAT URGENTLY REQUESTS CINC CENTCOM
PERSONALLY REPEAT PERSONALLY MEET LEAR FIVE-OH-SEVEN-
FIVE ON ARRIVAL MACDILL. ETA 1255. TORINE COL USAF.
```

"Got it, Jack. Hang on a minute."

"You're not going to tell me what the hell it's all about, Wes?"

"If I knew, I would. I don't," Suggins replied.

He pushed the key that would cause the message to appear on the screen of General Naylor's IBB.

The reply came in a second:

> ???????????????????????????????

The translation of that was, "What the hell?"
A moment later, there was another reply:

> OK

"Jack, reply that the CINC will do," Suggins said. "And the CINC autho-rizes the landing of the civilian airplane, if that's necessary. And for Christ's sake, keep this quiet."

"Why do I think you're not telling me everything you know?"

"Because I'm not," Suggins said. "Thanks, Jack."

Then Suggins picked up the telephone and ordered that the CINC's car be at the front door in five minutes.

[FIVE]

As the sleek white Bombardier/Learjet 45XR taxied up to the tarmac in front of Base Operations, General Allan Naylor could see the pilot. He knew him well. He was Major Carlos G. Castillo, U.S. Army. Naylor could also see who was sitting in the copilot's seat. He knew him well, too. He was Colonel Jacob Torine, USAF.

That figures, General Naylor thought. *A full goddamned Air Force colonel is flying copilot, and Charley—a lousy major—is in the pilot's seat.*

Naylor saw Castillo rise from the pilot's seat and leave the cockpit. A mo-ment later, the fuselage door began to unfold and in a moment Castillo appeared in the opening. He was in civilian clothing.

"Good afternoon, sir," Castillo called, politely. "Would you come aboard, please, sir? Alone?"

Now he's giving orders to a four-star general? Goddamn it!

"Wait here, please, Jack," Naylor said to the lieutenant colonel, his aide-de-camp, standing beside him, and then walked to the Lear and climbed up the stairs.

"Thank you, sir," Castillo said as Naylor entered the cabin.

"This had better be important, Charley."

"I thought it was, sir."

Naylor looked around the cabin. There were four men in it. One, Fernando M. Lopez, he knew well. The Lear belonged to one of the companies his family controlled.

The other three he did not know. One was an Asiatic, another a light-skinned African American, and the third looked like a high school kid.

"Who are these gentlemen, Charley?" Naylor asked.

"Special Agent Yung of the FBI, sir," Castillo answered, "Special Agent Britton of the Secret Service and Corporal Lester Bradley. Bradley's a Marine."

"Good afternoon, sir," Colonel Torine said from behind him.

"Hello, Jake," Naylor said and shook his hand.

None of them look smug, as if they've just pulled off something clever. They all look uncomfortable. As if whatever crazy operation they launched went the wrong way?

"I'm waiting, Charley," Naylor said.

Castillo pointed to the aisle at the rear of the cabin.

There was something there wrapped in what looked like sheets. And then Naylor knew what it was.

"Another body?" he asked, icily.

"Sir, those are the remains of Sergeant First Class Seymour Kranz," Castillo said. "He was KIA last night."

"What?"

"Garroted, sir," Castillo said.

"Garroted?"

"Yes, sir."

Castillo took the blue steel garrote from his pocket and extended it to Naylor.

"By who? Where?" Naylor blurted and then hurriedly added, as he pointed to Yung and Bradley: "Are these gentlemen privy to what happened? Or anything else?"

"They are aware of the Presidential Finding, sir. And they participated in the operation in which Kranz lost his life."

"And what was the operation?"

"We located Mr. Lorimer, sir. We staged an operation to repatriate him. We were in the middle of it when we were bushwhacked."

"By who?"

"I don't know, sir. Mr. Lorimer was killed during the attack as well as Sergeant Kranz."

"And the bushwhackers?"

"They were killed, sir."

"Where did this happen?"

"In Uruguay, sir."

"Uruguay?" Naylor asked, incredulously, and then verbalized what he was thinking. "The last thing I heard, you were in Europe. Hungary."

"We were, sir. But we tracked down Lorimer in Uruguay."

"And are the Uruguayan authorities already looking for you? Or will that come a little later?"

"So far as that aspect of the operation is concerned, sir, we came out clean."

"You came out with two bodies? And you call that clean?"

"We left Mr. Lorimer's body in Uruguay, sir," Castillo said. "What I meant to say is that I don't think we left anything behind that could tie the operation to us."

"And why did you come here? Why did you bring the sergeant's body here?"

"It was either here or Fort Bragg, sir—Washington was obviously out of the question—and we didn't have enough fuel to make Pope Air Force Base. And you were here, sir."

Naylor looked at him and thought, *Good ol' Uncle Allan will fix things, right?*

"Sir," Castillo added, "you are personally aware of my orders from the President. General McNab is not."

What's he doing, reading my mind?

And, dammit, he's right. Bringing the sergeant's body here was the right thing to do.

"When do you plan to go to Washington?"

"Just as soon as possible, sir. I'd be grateful if you would call Secretary Hall and tell him we're en route."

General Naylor looked for a long moment into Major Castillo's eyes. Then he walked to the door.

"Colonel," he called, "will you come in here, please?"

His aide-de-camp came quickly into the airplane.

"Colonel, you are advised that, from this moment, what you may see or hear is classified Top Secret Presidential."

"Yes, sir."

"Under that black plastic is the body of a sergeant . . ."

"Sergeant First Class Seymour Kranz," Castillo interrupted.

". . . who was killed," Naylor went on, "during the execution of a covert and clandestine operation authorized by a Presidential Finding. The officer in charge of this covert and clandestine operation has brought the sergeant's remains here for us to deal with. I confess I have no idea how to proceed with that."

"Sir, what is the sergeant's parent unit?" the lieutenant colonel asked Castillo.

Just in time, General Naylor stopped himself from saying the lieutenant colonel did not have to call Major Castillo "sir."

"Kranz was Gray Fox, out of Delta Force," Castillo answered.

"Sir, what about calling General McNab at Bragg? I suspect he has experience with a situation like this."

Oh, I bet Scotty McNab has! I'll bet this sort of thing is almost routine for good ol' Scotty!

"The first thing to do is cordon off this area," General Naylor said. "Then get an ambulance over here. Have the sergeant's remains taken to the hospital. Get a flag . . . No, have the ambulance crew bring a flag with them. Cover the remains with the national colors before they are moved. Arrange for the sergeant's remains to have a suitable escort from this moment. Understood?"

"Yes, sir."

"Is that satisfactory to you, Major Castillo?"

"Yes, sir. Thank you very much."

"Is there anything else you require?"

"No, sir."

"Then I will attempt to get General McNab on a secure line," Naylor said. He walked to the door, then turned.

"If this needs to be said, I am sure that all of you did your duty as you understood it. And I don't think I have to tell you how pleased I am that there was only the one casualty."

He was out the door before anyone could reply.

II

[ONE]
The Oval Office
The White House
1600 Pennsylvania Avenue NW
Washington, D.C.
1825 1 August 2005

The President of the United States was behind his desk. Across the room, Ambassador Charles W. Montvale, the director of National Intelligence, was sitting next to Secretary of State Natalie Cohen on one of two facing couches. Secretary of Homeland Security Matthew Hall was on the other couch.

Major C. G. Castillo, who was in civilian clothing, was nonetheless standing before the President's desk at a position close to at ease.

Or, Secretary Hall thought, *like a kid standing in front of the headmaster's desk, waiting for the ax to fall.*

For the past ten minutes, Castillo had been delivering his report of what had happened since he had last seen the President—aboard Air Force One in Biloxi, Mississippi—when the President had issued the Presidential Finding that had sent him first to Europe and ultimately to Estancia Shangri-La.

"And so we landed at MacDill, Mr. President," Castillo concluded, "where we turned over Sergeant Kranz's remains to Central Command, and then we came here. I took everyone involved to my apartment and told them nothing was to be said to anyone about anything until I had made my report, and that they were to remain there until I got back to them."

"Colonel Torine, too?" the President of the United States asked. "And your cousin, too? How did they respond to your placing them in what amounts to house arrest?"

"Colonel Torine knows how things are done, sir. I didn't *order* him . . . And Fernando, my cousin, understands the situation, sir."

"And that's about it, Castillo?" the President asked.

"Except for one thing, sir."

"Which is?"

"Howard Kennedy was at Jorge Newbery when I landed there from the estancia. Mr. Yung saw him."

"The FBI agent?"

"Who was there?" Ambassador Montvale asked.

"Howard Kennedy . . ." Castillo began.

"Who, it is alleged, is in the employ of Aleksandr Pevsner," the President said, drily.

"The Russian mobster?" Montvale asked, incredulously.

Both Castillo and the President nodded.

"I'm missing something here," Montvale said.

The President made a *fill him in* gesture with his hand to Castillo.

Secretaries Cohen and Hall, who knew the story, exchanged glances and quick smiles. Montvale wasn't going to like this.

"Sir, we have sort of reached an accommodation with Mr. Pevsner," Castillo began.

" 'We'?" Montvale interrupted. "Who's 'we'? You and who else? 'Accommodation'? What kind of 'accommodation'?"

" 'We' is Major Castillo and your President, Charles. Let Charley finish, please," the President said.

"He was very helpful in locating the stolen 727, Mr. Ambassador," Castillo said.

An American-owned Boeing 727 had disappeared from Luanda, Angola, on 23 May 2005, and when what the President described as "our enormous and enormously expensive intelligence community" was unable to determine who had stolen it, or why, or where it was, the president had come close to losing his temper.

He had dispatched Castillo, who was then an executive assistant to the secretary of the Department of Homeland Security, to Angola, his orders being simply to find out what the CIA and the FBI and the DIA and the State Department—and all the other members of the intelligence community—had come to know about the stolen airplane, and when they had come to know it, and to report back personally to him.

Castillo had instead gone far beyond the scope of his orders. He not only learned who had stolen the aircraft—an obscure group of Somalian terrorists—and what they planned to do with it—crash it into the Liberty Bell in Philadelphia—but he also had located the 727 in Costa Rica, where it was about to take off for Philadelphia. Castillo had—with the aid of a Delta Force team from Fort Bragg—stolen the aircraft back from the terrorists and, with Colonel Jake Torine in the pilot's seat, delivered it to MacDill Air Force Base.

This had endeared Castillo to the president but not to the CIA, the FBI, and the rest of the intelligence community, whose annoyance with him was directly proportional to the amount of egg the various directors felt they had on their faces.

"That's the first time I heard that," Montvale said.

"What part of 'Let Charley finish' didn't you understand, Charles?"

"I beg your pardon, Mr. President," Montvale said.

"Let me take it, Charley," the President said. "Perhaps there will be fewer interruptions that way. In a nutshell, Charles, there is no legal action of any kind against this fellow underway in an American court. He made contact with Charley shortly after I gave Charley the job of finding out why no one else in our intelligence community could find it. He was very helpful. He wanted something in return."

"I'll bet," Montvale said.

"Pevsner told Charley he thought the agency—which had quietly contracted for his services over the years—was trying to arrange his arrest by one of the countries that hold warrants for his arrest so that he could be locked up and his CIA contracts would not come to light. He went so far as to say he thought the agency would like to terminate him with extreme prejudice. Now, I know we don't do that anymore, but the man was worried.

"As a small gesture of my appreciation, I authorized Charley to tell him that I had ordered the DCI and the director of the FBI—this is before you became director of National Intelligence—to cease all investigations they might have underway and to institute no new investigations without my specific permission. What Pevsner thought was happening was that the CIA was looking for him abroad and the FBI inside the United States. If they located him, they would either arrest him here on an Interpol warrant or furnish his location to one of the governments looking for him.

"Such stay-out-of-jail status to continue so long as Pevsner does not violate any law of the United States and with the unspoken understanding that he would continue to be helpful."

"And has this chap continued to be helpful?" Montvale asked.

"He got me access to the helicopter I used to fly to Estancia Shangri-La," Castillo said.

"He's in Argentina?"

"I don't know where Pevsner is at this moment," Castillo said. "I ran into Howard Kennedy in Buenos Aires and he arranged for the helicopter."

That's not an outright lie. I just twisted the truth. For all I know, Alek might be in Puente del Este, Uruguay, not in Argentina.

"And Kennedy is?"

"A former FBI agent who now works for Pevsner," the President said.

"And what was he doing in Argentina?"

"He accompanied a 767 loaded with objets d'art sent by the Saudi royal family from Riyadh for the King Fahd Islamic Cultural Center in Buenos Aires and took back to Riyadh a load of polo ponies and saddles and other polo accoutrements for the royal family," Castillo said.

"The airplane no doubt owned by Pevsner?" Montvale asked.

"Probably, sir. I didn't ask."

"And this Kennedy fellow just turned over a helicopter to you because you asked him? Is that what you're saying, Major Castillo?"

"I would bet that he did so with Mr. Pevsner's permission, sir, but I didn't ask about that, either."

"I must say, Mr. President, that I find this whole situation amazing."

"What is it they say, Charles, about politics making strange bedfellows?"

"I don't understand why this Kennedy fellow was concerned that the FBI agent saw him," Montvale said.

"Kennedy is obviously paranoid," the President said. "He thinks the FBI is still looking for him, despite my specific orders that the search be called off, and that if they find him they will terminate him."

"That's absurd!"

"Oh, I agree. For one thing, terminating him would be illegal," the President said.

"Why would they want to?"

"Well," Castillo said, "Kennedy thinks—he was a senior agent in the Ethical Standards Division of the FBI before he left—it's because he knows where all the FBI's skeletons are buried."

"Charley," the President said, "correct me if I'm wrong, but wouldn't the secrecy provisions of the Finding extend to anything connected with what you were doing down there? I mean, even to who any of your people saw anywhere?"

"I made that point to Mr. Yung, sir."

"Well, that should do it," the President said. "But since the subject came up, Charles, why don't you check with the CIA and the FBI to make sure they haven't forgotten my specific orders? If they have, I'd really like to hear about it."

"I can't believe they would ignore any presidential order, Mr. President."

"Check, Charles, please," the President said.

"Yes, Mr. President."

"Charley, I didn't hear you say whether you found anything useful at this fellow's estancia."

"Sir, we found an address book, a coded address book. Agent Yung said it looks to him like a fairly simple code and that it should be breakable."

"That's underway?"

"No, sir. I came right here from the hotel, sir. And . . ."

"And what?"

"And frankly, sir, I thought it would be better to see if I still have a job, before going over to Fort Meade to—"

The President cut him off with a raised hand. "All you found at the estancia was this address book?"

"No, sir. We found written confirmation of what Agent Yung believed was the money Mr. Lorimer had in Uruguayan banks."

"A good deal of money? More than he could reasonably have socked away for a rainy day?"

"Fifteen-point-seven million dollars, Mr. President."

"What sort of evidence?" Ambassador Montvale asked. "Bankbooks? Certificates of deposit? What?"

The President flashed Montvale a very cold look, then looked at Castillo.

"Sir, what Mr. Lorimer did was in effect loan the banks the money. What we took from the safe . . . I have them with me."

"You have what with you?" Montvale asked.

"Let me ask the questions, Charles, please," the President said and made a *Give me whatever you have* gesture to Castillo with both hands.

Castillo somewhat awkwardly took a handful of colorfully printed documents from his briefcase and handed them to the President.

The President glanced at them, then said, "You're the linguist, Charley. I have no idea what these say."

"Sir, they're certificates signed by officers of the banks involved, essentially stating that a payment on demand loan has been made by Mr. Lorimer to their bank and that the bank will honor—pay—these things, like checks, once Mr. Lorimer has endorsed them. Sort of like bearer bonds, Mr. President, but not exactly."

"And these are unsigned?"

"Yes, sir. Right now they're as good as an unsigned check," Castillo said.

"And we have no idea where—specifically, I mean—Lorimer got all that money, do we?" the secretary of state asked.

"No, ma'am," Castillo said. "I think—hell, I know—it's oil-for-food proceeds, but I can't prove it. What I was hoping was that we could tie it somehow to one of the names in the address book—assuming we can get that decoded—or to one or more of the names I got from another source."

"What other source?" Ambassador Montvale asked.

"I'd rather not say, Mr. Ambassador," Castillo said.

"I'm the director of National Intelligence," Montvale said, icily.

"And I think Charley knows that," the President said. "If he'd rather not say, I'm sure he has his reasons." He paused. "Which are, Charley?"

"Sir, I promised I would not reveal the identity of that source or share what he gave me without his permission."

"That's absurd!" Montvale snapped.

"I was hoping to get his permission," Castillo said. "Before I fucked up in Uruguay."

"You did say '*screwed* up in Uruguay,' didn't you?" the President asked.

"I beg your pardon," Castillo said. "I'm very sorry, Madam Secretary."

"I've heard the word before, Charley," Natalie Cohen said.

"Is that about it, Charley?" the President asked.

"Yes, sir. Except to say, Mr. President, how deeply I regret the loss of Sergeant Kranz and how deeply I regret having failed in the mission you assigned."

The President did not immediately respond. He looked into Castillo's eyes a moment as he considered that statement, then said, "How do you figure that you have failed, Charley?"

"Well, sir, the bottom line is that I am no closer to finding the people who murdered Mr. Masterson and Sergeant Markham and shot Agent Schneider than I was before I went looking for Mr. Lorimer. Mr. Lorimer is now dead and we'll never know what he might have told us if I hadn't botched his . . ."

Castillo's voice trailed off as he tried to find the right word.

"Repatriation?" the President offered.

"Yes, sir. And now Sergeant Kranz is dead. I failed you, sir."

"Charles," the President said, "what about the long-term damage resulting from Major Castillo's failure? Just off the top of your head?"

"Mr. President, I don't see it as a failure," Secretary Hall spoke up.

"The director of National Intelligence has the floor, Mr. Secretary. Pray let him continue," the President said, coldly.

"Actually, Mr. President, neither do I," Montvale said. "Actually, when I have a moment to think about it, quite the opposite."

"You heard him," the President pursued. "This man Lorimer is dead. We have no proof that Natalie can take to the UN that he was involved in the oil-for-food scandal or anything else. And Castillo himself admits that he's no closer to finding out who killed Masterson and the sergeant than he ever was. Isn't that failure?"

"Mr. President, if I may," Montvale said, cautiously. "Let me point out what I think the major—and that small, valiant band of men he had with him—has accomplished."

"What would that be?"

"If we accept the premise that Mr. Lorimer was involved in something sordid, and the proof of that, I submit, is that he sequestered some"—Montvale looked to Castillo for help—"how many million dollars?"

"Fifteen-point-seven, sir," Castillo offered.

". . . Some sixteen million U.S. dollars in Uruguay, and that parties unknown tracked him down to Uruguay and murdered him to keep him from talking. After they abducted Mrs. Masterson and later murdered her husband."

"So what, Charles?" the President demanded.

"I don't seem to be expressing myself very well, Mr. President," Montvale said. "Let me put it this way: These people, whoever they are, now know we're onto them. They have no idea what the major may have learned before he went to South America. They have no idea how much Lorimer may have told him before they were able to murder him. If they hoped to obtain the contents of

Lorimer's safe, they failed. And they don't know what it did or did not contain, so they will presume the worst, and that it is now in our possession. Or, possibly worse, in the possession of parties unknown. They sent their assassins in to murder Lorimer and what we—what the major and his band—gave them in return were six dead assassins and an empty safe. And now that we know we're onto them, God only knows how soon it will be before someone comes to us."

"And rats on the rats, you mean?" the President asked.

"Yes, sir, that's precisely what I mean. And I'm not talking only about identifying the Masterson murderers—I think it very likely that the major has already 'rendered them harmless'—but the people who ordered the murders. The masterminds of the oil-for-food scandal, those who have profited from it. Sir, in my judgment the major has not failed. He has rendered the country a great service and is to be commended."

"You ever hear, Charles, that great minds run in similar paths? I had just about come to the same conclusion. But one question, Charles, is what should we do about the sixteen million dollars in the banks in Uruguay? Tell the UN it's there and let them worry about getting it back?"

"Actually, sir, I had an off the top of my head thought about that money. According to the major, all it takes is Lorimer's signature on those documents, whatever they're called, that the major brought back from the hideaway to have that money transferred anywhere."

"But Lorimer's dead," the President said.

"They have some very talented people over in Langley, if the President gets my meaning."

"You mean, forge a dead man's signature and steal the money? For what purpose?"

"Mr. President, I admit that when I first learned what you were asking the major to do, I was something less than enthusiastic. But I was wrong and I admit it. A small unit like the major's can obviously be very valuable in this new world war. And if sixteen million dollars were available to it—sixteen million untraceable dollars . . ."

"I take your point, Charles," the President said. "But I'm going to ask you to stop thinking off the top of your head."

"Sir?"

"The next thing you're likely to suggest is that Charley—and that's his name, Charles, not 'the major'—move the Office of Organizational Analysis into the Office of the Director of National Intelligence. And that's not going to happen. Charley works for me, period. Not open for comment."

Secretary Hall had a sudden coughing spasm. His face grew red.

Ambassador Montvale did not seem to suspect that Secretary Hall might be concealing a hearty laugh.

"Natalie, do you have anything to say before I send Charley out of here to take, with my profound thanks, a little time off? After he lets everybody in his apartment go, of course."

"I was thinking about Ambassador Lorimer, sir. He's ill and it will devastate him to learn what his son has been up to."

Ambassador Philippe Lorimer, Jean-Paul Lorimer's father, had retired from the Foreign Service of the United States after a lengthy and distinguished career after suffering a series of progressively more life-threatening heart attacks.

"Jesus, I hadn't thought about that," the President said. "Charley, what about it?"

"Sir, Mr. Lorimer is missing in Paris," Charley said. "The man who died in Estancia Shangri-La was Jean-Paul Bertrand, a Lebanese. I don't think anyone will be anxious to reveal who Bertrand really was. And I don't think we have to or should."

"What about his sister?" Natalie Cohen asked. "Should she be told?"

"I think so, yes," Charley said. "I haven't thought this through, but I have been thinking that the one thing I could tell Mrs. Masterson that would put her mind at rest about the threats to her children is that I know her brother is dead and, with his death, these bastards . . . excuse me . . . these *bad guys* have no more interest in her or her children."

"And if she asks how you know, under what circumstances?" the President asked.

"That's what I haven't thought through, sir."

"You don't want to tell her what a despicable sonofabitch he was, is that it?"

"I suspect she knows, sir. But it's classified Top Secret Presidential."

"Would anyone have objections to my authorizing Charley to deal with the Masterson family in any way he determines best, including the divulgence of classified material?"

"Splendid idea, Mr. President," Ambassador Montvale said.

"Do it soon, Charley. Please," Natalie Cohen said.

"Yes, ma'am."

The President stood up and came around the desk and offered Castillo his hand.

"Thank you, Charley. Good job. Go home and get some rest. And then think where you can discreetly hide sixteen million dollars until you need it."

[TWO]
Room 404
The Mayflower Hotel
1127 Connecticut Avenue NW
Washington, D.C.
2015 1 August 2005

When Major C. G. Castillo pushed open the door to his apartment—the hotel referred to room 404 as an "Executive Suite"; it consisted of a living room, a large bedroom, a small dining room, and a second bedroom—he found Colonel Jacob Torine sprawled on one of the couches watching *The O'Reilly Factor* on the FOX News Channel. Torine's feet were on the coffee table and his right hand was wrapped around a Heineken beer bottle, which rested on his chest.

Corporal Lester Bradley, USMC, sat beside him, feet on the floor, holding a half-empty bottle of Coca-Cola. He was puffing on a large dark brown cigar.

Well, I may not get cashiered, Castillo thought. *But if somebody sees him with that cigar, I'll certainly be charged with contributing to the delinquency of a minor.*

The obvious source of Bradley's cigar, Fernando Lopez, sat puffing on its twin across a chessboard from Special Agent David W. Yung, Jr., of the FBI. Special Agent Jack Britton of the Secret Service watched them with amused interest; it looked to him as if the kid was clobbering Lopez.

Major H. Richard Miller, Jr., in civilian clothing, sat in an armchair. His left leg, heavily bandaged, rested on the coffee table. Miller and Castillo had been classmates and roommates at West Point. They had served together several times during their careers, most recently with the "Night Stalkers," more formally known as the 160th Special Operations Aviation Regiment.

Everybody turned to look at Castillo.

"What happened to your cast?" Castillo asked, looking at Miller.

"They took pity on me and sawed it off. I am now down to two miles of rubberized gauze," Miller said.

"And how's the knee?"

"Time will tell," Miller said, disgustedly, then asked, "Well, how did it go with the President?"

"Well, I don't think we'll all wind up in Alaska counting snowballs," Castillo announced.

"You really didn't think something like that was going to happen, did you, Charley?" Torine asked.

"Actually, I bear a message from the commander in chief," Castillo said. "Quote, Good job. Thank you, End quote."

"What did you expect, Charley?" Torine pursued.

"We lost Kranz and they blew Lorimer away before we could talk to him," Castillo said. "How does that add up to a 'good job'?"

"You found the sonofabitch," Miller said. "And, in doing so, removed the threat to the Mastersons. That's a good job, Charley. In my book or anybody else's."

"Can Britton and I go home now, Gringo?" Fernando asked. "To try to salvage what we can from the ashes of our marriages?"

"Is that all the President had to say?" Torine asked.

"Montvale was there," Castillo said.

"And?"

"Hall and Natalie Cohen," Castillo said.

"How effusive was the ambassador in his praise for our little undertaking?" Torine said.

Castillo chuckled. "Actually, he called you—us—'the major and his small, valiant band of men.' "

"No kidding?" Torine said. "Well, I can live with that."

"He actually tried to take us—the Office of Organizational Analysis—over."

"Oh, shit!" Torine said.

"He didn't get away with it," Castillo said. "The President cut him off in midsentence."

"Leaving us where?" Miller asked.

"We're still in business," Castillo said. "The President was very clear about that." He looked at Miller. "Colonel Torine's brought you up to speed on everything, right, Dick?"

Miller nodded.

"David, we have something with Lorimer's signature on it, don't we?" Castillo asked.

Yung nodded.

"Well, as soon as possible, take it over to Langley," Castillo said. "That means right now. Something with Lorimer's signature on it, and the bearer bonds or whatever the hell they're called."

"Why?" Yung asked.

"So the agency's finest forgers can put Lorimer's signature on the bearer bonds and we can grab the money. It's now our operating budget."

"Lovely idea," Torine said. "Fifteen-point-seven million is a nice little operating budget. But what are you going to do when Montvale finds out about it? And he will."

"Actually, it was his idea," Castillo said. "Admittedly while he was still thinking he could bring us under his benevolent wing."

"Where am I supposed to put it?" Yung said.

"Good question," Castillo said.

"I've got an account in the Cayman Islands," Yung said. "At the Liechtensteinische Landesbank."

"You've got what?" Castillo asked, incredulously. "A pillar of the FBI, an expert in uncovering money laundering, and you're hiding your own money from the IRS in the Liechtensteinische Landesbank in the Cayman Islands?"

Yung was not amused.

"It was an investigative tool, Major," he said. "I opened the account both to see how that could be done and so that I could be kept abreast of any changes in their banking laws. As a depositor, I could ask questions that I could not ask otherwise."

"That's even better," Castillo said, delightedly. "The *FBI* has money in the Liechtensteinische Landesbank in the Caymans. Is nothing sacred anymore?"

"What the hell is that?" Britton asked. "Lickten-what?"

"Liechtenstein is a little country—run by a prince—about twenty miles long and five miles wide between Switzerland and Austria," Castillo said. "Landesbank means 'state bank.' The Liechtensteiners make their money growing cows and banking other people's money. "

"Actually, the funds in the bank are mine," Yung said. "Using my own money to open the account was easier than trying to get permission—and, of course, the money itself—from the FBI."

"And how much of your own money are you sequestering in your Liechtensteinische Landesbank account?"

"Twenty-five hundred dollars."

"How hard is it to open an account?" Castillo asked.

"Actually, it's quite simple. All they ask is a reference from your home banker and a cashier's check or a wire deposit. They won't take cash deposits," Yung answered.

"Well, then, that's what we'll do. But I want to get that money out of Uruguay before they find out Lorimer is dead."

"Bertrand," Yung corrected him. "The funds are in Bertrand's name."

"Okay. *Bertrand*," Castillo said. "Are any questions going to be asked when your secret little account suddenly grows by fifteen-point-seven million?"

"I'm not sure I want to do that," Yung said.

"Answer the question," Castillo said. "Is that going to make waves?"

"No questions are ever asked and they have stricter bank secrecy laws than even Switzerland. But, for the obvious reasons, I am uncomfortable transferring Bertrand's funds into my account."

"Then why did you tell us about your account?" Torine asked with a tone of impatience in his voice.

"I was going to suggest that you look into opening an account there. What Castillo's asking me to do is commit a felony. I'm an FBI agent, dammit!"

"Jesus H. Christ!" Torine said. "FBI rule number one: Always cover your ass. Right?"

"What I'm ordering you to do is carry out an order of the President of the United States," Castillo said.

"I don't believe you have the legal authority to give me an order. I'm in the FBI. I don't work for you."

Torine started to say something, then changed his mind and looked at Castillo.

Castillo said, "I suppose that's true, that you don't work for me. Right now, I guess your status is volunteer."

"Major, I thought—still think—you were doing the right thing when you staged that operation to kidnap Lorimer from Estancia Shangri-La. That's why I went with you. But that's not going to go over well at the J. Edgar Hoover Building when they hear about it. The FBI is supposed to investigate kidnappings, not participate in them."

"And you don't want to endanger your FBI career any more than you already have?" Torine asked, sarcastically.

Yung considered that and then nodded.

"Yung," Torine said, evenly, "if you're even thinking of running over to the J. Edgar Hoover Building and repeating even one word of this conversation or one detail of the operation we have just been on into some sympathetic FBI inspector's ear, I suggest you think again. That would constitute the divulgence of material classified Top Secret Presidential to persons not authorized access to such material. And that *is* a felony."

Castillo added, "And that includes telling anybody you bumped into Howard Kennedy in Buenos Aires."

Yung looked at him coldly.

"Let me be brutal," Castillo said. "Supposing you went to the FBI and confessed all and it was decided for a number of reasons not to try you for unauthorized disclosure, are you really naïve enough to think you'd be welcomed back like the prodigal son? Or is it more likely that you'd spend the rest of your FBI career investigating parking ticket corruption in Sioux Falls, South Dakota?"

The look on Yung's face showed that Castillo had struck home.

"Right now, the question seems to be that you don't think I have the authority to give you orders. Is that right?"

"I don't believe you have that legal authority," Yung said.

"What if I got it? Would that change things?"

"How could you do that?"

Castillo sat down on the couch next to Corporal Lester Bradley and picked up the telephone. He punched in a number from memory.

"This is C. G. Castillo," he announced a moment later. "Is Secretary Hall still with the President?

"Can you get him for me, please?

"Charley, sir. Sorry to interrupt.

"Yung would feel more comfortable dealing with that banking business we discussed earlier if he was assigned to the Office of Organizational Analysis and therefore under my orders. Is that going to be a problem?

"The sooner the better, sir. By the time the banks open in the morning. Tonight would be even better.

"He'll be with Miller. Here in my apartment, sir.

"Yes, sir."

There was a sixty-second period of silence.

"Yes, sir. Thank you very much, sir.

"No, sir. I'm going to go to Philadelphia and then to Biloxi. Maybe still tonight if there's a way to get from Philadelphia to Biloxi. In any event, as soon as I can, sir.

"Yes, sir. I'll let you and Secretary Cohen know how that went as soon as I can.

"Yes, sir, I will. Thank you very much, sir."

Castillo put the handset back in the cradle and looked at Yung.

"Secretary Hall tells me the President has put in a call to the director of the FBI. When he gets him, or his deputy, he will order that you be placed on duty with the Office of Organizational Analysis. Either the director or his deputy will call you here and tell you that. That will place you under my orders. Any questions?"

Yung shook his head.

"Let me take this opportunity to welcome you to the Office of Organizational Analysis, Mr. Yung," Castillo said, mock portentously. "We hope your career with us will last as long as the organization itself—in other words, maybe for the next two or three weeks."

Torine laughed. Others chuckled.

A smile—small but unmistakable—crossed Yung's lips.

"Just as soon as I can—within a day or two—I will open another account in the Liechtensteinische Landesbank," Castillo said. "We'll get the money out of your account as soon as possible."

Yung nodded.

"You ever been to Langley, Yung?" Miller asked.

Yung shook his head.

"I'll take you over there," Miller said and then had a second thought: "Better yet, Charley, Tom McGuire knows his way around there better than I do."

"You know where to find him?"

Miller nodded.

"Ask him to do that, please," Castillo said. "How hard is it going to be to get Vic D'Allessando on the horn?"

Miller held out a cellular telephone. Castillo went and took it from him.

"Autodial seven," Miller said.

"I don't know when I'll be able to get to Biloxi," Castillo explained. "But I want to see Vic before I see the Mastersons."

"It'll probably be in the very wee hours when we get there," Fernando said. "But if you go with me, I'll bet you'll get there sooner than if you went commercial."

"I want to go to Philadelphia first," Castillo said.

"So does Jack," Fernando said. "Jack's wife is with her mother in Philly. The planned itinerary is Reagan to Philly. Then, after you see your lady friend, Philly to Charleston, where we drop the colonel off. Then Charleston to San Antone. No problem to drop you off in Biloxi."

"You're going to Charleston by way of Philadelphia?" Castillo asked Torine. "You can't catch a plane from here?"

"The oldest member of this small, valiant band of men," Torine said, "having just returned from a tour of the world, is in no condition to pass through airport security, especially in possession of an Uzi and a case of untaxed brandy that I don't want to have to try to explain."

Castillo chuckled. "Untaxed brandy?"

"Fernando told me you had bought your grandmother a case of Argentine brandy at twelve bucks a bottle. I figured if it was good enough for your grandmother, it would be a suitable expression of my affection for my wife."

"It's really good brandy," Castillo said. "And, best of all, it's not French."

"It's a sad world, Charley, where boycotting the products of those who have screwed you interferes with your drinking habits, but that's the way it is."

Castillo chuckled.

"Okay, let's get this show on the road. While I call D'Allessando, somebody call the doorman and have him get us a couple of cabs."

"There's a big Yukon stationed at the National Geographic exit," Miller said. "And since I'm not going anywhere, you can use that."

"Great," Castillo said.

"Sir, what about me?" Corporal Lester Bradley asked.

Castillo looked at him a long moment before replying.

"You better come with me, Bradley," he said, finally.

"Sir, may I ask what I'm going to be doing?"

"You can ask, but I can't tell you because I haven't figured that out yet."

[THREE]
The Belle Vista Casino and Resort
U.S. Highway 90 ("The Magic Mile")
Biloxi, Mississippi
0405 2 August 2005

Inside the resort, as C. G. Castillo and Lester Bradley, in civilian clothing, approached the main entrance of the casino, a burly "host" came out from behind a small stand-up desk and not very politely asked Bradley how old he was and then, when told, shook his head and said he couldn't go in.

"Wait right here, Bradley," Castillo ordered. "I'll be right out."

"Yes, sir."

Castillo entered the casino and walked past rows of slot machines, at which maybe a quarter of them sat gamblers, most of them middle-aged and elderly women. Beyond the slot machines was an arch with a flashing GAMING sign on it. Castillo walked under it and found himself in a huge area filled with tables for the playing of blackjack, craps, and roulette.

Perhaps a third of them were in use. He saw Vic D'Allessando's totally bald head at one of the blackjack tables deep in the room. He walked toward the table and stopped six feet from it.

There was a sign on the table indicating the minimum bet was ten dollars. There were five stacks of chips in front of D'Allessando. He tapped them steadily with the fingers of his left hand as he watched the dealer deal.

Even if they were all ten-dollar chips—and they're obviously not, since each stack is a different color, which means they're worth even more—Vic is into this game big-time.

He watched a little longer, saw that Vic was playing two cards at a time, and then walked up behind him. D'Allessando sensed his presence and turned to see who was behind him. He gave no sign of recognition.

The dealer busted and passed out chips to both of the cards D'Allessando was playing.

"That'll do it," D'Allessando said, then slid a tip of two chips to the dealer and started to gather up the remainder of his chips. The dealer slid a rack to him.

"Thanks," D'Allessando said and put the chips in the rack.

"Oh, goody," Castillo said. "I brought you luck."

D'Allessando snorted. He arranged the chips in the rack and stood up. He was a short man whose barrel chest and upper arms strained his shirt.

"Cashier's over there," D'Allessando said, indicating the direction with a nod of his head.

On his retirement from twenty-four years of service—twenty-two of it in Special Forces—CWO5 Victor D'Allessando had gone to work for the Special Operations Command as a Department of the Army civilian. Theoretically, he was a technical advisor to the commanding general of the John F. Kennedy Special Warfare Center at Fort Bragg. What he actually did for the Special Operations Command was classified.

At the cashier's window, a peroxide blonde in her fifties counted the chips, then asked if D'Allessando wanted his winnings as a check.

"Cash will do nicely, thank you," D'Allessando said.

The peroxide blonde began to lay crisp new one-hundred-dollar bills in stacks, ten bills to a stack. There were four stacks. Then she started a fifth stack with fifties, twenties, a ten, and, finally, a five.

"Jesus Christ, Vic!" Castillo said. "You had a good night."

D'Allessando grunted again, stuffed the money in the inside pocket of his lemon-colored sports coat, and started for the door. Castillo followed him.

D'Allessando made a *Give it to me* gesture to the host, who had refused to let Bradley into the casino. The host unlocked a small drawer in the stand-up desk and tried to discreetly hand D'Allessando a Colt General Officers model .45 ACP semiautomatic pistol. The discretion failed. D'Allessando hoisted the skirt of his sports coat and slipped the pistol into a skeleton holster over his right hip pocket.

"They won't let you carry a weapon in there," D'Allessando said. "I guess losers have been known to pop the dealers."

Castillo chuckled. The host was not amused.

"Elevator's over there," D'Allessando said, again nodding to show the direction.

"I know."

"Oh, yeah. Masterson said you'd been here."

"You get to talk to him?" Castillo asked as they walked and Bradley followed.

"He'll be here at eight for breakfast."

When they reached the bank of elevators, D'Allessando took a plastic card key from his jacket pocket and swiped it through a reader. The elevator door opened. D'Allessando waved Castillo into it. Bradley started to get on.

"Sorry, my friend," D'Allessando said, "this elevator is reserved for big-time losers."

"He's with me," Castillo said.

D'Allessando shrugged and stepped out of the way.

When the door closed, Castillo said, "Bradley, this is Mr. D'Allessando. Vic, this is Corporal Lester Bradley. He's a Marine."

"You're in bad company, kid," D'Allessando said. "Watch yourself."

"He's a friend of mine, Vic."

"Even worse."

The elevator stopped and D'Allessando swiped the plastic key again. The door opened.

"Welcome to Penthouse C," D'Allessando said.

"Wow!" Bradley exclaimed.

They were in an elegantly furnished suite of rooms. Two walls of the main room were plate glass, offering a view of what was now an intermittent stream of red lights going west on U.S. 90, white lights going east. In the daylight, the view would be of the sugar white sand beaches and emerald salt water of the Mississippi Gulf Coast.

"My sentiments exactly, Bradley," Castillo said.

"You want a drink, Charley?" D'Allessando asked.

"At four o'clock in the morning?"

"It would not be your first drink at four in the morning," D'Allessando said.

"True," Castillo said. "What the hell, why not? There's wine?"

"There's a whole bin full of it behind the bar," D'Allessando said.

"You want something to drink, Bradley?" Castillo asked.

"I'm a little hungry, sir," Bradley said.

"So'm I," Castillo said. "There's round-the-clock room service, right, Vic?"

"Indeed."

Castillo picked up the telephone and punched a button on the base.

"What kind of steak can I have at this unholy hour?" he said into the phone. He was told.

"New York strip sounds fine."

Castillo looked at Bradley, who smiled and nodded, and then at D'Allessando, who said, "Why not? I can think of it as breakfast. Get mine with eggs."

"Three New York strips, medium rare. With fried eggs. Either home fries or French fries. And whatever else seems appropriate for two starving men and an old fat Italian who really shouldn't be eating at all."

D'Allessando gave him the finger as he hung up the phone.

"So tell me, Marine," D'Allessando said to Bradley, "how did this evil man worm his way into your life?"

"He saved my life, Vic," Castillo said.

D'Allessando looked at Bradley.

"Not to worry," he said. "You're a young man. In time, you'll be forgiven."

Castillo shook his head.

"You going to have a drink before or after you tell me what's going on, Charley?"

"Yes," Castillo said and went behind the bar in search of wine.

"If you promise not to tell your mother, Marine, you may also have a little taste," D'Allessando said.

"Leave him alone, Vic," Castillo said. "I wasn't kidding when I said he's a friend of mine."

"You also said he saved your life," D'Allessando said.

"He did."

"And how—not to get into 'Why in the name of all the saints?'—did he do that?"

"He took out two bad guys who were shooting submachine guns at me. With two head shots."

"I have this very odd feeling that you're not pulling my chain," D'Allessando said. "Forgive me, son, if I say you do not look much like the ferocious jarhead of fame and legend."

"Says the Special Operations poster boy," Castillo said.

"You always have had a cruel streak in you, Carlos," D'Allessando lisped as he put his hand on his hip.

Bradley chuckled.

"I have an idea, Charley," D'Allessando said. "Take it from the top."

Castillo held up a wineglass to Bradley.

"No, thank you, sir. Is there any beer?"

"Half a dozen kinds. Come over here and help yourself."

"And while you're doing that, Major Castillo is going to take it from the top."

"Okay," Castillo said. "Vic, this is Top Secret Presidential."

"Okay," D'Allessando said, now very seriously.

"You remember I told you here that Masterson had been whacked to make the point to his wife that these bastards were willing to kill to get to her brother?"

D'Allessando nodded. "The UN guy in Paris."

Castillo nodded. "What I didn't tell you is that there is a Presidential Finding, in which an organization called the Office of Organizational Analysis is founded—"

"C and c?" D'Allessando interrupted.

Castillo nodded.

"Covert and clandestine," he went on, "and charged with, quote, rendering harmless, end quote, those responsible for whacking Masterson, Sergeant Markham, kidnapping Mrs. Masterson, and wounding Special Agent Schneider."

"I figured there was something like that in the woodpile," D'Allessando said. "Who's running that?"

"I am."

D'Allessando considered that and nodded, then asked, "And you found out who these people are, huh?"

"I don't have a clue who they are."

"You're losing me, Charley."

"I figured the best way to find these people was to find Lorimer first. So we went looking for him. We found him in Uruguay."

"Uruguay?"

"Uruguay," Castillo confirmed. "We also found out that Mr. Lorimer was the bagman—*the* bagman—for the guys who got rich on the Iraqi oil-for-food scam. He knew who got how much, and what for."

"And they wanted to silence him," D'Allessando said. "But what's with Uruguay?"

"Uruguay and Argentina are now the safe havens of choice for ill-gotten gains."

"I knew Argentina and Paraguay, but this is the first I've heard about Uruguay."

"I really don't know what I'm talking about here, Vic. I always heard Argentina and Paraguay, too. But Uruguay is where we found Lorimer. He had a new identity—Jean-Paul Bertrand—a Lebanese passport, a Uruguayan residence permit, and an estancia. Everybody thought he was in the antiquities business."

"Clever," D'Allessando said.

"He also ripped off nearly sixteen million from these people."

"You never said who these people are."

"I don't have a fucking clue, Vic," Castillo said. "Anyway, once we found Lorimer I staged an operation to repatriate him."

"McNab sent people down there? I didn't hear anything about that. Who'd he send?"

"He didn't send anybody. I didn't have time to wait for anybody from the stockade. I went with what I had."

"Which was?"

"Kranz and Kensington were already down there, as communicators. So I used them. Plus two Secret Service guys, a DEA agent, an FBI agent, and Bradley."

D'Allessando pointed at Bradley, who was now sucking at the neck of a Coors beer bottle, and raised his eyebrows.

"Yeah. That Bradley," Castillo said and then went on: "The CIA station chiefs in Buenos Aires helped and I had an Argentine—ex-SIDE—with me. I thought it was, do it right then or don't do it all. If I could find Lorimer, so could the bad guys."

"Yeah. So what were you going to do with Lorimer when you found him?"

"Get him to the States."

"How?"

"I had the Lear—you saw it here?"

"You took that to South America?"

"By way of Europe," Castillo said.

"Across the Atlantic twice?" D'Allessando asked, incredulously.

"That was interesting," Castillo said. "But Jake Torine said we could do it and we did. I borrowed a JetRanger in Uruguay . . ."

"The last time you 'borrowed' a helicopter, you nearly went to Leavenworth," D'Allessando said. "Is Interpol looking for you, Charley?"

"No. I really borrowed this one from a friend."

"And he will keep his mouth shut when people start asking him questions?"

"It's in his interest to keep his mouth shut."

D'Allessando shrugged, suggesting he hoped this would be the case but didn't think so.

"The plan was to snatch Lorimer at his estancia, chopper him, nap of the earth, to Buenos Aires, put him on the Lear, and bring him to the States. The ex-SIDE guy had arranged for us get the Lear out of Argentina without questions being asked."

"But something went wrong, right? The best-laid plans of mice and special operators, etcetera?"

"We had just gotten him to open his safe when somebody stuck a Madsen through the window and let loose. Lorimer took two hits to the head and the SIDE guy took one in the arm. And then Bradley took the shooter out with a head shot from Kranz's Remington and then took out the shooter's pal. Both head shots. He saved my ass, Vic."

D'Allessando looked at Bradley.

"Consider all my kind thoughts about your touching innocence withdrawn," he said.

"Just doing my job, sir," Corporal Bradley said.

D'Allessando's eyebrow rose but he didn't say anything.

"And when Bradley was popping these people with Seymour's rifle, where was Seymour?"

"Getting himself garroted," Castillo said, softly.

"No shit? How the hell did that happen? Kranz was no amateur."

"Neither, obviously, were the bad guys. It was a stainless steel garrote, with handles."

"Well, who the hell were they?"

"I don't know, Vic. There ensued a brief exchange of small-arms fire, during which three more of the bad guys met their fate. Kensington found the last of them, number six, lying on the ground near Kranz. Seymour had gotten a knife into him before going down."

"And Kensington finished him off?"

Castillo nodded.

"Understandable—those two went way back together—but inexcusable. He should have remembered that dead people don't talk much."

"I mentioned that to him," Castillo said.

"So you hauled your ass out of wherever you were?"

"After Kensington took a 9mm bullet out of the ex-SIDE guy."

"And what was in the safe?"

"An address book and withdrawal slips for the money Lorimer had squirreled away in Uruguayan banks."

"You got the money? What did you say, sixteen million?"

"I think we should have it first thing in the morning."

"And what's in the address book?"

"It's in code. It'll be at Fort Meade at eight this morning. When they do their thing, I'll be able to have a good look. Anyway, we got the hell out of there and the hell out of South America."

"Seymour? You didn't leave him there?"

"We left Lorimer and the six bad guys there—no identification on any of them—and dropped Kranz off at MacDill on the way to Washington."

"And then you came here. Why?"

"I wanted your opinion, Vic."

"Well, that's a first."

"Mrs. Masterson told me the bad guys wanted Lorimer and that was why they executed Masterson, to make the point they were willing to kill to find him. Well, he's been found. The bad guys are going to hear that he's dead. Does that remove the threat from the Masterson family?"

"Unless the bad guys really want their sixteen million back."

"We don't know that it's the bad guys' sixteen million. Or that they know we have it. They may have been after Lorimer just to shut him up. . . ."

"Or both," D'Allessando said. "Whack him *and* get their money back."

"Or both," Castillo admitted. "Anything happen here to suggest they're watching her?"

"Not a thing. We have taps on all the phones, including the cellulars. Nothing. And no tourists at the plantation, either."

"I'd like to tell her I think the threat is gone."

"And I'd like to take my guys back to the stockade," D'Allessando said. "They're getting a little antsy. I didn't tell them why they're here, and they're starting to think of themselves as babysitters. Thank God the widow—and Masterson's father—are such good people."

What had once been the military prison—the stockade—at Fort Bragg now held the barracks and headquarters of Delta Force, the elite, immediate-response Special Forces unit. The same barbed wire that had kept prisoners in now kept people without the proper clearances out.

"How're you doing with people from China Post?"

Many former Special Forces soldiers, Marine Force Recon, Navy SEALs, Air Commandos, and other warriors of this ilk belong to China Post 1 in exile (from Shanghai) of the American Legion. Those wishing to employ this sort of people in a civilian capacity often have luck finding just what they want at "China Post."

"I guess you know General McNab called them?"

Castillo nodded. "He told me he was going to."

"That helped. I've got eight guys, good guys—I guess they're getting a little tired of commuting to Iraq and Afghanistan—lined up. They're going to be expensive, but Masterson said that wasn't a problem."

"It's not. How soon can they be up and running?"

"Forty-eight hours, tops, and they'll be on the job."

"I want to run this whole thing past Masterson—and the widow—but I don't think they'll object. How about first thing in the morning getting that going?"

"This is first thing in the morning."

Castillo looked at his watch. "Half past four, which means it's half past ten in Germany. Which brings me to this."

He walked to the bar, picked up a telephone, and punched in a long series of numbers from memory.

[FOUR]
Executive Offices
Gossinger Beteiligungsgesellschaft, G.m.b.H.
Fulda, Hesse, Germany
1029 2 August 2005

Frau Gertrud Schröder, a stocky sixty-year-old who wore her blond hair in a bun, put her head in the office door of Otto Görner, the managing director of Gossinger Beteiligungsgesellschaft, G.m.b.H. She had on a wireless headset.

"Karlchen is favoring you with a call," she announced, her hand covering the microphone.

"How kind of him," Görner replied. He was a well-tailored sixty-year-old Hessian whose bulk and red cheeks made him look like a postcard Bavarian. As he reached for one of the telephones on his desk, he added, "Well, at least he's alive."

Frau Schröder walked to the desk and Görner waved her into a chair opposite him.

"And how are things in South America?" Görner said into the handset.

"I have no idea, I'm in Mississippi. And I'm fine. Thank you for asking."

"May I ask what you're doing in Mississippi?"

"I'm in Penthouse C of the Belle Vista Casino in Biloxi about to have steak and eggs for breakfast."

"Why do I suspect that for once you're telling me the truth?"

"But speaking of South America, you might take a look at the Reuters and AP wires from Uruguay starting about now."

"Really?"

"I think both you and Eric Kocian might be interested in what might come over the wire."

"Well, I'll keep an eye out, if you say so."

"It might be a good idea."

"Is that why you called, Karl, or is there something else on your mind?"

"Actually, there is. How much trouble would it be for Frau Schröder to open a bank account for me in the Liechtensteinische Landesbank in the Cayman Islands?"

"Why would you want to do something like that?"

"And put, say, ten thousand euros in it?"

"Why would you want to do something like that?" Görner asked again.

"I've always been frugal. You know that, Otto. 'A penny saved,' as Benjamin Franklin said, 'is a penny earned.' "

"Gott!"

Frau Schröder shook her head and smiled. Görner gave her a dirty look.

"And tell them to expect a rather large transfer of funds into the account in the next few days, please," Castillo said.

"I really hate to ask this question, but didn't you just say you're in the penthouse of a casino?"

"In the Belle Vista Casino."

"And did you put the penthouse on the *Tages Zeitung*'s American Express card?"

"No. Actually, I'm staying here free."

"How much did you lose to get them to give you a free room? A penthouse suite?"

"Why do you think I lost?"

Görner exhaled audibly.

"When do you want this bank account opened?"

"How about today?"

"If you're telling the truth—and I would be surprised if you are—and you're trying to hide money from the IRS, you're probably going to get caught."

"Thank you for your concern. Just have Frau Schröder open the account and e-mail me the number so I can make a deposit. I'll worry about getting the money out later."

"All right, Karl. But I wish I really knew what you're up to this time."

"I'll tell you the next time I see you."

"And when will that be?"

"Maybe soon. I'm going from here to see my grandmother and then I'll probably come over there."

"I hope I can believe that."

"Tell Frau Schröder thanks, Otto. I've got to run."

The line went dead.

Görner put the handset in the cradle and Frau Schröder took off her headset.

"I wonder what that's all about?" he asked.

"Gambling? I never knew of his gambling."

"Not with money," Görner said. "The last I heard, when he was in Budapest with Eric and me, he was going—they were all going—to Argentina."

"I wonder what we're supposed to find on the South American wires?"

"He said 'Uruguay' wires."

"I wonder what we're supposed to find on the 'Uruguay' wires?"

Görner shrugged.

"Is there going to be any trouble with opening that account? Don't we have some money in the Liechtensteinische Landesbank?"

"Quite a bit, actually," she said. "I'll send them a wire and have them open an account for him. Shouldn't be any trouble at all." She paused. "The question is, though, in whose name do I open it?"

"I think we're supposed to cleverly deduce who he is right now."

"Shall I try to get him back and ask him?"

Görner thought that over for a moment and then said, "No. Open it for Karl W. Gossinger. That'll raise fewer questions than if we opened it for Carlos Castillo."

[FIVE]
Penthouse C
The Belle Vista Casino and Resort
U.S. Highway 90 ("The Magic Mile")
Biloxi, Mississippi
0835 2 August 2005

Vic D'Allessando, smiling and shaking his head, pointed to Corporal Lester Bradley, USMC, who was sitting sound asleep in an armchair.

Castillo smiled and then motioned for D'Allessando to go into the bedroom. He followed him in and closed the door.

"Jesus Christ, he's just a kid," D'Allessando said. "You going to tell me what he's doing here?"

"I didn't know what else to do with him," Castillo said.

"Meaning?"

"He's seen too much, he's heard too much, he's done too much. He's either eighteen or nineteen and I wonder if he can keep his mouth shut."

"Oh," D'Allessando said.

"I couldn't leave him in Buenos Aires," Castillo went on. "He's in the Marine Guard detachment at the embassy. I think he was the clerk. The detachment is run by a gunnery sergeant—good guy—but a gunnery sergeant who's going to ask, the moment he sees him, 'Lester, my boy, where have you been and what have you been doing?'"

"Yeah," D'Allessando agreed.

"As a rule of thumb, Marine corporals, when a gunny asks a question, answer it," Castillo said.

"Even if some Army major has told them to keep their mouth shut," D'Allessando said. "And since you can't have the gunny knowing what went down. . . . You have a problem, Charley."

"Yeah, compounded by the fact that Bradley not only saved my bacon but I really like him."

"Isn't his gunny going to wonder where the hell he is?"

"I told Alex Darby to tell the ambassador I exfiltrated Bradley with us. That'll hold off the gunny for a couple of days, but even if the ambassador and Darby tell the gunny not to get curious he will."

"So get him out from under the gunny. Get him transferred out. Can you do that?"

"Get him transferred where? 'Welcome to Camp Lejeune, Corporal Bradley. Where have you been, what have you been doing, and why have you suddenly been transferred here? What do you mean you can't tell me, it's classified Top Secret Presidential'?"

"Yeah," D'Allessando agreed again, chuckling. "Okay, stash him at Bragg. Call McNab and tell him the problem."

"A Marine corporal would stand out like a sore thumb at the Special Warfare Center."

"Not necessarily," D'Allessando said. "There's been some talk about taking some Marines—a lot of Marines, two or three thousand—into Special Operations. Another of Schoomaker's brainstorms, I think."

General Peter J. Schoomaker was chief of staff of the U.S. Army.

"Schoomaker's one of us, Vic," Castillo said.

"Yeah, I know. I knew him then, too. I was the armorer on his A-Team. Good guy. I wasn't saying it's a bad idea, just where I think it came from. Anyway, what they're doing right now is running some Marines—mostly from their Force Recon—through the Q course. So they can tell us what we're doing wrong, I guess. Anyway, we can stash the kid with them."

"Where Corporal Bradley would stand out like a sore thumb among the hardy warriors of Marine Force Recon," Castillo said. He chuckled. "Most of them have gone through that SEAL bodybuilding course on the West Coast and look like Arnold Schwarzenegger."

"That's my best shot, Charley. Take it or leave it."

"I'll take it. I'll call General McNab."

"I'll deal with McNab. Just leave the kid here with me. There will be a Special Ops King Air here around noon. I'll put him on it and it'll take him to Bragg."

"Thanks, Vic."

As they were walking out of the bedroom, there was a melodious chime and Vic D'Allessando walked to the door and pulled it open.

"Good morning, Mr. Masterson," he said. "Come on in."

"I'm sorry to be late," J. Winslow Masterson said. "It was unavoidable."

He was a very tall, very black sharp-featured man wearing a crisp, beautifully tailored off-white linen suit. He held a panama hat in his hand.

Castillo smiled as what his grandfather had said about linen suits—or, rather, about seersucker suits—popped into his memory: *The reason I wear seersucker suits is, they come from the tailor mussed and people expect that. When I put on a linen suit, it's mussed in ten minutes and people come up to me sure that I know where they can find dope or whores or both.*

"You're smiling, Charley," Masterson said, crossing the room with large strides to put out his hand. "There must be good news."

Castillo was finally able to get off the couch.

"Actually, sir, when I saw that beautiful suit I thought of something my grandfather said."

"I'd love to hear it," Masterson said.

Charley repeated his grandfather's trenchant comment.

Masterson laughed.

"Your grandfather had a way with words," he said. "Did you ever tell Mr. D'Allessando about Lyndon Johnson?"

"No, sir."

"Mr. Castillo had a magnificent bull registered as Lyndon Johnson. The animal, from the time it was a calf, had eaten heartily and therefore had droppings far above average. . . ."

"No kidding?" D'Allessando said, laughing. "I didn't know you knew Charley's grandfather."

"Not as well as I would have liked," Masterson said. He looked expectantly at Castillo.

"Yes, sir. I have news. Whether it's good or not is a tough call."

"May I help myself to your coffee?" Masterson asked.

"Oh, hell, excuse me," D'Allessando said. "Let me get it for you."

"I'm old but I can still pour my own coffee, thank you just the same."

As he walked to the wet bar, Masterson saw Corporal Lester Bradley for the first time. Bradley was dozing in an armchair. Masterson looked curiously at Castillo.

"That's Corporal Bradley of the Marine Corps, sir," Castillo said.

That woke Bradley up. He erupted from the armchair, saw Masterson, and quickly came to attention.

D'Allessando smiled and shook his head.

"At ease, Corporal," Castillo said. "This is Mr. Masterson's father, Bradley."

"Yes, sir," Bradley said.

"Bradley was involved in the protection of the family in Buenos Aires," Castillo said.

"How do you do, Corporal?" Masterson said, advancing on Bradley with his hand extended. "I'm very pleased to meet you."

God, he's really a gentleman, Castillo thought. *You'd never know from his face that's he's wondering what this boy could possibly have been doing on a protection detail. What he's doing is putting him at ease. That's class.*

"How do you do, sir?" Bradley said.

"Please, sit down," Masterson said.

Bradley looked at Castillo, who signaled for him to sit down.

Castillo waited until Masterson had poured the coffee.

"Sir," he began, "the President has authorized me to tell you and Mrs. Masterson anything I think I should. I'll tell you what I know and you can tell me how much I should tell her."

"Whatever you say."

"And I have to tell you, sir, that this is highly classified and is to go no further than yourself and Mrs. Masterson."

"There are two ladies so identified," Masterson said.

"I will trust your judgment with regard to both. And as far as that goes, with regard to Ambassador and Mrs. Lorimer."

"Thank you."

"Jean-Paul Lorimer," Castillo reported, "was shot to death by parties unknown at approximately 9:20 p.m. local time, 31 July, in Tacuarembó, Uruguay."

Masterson's eyebrows rose.

"You're sure of this?" Masterson said.

"Yes, sir, I was there," Castillo said. "As was Corporal Bradley. Bradley took out the men who killed Mr. Lorimer."

That got Masterson's attention. He looked first in uncontrollable surprise at Bradley and then shifted his curious look to Castillo. There was a question in his eyes. It hung in the air but was not asked.

"Mr. Masterson," Castillo said, carefully, "once I located Mr. Lorimer, it was my intention to repatriate him—willingly or otherwise. I had just identified myself to him when he was shot."

"I have two questions," Masterson said. "Who shot him? And what was he doing in Uruguay?"

"I have no idea who shot him. Every one of them—there were six men in the group who attacked us—were killed by my people. As to what he was doing in Uruguay, I believe he was trying to establish a new identity. Actually, he had established one. He had a Lebanese passport in the name of Jean-Paul Bertrand. He was legally—as Bertrand—a resident in Uruguay, where people believed he was a successful antiquities dealer."

"Antiquities dealer? Can you tell me—I have the feeling you know—why he was doing something like that?"

"Apparently, he was involved with the Iraqi oil-for-food scandal. Specifically, I believe, as *the* paymaster. He knew who got how much money, and when and what for. That could have been the reason he was killed. Additionally, I believe he skimmed some of the payoff money. He had almost sixteen million dollars in several bank accounts in Uruguay. He may have been killed as punishment for stealing the money."

"One is not supposed to speak ill of the dead," Masterson said, "but that explains a good deal. Greed would motivate Jean-Paul. Coupled with the delusion that he was smarter than those from whom he was stealing, that would give him motivation sufficient to overcome his natural timidity."

"I can't argue with that, sir, but I just don't know why he did what he did."

"How did you find him? And so quickly?"

"Good question, Charley," D'Allessando said.

Castillo flashed him a dirty look, then said, "I don't mean to sound flippant, but I got lucky."

"And the money? What happens to that money? Sixteen million, you said?"

"Yes, sir. We have it."

"Does anyone—everyone—know you have it?"

"No, sir."

"What are you going to do with it? Jesus! *Sixteen million!*" D'Allessando said, earning him another dirty look from Castillo.

"Mr. Masterson, do you remember me telling you the day we came here that the President had ordered Ambassador Montvale, and the attorney general, and the secretaries of state and Homeland Security—everybody—to give me whatever I needed to track down Mr. Masterson's murderers?"

Masterson nodded.

"That was the truth, but it wasn't the whole truth. In fact—and this carries the security classification of Top Secret Presidential, and, if I somehow can, I'd rather not make Mrs. Masterson privy to this—"

"I understand," Masterson interjected.

"In fact, there has been a Presidential Finding, in which the President set up a covert and clandestine organization charged with locating and rendering harmless those people responsible for the murders of Mr. Masterson and Sergeant Markham."

" 'Rendering harmless'? Is that something like the 'terminating with extreme prejudice' of the Vietnam era?"

"Just about," D'Allessando said.

"I would rather not answer that, sir," Castillo said.

"I understand. And who—if you can't answer, I'll understand—is running this 'covert and clandestine' organization? Ambassador Montvale? The CIA?"

"I am, sir. And that's something else I would rather not tell Mrs. Masterson."

Masterson nodded and pursed his lips thoughtfully.

"The money will be used to fund that activity, sir," Castillo said.

"Is that what they call poetic justice?" Masterson said. "A moment ago, I was worried about Ambassador Lorimer. . . ."

"Sir?"

"Jean-Paul's only blood kin are his parents and Betsy. That means unless he left a will bequeathing his earthly possessions to some Parisian tootsie, which I don't think is likely, they are his heirs. The ambassador would know there was no way Jean-Paul could have honestly accrued that much money. That would have been difficult for him. And God knows Betsy doesn't need it—and, of course, would not want it."

"Sir, Mr. Lorimer owned—and I don't think it was mortgaged—a large estancia—a farm—in Uruguay. And he owned—I know he owned—a nice apartment on rue Monsieur in the VII Arrondisement in Paris."

"Well, he lived in Paris, therefore he needed a place to live. Many people take insurance to pay off the mortgage on their apartments on their death. The same argument could be presented to the ambassador vis-à-vis the farm in Uruguay, which Jean-Paul could have acquired in anticipation of his ultimate retirement. The question is, how do we explain to the ambassador the circumstances of Jean-Paul's death?"

"That's what they call a multiple-part question," Castillo said. "Let me try to explain what we have. By now the local police in Tacuarembó have found out what happened. The question is, *what* have they found out?"

He let that sink in, then continued:

"We plastic-cuffed and blindfolded the servants that were in the house." He paused. "One of these was a young Uruguayan girl with whom Mr. Lorimer apparently had a close relationship."

He waited until he saw understanding and what could have been contempt in Masterson's eyes and then went on.

"We put her—and the estancia manager and his wife—to sleep. A safe narcotic, administered by someone who knew what he was doing.

"Now, everybody saw who did the cuffing: Spanish-speaking masked men wearing balaclava masks. You remember when the Alcohol, Firearms and Tobacco agents 'rescued' the Cuban boy in Miami? Their black ski masks?"

Masterson nodded. His face showed his contempt for that act.

"And everybody was wearing what are essentially black coveralls. That description will be reported to the police. When the police arrive—and by now they almost certainly have—they will have found six men in dark blue, nearly black coveralls. But no masks. Which poses a problem. . . ."

"Six *dead* men in coveralls," Masterson said.

"Yes, sir. Plus Mr. Lorimer, who they will have found lying on his office floor next to his safe. There are no valuables in the safe. The best possible scenario is that they will suspect a robbery by the same people who cuffed and needled the servants."

"But they're now dead?" Masterson said.

"Shot treacherously by one or more of their number so that whatever was stolen would not have to be split in so many shares," Castillo said.

"The local police won't know—or suspect—that someone else—you and your people—were there?"

"Well, we hope not," Castillo said. "There is a history of that kind of robbery—of isolated estancias—in Uruguay and Argentina. And Mr. Lorimer/Bertrand, a wealthy businessman, meets the profile of the sort of people robbed."

"You . . . left nothing behind that can place you there?"

"The only thing we know of—which is not saying I didn't screw up somewhere and they'll find something else—is blood."

"I don't understand," Masterson said.

"When we were bushwhacked by these people, we took casualties," Castillo said. "One was one of my men, who was garroted, and the other was an Argentine who was helping us. He lived, but he bled a lot."

"The guy the bastards got was a sergeant first class named Seymour Kranz," D'Allessando said. "Good guy. No amateur. Which makes me really wonder who these bad guys are."

"I'll get to that later, Vic," Castillo said.

"Do I correctly infer that the sergeant did not live?"

"Yes, sir."

"I'm really sorry to hear that. What happened to his body?"

"We exfiltrated it with us," Castillo said. "Now here the scenario gets very hopeful. If American police were investigating a crime like this, they would subject the blood to a number of tests. They would match blood to bodies, among other things. I'm hoping the police in rural Uruguay are not going to be so thorough; that they won't come up with a blood sample, or samples, that don't match the bodies."

"My God, seven bodies is a massacre. They won't ask for help from—what?—the Uruguayan equivalent of the FBI? A police organization that will be thorough?"

"I'm counting on that, sir. That's how it will be learned that Mr. Bertrand is really Mr. Lorimer."

"How will that happen?"

"Mr. Lorimer had a photo album, sir. One of the photographs was of Mr. Masterson's wedding. The wedding party is standing in front of a church—"

"Cathedral," Masterson corrected him. "Saint Louis Cathedral, on Jackson Square in New Orleans. Jack and Betsy were married there."

"The whole family—including Mr. Lorimer—is in the photo, sir. I'm almost sure that a senior police officer from Montevideo will recognize Mr. Masterson. Maybe even one of the local cops will. Mr. Masterson's murder was big news down there. It's what the police call a 'lead.' I can't believe they won't follow it up, and that will result in the identification of Mr. Bertrand. If they somehow get the photo to the embassy in Buenos Aires, a man there—actually, the CIA station chief who was in on the operation—is prepared to identify the man in the photo as Mr. Lorimer. He knew him in Paris."

"If the police are as inept as you suggest—and you're probably right—what makes you think they'll find, much less leaf through, Jean-Paul's photo album?"

"Because I left it open on Mr. Lorimer's desk, sir."

"You're very good at this sort of thing, aren't you?" Masterson said.

"No, sir, I'm not. There is a vulgar saying in the Army that really applies."

"And that is?"

Castillo hesitated a moment, then said: "'I'm up way over my ears in the deep shit and I don't know how to swim.'"

"Oh, horseshit, Charley," D'Allessando said. "You and I go back a long way. I know better."

"I agree that it's vulgar," Masterson said. "But I don't agree at all that it applies. You seem to have been born for duties like these and Mr. D'Allessando obviously agrees with me."

"Mr. Masterson, when I went to West Point what I wanted to do with my life was be what my father was, an Army aviator. At least twice a day, I curse the fickle finger of fate that kept me from doing that."

D'Allessando said, "The fickle finger's name, Charley, as you damned well know, is Lieutenant General Bruce J. McNab."

Masterson looked between them.

"The first time I ever saw Charley, Mr. Masterson, he was a bushy-tailed second lieutenant fresh from West Point. It was during the first desert war. General McNab—that was just before he got his first star, right, Charley?"

Castillo nodded.

"*Colonel* McNab, who was running Special Ops in that war, had spotted Charley, recognized him as a kindred soul, rescued him from what he was doing—probably flying cargo missions in a Huey; he wasn't old enough to be out of flight school long enough to fly anything else—and put him to work as his personal pilot."

"If we've reached the end of memory lane, Vic," Castillo said, "I would like to get on with this."

D'Allessando held up both hands in a gesture of surrender.

"Well, as a father," Masterson said, "I'm sure that your father is proud of what you do. He does know?"

"No, sir. My father died in Vietnam."

"I'm sorry, Charley," Masterson said. "I had no way of knowing."

"Thank you, sir. If I may go on?"

"Please."

"Once Mr. Lorimer is identified, there's a number of possibilities. For one thing, he was both an American citizen and a UN diplomat. God only knows what the UN will do when they find out he was murdered in Uruguay. We don't know what the UN knows about Mr. Lorimer's involvement with the oil-for-food business, but I'm damned sure a number of people in the UN do.

"They will obviously want to sweep this under the diplomatic rug. By slightly bending the facts—they can say Lorimer was on leave, somehow the paperwork got lost when we were looking for him to tell him about his sister getting kidnapped, and then about Mr. Masterson being murdered—they can issue a statement of shock and regret that he was killed by robbers on his estancia."

"Yeah," D'Allessando said, thoughtfully.

"Once it is established that Bertrand is, in fact, Lorimer, an American citizen, our embassy in Montevideo can get in the act. For repatriation of the remains, for one thing, and to take control of his property temporarily, pending the designation of someone—kin or somebody else—to do that. Which brings me to that.

"Do you think Ambassador Lorimer would be willing to designate someone to do that? The someone I have in mind is an FBI agent in Montevideo, who was in on the operation. Give him what would amount to power of attorney, in other words? I'd really like to really go through the estancia and see what can be found."

"I don't think he would have any problem with that. I don't think he would want to—in his condition—go there himself, nor do I think his wife or physician would permit it."

"And the same thing for the apartment in Paris?"

"I think so. Now that I have had a chance to think it over, they'd be pleased. Perhaps I can suggest it was offered as a courtesy to a fellow diplomat."

"The sooner that could be done, the better. Of course, we have to wait until the scenario I described unfolds. If it does."

"It'll work, Charley," D'Allessando said. "You've got all the angles covered."

"You never have all the angles covered, Vic, and you know it," Castillo said and then turned to Masterson. "This now brings us to the bad guys."

"I'm not sure I know what you mean," Masterson confessed. "We don't even know who they are, do we?"

"No, sir, we don't. I intend to do my best to find out who they are."

"And 'render them harmless'?" Masterson asked, softly.

Castillo nodded slightly but did not respond directly.

"What they did was find Mr. Lorimer, which among other things they've done suggests that they're professionals. And what they did was send an assault team to the estancia. I think it's logical to assume they wanted to make sure he didn't talk about what he knows of the oil-for-food business and possibly to get back the money he skimmed.

"By now, they have certainly learned that their operation succeeded only in taking out Mr. Lorimer. And that somebody took out their assault team. And they will have to presume the same people who took out their assault team have what was in the safe: money or information. They don't know who we are— we could be someone else trying to shut Lorimer up, somebody after the money, or Uruguayan bandits. I don't think it's likely that they'll think an American Special Operations team was involved, but they might.

"I think it's likely the people who bushwhacked us are the same people who killed Mr. Masterson, but of course I can't be sure. But if they are—or even if it's a second group—and they are professional, I think the decision will be to go to ground.

"They may be capable of—it wouldn't surprise me—of keeping an eye on her bank accounts, or yours, to see if they suddenly get sixteen million dollars heavier. But that's not going to happen.

"What I'm driving at is there is no longer a reason for them to try to get to Mrs. Masterson or the children. Lorimer is out of the picture and she has nothing they want to give them."

"You think we can remove Mr. D'Allessando's people, is that what you're saying?" Masterson asked.

"Well, they can't stay indefinitely," Castillo said. "And Vic tells me he's run the retired special operators from China Post past you."

"Very impressive," Masterson said.

"And very expensive?" Castillo asked.

"Uh-huh," Masterson said. "But what I was thinking was that the children—for that matter, Betsy, too—would probably be more at ease with them than they are now with all of Mr. D'Allessando's people. They must have grown used to private security people in Buenos Aires."

"The people I brought over here are good, Mr. Masterson," D'Allessando said. "And, frankly, a job like this is better than commuting to Iraq or Afghanistan, which is what they've all been doing."

"Okay, so that's what I'll recommend to Betsy," Masterson said. "When do you want to talk to her, Charley?"

"Now, if possible, sir. I'm on my way to Texas. I want to see my grandmother, and I can be with her only until they call me to tell me what's happened in Uruguay."

"I'll get her on the phone," Masterson said as he reached for it. "And I'll get you a car to take you to the airport."

"That's not necessary, sir."

"Biloxi? Or New Orleans?" Masterson asked.

"New Orleans, sir."

III

[ONE]
Office of the Legal Attaché
The Embassy of the United States of America
Lauro Miller 1776
Montevideo, República Oriental del Uruguay
1150 2 August 2005

The telephone on the desk of Assistant Legal Attaché Julio Artigas buzzed and one of the six buttons on it began to flash.

Artigas, a slim, olive-skinned Cuban American of thirty, who had been a

Special Agent of the Federal Bureau of Investigation for eight years and assigned to the Montevideo embassy for three, picked up the handset.

"Artigas."

"Julio, this is your cousin José," his caller said in Spanish.

Thirty-seven-year-old Chief Inspector José Ordóñez, of the Interior Police Division of the Uruguayan Policía Nacional, was not related to Julio Artigas, but they looked very much alike. They had several times been mistaken for brothers. That wasn't possible without the same surname, but it could have been possible for cousins, and cousins they had become. They also shared a sense of humor.

"And how goes your unrelenting campaign against evil, Cousin José?" Julio replied. He had arrived in Uruguay speaking Cuban-inflected Spanish fluently, and with only a little effort he had acquired a Uruguayan inflection. Many Uruguayans were surprised to learn he was not a native son.

"I would hope a little better than yours," José said. "How about lunch?"

"Is that an invitation? Or have you been giving your salary away at the blackjack tables again?"

"I will pay," José said. "I will put you on my expense sheet."

"Oh?"

"I hope you have, or can make, your afternoon free."

"If you are paying, my entire week is free."

"You are so kind."

"Where shall we meet? Someplace expensive, of course."

"I'm at the port. How about something from a *parrilla*?"

"Great minds travel similar paths. When?"

"Now?"

"Get out your wallet."

Artigas hung up. He opened a drawer in his desk, took from it a .38 caliber Smith & Wesson "Detective Special" revolver, then slipped the gun into a skeleton holster on his hip.

The pistol was his. It was smaller and lighter than the semiautomatic pistol prescribed for—and issued to—FBI agents, and, technically, he was violating at least four FBI regulations by carrying it.

But this was Montevideo, where his chances of ever needing a pistol ranged from very slight to none. Many of Artigas's peers simply went unarmed. The primary mission of the FBI in Uruguay was the investigation of money laundering.

It was a different story for the DEA guys, who often found themselves in hairy situations. While not necessarily successful in stopping the drug flow, they were very successful in costing the drug merchants lots of money and consequently were unpopular with the drug establishment. They went around heavily armed.

Artigas had chosen the middle ground. While it is true that you never need a pistol until you really need one, it was equally true there is no sense carrying a large and hard-to-conceal cannon when a less conspicuous means of self-defense is available.

Artigas walked across the large, open room to the open door of a glass-walled cubicle that was the office of Special Agent James D. Monahan, who was because of his seniority the de facto, if not the de jure, SAC, or Special Agent in Charge, and waited for him to get off the phone.

"Something, Artigas?" Monahan asked, finally.

"I have just been invited to lunch by Chief Inspector Ordóñez."

"Shit, I was hoping you were going to tell me you know where the hell Yung is."

FBI Special Agent David W. Yung, Jr., a fellow assistant legal attaché, was not held in high regard by his peers. He came to work late—or not at all—and left early. His research into Uruguayan bank records produced about half the useful information that came from the next least efficient of the others. And since he was still here—despite several informal complaints about his performance and back-channel suggestions that he be reassigned to the States—it was pretty clear he had friends in high places.

Another, less flattering rumor had it that Yung had been sort of banished to Uruguay because of his association with Howard Kennedy, the former Ethical Standards Division hotshot who had changed sides and was now working for some Russian mafioso. That rumor had some credence, as it was known that Yung had been assigned to the Ethical Standards Division.

It is a fact of life that people without friends in high places tend to dislike those who have them and that FBI agents do not like FBI agents whose personal integrity is open to question.

"Maybe still asleep?" Artigas asked. "It's not quite noon."

"I let his goddamned phone ring for five minutes. That sonofabitch!" Monahan paused. "Ordóñez say what he wanted?"

"Only that he hoped I could make my afternoon free."

"*Et tu*, Artigas?"

"He's got something on his mind, Jim," Artigas said.

"Ride it out," Monahan said. "But if you happen to run into Yung in a bar or a casino somewhere, would you please tell him that I would be grateful for a moment of his valuable time whenever it's convenient?"

"I will do that."

Artigas went out the front entrance of the embassy, found his car—a blue Chrysler PT Cruiser—got in, and drove to the gate.

The embassy, a four-story, oblong concrete edifice decorated with two huge satellite antennae on the roof, sits in the center of a well-protected compound overlooking the river Plate.

A heavy steel gate, painted light blue, is controlled by pistol-armed Uruguayan security guards wearing police-style uniforms. For reasons Artigas never understood, cars leaving the compound are subjected to just about as close scrutiny as those coming into the compound.

He waited patiently while security guards looked into the interior of the PT Cruiser, looked under it using a mirror mounted on the end of a long pole, and then checked his embassy identification before throwing the switch that caused the gate to slide open sideways.

He drove a hundred yards toward the water and then turned right on the Rambla, the road that runs along the coast from the port to the suburb of Carrasco where many embassy officers lived, including Artigas and the again-missing Yung.

Five minutes later, he pulled the nose of the PT Cruiser to the curb in front of what had been built sometime in the late nineteenth century to house cattle being shipped from the port. It now housed a dozen or more *parrilla* restaurants and at least that many bars.

He got a very dirty look from the woman charged with collecting parking fees on that section of the street. She had seen the diplomatic license plates on the car. Diplomats are permitted to park wherever they wish to park without paying.

In the interests of Uruguayan-American relations, Artigas handed her a fifty-peso note, worth a little less than two dollars U.S., and earned himself a warm smile.

He entered the building. With the exception of one or two women Julio could think of, there was in his judgment no better smell in the world than that of beef—and, for that matter, chicken and pork and a lot else—being grilled over the ashes of a wood fire.

As he walked to where he knew Ordóñez would meet him—one of the smaller, more expensive restaurants in the back of the old building—his mouth actually watered.

Chief Inspector Ordóñez was waiting for him and stood up when he saw Artigas coming.

They embraced and kissed in the manner of Latin males and then sat down at the small table. There was a bottle of wine on the table, a bottle of carbonated water, four stemmed glasses, a wicker basket holding a variety of bread and breadsticks, a small plate of butter curls, and a small dish of chicken liver pâté.

José poured wine for Julio and they touched glasses.

"There must be something on your mind," Julio said. "This is the good Merlot."

"How about seven males, six of them dressed in black, shot to death?"

Artigas thought: *I don't think he's kidding.*

He took a sip of the Merlot, then spread liver pâté on a chunk of hard-crusted bread and waited for Ordóñez to go on.

"You don't seem surprised," José said.

"I'm an FBI agent. We try to be inscrutable."

A waiter appeared.

Julio ordered a blue cheese empanada, *bife chorizo* medium rare, *papas fritas,* and an onion-and-tomato salad.

José held up two fingers, signaling the waiter he'd have the same.

"And where are these deceased Ninja warriors?" Julio asked.

José chuckled.

"On an estancia—called Shangri-La—near Tacuarembó."

Julio signaled with a quick shake of his head that he had no idea where Tacuarembó was.

"It's about three hundred sixty kilometers due north," José said. "On Highway 5." He paused. "I was hoping you might go up there with me."

"That's a long ride."

"Less long in a helicopter."

Julio knew the use of rotary-wing aircraft by Uruguayan police was not common, even for the movement of very senior officers.

"Am I being invited as a friend or officially?" Julio said.

"Why don't we decide that after we have a look around Estancia Shangri-La?" José replied.

"Okay." Julio paused. "Tell me, Cousin, would I happen to know—or even have met—the owner of Estancia Shangri-La?"

"You tell me. He is—was—a Lebanese dealer in antiquities by the name of Jean-Paul Bertrand."

Julio shook his head and asked, "And had you a professional interest in Señor . . . what was his name?"

"Jean-Paul Bertrand," José furnished.

". . . *Bertrand* before he was killed?"

José shook his head. "He was as clean as a whistle, so far as I have been able to determine."

The waiter returned with their empanadas, and they cut off their conversation. They might have returned to it had not two strikingly beautiful young women come in the restaurant.

They didn't hurry their lunch, but they didn't dawdle over it, either. Twenty-five minutes after Julio had taken his first sip of the Merlot, the bottle was empty and José was settling the bill with the waiter.

When they left the former cattle shed, they walked across the street to the Navy base. Julio saw—with some surprise—that the helicopter waiting for them was not one of the somewhat battered Policía Nacional's Bell Hueys he expected but a glistening Aerospatiale Dauphin. The pilot was a Navy officer. Julio suspected it was the Uruguayan president's personal helicopter.

That meant, obviously, that someone high in the Uruguayan government— perhaps even the president himself—considered what had happened at Estancia Shangri-La very important.

[TWO]
Estancia Shangri-La
Tacuarembó Province
República Oriental del Uruguay
1405 2 August 2005

As the Dauphin fluttered down onto a field, Julio saw that there were a dozen police vehicles and two ambulances parked unevenly around the main building of the estancia and that there were twenty-five or thirty people—many in police uniform—milling about.

Julio had an unkind thought: *Well, so much for preserving the crime scene.*

Two portly senior police officers walked warily toward the helicopter. Both saluted Chief Inspector Ordóñez as he stepped down from the chopper. He returned their salutes with a casual wave of his hand. Julio remembered seeing him in uniform only once, when Fidel Castro, a year or so before, had come to Montevideo and Ordóñez had been head of the protection detail.

"This is Señor Artigas," Chief Inspector Ordóñez said. "You will answer any questions he puts to you."

Both of the policemen saluted. Julio responded with a nod and offered them his hand.

"I ordered that nothing be touched?" Ordóñez questioned.

"We have covered the bodies, Chief Inspector, but everything else is exactly as it was when we first came here."

Ordóñez met Artigas's eyes. It was clear to both they were thinking exactly the same thing: *The curious had satisfied their curiosity. The crime scene had been trampled beyond use.*

Ordóñez gestured with his hand that he be shown.

There were two bodies on a covered veranda. They were covered with heavy black plastic sheeting. Artigas wondered if that was the local version of a body bag or whether the sheeting had just been available and put to use.

A large pool of blood, now dried black, had escaped the plastic over the first body. When, at Ordóñez's impatient gesture, the plastic sheeting was pulled aside, the reason was clear. This man had died of a gunshot wound to the head. There is a great deal of blood in the head.

And not a pistol round, either, I don't think. His head had exploded.

The body was dressed in dark blue, almost black, cotton coveralls, the sort worn by mechanics.

What looked like the barrel of a submachine gun was visible in the pool of dried blood. The dead man had fallen on his weapon.

Artigas felt a gentle touch on his arm and looked down to see that Ordóñez was handing him disposable rubber gloves.

"This has been photographed?" Ordóñez asked.

"Yes, Chief Inspector, from many angles."

Ordóñez squatted and pulled the weapon out from under the body. It *was* a submachine gun, its stock folded. He held it out for Artigas to see.

"Madsen, right?" he asked.

"Yes," Artigas said. "That's the 9mm, I think."

Ordóñez raised the barrel so that he could see the muzzle, then nodded.

Artigas looked around and saw a glint in the grass just beyond the veranda. He walked to it. It was a cartridge case.

"Have you got a position on this? And photographs?"

"My sergeant must have missed that, señor," the heftier of the two local police supervisors said and angrily called for the sergeant.

When Artigas went back on the veranda he saw that Ordóñez had replaced the black plastic over the body and had moved ten meters down the veranda, where another police officer was pulling the plastic off another body. This one, too, was dressed in nearly black coveralls.

Another large pool of dried black blood from another exploded head.

As he squatted by the body, Ordóñez looked at Artigas and asked, "What did you see?"

"A cartridge casing. Looks like a 9mm."

"I wonder where this one's weapon went to?" Ordóñez asked, studying the body.

He pointed to a disturbance in the blood that could have been the marks left when someone had dragged a weapon from it.

"Looks like somebody took it," Artigas agreed.

"Yeah, but who?"

The implication was clear. Ordóñez would not have been surprised if one of the local cops had taken it, for any number of reasons having nothing to do with the investigation of a multiple homicide.

I'm not going to comment on that, Ordóñez thought.

"Both head shots," Artigas said.

Ordóñez nodded and then, raising his voice, asked, "Where's the other five?"

The second police supervisor made a vague gesture away from the house.

"Four out there, Chief Inspector," he said. "Señor Bertrand's body is in the house, in his office."

Ordóñez gestured for him to lead the way into the house.

The body lying on its back behind a large, ornate desk and next to the open door of a safe was that of a somewhat squat, very black man in his late forties. There were two entrance wounds in the face, one on the right side of the forehead, the second on the upper lip.

A section of the skull had been blown outward. There was brain tissue on the safe and on the wall beside it.

Artigas sensed Ordóñez's eyes on him.

"Two entrance wounds that close," Artigas said, "maybe a submachine gun?"

Ordóñez nodded.

"But from a distance," he said, pointing to the window. One of the panes was broken. "If he had been shot in here, for example, the moment he obligingly opened the safe, I think there would have been powder burns on the face."

"Yeah," Artigas said.

"The photo album?" Ordóñez asked.

"On the desk, Chief Inspector," the police supervisor said.

"While Captain Cavallero was leaving everything exactly as it was when he first came here," Ordóñez said, drily, "he happened to notice and then scan through a photo album. I think you may find it interesting."

The Moroccan leather-bound photo album on the desk was open to an eight-by-ten-inch color photograph of a wedding party standing on the steps of a church large enough to be a cathedral. Everyone was in formal morning clothing. Señor Bertrand was standing at the extreme right. The bride, a tall, slim woman, was standing beside an extraordinarily tall, broadly smiling young man.

"Julio," Ordóñez asked, softly, "do you think the bridegroom is who Captain Cavallero thought it might be?"

Well, Artigas thought, *now I know why I'm here.*

"That's Jack the Stack, all right. No question about it," he said.

" 'Jack the Stack'?"

"Before he was J. Winslow Masterson of the United States State Department, he was Jack the Stack of the Boston Celtics," Artigas said.

"Really? A professional basketball player? I didn't know that. From the Celtics to the State Department?"

"He got himself run over by a beer truck as he was leaving a stadium," Artigas said. "No more pro ball. And the settlement—the truck driver had been sampling his wares—made Jack the Stack a very wealthy man. I heard sixty million dollars."

"Now that I think about it, I remember hearing that story. But I didn't connect it with an American diplomat in Buenos Aires," Ordóñez said and then asked, "I wonder what Señor Bertrand's relationship to Señor Masterson was?"

"That's not all I'm wondering about Señor Bertrand," Artigas replied.

[THREE]
Office of the Ambassador
The Embassy of the United States of America
Lauro Muller 1776
Montevideo, República Oriental del Uruguay
2035 2 August 2005

The Honorable Michael A. McGrory, minister extraordinary and plenipotentiary of the President of the United States to the Republic of Uruguay, was a small, wiry well-tailored man of fifty-five with a full head of curly gray hair. He was held in varying degrees of contempt by many members of the "embassy team," the very ones who referred to him—behind his back, of course—as "Señor Pompous."

This was especially true of those members of the embassy team who were not members of the Foreign Service of the United States. These included the twenty-one employees of the Justice Department assigned to the Montevideo embassy. Fourteen of them carried the job description of "Assistant Legal Attaché," although they were in fact special agents of the Federal Bureau of Investigation. The other seven were special agents of the Drug Enforcement Administration.

There were others—the CIA station chief, for example, representatives of the Federal Aviation Agency, the Department of Homeland Security, and even employees of the Department of Agriculture—assigned to the embassy. The latter were charged with ensuring that Uruguayan foodstuffs exported to the United States—primarily, meat and dairy products—met the high standards of purity established by the U.S. government.

Although all of these specialists enjoyed diplomatic status, they were not *really* diplomats—and this was often pointed out to them in varying degrees of subtlety by Señor Pompous.

All the specialists would, after several years, return to the States and whatever governmental agency had, so to speak, loaned them to the Department of State.

The Foreign Service people, on the other hand, regarded themselves as professionals trained in the fine art of diplomacy who could look forward to other foreign assignments after Uruguay and to increasingly senior positions within the Department of State. Presuming, of course, that the hired hands from the Justice Department or the FAA or—especially—the CIA didn't do something violating the rules of diplomatic behavior that would embarrass the embassy and the Foreign Service personnel who were supposed to keep the hired hands under control.

Ambassador McGrory, for example, had begun his Foreign Service career as a consular officer in Nicaragua. As he over the years had moved from one United States embassy to another in South America, he had risen—somewhat slowly but steadily—upward in the State Department hierarchy. He had been a commercial attaché in Peru, a cultural attaché in Brazil, and, before his appointment as ambassador to Uruguay, he had been deputy chief of mission in Asunción, Paraguay.

With the exception of the Agriculture Department people—who did their job, kept him abreast of what was going on, and stayed out of trouble— Ambassador McGrory had trouble with just about everyone else who was not a bona fide diplomat.

There were several reasons for this, and, in Ambassador McGrory's opinion, the most significant was their inability to understand that they were in fact answerable to him. The regulations were clear on that. As the senior official of the United States government in Uruguay, all employees and officers of the United States were subject to his orders.

Many—perhaps most—of the problems caused were by the DEA agents, whom McGrory privately thought of as hooligans. They often went around "undercover," which meant that not only were they unshaven and unshorn but dressed like Uruguayan drug addicts. And under their shabby clothing they carried a variety of weaponry. It was only a matter of time, in McGrory's professional opinion, before they shot some Uruguayan and he would have to deal with all the ramifications.

He had issued an order a year before that required that the DEA agents go armed only when necessary. When it became apparent that the DEA agents considered it was necessary all the time, he had modified the order so that they would have to have his permission before arming themselves on any specific occasion. That order had been in effect fewer than seventy-two hours when the assistant secretary of state for Latin America had telephoned him to politely but firmly order him to refrain from interfering with the DEA agents' rights to defend themselves.

The FBI agents were far better dressed than those of the DEA but, if anything, less willing to keep him abreast of what they were doing and when. Their primary function was the detection of money laundering. Uruguay was known as the South American capital of money laundering. McGrory was naturally interested to know what they were doing, but they rarely told him any specifics.

And half of them, at least, also went about armed to the teeth.

Ambassador McGrory was thus concerned when the senior of the FBI agents, a man named James D. Monahan, telephoned him as he was about to leave the embassy and requested an immediate audience.

"Will this wait until the morning, Monahan?"

"Sir, I really think you should hear this now."

"Very well," the ambassador replied. "You may come up."

Monahan and Julio Artigas arrived at McGrory's office three minutes later. The ambassador did not offer them chairs.

"Artigas has run into something I thought should be brought to your attention as quickly as possible, Mr. Ambassador," Legal Attaché James D. Monahan said, politely.

"Really?" McGrory replied and looked at Assistant Legal Attaché Artigas.

"Ordóñez called me just before lunch—"

McGrory raised his hand to stop him, and asked, "Ordóñez is?"

"Chief inspector of the Interior Division of the Policía Federal, Mr. Ambassador."

McGrory nodded and waved his fingers as a signal for Artigas to go on.

"And asked that I meet him for lunch. I did so, and almost immediately he told me there had been a multiple murder—"

"*Multiple* murder?" McGrory interrupted. "How many did he mean by *multiple?*"

"Seven, Mr. Ambassador."

"Seven?"

"Yes, sir. Seven."

"And this massacre occurred here in Montevideo?"

"No, sir. On an estancia near Tacuarembó."

"And where, refresh me, is 'Tacuarembó'?"

"It's about three hundred sixty kilometers north of Montevideo, Mr. Ambassador."

"Never heard of it," the ambassador said. "Go on, Artigas."

"Yes, sir. Chief Inspector Ordóñez asked me if I would be willing to go there with him—"

"I don't think that's a very good idea, Artigas," the ambassador said. "Do you, Monahan? We don't want the embassy splattered with the water from Uruguay's dirty laundry, do we?"

"Sir, I accepted Ordóñez's invitation. I went there," Artigas said.

"And who did you check with before you did so? I can't believe Monahan would give you the go-ahead to do something like that. You didn't, Monahan, did you?"

"I didn't check with anyone, sir. I wasn't aware that I was required to."

"There is a difference, Artigas, between a requirement and the exercise of prudent conduct," the ambassador said. "Perhaps you should keep that in mind."

"Yes, sir."

"Go on."

"We flew to Tacuarembó in what I believe was the president's helicopter," Artigas said. "Which suggested to me that someone very senior in the Uruguayan government was really interested to see that Inspector Ordóñez got there in a hurry, that there was interest at high levels in whatever had transpired at Tacuarembó."

"Several things, Artigas," the ambassador said. "First, I thought you said *Chief* Inspector Whatever . . ."

"It is Chief Inspector Ordóñez, sir."

"Second, what makes you think you went flying in the president's helicopter?"

"It was a nearly new Aerospatiale Dauphin, sir. The police have old Hueys."

"In which you have flown?"

"Yes, sir. Many times."

"I wasn't aware of that," the ambassador said. "Were you, Monahan?"

"Yes, sir, I was. We try very hard to work closely with the Uruguayan authorities and—"

"Working closely with the Uruguayan authorities, of course, is a good idea. But riding in their helicopters? I shudder when I think of how well they are maintained. Or not maintained. I'll have to give that some thought. And until I have had the chance to do just that, I don't think there should be any more helicopter joyrides. Pass that word, won't you, Monahan?"

"Yes, sir."

"You flew to *Tacuarembó*, is that what you're saying, Artigas?"

"Yes, sir."

"And why did Chief Inspector Ordóñez want you to do that, do you think?"

"He wanted to show me a photograph of one of the dead men, Mr. Ambassador."

"And why would he do that?"

"Probably because the photograph was of one of the dead men standing in a wedding party with J. Winslow Masterson."

"I beg your pardon?"

"Probably because the photograph was of one of the dead men standing in a wedding party with J. Winslow Masterson."

Now I have your attention, Artigas thought, *you pompous little asshole!*

"That's difficult to believe," Ambassador McGrory said after a moment. "You're sure it was our Mr. Masterson?"

"Yes, sir, it was Jack the Stack, all right."

"The late Mr. Masterson's athletic accomplishments are long past. You don't think it is disrespectful of you to refer to him that way?"

"No disrespect was intended, sir. I was a great admirer of Mr. Masterson."

"Still, Artigas . . ." McGrory said, disapprovingly. He went on: "Do we know the name of the man in the photograph with Mr. Masterson?"

"Chief Inspector Ordóñez identified him to me as Señor Jean-Paul Bertrand, the owner of the estancia, sir."

"And he was dead, you said?"

"Shot twice, sir. In the head."

"By whom?"

"I have no idea, sir."

"And you think your good friend Chief Inspector Ordóñez, if he had suspects in the case, would confide them to you?"

"Yes, sir, I think he would."

"But he has not done so, has he?"

"What the chief inspector has done, sir, is to request our assistance."

"What kind of assistance?"

"There were seven dead men in all, sir. Señor Bertrand and six others."

"Who were they? Who killed them?"

"We have no idea, sir. There was no identification of any sort on their bodies. What the chief inspector has asked me to do, Mr. Ambassador, is to send their fingerprints to Washington to see if the FBI has them on file."

Ambassador McGrory thought that over for a moment.

"I can see no problem with doing that," he said, finally. "But what makes you—or Chief Inspector Ordóñez—think their fingerprints would be in the FBI's files? These are not Americans, presumably."

"We don't know that, sir."

"Is there any reason to think they might be?"

"No, sir. I don't think there is. On the other hand, there is no reason to presume they are not."

Ambassador McGrory considered that a moment.

"Do we know anything about the murdered man? The murdered man in the photograph?"

"His name was Bertrand, sir. Jean-Paul Bertrand."

"You already told me that," McGrory said. "My question was: Do we know anything about the murdered man?"

"He was Lebanese, sir, resident in Uruguay. Chief Inspector Ordóñez told me that. He was an antiquities dealer."

"And for the third time, do we—as opposed to your friend the chief inspector—know anything about the murdered antiques dealer?"

Monahan said, "Special Agent Yung is maintaining a file on him, sir."

"And what does the file say?"

"I don't know, sir. The file is not in the file cabinet."

"Well, where is it?"

"I don't know, sir," Monahan said. "Possibly Yung took it home with him."

"He took an official file home with him?"

"I don't know that, sir. It is possible."

"Well, get him on the phone and tell him to bring the file to my office immediately."

"I tried to call him, sir. He doesn't answer the telephone at his apartment."

"Well, where is he?"

"I don't know, sir."

"You don't know?" Ambassador McGrory parroted, incredulously.

"He didn't come in today, sir. Possibly he's in Puente del Este."

"He had the day off, in other words?"

"I meant to say he may be working in Puente del Este, sir."

"But you don't know?"

"No, sir. I don't."

"What you're going to do, Monahan, while Artigas is preparing his draft report on this matter, is find Special Agent Yung and have him bring his files here."

"Yes, sir."

"I must say, Monahan, that until just now I thought you ran a tighter ship than is apparently the case."

[FOUR]
Office of the Ambassador
The Embassy of the United States of America
Lauro Muller 1776
Montevideo, República Oriental del Uruguay
0805 3 August 2005

Special agents/assistant legal attachés James D. Monahan and Julio Artigas were sitting on the chrome-and-leather couch outside the office of the minister extraordinary and plenipotentiary of the President of the United States to the Republic of Uruguay when the ambassador arrived.

They both looked worried. The Honorable Michael A. McGrory took no pity on them. Without speaking, he waved them somewhat imperiously into his office. He went to his desk, sat down, and, with another grand gesture, gave them permission to seat themselves in the two chairs facing his desk.

"Well," McGrory said, "what more do we know about the massacre in Tacuarembó than we did when last we met? Have you heard, for example, Artigas, from your good friend, Chief Inspector Ordóñez?"

"I spoke with him last night, sir, to report that I had faxed the fingerprints to the bureau. But he didn't pass on any other information to me."

"I cannot help but wonder if your good friend has learned—or perhaps already knew—something he has elected not to pass on to you."

"I really don't think that's the case, Mr. Ambassador," Artigas replied.

"And you, Monahan? What have you to contribute?"

McGrory really disliked Monahan. The only reason he wasn't absolutely sure that Monahan was the so-called wit who had installed a decalcomania of an Irish leprechaun named McGrory in a urinal in the visitor's men's room was that he couldn't believe one Irishman would do that to another.

"Sir . . ." Monahan began uncomfortably. He cleared his throat and began again. "Sir, I have been unable to locate Mr. Yung. I even went to Puente del Este last night and checked all the hotels where he usually stays."

"That's probably because Mr. Yung is no longer with us," the ambassador said.

"Sir?"

"I received, at the residence, a telephone call at half past nine last night from the assistant director of the FBI. He said that it had been necessary to recall Mr. Yung to Washington. He informed me that Mr. Yung had actually already left Uruguay. It apparently has something to do with Mr. Yung being needed to testify in court. The assistant director said he was reluctant to get into details on a nonsecure telephone connection."

"I wonder what that's all about?" Monahan mused aloud.

"And so do I. I'm sure the assistant director will explain the situation to me when he calls, which he has promised to do as soon as he gets to a secure telephone in his office this morning."

"That won't be before ten-thirty our time," Monahan said. "There's a one-hour difference between here and D.C. and I never knew an assistant director who came to work before nine-thirty."

"And whenever he calls, I won't be here. *We* won't be here."

"Sir?"

"When thinking this matter through last night, I decided I should, as soon as possible, bring it to the attention of Ambassador Silvio in Buenos Aires. The late Mr. Masterson was, after all, the chief of mission there."

"Yes, sir."

"I decided (a) that I should do so personally and (b) that you, Artigas, should come with me. I can see no reason for you to go to Buenos Aires, Monahan. Can you?"

"No, sir."

"We are on the nine-ten Austral flight," McGrory said. "Mr. Howell will be going with us. He has some cultural business to transact in Buenos Aires, if you take my meaning."

"I understand, sir," Artigas said.

Mr. Robert Howell was the cultural attaché of the embassy. That he was also the CIA station chief was just about as much of a secret as was the identity of the Irish FBI agent who had put the McGrory leprechaun decal in the urinal.

"While we are gone, Monahan, I want you to do two things," the ambassador went on. "One, keep yourself available to take the call from the assistant director. Tell him where I am and ask him to call me at the embassy in Buenos Aires."

"Yes, sir."

"Two, it will probably be a waste of your time, but see if you can find out anything else from Artigas's friend, Chief Inspector Ordóñez, or anyone else."

"Yes, sir."

[FIVE]
Office of the Ambassador
The Embassy of the United States of America
Avenida Colombia 4300
Palermo, Buenos Aires, Argentina
1025 3 August 2005

"Please come in, Mr. Ambassador," Ambassador Juan Manuel Silvio, the American ambassador in Buenos Aires, said to Ambassador Michael McGrory. "It's always a pleasure to see you."

Silvio was a tall, lithe, fair-skinned, well-tailored man with an erect carriage and an aristocratic manner. He was younger than Ambassador Michael McGrory and, despite five years less service in the Foreign Service than McGrory, had a far more important embassy. McGrory didn't like him.

He was honest enough to admit to himself, however, that his rationale for bringing the Tacuarembó whatever it was to Silvio went beyond the fact that he had a photograph of the late Mr. Masterson, who had been Silvio's deputy. He suspected that, whatever it was, he was liable to see egg on his face when the matter got to the State Department. McGrory knew it was better that there be egg on two faces rather than his alone.

The two shook hands.

Silvio then offered his hand to Julio Artigas and said, "I don't believe I've had the pleasure?"

"My name is Artigas, sir. How do you do?"

"Artigas is one of my legal attachés," McGrory said. "And this is my cultural attaché, Mr. Howell."

"We've met," Silvio said. "Nice to see you again, Mr. Howell. I know you know Alex, but I'm not sure if Mr. Artigas does."

"No, sir," Artigas said and shook hands with a small, plump man with a pencil-thin mustache.

"Alex Darby," the man said.

"And I know Howell and Darby know each other," Silvio said. "What is it that they say about birds of a feather?"

McGrory thought: *He might have just as well come out and said, "These two are CIA."*

"Hey, Bob," Darby said. "Long time no see."

"Too long," Howell replied. "We're really going to have to get together."

Silvio's secretary rolled in a coffee tray.

"Unless it's someone important like my wife or the secretary, no calls, please," Silvio said.

When the door had closed, Silvio went on: "You said you'd come across something that might have a bearing on what happened to Jack Masterson, Mr. Ambassador?"

"Artigas," McGrory ordered, "show Ambassador Silvio the picture."

Artigas opened his briefcase and took out the photograph of the wedding party. He stood up, walked over to Silvio, and handed it to him. Silvio looked at it, then handed it to Darby.

"Where'd you get this?" Darby asked.

"Do you recognize the people?" McGrory said.

"Yeah, I do. That's Jack and Betsy at their wedding. And her parents, and Jack's, and her brother."

"You know who that man is?" McGrory asked.

"Yes, I do," Darby said. "He's Betsy Masterson's brother. Where did you get this?"

"Artigas," McGrory ordered.

"Yes, sir. It's from an estancia called Shangri-La in Tacuarembó. I was taken there by an officer of the Interior Police Division of the Uruguayan Policía Nacional."

"Why did he do that?" Darby asked.

"I now believe it was because a Uruguayan police officer on the scene recognized Mr. Masterson," Artigas said. "The photo was in a scrapbook at the scene."

"You've used the word 'scene' twice," Darby said. "Is there an implication that something had happened at this estancia, that it was, maybe, a *crime scene?*"

"That's something of an understatement, Darby," McGrory said. "According to Artigas, there were seven bodies at that estancia."

"Seven bodies?" Darby asked. *"Seven bodies?"*

"Seven bodies, including that of the man in the photograph," McGrory said. "All shot to death."

"And who were the others?" Darby asked.

Artigas saw that Darby was looking at Howell. The hair on Artigas's neck curled.

"That seems to be the mystery," McGrory said.

"You don't know who they are?" Darby asked.

"According to Artigas, none of them had any identification on them, and they were all dressed in black."

"Really?" Darby said and looked at Howell again—not for long, but long enough for Artigas to see it. "That sounds like something from a James Bond movie."

"Or a Ninja movie," Howell said. "All dressed in black."

"Well, who shot them?" Darby asked.

"No one seems to have any idea," Artigas said.

"No one seems to have any idea?" Darby parroted, incredulously.

Artigas suddenly had a number of thoughts, one right after the other:

You know all about this, don't you, Mr. Darby?

Did Howell call you last night, after McGrory told Howell?

The CIA sticks together?

Jesus, did Howell know about this before McGrory told him?

Did they both know about it?

Were they both involved?

You're letting your imagination run away with you, Julio!

You've seen too many spy movies—bad spy movies.

Yeah. But you always were a good interrogator, able to pick up things like the looks between Darby and Howell.

What the hell is going on here?

"According to Artigas, the Uruguayan police have no idea, either," Howell said.

"What do you think it was, Mr. McGrory?" Darby asked. "A robbery? An attempted kidnapping?"

That's "Mr. Ambassador," thank you very much, Darby!

"I have no idea what it was," McGrory said. "The question, it would seem to me, is, what do we do about this photograph?"

"Alex?" Silvio asked.

"I would suggest, Mr. Ambassador . . ."

Silvio is Mr. Ambassador, McGrory thought, and I'm not? You sonofabitch!

". . . that we get this information into the hands of Mr. Castillo. Or that Mr. McGrory should. The photo turned up in Uruguay. On Mr. McGrory's watch, so to speak."

"Who's Castillo?" McGrory asked.

"This is classified information, Mr. Ambassador," Silvio said. "When Mrs. Masterson was abducted, the President told me he had appointed Mr. Castillo to supervise the investigation. And later, the President charged him with the security of the Masterson family and with their repatriation to the States."

"Who's he?"

"He's the President's agent."

"What does that mean?"

"I can only tell you what the President told me," Silvio said.

"Is that the same man who came to Montevideo to see Special Agent Yung?"

"Yes, I believe so."

"What's his connection with Yung?" McGrory asked.

Silvio shrugged.

Artigas wondered: *And what's the connection between this and Yung suddenly being ordered to the States?*

"What we can do, if you'd like, Mr. Ambassador," Silvio said, "is send the photograph to the secretary, together with the information that Darby positively identified this man as Mrs. Masterson's brother. You are sure, are you not, Alex?"

"Yes, sir, I'm sure. I met him several times when Jack and I were in Paris."

Just in time, McGrory stopped himself from saying he would take care of notifying the secretary, thank you just the same.

I am not going to be twisting alone in the wind, he thought.

"Yes, I think that's the way to go," he said.

Artigas thought: *Señor Pompous, I think you're wondering if, without having any idea why, you're in the deep do-do.*

God, I hope so.

[SIX]
Hacienda San Jorge
Near Uvalde, Texas
1330 3 August 2005

Major C. G. Castillo stood by a barbecue grill constructed from a fifty-five-gallon barrel, his eyes stinging from the smoke of the mesquite fire. He had a long, black cigar clamped in his teeth and was attired in khaki pants, a T-shirt printed with the legend YOU CAN ALWAYS TELL A TEXAS AGGIE, BUT NOT MUCH, battered western boots, and an even more battered Stetson hat, its brim curled.

He saw Estella, a short, massive, swarthy woman who had been helping at the ranch as long as he could remember, come out of the big house carrying a walk-around telephone and he had the unpleasant premonition that the call was going to be for him.

But then Estella gave the phone to Abuela and he saw her smile and say, "How good it is to hear your voice," and he returned his attention to the steaks broiling on the grill.

He had just annoyed Maria, his cousin Fernando's wife, by solemnly proclaiming that only males could be trusted to properly grill a steak and challenged her to name one world-class female chef. Or, for that matter, one world-class female orchestra leader.

Castillo didn't believe any of this, but there was something in Maria that had always made him really like to ruffle her feathers. He thought of her as his sister-in-law, but technically that wasn't accurate. Fernando was his cousin, not his brother. But if there was a term to describe the wife of your cousin, who was really more like your brother, he didn't know it.

He felt a tug at his trouser leg and looked down to see Jorge Carlos Lopez, who was seven, his godchild and the fourth of the five children of Fernando and Maria. Jorge was holding up a bottle of Dos Equis beer to him.

"You have saved my life, Jorge," Charley said solemnly, in Spanish. "You will be rewarded in heaven."

He looked around, saw Fernando standing by the table set for lunch on the shaded veranda of the big house, and gave him a thumbs-up to express his appreciation for the beer.

He then surreptitiously reached in his trousers pocket and came out with a small computerized meat thermometer, which gave an almost immediate and very accurate indication of temperature.

There was nothing wrong in getting scientific confirmation of what your thumb suggested when pressed into a broiling steak, especially if no one saw you use the device and remained convinced you had an educated thumb.

He stabbed each of the steaks with the thermometer—there were eight inch-and-a-half-thick New York strips—and saw they all had interior temperatures of just over 140 degrees Fahrenheit.

He put the thermometer back in his pocket, then turned and faced the veranda.

"I proclaim these done!"

Fernando applauded, and several of the rugrats joined in.

At that point, Charley saw Abuela advancing on him holding out the walk-around telephone.

"It's for you," she said. "Dick."

Shit! I knew it.

"Thank you," he said. "Wait until I get the steaks on the platter."

Abuela laid the telephone on the table beside the grill, then picked up the platter—a well-used, blood-grooved wooden board with horseshoe handles—and held it out for him to put the steaks on it. Then she started for the veranda.

"I'll carry that, Abuela," he called after her.

"I am old, tired, and decrepit, but I can still carry this," she said.

Charley picked up the telephone.

"Why do I think I'm not going to like this?" he asked by way of greeting.

"Doña Alicia was glad to hear my voice," Major H. Richard Miller, Jr., said. "She told me."

"As you well know, she is too kind for her own good, especially where cripples are concerned. What's up?"

"I think you better get back here, Charley."

"Jesus, I haven't been here thirty-six hours."

And not only that, I really wanted to have a closer look at that Gulfstream.

Surprising Charley, Fernando had met him at San Antonio International Airport.

"To what do I owe the honor?" Castillo said.

"I want to show you something."

"And it wouldn't wait until we were at San Jorge?"

"No. You have any checked luggage?"

Castillo shook his head.

Fernando's car, a new twelve-cylinder black Mercedes-Benz S600, was in the short-term parking lot. Castillo remembered reading in a magazine that the sedan had a sticker price somewhere north of $140,000.

"Is this what you wanted to show me?"

"No."

"Nice wheels."

"It's Maria's," Fernando said.

"You must have been a really bad boy."

"Fuck you, Gringo."

"What exactly did you do wrong?"

"Well, for example, I went to Europe and South America without taking her along."

"She didn't like that?"

"No, she did not."

"I can't understand that."

Fernando shook his head but didn't reply.

He then drove them around the airport to Lemes Aviation, a large business-aviation operation.

"Don't tell me you pranged the Lear?"

"No. But it's in here for a hundred-hour maintenance a lot sooner than I thought it would be."

"You'll get a check, eventually, from the Secret Service. You know the deal: They chartered it."

"I know the deal," Fernando said.

He pulled the Mercedes into a parking slot at the Lemes building and they got out. But instead of going in the building, Fernando marched purposefully toward a hangar. Castillo followed him expecting to see the Lear, on which he was sure Fernando was going to show him something that had happened that was going to require expensive repair.

The Lear wasn't in the hangar. There were four Beechcraft turboprops and one jet, a Gulfstream III.

"What are we looking at?" Castillo asked.

Fernando pointed to the Gulfstream.

"Jesus, don't tell me you bought that!"

"I didn't. I think maybe you should," Fernando said.

A smiling man wearing a leather aviator's jacket and aviator's sunglasses walked quickly up to them before Castillo had a chance to respond.

"How are you, Mr. Lopez?" he asked.

"Do you know my cousin, Charley Castillo?"

"I have not had that privilege," the man said. "Brewster Walsh, Mr. Castillo."

He enthusiastically pumped Castillo's hand.

"She's a beauty, isn't she?" Mr. Walsh inquired, then added, "And a steal at seven million nine ninety-nine."

"In other words, eight million, right?" Castillo asked, innocently.

"Can we have a look inside?" Fernando asked.

"It would be my pleasure," Mr. Walsh said.

Castillo, who was tired and wanted to get out to Hacienda San Jorge, was just about to politely decline the offer when he remembered what Fernando had said: *"I didn't. I think maybe you should."*

He meant that. He thinks I should buy this with Lorimer's money.

He wouldn't have said that unless he meant it. Jesus!

Castillo allowed himself to be waved up the stair door. He looked into the cockpit.

"Are you a pilot yourself, Mr. Castillo?" Mr. Walsh inquired, and, when Castillo nodded, went on, "Well, then you'll really appreciate that panel."

Castillo examined the flight instruments carefully. It was a nice panel, mostly Honeywell and Collins. It wasn't on a par with the panel in the Lear, but then the Lear was nearly brand-new and this wasn't.

"How old is this?" Castillo asked.

"I'm sure you're aware that it isn't how old an airplane is but rather how hard it's been ridden."

"Which makes it how old?"

"Total time, just over eight thousand hours," Mr. Walsh replied. "Just over forty-five hundred landings, which means the average flight was less than two hours. And—*and*—the engines were replaced at eight thousand hours and are practically brand-new."

"Which makes it how old by the calendar?" Castillo pursued.

"Twenty-three years," Mr. Walsh replied, somewhat reluctantly. "Hard to believe looking at it, isn't it?"

Yeah, it is. Jesus, it doesn't look that old. It looks practically brand-new.

"And there was a complete refurbishment of the interior just six months ago," Mr. Walsh added.

"Does 'refurbished' mean cleaned and shined?"

"Everything that showed the slightest signs of wear was replaced," Mr. Walsh said.

Castillo looked down the luxuriously fitted-out passenger compartment. When he breathed in, he smiled at the rich smell of fine glove leather.

"It looks new," he admitted.

"It has a maximum range of thirty-seven hundred nautical miles," Mr. Walsh offered, "at four hundred fifty knots."

"That would get you across the Atlantic in a hurry, wouldn't it?" Fernando asked, over Mr. Walsh's shoulder. "I mean, if a person had some reason to go to Europe. Me, if I had my way, I'd never leave Texas, much less the good ol' USA."

"Well, if you wanted to go to Europe," Mr. Walsh said, "this little beauty would take you and twelve of your friends—*and* their golf clubs and their overnight bags."

"In case you wanted to play a quick round at St. Andrews, for example, Carlos," Fernando said, and then looked at Mr. Walsh. "Ol' Carlos is quite a golfer."

"Me, too," Mr. Walsh said. "I just love the game."

"Anytime anyone's looking for ol' Carlos, I just tell them to check out the nearest golf club," Fernando said.

"What business are you in, Mr. Castillo? If you don't mind my asking?"

"Investments," Castillo said.

"Buy low and sell high, right, Carlos?" Fernando asked.

"I try."

"Word of a steal like this gets around quickly," Mr. Walsh said. "Frankly, I've got several people really interested."

"Well, Mr. Walsh, if you can get somebody to give you eight million for this old airplane I suggest you take the offer. On the other hand, if you'd be willing to shave half a million off your asking price I *might* be interested. With several other caveats."

"For example, Mr. Castillo?"

"My golfing buddy, Jake Torine, is a much better pilot than I am. I'd have to have him check it out. He lives in Charleston."

"We'd be happy to have your friend fly here at our expense and give him a test hop. He's checked out in the Gulfstream, I presume?"

"Yes, he is."

"But so far as lowering the price is concerned . . ."

"What I meant was, you would take the airplane—and Fernando—to Charleston and let my friend fly it there," Castillo said. "But if you can't lower the price, I guess that doesn't matter."

"Perhaps—one never knows what will happen, does one?—something could be worked out. If you'd be willing to pay the standard hourly charter rate for the G-III, for example, for the hours it took to fly to Charleston . . ."

"Which is how much?"

"Ballpark figure, about three thousand an hour."

"Since we're playing what-if," Castillo said, "what if you flew this airplane to Charleston, gave my friend a test hop, all at three thousand an hour, and what if he said the old bird was worth the money, and what if I said, 'Okay, I'll buy it,' you'd take how many hours at three thousand per it came to off your price of seven million five, right?"

"Mr. Castillo, I'm not at all sure I can shave the price even a little, much less half a million dollars."

"I understand," Castillo said. "You go ahead and sell to whoever is willing to pay that much money for a twenty-four-year-old airplane. Thanks for letting me have a look."

"It's only twenty-three years old, Mr. Castillo."

"Okay. Twenty-*three*-year-old airplane."

"At the risk of repeating myself," Mr. Walsh said, "one never knows what's going to happen. How would I get in touch with you, Mr. Castillo, if—"

"Fernando usually knows where I'm swatting the ol' ball around at any given time, so just call him. You have his number, right?"

When they were on the highway to Uvalde, Fernando said, "I wonder if he'll call today or wait until tomorrow."

"I hope he waits longer than that," Castillo said. "That looks like such a good deal, I can hear Grandpa say, 'Anytime you're offered a really good deal you'd be a fool to turn down, take a cold shower every day for a week and then have another look, a very *close* look.'"

Fernando chuckled.

"I have something serious to say, Gringo."

"Uh-oh."

"I really should not be playing James Bond with you as much as I have been."

"And is the rest of the sentence 'and I won't in the future'?"

"Hey, Gringo. You need me, I'm there. You know that. But I have Maria and the kids and Abuela to think of."

"Touché."

"All I'm saying is you now have people working for you. Please don't call me unless you really need me."

"Done."

"And you need an airplane. Maybe not that G-III, but an airplane. A bigger one than the Lear. And not just because Maria and Abuela are not only going to smell a rat if you keep using the Lear but are going to start nosing around. Neither of us wants that."

"You're right. So to hell with Grandpa's advice. Let's hope Smiley calls you tonight instead of tomorrow."

"I don't like the way you're agreeing with me so easily."

"What should I do, agree with you hardly? You're right, Fernando, it's as simple as that. I wasn't thinking."

"You're making me feel like a shit, you know that?"

"What I was just thinking was how lucky I am to have you as my brother."

"I'm not your brother, Cuz."

"If you won't tell, I won't."

"What I want from you, Gringo, is your word that when you need me you'll call me."

"Done."

"No rest for the weary," Dick Miller now said over the phone. "You never heard that?"

"Something specific?" Castillo asked.

"Well, how about the secretary of the Department of Homeland Security sticking his head in the door and saying, 'I really hate to do this to him, but I think you better get Charley on the horn and tell him to get back here as soon as he can.' "

"Well, that's certainly specific enough. Did he say why?"

"No. But it may have something to do with General Naylor having called him five minutes before—they put that call on your line by mistake."

"I wonder what he wants?"

"Or it may have something to do with our new liaison officer," Miller said.

"Our new what?"

"Ambassador Montvale has been kind enough to assign a liaison officer to the Office of Organizational Analysis. He was here first thing this morning, just bubbling over with enthusiasm to get right to work liaising things."

"That's the last thing we need! Montvale's surrogate's nose in our business."

"Or it may have something to do with what Mr. Ellsworth—our new liaison officer's name is Truman C. Ellsworth—brought with him when he came over this morning to start liaising."

"Which is?"

"This isn't even classified. It's just a standard interoffice memorandum from the director of National Intelligence to the chief of the Office of Organizational Analysis. It says that he thought you might be interested to know that he has learned from, quote, Central Intelligence Agency officers in Montevideo, Uruguay, and Buenos Aires, Argentina, end quote, that a man named Bertrand who was murdered in the course of a robbery in Uruguay has been tentatively identified as really being a UN diplomat named Lorimer and that Mr. Lorimer was the brother-in-law of the late J. Winslow Masterson."

"That's interesting, isn't it?" Castillo said. "Did the memo say anything about who might have robbed or murdered this man?"

"It says that, quote, the aforementioned officers have been directed to investigate this matter and to report their findings to the undersigned, end quote."

Castillo considered that a minute, then asked, "What do we hear about the world of high finance?"

"There's been a very nervous Chinaman asking about you every hour on the hour. I think he thinks he is about to be swooped upon by the IRS and carried off to Leavenworth for having too much money in his offshore account."

Castillo chuckled. "Given all that, yeah, I better come back. I don't know when I can catch a plane."

"If you can fit it into your busy schedule, you have a reservation on Continental 5566 departing San Antone at five forty-five. It will put you into Dulles, after only three stops and one change of planes, at half past eleven."

"Oh, shit!"

"Just a little jerk on your chain, Charley. Relax. It's nonstop. Mrs. Forbison got the reservation for you."

"Okay. I will be sure to wake you when I come in, presuming I can get a cab at Dulles within three or four hours."

"You will be met by your own personal Yukon," Miller said. "She set that up, too. Look for a heavily armed man wearing a strained smile."

"You can call that off. I can catch a cab."

"Actually, Tom McGuire told Mrs. F. to set it up. Get used to it, hotshot. You now really are a hotshot."

"I'll see you shortly, Dick. Thank you."

He broke the connection and carried the telephone to the veranda. Everyone there was waiting, patiently, sitting with a steak on a plate before him.

"What'd Dick want?" Fernando asked.

"Enjoy your steak. You're going to need your strength for the trip."

"Fernando, you're not going anywhere," Maria announced, firmly.

"You're going to leave him here when you go home?" Castillo asked, innocently.

"He's not going anywhere with you, period," Maria said.

"Who said anything about him going anywhere with me, question mark? I was thinking of the trip between here and Casa Lopez, period. What are you talking about, question mark?"

Fernando chuckled.

"You've been zinged, my dear," he said.

"Jorge, comma," Fernando M. Lopez, Jr., aged ten, asked his brother, "would you please pass the butter, question mark?"

"No, comma, I won't, exclamation point!" Jorge Lopez replied and giggled

Abuela, who had been frowning, now smiled.

"I don't know why I even try," Maria said. "I should know better. I should just sit here and let Carlos make a fool of me while my husband and children laugh at me."

"The Gringo only makes fools of people he loves," Fernando said.

"Please don't call him that," Fernando Junior and Jorge said in unison, looking at their great-grandmother. "You know I don't like it."

Immediately, Fernando Junior added, "I don't like it, exclamation point!"

"My father warned me I was making a mistake marrying into this family," Maria said, but she was smiling.

When the car came, Abuela went out to it with him.

It was a silver Jaguar XJ8.

"Nice wheels, Abuela," Charley said. "New, huh?"

"Fernando sent a Mercedes out here," she said. "A twelve-cylinder one. Black. I made him take it back. I felt like a Mafia gangster. This one I can drive myself."

"Ah, the truth about how Maria came into her Mafiamobile!"

"Well, it just made sense to let Maria have it. Otherwise, he would have lost a lot of money. You just can't turn a new car back in."

"And Maria doesn't mind feeling like a Mafia gangster?"

"I'm glad this didn't come up while she was here," Abuela said. "Darling, do you really have to tease her all the time?"

"Hey, I saw you smiling when the boys started to speak the punctuation."

"They are clever, aren't they? They remind me so much of you and Fernando."

"That should be a frightening prospect."

She didn't respond to that.

"That's what you need, Carlos. Boys of your own. A nice family."

"I have a nice family. I just don't have a wife."

"And there have been no developments along that line that you'd like to tell me about?"

"Has Fernando been running off at the mouth again?"

"How is the lady Secret Service agent?"

"She has her jaws wired shut. If I can get her to agree to leave the wires in, maybe something could be worked out."

"I don't think that's funny, Carlos."

He looked down at his feet.

"The wires in her jaw aren't," he said. "I'm sorry I said that."

"You should be."

He looked Abuela in the eyes.

"I'm going to have to go to Europe for a couple of days. I'll go from New York and stop off in Philadelphia to see her."

"Fernando said she's very nice."

"She is."

She nodded at him, then leaned up and kissed him.

"Via con Dios, mi amor," she said.

He got in the front seat with the driver.

As the car rolled away from the sprawling, red-tile-roofed Spanish-style big house, he turned in the seat and looked out the back window. Abuela was standing where he had left her.

She's right. I do need boys like Fernando's, and a wife—a family.

He watched Abuela until the road curved and then he thought of Betty Schneider.

Maybe the time has come. God knows I've never felt about any other woman the way I feel about Betty.

IV

Castillo smiled when he came out of the Jetway and entered the terminal. There waiting for him was indeed a heavily armed man wearing a strained smile. He was standing behind a wheelchair on which sat, one leg supported vertically in front of him, Major H. Richard Miller, Jr.

He wondered for a moment how they'd got into the security area, then felt a little foolish when the answer came to him: *Wave your Secret Service credentials and you can go anywhere in an airport you want.*

"Mr. Castillo," the Secret Service agent said, "Major Miller said he didn't think you would have any checked baggage."

That's interesting. Mister *Castillo and* Major *Miller. We're both majors. And this guy has to know that.*

What did Dick say on the phone? "Get used to it, hotshot. You now really are a hotshot."

"I don't," Castillo said, smiling. He put out his hand. "I don't think we've met, have we? I'm Charley Castillo."

The Secret Service agent gave him a firm but very quick handshake, and said, "Special Agent Dulaney, sir."

Castillo looked at Miller and saw that he was smiling at him.

Special Agent Dulaney spoke to his lapel microphone.

"Don Juan is out. No luggage. We're on our way."

"I'll push the cripple, Dulaney," Castillo said.

"Yes, sir. The Yukon's right outside, sir."

"What happened to the Pride of the Marine Corps?" Miller asked as they moved through the airport.

"Vic D'Allessando arranged to stash him at Bragg until I figure out what to do with him."

"How much help do you need to get into this?" Castillo asked when they were at the Yukon.

"None. But you can put the wheelchair in," Miller said.

He came nimbly off the wheelchair, stood on one leg, pulled the door open, and then sort of dove into the rear. Castillo saw that the middle seat had been folded flat against the floorboard, and, when he looked again, Miller was already sitting up in the far backseat, his leg stretched out in front of him on the folded-down seat.

"*Now* is when you put the wheelchair in," Miller said.

"Can I help you with that, sir?" Special Agent Dulaney asked.

"I'm all right, thanks," Castillo said, somewhat struggling with collapsing the wheelchair.

Sixty seconds later, Miller asked, "You're not very good at that, are you?"

"There's a lever on the side here, sir, that lets you fold it," Special Agent Dulaney said. "Let me show you."

"Thank you," Castillo said and got in the Yukon.

Thirty seconds later, the Yukon pulled away from the curb.

Special Agent Dulaney spoke again to his lapel microphone.

"Don Juan aboard. Headed for the nest."

"Who is he talking to?" Castillo asked, softly.

"I asked him that," Miller said. "He said, 'The Secret Service has a communications system,' and then I said, 'Yeah, but who are you talking to?' And he said, 'The communications system.' "

"Well, ask a dumb question," Castillo said, grinning. Then he added, "You didn't have to ride all the way out here, Dick."

"I had my reasons. Two of them, to be precise. The first was that it was a pleasant change from my usual routine, which is to go from the hotel to the Nebraska Avenue Complex, then back again, sometimes stopping off at the lobby bar on the way home to have a drink to recuperate from my journey."

"And the second?"

"I thought you might have had it in your head to stop off in the lobby bar en route to the room tonight."

"You're psychic! And I'll even buy."

"And I thought I should warn you what you're liable to find in there if you do," Miller said, paused, then added, "The former CIA regional director for Southwest Africa."

"No kidding?"

"Yes, indeed. I was having a little nip about this time night before last in the lobby bar when I sensed death rays aimed at me. I looked around and there she was, Mrs. Patricia Davies Wilson, in the flesh. And very nice flesh it was, I have to admit, spilling out of her dress."

"So what happened?"

"Nothing happened. She was with a fellow I strongly suspect was not Mr. Wilson. He was even younger than you or me."

"You're sure she made you?"

"The death rays made it clear that she did. They froze my martini solid. I had to chew it, like ice cubes."

"Well, she probably blames you for getting her fired."

"That thought occurred to me," Miller said, "shortly followed by a possible worse scenario, that she didn't get fired."

"You think that's possible?"

"You know the agency better than I do," Miller said. "Firing somebody is an admission that the agency is less than perfect."

"Can we find out? Maybe ask Tom McGuire to ask a few discreet questions?"

"I'm way ahead of you, Charley," Miller said. "As a devout believer in Know Thy Enemy, the first thing the next morning, I called Langley, identified myself as chief of staff to the chief of the Office of Organizational Analysis . . ."

"You're not kidding, are you?"

"Oh, no," Miller said. "And I asked, did they happen to have an employee named Patricia Davies Wilson and, if so, what was she doing for them?"

"And they told you?"

"Has anyone told you, Chief, that we now have a 'contact officer' in most of the important agencies, under orders to give us anything we ask for?"

"No, nobody told me."

"You should spend more time in the office, Chief. All sorts of things are happening. But your question was, 'And they told you?' Yes, they did. And what they told me—you're going to love this—is that Mrs. Wilson is a senior analyst in the South American Division's Southern Cone Section."

"Jesus Christ!"

"Yeah," Miller said. "Where, one would presume, she would have access to everything that the agency hears—more important, *does*—down there."

"Well, I'll have to do something about that," Castillo said, almost to himself.

"Short of rendering her harmless, Charley, what?"

"I don't know. But I don't want that woman's nose in what's happened down there or what may happen."

"Her nose doesn't bother me nearly as much as her mouth."

"Did you say anything to anybody?"

Miller shook his head.

"I'll go see Matt Hall first thing in the morning," Castillo said.

"First thing late tomorrow afternoon," Miller said. "He's in Saint Louis, and from there he's going to Chicago. He's due back here at five-thirty. There's a reception at the White House—command performance for him."

"Okay, first thing late tomorrow afternoon," Castillo said. "Damn! I'm on my way to Europe and I wanted to see Betty in Philadelphia before I left. Now I either don't get to see her or I leave a day later."

"Does this mean you're not going to buy me a drink?"

"I will buy you two drinks," Castillo said. "Maybe more."

"In the lobby bar?"

"As I recall that encounter, we were the innocent victims. Why should we be afraid of running into the villain in a bar?"

"Come on, Charley! You know damned well why."

"I have the strength of ten, because in my heart I'm pure. I am not going to let that 'lady,' using the term loosely, run me out of a bar."

Miller snorted.

[TWO]
Office of Organizational Analysis
Department of Homeland Security
Nebraska Avenue Complex
Washington, D.C.
0825 4 August 2005

Mrs. Agnes Forbison, deputy chief for administration of the Office of Organizational Analysis, Major H. Richard Miller, Jr., chief of staff to the chief of the Office of Organizational Analysis, and the chief himself, Major C. G. Castillo, were standing on the carpet in just about the center of the latter's office. Major Miller was supporting himself on a massive cane.

It was an office befitting a senior executive of the federal government. There was an oversized, ornately carved antique wooden desk, behind which sat a red leather, high-backed "judge's chair."

On the desk were two telephones, one of them red. It was a secure line, connected to the White House switchboard. There were two flags against the wall, the national colors and that of the Department of Homeland Security. In front of the desk were two leather-upholstered straight-backed chairs. There was a coffee table, with two chairs on one side of it and a matching couch on the other. There were two television sets, each with a thirty-two-inch-wide screen, mounted on the walls.

"And that completes the tour," Mrs. Forbison said. "Say, 'Good job, Agnes.' "

Mrs. Forbison, a GS-15—the highest rank in the General Service hierarchy—was forty-nine, gray-haired, and getting just a little chubby.

"Jesus Christ, Agnes!" C. G. Castillo said.

"You like?"

"I don't know what the hell to say," Castillo said. "What am I supposed to do with all this?"

The tour had been of the suite of offices newly assigned to the Office of Organizational Analysis of the Department of Homeland Security in the Nebraska Avenue Complex, which is just off Ward Circle in the northwest section of the District of Columbia. The complex had once belonged to the Navy, but it had been turned over in 2004 by an act of Congress to the Department of Homeland Security when that agency had been formed after 9/11.

"You need it now," she said. "And the way things are going, I don't think it will be long before we'll be cramped in here."

Until very recently, Mrs. Forbison had been one of the two executive assistants to Secretary of Homeland Security Matt Hall. When the Office of Organizational Analysis had been formed within the Department of Homeland Security, Mrs. Forbison had been—at her request—assigned to it.

She had known from the beginning that the Office of Organizational Analysis had nothing to do with organizational analysis and very little to do with the Department of Homeland Security. Secretary Hall had shown her the Top Secret Presidential Finding the day after it had been issued.

Agnes, who had been around Washington a long time, had suspected that Secretary Hall was going to have to have an in-house intelligence organization—Homeland Security was the only department that didn't have one—if for no other reason than to do a better job than she and her staff were capable of doing, sorting through the daily flood of intelligence received from the entire intelligence community.

And she had suspected, when the President had gone to Biloxi to meet the plane carrying the bodies of Masterson and the sergeant and given his speech—*". . . to those who committed the cowardly murders of these two good men, I say to you that this outrage will not go unpunished . . ."*—that Charley Castillo was going to be involved in that punishment. He not only had found the stolen 727 when the entire intelligence community couldn't, but had stolen it back from the terrorists.

It would have been in character for the President to send Charley off as his agent to find the people who had killed Masterson and the sergeant, much as he'd sent him off to locate the stolen 727.

But she hadn't expected the Presidential Finding. With a stroke of his pen— actually, the secretary of state's pen—the President had given Castillo a blank check to do anything he thought he had to do "to render harmless" the people responsible for the murders. And he had to answer to the President alone, not even Secretary Hall. And the Finding had given him an organization to do it with.

When Secretary Hall had shown her the Finding, she'd read it, then handed it back and said, "Wow!"

"You don't think he's up to it?" Hall had asked.

"I think he can handle the terrorists, but I'm not so sure about Washington," she said. "Top Secret Presidential or not, this is going to get out, and as soon as it does so do the long knives. The FBI and the CIA are going to have a fit when they hear about this. And Montvale—especially Montvale—he is not going to like this at all."

"Would you, if you were the ambassador? He's supposed to be in charge of all intelligence and the President makes an exception—for a young major answerable only to him?"

"Montvale can take care of himself," she said. "It's Charley I'm worried about."

"You think he needs some mentor, wise in the ways of Washington backstabbing? Like you, for example?"

"Like *you*, of course," she said. "But, yeah, like me, too."

"Then you would not consider being transferred to the Office of Organizational Analysis as, say, deputy chief for administration, as an indication that I was less than satisfied with your performance of your duties and, since I couldn't fire you, promoted you out?"

"That has a nice ring to it, 'Deputy Chief for Administration,' " Agnes said.

"Then, since I have no authority over this new organization—or him—I will *suggest* that to Charley."

Agnes now said to Castillo, "What I did, boss—"

"I'd rather be called Charley," Castillo said.

"I'd rather be called 'My Beauty,' 'My Adored One,' but this isn't the place for that. This is where the boss gets called 'boss' or 'sir.' Your choice."

"Okay, okay."

"What I did, *boss*, was move everybody off the floor but the secretary's office. And since he uses that for about twenty minutes once a month, that means there will not be a stream of curious people getting off the elevator. I'm also having the engineer put in one of those credit-card-swipe gadgets in the lobby and in the garage, for what will be *our* elevator. When he gets that in, he'll rig the other elevators so they can't come up here."

"You're amazing," Charley said.

"And, as we speak, they're putting in additional secure telephones. You and Dick and I will have our own, of course, and so will Tom McGuire. And there will be one in the conference room. I told our new liaison officer, Mr. Ellsworth, that I will get him one just as soon as I can. No telling how long that will take."

"What do you think of Mr. Ellsworth?"

"He's smart, tough, and experienced, which is to be expected of someone who has worked for Ambassador Montvale for a long time."

Miller snorted.

"Why am I not surprised?" Castillo asked.

"And he requests an audience with you, boss, as soon as you can fit him in."

"Can I stall him for today? I'm going to Europe—Paris, Fulda, and Budapest, and maybe Vienna—tomorrow. Maybe by the time I get back, I'll have thought of some clever way to send him back to Montvale."

"I can stall him," she said. "But not indefinitely. How long will you be gone?"

"Just a couple of days. I'd go right now, but I have to talk to Hall. He sent for me, but he won't be back until late this afternoon." He paused. "The silver lining in that black cloud is that maybe I can talk to him about this Mr. Ellsworth."

"Charley," Agnes said, hesitantly, and then went on: "Charley, you're going to have to understand that you don't work for Matt Hall any longer."

"If Matt Hall says he wants to see me, he will see me standing there at attention."

"That's your choice. But you don't *have* to. And the black lining in that silver cloud is that it wouldn't really be fair of you to ask Hall to fight your battles with Montvale. Since he no longer has authority over you, he has no responsibility for you."

"She's right, Charley," Miller said. "Like I said, get used to being a hotshot, hotshot."

"Oh, Jesus," Castillo said.

"And you're going to have to get used to, as of yesterday, playing that role," Agnes said. "That's the reason for the fancy office and the Secret Service Yukon. Those are D.C. status symbols, Charley. Middle-level bureaucrats get a parking space with their name on it. One step up from that is getting to ride around town in a government car, but not back and forth to work. One up from that is having a Yukon but your people drive it, not the Secret Service. At the top of the heap is a Secret Service Yukon at your beck and call. That's why Tom McGuire set that up. He knows how the game is played and you better learn quick."

Castillo shook his head, then asked, "Where is Tom?"

There was no time for a reply. There was a tinkling sound and a red light on the red telephone began to flash.

"That one you answer yourself," Agnes said.

Castillo walked over to the huge desk and picked up the telephone.

"Castillo."

"Natalie Cohen, Charley."

"Good morning, Madam Secretary."

"I just got off the phone with Ambassador Lorimer," she said. "I called Mr. Masterson first and told him that Mr. Lorimer had been found, and the circumstances, and asked how a call from me would be received."

"Yes, ma'am?"

"He told me that someone from our embassy in Montevideo had called the ambassador—as next of kin—and told him what had happened."

"I didn't even think about that," Castillo said.

"There's a procedure in cases like this and it kicked in when Mr. Lorimer was identified," she said. "And they had no way of knowing, of course, that he had a heart condition, or, indeed, that he is a retired ambassador."

"How did he take it?"

"Well. And he and Mr. Masterson both expressed their appreciation for your offer to look after Mr. Lorimer's affairs in Uruguay and France. That was a nice thing for you to do, Charley."

"The truth is, I wanted a legal reason to get into his apartment in Paris and the Uruguay estancia to see what I could find. And maybe keep quiet some questions being asked about Lorimer's bank accounts in Uruguay."

She took that without breaking stride.

"And how did that go?"

"Special Agent Yung had an account in the Liechtensteinische Landesbank in the Caymans—in connection with what he was doing for the FBI down there. Getting it in there went smoothly. The next step is getting it out of that account and into one that was supposed to be opened for me. I'm going to see if I can do that this morning."

"The reason I asked is the same standard procedures that come into play when an American dies abroad that require the notification of the next of kin also require the protection of assets. Even if you got it out of Uruguay, obviously, it was after his death. There will probably be some questions asked."

"Damn!"

"Yeah. Well, maybe we'll have a chance to talk about that tonight."

"I beg your pardon?"

"You're not going to be at the White House?"

"No, ma'am. I know Secretary Hall will be there, but I won't."

"Okay. Well, I will ask some discreet questions about that problem, and if I come up with anything I'll let you know."

"I would very much appreciate that."

"Talk to you later, Charley," the secretary of state said and hung up.

Castillo put the handset back in its cradle.

"Priority one is to get that money out of Yung's account and into mine," he said. "And to do that, I have to have the numbers of my new account and somebody has to tell me how to move money around in an offshore bank."

"Who has the numbers?" Agnes asked.

"Otto Görner at the *Tages Zeitung*. More probably Frau Schröder."

"Would they give them to me if I called?"

"Probably not now, but after I call them this time they will. How do I dial an international number?"

"If you know it," Agnes said, "punch it in. *After* you give it to me."

Transferring nearly sixteen million dollars between two accounts in the Liechtensteinische Landesbank in the Cayman Islands proved to be even more difficult and time-consuming than Charley thought it would be.

Since no one wanted to be out of the office when yet another call involving their furnishing of just one more detail came from either Fulda or the Cayman Islands, luncheon was hamburgers from Wendy's. Special Agent Yung, who was apparently willing to make any sacrifice required to get the money out of his account, volunteered to go get them.

Yung's relief when, shortly after two P.M., the Liechtensteinische Landesbank reported that the funds were now in the account of Karl W. von und zu Gossinger—and thus out of his account—was palpable but short lived.

Just about as soon as Castillo had hung up, Miller wondered aloud—Castillo thought he was probably doing it on purpose; he knew Miller didn't like Yung—what the boys at Fort Meade were going to do with their intercepts of the many telephone calls they had made.

Fort Meade, Maryland, near Washington, houses the National Security Agency, the very secretive unit that "intercepts" telephone conversations and other electronic transmission of data or text, such as e-mails.

"You know how that works, don't you, Yung?" Miller asked.

"I have a general idea, of course," Yung said.

"Well, in simple terms, what they do is record practically everything coming out of Washington," Miller began. "Then they run what they've recorded though high-speed filters looking for words or names or phrases in which there is interest. With all the interest in money laundering, as you of all people should know, the Liechtensteinische Landesbank is sure to be one of those phrases. And so is 'millions of dollars.'

"So by now, there's probably at least one NSA analyst sitting over there wondering whether that transfer was simply a legitimate transfer or whether some drug lord or raghead is making financial transactions inimical to the interests of the United States. I don't think the IRS is on their distribution list, but I know Langley and the FBI are."

Castillo restrained a smile as Yung's face reflected the implications for him of what Miller was saying.

And then, suddenly, Castillo realized that what had started as a joke was potentially a serious problem.

"Which means we're going to have to do something and right now," he said, "before somebody starts a file on this."

Miller misread him. He thought Castillo had decided to add to Yung's discomfiture.

"Charley, you know as well as I do that once those NSA people latch on to something, they're like dogs with a meaty bone," Miller said.

"Agnes," Castillo said, "I want Yung on the next plane to Buenos Aires."

"You mean today?" Yung asked.

"I mean in an hour, if that's when the next plane leaves."

"What am I going to do in Buenos Aires?"

"In *Montevideo*, you are going to make sure that whatever information the embassy has turned up there about recent wire transfers out of the accounts of Señor Jean-Paul Bertrand is not reported to the State Department and that they don't turn up anything more that will be reported."

"Good God, you go to prison for destroying evidence!" Yung said.

"You're not going to destroy evidence," Castillo said. "You're going to collect that evidence and get it to Mrs. Forbison, who will establish and maintain a classified file on that money from step one."

He leaned forward in the high-backed judge's chair and pulled the red telephone to him.

"Which of these buttons is Natalie Cohen's?" he asked, looking at Mrs. Forbison.

"Five," she said.

He pushed the fifth button.

"Castillo, Madam Secretary," he said. "Can you give me a moment?"

Castillo explained the situation, then listened to her thoughts.

"Thank you very much, Madam Secretary. I think this will handle the problem. I'll keep you advised," Castillo said.

He put the handset back in the cradle and looked at Special Agent Yung.

"You should have picked up on that, Yung," Castillo said. "But, in case you didn't, the secretary of state will message the ambassador in Montevideo that she is dispatching an FBI agent with special knowledge of the situation—you—down there to investigate the financial affairs of Mr. Lorimer/Bertrand, that they are to turn over to you whatever they have developed so far, and that you will make your report directly to her."

"Okay," Yung said.

"You will make two reports," Castillo said.

"Two?"

Castillo nodded.

"One will be a complete report of everything you know, what the other FBI guys know, and the details of the wire transfers of the money from his account to yours. You will take that one, by hand, to the embassy in Buenos Aires, and give it to Alex Darby, who will be expecting it and who will send it to Mrs. Forbison in a diplomatic pouch. That will take a day longer, but we won't get involved with encryption."

"I don't understand that, Charley," Mrs. Forbison said. "Why not encrypt it?"

"Whenever you encrypt anything, two more people, the encryptor and the de-cryptor, are in on the secret."

"I never thought about that," she said. "You don't trust cryptographers?"

"I trust them more than most people I know. I'm just being careful."

When she nodded her understanding, he turned back to Yung.

"The second report will include what the other FBI guys down there have found out and a sanitized version of what you know. No details of how much money was in those accounts before we made the transfers, just how much we left in them. And, of course, no mention of the wire transfers. This one you will give to the ambassador in Montevideo, requesting that he have it encrypted and transmitted to the secretary of state. Got it?"

"You're asking me to officially submit a report I know to be dishonest. I'm not sure I can do that."

"What I am ordering you to do is submit a report less certain details that are classified Top Secret Presidential. There's a difference. There was no reason for the ambassador to be told about the Finding and he has not been told. He does not have the Need to Know about that money or what we have done with it."

"I was always taught that the ambassador has the right to know what any agency of the U.S. government is doing in his country."

"Try to understand this, Yung. It would be a violation of the law for you to pass information to the ambassador that he is not entitled to have because he doesn't have the proper security clearance. There are only two people who can give him that clearance: the President and me. The President has not done so and I can't see any good reason that I should." He paused and then asked, "Are you going to do this, Yung, or not?"

Yung didn't reply for thirty seconds, which seemed much longer.

"When you put it that way . . ." he began, then paused a moment. "You have to understand I've just never had any experience with . . . this sort of business."

"Are you going to do it or not?"

"Yes. Yes, of course."

"I don't have any idea what kind of an oath you FBI people take, but the oath an officer takes when he is commissioned has a phrase in it: *without any mental reservations whatsoever.*' Are you harboring any mental reservations?"

Yung cocked his head as he thought that over, then shook his head and said, "No, I guess I'm not."

"Okay, we'll be in touch. I'll probably see you down there."

"Come with me," Agnes said to Yung, "and we'll see what we can do with the travel agency." Then she looked at Castillo. "I don't know what else you have planned for right now, but Tom McGuire and Jack Britton are waiting to see you."

Castillo waved as a signal for her to send them in. They came in immediately.

Supervisory Special Agent Thomas McGuire of the Secret Service was a large, red-haired Irishman in his forties. Until the reorganization following 9/11, the Secret Service had been under the Treasury Department. He and Supervisory

Special Agent Joel Isaacson had been assigned to the Presidential Protection Detail.

When the Secret Service had been assigned to the Department of Homeland Security, McGuire and Isaacson became the first members of the secretary's protection detail. And when McGuire had learned of the Presidential Finding and the formation of the Office of Organizational Analysis, he had gone to Secretary Hall—who was now the de facto head of the Secret Service—and asked that he be assigned to it.

"I'm a cop at heart, boss," he'd said. "It looks to me like Charley is going to need somebody like me, and you don't really need both Joel and me."

Secret Service Special Agent Jack Britton, a tall black man with sharp features, was new to the Secret Service. He had been a Philadelphia Police Department detective assigned to the Counterterrorism Bureau. Castillo and Miller had met him while trying to find the stolen 727. The first time they spoke, Britton had "come in" from his undercover assignment—keeping track of what he, political correctness be damned, called the AAL, which stood for "African American Lunatics."

He had been wearing a scraggly beard, a dark blue robe, sandals, had his hair braided with beads, and was known to his brother Muslims in Philadelphia's Aari-Teg mosque as Ali Abid Ar Raziq.

Impressed with Britton for many things, including his courage and dedication as well as his intimate knowledge of the Muslim world in the United States—both bona fide and AAL—Isaacson had recruited him for the Secret Service, together with another Philadelphia Police Department officer, Sergeant Elizabeth Schneider, of the Intelligence and Organized Crime unit.

Isaacson hadn't been thinking of the Office of the Secretary of Homeland Security, and certainly neither of them working with or for C. G. Castillo. He had recruited Britton and Schneider for the Secret Service, knowing of twenty places around the country that could really use Britton's talents and thinking of Betty Schneider as a likely candidate for duty on one of the protection details.

That hadn't happened. Both had just about completed Secret Service training when Mrs. Elizabeth Masterson had been kidnapped. Castillo had had Britton and Schneider flown to Buenos Aires to assist in the investigation of the kidnapping and murders.

"Parties unknown" had ambushed the embassy car taking Special Agent Schneider from the Masterson home, killing the Marine driver and seriously wounding Schneider.

Once the Presidential Finding had been made, it had simply been assumed that Britton was assigned to the Office of Organizational Analysis and that when Special Agent Schneider recovered from her wounds and returned to duty she would be, too.

"It's all right this time," Castillo greeted McGuire and Britton, "but when you come to the throne room in the future please take off your shoes and wear white gloves."

Miller and McGuire laughed.

"I'm impressed, Charley," McGuire said.

Britton didn't say anything, and his smile was strained.

I wonder what's the matter with him? Castillo thought.

"I don't know, Jack," Castillo said. "Now that I think about it, you really didn't look so bad in your blue robe and the beads in your hair."

That got another chuckle from McGuire and Miller.

"I'd really like to see you in private, Charley," Britton said. "Why don't I come back in ten minutes?"

He wants a favor. Madam Britton wants him to spend a little time at home. Maybe somebody is sick. Maybe somebody at the school wants a real cop for a teacher and he doesn't want that.

"Something personal, Jack?" Castillo asked.

Britton visibly thought that over before replying, "Yeah, in a way. But, no, not really personal."

"Something to do with what's going on here?"

Britton nodded.

What the hell doesn't he want Miller and McGuire to hear?

I can't have that.

"Jack, let me tell you how we're going to work around here," Castillo said. "Or how we're not going to work. Around here, I don't want anyone to be in the dark about anything that's going on."

He swept his hand to indicate he meant everybody in the office, then added, "And that includes Mrs. Forbison. I can't see how we can work any other way."

"Permission to speak, sir?" Miller asked.

Now, what the hell is the matter with him?

"If you're being clever, Dick, now is not the time," Castillo said.

"I'm asking if you're open to a comment or a question?"

"Ask it."

"Does 'anyone' include Special Agent David William Yung, Jr.?" Miller asked, then looked at McGuire and explained, "When Charley told him he was sending him to Uruguay to keep the details of Lorimer's bank accounts from becoming public knowledge, Yung had to think it over carefully."

"Oh, shit!" McGuire said. "And that's not the first time he's had 'reservations,' is it?"

"Say it out loud, Dick," Castillo said.

"I think it's only a matter of time before his conscience overwhelms him about the 'irregular' things you're having him do and/or he really gets homesick for the purity of the FBI and decides to come clean," Miller said.

He let that sink in, then finished, "And the more he knows, the more he will have to tell."

"He's right, Charley," McGuire said. "There's a Puritan streak in the FBI. They like to hire pure people. They start working on them at Quantico that the book is holy, that they have to go by it, and they keep it up afterward. Even before Dick brought it up, I wondered if Yung belonged in here. I'd say send him back to the FBI, but that would remind him even more that we are ignoring the book and he already knows too much to take the risk that he would confess all."

"So, me sending him down there was a mistake?" Castillo asked.

"Not a mistake but risky," McGuire said. "And who else could you have sent?"

"Well, I guess the thing to do is bring him back and sit on him *after* he makes sure that what we've done with Lorimer's money doesn't get out," Castillo said. "The only comment I have is that I agree that Yung is . . . what? Highly moral? What's wrong with that? And I think he would love nothing better than to go to somebody in the FBI and tell them what's going on around here. But it is that morality that keeps him from doing that."

"Run that past me again," Miller said.

"You were here, Dick. I asked him if he had any mental reservations and he said—after thinking about it—that he didn't. I think he meant that."

"Keep your fingers crossed, Charley," Miller said, doubtfully.

"But you're right. We can't afford to have him in the loop," Castillo said. "We'll tell him as little as possible." He turned to Britton. "You're in the loop, Jack. We all need to know what you have to say."

Britton shrugged, then said, "Okay. This is one of those damned if you do, damned if you don't things. I heard something in Philadelphia that is probably about as far off the wall as anything ever gets, that logic tells me to dismiss but which I thought I should pass on to you."

"Let's have it," Castillo said.

"I went to see Sy Fillmore in the hospital while I was there. I got it from him."

"Who's he?

"A counterterrorism detective. He was doing what I used to do. He went around the bend and they've got him in the loony bin in Friends Hospital on Roosevelt Boulevard. So my source is somebody they're keeping in a padded room."

"What did he have to say?"

"The brothers in his mosque believe they are about to get their hands on a nuclear bomb."

"That does sound a little incredible," Miller said. "Where are they going to get it?"

Britton shrugged. "He didn't know. What he did know was they have just bought a farm in Durham."

"North Carolina?" McGuire asked.

"Pennsylvania," Britton replied. "Bucks County. Upper end of the county. A couple of miles off the Delaware River. The reason they bought the place is because of the old iron mines on it."

"Iron mines?"

"They're going to use them as bomb shelters when the nuclear bomb takes out Philadelphia. They're stocking them with food, etcetera."

"Tell me about the iron mines," McGuire said.

"Well, they've been there forever," Britton said. "You remember when Washington crossed the Delaware?"

"I've heard about it. I'm not quite that old," McGuire said.

"He crossed the Delaware in a Durham boat. They were called Durham boats because they moved the iron ore from the iron mines in Durham down the Delaware. They haven't taken any ore out of them for, Christ, two hundred years, but the mines, the tunnels, are still there, because they were hacked out of solid rock."

"You believe this story, Jack?" Miller asked.

"I don't want to believe it, logic tells me not to believe it, but Sy Fillmore tells me the brothers believe it. And I'd like to know where they got the money to buy a hundred-odd-acre farm. That's high-priced real estate up there. They didn't pay for it with stolen Social Security checks."

"Stolen Social Security checks?" Castillo asked.

"That—and ripping off the neighborhood crack dealers—was their primary source of income when I was in the mosque."

"And the cops in Philadelphia?" Castillo asked. "Chief Inspector Fritz Kramer, for example. What do they say?"

"They found Cy wandering around North Philly babbling to himself," Britton said. "It was three days before they even found out he was a cop. And he's been in Friends Hospital ever since, with a cop sitting outside his door, as much to protect Sy from himself as from the AALs. No, Chief Kramer doesn't believe it. He didn't even pass it on to the FBI."

"Where are they going to get a nuke?" Miller asked. "How are they going to move it around, hide it?"

"There were supposed to be thirty-odd suitcase-sized nukes here, smuggled in by the Russians." McGuire said. "They wouldn't be hard to move around or hide."

"You think there's something to this, Tom?" Castillo asked.

"No. But I'm like Jack. Sometimes there's things you just shouldn't ignore because they don't make sense."

"So what do we do, tell the FBI?" Castillo asked.

"Why don't you send Jack back to Philly?" McGuire asked. "I'll call the Secret Service there—the agent in charge is an old friend of mine—and tell him we're interested in why a bunch of American muslims from Philadelphia bought that farm, where they got the money to buy it, and what they're doing with it. And I'll tell him we can't say why we're interested. If and when we get those answers, we can think about it some more."

"Okay, do it," Castillo ordered. "Has anyone else got anything for me?"

Everybody shook their heads.

Castillo went on: "What I am going to do now is go to my apartment and pack. Then I'm going to the Old Executive Office Building to wait for Hall. I was going to ask him what to do about our new liaison officer, but Dick and Agnes have told me that's my problem. Then as soon as he lets me go, I'm going to Philadelphia to see Betty Schneider and then, somehow, I'm going to go to Paris, either tonight or as soon as I can."

"I didn't know anybody went to Paris on purpose," Miller said. "What are you going to do there?"

"Thank you for asking, and I'm not being sarcastic. I want everybody to know what I'm doing," Castillo said. "The agency guy in Paris—Edgar Delchamps—is a good guy, a real old-timer. I'm going to ask him to go with me to Lorimer's apartment. The embassy has been informed that I'm going to look after Lorimer's property for Ambassador Lorimer. Then I'm going to tell him what happened at Lorimer's estancia and see if he has any ideas who the guys who bushwhacked us were or who they were working for.

"Then I'm going to Fulda to make sure there's no problems with all that money in my Liechtensteinische Landesbank account in the Caymans. Maybe there's a better place to have it.

"Then I'm going to Budapest to see a journalist named Eric Kocian, who gave me some names of people in the oil-for-food business. I promised him I wouldn't turn them over to anyone. I want to get him to let me use the names. See if we can figure out where I might have got them, other than from him. I'm also going to ask him to guess who was paying the guys who bushwhacked us.

"Then, maybe a quick stop in Vienna to see what I can pick up there about the guy who was murdered just before Lorimer decided to go missing. Before I come back here, I'm probably going to go to Uruguay and Argentina. I want to go through Lorimer's estancia to see what I can come up with.

"Which reminds me of something else that I probably would have forgotten: Dick, get on the horn to somebody at Fort Rucker, maybe the Aviation Board, and find out the best panel and black boxes available on the civilian market for a Bell Ranger. Get a set of it, put it in a box, and ask Secretary Cohen to send it under diplomatic sticker to Ambassador Silvio in Buenos Aires."

"What the hell is that all about?"

"You wouldn't believe the lousy avionics in the Ranger I borrowed down there. The new stuff is payment for the use of the chopper. And it will be nice to have if I need to borrow the Ranger again."

No one spoke for a moment, then Miller said, "Charley, those avionics are going to cost a fortune."

"We'll have a fortune in the Liechtensteinische Landesbank. So far as I'm concerned, that's what it's for."

Miller gave him a thumbs-up.

"I'll be in touch," Castillo said and walked toward his office door.

He turned.

"Dick, can you come with me? Sure as Christ made little green apples, I've forgotten something."

[THREE]
Room 404
The Mayflower Hotel
1127 Connecticut Avenue NW
Washington, D.C.
1630 4 August 2005

Major H. Richard Miller, Jr., was sprawled on the chaise longue in the master bedroom, his stiff leg on the chair, his good leg resting, knee bent, on the floor. A bottle of Heineken beer was resting in his hand on his chest.

Major C. G. Castillo was standing by the bed, putting clothing into a hard-sided suitcase.

"If I was just coming back here," he said, "I could get by with a carry-on. But if I take just a carry-on, I'll find myself in the middle of winter in Argentina."

"And if you take the suitcase, it will be misdirected to Nome, Alaska," Miller said, lifting his bottle to take a sip of beer. "It is known as the Rule of the Fickle Finger of Fate."

Castillo closed the suitcase and set it on the floor.

"So tell me about that," Castillo said, pointing to Miller's leg. "What do they say at Walter Reed?"

"I am led to believe that my chances of passing an Army flight physical range from zero to zilch. I have been 'counseled' that what I should do is take retirement for disability. One bum knee is apparently worth seventy percent of my basic pay for the rest of my life."

"Oh, shit," Castillo said.

"What really pisses me off is that I have reason to believe that all I have to do to reactivate my civilian ticket—"

"Reactivate?"

"Yeah. It went on hold when I didn't show up for my annual physical. I didn't think I could pass it wearing twenty pounds of plaster of paris on my leg. So my ticket became inactive. They didn't pull it, which is important, but declared it inactive, pending the results of a flight physical. I've looked into that. What that means is I find some friendly chancre mechanic. He sees the scars and I tell him they are from a successful knee operation and show him how I can bend my knee. He will make a note of that for the examiner giving me my flight test. In other words, 'Did his knee operation result in a physical limitation that makes him unsafe in a cockpit?' The examiner will see that I can push the pedals satisfactorily. My tickets as an instrument-qualified pilot in command of piston and jet multiengine fixed- and rotary-wing aircraft is reactivated. Which means I can then fly just about anything for anybody but the Army."

"Can you 'push the pedals satisfactorily'?" Castillo asked.

"I think so. I would hate to believe that all the fucking exercise I've been doing flexing the sonofabitch has been in vain. So what I've been thinking of doing is going to Tampa and see if I can't find reasonably honest work as a contractor."

"Flying worn-out Russian helicopters on some bullshit mission in the middle of nowhere?"

"The pay is good."

"What's wrong with staying right where you are?"

"Working for you?"

"Is something wrong with that?"

"It would look like—would be—cronyism."

"Think of it as affirmative action," Castillo said. "The Office of Organizational Analysis is offering employment to somebody who meets all the criteria. You're ignorant, physically crippled, mentally challenged, and otherwise unemployable."

"And black. Don't forget that."

"And black. I'll talk to McGuire. Maybe he can get you hired by the Secret Service."

"I don't think I could pass their physical."

"We'll work something out. I really hate to tell you this, but I need you, Dick."

"If I thought you really meant that, Charley . . ."

"Have I ever lied to you?"

"You really don't want me to answer that, do you?"

"In this case, I'm going to need somebody—you—to protect my back from this goddamned liaison officer Montvale is shoving down my throat. And that's the truth."

"You just can't say, 'Thank you just the same but I don't need a liaison officer'?"

"To Ambassador Charles Montvale, the director of National Intelligence? He's not used to being told no, especially when all he's trying to do is be helpful."

"What's he really after?"

"He doesn't like the whole idea of a presidential agent. If he can't take me over—and I'm sure he's working on that—he wants to put me out of business."

"So what? What are they going to do, send you back to the Army? What's wrong with that? Goddamn, I wish that was one of my options."

Castillo didn't respond to that. Instead, he asked, "When is all this going to happen?"

"I'll have thirty days from the time I'm restored to limited duty, which should be in the next week to ten days. I then have to tell them I'll accept permanent limited-duty status—which means I would wind up in a recruiting office or a mess-kit-repair battalion—or take the medical retirement."

"Then we have time," Castillo said. "Just forget that contractor bullshit, okay?"

Miller nodded.

"Thanks, Charley," he said.

"Jesus, that beer looks tempting," Castillo said.

"Give in," Miller said.

"I will. Stay there. I'll go get one. You want another?"

Without waiting for an answer, he went into the living room and to the wet bar. As he was taking two bottles of beer from the refrigerator, he heard the telephone ring and when he went back into the bedroom Miller was holding out a handset to him.

"Your guardian angel, saving you from temptation," Miller said.

Castillo took the phone. "Castillo," he said.

"Matt Hall, Charley."

"Yes, sir?"

"Two changes in the plan," Hall said.

What plan?

"Yes, sir?"

"I'll pick you up there at half past seven, not eight."

"Excuse me?"

"I said I'll pick you up at half past seven, not eight."

"Where are we going, sir?"

"To the White House. I told you."

Oh no you didn't. You told me that you *were going to the White House.* I *was going to be on the Metroliner on the way to Philadelphia at seven-thirty.*

"That message must have come through garbled, sir."

"Obviously," Hall said. There was a suggestion of annoyance in his tone. "And the second change is that the President wants you to wear your uniform."

"Excuse me?"

"The President said about ten minutes ago, quote, Tell Charley to please wear his uniform, end quote."

"What's that all about?" Castillo blurted.

"The commander in chief did not choose to share with me any explanation of his desire," Hall said. "The Seventeenth Street entrance, seven-thirty. Brass and shoes shined appropriately. Got to go, Charley."

The line went dead.

Castillo said, "Sonofabitch!"

"Good news, huh?"

Castillo didn't reply. He went to the walk-in closet.

Miller heard him say, "Thank you, West Point."

Castillo came out of the closet, carrying a zippered nylon bag.

" 'Thank you, West Point'?" Miller parroted.

"Yeah," Castillo said. "The first thing I learned on the holy plain was that when you fuck up the only satisfactory excuse is, 'No excuse, sir.' The second thing I learned was to get your uniform pressed the minute you take it off because some sonofabitch will order you to appear in it when you least expect it and it had better be pressed."

"And in this case, the sonofabitch is the Honorable Matthew Hall? Why does he want you to put on your uniform?"

"Worse," Castillo said, as he unzipped the bag. "The President does."

"What's that about?"

"I have no fucking idea," Castillo said. "But like the good soldier I used to be, I will show up at the appointed place at the appointed hour in the prescribed uniform."

"What is the appointed place and the appointed hour?"

"Nineteen-thirty at the Seventeenth Street entrance, from which Hall will convey me to the White House for reasons unknown."

Castillo started taking off his clothing, laying his suit, shirt, and tie neatly on the bed so that he could change back into it as soon as he could get away from whatever the hell was going on at the White House.

The lobby of the Mayflower Hotel runs through the ground floor from the Connecticut Avenue entrance to the Seventeenth Street entrance. The elevator bank is closer to Connecticut Avenue, and it is some distance— three-quarters of a city block—from the elevators to the Seventeenth Street entrance.

Nevertheless, Major C. G. Castillo, now attired in his "dress blue" uniform, saw her just about the moment he got off the elevator. She was wearing a pale pink summer dress and a broad, floppy-brimmed hat. He decided she was either waiting for someone to meet her there or was waiting, as he would be, for someone to pick her up.

She didn't see Castillo until he was almost at the shallow flight of stairs leading upward to the Seventeenth Street foyer and doors. Then she looked at him without expression.

When he came close, Castillo said, "Good evening, Mrs. Wilson."

She said, softly but intensely, "I thought it was you, you miserable sonofabitch."

"And it's nice to see you again, too," Castillo said, put his brimmed uniform cap squarely on his head, and pushed through the revolving door onto Seventeenth Street, then walked to the waiting Secret Service GMC Yukon XL.

He did not look back at the lobby, but as the Yukon pulled away from the curb he took a quick look.

Mrs. Patricia Davies Wilson still was standing there, her arms folded over her breasts, glaring at the Yukon.

He remembered what Miller had said about her death rays freezing his martini solid.

[FOUR]
The White House
1600 Pennsylvania Avenue NW
Washington, D.C.
1950 4 August 2005

Castillo recognized the Marine lieutenant colonel standing just inside the door in the splendiferous formal uniform, heavily draped with gold braid and the aiguillettes of an aide-de-camp to the commander in chief. He had last seen him on Air Force One at Keesler Air Force Base in Mississippi. He even remembered his name: McElroy.

"Good evening, Mr. Secretary, ma'am," Lieutenant Colonel McElroy said to Secretary and Mrs. Matthew Hall, "The President asks that you come to the presidential apartments."

Then he looked at Castillo, who thought he saw recognition come slowly to McElroy's eyes.

"And you're Major Castillo?" Lieutenant Colonel McElroy asked.

"Yes, sir," Castillo said and, smiling, pointed to his chest to the black-and-white name tag reading CASTILLO.

"The President desires that you go to the presidential apartments, Major," Lieutenant Colonel McElroy said. It was evident he did not appreciate Castillo having pointed to his name tag.

Well, fuck you, Colonel. All you had to do was look.

"Yes, sir," Castillo said.

"The elevator is there, Mr. Secretary," Lieutenant Colonel McElroy said, gesturing.

"Thank you," Hall said.

The First Lady was in the sitting room of the presidential apartments but not the President. So were three other people whose presence did not surprise Castillo—Secretary of State Natalie Cohen; Ambassador Charles W. Montvale, the director of National Intelligence; and Frederick K. Beiderman, the secretary of defense—and one, General Allan Naylor, whose presence did. There was a photographer standing in a corner with two Nikon digital cameras hanging around his neck.

I wonder what is about to be recorded for posterity?

Montvale, Beiderman, and Hall were wearing dinner jackets. Naylor was wearing dress blues.

"He'll be out in a minute," the First Lady announced, and then added, "Hello, Charley, we haven't seen much of you lately."

"Good evening, ma'am."

The men nodded at him but no one spoke.

The President came in a moment later, shrugging into his dinner jacket.

There was a chorus of, "Good evening, Mr. President."

The President circled the room, first kissing the women, then shaking hands with the men, including Charley.

"Okay, General," the President ordered. "As usual, I'm running a little late. Let's get this show on the road."

Naylor took a sheet of paper from his tunic.

"Attention to orders," he read. "Department of the Army, Washington, D.C. Extract from General Order 155, dated 1 August 2005. Paragraph eleven. Major Carlos G. Castillo, 22 179 155, Special Forces, is promoted Lieutenant Colonel, with date of rank 31 July 2005. For the Chief of Staff. Johnson L. Maybree, Major General, the Adjutant General."

I'll be a sonofabitch!

"And as soon as the colonel comes over here so General Naylor and I can put his new shoulder boards on him," the President said, motioning for Castillo to join him, "I will have a few words to say."

The photographer came out of his corner, one camera up and its flash firing. Castillo, without thinking about it, came to attention next to the President.

"How do we get the old ones off?" the President asked, tugging at Castillo's shoulder boards.

"Let me show you, Mr. President," General Naylor said. He handed something to the President and put his hands on Castillo's shoulders.

Castillo glanced down to see what Naylor had handed the President.

Of course, light bird's shoulder boards.

But they're not new.

Christ, they're his.

Castillo felt his eyes water.

"And these slip on this way," Naylor said, demonstrating.

The photographer bobbed around, clicking the shutter of his Nikon every second or so as the President got one shoulder board on and then Naylor got the other one on, and as they stood side by side, and then as the President and then Naylor shook Charley's hand, and then as the others in the room became involved. Charley's hand was shaken by the director of National Intelligence and the secretary of defense. His cheek was kissed by the First Lady, the secretary of state, and Mrs. Hall. A final series of photos including everyone was taken.

"And now I have something to say," the President said. "As some of you may know, I am the commander in chief. Until the promotion of Colonel Castillo came up, I naïvely thought that meant I could issue any order that I wanted and it would be carried out. I learned that does not apply to the promotion of officers.

"When *Colonel* Castillo found and returned to our control the 727 the terrorists had stolen in Angola—when the entire intelligence community was still looking for it, when we learned how close the lunatics had actually come to crashing it into the Liberty Bell in downtown Philadelphia after the entire intelligence community had pooh-poohed that possibility—I thought that a promotion would be small enough reward for Castillo's extraordinary service to our country.

"Then-Major Castillo had already been selected, Matt Hall told me, for promotion to lieutenant colonel, not only selected but selected for quick promotion because of outstanding service.

"So I asked General Naylor, 'How soon can I promote him?' and General Naylor said, in effect, that I couldn't, that it doesn't work that way. Well, I thought that might well be because General Naylor and Colonel Castillo have a close personal relationship and he didn't want it to look like Charley was getting special treatment. So I went to the chief of staff of the Army and said I knew of an outstanding major, a West Pointer, and a Green Beret, like the chief of staff, who not only had been selected for promotion to lieutenant colonel on what I now knew to be the 'five percent list' but had rendered a great service to his country, and I would like to know why he couldn't be promoted immediately. And the chief of staff said that it didn't work like that, and, as a West Pointer and a Green Beret, the major to whom I was referring would understand that. The clear implication being, so should the commander in chief.

"So the commander in chief backed off, except to phone General Naylor, and order him the moment he learned that the slowly grinding wheels of the Army promotion system had finally ground out that it was time to promote Major Castillo to let me know immediately. Which he did the day before yesterday."

He turned to Castillo, shook his right hand, and put his left on Castillo's shoulder.

"So you, *Colonel* Castillo, are going to have to be satisfied with better late than never. Congratulations, Charley."

"Thank you, sir."

There was polite laughter, applause, and another round of handshaking.

"Over the objections of the secretary of state, who fears that after one drink I will give the country away to our guests tonight, we will now toast Colonel Castillo's new rank," the President said.

A white-jacketed steward appeared with a tray of champagne glasses and distributed them.

"Ladies and gentlemen," the President said, his glass raised, "Lieutenant Colonel C. G. Castillo."

The President had just put his glass to his lips when a steward motioned that he had a telephone call.

"Natalie and I have been expecting that," the President said. "Will you excuse us, please?"

He and the secretary of state left the room.

General Naylor walked up to Charley.

"Thank you for the shoulder boards, sir," Charley said.

"My pleasure, Colonel," Naylor said. "And if you have no further need for your old ones, Allan's on the major's list."

"I'd be honored to have Allan wear them, sir."

Ambassador Montvale joined them. He laid an almost paternal hand on Castillo's shoulder.

"I think you were genuinely surprised by this, weren't you, Colonel? I agree with the President that it's overdue."

An alarm bell went off in Castillo's mind:

Why is this sonofabitch charming me?

Because the President made that little speech? Set up this ceremony in the first place?

No. He wants something. What?

He doesn't want me complaining about his goddamned liaison officer. That's what it is. He knows that right now, the President is in a mood to give me just about anything I ask for.

If I don't bite the bullet now about that—and doing so now would ruin this "we're all pals" ambiance—by the time I get back, and God only knows when that will be—I'll permanently be stuck with Mr. Truman Ellsworth.

"General Naylor told me a long time ago that waiting for a promotion is like watching a glacier," Castillo said. "For a long time, absolutely nothing—and then all of a sudden a great big splash."

Montvale and Naylor chuckled.

What's that line from Basic Tactics 101?

The best defense is a good offense.

"Mr. Ambassador," Charley said, "I'd like a few minutes of your time, if that would be possible."

Naylor's surprise was evident on his face.

"Certainly," Montvale said. "Sometime tomorrow afternoon?"

"Sir, just as soon as I can I'm going to be on a plane to Paris."

"You mean now?"

"If that would be possible, sir."

"Actually, I've been wanting to have a private word with you, too," Montvale said, thoughtfully. "And this would seem to be one of those fortuitous circumstances."

"Thank you, sir," Castillo said.

"Especially since General Naylor is here," Montvale went on.

"Excuse me?" Naylor said.

"We could go to the situation room and use the bubble, but I'm afraid that the three of us going there would attract attention. Wouldn't you agree, General? Someone would decide that something is going on that they should know about."

"Mr. Ambassador," Naylor said, "my aide is waiting outside with a car to take me to Andrews. Just as soon as I can get away from here I'm going back to Tampa."

"So far as getting away from here is concerned," Montvale said, "our role in tonight's events is over. The President has moved on to other things on his agenda. And if something unexpected comes up, he knows how to find us. I really don't want to waste the next couple of hours smiling at people I don't really like."

"I was just thinking the same thing," Naylor confessed, smiling.

"I know," Montvale said. "The Army and Navy Club. We could talk there. Could I impose and suggest we go there?"

"Mr. Ambassador, I really have to get back to Tampa," Naylor said.

"General, I just saved us from two hours—at least—of smiling at people we don't like. Can't you spare me thirty minutes? I'd really like for you to be there when the colonel and I have our little chat."

"Yes, of course," Naylor said.

"Playing the game, I suggest we leave in our own vehicles," Montvale said as they approached the portico.

"Secretary Hall brought me here," Castillo said. "May I ride with you, General?"

"You can use the pool," Montvale said.

"Sir?"

Montvale answered by speaking to one of the Secret Service uniformed police guards at the door.

"We'll need my car, General Naylor's, and Colonel Castillo will need one from the pool," he ordered.

"Yes, sir," the guard said. Then he spoke to his lapel microphone. "Send up Big Eye's car, Tampa One's car, and one from the pool for Don Juan." Then he turned to Montvale. "They'll be right here, sir," he said.

Thirty seconds later, a dark blue GMC Yukon XL pulled up.

"I'll wait for you in the lobby," Montvale said to Naylor. "All right?"

"That'll be fine."

As Montvale got in the Yukon, a dark blue Chevrolet Suburban pulled up behind it.

A full colonel wearing the insignia of an aide-de-camp got out of the front passenger's seat as a staff sergeant came out from behind the wheel to snatch the covers from the four-star bumper plates.

Castillo, as a reflex action, saluted the colonel.

"Jack, take the car to the Army-Navy Club," Naylor said. "I'll ride with Maj . . . Colonel Castillo."

"Yes, sir," the colonel said.

Another dark blue Yukon came up the drive and pulled in ahead of the Chevrolet as the sergeant put the covers back over Naylor's four-star plates. A Secret Service agent got out of the front passenger's seat and opened the rear door.

Naylor climbed in and Castillo followed him. The Secret Service agent closed the door, got in front, and turned to look in the back.

"Where to, sir?"

"The Army-Navy Club, please," Castillo said.

"Yes, sir," the Secret Service agent said and then spoke to his microphone. "Don Juan, with Tampa One aboard, leaving the grounds for the Army-Navy Club."

The Yukon started down the drive toward Pennsylvania Avenue.

" 'Don Juan, with Tampa One aboard'?" Naylor parroted.

"Don Juan is Joel Isaacson's idea of humor," Charley said.

"Charley, I've got something to say. And I think I better say it before we get there."

"Yes, sir."

"What I was thinking tonight—and don't misunderstand me, you earned that promotion—was that I really wish I hadn't sent you to work for Matt Hall."

"Me, too."

"I wonder if you mean that," Naylor said. "This is pretty heady stuff, Charley. A Secret Service car, a Secret Service code name. I am reminded of Lieutenant Colonel Oliver North and that worries me."

Castillo didn't reply.

"I would have been much happier if your promotion meant you now would take command of some battalion," Naylor said.

"I would, too, sir. I didn't ask for this job. And I asked to be relieved."

"Well, that's not going to happen and that's what worries me," Naylor said, then suddenly shifted subjects: "Do you have any idea why Montvale wants me at the club?" Then, before Castillo could reply, he asked another: "Why did you want to talk to him?"

"I have no idea why he wants you there, but the reason I want to talk to him is because he sent me Truman Ellsworth to be his liaison officer—read spy . . ."

"Truman Ellsworth is a former under secretary of state," Naylor interrupted. "A liaison officer with that background?"

"Yes, sir. I thought of that. And I don't want him. I want to get rid of him now before he chains himself to my desk."

"I don't think I have to tell you that Montvale is a powerful man. And a dangerous one."

"I've already figured that out," Castillo said.

"In North Africa," Naylor said, almost to himself, "when Eisenhower sent Omar Bradley to Patton as his liaison officer—read spy—Patton outwitted Eisenhower by asking that Bradley be assigned as his chief of staff. That put Bradley under Patton's orders. That kept him from communicating anything to Eisenhower without Patton knowing about it and *not* communicating anything Patton didn't want communicated."

"I've heard that story," Charley said.

"I don't think you want this fellow Ellsworth as your chief of staff," Naylor said. "Ellsworth is not Bradley; he works for Montvale and that's not going to change. And you're not Patton, who had as many stars as Bradley. You're a lowly lieutenant colonel and Ellsworth is . . . a former under secretary of state."

"That's what worries me," Castillo said.

"The difference here is that Patton worked for Eisenhower. You don't work for Montvale. But that's what he's after. If he can't get that right now, he'll use Ellsworth as your puppet master."

"That's what it looks like to me, sir," Charley agreed.

"Goddamn it, I hate Washington," Naylor said.

[ONE]
The Daiquiri Lounge
The Army and Navy Club
901 Seventeenth Street NW
Washington, D.C.
2105 4 August 2005

Ambassador Montvale was waiting for them in the lobby. They all walked up the stairs to the second floor, then into the Daiquiri Lounge, taking a table in the bar where Castillo knew he and General Naylor could smoke cigars.

It immediately became apparent that before their conversation could begin, they were going to have to deal with other guests in the lounge.

The commander in chief of Central Command was not only known to—that is to say, a friend of—half a dozen officers and their wives having after-dinner drinks there but, as one of the most powerful officers in the Army, was someone to whom it was necessary to "make manners."

Once the first old friend walked over to shake General Naylor's hand, everyone else decided that it was not only all right for them to do so but expected of them.

Each visit—however brief—required that both Ambassador Montvale and Lieutenant Colonel Castillo be introduced. And Lieutenant Colonel Castillo was not used to—and thus made a little uncomfortable by—being addressed by his new title.

Finally, it was over, and the waiter, who had hovered in the background awaiting its end, came to the table.

"Gentlemen, what can I get for you?"

"I'm a scotch drinker," Montvale answered, looking at Naylor. "Nothing fancy, no single malt. Something like Chivas Regal. That okay with you?"

"Fine," Naylor said.

What is he trying to do, establish the pecking order by telling Naylor what to drink?

And why did Naylor go along?

Castillo looked at the waiter. "Yes, please," he said.

When the waiter had left, Montvale asked, "What are you going to do in Paris?"

"Sir, I'm still looking for the people who murdered Mr. Masterson," Castillo said.

"That's what you wanted to talk to me about?"

"No, sir."

"Maybe you should. Maybe there's something I could do to help."

Castillo didn't reply.

"Well," Montvale continued, "if you didn't want my help, then what is it that you wish to talk about?"

"Mr. Ellsworth, sir."

"Truman Ellsworth. A good man. What about him?"

"I'm sure he is, but I don't want a liaison officer."

"Oh! Right to the bottom line!"

"Yes, sir."

"I could offer any number of reasons why a liaison officer who enjoys my trust could be very useful to you."

"I'm sure you could. But, thank you very much just the same, I don't want Mr. Ellsworth."

"Because you think he would be spying on you for me?"

Castillo didn't reply. But he thought of something that might provide an excuse for him not to do so immediately.

Maybe I'll think of something.

"Sir, excuse me. I have to make a call."

Montvale looked at him impatiently. Naylor looked at him curiously.

Castillo punched an autodial number on his cellular telephone.

"Dick," he said a moment later, "I think I can make the 2330 Air France flight to Paris. Can you send my luggage—and the suit and shirt and tie I left on the bed, and my laptop case—to the Army-Navy Club? Just tell the driver to wait outside."

Castillo listened for a moment, then said, "Actually, I'm having a drink with General Naylor and Ambassador Montvale." He paused. "Yes, I will. Thanks, Dick. I'll check in from Paris."

He pushed the CALL END button and turned to General Naylor.

"Major Miller's compliments, sir," he said.

Naylor nodded.

"What's your objection to having Mr. Ellsworth work with you?" Montvale asked, resuming the conversation as if there had been no interruption.

Castillo met his eyes for a moment.

I might as well go down fighting.

"I've been thinking about that, sir," Castillo said. "I certainly can't order you to do anything. But if you elect to keep sending Mr. Ellsworth to the Nebraska Complex, I'm afraid what he's going to be doing is sitting in an office all day without very much to do at all."

"What the hell are you talking about?"

"Unless Mr. Ellsworth has access to the Presidential Finding establishing the Office of Organizational Analysis, there's nothing I can tell him about what we're really doing."

"That's ridiculous and you know it," Montvale snapped. "Ellsworth has had the highest-level security clearances for years."

Again Castillo didn't reply and again Montvale took his meaning.

"You're not actually suggesting, Castillo, that you're not going to give *Truman Ellsworth* the necessary security clearance, are you?"

"Sir, I don't see where Mr. Ellsworth has the Need to Know about the Presidential Finding and my mission."

"I'll clear him for the Finding!"

"Sir, I don't believe you have that authority," Castillo said. "As I understand it, only the President and I do."

"I can't believe what I'm hearing! Just who the hell do you think you are? I'm the director of National Intelligence. *I* decide who is cleared for what."

"Ambassador, you don't have the authority to clear anyone for that Presidential Finding," Castillo said.

"Well, I guess we'll just have to see what the President has to say about that," Montvale said, "and about your attitude."

"Yes, sir. I guess we will," Castillo said.

"Before this gets out of hand, gentlemen," General Naylor said, "I'm going to say that neither one of you wants this disagreement to go any further."

"Nothing is going to get out of hand, thank you very much, General," Montvale said.

"Good," Naylor said, "because it would not be in the best interests of the country—or either of you—if it did."

Montvale looked icily at him.

"Frankly, General, I was hoping that you would help me reason with Major Castillo, help him to understand where he fits into the system."

"It's now Colonel Castillo, Mr. Ambassador," Naylor said.

"*Lieutenant colonel,* I believe," Montvale said. "Like Lieutenant Colonel Oliver North, who was also a junior officer given more authority than he was equipped to handle. You remember *Lieutenant* Colonel North, don't you, General?"

"I don't have the feeling, Mr. Ambassador," Naylor said, "that the President thinks he has given Colonel Castillo more authority than he can handle. Do you?"

Montvale didn't respond.

"Let me suggest a scenario, Mr. Ambassador," Naylor said, glancing around the lounge, then, satisfied no one was trying to follow their conversation, continued in a lower voice: "This dispute comes before the President. That would force him to choose between you two. From what I have seen of the President, he doesn't like to be forced to do anything."

"Nevertheless . . ."

"Obviously," Naylor went on, "you are of far greater importance to the government, to the country, than is Colonel Castillo. Colonel Castillo would be relieved. But he would be replaced, because we know the President likes having an agent—a presidential agent, if you will—answerable only to him. And you and I both know that his replacement would not be anyone you might suggest, however well qualified he might be. That would be giving you too much of a victory.

"So it would be another military officer. And I put it to you, sir, that no matter how well that officer might do, his performance would be compared by the President against that of Colonel Castillo and found wanting. Partially because in the two successful operations Colonel Castillo has run as the President's agent he was—as he is well aware—incredibly lucky. And partially because it wasn't *all* luck. Colonel Castillo has demonstrated that he is obviously extremely well qualified for the duties the President has chosen to give him.

"And I put it to you further, Mr. Ambassador, that always—*always*—the President is going to be thinking, *If Montvale hadn't gotten on his high horse and forced me to get rid of Castillo, things would have turned out better.* You were there. He did everything but beatify Charley in that little post-promotion speech he gave."

Naylor turned to Castillo.

"And you, *Colonel,* are going to have to learn something that is not taught at West Point. An accommodation is not a surrender. You are going to have to come to some arrangement, an accommodation, with Ambassador Montvale. And he with you. Or you will both be failing the President, and I'm sure neither of you wants that."

Montvale was about to reply when the waiter delivered their drinks, stopping the conversation.

After he'd gone, Montvale stirred his for several seconds, then extended the plastic stirrer to Castillo.

"Take it," the director of National Intelligence said. "Think of it as an olive branch."

"Make love, not war?" Castillo asked as he took the stirrer. It earned him a dirty look from Naylor.

"I really don't want to get in a war with you, Charley," Montvale said.

"Charley"? Not "Castillo"? Not "Colonel"? Or even "Major"?

I'm being charmed again and that's dangerous.

"Nor I with you, Mr. Ambassador."

"Shall we lay our cards on the table?"

"I have only one card to play: going to the President and telling him I can't function with Mr. Ellsworth looking over my shoulder and reporting to you everything I'm doing or planning on doing."

"I don't understand why my being kept aware of what you're doing is wrong," Montvale said. "Certainly, you confide in General Naylor."

"He does not," Naylor said, flatly. "I frankly hoped he would, but he has not."

Montvale raised an eyebrow. "You both realize, I'm sure, that would put another arrow in my quiver if I have to go to the President? 'Mr. President, he doesn't even tell General Naylor what he's doing. Remember Ollie North?' "

Naylor said, "To which the President might well reply, 'That's because Colonel Castillo doesn't work for General Naylor, he works for me.' "

"Point well taken," Montvale said after a moment with a smile.

"Are you going to the President, Mr. Ambassador?" Castillo asked.

"Probably, but not right now. That one card of yours—at this moment—is the ace of all spades. General Naylor is right. If the President was the pope, after that session in the apartment tonight you would now be Saint Carlos the Savior of His Country."

Both Naylor and Castillo chuckled.

"So you are going to find something else for Mr. Ellsworth to do?" Castillo asked.

"Let me show you my cards," Montvale said. "Okay?"

Castillo nodded.

"I'm very impressed with you."

"Is that what they call the 'flattery card'?"

"Hear me out. All it will cost you is a little time."

"My standard tactic when I'm dealing with someone I know is smarter than me is to run," Castillo said.

"Is that *your* flattery card?"

"I am out of my class with you and I know it. Just because it may be flattering doesn't mean it isn't true," Castillo said.

"Then why does it have to be untrue that I'm impressed with you?"

"That would depend on why you're impressed."

"Like the President, I think you did one hell of a job finding that airplane and then finding this Lorimer fellow. The major problem I have with you—other than that the President thinks you should be beatified—is that I think you should be working for me."

"Mr. Ambassador, I don't want to work for you."

"At the moment, that's a moot question, isn't it? The President is very happy with his presidential private agent."

"All I want from you, sir, is to be left alone to do what the President wants me to do."

"Until you said that, I was beginning to think you might really be as smart as the President thinks," Montvale said.

"Excuse me?"

"You can't afford to be alone, Charley," Montvale said. "You need me. My assets. My authority. My influence. Think about it. They use your face as a dartboard in Langley and in the J. Edgar Hoover Building. The FBI is starting to hate you as much as they do your friend Howard Kennedy."

"I wasn't sure you believed that story," Castillo said.

"I checked on it," Montvale said. "I have some friends in the bureau. To a man, they would like to see Kennedy dragged apart by four horses after he was disemboweled."

Curiosity overwhelmed General Naylor. "Who is this fellow? What did he do?"

Montvale smiled, more than a little condescendingly.

"As Charley told me—and my friends confirmed—after being made privy to the darkest secrets of the FBI, Mr. Kennedy went to work—presumably at a far more generous salary—for a notorious Russian mafioso, a chap named Aleksandr Pevsner, taking with him all the darkest secrets." He paused. "The reason they hate our friend Charley is because when they sent an inspector to tell him they expected him to notify them immediately of any contact with Kennedy, our friend Charley told them not to hold their breath. They also suspect—correctly—that Charley was behind the President's order to them to immediately cease and desist looking for Mr. Kennedy."

"Pevsner and Kennedy have been useful to me in the past," Castillo said. "And almost certainly will be useful to me in the future."

Charley saw the look on Naylor's face.

It's a look of . . . sympathetic resignation.

He's thinking I'm going down Ollie North's path.

And that I have just lost this confrontation.

Well, what the hell did I expect?

Montvale's right. I am *a junior officer given more authority than I am equipped to handle.*

A very small fish in a large pond about to be eaten by a very large shark.

"What are you suggesting, Mr. Ambassador?" Castillo asked.

"Until such time as I can convince the President—and that's a question of *when,* not *if*—that the Office of Organizational Analysis should be under me, I suggest that it would be in our mutual interest to cooperate."

"Cooperate how?"

"On your part, primarily by keeping me informed of what you're doing. I really don't like walking into the Oval Office to have the President greet me with, 'Charles, you're not going to believe what Castillo has done,' and have no idea what the hell he's talking about. I want to be able to tell him that I knew what you would be going to try to do and that I did thus and so to help you do it."

"I'm sorry," *he said, just before he was shot down in flames,* "but if that means you will insist on your liaison officer, no deal."

The look on the general's face now means I have really just shot myself in the foot.

"That's negotiable," Montvale said.

"Negotiable?" Castillo blurted. It was not the response he expected.

"That means you offer me something in lieu thereof and I decide if I'm willing to take it."

"That telephone call I made just now? It was to my chief of staff, Major Richard Miller."

"What about him?"

"You take Mr. Ellsworth out of my office and I will instruct Major Miller to tell you—promptly—everything he can, without putting the lives of my men at risk, about what I'm doing and why."

"We are, I presume, talking about the same Major Miller who comes to my mind?"

"Excuse me?"

"The general's son? The man whose life you saved—at considerable risk to your life and career—in Afghanistan? The man whom Mrs. Wilson accused of making improper advances to her when she was in fact at the time making the beast with two backs in your bed? *That* Major Miller?"

"Yes, sir. That Major Miller."

"Deal," Montvale said and got half out of his chair and put out his hand.

Jesus H. Christ!

This is too easy.

When does the other shoe drop?

Montvale's grip was firm.

"Our new relationship will probably be a good deal less unpleasant for you than I suspect you suspect it will be," Montvale said, smiling.

"Yes, sir," Castillo said.

"Okay, why are you going to Paris?" Montvale asked, retaking his seat.

Okay, a deal is a deal. I'll live up to my end of it.

"I got Ambassador Lorimer, Mr. Lorimer's father, to give me sort of power of attorney to settle his affairs in Paris and Uruguay. I want to see what I can turn up in his apartment and at his estancia."

"You're also going to Uruguay?"

"Yes, sir."

"And you think you are qualified to perform searches of that nature?"

"No, sir, I don't. I'm going to enlist the CIA station chiefs in both places to help me."

"What makes you think they will?"

"Because I have already dealt with them, sir. They'll help."

Montvale nodded.

"Anything else I should know?"

"I have a source in Budapest. I'd rather not identify him. He gave me a list of names of people involved in the oil-for-food business, with the caveat that I do not turn them over to the agency or anyone else. I'm going there to see if I can get him to release me from that agreement."

"And if he doesn't?"

"Then I will have to see if I can get another list from someone else."

Montvale nodded but did not respond directly, instead asking, "What's happened to the money?"

"We got it out of Uruguay, first into an account an FBI agent there had opened in the Caymans . . ."

"Yung? The one who was with you when Lorimer was terminated?"

"Yes, sir. I'm sending him back to Uruguay to cover our tracks."

"He'll be able to do that?"

"I think so, sir."

"He would probably be useful permanently assigned to you," Montvale said. "Have you thought about that?"

"Yes, sir. I have. Secretary Hall arranged it."

"Well, fine. But the next time something like that comes up, I suggest you come to me with it."

What is he doing, trying to cut Matt Hall out of the loop?

"Yes, sir."

"You said 'first' into Yung's account?" Montvale pursued.

"And then I moved it into an account I opened in the same bank, the Liechtensteinische Landesbank. That took place today."

"In your name?"

"In the name of an identity—that of a German national—I use sometimes. I thought that would be best."

"And you can trust the people at Gossinger Beteiligungsgesellschaft, G.m.b.H., to keep their mouths shut?" Montvale asked.

"Yes, sir," Castillo said, as the realization dawned, *Jesus Christ, he knows about that, too. And he asked the question in absolutely fluent German.*

Montvale switched back to English.

"Goddamn, he is good, isn't he, General?" Montvale asked.

Naylor didn't reply. Instead, he asked, "Am I permitted to ask, 'What money?'"

"You can ask, of course," Montvale said, smiling. "But getting an answer would depend on the colonel, as he correctly pointed out he and the President are the only ones with the key to the Finding. It would be a felony for me to tell you."

What's he doing now? Playing with me? With General Naylor? With both of us?

"General," Castillo said. "Lorimer had nearly sixteen million dollars in several banks in Uruguay. We took it over. It is now the operating fund for the Office of Organizational Analysis."

"How did you manage to do that?" Naylor asked.

"He doesn't need to know that, does he, Colonel?" Montvale asked.

"No, I don't," Naylor answered for him. "And I don't think I want to."

"I have access to business jets in Europe and in Brazil," Montvale said. "Would it facilitate your travel if I made them available to you?"

"It would probably draw attention to me," Castillo replied.

"They're agency assets, actually," Montvale said. "The agency owns two charter companies in Europe and one in Brazil. Sort of an aerial version of the Town Car limos that prowl the streets of Manhattan. I don't think taking a ride in one would draw undue attention to you. All I would really be doing—unless you needed a plane for more than carrying you from point A to point B—would be ensuring you went to the head of the line."

"Can I have a rain check?"

"When we shook hands, you got your rain check," Montvale said. "Good for as long as you hold up your end of our deal."

He took a large wallet from his jacket, took a card from it, and laid the card on the table. Then he took an electronic notebook from another pocket, consulted it, and wrote several numbers on the card. He handed the card to Castillo.

"By the time you get to France, the aerial limo services will understand that when you call, you go to the head of the line. The bottom number on there is mine. Use it if you ever need anything you think I can provide and can't get through to me through the White House switchboard."

"Thank you," Castillo said.

"Can you think of anything else I can do for you?" Montvale asked.

"Mrs. Wilson is a now a senior analyst in the agency's South American Division's Southern Cone Section," Castillo said.

Montvale pursed his lips thoughtfully.

"I knew she managed not to get fired, but I didn't know that," he said. "We can't have that, can we?"

"Miller and I ran into her in the lobby of the Mayflower earlier tonight," Castillo said. "She called me a miserable sonofabitch."

"Well, I can see how she might feel that way," Montvale said. "I'll deal with it first thing tomorrow."

"Thank you."

"Anything else?"

"No, sir, I can't think of anything else."

"Well, in that case, I'm afraid I'm going to have to be going," Montvale said.

He stood up, drained his drink, and offered his hand to Naylor, who had risen to his feet.

"It's always a pleasure, General Naylor," he said.

Then he turned to Castillo, shook his hand, and patted his shoulder.

"This turned out better than either of us thought it would, didn't it?" he asked. "Keep in touch, *Colonel.*"

"Yes, sir, I will."

Montvale walked out of the room and Naylor and Castillo sat down.

"Jesus Christ!" Charley said. "Why does his being so cheerful, charming, and accommodating make me so uncomfortable?"

"Maybe because you weren't asleep when they were lecturing about never underestimating your enemy?"

Castillo chuckled.

"I'm sorry I said that," Naylor said thoughtfully a moment later. "That was a hell of a session, but I'm not so sure he doesn't mean exactly what he said. The bottom line is that he got what he wanted."

"Which was?"

"If you succeed, he can claim credit. If you fail, he can say it wouldn't have happened if you worked for him."

Castillo grunted.

"And he was right," Naylor went on. "You do need his influence and authority. The FBI and the CIA—and everybody else—are afraid of him. And with good reason. Once it becomes known, as it soon will, that he's standing behind you, people will think very carefully before knifing you in the back."

"I thought I had the President standing behind me," Castillo said.

"You do. But the President is a decent fellow. The ambassador, on the other hand, is well known as a follower of the Kennedy philosophy."

"Sir?"

"Don't get mad, get even," Naylor said. "He is not a man to be crossed. But on the other hand, I think he's a man of his word."

Castillo looked at his wristwatch.

"I've got to change out of my uniform and get out to Dulles," he said. "But before I do, I really would like another drink."

"After that, we both need one," Naylor said. "But there's one thing you have to do before that."

"Sir?"

Naylor took out his cellular telephone and punched an autodial number.

"Allan Naylor, Doña Alicia," he said a moment later. "I'm sitting here in the Army-Navy Club in Washington with Lieutenant Colonel Castillo and we thought we'd call and say hello."

There was a pause.

"Yes, ma'am, that's what I said."

He handed the cellular to Castillo.

"Your grandmother would like a word with you, Colonel."

An hour and a half later, as Air France flight 9080 climbed to cruising altitude somewhere over Delaware, Herr Karl Gossinger, the Washington correspondent of the *Tages Zeitung*, accepted a second glass of champagne from the first-class cabin attendant—and suddenly startled her by bitterly exclaiming, "Oh, *shit*!"

It had just occurred to him that he had not only not gone to see Special Agent Elizabeth Schneider in her hospital bed but had not even called her to tell her why he couldn't.

[TWO]
Suite 222
InterContinental Paris
3 rue de Castiglione
Paris, France
1230 5 August 2005

The bellman placed Castillo's suitcase on the nicely upholstered stand next to the dresser, graciously accepted his tip, and left, pulling the door to the suite quietly closed behind him. Castillo made a beeline for the toilette, voided his bladder, then sat down on one of the double beds. He picked up the telephone and dialed a number from memory.

"United States embassy," a woman's pleasant voice answered.

"Monsieur Delchamps, s'il vous plaît."

The Paris CIA station chief answered on the second buzz: "Delchamps."

"My name is Gossinger, Mr. Delchamps. Perhaps you remember we met recently in the Crillon?"

Delchamps hesitated just perceptibly.

"Oh, yes. Mr. *Gossinger,* is it? I've been expecting your call. You're in the Crillon again?"

"The Continental. I was wondering if you were free for lunch."

"Yes, I am. How does a hamburger sound?"

"You're not suggesting McDonald's?"

"No. What you get in McDonald's is a frenchified hamburger. You can still get a real hamburger in Harry's New York Bar. It's right around the corner from the Continental. You want to meet me in the lobby? I can leave here right now."

"A real hamburger sounds fine. I'll be waiting. Thank you."

"Your wish is my command, Herr Gossinger," Delchamps said and hung up.

Delchamps—a nondescript man in his late fifties wearing a somewhat rumpled suit—came around the corner from the rue de Rivoli ten minutes later.

He offered Castillo his hand.

"Nice to see you again, Mr. Gossinger. How may I be of service?"

"Why don't we wait until we get to Harry's?" Castillo replied.

"Whatever you wish, sir," Delchamps said.

Castillo eyed him a moment. *My chain is being pulled. What's he up to?*

"The Continental has an interesting history, Mr. Gossinger," Delchamps said as they started down rue de Castiglione toward the Ritz and the Place de l'Opera. "Are you interested?"

"Fascinated," Castillo said, smiling and playing along.

"There was once a monastery where it now stands," Delchamps said. "Louis XVI and his girlfriend—'Let them eat cake' Marie Antoinette—were staying there just before they were taken over to the Place de la Concorde and had their heads removed in the name of liberty."

"You don't say?"

"It's absolutely true."

"Thank you for sharing that with me."

"My pleasure, sir," Delchamps said. "But let me continue since you seem to find this of interest."

"Please do," Castillo said.

The conversation was momentarily interrupted by the sight of an incredibly beautiful, long-legged blonde coming out of the Hotel Ritz. She was surrounded by four muscular men who might as well have had SECURITY stamped on their large foreheads. She got into the rear seat of a Maybach, in the process revealing a good deal of thigh. One of the gorillas with her got in the front seat of the car, another trotted quickly to a Mercedes in front of it, and the other two trotted to an identical Mercedes behind it. The convoy rolled majestically away toward the rue de Rivoli.

"I regret being unable to identify that young woman for you, Mr. Gossinger, as I can see you are really interested," Delchamps said after they had passed the entrance to the Ritz. "But I'm sure she's someone famous."

"Either that or a high-class hooker," Castillo said.

"The two possibilities are not mutually exclusive," Delchamps said.

Castillo chuckled.

"But I was telling you about the Continental, wasn't I?" Delchamps asked and then went on without waiting for a reply. "And it was in the Continental— I seem to remember in 1880, but don't hold me to that—that what many regard as the advertising coup of all time took place."

"I've always been interested in advertising," Castillo said. "Tell me about that."

"Tourism was just beginning to blossom and become big business,"

Delchamps said. "The British, the Italians, the Germans, and of course the French were in hot competition for the Yankee tourist dollar. There was hardly a building on Manhattan Island without a billboard urging the Yankees to come to England, Italy, Germany, or France. There were so many of them that not one of them really caught people's attention. And the advertising was really expensive, which really bothered the French.

"The matter was given a great deal of thought, and, in studying the problem the French realized that the ideal advertisement would be something that incorporated novelty. Edison had just given us the lightbulb, you will recall, so the new advertisement had to include one of those. Yankees, the French knew, also liked amply bosomed females, so the advertisement would have to have one of those, too. How about an amply breasted woman holding an electric light over her head?"

Castillo laughed aloud.

"You sonofabitch, you had me going. The Statue of Liberty."

Delchamps smiled and nodded.

"And if we give it to the Yankees, the clever Frogs realized, call it a 'gift of friendship' or something, not only will the Yankees never take it down but—desperate as they are to have people like them—they'll put it someplace where it can't be missed. And if we give it to them, they'll pay to maintain it. If we play our cards right, we can probably even get them to pay for part—maybe most—of it."

"God, isn't history fascinating?" Castillo said.

"That meeting took place right in your hotel," Delchamps said. "And here we are on rue Danou, site of the legendary Harry's New York Bar. Would you be interested to learn that Ernest Hemingway used to hang around in Harry's?"

"Absolutely," Castillo said as Delchamps held open the door to the bar for him.

"Paris was known in those days as the intellectual center of the world. The truth is that before we sent Pershing over here to save their ass, they had emptied the French treasury and wiped out a generation of their male population in a standoff with the Krauts . . ."

He paused to direct Castillo, pointing to the stairway to the basement. When he had followed Castillo down the narrow, winding stairway and they had taken stools at the bar, he picked up where he had left off.

"And, presuming you had the Yankee dollar, it was one of the cheapest places to live. Not to mention that since most of the young Frogs had been killed in the trenches, there was no shortage of places for you to hide your salami."

The bartender appeared.

"They have other stuff, but they make a really good hamburger," Delchamps said.

"Sounds fine," Castillo said.

Delchamps ordered—in fluent Parisian French, Castillo noted—the hamburgers, medium rare, and two bottles of Dortmunder Union beer.

"Do you find it interesting, Herr Gossinger, that your tail is resting where very possibly Hemingway's tail once rested?"

"Yes, I find that interesting," Castillo said.

"And would you be interested in hearing the true story of Hemingway's war service as an officer?"

"I would be interested."

"He drove an ambulance in the Italian Army Medical Corps," Delchamps said. "Normally, as you know, Herr Oberst, ambulance drivers are privates. Oh, every once in a while there's a PFC, and maybe even a corporal after long and faithful service, but usually a private."

"I suppose that's true," Castillo said.

"Hemingway was a lieutenant," Delchamps said. "The Italian government decided it wouldn't be good if all the starry-eyed American boys who rushed to do their part in the war to end all wars wrote home to Mama about how privates driving ambulances in the Italian Army were treated and fed, so they made them all second lieutenants."

"Really?"

"True story. You found it interesting, I hope?"

"Absolutely! But you know what I would really find interesting to know?"

"And what is that?"

"Please tell me if you deliver these fascinating, *interesting* lectures on little-known facts of history to everyone who comes to Paris or if you have some interesting—possibly nefarious—purpose in relating them to me."

"In your case, Herr Oberst Gossinger, I was ordered to do so," Delchamps said as he took a sheet of paper from his pocket.

That's the second time he called me "Herr Oberst." I wonder what's that all about?

"This came in at six this morning, Colonel," Delchamps said, handing the paper to Castillo, "making it necessary for me to get out of bed at that obscene hour and go to the fucking embassy to get it. I was, as you can imagine, more than a little pissed, for several reasons."

Castillo unfolded the sheet of paper and read it.

TOP SECRET

URGENT

DUPLICATION FORBIDDEN

DELIVER IMMEDIATELY TO EDGAR J. DELCHAMPS ONLY AND
REPORT TIME OF DELIVERY OR REASONS FOR FAILURE TO DO SO

FROM: DIRECTOR NATIONAL INTELLIGENCE

TO: EDGAR J. DELCHAMPS

CIA STATION CHIEF PARIS

COPIES TO: (EYES ONLY) SECSTATE, SECHOMELANDSEC; DIRCIA

COLONEL C.G. CASTILLO, USA, IS PRESENTLY EN ROUTE PARIS
ON A MISSION FOR THE PRESIDENT OF THE UNITED STATES
WHICH HE MAY AT HIS SOLE DISCRETION ELECT TO CLARIFY
FOR YOU.

COLONEL CASTILLO WILL BE FURNISHED WHATEVER ASSISTANCE
AND INTELLIGENCE HE REQUESTS, TO INCLUDE, BUT NOT
LIMITED TO, ACCESS TO AGENCY-OWNED AVIATION ASSETS.
FURTHER, IT IS DIRECTED THAT YOU FURNISH HIM WITH ANY
INTELLIGENCE NOT SPECIFICALLY REQUESTED BUT IN WHICH
YOU FEEL HE MAY BE INTERESTED.

CHARLES W. MONTVALE

DIRECTOR OF NATIONAL INTELLIGENCE

TOP SECRET

"When Montvale called the last time you came here, he told me you were a major, Ace," Delchamps said, accusingly.

"I'm a *lieutenant* colonel as of yesterday," Castillo said.

"Then permit me to be among the very first to congratulate you."

"I didn't have anything to do with this," Castillo said, handing the message back. "But it does explain the interesting history lectures, doesn't it?"

"You going to tell me about this presidential mission you're on or are we going to fuck around with each other in the dark?"

"It's more than a mission. There's been a Presidential Finding," Castillo said. "The bottom line of which is, I'm supposed to find and 'render harmless' whoever whacked Jack the Stack Masterson in Buenos Aires."

"And you're working for who? Montvale directly?"

"The President directly. Montvale thinks I should be working for him."

"Well, that explains that little middle-of-the-night *billet-doux,* doesn't it?"

"He makes me feel like a sixteen-year-old virgin with some thirty-year-old guy chasing me who won't take no for an answer."

"I take your point, even if I don't think you were ever a sixteen-year-old virgin," Delchamps said. "The UN notified the embassy that Lorimer was killed during a robbery in Uruguay, of all goddamned places. That's obviously bullshit. You have the real skinny on that?"

"He was whacked, with a Madsen, at an estancia he owned down there."

"Your source reliable?"

"I was there. I had just told Lorimer he was about to be returned to the bosom of his family when somebody stuck a Madsen through the window, put two bullets in his head, and wounded one of the guys with me."

"You do get around, don't you, Ace?"

"The bad guys also garroted one of my guys, a Delta Force sergeant who wasn't easy to get to. They were real professionals."

"Who all unfortunately left this vale of tears before they could tell you who they worked for?"

Castillo nodded. "There were six of them, all dressed in black, no identification."

"Sounds like Spetsnaz or Mossad," Delchamps said. "Or maybe even Frogs from Rip-em."

"From where?"

The bartender delivered their Dortmunder Union. Delchamps waited until he was out of earshot before answering.

"Le premiere Régiment de Parachutistes d'Infanterie de Marine," Delchamps explained. "Rip-em, from the acronym, are pretty good. The French version of the English SAS, which is where they got started. Rumor has it that they've got a bunch of ex-Spetsnaz. From Spetsnaz to Légion Etrangère to Rip-em."

"French?" Castillo thought aloud.

"Why not? The Frogs were up to their ears in the oil-for-food business and, from what I hear, Lorimer knew which ones."

"I never even thought of the French," Castillo admitted.

"You didn't learn anything from Lorimer? Jesus, how the hell did you find him? In Uruguay?"

"I did find what we believe to be almost sixteen million skimmed from the bribe funds, but, as you put it, he passed from this vale of tears before I could ask him about it."

"Sit on that, and see who tries to get it."

"We've got it," Castillo said.

"Good for you!" Delchamps said and took his beer glass and, in a toast, clinked it against Castillo's.

Delchamps took a sip, then continued: "You were going to tell me how you found Lorimer. I was convinced—as I told you—that he was feeding the fish in either the Seine or the Danube."

"I have a source, a reporter, who's been running down the transfer of money from oil-for-food profits from Germany to South America—Uruguay and Argentina—and I got some names from him. I was showing them to an FBI agent in Montevideo who was working money laundering. He opened one of his files and Jean-Paul Lorimer's picture was in it. He had another identity—Jean-Paul Bertrand, Lebanese passport, antiquities dealer—and what I'm guessing is that when they stopped looking for Lorimer, he was going to move elsewhere . . . with the sixteen mil."

"Reporter from where?"

"A German newspaper."

"That makes me wonder about Gossinger," Delchamps said.

"I was born in Germany to a German mother. So far as the Germans are concerned, that makes me a German forever and eligible for a German passport. It's a handy cover."

"You going to tell me who Castillo is?"

"My father was a Huey pilot who got killed in Vietnam before he got around to marrying my mother. When I was twelve, my father's parents found out about me and off I went to the States, with my father's name on my American passport."

Delchamps met his eyes for a moment but didn't respond directly. Instead, he said, "I would say that maybe the KSK is involved, but—"

"The KSK?"

"Die Kommando Spezialkräfte, KSK, German Special Forces. You didn't know?"

His German pronunciation is perfect. He sounds like he's a Berliner. Well, he told me he'd done time in Berlin.

"Two of the guys in black were black-skinned," Castillo said. "I never even thought they might be German."

Which was pretty goddamned stupid of me.

Delchamps looked as if he had been going to say something but had changed his mind.

"Say it," Castillo said.

Delchamps looked at him for a moment, then shrugged.

"Some of the kids—hell, thousands of them—in situations like yours had black fathers whose family didn't take them to the States. When they grew up—and being a black bastard in Germany couldn't have been a hell of a lot of fun—they found getting jobs was hard, but they were German citizens and could join the army. A lot of them did. And, by and large, most of them weren't fans of anything American."

"I should have thought of that," Castillo said.

"That said, I think it's unlikely that KSK would be involved in anything like what happened in Uruguay. Unlikely but not impossible. They keep them on a pretty tight leash."

"There were some German Special Forces people in Afghanistan," Castillo said. "I didn't see any black ones."

"So what do you want to do in Paris?"

"Can you get me into Lorimer's apartment?"

"I can, but you're not going to find anything there," Delchamps said. "The Deuxième Bureau and the UN guys went through it as soon as he turned up missing. And so did I, when I learned there was interest in the bastard."

He's right. This has been a wild-goose chase.

Inspector Clouseau fucks up again.

"I just remembered," Delchamps went on, "that I'm the guy who assured you that Lorimer had already been taken care of. So, okay. We'll have another look. You looking for anything special?"

"Nothing special. Anything that'll point me in the direction of whoever whacked Masterson."

"And that's all you came to Paris for?"

Castillo nodded.

"Where are you going from here, to see the German reporter?"

"To his newspaper. I want to talk to his editor."

"Where's that?"

"Fulda."

"Well, I can't get you in the apartment until after dark. So what I suggest is that when we finish our hamburgers—if we ever get them—we go over to the embassy and have another look at what I've got. Maybe you'll see something I don't. You've got your American passport?"

Castillo nodded.

"And while we're there, I'll get on the horn to Brussels and have Eurojet taxi pick you up at Charles de Gaulle in the morning. What's closest to Fulda, Rhine-Main?"

Castillo nodded. "But it's no longer Rhine-Main; we gave it back to the Germans a couple of weeks ago. It's now all Frankfurt International."

"The old order changeth and giveth way to the new. Write that down."

Castillo chuckled. "Ed, I'm not sure about using that Eurojet whatever you said. Why don't I catch a train after we do the apartment?"

"Worried about owing Montvale?"

Castillo nodded.

"On the other hand, if he hears you used his airplane—and he will—he'll presume he has you in his pocket. Having him think that is known as disarming your enemy."

"Why do you make me feel so stupid, Delchamps?"

"You're not stupid, Ace. A little short on experience, maybe, but not stupid."

"I don't suppose you'd be interested in reasonably honest employment in our nation's capital, would you?"

Delchamps met his eyes for a long moment.

"Why don't we talk about that again, Ace, after you find out who these people are?"

"That presumes I will."

"Rephrase: After you have your best shot at it. The first thing a wise spook has to admit is that failure is the norm. You seem to have learned that, so maybe there is some hope for you in this business."

[THREE]
The Residence of the Ambassador of the United States
of America
1104 La Rambla
Carrasco, República Oriental del Uruguay
0805 5 August 2005

As the Honorable Michael A. McGrory, still in his bathrobe, was sipping at a cup of coffee while looking somewhat glumly out his dining-room window at what looked like a drizzle that would last all day, Theodore J. Detweiller, Jr., his chief of mission, telephoned.

"I'm sorry to bother you at home, Mr. Ambassador, but I thought I should bring this to your attention immediately."

"What's up, Ted?" McGrory responded.

There were two ways to look at a chief of mission who would not take any action without being absolutely sure it was what the ambassador wanted.

On one hand, Ambassador McGrory thought it was a good thing. He didn't have to spend much time or effort rescinding Detweiller's bad decisions and re-pairing the collateral damage they may have caused because Detweiller rarely—almost never—made any decisions on his own.

On the other, having a de facto deputy ambassador who would not blow his nose until he found in the Standing Operating Procedure when and under what circumstances doing so was specifically authorized or, failing that, until he had asked permission of the ambassador to do so was often a pain in the you-know-where.

Detweiller, too, often considered things that could well wait until the next day—or the next week—important enough to bring them to the ambassador's immediate attention, even if that meant disturbing the ambassador's breakfast, lunch, or golf game.

"I just now had a telephone call from Deputy Foreign Minister Alvarez, Mr. Ambassador."

"At your home, presumably?"

"Yes, sir. At my home."

"And what did Deputy Foreign Minister Alvarez want?"

"He asked if I was going to be in the office about nine," Detweiller reported, "and, if so, if I would be kind enough to offer him a cup of coffee."

McGrory stopped himself just in time from saying, "Well, give him one, Ted. And offer my best regards."

Instead, he asked: "He didn't say what he wanted, huh?"

"No, sir. He didn't. And I thought the call to my home, at this hour . . ."

"A bit unusual, isn't it?"

"Yes, sir, I thought so."

"You did tell Deputy Foreign Minister Alvarez that you'd give him a cup of coffee, Ted, didn't you?"

"Yes, sir, I did. Mr. Ambassador, may I give you my gut feeling?"

"Of course."

"I have the feeling, sir, that this is not a social call, but that Alvarez wants to keep it unofficial, if you take my meaning."

"I see. And why would he want to do that?"

"I haven't a clue, but that's my gut feeling and I thought I should mention it."

"And you should have. And just as soon as you find out what he wanted, if anything, besides a cup of coffee, let me know."

"Yes, sir, of course."

"Anything else, Ted?"

"No. That's it. Again, sorry to have to disturb you at home, Mr. Ambassador."

"Not at all, Ted," Ambassador McGrory said and hung up.

The ambassador picked up his coffee cup, took a sip, and found that it was tepid.

"Goddamn it," he exclaimed, then returned the cup to the table with a bang and walked briskly out of the dining room and to his bedroom to get dressed.

Since he really wanted a cup of fresh hot coffee when he got to his office, McGrory was not surprised to find that Señora Susanna Obregon, his secretary, had not yet prepared any.

He did not remonstrate with her. It would be a waste of his time. She would have some excuse, ranging from she liked to time the preparation of it so that it would be fresh and hot when he got to the office (and today he was almost an hour early) to the fact that her second cousin's wife had just given birth to quadruplets.

He went into his office and sat at his desk. There was only one sheet of paper in his in-box, which meant that for a change there had not been radioed overnight at least a dozen friendly suggestions from the under secretary of state on how he could better do his job.

Having nothing else to do until his coffee arrived, he reached for the message in the in-box, slumped back in his chair, and began to read it.

SECRET

ASLA 3445-4 1745 4AUG05

FROM: DEPUTY ASSISTANT SECRETARY OF STATE FOR
LATIN AMERICA

TO: US EMBASSY, MONTEVIDEO, URUGUAY
    PERSONAL ATTENTION: AMBASSADOR MCGRORY

CONFIRMING TELECON BETWEEN ASSTSECTLATAM AND THEODORE
J. DETWEILLER, JR., C/M USEMB MONTEVIDEO 1705 4 AUGUST
2005

MR. DAVID W. YUNG, JR., A SPECIAL AGENT OF THE FBI ON
THE PERSONAL STAFF OF SECSTATE, IS CURRENTLY EN ROUTE
TO MONTEVIDEO AND SHOULD ARRIVE THERE AFTERNOON 5
AUGUST 2005.

SECSTATE COHEN HAS DIRECTED AND AUTHORIZED MR. YUNG TO
ASSUME AND DISCHARGE ALL CONSULAR DUTIES RELATING TO
THE LATE DR. JEAN-PAUL LORIMER INCLUDING BUT NOT
LIMITED TO REPATRIATION OF THE REMAINS AND THE
PROTECTION OF ASSETS.

SECSTATE FURTHER DIRECTS USEMB MONTEVIDEO TO PROVIDE
MR. YUNG WITH WHATEVER ASSISTANCE HE REQUIRES,
INCLUDING BUT NOT LIMITED TO TURNING OVER TO HIM ANY
AND ALL USEMB RECORDS AND FILES CONCERNING MR. LORIMER
AND ANY AND ALL MATERIAL REGARDING JEAN-PAUL BERTRAND
WHOSE IDENTITY MR. LORIMER HAD APPARENTLY ASSUMED. THIS
SPECIFICALLY INCLUDES ALL INFORMATION REGARDING THE
CIRCUMSTANCES OF MR. LORIMER'S DEATH KNOWN TO EMB
AND/OR OBTAINED FROM URUGUAYAN GOVERNMENT SOURCES.

SECSTATE AUTHORIZES AND DIRECTS MR. YUNG TO, AT HIS
DISCRETION, SHIP ALL SUCH MATERIALS VIA DIPLOMATIC

```
POUCH TO STATE DEPT, PERSONAL ATTENTION SECSTATE, OR TO
MAKE SUCH OTHER ARRANGEMENTS FOR THEIR SHIPMENT TO
SECSTATE AS HE DESIRES.


BARBARA L. QUIGLETTE


DEPUTY ASSISTANT SECRETARY OF STATE FOR LATIN AMERICA


SECRET
```

The sonofabitch interrupts my breakfast to tell me the deputy foreign minister wants to talk to him unofficially and didn't mention this?

Goddamn him! He should have called me the moment he got off the phone from talking to the under secretary! Last night!

McGrory pushed himself out of his high-backed, blue-leather-upholstered chair and walked quickly to his office door, still holding the radio teletype printout.

"Susanna," he ordered, "I want to see, right now, in this order, and separately—in other words, one at a time—Mr. Detweiller, Mr. Monahan, and Mr. Howell."

"Yes, sir," Señora Obregon replied.

Three minutes later Señora Obregon reported that neither Mr. Detweiller nor Mr. Howell had yet come in but that Mr. Monahan was on his way to the ambassador's office and asked if she should send him in or make him wait until he'd seen the others.

"Send him in, please," McGrory ordered.

Monahan appeared at the office door moments later.

"You wanted to see me, Mr. Ambassador?"

McGrory waved him into the office but not into one of the chairs in front of his desk.

"I'm a little curious, Monahan, why you did not elect to tell me Yung is on the personal staff of the secretary of state," McGrory said.

"Excuse me?"

"You are the special agent in charge, are you not? And you were aware, were you not, of Yung's status?"

"That's two questions, Mr. Ambassador."

"Answer them one at a time."

"I'm the *senior* FBI agent here, Mr. Ambassador, but not the SAC."

"What's the difference?"

"A SAC is in charge of the special agents," Monahan replied and then clarified: "It stands for Special Agent in Charge."

"And you're not?"

"No, sir. I'm the *senior* agent. I've been with the bureau longest. But I was never appointed the SAC."

"You're telling me you're not in charge of the other FBI agents? Is that what you're saying?"

"Yes, sir. I'm sort of in charge, because, like I say, I'm the senior agent. But not *really*, if you take my meaning."

"If you're not *really* in charge, Monahan, who is?"

Monahan seemed puzzled by the question for a moment, then answered it: "You are, Mr. Ambassador."

McGrory thought: *Sonofabitch! Is he stupid or just acting that way?*

He went on: "And Special Agent Yung, who does he work for?"

"When he was here, he worked for you, sir."

"Not the secretary of state?"

"Up the chain of command, maybe," Monahan said. "I never thought about that. I mean, he worked for you and you work for the secretary of state, if you follow me. In that sense, you could say he worked for the secretary of state."

Señora Obregon put her head in the door.

"Mr. Howell is here, Mr. Ambassador."

McGrory thought, *There's no sense going any further with this.*

He said, "Monahan, I have to see Mr. Howell right now. Please keep yourself available."

"Yes, sir."

"Ask Mr. Howell to come in, please, Señora Obregon," McGrory said.

"Interesting," Cultural Attaché Robert Howell said, handing the message back to McGrory. "I wonder what it means?"

"I was hoping you could tell me," McGrory said.

"Well, all I can do is guess. Mr. Masterson's father-in-law is a retired ambassador. We heard in Buenos Aires that the father-in-law has heart problems and perhaps Secretary Cohen—"

"I mean about Yung being on the personal staff of the secretary," McGrory interrupted.

"Mr. Ambassador, you never elected to tell me about that. I simply presumed Yung was one more FBI agent."

"I didn't know he was on the secretary's personal staff, Robert," McGrory said.

"You didn't? Even more interesting, I wonder what he was doing down here that even you didn't know about? Does Monahan know?"

McGrory didn't answer the question.

Instead, he said, "Deputy Foreign Minister Alvarez telephoned Ted Detweiller at eight this morning. He wanted to know if Detweiller would be in his office at nine and, if so, if Detweiller would be kind enough to offer him a cup of coffee."

"I wonder what that's all about?" Howell said.

"I intend to find out. As soon as Detweiller gets here, I'm going to tell him he has the flu and is going home. Since he is unfortunately not able to give Deputy Foreign Minister Alvarez his cup of coffee, I will. And I want you to be here when I do so."

"Yes, sir."

"Mr. Ambassador," Señora Obregon announced from his door, "Deputy Foreign Minister Alvarez and another gentleman to see you."

McGrory rose quickly from his desk and walked quickly to the door, smiling, his hand extended.

"Señor Alvarez," he said. "What an unexpected pleasure!"

Alvarez, a small, trim man, returned the smile.

"Mr. Detweiller has developed a slight case of the flu," McGrory went on, "which is bad for him, but—perhaps I shouldn't say this—good for me, because it gives me the chance to offer you the cup of coffee in his stead."

"It's always a pleasure to see you, Mr. Ambassador," Alvarez said, enthusiastically pumping McGrory's hand. "I only hope I am not intruding on your busy schedule."

"There is always time in my schedule for you, Señor Alvarez," McGrory said.

"May I present my friend, Señor Ordóñez of the Interior Ministry?" Alvarez said.

"A privilege to make your acquaintance, señor," McGrory said, offering Ordóñez his hand. "And may I introduce my cultural attaché, Señor Howell?"

Everybody shook hands.

"I understand from Señor Detweiller that this is a purely social visit?" Mc-Grory asked.

"Absolutely," Alvarez said. "I knew Ordóñez and I were going to be in the area, and since I hadn't seen my friend Detweiller for some time I thought he might be kind enough to offer me a cup of coffee."

"He was really sorry to miss you," McGrory said.

"Please pass on my best wishes for a speedy recovery," Alvarez said.

"Since this is, as you say, a purely social visit, may I suggest that Señor Howell share our coffee with us?"

"Delighted to have him," Alvarez said.

"Please take a seat," McGrory said, waving at the chairs and the couch around his coffee table. Then he raised his voice, "Señora Obregon, would you be good enough to bring us all some coffee and rolls?"

Howell thought: *Whatever this is—it almost certainly has to do with the blood bath at Tacuarembó—it is not a purely social visit and both Alvarez and McGrory know it.*

Alvarez knows that Detweiller "got sick" because McGrory wanted to talk to him himself, which is probably fine with Alvarez. He really wanted to talk to him, anyway, but the deputy foreign minister couldn't call the American ambassador and ask for a cup of coffee.

That's known as protocol.

Ordóñez is not just in the Interior Ministry; he's chief inspector of the Interior Police Division of the Uruguayan Policía Nacional and McGrory knows that.

And Ordóñez knows—and, since he knows, so does Alvarez—that I'm not really the cultural attaché.

I know just about everything that happened at Tacuarembó, but Señor Pompous doesn't even know that Americans—much less his CIA station chief—were involved, because Castillo decided he didn't have the Need to Know and ordered me—with his authority under the Presidential Finding—not to tell him anything at all.

Everybody is lying to—and/or concealing something from—everybody else and everybody either knows or suspects it.

That's known as diplomacy.

I wonder how long it will take before Alvarez decides to talk about what he wants to talk about?

It took less time—just over five minutes—than Howell expected it to before Alvarez obliquely began to talk about what he had come to talk about.

"While I'm here, Mr. Ambassador," Alvarez said, "let me express my per-

sonal appreciation—an official expression will of course follow in good time—
for your cooperation in the Tacuarembó matter."

"Well, no thanks are necessary," McGrory replied, "as we have learned
that the poor fellow was really an American citizen. We were just doing
our duty."

Alvarez smiled as if highly amused. McGrory looked at him curiously.

"Forgive me," Alvarez said. "My wife is always accusing me of smiling at the
wrong time. In this case, I was smiling at your—innocent, I'm sure—choice
of words."

"What words?" McGrory said.

" 'The poor fellow,' " Alvarez said.

"I'm not sure I follow you, Señor Alvarez," McGrory said.

"What is that delightful American phrase? 'Out of school'?"

"That is indeed one of our phrases, Señor Alvarez. It means, essentially, that
something said was never said."

"Yes. All right. Out of school, then. Actually, two things out of school, one
leading to the other."

"There's another American phrase," McGrory put in. " 'Cross my heart
and hope to die.' Boys—and maybe girls, too—say that to each other as they
vow not to reveal something they are told in confidence. Cross my heart and
hope to die, Señor Alvarez."

Howell thought: *My God, I can't believe you actually said that!*

"How charming!" Alvarez said. "Well, Señor Ordóñez, who is really with
the Policía Nacional—he's actually the chief inspector of the Interior Police
Division—was telling me on the way over that Mr. Lorimer—or should I say
Señor Bertrand?—was a very wealthy man until just a few days ago. He died
virtually penniless."

"Oh, really?" McGrory said. "That's why you smiled when I called him a
'poor fellow'?"

Alvarez nodded. "And I apologize again for doing so," he said, and went on:
"Señor Ordóñez found out late yesterday afternoon that Señor Bertrand's bank
accounts were emptied the day after his body was found."

"How could that happen?" McGrory asked. "How does a dead man empty
his bank account?"

"By signing the necessary withdrawal documents over to someone several
days before his death and then having that someone negotiate the documents.
It's very much as if you paid your Visa bill with a check and then, God forbid,
were run over by a truck. The check would still be paid."

"Out of school, was there much money involved?" McGrory asked.

"Almost sixteen million U.S. dollars," Ordóñez said. "In three different banks."

This was the first Howell had heard anything about money.

When Alex Darby, the Buenos Aires CIA station chief who had driven Howell's "black" Peugeot to Tacuarembó so that it could be used to drive Castillo and Munz to the estancia, returned the car to Howell in Montevideo, he had reported the operation had gone bad.

Really bad, but not as bad as it could have been.

Darby's report of what had happened at Hacienda Shangri-La had been concise but complete—not surprisingly, he had been a CIA agent, a good one, for a long time.

But no mention at all of any money.

Hadn't Darby known?

Hadn't he been told?

Or had he been told, and decided I didn't have the Need to Know?

Jesus Christ, sixteen million dollars!

Did Castillo get it?

Or the parties unknown—parties, hell, with that kind of money involved, it was probably a government—who had sent the Ninjas after Lorimer?

"My God!" McGrory said. "Out of school, who was the someone to whom Mr. Lorimer wrote the checks?"

"We don't know," Alvarez said. "They were presented to the Riggs National Bank in Washington. All three of the banks here use Riggs as what they call a 'correspondent bank.' "

"Let me see if I have this right," McGrory said. "Somebody walked into the Riggs National Bank in Washington, handed over whatever these documents were, and they handed him sixteen million dollars?"

Ordóñez said, "What the Riggs Bank did was send—they have a satellite link—photocopies of the promissory notes to the banks here to verify Señor Bertrand's signature. When the banks had done that, they notified the Riggs Bank that the signature was valid and the transaction had been processed."

"So *then* they handed the man in Washington sixteen million dollars?"

"No. What the man in Washington wanted was for the money to be wired to his account in the Liechtensteinische Landesbank in the Cayman Islands. That was done. It takes just a minute or two."

"And what was this fellow's name?"

"We don't know. For that matter it could just as easily have been a woman. The money went into a numbered account."

"But it was Lorimer's signature on the promissory notes? You're sure of that?"

"There was no question at any of the banks—and, with that kind of money involved, you can imagine they were very careful—that Señor Bertrand had indeed signed the promissory notes."

"I'm baffled," McGrory said.

"So are we," Alvarez said.

"Can we find out from the bank in the Cayman Islands . . . what did you say it was?"

"The Liechtensteinische Landesbank," Ordóñez furnished.

"Can we find out from them who owns the numbered account?" McGrory pursued.

"I don't think that will be easy," Ordóñez said. "They have stricter banking secrecy laws in the Cayman Islands than in Switzerland."

"Well, perhaps I can do something," McGrory said, looking at Howell. "I'll ask Washington."

"We would of course appreciate anything you can do, Mr. Ambassador. Officially or otherwise," Alvarez said.

"I suppose if you had any idea who murdered Mr. Lorimer, you would tell me?"

"Of course," Alvarez said. "Who murdered Mr. Lorimer or who was responsible for the deaths of the other men we found at Estancia Shangri-La."

"We're working very hard on it," Ordóñez said. "I think in time we'll be able to put it all together. But it will take time and we would appreciate anything you could do to help us."

"But so far, nothing, right?" McGrory asked.

"There are some things we're looking into that will probably be valuable," Ordóñez said. "For one thing, we are now pretty sure that a helicopter was involved."

"A helicopter?" Howell asked.

"A helicopter," Ordóñez said. "Not far from the farm, we found barrels of jet fuel. And, beside it, the marks of . . . what's the term for those pipes a helicopter sits on?"

"I don't know," McGrory confessed after a moment.

"Skids," Howell furnished, earning him a dirty look from McGrory.

"Right," Ordóñez said. "There were marks in the mud which almost certainly came from a helicopter's *skids*. Strongly suggesting that the helicopter came some distance to the estancia and that the fuel was placed there before the helicopter arrived."

"Where would a helicopter come from?" Howell asked. "Brazil?"

"Brazil or Argentina," Ordóñez said. "For that matter, from Montevideo. But I'm leaning toward Argentina."

"Why?" McGrory asked.

"Because that's where the fuel drums came from," Ordóñez said. "Of course, that doesn't mean the helicopter came from Argentina, just that the fuel did. The helicopter could just as easily have come from Brazil, as you suggest."

"You haven't been able to identify any of the bodies?" McGrory asked.

"The only thing we have learned about the bodies is that a good deal of effort went into making them hard to identify. None of them had any identification whatever on them or on their clothing. They rented a Mercedes Traffik van at the airport in Carrasco—"

"Don't you need a credit card and a driver's license to rent a car?" Howell asked. "And a passport?"

That earned him another dirty look from McGrory.

And when this is over, I will get a lecture reminding me that underlings are not expected to speak unless told to by the ambassador.

Sorry, Mr. Ambassador, sir, but I didn't think you were going to show any interest in that, and it damned well might be useful in finding out who the Ninjas were and where they came from.

"Both," Ordóñez said. "The van was rented to a Señor Alejandro J. Gastor, of Madrid, who presented his Spanish passport, his Spanish driver's license, and a prepaid MasterCard debit card issued by the Banco Galicia of Madrid. The Spanish ambassador has learned that no passport or driver's license has ever been issued to anyone named Alejandro J. Gastor and that the address on the driver's license is that of a McDonald's fast-food restaurant."

"Interesting," Howell said.

He thought: *Ordóñez is pretty good.*

I wonder if anyone spotted my car up there?

Or the Yukon from the embassy in Buenos Aires that took the jet fuel there?

We put Argentinean license plates on it.

Is that another reason Ordóñez is "leaning toward Argentina" as the place the chopper came from?

"And so is this," Ordóñez said, and handed Howell a small, zipper-top plastic bag. There was a fired cartridge case in it.

"This is one of the cases found at the estancia," Ordóñez went on. "There were, in all, one hundred and two cases, forty-six of them 9mm, seventy-five .223, and this one."

"Looks like a .308 Winchester," Howell said, examining the round through the plastic, then handed the bag to McGrory, who examined it carefully.

Howell watched with masked amusement. *Señor Pompous doesn't have a clue about what he's looking at.*

Ordóñez did not respond directly to the .308 comment.

Instead, he said, "The 9mm cases were of Israeli manufacture. And the .223 were all from the U.S. Army. Which means, of course, that there is virtually no chance of learning anything useful from either the 9mm or the .223 cases. Or from the weapons we found on the scene, which were all Madsen submachine guns of Danish manufacture. We found five submachine guns, and there were six men in the dark coveralls. There were also indications that something—most likely a sixth Madsen, but possibly some other type of weapon taken because it was unusual—was removed from under one of the bodies found on the veranda.

"I think it's reasonable to assume this casing came from the rifle which killed the two men we found on the veranda. They were both shot in the head. We found one bullet lodged in the wall—"

"I'm afraid I'm missing something," McGrory interrupted. "Is there something special about this bullet?"

There you go again, McGrory! The bullet is the pointy thing that comes out the hole in the barrel after the "bang."

What you're looking at is the cartridge case.

"Mr. Ambassador, what you're holding is the cartridge case, not the bullet," Ordóñez said. "And, yes, there is something special about it."

Now I know I like you, Chief Inspector Ordóñez. You're dangerous, but I like you.

"And what is that?" McGrory asked, his tone indicating he did not like to be corrected.

"If you'll look at the headstamp, Mr. Ambassador," Ordóñez said.

"Certainly," McGrory said, and looked at Ordóñez clearly expecting him to hand him a headstamp, whatever that was.

"It's on the bottom of the cartridge casing in the bag, Mr. Ambassador," Ordóñez said.

That's the closed end, Señor Pompous, the one without a hole.

McGrory's lips tightened and his face paled.

With a little bit of luck he's going to show everybody his fabled Irish temper. Does hoping that he does make me really unpatriotic?

"What about it?" McGrory asked, holding the plastic bag with his fingers so he could get a good look at the bottom of the cartridge casing.

"The headstamp reads 'LC 2004 NM,' Mr. Ambassador," Ordóñez said. "Can you see that, sir?"

Oh, shit! I didn't see that.

I didn't look close at the case because I knew what it was and where it had come from: the sniper's rifle.

That's an explanation, not an excuse.

Darby said the kid fired only two shots, so why didn't they pick up both cases? Is that one lousy cartridge case going to blow the whole thing up in our faces?

McGrory nodded.

"If I'm wrong," Ordóñez said, "perhaps you can correct me, but I think the meaning of that stamping is that the cartridge was manufactured at the U.S. Army Lake City ammunition plant—I believe that it's in Utah—in 2004. The *NM* stands for 'National Match,' which means the ammunition is made with a good deal more care and precision than usual because it's intended for marksmanship competition at the National Matches."

McGrory looked at him but didn't say anything.

"That sort of ammunition isn't common, Mr. Ambassador," Ordóñez went on. "It isn't, I understand, even distributed throughout the U.S. Army. The only people who are issued it are competitive marksmen. And snipers. And, as I understand it, only Special Forces snipers."

"You seem to know a good deal about this subject, Chief Inspector," McGrory said.

"Only since yesterday," Ordóñez said, smiling. "I called our embassy in Washington and they called your Pentagon. Whoever they talked to at the Pentagon was very obliging. They said, as I said a moment ago, that the ammunition is not issued to anyone but competitive marksmen. And Special Forces snipers. And has never been sold as military surplus or given to anyone or any foreign government."

"You are not suggesting, are you, Chief Inspector," McGrory asked, coldly, "that there was a U.S. Army Special Forces sniper in any way involved in what happened at that estancia?"

"I'm simply suggesting, sir, that it's very unusual . . ."

The storm surge of righteous indignation overwhelmed the dikes of diplomacy.

"Because if you *are*," McGrory interrupted him, his face now flushed and his eyes blazing, "please let me first say that I find any such suggestion—any hint of such a suggestion—personally and officially insulting."

"I'm sure, Mr. Ambassador, that Chief Inspector Ordó—" Deputy Foreign Minister Alvarez began.

"Please let me finish, Señor Alvarez," McGrory said, cutting him off. "The way the diplomatic service of the United States functions is the ambassador is the senior government official in the country to which he is accredited. Nothing is done by any U.S. government officer—and that includes military officers—without the knowledge and permission of the ambassador. I'm surprised that you didn't know that, Señor Alvarez.

"Further, your going directly to the Pentagon via your ambassador in Washington carries with it the implication that I have or had knowledge of this incident which I was not willing to share with you. That's tantamount to accusing me, and thus the government of the United States, of not only conducting an illegal operation but lying about it. I am personally and officially insulted and intend to bring this to the immediate attention of the secretary of state."

"Mr. Ambassador, I—" Alvarez began.

"Good morning, gentlemen," McGrory said, cutting him off again. "This visit is terminated."

Alvarez stood up, looking as if he was going to say something else but changing his mind.

"Good morning, Mr. Ambassador," he said, finally, and walked out of the office with Ordóñez on his heels.

Howell thought: *Well, that wasn't too smart, McGrory. But, on the other hand, I think both Alvarez and Ordóñez walked out of here believing that you know nothing about what happened at Tacuarembó. The best actor in the world couldn't turn on a fit like you just threw.*

That doesn't mean, however, that Ordóñez thinks I'm as pure as the driven snow.

"I regret that, of course, Howell," McGrory said. "But there are times when making your position perfectly clear without the subtleties and innuendos of diplomacy is necessary. And this was one of those times."

"Yes, sir," Howell said.

"If this has to be said, I don't want what just happened to leave this room."

"I understand, sir."

"What is your relationship with Mr. Darby?" McGrory asked.

"Sir?"

"Are you close? Friends? If you asked him, would he tell you if he knew anything about anything that went on at that estancia?"

"We're acquaintances, sir, not friends."

"But you both work for the CIA. Don't you exchange information?"

"As a courtesy, sir, I usually send him a copy of my reports to the agency— after you have vetted them, sir. And he does the same for me."

"Nevertheless, I think you should ask him about this. I'm going to catch the next plane to Buenos Aires to confer with Ambassador Silvio. I want you to go with me."

"Yes, sir, of course."

"I don't want to go to Washington with this until I hear what Ambassador Silvio has to say."

"Yes, sir."

Why do I think that you're having second thoughts about throwing Alvarez out of your office?

[FOUR]
Office of the Director
The Central Intelligence Agency
Langley, Virginia
1205 5 August 2005

John Powell, the DCI, a trim fifty-five-year-old who had given up trying to conceal his receding hairline and now wore what was left of his hair closely cropped to his skull, rose from behind his desk and walked across his office with his hand extended to greet his visitor.

"It's good to see you, Truman," he said as they shook hands. "We haven't been seeing much of each other lately."

"The ambassador keeps me pretty busy," Truman Ellsworth replied. He was also in his midfifties but with thirty pounds and six inches on Powell. He also had a full head of carefully coiffured silver hair. "Thank you for seeing me on such short notice."

Powell gestured to indicate thanks were not necessary.

"And your coming gave me a much nicer alternative to eating alone or with five people with an agenda, not food, in mind. I ordered grilled trout *avec beurre noir*. How does that sound?"

"It sounds wonderful," Ellsworth said and obeyed the DCI's gesture to precede him into the DCI's private dining room.

The table, with room for eight, had been set for two, across from one another, at the head of table.

A waiter in a stiffly starched jacket asked what they would like to drink.

"Unsweetened iced tea, please," Ellsworth said.

"The same," the DCI ordered.

"So what can I do for you, Truman? Or the ambassador?" the DCI asked when the trout had been served and the waiter had left the room.

"The president has taken a personal interest in the Argentine affair," Truman said.

"There's a rumor that there has even been a Presidential Finding," the DCI said.

"One wonders how such rumors get started," Ellsworth said. "And, consequently, the ambassador has taken a very personal interest in that unfortunate business."

"You don't want to tell me about the Finding?" the DCI asked.

"If there is a Finding, John, I really don't think you would want to know the details."

The DCI pursed his lips thoughtfully but didn't respond.

"And as the ball bounces down from the pinnacle, I now have a personal interest in the Masterson affair," Ellsworth said.

"Well, that's certainly understandable," the DCI said.

"I don't suppose there have been any developments in the last couple of hours?"

"No. And since I have made it known that I also have a personal interest in this matter, I'm sure I would have heard," the DCI said.

"Yes, I'm sure you would have," Ellsworth said. "That's one of the reasons I'm here. Should there be any developments—and I'm sure there will be—the ambassador would like to hear of them immediately after you do. I mean immediately, not through the normal channels."

"Consider it done, Truman."

"If the ambassador is not available, have the information passed to me."

The DCI nodded.

"Does the name Castillo ring a bell, John?"

"Major C. G. Castillo?"

Ellsworth nodded.

"Oh yes indeed," the DCI said. "The chap who stumbled upon the missing 727. Odd that you should mention his name. That rumor I heard about a Finding said that he was somehow involved in the Masterson business."

"Well, if there were a Finding, I wouldn't be surprised. The ambassador was at the White House last night where Castillo was promoted to lieutenant colonel by the President himself. Not to be repeated, entre nous, the ambassador told me that if the President were the pope he would have beatified Colonel Castillo at the ceremony."

"How interesting!" the DCI said. "I wonder why that brings to mind Lieutenant Colonel Oliver North?"

"Possibly because they are both good-looking, dashing young officers who somehow came to bask in the approval of their commander in chief," Ellsworth said.

"That's probably it."

"The ambassador is personally interested in Colonel Castillo," Ellsworth said. "I have the feeling he likes him and would like to help him in any way he can."

"Is that so?"

"Now, to help him—which would also mean keeping him from getting into the same kind of awkward situation in which North found himself—the more the ambassador knows about where the colonel is and what he's up to, the better. Even rumors would be helpful."

"I understand."

"The problem, John, is that both Colonel Castillo and the President might misinterpret the ambassador's interest. It would be best if neither knew of the ambassador's—oh, what should I say?—*paternal* interest in Colonel Castillo and his activities."

"Well, I certainly understand it. And I hear things from time to time. If I hear anything, I'll certainly pass it on to you. And I'll spread the word, discreetly of course, of my interest."

"Not in writing, John. Either up or down."

"Of course not. Have you any idea where Colonel Castillo might be?"

"The last I heard, he was on his way to Paris. And he's liable to go anywhere from there. Germany. Hungary. The Southern Cone of South America."

"He does get around, doesn't he?"

"Yes, he does."

"Well, as I said, I'll keep my ear to the rumor mill and keep you posted."

"Thank you. I know the ambassador will be grateful."

"Happy to be of whatever assistance I can. Is that about it?"

"There's one more thing, John. For some reason, the ambassador thinks your senior analyst in the South American Division's Southern Cone Section may not be quite the right person for the job."

"Oh really? Well, I'm sorry to hear that. And you can tell the ambassador I'll have a personal look at the situation immediately."

"Her name is Wilson. Mrs. Patricia Davies Wilson," Ellsworth said.

"You know, now that I hear that name, I seem to recall that it came up not so long ago in connection with Castillo's."

"Really?"

"I seem to recall something like that."

"I think the ambassador would be pleased to have your assurance that you're going to put someone quite top-notch in that job and do so in such a manner that, when she is replaced, Mrs. Wilson will have no reason to suspect the ambassador—or even the DCI—was in any way involved with her reassignment."

"Of course."

"And I think he would be even more pleased if I could tell him you said that that would be taken care of very soon."

"How soon is 'very soon,' Truman?"

"Yesterday would be even better than today."

The DCI nodded but didn't say anything.

[FIVE]
Restaurante Villa Hipica
The Jockey Club of San Isidro
Buenos Aires Province, Argentina
1340 5 August 2005

Ambassador Michael A. McGrory was not at all pleased with where Ambassador Juan Manuel Silvio had taken him for lunch.

McGrory had suggested they go somewhere they could have a quiet, out-of-school conversation. If Silvio had made a similar suggestion to him in Montevideo, he would have taken Silvio either to his residence or to a restaurant where they could have a private room.

Instead, he had brought them all the way out here—a thirty-minute drive— to a wide-open restaurant crowded with horse fanciers.

Well, perhaps not wide open to every Tom, Dick, and José, McGrory thought, surveying the clientele. *I suspect membership in the Jockey Club is tied in somehow with the restaurant.*

Their table by a window provided a view of the grandstands and there was a steady parade of grooms leading horses—sometimes four or five at a time— right outside the window.

Certainly, a fine place to have lunch if you're a tourist—if they let tourists in— but not the sort of place to have a serious conversation about the business of the United States government!

A tall, well-dressed man with a full mustache approached the table with a smile and a bottle of wine.

"Your Excellency, I was just now informed you are honoring us with your presence," he said, in Spanish.

"I've told you, Jorge," Silvio replied, "that if I want you to call me that, I will wear my ermine robes and carry my scepter." He shook the man's hand and then said, "Jorge, may I present Ambassador Michael McGrory, who came here from Uruguay to get a good meal? Mike, this is Señor Jorge Basto, our host."

"My little restaurant is then doubly honored," Basto said. "It is an honor to meet you, Your Excellency."

"I'm happy to be here and to make your acquaintance," McGrory replied with a smile.

"And look what just came in this morning," Basto said, holding out the bottle.

"You're in luck, Mike," Silvio said. "This is Tempus Cabernet Sauvignon. Hard to come by."

"From a small bodega in Mendoza," Basto said. "May I open it, Mr. Ambassador?"

"Oh, please," Silvio said.

Goddamn it, McGrory thought, *wine! Not that I should be drinking at all. I am—we both are—on duty. But these Latins—and that certainly includes Silvio— don't consider drinking wine at lunch drinking, even though they know full well that there is as much alcohol in a glass of wine as there is in a bottle of beer or a shot of whiskey.*

I would really like a John Jamison with a little water, but if I ordered one I would be insulting the restaurant guy and Silvio would think I was some kind of alcoholic, drinking whiskey at lunch.

A waiter appeared with glasses and a bottle opener. The cork was pulled and the waiter poured a little in one of the glasses and set it before Silvio, who picked it up and set it before McGrory.

"Tell me what you think, Mike," he said with a smile.

McGrory knew the routine, and went through it. He swirled the wine around the glass, stuck his nose in the wide brim and sniffed, then took a sip, which he swirled around his mouth.

"Very nice indeed," he decreed.

McGrory had no idea what he was supposed to be sniffing for when he sniffed or what he was supposed to be tasting when he tasted. So far as he was concerned, there were two kinds of wine, red and white, further divided into sweet and sour, and once he had determined this was a sour red wine he had exhausted his expertise.

The waiter then filled Silvio's glass half full and then poured more into Mc-Grory's glass. Silvio picked up his glass and held it out expectantly until McGrory realized what he was up to and raised his own glass and touched it to Silvio's.

"Always a pleasure to see you, Mike," Silvio said.

"Thank you," McGrory replied. "Likewise."

Silvio took a large swallow of his wine and smiled happily.

"The wines here are marvelous," Silvio said.

"Yes, they are," McGrory agreed.

"Don't quote me, Mike, but I like them a lot better than I like ours, and not only because ours are outrageously overpriced."

"I'm not much of a wine drinker," McGrory confessed.

" 'Use a little wine for thy stomach's sake,' " Silvio quoted, " 'and thine other infirmities.' That's from the Bible. Saint Timothy, I think, quoting Christ."

"How interesting," McGrory said.

The waiter handed them menus.

McGrory ordered a *lomo con papas fritas*—you rarely got in trouble ordering a filet mignon and French fries—and Silvio ordered something McGrory had never heard of.

When the food was served, McGrory saw that Silvio got a filet mignon, too.

But his came with a wine-and-mushroom sauce that probably tastes as good as it smells, and those little potato balls look tastier—and probably are—than my French fries will be.

"You said you wanted to have a little chat out of school, Mike," Silvio said after he had masticated a nice chunk of his steak. "What's on your mind?"

"Two things, actually," McGrory said, speaking so softly that Silvio leaned across the table so that he would be able to hear.

McGrory took the message about FBI Special Agent Yung and handed it to Silvio, who read it.

"Isn't this the chap you sent here when Mrs. Masterson was kidnapped?" Silvio asked.

"One and the same."

"You never said anything to me, Mike, about him being on Secretary Cohen's personal staff."

"I didn't know about that," McGrory confessed.

Silvio pursed his lips thoughtfully but didn't say anything.

"Something else happened vis-à-vis Special Agent Yung," McGrory went on. "The same day—the night of the same day—that the bodies were found at what turned out to be Lorimer's estancia, I received a telephone call from the assistant director of the FBI telling me that it had been necessary to recall Yung to Washington, and that he had, in fact, already left Uruguay."

"He say why?"

"We were on a nonsecure line and he said he didn't want to get into details. He gave me the impression Yung was required as a witness in a trial of some kind. He said he would call me back on a secure line but never did."

Silvio cut another slice of his steak, rubbed it around in the sauce, and then forked it into his mouth. When he had finished chewing and swallowing, he asked, "Did you try to call him?"

"I was going to do that this morning when that message came and then I found out the deputy foreign minister, Alvarez, had called my chief of mission and asked if he could come by the embassy for a cup of coffee."

"Sounds like he wanted to have an unofficial chat," Silvio said.

"That's what I thought. So when he showed up, I told him that my man had the flu and I would give him his coffee."

"What did he want?"

"He had Chief Inspector Ordóñez of the Interior Police with him," McGrory said. "The man in charge of the investigation of what happened at that estancia. After they beat around the bush for a while, he as much as accused me of not only knowing that there were Green Berets involved in the shooting but of not telling them."

"Were there?" Silvio asked.

"If there were, I have no knowledge of it."

"And as the ambassador, you would, right?"

"That's the way it's supposed to be, Silvio. We're the senior American officers in the country to which we are assigned and no government action is supposed to take place that we don't know about and have approved of."

"That's my understanding," Silvio agreed. "So where did he get the idea that Green Berets were involved?"

"He had two things," McGrory said. "One was a—I don't know what you call it—what's left, what comes out of a gun after you shoot it?"

"A bullet?" Silvio asked.

"No, the other part. Brass. About this big."

He held his fingers apart to indicate the size of a cartridge case.

"I think they call that the 'cartridge case,' " Silvio said.

"That's it."

"What was special about the cartridge case?"

"It was a special kind, issued only to U.S. Army snipers. And the reason he knew that was because he called the Uruguayan ambassador in Washington, who called the Pentagon, who obligingly told them. They didn't go through me. And when a foreign government wants something from the U.S. government, they're supposed to go through the ambassador."

"On the basis of this one cartridge case, they have concluded that our Green Berets were involved? That doesn't make much sense, does it?"

"They also found out that a helicopter was involved. People heard one flying around and there were tracks from the skids—those pipes on the bottom?—in a nearby field, where it had apparently been refueled. You don't have a helicopter, do you?"

"I have an airplane—the Army attaché does, an Army King Air—out at Campo Mayo, but no helicopter. The King Air is so expensive to fly that most of the time it just sits out there."

How come Silvio's Army attaché gets an airplane, McGrory thought, *and mine doesn't?*

He said, "Well, according to them, whoever left all the bodies had a helicopter. And they think it was a Green Beret helicopter."

"Maybe they're just shooting in the dark," Silvio said. "They must be getting pretty impatient. Seven people killed and they apparently don't know why or by whom."

"Do you have any idea what that massacre was all about?"

Silvio shook his head, took a sip of wine, then said, "What I'd like to know is what this Lorimer fellow was doing with a false identity in Uruguay. Do you have any idea?"

McGrory shook his head. "No, I—oh, I forgot to mention that. Lorimer had a fortune—sixteen million dollars—in Uruguayan banks. It was withdrawn—actually, transferred to some bank in the Cayman Islands—the day after he was killed. By someone using the Riggs National Bank in Washington."

"Really? Where did Lorimer get that kind of money?"

"Most of the time, when large sums of money like that are involved, it's drug money," McGrory confided.

"Do they know who withdrew it?"

"*Transferred* it. No, they don't."

"Well, if you're right, Mike, and I suspect you are, that would explain a good deal, wouldn't it? Murder is a way of life with the drug cartels. What very easily could have happened at that estancia is that a drug deal went wrong. The more I think about it . . ."

"A fortune in drug money, a false identity . . ." McGrory thought aloud. "Bertrand, the phony name he was using, was an antiques dealer. God knows, being an established antiques dealer would be an easy way to move a lot of cocaine. Who would look in some really valuable old vase, or something, for drugs?"

"I suppose that's true," Silvio agreed.

"I'm thinking it's entirely possible Lorimer had a room full of old vases stuffed with cocaine," McGrory went on, warming to his new theory. "He had already been paid for it. That would explain all the money. When his customers came to get it, some other drug people—keeping a secret like that is hard—went out there to steal it. And got themselves killed. Or maybe they did steal it themselves. Maybe there were more than six guys in black overalls. The ones that weren't killed loaded the drugs on their helicopter and left, leaving their dead behind. They don't care much about human life, you know. They're savages. Animals."

"So I've heard."

Ambassador McGrory sat thoughtfully for a long moment before going on: "If you were me, Juan, would you take the insult to the department?"

Silvio paused thoughtfully for a moment before answering.

"That's a tough call, Mike," he said. "If I may speak freely?"

"Absolutely," McGrory said.

"Alvarez's behavior was inexcusable," Silvio said. "Both in not going through you to get to the Pentagon and then by coming to your office to as much as accuse you of lying."

"Yes, it was."

"Incidents like that in the past have been considered more than cause enough to recall an ambassador for consultation, leaving an embassy without an ambassador for an extended period."

"Yes, I know. Insult the ambassador of the United States of America at your peril!"

McGrory heard himself raising his voice and immediately put his wineglass to his lips and discreetly scanned the restaurant to see if anyone had overhead his indiscretion.

"The question is," Silvio said, reasonably, "you have to make the decision whether what happened is worth, in the long haul, having you recalled for consultation. Or if there is some other way you can let them know you're justifiably angry."

"They left my office, Juan, let me tell you, knowing that I was pretty damned angry."

"Oh?"

"Yes, they did. I told Alvarez in no uncertain terms that what they had done was tantamount to accusing me, and thus the government of the United States, of not only conducting an illegal operation but of lying about it and that I was personally and officially insulted, and then I said, 'Good morning, gentlemen, this visit is terminated.'"

"Well, that certainly let them know how you felt," Silvio said.

"And they're really going to be embarrassed when they finally realize that what happened out there was drug connected and their idea that Green Berets were involved was simply preposterous."

"If that's what happened, Mike, you're right."

"And if I take this to Washington," McGrory said, "by the time they actually get around to recalling me for consultation Alvarez more than likely will come to me with his tail between his legs to apologize. I'll accept it, of course, but I'll be one up on him, that's for damned sure. There's no sense bothering the secretary with this."

"I agree," Silvio said and picked up the bottle of Tempus and poured wine into both their glasses.

When they tapped glasses again, McGrory said, "I really appreciate your advice, Juan. Thank you."

[SIX]
Office of the Ambassador
The Embassy of the United States of America
Avenida Colombia 4300
Palermo, Buenos Aires, Argentina
1605 5 August 2005

"That's essentially what Howell told me, sir," Alex Darby said to Ambassador Silvio, "that Ordóñez found the cartridge casing, put it together with the chopper's skid marks and all those bodies, and decided it was something more than a robbery."

"Ambassador McGrory is now just about convinced it was a drug shoot-out," Silvio said. "I sowed the seed of that scenario and he really took it to heart. Between you and me, Alex, I felt more than a little guilty—ashamed of myself."

"Sir, you didn't have much of an option," Darby said. "Castillo was operating with the authority of a Presidential Finding. He had the authority to do what we did and not tell McGrory about it."

"Granting that," Silvio said, "I still felt very uncomfortable."

"You shouldn't feel that way, sir. With all due respect to Ambassador McGrory, can you imagine how out of control things would get if he knew? Or worse, if Castillo had gone by the book and asked his permission?"

Silvio didn't respond to that. Instead, he asked, "Where in the world did Castillo get that helicopter? I asked him, but he evaded the question."

"So did I and he wouldn't tell me, either. I didn't know about the money either."

"You don't think that it will be traceable?"

"The money or the helicopter?"

Silvio chuckled and shook his head. "Both. Neither."

"The helicopter, no. Castillo filed a local flight plan from Jorge Newbery to Pilar, closed it out over Pilar, and then flew over there about five feet off the water. He came back the same way, then got on the horn over Pilar and filed a local flight plan to Jorge Newbery. Nothing suspicious about that."

"If somebody had the helicopter's numbers," Silvio said, "it wouldn't be hard to learn whose machine it is, would it?"

"I thought about that, sir, and decided it was information I would just as soon not have."

Silvio nodded. "You're right, of course. What about the money?"

"Before this happened, Yung was working on finding Americans—and other people—who had decided to secretly invest money down here. I don't know who he was doing that for, but he wasn't just looking for dirty money being laundered. He is therefore an expert on how to move large amounts of money around without anyone knowing. I suspect the reason Castillo sent him back down here was to make really sure there are no tracks."

"I think Ambassador McGrory is going to give him a hard time when he gets to Uruguay. For concealing his special status from him. And I find myself thinking McGrory has the right to be annoyed."

"He shouldn't be annoyed at Yung," Darby said. "Yung was just following orders."

"That 'just following orders' philosophy covers a lot of sins, doesn't it?"

"Mr. Ambassador, I'm pretty sure before you tell somebody something, you consider who you're telling it to, how trustworthy they are. And that's how it should be. I've never understood why people don't seem to understand that works both ways."

"I'm not sure I follow you, Alex."

"How much the guy in charge—a corporal in a rifle squad, a station chief in the agency, an ambassador—gets told, official rules be damned, depends on how much the underling thinks the guy in charge can be trusted."

Silvio considered that a moment and then said, "I have to ask, Alex. How much do you tell me?"

"When I got here, Mr. Ambassador, based on my previous experience with people in your line of work, I was careful when I told you what time it was. After a while, when I got to know you, I started telling you everything."

"Thank you," Silvio said, simply.

"Mr. Ambassador, I'd like to get on a secure line and let Castillo know what's happened in Montevideo and here."

"He should know, of course, and right away. But I can do it, Alex. You don't have to."

"Why don't you let me do it, sir?" Darby replied. "I don't feel guilty about going behind McGrory's back."

"Ouch!" Ambassador Silvio said. He paused thoughtfully. "Obviously what has happened, Alex, is that my close association with you has corrupted me. I just realized that I was happy that you offered to make the call. Thank you."

He pushed the secure phone toward Darby.

VI

[ONE]
Executive Offices
Gossinger Beteiligungsgesellschaft, G.m.b.H.
Fulda, Hesse, Germany
1105 6 August 2005

Otto Görner, managing director of Gossinger Beteiligungsgesellschaft, G.m.b.H., reached for his private line telephone with his right hand without taking his eyes off the editorial on his desk. It was anti-American, blasting the President of the United States of America personally and the policies of the U.S.A. generally.

He had known from the first couple of sentences that he would not permit it to run in any of the *Tages Zeitung* newspapers. The author would then think—and more than likely share with his peers—unkind thoughts about the *Amizaertlich* editor in chief of the *Tages Zeitung* newspapers for killing a well-thought-out piece about what the *Gottverdammt Amis* had done wrong again.

By the fourth paragraph, Görner had realized—with some relief—that he would have killed the piece anyway based on its departure from what he re-

garded as the entirely Germanic editorial principles of the newspaper chain—
in essence, to be fair—and not solely because running it would have offended
the *Ami* who was the sole stockholder of Gossinger Beteiligungsgesellschaft, G.m.b.H.

"Görner," he growled into the telephone.

"Have you got any influence with the storm trooper guarding the parking
lot?" a very familiar voice inquired in English. "He won't let me in."

"Speak of the devil," Görner said.

"Is that a yes or a no?"

"Put him on, Karlchen," Görner said as he rose quickly from his desk and
went to his window, which overlooked the parking lot.

Carlos Guillermo Castillo, born Karl Wilhelm von und zu Gossinger, was
standing by the red-and-white-striped barrier pole to the parking lot and extending a cellular telephone to the guard thereof.

As the guard somewhat suspiciously put the cellular to his ear, Castillo
looked up at the window, saw Görner, and blew him a kiss. The guard followed
that gesture, too, with interest.

"In the future," Görner said to the telephone, "you may admit Herr von und
zu Gossinger to our parking lot at any time, even if his car doesn't have an identification sticker."

"Jawohl, Herr Görner," the guard said.

He handed the cellular back and hurried to the switch that would cause the
barrier pole to rise.

Castillo bowed toward the window and then got in his car, a Mercedes-Benz
220, which Görner decided he had rented at an airport.

Görner had mixed feelings on seeing Castillo. On one hand, he was—and
had been since Castillo's birth—extremely fond of the boy born to the sister of
his best friend. He had long ago realized that there was little difference between
the paternal feelings he had for Karlchen—"Little Karl"—and those he felt for
his own children.

If Erika von und zu Gossinger would have had him, either when it first became known that the seventeen-year-old girl was pregnant with the child of an
American helicopter pilot she had known for only four days or, later, until the
hour of her death twelve years later, he would have married her and happily
given the child his name.

But Erika would not have him as her husband, although she had been perfectly willing for him to play *Oncle* Otto to the boy as he grew up.

And over the last three or four days, Görner had been genuinely concerned
about Castillo's safety—indeed, his life. Karlchen had called from the States and

suggested Görner "might take a look at the Reuters and AP wires from Uruguay starting about now."

Görner had done so, and the only interesting story—about the only story at all—from Uruguay had been a Reuters report that the Lebanese owner of a farm, a man named Jean-Paul Bertrand, and six other men, unidentified, had been found shot to death on Bertrand's farm.

There had been no question at all in Görner's mind that Bertrand was Jean-Paul Lorimer, for whom he knew Karlchen had been looking. Confirmation of that had come yesterday, with an Agence France-Presse wire story that Dr. Jean-Paul Lorimer, Chief, European Directorate of UN Inter-Agency Coordination in Paris, had been murdered during a robbery while vacationing in Uruguay.

He had not been surprised to learn that Lorimer was dead. He had been in Budapest with Karlchen when Billy Kocian had told both of them that he thought Lorimer was probably fish food in either the Danube or the Seine and he didn't believe the robbery spin at all. Lorimer had been killed because he knew too much about the oil-for-food scandal.

But Uruguay? What was that all about?

He wondered how Karlchen had learned what had happened to Lorimer so quickly.

His thoughts were interrupted when Frau Gertrud Schröder put her head in the door and cheerfully announced, "Karlchen's here. They just called from the lobby."

"Warn my wife, lock up anything valuable, and pray," Görner said.

"You're as glad to see him as I am," she said.

"Yes. Of course," Görner agreed with a smile.

That's only half true. I am glad to see him, but I don't think I'm going to like what he tells me, or giving him what he asks for.

Castillo came to the door forty-five seconds later.

He hugged Frau Schröder and kissed her wetly on the forehead.

She beamed.

"Do I call you 'colonel'?" Görner said.

"Not only do you call me colonel but you pop to attention, click your heels, and bow," Castillo said as he went to Görner and hugged him. He would have kissed him on the forehead, too, had Görner not ducked. Then he added, "How did you hear about that?"

"You're an *oberst*, Karlchen?" Frau Schröder asked.

"Oberst*leutnant,* Frau Schröder," Castillo said.

Görner went behind his desk and sat down.

The old man was Oberstleutnant Hermann Wilhelm von und zu Gossinger at

Stalingrad. The first time I met him, I was terrified of him. And now his grand-
son is one. In the American Army, of course. But an oberstleutnant. The old man
would have been ecstatic.

"I'm so proud of you, Karlchen!" Frau Schröder said.

"Thank you," Castillo said.

He looked at Görner and asked again, "How did you hear about that?"

"The American embassy called. A man who said he was the assistant con-
sul general said he had reason to believe Lieutenant Colonel Castillo would be
coming here and, if you did, would I be good enough to ask you to call?"

"We have a name and a number?"

Görner nodded, lifted the leather cover of a lined tablet on his desk, and
then flipped through several pages. By the time Frau Schröder had walked to
the desk, he had found what he was looking for and had his finger on it.

She punched in numbers on one of the three telephones on Görner's desk.

A moment later, she said in almost accentless English, "I have Colonel
Castillo for you, Mr. Almsbury. Will you hold, please?"

She handed the handset to Castillo.

He spoke into it:

"My name is Castillo, Mr. Almsbury. I'm returning your call.

"My father's name was Jorge Alejandro Castillo.

"Who's it from?

"The *sender* is classified?

"Well, how do I get to see this message?

"And if I can't come to Berlin, then what?

"Well, then, I guess I just won't get to see it.

"Yes, I'll take your assurance that the sender is a very important person. But
I still can't come to Berlin and I won't be here long enough for you to come deliver the message.

"I'd rather not share that with you, Mr. Almsbury. What I suggest you do
is send a message to the sender that you couldn't get the message to me and that
if the message is important that they try to send it to me through my office.

"Yes, I'm sure they know how to get in contact with my office.

"Yeah, I'm sure that this is the way I wish to handle this. Thank you very
much, Mr. Almsbury. Good-bye."

He hung up.

"That sonofabitch," he said, shaking his head.

"I don't suppose you're going to tell us what that was all about, Karl?"
Görner asked.

Castillo looked between them and then said, "A couple of years ago—maybe longer—somebody said—maybe wrote a book—saying, 'The medium is the message.' "

"I don't understand," Görner confessed.

"For the first time, I understand what that means," Castillo said.

"You're talking in tongues, Karl."

"Mr. Almsbury, who is more than likely the CIA station chief in Berlin, has a message for me. For a number of reasons, I think that message is from Ambassador Charles Montvale. You know who he is?"

Görner nodded.

Frau Schröder said, "Your new chief of intelligence?"

"Close," Castillo replied. "He's the new director of *National* Intelligence."

"You work for him? Can I ask that?" Görner said.

"You can ask. No, I don't work for him. He wishes that I did. The President told him no, I told him no, but Montvale doesn't like no for an answer—"

"Karl," Görner interrupted and then stopped.

Castillo smiled at him. "I read minds, you know. What you were about to ask is, 'Why are you telling us this?' And/or, 'Aren't you liable to get in trouble talking so freely to us?' Am I close?"

Görner shook his head in disbelief and then nodded in resignation.

"I'm telling you because I think you should know certain things, and because both of you are on my short list"—he held up his left hand with the fingers spread widely and his right hand with three fingers held upward—"of people I trust absolutely. And, no, I won't get in trouble. The President gave me the authority to tell anyone anything I want to tell them."

Görner met his eyes for a moment and thought: *He means that. He's telling the truth. But I now understand there is a third reason. Karlchen has just put both* Onkle *Otto and* Tante *Gertrud in his pocket. And I think he knows that. My God, he's so much like the old man!*

"And the final reason I'm going to tell you about what I'm doing is because I'm going to need your help and I want you to understand why I need that help; why you're doing what I'm going to ask you to do."

Görner started to speak, then stopped—*Goddamn it, I have to say this*—then said what was on his mind: "Karl, what we do here is publish newspapers, newspapers started by your great-great-grandfather. I can't stand idly by while you turn it into a branch of the CIA."

"The simple answer to that, Otto," Castillo said, "is you're right. It's a newspaper. But let's not forget, either, that I own Gossinger Beteiligungsgesellschaft, G.m.b.H." He let that sink in a moment, then went on: "A more complicated answer is that I've thought about *Grosspappa*. And the *Tages Zeitung* newspapers. I'm not turning them into a CIA asset. For one thing, I don't work for the CIA. And from all I remember about him, all I've heard about him, he was a very moral man. I think he would be as annoyed—as disgusted—with the greedy bastards behind this oil-for-food scandal as Eric Kocian is. And I think if he was still alive and Ignatz Glutz came to him with CIA tattooed on his forehead and said he was trying to do something about those greedy, murderous bastards, *Grosspappa* would have helped. Within certain boundaries, of course. Anyway, that's the way I'm going to play it. Carlos Castillo is going to ask certain things of the *Tages Zeitung* and if Karl von und zu Gossinger thinks his grandfather would have given Castillo what he's asking for, the *Tages Zeitung* is going to give it to him."

"It says in the Bible, Karlchen, that a man cannot serve two masters," Görner said.

"It also says in the Bible that Jonah was swallowed whole by a whale and lived through it," Castillo said. "Aren't you the man who told me to be careful about what you read? Not to believe something just because it's in print?"

" 'Within certain boundaries' covers a lot of ground, Karl," Görner said, softly. "Who defines those boundaries?"

"I do. But it should also go without saying that if I step over the line, you are free to tell me how I am over that line."

Görner stared at him intently for a long moment.

"The older I get, the more I believe in genetics," he said, finally. "So I'm going to go with my gut feeling that there's a hell of a lot more of Oberst Hermann Wilhelm von und zu Gossinger running through your veins than there is Texas cowboy, Colonel Carlos Castillo."

Castillo didn't reply.

"Tell me about Ambassador Montvale and his message," Görner said.

"I have no idea what's in Montvale's message, but if it was really important he would have gotten it to me."

"I don't understand," Frau Schröder said.

"If I go to Berlin to get the message, I'm a cute little dachshund answering its master's whistle. Which is what he wants."

"Oh," she said, and then a moment later said, "But what if there is something important in the message?"

"If something important happened, Dick Miller would know what it was and he would have gotten through to me. But just to be sure, as soon as we get the money straightened out, I'm going to give Dick a call."

"Is that why you're here?" Görner asked. "About that money in the Liechtensteinische Landesbank?"

"Mostly."

"What else?"

"I want all your notes, all your reporters' notes, on oil for food," Castillo said. "They will go no further than me. I really don't work for the CIA, Otto. Or anybody but the President."

Görner didn't reply.

"Am I crossing the line, Otto?" Castillo asked, softly.

"Not with that," Görner said, simply. "I think the Old Man would have given your Mr. Ignatz Glutz his reporter's notes. I'll reserve judgment about the money until I hear whatever you think you can tell me about it."

"I'll tell you everything about it," Castillo said. "We found out that Lorimer had it in three banks in Uruguay. It seems logical to assume that he stole it—the American phrase is 'skimmed it'—from his payoff money. We also found out that it was not on deposit but rather in the form of on-demand notes issued by the bank, something like bearer bonds. We got the notes, and took the money. It's going to be spent finding who killed Mr. Masterson and Sergeant Markham and for other noble purposes, including finding out who sent the men to murder Lorimer."

"You certainly found out about that quickly," Görner said.

"I was there, Otto. I was just about to tell Lorimer that he was about to be returned to the bosom of his family when somebody stuck a submachine gun through the window. They killed Lorimer and wounded a man with me. Other bad guys killed one of my sergeants by garroting him."

"Karlchen!" Frau Schröder exclaimed.

"Who were they?" Görner asked.

"I don't know. I intend to find out. The only thing I know for sure was they were not Uruguayan bandits. Spetsnaz, possibly. Maybe Mossad. Maybe even French, from Le Première Régiment de Parachutistes d'Infanterie de Marine, known as Rip-em. There's even been a suggestion that they might be from Die Kommando Spezialkräfte. Whoever they were, they were damned good."

"And, I suppose you realize, damned dangerous?" Görner asked.

"That thought has run through my mind. Let me tell what I'd like to do about the money, then Frau Schröder can explain why that's not possible."

Görner realized that although it was the last thing he wanted to do, he was smiling.

Castillo said, "I have—that is, Lopez Fruit and Vegetables Mexico has—an account with the Banco Salamander Mexicano in Oaxaca."

"Say that again, slowly," Frau Schröder said as she picked up Görner's leather-covered legal pad and a pencil. "And you better spell it, too. I don't speak Spanish."

"You don't?" Castillo asked as if deeply shocked. "I thought everybody spoke Spanish."

Görner realized that he was smiling again at the look on Frau Schröder's face before she realized she was being teased.

Castillo went into his laptop case and took out a sheet of paper and handed it to her.

"Everything's on there," he said, "including account numbers. Fernando tells me we run a lot of money through there."

"That's the Bahias de Huatulco ranch?" Otto asked.

"Used to be cattle, now it's mostly grapefruit," Castillo confirmed. "Anyway, a wire transfer of ten million dollars wouldn't set off alarm bells, particularly if we spend most of it right away to buy an airplane."

"Excuse me?" Görner asked.

Castillo went back to his briefcase and took out a photocopy of what Görner recognized after a moment as an aircraft specification sheet.

"A twenty-three-year-old Gulfstream III," Castillo said. "Just the sort of airplane that would be owned—or leased—by a successful Mexican farming operation trying to peddle its wares in Europe and Latin America. And a bargain, Fernando tells me, at seven million five, as it has new engines and all the maintenance is up-to-date. And its new glove-leather interior is sort of the cherry on the cake."

"Why do you need an airplane like that?" Frau Schröder asked.

"We flew Fernando's plane—the Bombardier/Learjet—over here, then to South America, and then from Buenos Aires to the States. Two things wrong with that. It's not designed for long flights—over-the-ocean flights—like that. And, as a corollary, attracts attention when it does. And then when Ambassador Montvale kindly put the CIA's private airlines at my disposal, I knew I had to have an airplane, the pilot of which is not going to make hourly reports of my location to the ambassador."

"You're going to be doing a lot of that, flying across oceans?" Görner asked.

"I'll be going wherever I have to go and I want to do it quickly, safely, and as invisibly as possible."

"Can you just go out and buy an airplane like that? And who's going to fly it?"

"That's a moot question until Frau Schröder tells me whether I can move the ten million to the account in Mexico."

He looked expectantly at Frau Schröder.

"That can be done with a telephone call," she said. "You can count on the money being available within the hour."

"Well, let's do that and then we'll get on the horn to Dick Miller," Castillo said. "The sooner we get the money into Salamander, the sooner I can—as an officer of Lopez Fruit and Vegetables Mexico—wire-transfer out of it to my account at the Riggs Bank in Washington. I already know how to do that."

"Couple of questions," Frau Schröder said, now all business. "You want to put the Liechtensteinische Landesbank money in a special account or just deposit it?"

"Just deposit it," Castillo said. "Fernando's going to report it as ordinary business receipts."

"Is that what they call 'money laundering'?" Görner asked, drily.

"This is in a good cause," Castillo replied.

Görner shook his head. Frau Schröder picked up the telephone.

Three minutes later, she announced, "Ten million dollars will be available in the Lopez account within twenty minutes."

"Thank you, and now see if you can get Dick Miller on there, will you, please? And put it on the speakerphone, please."

"I think I should point out, Karl," Görner said, "that it's now about half past six in the morning in Washington."

"Until they take the bandages off his leg, Dick's sleeping in the office," Castillo replied. "He'll be there."

Frau Schröder punched in numbers on one of Görner's telephones and then pushed the button that activated the speaker.

The phone rang twice and then Major H. Richard Miller, Jr., answered it. "Miller."

"Good news, sweetheart, we won't have to sell the dogs and move in with your mother. The money's in the bank."

"That was quick."

"They don't call me Speedy Gonzales for nothing," Castillo said. "Any word from Jake about the new toy?"

"He and Fernando and the salesman brought it in here, to BWI, last night. Jake said it would have made waves taking it into Reagan. Jake says the bird's okay and where do you want to keep it?"

"Let me think about that. Ask Jake what he recommends. Transfer nine really big ones from Salamander to my account in Riggs and then pay for it."

"That check's not going to bounce, is it?"

"Nope. I have Frau Schröder's personal guarantee. Say, '*Danke schön, Frau Schröder.*'"

"*Danke shön, Frau Schröder,*" Miller said.

"How are you, Dick?" she replied.

"Aside from having more gauze bandage on my leg than a mummy, I'm just fine. Say hello to Otto for me when you see him."

"How are you, Dick?" Görner said.

"You weren't listening in, were you, Otto? If so, did the colonel make you stand at attention?"

"And click my heels," Görner said.

"God, he's going to be hard to live with."

"He's always been hard to live with."

"Jesus," Miller suddenly said, "before I forget, Charley, remember that you were here all day yesterday."

"Why?" Castillo said.

"Because yesterday, Colonel, Colonel Torine gave you a check ride in the C-20, which you passed, and which will be recorded on your FAA records this morning."

"Oh, that's great," Castillo said.

"Anything else, Charley?"

"Have you any idea why the ambassador would send me a message? To Berlin?"

"No. But he was fascinated to hear that we have people looking into brief-cases in suburban Philadelphia. He can't imagine why you didn't share that with him."

"Because, as far as we know, that's fantasy. Did you tell him that?"

"I did. He didn't seem very impressed. What did the message say?"

"I don't know. I'm not going to Berlin to read it."

"You want to tell me where you are going?"

"Paris was a waste of time. Lorimer's apartment had been searched by the Deuxième Bureau and the UN before my friend there could get in. I had a look. Nothing useful. And I'm just about finished here. All I have left to do is go see Billy Kocian in Budapest. I don't think that will take long . . ."

He stopped when he saw Görner holding up his hand.

"Hold it a second, Dick," Castillo said and gestured for Görner to speak.

"I don't think going to see Billy Kocian right now is going to be profitable," Görner said.

"Why not?" Castillo asked.

"He's in the Telki Hospital with a broken ankle."

"What happened?"

"He fell down the stairs in his apartment."

"How do you know he broke his ankle?"

"He called and told me."

"He called and told you," Castillo repeated, softly, and then, raising his voice slightly for the speakerphone, asked, "Dick, where's Torine?"

"In your place. He and Fernando."

"Get on another line and ask him if there's any reason he can't bring the G-III to Budapest right away."

"I can think of one," Miller replied. "You don't own it yet."

"Call Jake, and ask him if the airplane is ready to cross the Atlantic. I'll hold."

Castillo felt Görner's eyes on him.

"You think something happened to Billy," Görner said.

"What I'm thinking is that it's unlikely that Billy would call to tell you he fell down. More than likely, he called you to tell you that because he didn't want you to know what really happened to him in case you heard he was in the hospital."

Görner's eyebrows went up but he didn't say anything.

Miller's voice came over the speaker.

"I have Colonel Torine on the line for you, Colonel Castillo," Miller's more than a little sarcastic voice announced.

"What's up, Charley?" Torine's voice came over the speaker.

"If Dick gave the guy who came with the Gulfstream a cashier's check for the airplane as soon as the Riggs Bank opens, how soon could you get it to Budapest?"

"You mean handle the paperwork later?"

"Right."

"If he goes along with the cashier's check, it would take me maybe an hour and a half to go wheels-up at Baltimore. I can't make it nonstop. I'd have to re-fuel someplace, maybe Rhine-Main—"

"That's now Frankfurt International. Hadn't you heard? No more Rhine-Main."

"And didn't that make you feel old?" Torine replied. "Figure nine hours total flight time, an hour to refuel. Figure twelve hours from the time Dick gives the owner's guy the check, presuming he's willing to go along. If he's not?"

"Give him the check anyway and don't tell him where you're going on your final test flight."

"One more problem. I'll have to bring Fernando along to fly the right seat. He's not going to like that."

"Do you really need someone in the right seat?"

Torine hesitated before replying, "You know, I've never landed an airplane anywhere where someone counted the pilots. You have a reason you don't want Fernando to come?"

"I want Fernando to go home to Texas and keep the home fires burning."

"Okay, Charley. Not a problem."

Fernando's voice came over the loudspeaker: "I'll fly the goddamned airplane to Budapest, Gringo, and then go home."

"You're sure?"

"I'm sure."

"Thanks," Castillo said. "Both of you. I'll get us rooms at the Gellért."

"See you in the wee hours tomorrow," Torine said and hung up.

"Anything else before I have my breakfast, Charley?" Miller asked.

"You ever get the avionics for the Ranger?"

"They're on their way to Buenos Aires."

"Okay. Great. I'll be in touch, Dick."

"Do I tell the ambassador where you're going?"

"You might as well. He'll know anyway."

"Run that past me again?"

"I'm going to use his aerial taxi to get me there," Castillo said. "He'll know."

"I don't quite understand that, but, what the hell. I probably don't have the Need to Know. Watch your back, buddy."

Castillo switched off the telephone and went back into his computer case, retrieved a business card, and held it in his hand as he punched in numbers on the telephone.

"Now what?" Otto Görner asked.

"I'm calling an aerial taxi to take me to Budapest."

"You sure you can get one? And is the *Tages Zeitung* going to have to pay for it?"

"I'm sure I can get one. The CIA owns the taxi service and Ambassador Montvale told them I go to the head of the line. And, no, the Lorimer Charitable and Benevolent Fund will pay for it."

"Get two seats," Otto said.

Castillo looked at him curiously.

"You're right. Eric's story was a little too detailed," Görner said. "He said he fell over his dog going down the stairs. If he had fallen over that goddamned dog, he wouldn't have told me. In fact, if he'd fallen down, period, he wouldn't have told me. Now I really want to know what's going on."

"This is Colonel Castillo," Charley said to the telephone. "I'm in Fulda, Germany, and I—and one other—have to get to Budapest as soon as possible. How's the best way to do that?"

Thirty seconds later, he put down the phone.

"Our taxi will be at Leipzig-Halle in ninety minutes," he said.

[TWO]
Office of the Ambassador
The Embassy of the United States of America
Lauro Miller 1776
Montevideo, República Oriental del Uruguay
1005 6 August 2005

"There's something going on around here, Robert," Ambassador McGrory said to Robert Howell, "that has the smell of rotten eggs and you and I are going to get to the bottom of it."

"I'm not sure that I know what you mean, Mr. Ambassador."

"I really would have thought, Robert, that someone in your line of business would be curious about Mr. Yung. His being suddenly called to the States and then coming back here to handle the Lorimer matter."

"I admit I wondered about that," Howell said.

"It could, of course, have just happened. But I don't think so."

"What do you think it is, Mr. Ambassador?"

"That, I don't know. That is what you and I are going to find out," Mc-Grory said.

"What is it you would like me to do, sir?"

"So long as he's here, I want you to keep a very close eye on him. I want to know where he goes, who he talks to, etcetera. I suspect he has some connection with what happened at that estancia and I want to know what that connection is."

"Is there some reason you think he has . . . 'some connection' . . . with what happened at Estancia Shangri-La?"

"Intuition," McGrory said. "When you have been in this game as long as I have, you develop an intuition."

"I'm sure that's true, Mr. Ambassador."

"So I want you to watch him very closely."

Howell nodded. *I think I have just become the fox placed in charge of the chicken coop.*

"Yung will be here in few minutes," McGrory said. "I want you to be here when I talk to him."

"Yes, sir."

"Mr. Yung just came onto the compound, Mr. Ambassador," Señora Susanna Obregon reported from Ambassador McGrory's office door.

"When he gets up here, make him wait five minutes and then show him in," McGrory replied, and then added: "And don't give him any coffee."

He looked significantly at Howell.

"Making Special Agent Yung twiddle his thumbs for a while, Robert, will make the point that his being on the personal staff of the secretary or not, I am the senior officer of the United States government here."

"I understand, sir."

Fifteen minutes later, when Yung had not appeared, McGrory was about to reach for his telephone to find out where the hell he was when Señora Obregon stepped into his office, closed the door behind her, and asked, "Mr. Yung just came in. What shall I do with him?"

"Ask him to wait, please," Ambassador McGrory replied and held up his hand, fingers and thumb extended, to remind her of how many minutes he wanted Yung to wait.

He then punched a button on his chronometer wristwatch, starting the timer.

"The ambassador will see you now, Mr. Yung," McGrory's secretary announced.

Yung got up off the chrome-and-plastic couch, laid on the coffee table the *Buenos Aires Herald* he had been reading, and walked to McGrory's door.

"Good morning, Mr. Ambassador."

"Welcome back to Uruguay, Yung," the ambassador said, waving him first into the room, then into one of the chairs facing his desk. "You know Mr. Howell, of course?"

"Yes, sir. Good to see you, Mr. Howell."

"May I offer you some coffee?" McGrory asked.

"Thank you, sir."

McGrory flipped the switch on his intercom and ordered coffee.

"Long flight?" McGrory inquired as they waited.

"It didn't seem as long, sir, as the ride from Ezeiza to Jorge Newbery. The *piqueteros* had the highway blocked. It took the taxi two hours to get downtown, moving five meters at a time."

That was more information than McGrory wanted or needed.

"Well, you know the pickets," he said. "Closing highways and bridges gives them something to do."

"Yes, sir. I suppose that's so."

Señora Obregon served the coffee. McGrory waited until she had left the office, then asked, "I understand, Yung, that when you were here before you weren't doing exactly what everyone—including Mr. Howell and I—thought you were doing."

Yung didn't reply.

"What, exactly, were you doing?" McGrory said, pointedly.

"With the exception, sir, that I was responding to specific requests for information from the State Department and answering those queries directly to the department rather than through the embassy, I was looking into money laundering like every other FBI agent here."

"Why do you suppose that was necessary? And that I was not informed?"

"Sir, I have no idea. I'm pretty low on the totem pole. That's what I was told to do and I did it."

"Who told you to do it?"

"Mrs. Quiglette," Yung said, simply.

"You're referring to Deputy Assistant Secretary of State for Latin America Quiglette?"

Yung nodded. "Nice lady."

"It was Mrs. Quiglette who told you to tell me nothing of your special orders?"

"What special orders is that, sir?"

"The ones to keep me in the dark about what you were actually doing down here?"

"Yes, sir. But it wasn't a question of not telling you specifically, sir. I was told that no one was to know what I was doing."

"But you were aware that was highly extraordinary?"

"No, sir. I didn't think anything about it. I've had other assignments where no one knew what I was really doing."

"Such as?"

"Sir, I really can't discuss anything like that."

"And can you discuss why you were suddenly ordered out of here?"

"No, sir," Yung said.

"Deputy Assistant Secretary Quiglette messaged me that you were coming back here, to take over the late Mr. Lorimer's body, his assets, etcetera. Are you aware of that?"

"Yes, sir."

"Then, presumably, you are aware of the circumstances of Mr. Lorimer's death?"

Yung looked at the ambassador. *Now, here's where I'm going to have to start being deceptive and dishonest. Goddamn Castillo for getting me into this!*

"I know he was murdered, sir, and that he was Mr. Masterson's brother-in-law, but that's about all."

"I'm curious why the State Department felt it necessary to send someone down here to do what we're perfectly capable of doing ourselves?" McGrory asked, but it was more of a statement than a question.

Yung answered it anyway: "I was given the impression, sir, that that came from the secretary herself."

"You didn't deal with the secretary herself?"

"No, sir. But I was led to believe that it was personal courtesy—maybe professional courtesy—probably both—on her part to Mr. Lorimer's father, who is a retired ambassador."

"But why you, Yung?"

"Because I was here, I suppose. I know Uruguay and the banks and people at the embassy."

McGrory appeared to think that over, then nodded.

"That may well put you in a very delicate situation, Yung," McGrory said.

"Sir?"

"As it does me, frankly, Yung," McGrory said. "Could we go off the record a moment, do you think?"

"Yes, sir. Of course."

"Not that you're really keeping a record, of course. Just as a manner of speaking."

"Yes, sir."

"Now—bearing in mind that I don't know this for sure, but I've been in this diplomatic game for many years now, and believe me you acquire a certain insight into things . . ."

"I'm sure you have, sir."

"One of the things you learn is that people who would have you think they have a certain influence with the upper echelons of something—like the State Department, for example—don't really have much influence at all."

"I suppose that's true," Yung said.

"And ying yong," McGrory said, significantly.

"Excuse me?"

"Ying yong," McGrory repeated, and then when he saw on Yung's face that he didn't understand went on: "I thought, as an Oriental, you would understand. That's Korean, I believe."

"I'm Chinese, Mr. Ambassador," Yung said. "My family came to this country—to the United States—in the 1840s. I don't speak Korean."

"It means everything evens out," McGrory explained. "Sort of like the law of physics which says every action has an immediate and exactly opposite reaction."

"Yes, sir?"

"In this case, Yung, it would mean that someone who goes to some effort to suggest he has little influence—is 'pretty low on the totem pole,' to use your phrase—may in fact have a good deal of influence."

What the hell is McGrory talking about? Is he suggesting I have influence?

"I'm not sure I follow you, Mr. Ambassador."

"I understand, of course," McGrory said.

McGrory gave Yung time for that to sink in, then went on: "As I was saying, we are both in a somewhat delicate position vis-à-vis Mr. Lorimer."

"How is that, sir?"

"Like the secretary, I am concerned with Ambassador Lorimer. I never met him, but I understand he is a fine man, a credit to the diplomatic service."

"That's my understanding, sir."

"And Ambassador Silvio, in Buenos Aires, told me in confidence that Ambassador Lorimer has certain health problems . . . his heart."

"So I understand," Yung said.

"Let me tell you, Yung, what's happened here. Off the record, of course."

"Yes, sir."

"As incredible as this sounds, Deputy Foreign Minister Alvarez came to my office. He had with him a Señor Ordóñez, who I have learned is the chief inspector of the Interior Police Division of the Uruguayan Policía Nacional. Not an official visit. He just 'happened to be in the neighborhood and wanted to chat over a cup of coffee.' "

"Yes, sir?"

"And he suggested not only that what really happened at Estancia Shangri-La was a shoot-out between persons unknown and United States Special Forces, but also that I knew all about it."

Yung looked at Howell but did not reply.

McGrory continued: "The accusation is patently absurd, of course. I don't have to tell you that no action of that kind could take place without my knowledge and permission. As ambassador, I am the senior U.S. officer in country. And Mr. Howell—who as I'm sure you suspect is the CIA station chief—assures me that he knows of no secret operation by the intelligence community. And he would know."

"I'd heard the rumors that Mr. Howell was CIA, sir . . ."

"Well, that's classified information, of course," McGrory said. "I never told you that."

"Yes, sir. I understand, sir. Where do think Mr. Alvarez got an idea like that? About a Special Operations mission?"

McGrory did not reply directly.

Instead, he said, "The question is, why would he make such an absurd accusation? That was the question I asked myself, the question that kept me from immediately reporting the incident to the department. I did, however, just about throw him out of my office."

"Did he offer anything to substantiate the accusation?" Yung asked.

"He showed me a . . . thingamabob . . . the shiny part of a cartridge, what comes out of a gun after it's fired?"

"A cartridge *case,* sir?"

"Precisely. He told me it had been found at the estancia. And he told me he had gone directly to the Uruguayan embassy in Washington and they had gone to the Pentagon and the Pentagon had obligingly informed them that it was a special kind of bullet used only by U.S. Army competitive rifle shooters *and* Special Forces."

"A National Match case, sir? Did the case have *NM* stamped on it?"

If it did, it almost certainly came from that Marine high school cheerleader's rifle.

McGrory pointed his finger at Yung and nodded his head.

"That's it," he said.

"That's not much proof that our Special Forces were involved," Yung said.

"Of course not. Because they were not involved. If there were Special Forces involved, Mr. Howell and I would have known about it. That's a given."

"Yes, sir."

"My temptation, of course, was to go right to the department and report the incident. You don't just about call the American ambassador a liar in his office. But as I said before, Yung, I've been in the diplomatic game for some time. I've learned to ask myself why somebody says something, does something. I realized that if I went to the department, they'd more than likely register an official complaint, possibly even recall me for consultation. And I thought maybe that's what the whole thing was all about. They wanted to cause a stink, in other words. Then I asked myself, why would they want to do that? And that answer is simple. They were creating a diversion."

"To take attention from what, sir?"

"What really happened at that ranch, that estancia."

"Which is, sir?"

"Think about this, Yung," McGrory replied, indirectly. "Bertrand—Lorimer—had nearly sixteen million dollars in banks here. Did you know about that?"

Yung didn't answer directly. He said, "Sixteen million dollars?"

McGrory nodded.

"That's a lot of money."

"Yes, it is," McGrory agreed. "And the United Nations—although their pay scales are considerably more generous than ours—wasn't paying him the kind of money—even if he lived entirely on his expense account, which I understand a lot of them do—for him to have socked away *sixteen million* for a rainy day. So where, I asked myself, did he get it?"

He looked expectantly at Yung, who looked thoughtful, then shrugged.

"You've been looking into money laundering," McGrory said, somewhat impatiently. "Where does most of that dirty money come from?"

"Embezzlement or drugs, usually," Yung said.

"And there you have it," McGrory said, triumphantly. "Lorimer was a drug dealer."

"You really think so, sir?"

"Think about it. Everything fits. With his alter ego as an antiques dealer, he was in a perfect position to ship drugs. Who's going to closely inspect what's stuffed into some old vase—some old, very valuable vase? You can get a lot of heroin into a vase. And where did Lorimer get his new identity and permission to live in Uruguay? The best face they could put on that was they were surprised that he was dealing drugs right under their noses. He had probably paid off a half dozen officials. That would come out, too."

"It's an interesting theory, Mr. Ambassador," Yung said.

"I thought you might think so, Yung. What happened at the estancia was that a drug deal, a big one, a *huge* one—we're talking sixteen million dollars here—went wrong. You know, probably better than I do, that murder is a way of life in that business. Those drug people would as soon shoot you as look at you."

"Yes, sir, that's certainly true."

Does he really believe this nonsense?

"Well, I'm not going to let them get away with it, I'll tell you that. I'm not going to give them the diversion they want. No official complaint to the State Department."

"I understand, sir."

"I'm just going to bide my time, leaving them to swing in the breeze as they realize I'm not going to be their patsy." He paused, then went on: "However, I think that the appropriate people in the State Department should be made aware of the situation. That's more or less what I was getting into when I said you and I—and even the secretary herself—are in a delicate position. If it wasn't for Ambassador Lorimer, I'd be perfectly happy to call a spade a spade, but in view of the ambassador's physical condition . . ."

"I understand, sir."

"None of us wish to spoil what I'm sure is his cherished memory of his son, much less give him a heart attack, do we?"

"No, sir, we certainly don't."

"On the other hand, I think the secretary should know about this, don't you? Even if the information comes quietly from someone pretty low on the totem pole."

"I take your point, sir."

"I was sure you would," McGrory said.

He stood up, leaned across his desk, and offered Yung his hand.

They shook, then he sat back down.

"Now, getting to the business you're here for. Is there anything I can do, anyone on my staff can do, to facilitate the return of Mr. Lorimer's remains to the United States, and the rest of it?"

"I'm sure there will be something, sir."

"I'll pass the word that you are to be given whatever assistance you need, and if you think anyone needs a little jogging, I'm as close as your telephone."

"Thank you, sir."

"Specifically, what I'm going to do is ask Mr. Howell to ask Mr. Monahan to assign Mr. Artigas to assist you in whatever needs to be done so long as you're here."

"Mr. Artigas?"

"He can fill you in on what happened at Estancia Shangri-La," McGrory explained. "He's been up there. Chief Inspector José Ordóñez of the Interior Police Division of the Uruguayan Policía Nacional flew him up there in a helicopter the day after it happened."

Yung thought: *I've been sandbagged. The last thing I need is Julio Artigas looking over my shoulder and taking notes so that he can report to McGrory.*

"I appreciate the thought, sir, but I'm not sure that will be necessary."

"Nonsense," McGrory said. "I'm sure he'll be very helpful to you."

"Yes, sir."

McGrory stood up again.

"If you can find time while you're here, why don't we have lunch?"

Yung understood the meeting was concluded.

"I'd like that very much, sir," Yung said and stood up.

McGrory offered his hand again. Yung shook it, then offered his hand to Howell.

"Why don't we go see Mr. Monahan right now, Yung?" Howell asked.

"Good idea," McGrory said.

"Thank you," Yung said.

As he walked out of the ambassador's office, Yung had several thoughts, one after the other:

Unbelievable! Surreal!

Wait till Castillo hears that nonsense about Lorimer being a drug dealer!

Thank God that pompous moron—no wonder they call him Señor Pompous!—wasn't told what we were up to! He would have ordered all of us out of the country and told the Uruguayans why.

But he's not as stupid as he appears. He's going to have Artigas watch me and Howell watch both of us. I have to keep that in mind.

Just as soon as I can, I'm going to have to go to Buenos Aires and get on a secure line to Castillo.

"I'm going to have to stop in here," Yung said to Howell as they approached the door to a men's room.

Howell followed him inside and stood at the adjacent urinal.

"Well," Howell said. "That was interesting, wasn't it?"

"Does he actually believe that drug dealer business or is he being clever?"

"He believes it. He also believes he's smelling rotten eggs."

"Artigas is smart and he doesn't like me," Yung said.

"And he and Chief Inspector Ordóñez are pals."

"So what do I do?"

"Make sure Artigas doesn't learn anything Ordóñez would like to know."

"And how do I do that?"

"Be very careful, Yung. Very careful."

[THREE]
Office of the Legal Attaché
The Embassy of the United States of America
Lauro Miller 1776
Montevideo, República Oriental del Uruguay
1035 6 August 2005

Generally speaking, there is little love lost between the Federal Bureau of Investigation and the Central Intelligence Agency, and in the United States embassy in Montevideo there was little lost between James D. Monahan, the senior FBI agent, and Robert Howell, the cultural attaché rumored to be the CIA station chief.

Monahan privately thought of Howell as a typical CIA asshole who couldn't find his ass with both hands and Howell privately thought of Monahan as someone far better suited to be walking a beat in Chicago eating a stolen apple while preserving law and order with his billy club than holding his present position.

They were, of course, civil to each other.

"Can we come in a moment, Jim?" Howell asked.

"Absolutely. What's on your mind, Bob?"

"Hello, Monahan," Yung said.

"I heard you'd been recalled to the bureau," Monahan said. "You're back?"

"Temporarily," Yung said. "They sent me back to handle the affairs of Mr. Lorimer. Return of the remains, conservation of assets, etcetera."

"The *bureau* sent you back to do that?"

"Actually, it was the State Department that sent me."

"Oh, that's right. You work for the State Department, don't you? A little something you never got around to telling me."

"You didn't have the Need to Know," Yung said, more than a little lamely.

"Jim," Howell said, quickly, "the ambassador would like you to have Julio Artigas work with Yung on this."

"Work with Yung on what?"

"Repatriation of Mr. Lorimer's remains, for one thing, safeguarding his assets and having a look at Lorimer's estancia."

"The ambassador wants this?" Monahan asked.

"Yes, he does."

Monahan picked up his telephone and punched in a number.

"Julio, can you come in here a minute?"

Legal Attaché Julio Artigas was surprised to see Yung in Monahan's office. In thinking about what had happened at Estancia Shangri-La and his gut feeling when he had gone with Ambassador McGrory to Buenos Aires that Howell and Darby, the Buenos Aires CIA station chief, knew all about what had happened there, he had concluded that Yung was also probably involved.

The story that Yung had been suddenly recalled to the States to testify in some court case smelled. Artigas had thought it even possible that Yung had been at the estancia during the firefight and had been wounded and taken out of the country by whoever had been at the estancia and won the gun battle. It seemed logical to presume that at least some of the Americans involved had been wounded or even killed—and there was little question in his mind that Americans were involved. Getting Yung out of the country, even with a fishy, hastily concocted story, made more sense than trying to explain how and where he had been wounded.

Artigas had kept his thoughts to himself. His opinion of James D. Monahan was that his greatest skill was covering his own ass. Monahan liked being the senior FBI agent in the embassy, which allowed him to order the other agents around. But whenever he should have stood up and defended the other agents from one of McGrory's stupid orders, he was quick to argue that he wasn't the SAC and that sort of thing wasn't his business.

Artigas knew that if he had said anything of his suspicions to Monahan, there was no question that Monahan would have run with it right to McGrory—or, more likely, to Theodore J. Detweiller, Jr., the chief of mission.

"I think I should tell you, Ted, what a wild idea Artigas came to me with."

"What can I do for you, Jim?"

"It's what you can do for Yung," Monahan replied. "Or, more accurately, for the State Department."

"You're back, huh, Yung?" Artigas asked.

"Yung was sent back," Howell answered for him, "by the secretary of state to handle the return of Lorimer's remains and to protect his assets."

"And to compile a report for the secretary about what happened at Lorimer's estancia," Yung added.

Artigas looked at Yung. *Or maybe, since you know goddamned well what happened, to see how much we know? Or the Uruguayans know?*

"You're a little late to protect his assets," Artigas said. "Parties unknown emptied his bank accounts. Of sixteen million dollars."

He thought, *As you almost certainly know.*

"I've heard something about that," Yung replied, "and I'd like a full report on that. What we know for sure. Ambassador McGrory told me there is some reason to think he was into drugs. But first things first. Where is the body?"

"In the cooler, in the British Hospital on Avenida Italia. It was taken there for an autopsy. Chief Inspector Ordóñez of the federal police has promised me a copy of the autopsy report sometime today."

"I'd like a copy of that, too, of course. And is there going to be any kind of a problem getting into the estancia?"

"Ordóñez has the estancia pretty well sealed off. He'd be the man to ask about that."

"Well," Howell suggested, "why don't we go to my office, see if we can get him on the phone? And get out of Jim's hair."

"Just to be sure I know what's going on here, this has the blessing of the ambassador, right?" Artigas asked.

"Yes, it does," Howell said. He nodded toward the door. "Shall we go?"

"I'd like a brief word with you, Artigas," Monahan said, then added for Howell, "It'll take just a couple of seconds, Bob."

"Certainly," Howell said, smiling, and walked out of Monahan's office. Yung followed him.

Both heard Monahan say, "Close the door, Jim," and exchanged glances.

"I suspect Monahan just told him to report everything we do," Howell said. "Does that make me paranoid?"

[FOUR]
Office of the Cultural Attaché
The Embassy of the United States of America
Lauro Miller 1776
Montevideo, República Oriental del Uruguay
1055 6 August 2005

There was no reason for Julio Artigas to report the substance of his conversation with Chief Inspector Ordóñez to Howell and Yung. Howell had punched the speakerphone button on his telephone and they had heard the entire conversation.

Howell spoke first: "Chief Inspector Ordóñez is certainly obliging, isn't he?"

"Uruguayan courtesy," Yung said. "Or professional courtesy. Maybe—probably—both."

"I thought his offer of a Huey to fly us to the estancia was more than generous," Howell said.

"And volunteering to go with us. That was rather nice of him," Yung said.

"My cousin José is a very charming man," Artigas said. "But what I think you two have to keep in mind is that he's one smart cop."

"Why do you think we should we keep that in mind, Julio?" Howell asked.

"Oh, come on," Artigas said.

"Oh, come on what?" Howell replied.

"Something is going on here. I have no idea what. But you two do."

"Really?" Howell asked. "What do you think is going on, Julio?"

"What I don't think is that Lorimer was a drug dealer who got himself killed when a deal went wrong. And neither does José Ordóñez."

"He told you that?" Yung asked.

"He didn't have to. I know him pretty well."

"What does he think, do you know? Or can you guess?" Howell asked.

"I know he's fascinated with several things," Artigas said. "First, that he can't identify the Ninjas at the estancia. If they were Uruguayans, Argentines, or Brazilians, by now he would have. Second, that National Match cartridge case. And the cleaning out of Lorimer's bank accounts. He's trying to tie those unknowns together. If he can, he'll know what really happened at Estancia Shangri-La."

"What do you know about Presidential Findings, Julio?" Howell asked.

"Jesus," Yung muttered.

Howell looked at him and shrugged, as if to say, *What choice do we have?*

"Not much," Artigas admitted. "I've heard the term."

"Well—just talking, you understand—what *I've* heard about Presidential Findings is that they are classified Top Secret Presidential. The only persons cleared to know any details of a Presidential Finding are those cleared by the President himself or by the officer the President has named to do whatever the Presidential Finding calls for."

"You've got my attention," Artigas said.

"So hypothetically speaking, of course," Howell went on, obviously choosing his words carefully, "if there were people privy to a Presidential Finding and it happened that a professional associate of theirs—an FBI agent, for example, or an ambassador for that matter, someone with all the standard security clearances—became interested in something touching on the details of the Finding and went to one of these people and asked them about it, they just couldn't tell him no matter how much they might like to, not even if telling that person would facilitate their execution of their assignment."

"That would apply to an ambassador, too? I mean, there's the rule that nothing is supposed to happen in a foreign country that the ambassador doesn't know about and approves of."

"That's my understanding," Howell said. "Is that your understanding, too, of how a Presidential Finding works, Yung?"

"From what I've heard," Yung said.

"And from what I understand," Howell went on, "it would be a serious breach of security for someone privy to a Presidential Finding to even admit his knowledge of any detail of a Presidential Finding. He couldn't say, for example, 'I'm sorry, Mr. Ambassador, but that touches on a Presidential Finding for which you are not cleared.' He would have to completely deny any knowledge of even knowing there was a Presidential Finding."

"Fascinating," Artigas said. "Can I ask a question?"

"You can ask anything you want," Yung said.

"But I may not get an answer? Is that it?"

"Ask your question," Howell said.

"Just between us, hypothetically speaking, where do you suppose Lorimer got sixteen million dollars?"

"The ambassador thinks it was from drugs. I'm not about to question the ambassador's judgment," Howell said. "But, hypothetically speaking of course, it could have come from somewhere else. Embezzlement comes to mind. It could even, I suppose, have something to do with the oil-for-food scandal. I heard somewhere there was really a lot of money involved in that."

"You know, that thought occurred to me, too."

"Did it?" Howell asked.

"One more question?" Artigas asked.

"Shoot."

"Monahan just now told me I was to tell him everywhere Yung went, who he talked to, what he said—everything."

"How interesting," Howell said. "The ambassador told me to do exactly that about Yung."

"I'm wondering whether that would mean I should tell him about this little discussion of ours."

"What discussion was that?"

"About Presidential Findings."

"I don't remember any discussion of Presidential Findings, do you, Yung?" Howell asked.

"No, I don't remember any discussion like that."

Artigas stood up.

"We'd better be getting over to the British Hospital," he said. "We wouldn't want to keep Ordóñez waiting, would we? Since he's being so helpful?"

[FIVE]
Camp Mackall, North Carolina
0930 6 August 2005

Sergeant Major John K. Davidson's job description said he was the Operations Sergeant of the Special Forces training facility. He was, but he actually had two other functions, both unwritten and both more or less secret. It was not much of a secret that he was the judge of the noncommissioned officers going through the basic qualification course—the "Q course." He was the man who, with the advice of others, decided which trainee was going to go on to further, specialized training and ultimately earn the right to wear the blaze of a fully qualified Special Forces soldier on his green beret and which trainee would go back to other duties in the Army.

Far more of a secret was that he was also the judge of the commissioned officers going through the Q course.

Jack Davidson had not wanted the job—for one thing, Mackall was in the boonies and a long drive from his quarters on the post, and, for another, he thought of himself as an *urban* special operator—as opposed to an out in the boonies eating monkeys and snakes and rolling around in the mud *field* special operator—and running Mackall meant spending most of his time in the boonies.

But two people for whom he had enormous respect—he had been around the block with both of them: Vic D'Allessando, now retired and running the Stockade, and Bruce J. "Scotty" McNab, whom Davidson had known as a major and who was now the XVIII Airborne Corps commander and a three-star general—had almost shamelessly appealed to his sense of duty.

"Jack, you know better than anybody else what it takes," Scotty McNab had told him. "Somebody else is likely to pass some character who can't hack it and people will get killed. You want that on your conscience?"

Sergeant Major Davidson was not surprised when he heard the peculiar *fluckata-fluckata* sound the rotor blades of MH-6H helicopters make as they came in for a landing. And he was reasonably sure that it was either D'Allessando or the general, who often dropped in unannounced once a week or so, and neither had been at Mackall recently.

But when he pushed himself out of his chair and walked outside the small, wood-frame operations building just as the Little Bird touched down, he was surprised to see that the chopper held both of them. That seldom happened.

He waited safely outside the rotor cone as first General McNab—a small, muscular ruddy-faced man sporting a flowing red mustache—and then Vic D'Allessando ducked under the blades.

He saluted crisply.

"Good morning, General," he said, officially. "Welcome to Camp Mackall. May the sergeant major ask the general who the bald, fat old Guinea is?"

"I told you it was a bad idea to teach the bastard how to read," D'Allessando said, first giving Davidson the finger with both hands and then wrapping his arms around him.

"How are you, Jack?" McNab asked.

"Can't complain, sir. What brings you to the boonies?"

"A bit of news that'll make you weep for the old Army," McNab said. "Guess who's now a lieutenant colonel?"

"Haven't the foggiest."

"Charley Castillo," Vic D'Allessando said. "Make you feel old, Jack?"

"Yeah," Davidson said, thoughtfully. "I remember Charley when he was a second john and driving the general's chopper in Desert One. *Lieutenant Colonel* Castillo. I'll be damned." He paused, thought about that, then added, "I think he'll be a good one."

"And I want to see Corporal Lester Bradley of the Marines," McNab said.

"You heard about that, did you, General?" Davidson said.

"Heard about what?"

"The goddamned Marines pulling our chain."

"How pulling our chain?"

"I'm responsible," Davidson said.

"What are you talking about?"

"I went to Quantico and talked to the jarheads about the people they're starting to send here. The master gunnery sergeant of Force Recon there—an Irishman named MacNamara—was a pretty good guy. We hit it off. We had a couple of tastes together. And while we were talking, I asked him if he had any influence on who they were sending here. He said he did. So I asked him as a favor if he could send us at least one who wasn't all muscles, especially between the ears, and could read and write."

He stopped when he saw the look on McNab's face.

"General," he went on, "they send all their Force Recon guys through the SEAL course on the West Coast. They run them up and down the beach in the sand carrying telephone poles over their heads. By the time they finish, they all look like Arnold Schwarzenegger. They're more into that physical crap than even the goddamned Rangers."

"And?" McNab asked.

"So I forgot about it," Davidson said. "I'd pulled MacNamara's chain a little and I was satisfied. And then Bradley appeared."

"And?" McNab pursued.

"Well, not only can he read and write—he talks like a college professor, never using a small word when a big one will do—and not only is he not all muscle, he's no muscle at all. And he's eighteen, nineteen years old and looks fifteen. I have to hand it to Master Gunnery Sergeant MacNamara. He had to look all over the Marine Corps to find this guy."

"And where is this stalwart Marine warrior?"

"In the office. I've got him typing. He didn't even—I forgot to mention this—have orders. What I'm doing now is hoping that MacNamara's going to call me and go, 'Ha-ha! Got you good, my doggie friend. Now you can send him back.' "

"I think that's unlikely, Jack," General McNab said and walked toward the small frame building, where he pushed open the door.

A voice inside, in a loud but somewhat less than commanding voice, cried, "Attention on deck!"

Mr. D'Allessando and Sergeant Major Davidson followed General McNab into the building.

Corporal Bradley was standing at rigid attention behind a field desk holding a notebook computer.

General McNab turned and looked at Sergeant Major Davidson.

"Never judge a book by its cover," he said. "You might want to write that down, Jack."

Then he looked at Corporal Bradley.

"At ease," he said, softly.

Bradley shifted from his rigid position of attention to an equally rigid position, with his hands in the small of his back, his legs slightly spread.

"Unless I'm mistaken, son," General McNab said, "you are now standing at parade rest."

"Sir, the corporal begs the general's pardon. The general is correct, sir," Bradley said, let his body relax, and took his hands from the small of his back.

"So you're the sniper, are you, son?" McNab asked.

"Sir, I *was* a *designated marksman* on the march to Baghdad."

"Thank you for the clarification."

"With all respect, sir, my pleasure, sir."

"Tell me, son, how would you describe your role in the assault on that wonderfully named Estancia Shangri-La?"

"With all respect, sir, I am under orders not to discuss that mission with anyone."

"Can you tell me why not?"

"Sir, the mission is classified Top Secret Presidential."

General McNab looked at Sergeant Major Davidson but didn't say anything.

Vic D'Allessando said, "It's okay, Lester. The general and the sergeant major are cleared."

"Yes, sir," Lester said.

"Well, son? What did you do on that mission?"

"Sir, Major Castillo, who was in command, assigned me to guard the helicopter."

"For your information, Corporal, Major Castillo has been promoted to lieutenant colonel," McNab said.

"If it is appropriate for me to say so, sir, it is a well-deserved promotion. Maj . . . *Lieutenant Colonel* Castillo is a fine officer under whom I am proud to have served."

Vic D'Allessando was smiling widely at a thoroughly confused Sergeant Major Davidson.

"So you guarded the helicopter?" McNab pursued.

"Yes, sir. Until the situation got a bit out of control, when I realized it had become my duty to enter the fray."

" 'The fray'? Is that something like a firefight?" McNab asked.

"Yes, it is, sir. Perhaps I should have used that phrase."

"How exactly did you enter the fray, Corporal?" McNab asked. "When the situation got a bit out of control?"

"Sir, when it became evident that one of the villains was about to fire his Madsen through a window into a room into which Maj . . . *Lieutenant Colonel* Castillo had taken the detainee, I realized I had to take him out. Regrettably, he managed to fire a short burst before I was able to do so."

"How did you take him out?"

"With a head shot, sir."

"You didn't consider that it would be safer to try to hit him in the body?"

"I considered it, sir, but I was no more than seventy-five meters distant and knew I could make the shot."

"Is that all you did, Corporal?"

"No, sir. I took out a second villain perhaps fifteen seconds later."

"With another head shot?"

"Yes, sir."

"Just to satisfy my curiosity, Corporal," McNab asked, "were you firing offhand?"

"Yes, sir. There just wasn't time to adjust a sling and get into a kneeling or prone position, sir."

"Colonel Castillo has told Mr. D'Allessando that there is no question you saved his life. Sergeant Major Davidson and myself are old friends of Colonel Castillo's and we are grateful to you, aren't we, Sergeant Major?"

"Yes, sir. We certainly are."

"Just doing my duty as I saw it, sir."

"They are going to bury Sergeant Kranz at sixteen hundred today in Arlington. If Sergeant Major Davidson can spare you from your duties here, I thought perhaps you might wish to go there with Mr. D'Allessando and me."

"Yes, sir. I would like very much to pay my last respects."

"Have you a dress uniform?"

"Yes, sir. But I'm afraid it's not very shipshape, sir."

"Well, I'm sure Sergeant Major Davidson will be happy to see that it's pressed and that you're at Pope at twelve hundred, won't you, Jack?"

"My pleasure, sir," Sergeant Major Davidson said.

VII

[ONE]
Ferihegy International Airport
Budapest, Hungary
1655 6 August 2005

Hungary is not a member of the European Union. It was therefore necessary for Otto Görner and Karl W. von und zu Gossinger to pass through immigration and customs when the Eurojet Taxi deposited them before the small civil-aviation building.

But it was just the briefest of formalities. Not only were their passports quickly stamped by the officer who came aboard the twin-engine jet aircraft but he volunteered the information, "Your driver is waiting, Úr Görner."

Then he left without even looking at the luggage the pilot and copilot had carried down the stair door.

"Thanks for the ride and the cockpit tour," Castillo said, in English, offering his hand to the pilot.

"My pleasure, Colonel," the pilot replied, also in English—American English.

"Maybe we can do it again."

"Any time. You've got our number."

There had been no other passengers on the flight from Leipzig, which made Castillo wonder if that was coincidence or whether the Cessna Citation III had been sent to pick him up because there would be no smaller aircraft available for some time and Montvale had ordered them to put him at the head of the line.

Just after they had gone wheels-up, he had made his way to the cockpit and asked, in English, "How's chances of sitting in the right seat and having you explain the panel to me?"

The copilot had exchanged glances with the pilot, who nodded, and then wordlessly got up.

"Thanks," Castillo said to the pilot as he sat down and strapped himself in.

"Anything special you want to see, Colonel?" the pilot had asked, in English, making it clear that there was no reason to pretend he was anything but an employee of the agency or that Castillo was a German businessman named Gossinger availing himself of Eurojet Taxi's services.

"How long do you think it would take to show a pilot—several hundred hours in smaller business jets—enough to make him safe to sit in the right seat?"

"These are nice airplanes," the pilot said. "They come in a little hot, and sometimes, close to max gross, they take a long time to get off the ground, but aside from that they're not hard to fly. How long it would take would depend on the IP and the student. But not long."

"I'd really be grateful to be able to sit here and watch until you get it on the ground in Budapest. Is that possible?"

"You know how to work the radios?" the pilot asked and when Castillo nodded the pilot motioned for him to pick up the copilot's headset and, when Castillo had them on, pointed out on the GPS screen where they were—over the Dresden–Nürnberg Autobahn, near Chemnitz.

I think Montvale will learn that I wanted to sit in the cockpit, but I don't think he'll think it's anything but my boyish enthusiasm for everything connected with flying.

"Good afternoon, Úr Görner," Sándor Tor greeted them inside the civil-aviation building. "The car's right outside."

"Sándor, this is Herr von und zu Gossinger," Görner said. "And this, Úr von und zu Gossinger, is Sándor Tor, who was supposed to keep Kocian from falling over his goddamned dog and down the stairs."

"Úr Görner . . ." Tor began, painfully embarrassed.

"And also, incidentally, to telephone me immediately, at any time, if anything at all out of the ordinary happened to Úr Kocian."

"Úr Görner . . ." Tor began again, only to be interrupted again by Görner.

"Why don't we wait until we're on our way to the hospital?" Görner said. "Then you can tell us everything."

"I wish God had put me in that hospital bed instead of Úr Kocian," Tor said, emotionally.

I think I like you, Sándor Tor, Castillo thought.

In 2002, Otto Görner had reluctantly concluded Eric Kocian, in his eighties, needed protection—protection from himself.

The old man was fond of American whiskey—Jack Daniel's Black Label in particular—and driving fast Mercedes-Benz automobiles. A combination of the former and his age-reduced reflexes and night vision had seen him in half a dozen accidents, the last two of them spectacular. The final one had put him in hospital and caused the government to cancel his driver's license.

Otto Görner had come to Budapest and sought out Sándor Tor right after he'd been to Kocian's hospital room.

"We're going to have to do something or he's going to kill himself," Görner had announced. "It won't take him long to get his driving license back—he knows where all the politicians keep their mistresses. We have to get this fixed before that happens."

"You mean get him a chauffeur?"

Görner nodded.

"Good luck, Úr Görner," Tor had said. "I'm glad I'm not the one who's going to have to tell him that."

Görner had smiled and, obviously thinking about what he was going to say, didn't reply for a moment.

Then he said, "Let me tell you what he said in the hospital just now. Not for the first time, he was way ahead of me."

Tor waited for Görner to go on.

" 'Before you say anything, Otto,' he said, the moment I walked in the door, 'let me tell you how I'm going to deal with this.' "

"I can't wait to hear this," Tor said.

" 'Sándor Tor will now drive me around,' " Görner quoted.

"No," Tor said, quickly and firmly, not embracing the idea at all.

"I told him you were the director of security, not a chauffeur," Görner said. "And?"

" 'Did you think I don't know that?' " Görner quoted. " 'As director of security, he carries a gun. I'm getting too old to do that anymore, too. Furthermore, Sándor can be trusted to keep his mouth shut about where I go and who I talk to. I don't want some taxi driver privy to that or listening to my conversations. And, finally, Sándor's a widower. Driving me around may interfere with his sex life, but at least he won't go home and regale his wife with tales of what Kocian did today and with whom.' "

"No, Úr Görner," Tor repeated, adamantly.

"I told him you would say that," Görner said. "To which he replied, 'I'll handle Tor.' "

"No. Sorry, but absolutely not."

"Do you know, Sándor, how far back Eric Kocian goes with Gossinger, G.m.b.H.?"

"Not exactly. A long time, I know that."

"He was with Oberstleutnant Hermann Wilhelm von und zu Gossinger at Stalingrad," Görner said. "They met on the ice-encrusted basement floor of a building being used as a hospital. Both were very seriously wounded."

"I've heard that the Herr Oberst had been at Stalingrad . . ."

"Eric was an eighteen-year-old *Gefreite*," Görner went on. "He and the colonel were flown out on one of the very last flights. The colonel was released from hospital first and placed on convalescent leave. He went to visit a friend in the Army hospital in Giessen and ran into Kocian there. Eric had apparently done something for the colonel in Stalingrad—I have no idea what, but the colonel was grateful—so the colonel arranged for him to be assigned to the POW camp he was going to command. The alternative for Kocian was being sent back to the Eastern Front.

"They ended the war in the POW camp and became prisoners themselves. Kocian was released first. He went home to Vienna and learned that the American bombs that had reduced St. Stephen's Cathedral and the Opera to rubble had done the same to his family's apartment. All of his family, and their friends, were dead."

"Jesus!" Tor exclaimed, softly.

"His only friend in the world was the colonel. So he made his way back to Germany and Fulda. The presses of the *Fulda Tages Zeitung* were in the basement of what had been the building. Eric arrived there a day or so after the colonel had been given permission by the Americans to resume publishing. They had found his name on a list the SS had of people they were going to execute for being anti-Nazi and defeatist and he was thus the man they were looking for to run a German newspaper.

"The problem was the presses were at the bottom of a huge pile of rubble that had been the *Fulda Tages Zeitung* building. Eric Kocian began his journalistic career making one whole Mergenthaler Linotype machine from parts salvaged from the dozen under the rubble.

"A year later, when the *Wiener Tages Zeitung* got permission from the Americans to resume publishing, Eric was named editor in chief primarily because he had already been cleared by the de-Nazification courts and also because their Linotype machines had to be rescued from the rubble of the *Wiener Tages Zeitung* building. It was understood that Eric was to be publisher and editor in chief only and that older, wiser, bona fide professional journalists would really run things.

"When the colonel went to Vienna for the ceremonies marking the first edition, he found that Eric had fired the older, wiser, etcetera people, hired his own, and was sitting at the editor in chief's desk himself."

"That sounds like him," Tor said, chuckling.

"Well, he kept the job and now he's the oldest employee of Gossinger, G.m.b.H. Further, I learned that when the colonel and his brother were killed it was Eric who went to the colonel's daughter and got her to give me the job of running the business. So I think I owe him."

"I understand."

"I realize you don't owe him a thing—"

Tor held up his hand.

"When my wife was dying, he held my hand, and, later, he got me off the bottle," Tor said. "Okay, until I can get somebody he can live with, and vice versa—but only until then, understand—I'll keep an eye on him."

Somebody Eric Kocian could live with had never appeared. And Tor learned somewhat to his surprise that he actually had time to both serve as director of security for the *Tages Zeitung* and keep an eye on the old man.

The job now was more than keeping Kocian from behind the wheel of his Mercedes. A year before, Kocian had begun investigating Hungarian/Czech/German involvement in the Iraqi oil-for-food scandal. It personally outraged him.

And when those who had been engaged in it learned of Kocian's interest in them, they were enraged. There had been a number of threats by e-mail, postal mail, and telephone. Eric Kocian grandly dismissed them.

"Only a fool would kill a journalist," he said. "The slime of the world need darkness. Killing a journalist would turn a spotlight into their holes and they know it."

Sándor Tor didn't believe this for a minute, but he knew that arguing with the old man would be futile. Instead, he had gone to Otto Görner with his fears.

Tor had said, "I think we had better have someone keeping an eye on him around the clock."

"Do it," Görner had replied.

"That's going to be expensive, Úr Görner. I'm talking about at least one man—probably two—in addition to myself, plus cars, around the clock."

"The cost be damned, Tor. And, for God's sake, don't let the old man know he's being protected. Otherwise, we'll have to find him to protect him."

"I'm pleased to meet you," Castillo said, in Hungarian, as he offered his hand. "And you should consider that Úr Görner is even more fond of Billy Kocian than I know you are and is therefore even more upset than you or I about what's happened."

"Before God, no one is more sorry than me," Sándor Tor said. "I love that old man."

Now I know I like you.

[TWO]
Room 24
Telki Private Hospital
2089 Telki Kórház Fasor 1
Budapest, Hungary
1730 6 August 2005

There was a heavyset man in his fifties sitting in a heavy well-worn captain's chair in the corridor beside the closed door to room 24. He watched as Görner and Castillo walked down the corridor, and then, when it became clear that Castillo was going to knock at the door, announced, "No visitors."

That's a cop, Castillo thought, *or my name really is Ignatz Glutz.*

"It's all right," Otto said. "We're from the *Tages Zeitung.*"

He took a business card from the breast pocket of his suit and handed it to the man. The man read it.

"He said, 'No visitors,' Úr Görner."

"Why don't I tell him I'm here?" Görner said and reached for the door handle.

"He's got his dog in there," the man said.

Görner opened the door just a crack and called, "Eric, get your goddamned dog under control. It's Otto."

"Go away, Otto Görner!" Kocian called out.

"Not a chance!" Otto called back. "Put that *Gottverdammthund* on a chain. I'm coming in."

The response to that was animal—a deep, not too loud but nevertheless frightening growl.

"Got a little cough, have you, Oncle Erik?" Castillo called.

"Goddamn, the plagiarist!" Kocian said.

Görner pushed open the door to room 24.

Eric Kocian was sitting against the raised back of a hospital bed. A large, long black cigar was clamped in his jaw. A roll-up tray was in front of him. It held a laptop computer, a large ashtray, several newspapers, a cellular telephone, a pot of coffee, and a heavy mug. Kocian's somewhat florid face, topped with a luxuriant head of naturally curling silver hair, made him at first look younger than he was, but his body—he was naked above the waist—gave him away.

What could be seen of his arms and chest—his left arm was bandaged and in a sling and there was another bloodstained bandage on his upper right chest—was all sagging flesh. There were angry old scars on his upper shoulder and on his abdomen.

Görner had two thoughts, one after the other, in the few seconds before Max, now growling a mouthful of teeth, caught his attention.

My God, he's nearly eighty-two.

God, even the damned dog is bandaged.

Görner, who usually liked dogs, hated this one and was afraid of him.

Castillo was not.

He squatted just inside the door, smiled, and said, conversationally in Hungarian, "You're an ugly old bastard, aren't you? Stop that growling. Not only don't you scare me but that old man in the bed is really glad to see us."

The dog stopped growling, sat on its haunches, and cocked his head.

"Come here, Fatso, and I'll scratch your ears."

"His name is Max," Kocian said.

"Come, Max," Castillo said.

Max got off his haunches and, head still cocked, looked at Castillo.

"Watch out for him, Karl!" Görner exclaimed.

"Come, dammit!" Castillo ordered.

Max took five tentative steps toward Castillo.

Castillo held out his left hand to him.

Max sniffed it, then licked it.

Castillo scratched Max's ears, close to the bandage. Max sat down again, pressing his massive head against Castillo's leg, and licked his hand again.

"Max, you sonofabitch," Kocian said. "You're supposed to take his hand off, not lick it like a Kartnerstrasse whore!"

"He knows who his friends are," Castillo said. "So who shot you, Eric? More important, who shot Max?"

"He wasn't shot," Kocian said. "One of the bastards clipped him with his pistol."

"One of your readers, disgruntled with your pro-American editorials?"

"That from a shameless plagiarist?" Kocian asked.

"Am I never to be forgiven?" Castillo asked.

The reference was to Castillo's habit—to lend authenticity to his alter ego, Karl W. von and zu Gossinger, Washington correspondent for the *Tages Zeitung* newspapers—of paraphrasing articles from *The American Conservative* magazine and sending them to Fulda to be published under his byline in the *Tages Zeitung* newspapers. Kocian had caught him at it.

"Not in this life," Kocian said, looking incredulously at Castillo and Max, who was now on his back getting his chest scratched.

"Where did you come from, Max?" Castillo asked. "An illicit dalliance between a boar and a really horny dachshund?"

"That's a Bouvier des Flandres," Kocian said.

" 'Bouvier' was Jacqueline Kennedy's maiden name," Castillo said.

"I don't think so! Jesus Christ!" Kocian said.

"I could be wrong," Castillo said.

"One *Bouvier des Flandres* bit Corporal Adolf Schickelgruber when he was in Flanders," Kocian said.

"I told you, he's a marvelous judge of character," Castillo said. "What do you mean, one of them bit Hitler?"

"One of them bit Hitler in Flanders in the First World War," Kocian repeated. "I've always wondered if that's what really happened to *Der Führer's* missing testicle. Anyway, Adolf was really annoyed. When the Germans took Belgium in 1940, one of the first things he did was order the breed wiped out."

"Why do I believe that?" Castillo asked.

"Because I'm telling you," Kocian said. "*I'm* not a plagiarist. I can be trusted."

"Particularly when you're telling me how you came to be in hospital," Görner said. "Falling over the dog and down the stairs! Jesus, Eric!"

"It was the best I could think of at the time," Kocian said, completely unembarrassed, and then returned to the subject at hand. "I heard the story of the Bouvier taking a piece out of Adolf in Russia and, when I had the chance, I checked it out and I knew I had to have one. So I went to Belgium and bought one. That's Max VI. Maxes I through V never betrayed me the way that one's doing."

"They didn't know me," Castillo said.

"So aside from corrupting my dog, what brings you to Budapest, Karlchen?"

"That's *Herr Oberstleutnant* Karlchen," Görner said.

"God, the Herr Oberst must be spinning in his grave!"

"If he is, it's from pride," Görner said, sharply.

Kocian considered that and nodded.

"I shouldn't have said that. The Herr Oberst would have been proud of his grandson being Oberstleutnant, Karlchen."

"Thank you," Castillo said.

"You were about to tell me what brings you to Budapest," Kocian said.

"I'll tell you if you tell me—the truth—about what happened to you."

"Okay," Kocian said after a moment. "You first."

"I want to be released from my promise to keep the list of names you gave me to myself."

Kocian didn't reply directly. Instead, he asked, "By now, I assume you've heard that they got to your man Lorimer? In Uruguay, of all places?"

"I was there when he was shot," Castillo said.

Kocian pursed his lips thoughtfully, then asked, "Who done it?"

"One of the six guys in dark blue coveralls who went to Lorimer's estancia to do it."

"How come they didn't get you, too, if you were there?"

"I couldn't ask them. They were all dead."

"Not identifiable?"

"No."

"Sounds like the people who got me," Kocian said. "Max and I were taking a midnight stroll on the Franz Joséf Bridge—"

"The where?" Görner asked.

"They now call it the *Szabadság híd*, Freedom Bridge. I don't. Freedom has many meanings. Franz Joséf means Franz Joséf. I remain one of his admirers."

"Going off at a tangent," Castillo said. "There's a country club called Mayerling outside Buenos Aires."

"Really?" Kocian asked.

"Yeah, really."

"Well, I'll have to have a look at it when I go to Argentina," Kocian said.

"What are you two talking about? What's Mayerling?" Görner asked. "What do you mean, when you go to Argentina?"

"Mayerling was the Imperial Hunting Lodge outside Vienna," Castillo said, "where Crown Prince Rudolph, heir to the throne of Austria-Hungary, on being told he had to give up his sixteen-year-old tootsie, shot her and then shot himself."

"According to my father, it's where Franz Joséf had him shot on learning he had been talking to people about becoming king of Hungary," Kocian said.

"My aunt Olga told me that version, too," Castillo said.

"A great lady," Kocian said. "And you remember? I'm impressed. You were only a kid—seven, eight, maybe nine—when she died."

"And what do you mean, when you go to Argentina?" Castillo said.

"Don't interrupt me when I'm telling you what happened to me," Kocian said. "Max and I were coming back from taking a midnight snack across the river. We were about halfway across the Franz Joséf Bridge when I sensed there were people approaching us from behind. That happens often. You'd be surprised how many young Hungarians think robbing old men out walking late at night is a lot more fun than getting a job. Max loves it. He gets to growl a little, show them his teeth, and after they wet their pants, drop their knives or whatever they had planned to hit me in the head with, he gets to chase them off the bridge."

Castillo chuckled.

"This time, it wasn't young men. This time, it's two full-grown men, with a third man driving a Mercedes. And the guy who got pretty close before Max grabbed him wasn't carrying a knife. He had a hypodermic needle in his slimy little hand. Had had. By the time I saw it, Max was chewing on his arm and he'd dropped it."

"My God!" Görner exclaimed.

"The second thug pulled out a pistol and started beating Max on the head with it. I jumped on him and then the Mercedes pulled up and the second guy got away from me and got in it. Off they drove. They stopped ten meters away, maybe a little more, and started shooting at me through an open window. And then they drove off for good. The license plates, it turned out, they'd stolen off a Ford Taurus."

"What happened to the guy with the hypo?" Castillo asked.

"He was begging—in German—for me to get Max off him."

"What happened to the needle?" Castillo asked.

"The cops have it."

"By any wild coincidence was it loaded with bupivacaine? Or something similar?"

"This one was loaded with phenothiazine," Kocian said. "I have been told they use it on lunatics. What's the wild coincidence you were hoping to find?"

"When Masterson's wife—"

"Masterson being your murdered diplomat in Buenos Aires?" Kocian interrupted.

Castillo nodded. He went on: "When she was kidnapped in a restaurant parking lot, they jabbed her in the buttocks with a hypo full of bupivacaine."

"Very interesting," Kocian said. "But, sorry. No match."

"What about the guy this adorable puppy almost ate?"

"He's in jail. His story, which I think he may get away with, is that he's a vacationing housepainter from Dresden who was walking on the bridge when I made an indecent proposal to him, attempted to fondle his private parts, and when he resisted and pushed me away my dog attacked him."

"How did he explain the hypo?"

"He never saw it before; therefore, it probably belongs to the old pervert." He paused and looked at Otto. "That's why I told you I fell over Max, Otto. I knew you'd be delighted to accept the old pervert story."

"My God, Eric!"

"What's going to happen to this guy?"

"I told the cops—in particular, the police commissioner, who is an old pal of mine—to see if he can connect him with Stasi . . ."

"They're out of business, aren't they?"

"You can ask a question like that and still get promoted as an intelligence officer?"

"You have all the answers, you tell me," Castillo said.

"Did you ever think about it, Karlchen?" the old man asked and Castillo had a sudden insight: *From now on, when he calls me Karlchen it will be because he has decided I am either impossibly ignorant or have done something monumentally stupid.*

"Think about what?"

"What happened to the better agents of the Ministry for State Security of the German Democratic Republic, commonly known as Stasi, when the Berlin Wall came tumbling down and peace and loving-kindness descended on our beloved Germany?"

"Frankly, I never gave it much thought."

"Maybe you should have, Karlchen," Kocian said. "Well, I'll tell you this, very few of them became bakers, cobblers, or took Holy Orders."

"Okay, so what are they doing? For whom? Who's paying them?"

"If you have to ask that, you must believe that once democracy came to the former Soviet Union, Russia really became the 'friendly bear' your President Roosevelt always thought it was. While you're here in Budapest you should go over to Andrassy Ut 60. Broaden your professional horizons."

"I'll bite. What's at Andrassy Ut 60?"

"Now it's a museum. It used to be the headquarters of the AVO, and then the AVH. The Allamvedelmi Osztaly and the Allamvedelmi Hatosag. I don't suppose you have any idea what that means."

"I didn't know the address," Castillo said, "or that they had turned it into a museum."

"Great museum. They not only have a ZIS-110 in the lobby . . ."

"What's a ZIS-110?" Görner asked.

". . . Formerly the limousine of the head of the AVH . . ." Kocian continued, only to be interrupted again.

"A Russian copy of the 1942 Packard Super Eight," Castillo said. "Stalin showed up in Yalta in one. Reserved for really big shots."

"Maybe the plagiarist isn't as ignorant as he sometimes sounds," Kocian said. "And the walls are covered with pictures of people the bastards garroted in the basement. The garrote gallows is also in the basement."

"Now, that's interesting," Castillo said. "I'd forgotten that."

"You forgot what?" Görner asked.

"The NKVD's preferred method of execution was a pistol bullet in the back of the head," Castillo explained. "The People's Court found you guilty and then they marched you straight into a room in the basement and shot you in the base of the skull. Stasi and the Hungarian State Security Bureau—AVO and AVH—weren't that nice. They . . ."

My God, Görner thought, *he's lecturing me like a schoolboy. But, it would seem that my little Karlchen really is knowledgeable. I'm a journalist, I'm supposed to know these things. And I didn't. More than that, he sounds like, acts like, an intelligence officer who knows his profession.*

". . . took you into the basement," Castillo went on, "stood you on a stool under the garrote gallows, put the rope around your neck, and then kicked the stool away."

"You mean to say they hung their . . . prisoners?" Görner asked.

"No. Hanging is when they drop the . . . *executee* . . . through a trap in a gallows. The rope around the neck usually has a special knot designed to break the executee's neck with the force of the fall."

He mimed a knot forcing his head to one side.

"That usually causes instant death as the spinal cord is cut," Castillo went on. "Garrote *executees* don't fall far enough to break their neck. The rope is just a loop around their neck, so they die of strangulation. It takes some time."

"And you find this fascinating, Karlchen?" Görner asked, more than a little horrified.

"They also had the habit, when taking out people they didn't like, and wanted it known that Stasi or the AVO/AVH had done it, to garrote them. Sort of a trademark."

"Fascinating!" Görner said, sarcastically.

"What's fascinating is that one of the men with me at Estancia Shangri-La, who had been around the block a lot of times, was garroted."

"Estancia *Shangri-La*?" Kocian asked. "How picturesque!"

"Lorimer's farm in Uruguay," Castillo explained. "They took out my guy by garroting him and they used . . ."

He stopped in midsentence as the door opened.

A small, slight man in his middle fifties, wearing a white hospital tunic, came into the room followed by a younger man—also a doctor, Castillo decided—and a nurse.

"You're not supposed to be smoking," the first doctor announced. "And you promised to get that dog out of here."

"Four people have tried to take Max out of here," Kocian replied. "He took small nips out of each of them. You're welcome to try. And I have been smoking longer than you're old and I am not about to stop now. Say hello to my boss."

The doctor put out his hand to Görner.

"No. The young one," Kocian said, switching to German. "Karl Wilhelm von und zu Gossinger. The fat one's another of his flunkies."

"I never know when to believe him," the doctor confessed, putting out his hand to first Görner and then Castillo. "I'm Dr. Czerny. I'm the chief of staff."

"If you're treating him, Doctor, you have my sympathy," Castillo said, in Hungarian.

"You're Hungarian?" Dr. Czerny asked, surprised.

"I had a Hungarian aunt."

"He's mostly German and Hungarian, with a little Mexican thrown in," Kocian said. "Tell us about . . . what was the name of that drug in Argentina, Karlchen?"

"Bupivacaine," Castillo furnished.

"Tell us about bupivacaine, please, Doctor," Kocian said.

The doctor shook his head.

"What do you want to know about bupivacaine? And why?"

"I'm an old man. Indulge me. What would have happened if the house-painter's hypodermic had been loaded with bupivacaine and he had succeeded in sticking it into my rump?"

Dr. Czerny smiled.

"You're amused?" Kocian demanded, indignantly.

Dr. Czerny nodded, then explained: "Your rump would have gone numb for, oh, two hours or so. Bupivacaine is a drug commonly used by dentists to numb the gums."

"You're sure, Doctor?" Castillo asked.

Czerny nodded.

"If you're ever going to be a decent journalist, Karlchen, you're going to have to start checking your facts," Kocian said, triumphantly. "And, of course, stop plagiarizing."

"The doctor in the German hospital in Buenos Aires," Castillo said as much to himself as to them, "told me it was bupivacaine."

"That's something else you should keep in mind, Karlchen. Never trust what a doctor tells you. They only tell you what they think you should know. Isn't that right, Czerny?"

"My father used to say you were the most difficult person he had ever known," Dr. Czerny said, smiling.

"How long are you going to have to put up with him, Doctor?" Castillo asked.

"Well, once he regains his sanity, there's no reason he couldn't leave here in a day or two."

"His general sanity? Or is there something specific?" Görner asked.

"When I walked in here this morning, I thought he was having a heart attack," the doctor said. "But what it was, he was on the telephone and Air France had just told him they would not carry that animal to Buenos Aires."

"Aerolineas Argentina will be happy to accommodate Max," Kocian said. "But I'll have to take the damned train to Madrid. They don't fly into Budapest. And Max doesn't like trains."

"I have no idea why he wants to go to Argentina," Dr. Czerny said. The implication was that it was one of the reasons he doubted Kocian's sanity. "And he won't tell me."

"That's because it's none of your damned business," Kocian explained.

"What is my business, Eric, personal and professional, is that you're getting pretty long in the tooth and you have just been shot—twice—and I'm not going to stand idly by while you go halfway around the world, alone and in bandages. And with that damned dog."

"Your father, may his soul rest in peace, Fredric, could call me by my Christian name. I don't recall giving you that privilege," Kocian said. "And don't call Max 'that damned dog.'"

"I beg your pardon," Dr. Czerny said.

"Doctor, for the sake of argument, supposing he could get someone to go with him to Argentina," Castillo asked, carefully, "and stay with him while he's there, would that be all right? I mean, could he stand the strain?"

"In a couple of days, why not?" Dr. Czerny said.

It was clear that Dr. Czerny had concluded that Castillo had come up with a way to calm Kocian down and that Otto Görner had concluded that Castillo had lost his mind.

"Well, let's have a look at you, Úr Kocian," Dr. Czerny said. "Will you excuse us a moment, please?"

He started to draw a curtain around the bed. Max stood up, showed his teeth, and growled softly but deeply.

"Come on, Max," Castillo said. "Let's go terrorize people in the corridor."

Max looked doubtful for a moment, then followed Castillo out of the room.

As soon as he had closed the door to room 24, Otto Görner grabbed Castillo's arm.

"You're not actually thinking about taking him to Argentina, are you, Karl?"

"For one thing, do you think we'd be able to stop him from going to Argentina?" Castillo replied, and then went on without giving Görner a chance to reply: "The people who tried to kill him—the needle full of phenothiazine makes me think they were going to question him, which means torture him, to see what he knew before killing him—are almost certainly going to have another try at him. I can protect him a lot better in Argentina than I can here. And if I take him on the Gulfstream, there will be no record of him having bought a ticket to go anywhere. That'll take them off his trail for at least a few days."

Görner considered that for thirty seconds, then asked: "When will your airplane be here?"

Castillo thought out loud: "It was probably ten, Washington time, by the time Dick had the cashier's check from the Riggs Bank. Torine said twelve hours from then. That would make it ten tonight, and how far ahead of Washington is Budapest? Five hours this time of year?"

"Six," Görner furnished.

"That'll put them into Ferihegy at four tomorrow morning. Figure an hour—maybe a little more—to clear customs and get to the Gellért. Five o'clock. I think we'd better spend a day here, both to give Billy a chance to get his stuff together and for Torine and Fernando to get some rest."

Görner nodded.

"You can protect him in Argentina?" he asked.

Castillo nodded. "But I'm a little worried about here. That one cop doesn't look like much protection. Can you do something about that?"

Görner took his cellular telephone from his pocket and punched an auto-dial button.

Thirty seconds later, he said, "As soon as someone wakes up long enough to answer the goddamned telephone at the *Budapester Tages Zeitung,* there will be people from the security service here within fifteen minutes."

"Can they be trusted?"

"Eric trusts them," Görner said and then turned his attention to his cellular telephone: *"Hier ist Generaldirektor Görner . . ."*

[THREE]
Room 24
Telki Private Hospital
2089 Telki Kórház Fasor 1
Budapest, Hungary
1750 6 August 2005

Doctor Fredric Czerny put his head into the corridor and, shaking his head in what was obviously resignation, signaled for Castillo and Görner to come into Eric Kocian's room.

"Úr Kocian and I are *negotiating* his release from the hospital," he said. "He wishes you to participate."

Max trotted after them, sat on his haunches by the bed, and offered Kocian his paw.

"Traitor!" Kocian said but took the paw and then caressed Max's massive head.

"What are the points in dispute?" Castillo asked.

"I told him I would release him *probably* tomorrow afternoon, as I think he needs another day of bed rest," Czerny explained.

"And I said if I have to spend another day in bed, I would prefer to do so in my own bed instead of on this Indian bed of nails," Kocian said. "Starting right now."

"My counteroffer was to release him after breakfast tomorrow, with the caveat he will actually go to his bed and stay there for twenty-four hours. He said that whether he stays in bed depends on when you plan to leave for Argentina."

"Very early in the morning, the day after tomorrow," Castillo said.

"Why then?" Kocian asked.

"Because that's when the plane leaves," Castillo said.

"You understand Max is going?"

"I understand Max is going," Castillo said. "I couldn't leave him; we're pals."

Kocian snorted, then said: "You see, Fredric? We have reached agreement. I will leave your charnel house in the morning. Before breakfast, as the food you serve in here would poison an oxen."

"You will leave *after* breakfast and *after* I have another look at you in the morning, and then only if Úr Gossinger will guarantee that you will go directly from here to your apartment and get in bed and stay there."

"Will I be paroled, Karlchen, to have a bath and attend to necessary bodily functions?"

"As long as you're quick about it and the bath is in your bathroom," Castillo said. "Doctor, I'll see that he stays in bed if I have to chain him to it."

"You may well find yourself doing just that," Dr. Czerny said, quickly shook Castillo's and Görner's hands, and walked out of the room.

"There will be security people from the *Tages Zeitung* here in a couple of minutes," Otto Görner announced. "And I will arrange with them to take you from here to your apartment in the morning."

"Do you ever think before you act, Otto?" Kocian asked.

"Something's wrong?" Görner said.

"Max dislikes security people," Kocian explained. "They apparently have a special smell. Max tends to bite people he dislikes and the security people know it. They may go on strike."

Castillo said, "I want you alive, so you can talk to me. These people will keep you alive until I can get you on the airplane." He paused. "What about the cop at the door? Max has no problem with him."

"There is an exception to every rule," Kocian said. "And I suspect the cop—his name is Kádár—has been feeding Max leberwurst. Max likes leberwurst."

"So we will get the security people a supply of leberwurst," Castillo said.

Kocian considered this a moment.

"No. Hanging around my bed of pain is no fun for Max," he said, finally. "And the cop at the door has already been there too long. So when my security people arrive, I will send him away. And you will take Max to my apartment. You may stay with him, providing you take him for a late-night walk."

"Two questions," Castillo said. "Where is your apartment? And will they let me into it?"

"On the top floor of the Hotel Gellért," Kocian replied, the expression on his face making it obvious he thought Castillo should have known where he lived. "And if you're with Max, of course they will. You will find dog food in the kitchen, and there will be some beef bones in the refrigerator. He gets one large, or two small, *only* after he eats his dog food."

"Yes, sir. And what does he like for dessert?"

"There is a dish of chocolates beside my chair. He gets two only."

"Okay."

"For reasons I can't imagine, chocolate is supposed to be bad for dogs. In Max's case, too much chocolate causes flatulence—and he can clear a room with it—so be wise and strong when he begs for more. He's a very appealing beggar."

"I'll remember."

"There's a leash hanging from the door handle," Kocian said. "You'd better put him on it. Unless I am there, Max tends to go pretty much where he wants to."

Two minutes later, there was a knock at the door and two burly men—obviously armed under their suits—came into the room, saw Max, and stayed close to the door. Max growled softly but deeply and showed a thin but impressive row of teeth.

"What did I tell you?" Kocian asked.

"How many of you are there?" Castillo asked.

They looked at him but didn't answer, looking instead at Görner.

"You can tell him," Kocian said. "That's Herr Karl von und zu Gossinger."

"There are three of us, Herr Gossinger," one of the men said, in German.

"You heard what happened to Mr. Kocian?" Castillo asked, in Hungarian.

Both nodded. The same man said, "Mr. Kocian was assaulted on the Szabadság híd."

"It was not a robbery. It was far more serious and it may well happen again," Castillo said.

They both nodded again.

"I want two men outside this door at all times," Castillo ordered. "And I want at least two more close by."

"I can have another man—as many men as you would like, sir—here in fifteen minutes."

"Get two," Castillo ordered. "Do you know how to use your pistols?"

"They're all retired policemen, Úr Gossinger," Kocian answered for them.

"Everyone has cellular telephones?" Castillo asked.

They nodded.

"If anything at all suspicious happens, you notify first the police and then me. That means you will have to give me one of your telephones. I will be in Úr Kocian's apartment."

The man who had spoken gestured for the other to give Castillo his cellular telephone.

"Thank you," Castillo said, examining it. "And how do I call you with this?" The man showed him.

"In the morning, we are going to move Úr Kocian from here to his apartment. We don't want anyone to know we're doing that, which means we don't want anyone to see him leaving the hospital or entering the hotel. He will be in a wheelchair. Suggestions, please?"

"I will not be in a wheelchair," Kocian announced.

"Úr Kocian will be in a wheelchair," Castillo repeated.

"We could get a van from the *Tages Zeitung,* sir. Back it up to the loading dock in the basement of the hospital and then do the same thing at the Gellért."

"I want one of you to drive the van," Castillo ordered. "And when you are prepared to leave, I want you to call me. You will say, 'Úr Kocian is having his breakfast and waiting for the doctor.' "

The man nodded and smiled.

"Did I say something amusing?" Castillo asked. "You're smiling."

"Excuse me, sir. I was just thinking you sound more like a policeman than a newspaper publisher."

"Think what you like about me, but don't repeat what you're thinking."

"No offense intended, sir."

"None taken," Castillo said.

"Sir," the man said. "We will take good care of Úr Kocian and get him safely and discreetly to the Gellért in the morning."

"Good," Castillo said.

He meant that. Obviously, he really likes Eric. Why should that surprise me?

"There is one thing, sir . . ."

"Which is?"

"The dog, sir. Sometimes he can be difficult . . ."

"What it is," Kocian said, "is that you smell like leberwurst."

"I'm taking Max with me," Castillo said.

The man's face registered both surprise and relief.

"I think that would be best, sir."

Sándor Tor was waiting with the silver Mercedes-Benz S500 when Görner and Castillo walked out of the hospital door. Max lunged toward it, towing Castillo after him.

"I called the office and had them send other security people over," Görner said.

"I saw them," Tor said. "He ran off the people I had placed in the corridor." He paused, then asked, "How is he?"

"He's all right," Görner said. "The hospital will never be the same, but Úr Kocian is fine."

"He also ran me off," Tor said. "He said I made him nervous."

"Having you around would be like admitting he needed your protection," Castillo said.

"After you drop us at the Gellért, you can come back here and go see him. Your excuse will be that Úr Gossinger"—he nodded at Castillo—"suggested you drive the van in the morning."

"The van in the morning?"

"We're going to move him, very quietly, to the Gellért in the morning," Castillo said. "Tell him I just put you in charge of the movement."

"Thank you very much, Úr Gossinger."

Tor opened a rear door of the Mercedes.

Max, nearly knocking Castillo off his feet, jumped in and sat up on the seat.

"Jesus," Castillo said, letting go of the leash and tossing it into the car. "Go ahead, Otto. I'll get in front."

Görner started to get in the back. Max announced he didn't think that was the way things should be by showing a thin row of teeth and growling.

"Damn that dog!" Görner said and got in the front passenger's seat.

Castillo got in the back. Max showed he thought that was a very good idea by leaning over and lapping Castillo's face.

"The Gellért, right, Úr Görner?" Tor asked when he was behind the wheel.

"No," Castillo said. "Take us to the American embassy, please."

Görner looked at him in surprise but didn't say anything.

[FOUR]
The Embassy of the United States of America
Szabadság tér 12
Budapest, Hungary
1825 6 August 2005

There was a Marine sergeant on guard behind a bulletproof-glass window in the lobby of the seven-story century-old mansion housing the United States embassy.

"Sir, you can't bring a dog in here," the sergeant said.

"Think of him as a friend of man, like a Seeing Eye dog," Castillo replied.

The sergeant smiled, but said, "Sir, that's the rules."

Otto Görner watched as C. G. Castillo slid his Secret Service credentials through the slot under the glass. The sergeant examined them carefully, then returned them.

"Why don't we get the ambassador on the horn and see if he won't make an exception for my puppy?" Castillo asked.

"Sir, the ambassador's not in the embassy."

"Well, then get the duty officer down here," Castillo said. "And I'm going to have to speak to the ambassador, so why don't you, one, call the duty officer and, two, get the ambassador on that phone for me?"

He pointed to a telephone on the counter.

The Marine guard picked up the change of tenor in Castillo's voice—from *We're joking with each other* to *That's a command.*

"One moment, sir," he said and picked up his telephone.

The ambassador came on the line very quickly.

"And how are you, Mr. Castillo?" he asked. "Actually, I've been expecting you."

"A little bird named Montvale told you I was coming?"

"And that he wants to speak to you."

"I need a secure line, sir, to do just that," Castillo said.

"Not a problem. Tell the Marine guard to pick up."

"And I need a waiver, sir, of your no-canines-on-the-property rule."

"You've got a dog with you?"

"Yes, sir. A sweet puppy who whines piteously when I tie him to a fence or something and leave him."

The ambassador laughed. "Okay. The Marine can handle that, too."

"And I need to see the man who gets his pay from Langley."

"That's not a problem at all. He's probably with my duty officer, waiting for you to show up so he can tell you personally that Ambassador Montvale wishes to speak with you."

Two men came into the lobby through the metal-detector arch. They were both in their forties and both were wearing dark gray summer-weight suits that Castillo suspected had come from Brooks Brothers.

"I think they have both just walked into the lobby, Mr. Ambassador."

"Hand the phone to one of them," the ambassador said.

"Thank you very much, sir."

"Happy to be of service," the ambassador said.

Castillo handed the phone to the nearest of the two Americans.

"The ambassador," he said.

The second man said, "Sir, the embassy has a rule about dogs."

Max growled. The second man looked very uncomfortable.

"I have just been granted a waiver," Castillo said.

The man holding the telephone said "Yes, sir" into it a half dozen or so times, then handed the phone to Castillo. "The ambassador wishes to speak with you, Mr. Castillo."

"Yes, sir?" Castillo said into the handset.

"If there's anything else you need, Mr. Castillo, just call me."

"Thank you very much, sir."

"Get the Marine guard on the line, please. If I tell him you're to have the keys to the kingdom, it'll be easier."

"Thanks again, sir," Castillo said and motioned for the guard to pick up his telephone.

"Why don't we go inside?" the man who had been talking to the ambassador asked, gesturing to the metal-detector arch.

Otto Görner asked with his eyes what he was supposed to do. Castillo, making no effort to hide the gesture, motioned for him to go through the metal detector.

"And this gentleman is, Mr. Castillo?" the man who had talked with the ambassador asked, looking at Görner.

"This is Mr. Smith. He's with me."

"I really have to have a name, Mr. Castillo."

"You'd really *like* to have a name, so that you can tell Ambassador Montvale who I had with me. That's not quite the same thing."

"And this gentleman is, Mr. Castillo?" the man repeated.

Okay, so you're the resident spook. I sort of thought you might be.

"Sergeant, will you get the ambassador on the horn again?" Castillo said, raising his voice.

The two locked eyes for a moment. Then the man said, "That won't be necessary, Sergeant. If you'll follow me, gentlemen, please?"

They passed through the metal-detector arch. As the man Castillo had decided was the CIA station chief went through it, the device buzzed and a red light began to flash.

Why does that make me think you're carrying a gun?

So thank you, metal detector, for bringing that to mind.

An elevator took them all to the basement, where the second man walked ahead of them to a heavy steel door and opened it with a key.

Inside was a bare room, with four unmarked doors leading off it.

"Mr. Castillo," the CIA man announced, "I have been instructed to tell you that Ambassador Montvale wants to talk with you as soon as possible."

"And behind one of these doors is a secure phone?" Castillo asked.

The CIA man nodded.

"Okay," Castillo said. "And while I'm talking to Montvale, please get me a weapon. Black. Preferably an Uzi, with a spare magazine."

Görner's eyes widened for an instant.

"I'm not sure that I can do that, Mr. Castillo," the CIA man said.

"You don't have a Uzi?"

"Provide you with a weapon."

"You can either check that out with the ambassador or wait until I have Ambassador Montvale on the line and he will tell you that you can."

"May I ask why you need a weapon?"

"No," Castillo said, simply.

The two locked eyes again for a moment, then the CIA man took a ring of keys from his pocket and unlocked one of the steel doors. It opened on a small room furnished with a table and a secretary's chair. On the table were two telephones—one of them with a very heavy cord—a legal tablet, a water glass holding half a dozen pencils, and an ashtray. Hanging from a nail driven into a leg of the table were a dozen or more plastic bags of the sort used by grocery stores. BURN was printed all over them in large red letters.

The CIA man waved Castillo into the room and, when Castillo had sat down, picked up the telephone with the heavy cord.

"This is Franklin," he said. "I am about to hand the phone to Mr. Castillo, who has been cleared to call anywhere."

He handed the telephone to Castillo.

"Thank you," Castillo said. "Please close the door."

"Certainly."

And don't let the doorknob hit you in the ass.

If I were this guy, I would now go into the commo room, which is certainly behind one of those other doors, put on a set of earphones, turn on a recorder, and listen to what this Castillo character is going to talk to Montvale about.

Fuck him. Let him listen. The only thing he's going to learn from this conversation is that I don't work for Ambassador Charles W. Montvale.

Castillo waited fifteen seconds and then put the handset to his ear.

"You on there, Franklin?" he asked, conversationally.

There was no reply. Castillo hadn't expected one.

But he was doing more than giving Franklin a hard time. If Franklin was listening and recording the conversation—and the more he thought about it, the more convinced he was that Franklin would be—he was almost certainly using one of the recorders in the commo room. Castillo was familiar with most of the recorders used. They shared one characteristic. The recordings were date- and time-stamped, down to one-tenth of a second. That data could not be changed or deleted.

Franklin, therefore, could not pretend if he played the recording for someone—or, more likely, sent it to Langley, or, even more likely, to Montvale himself—that he had not been asked if he was listening. The embassy was U.S. soil; therefore, the laws of the United States applied. Without a wiretap authorization issued by a federal judge, it is a felonious violation of the United States Code to record a conversation unless one of the parties to the conversation is aware that the conversation is being recorded.

He could of course make a written transcript of the conversation, leaving out the "You on there, Franklin?" That not only would look odd but he would be asked, "What happened to the recording itself?"

"If you are on there, Franklin," Castillo said, still conversationally, "you should not be. You are advised that this communication is classified Top Secret Presidential and you do not have that clearance."

"Sir?" a male voice came on the line.

Castillo knew it had to be whoever was in charge of the communications room.

"My name is C. G. Castillo. Get me the White House switchboard on a secure line, please."

"One moment, sir."

"White House."

"This is the U.S. embassy, Budapest," the male voice said. "Please confirm we are on a secure line."

"Confirm line is secure."

"Go ahead, Mr. Castillo," the communications room man said.

"C. G. Castillo. Can you patch me through to Ambassador Montvale, please?"

"Colonel, Secretary Hall wishes to speak with you."

Colonel? Boy, that news got around quick, didn't it?

"Secretary Hall first, please. On a secure line, please."

"One moment, sir."

"Secretary Hall's secure line. Isaacson."

"Hey, Joel. Charley. Is the boss around?"

"Oh, he is indeed, *Colonel,*" Isaacson said. "Hold on."

Charley faintly heard "Charley for you, boss," then Hall's reply, also faint, "Finally."

And then the Honorable Matthew Hall, secretary of the Department of Homeland Security, came clearly on the line.

"Hello, Charley. Where are you?"

"Budapest, sir."

"You didn't go to Berlin, I gather?"

He knows about that?

"No, sir."

"Why not?"

Oh, I don't want to answer that.

How the hell can I say "Because I didn't want Montvale ordering me around" without sounding as if I am very impressed with myself?

Hall, sensing Castillo's hesitation, added: "I understand you had a couple of sips at the Army-Navy Club to celebrate your promotion."

Obviously, Naylor told Hall about that.

Thank God!

"Yes, sir, I did."

"He's been on the phone several times . . ."

He who? Naylor or Montvale?

". . . the first time to tell me the two of you had come to an understanding . . ."

Okay, he means Montvale.

". . . and that you were going to keep him in your loop. The last several calls, he wondered where you were, since you told somebody you wouldn't be going to Berlin."

"I think by now he knows where I am, sir."

"You've spoken to him?"

"I used an air taxi with which he has a connection."

There was a pause. After a moment, Hall said, "Okay. I get it. And the last several times, he's been very interested in explosive briefcases. Asked me if I had heard about them. I told him I hadn't."

"There's nothing to tell, sir."

"Later, Joel told me Tom McGuire had told him about it. I understand. But our mutual friend seemed very surprised that you hadn't passed this information on to him or me."

"Dick Miller told him about the briefcases. I told him to tell him."

Why are we talking in verbal code on a secure line?

Because Hall thinks it's entirely possible that "our mutual friend" has told the friendly NSA folks at Fort Meade that it might be a good idea to scan Hall's calls for names like "Montvale." And he could easily do that. The National Security Agency works for him. No problem, either, with decrypting a White House secure line. NSA provides the encryption code to the White House.

"Dick told me. Just consider that a heads-up, Charley."

"Yes, sir. I will."

"What are you doing in Budapest?"

"I'm trying to get a source to relieve me from a promise that I wouldn't pass a list of names he gave me to anyone else," Castillo said. "I'm going to tell our mutual friend that when I talk to him. Which I will do as soon as we're finished."

"And where do you go from Budapest?"

"Sir, do you really want to know?"

Hall perceptibly thought that over before replying: "No, I don't. You don't work for me anymore. There's no reason you should tell me. But, Charley, I suspect our mutual friend is going to ask you the same question."

"I don't work for our mutual friend, either, sir."

There was another pause before Hall responded: "Charley, can you handle your arrangement with our mutual friend?"

"I really hope so, sir."

"Another of our mutual friends, an old friend of yours . . ."

That has to be General Naylor.

". . . doesn't think so. The way he put it was he always thought David got awful lucky with that slingshot."

What the hell does that mean?

Oh! David, as in David and Goliath.

"Sir, I'm not going to try to bring Goliath down. All I want him to do is leave me alone."

"That was Jefferson Davis's philosophy in the Civil War. He didn't want to defeat the North. All he wanted was for the North to leave the South alone. You know how that turned out."

"Yes, sir."

"There's one more option, Charley," Hall said.

"Prayer?"

Hall chuckled, then said, "I'll have a word with the President, get him to get him off your back."

When Castillo didn't immediately reply, Hall added: "That's my idea, Charley. Not our friend's."

After a long moment, Castillo said, "Why don't we wait and see how it goes?"

Hall didn't respond directly. Instead, he said, "His tactic is going to be damning you by faint praise. He's already started. 'You're a fine young man but inexperienced. You need a wise, guiding hand on your shoulder, to keep you from doing something impulsive and unwise.' He's going to keep repeating that—or something like it—until one day you're going to do something impulsive and unwise. And then the President will tell you something like, 'Before you do something like that again, you'd better check that with Mon . . . our friend.' And that will put you in our friend's pocket."

"When I worked for you, I had one," Castillo replied. "A wise hand on my shoulder."

"That's not true but thank you."

"I guess I'm going to have to be careful not to act unwisely on an impulse."

"That's an open offer, Charley. Nonexpiring, in other words."

"Thank you," Castillo said, very seriously, and then chuckled.

"Speaking of the Civil War, sir, you remember what Lee said at Appomattox Court House? 'I would rather face a thousand deaths, but now I must go to treat with General Grant.' I would rather face a thousand deaths, but now I have to get our friend on the horn."

That made Hall chuckle and then he said, "There's a big difference, Charley. You're not going there with the intention of handing him your sword, are you?"

"No. But, on the other hand, I was never very good with a slingshot, either."

Hall laughed.

"Keep in touch, Charley."

"I will. Thank you."

Castillo tapped the telephone switch several times.

"White House."

"Will you get me Ambassador Montvale, please? And verify that the line is secure, please."

"One moment, please."

"Director Montvale's secure line. Truman Ellsworth speaking."

"Colonel Castillo on a secure line for Director Montvale," the White House operator said.

"I'll take it."

Like hell you will, Castillo thought.

He said, "Mr. Ellsworth?"

"How are you, Colonel? We've been expecting to hear from you."

"Would you take a message to Ambassador Montvale for me?"

"Certainly."

"Please tell him that I'll be in the U.S. embassy in Budapest for the next fifteen minutes if he wants to talk to me."

"I'm not sure the ambassador will be available within that time frame, Colonel."

"That's all the time frame I have available."

"You understand, I hope, Colonel, that anything you'd like to say to the ambassador you can say to me."

"I'm calling because I understand the ambassador has a message for me."

"You're talking about the message sent to Berlin?"

"I know there was a message sent to Berlin for me, but I haven't seen it. The man who called me was unwilling to tell me what the message said, only that there was a message I could have only if I went to Berlin. I didn't have time to do that. Can you give it to me?"

"I see. Well, Colonel, the idea was that you would go to Berlin and, once you'd received the ambassador's message, get on a secure line at the embassy there."

"Okay. Well, that's moot. When I walked in the embassy here, Mr. Franklin gave me a similar message. Which is the reason I placed the call. I'll be available here if the ambassador becomes available in the next"—he paused and checked his watch—"fourteen minutes. Thank you very much, Mr. Ellsworth."

Castillo tapped the switch of the telephone several times, said, "Break it down, please," and hung up.

Castillo exhaled audibly, then took a cigar from his briefcase and very carefully unwrapped it, carefully nipped one end with a cutter, and carefully lit the other end.

He tried to blow a smoke ring but failed.

That's funny. This room is sealed, and if the air conditioner is working I can't feel it. I should have been able to blow a nice ring.

Possibly, Colonel, that is because you're just a little nervous.

David obviously managed to hit Goliath Junior just now. Probably right between the eyes. But the projectile didn't blow him away—it just bounced off, making Goliath Junior mad.

And when Goliath Junior reports what just happened to Goliath Senior, Goliath Senior is going to be even angrier.

Which is probably happening at this very moment.

Goliath Senior, like everyone else on the White House secure circuit, is never supposed to be more than ninety seconds from picking up the phone—and fifteen seconds is preferred.

It is of course possible that Goliath Senior was taking a leak. It is far more likely that he was in his office all the time. He has Ellsworth answer his phone to make the point that he is too important to answer his own phone, even when the President might be calling.

And he especially wanted to make that point to me. He was going to make me wait.

And if I hadn't hung up when I did, it's more than likely that Ellsworth—when signaled to do so, of course—would have cheerfully announced, "Well, the ambassador just walked in," and Goliath Senior would have come on the line.

Castillo took several puffs on his cigar, held the last one for a moment, then very carefully tried to blow a smoke ring.

This time it worked.

He watched it until it bounced off the wall and disintegrated.

Fuck it! One of two things is going to happen. Goliath Senior is going to call back. Or he isn't.

If he does call back, let him wait for me.

He stood up, put the cigar in his mouth, opened the door, and left the room.

"Why don't we go have a look at your arsenal, Mr. Franklin?" Castillo said.

Franklin obviously didn't like the suggestion very much, but he nodded and said, "It's one floor down. Are you through here?"

"I don't know."

"Colonel, smoking is forbidden in the embassy," the second man said.

Colonel? How did you know that?

What did they do, put my conversation on speakers while they were eavesdropping?

"Is it?" Castillo replied and took another puff.

He looked at Franklin, who hesitated a moment and then said, "This way, Mr. Castillo."

"Why don't you wait here with this gentleman," Castillo said to Otto Görner, in English. "I'll come back and fetch you."

Görner nodded.

The weapons locker was a gray metal two-door cabinet in a small narrow room that also held rows of gray filing cabinets, each of them securely locked with steel bars and padlocks. Castillo idly wondered how much of the obviously classified material they held would be of real intelligence value.

Franklin took the padlock from the door and swung the double doors open for Castillo.

There wasn't much in it, and most of what was there were ordinary American weapons, ranging from M-16 rifles to an assortment of handguns, both revolvers and semiautomatics. There were some odd pistols, including two Russian Makarovs and four German Walther PPs.

Castillo was familiar with both of the Makarov semiautomatics and liked neither. The Russians had basically copied the Walther when they had replaced their Tokarev pistol. The basic difference was a larger trigger guard on the Makarov to accommodate a heavily gloved trigger finger.

The Walthers fired a 9mm Kurz cartridge, virtually unchanged since Colt had introduced it as the .380 ACP cartridge for their sort of scaled-down version of the Colt 1911 .45 ACP. The cartridge had never been successful in the United States but had enjoyed wide popularity in Europe.

The reason it had not been very successful was the reason Castillo disliked it. It didn't have anywhere near the knockdown power of the .45 ACP.

There were a half dozen cardboard cartons on the floor of the locker, one long rather thin one and two larger thick ones. Castillo picked up the long thin one and one of the thick ones and laid them atop one of the filing cabinets. He opened the long thin one first.

It held what looked like a target pistol, and, indeed, that's what it had been before Special Forces armorers had worked their magic on it years before. Their version of the target pistol, chambered for the .22 Long Rifle round, was now known as the Ruger Mk II Suppressed.

"Just what the doctor ordered," he said.

Franklin did not seem to share Castillo's enthusiasm.

There really is no such thing as a "silenced" weapon for a number of reasons, heavy among them the fact that almost all bullets exit the barrel at greater than the speed of sound and it is impossible to silence the noise they make when they do. There are "suppressed" weapons, the best of which make no more sound than a BB gun. Of these, Castillo thought the Ruger Mk II to be among the very best.

The one before him looked brand-new, and it looked as if it was a "manufactured" weapon rather than one modified by the weapons wizards at Bragg.

Castillo examined the weapon carefully and liked what he found.

"I'll take this," he announced.

"Colonel . . ."

There goes "Colonel" again. The sonofabitch did listen.

" . . . I'm going to have to get authority to let you take that," Franklin said.

"As soon as we see what else you have, we'll get on the horn to the ambassador," Castillo replied and then opened the larger box.

I got lucky again.

The box held a Micro Uzi submachine gun, the smallest and, as far as Castillo was concerned, the most desirable of the three variants of the Uzi.

Seeing the Uzi triggered a series of connects in his brain:

The Uzi is named after its designer, Lieutenant Colonel Uziel Gal, of the Israeli Army . . . CONNECT . . . My God, now I'm a lieutenant colonel! . . . CONNECT . . . Gal retired and lived in Philadelphia until he died a couple of years ago . . . CONNECT . . . Chief Inspector Dutch Kramer of the Philly P.D. Counterterrorism Bureau told me that . . . CONNECT . . . Betty Schneider used to work for Kramer . . . CONNECT . . . No, she worked for Captain Frank O'Brien in Intelligence and Organized Crime . . . CONNECT . . . And I didn't call her before I came over here. Or since . . .

What the hell's the matter with me?

Well, it's not as if I've been sprawled in a chair watching TV and sucking on a beer.

I'll call her the first chance I get and explain. As soon as I get to the hotel. She'll understand.

He turned his attention to the Micro Uzi and took it from its box. It looked almost brand-new.

Castillo had had a lot of experience with the Uzi in the three common variants—Standard, Mini, and Micro—which all fired the 9mm Luger Para bellum cartridge, which was a much better cartridge than the 9mm Kurz .380 ACP.

The Standard Uzi, with a full magazine, weighed about eight pounds, just about what the standard M-16 rifle weighed. The Mini Uzi weighed just under six pounds, about half a pound more than the Car-4 version of the M-16. The Micro weighed about three and a half pounds. There was no equivalent version of the M-16.

Which was one of the reasons why the Micro was a favored weapon of special operators. Another was that it had a much higher rate of fire, 1,250 rounds per minute, double that of the Standard and 300 rpm more than the Micro. In Castillo's mind, using the Micro was like having a shotgun in your hand, with nowhere near the bulk, weight, or recoil of a 12-gauge shotgun.

"At the risk of repeating myself," Castillo said, "just what the doctor ordered."

Franklin looked at him uncomfortably but didn't say anything.

"Let's go get you off hook and get the ambassador on the horn," Castillo said.

"Why don't we?" Franklin said, and added, "Let me carry those for you, Mr. Castillo."

Does he think I'm going to grab them and run out of the embassy?

"Thank you," Castillo said. "And I'll need ammunition. A couple of boxes of 9mm Parabellum and a box of .22 Long Rifle, please."

Franklin nodded, went into a cabinet inside the locker, and came out with the ammunition.

A fat man in a white shirt limp with sweat was coming heavily down the stairwell as they went up.

"There's a call from the White House switchboard for Colonel Castillo, Mr. Franklin," he announced in awe.

"Come into the phone room with me, please, Mr. Franklin," Castillo said. "If that's who I think it is, maybe we won't have to bother the ambassador."

"We have Colonel Castillo on a secure line for you, Director Montvale," the White House operator announced.

"Director Montvale is ready for the colonel," Montvale said.

"Good afternoon, sir," Castillo said.

"I'm glad I caught you, Colonel. We seem to be having communications problems."

"It seems that way, sir. Sir, before we get into this, I have Mr. Franklin with me . . ."

"Who?"

"He's the CIA station chief, sir."

"What's that about?"

"I need a weapon—weapons—sir, and he seems uncomfortable giving them to me."

"Why do you need a weapon?"

Castillo didn't reply. After ten seconds, which seemed much longer, Ambassador Montvale said, a touch of resignation in his voice, "'Put him on the line."

"Is there a speakerphone on this?" Castillo asked Franklin.

"There's a switch on the wall," Franklin said, then went to it and pushed a button.

"Nathaniel Franklin, sir," he announced.

"Do you know who I am?" Montvale asked.

"Yes, sir. We've spoken before. You're Ambassador Montvale, the director—"

" 'Yes, sir' would have been sufficient," Montvale interrupted him. "Now, there's two ways we can deal with Colonel Castillo's request. You can give him whatever he asks for. Or I will call the DCI and in a couple of minutes he will call you and tell you to give the colonel whatever he asks for. What would you like to do?"

"Your permission is all I need, Mr. Ambassador," Franklin said.

"Thank you, Mr. Franklin. Nice to talk to you."

Castillo looked at Franklin and then waited until Franklin had left the small room and closed the door before going on.

"Elvis has left the theater, Mr. Ambassador," he said.

He had just enough time to decide *That was a dumb thing to say* when he heard Montvale laugh.

"I told you, Charley, I can be useful," he said. "If I had had to call John Powell, then the DCI would want to know why you wanted his weapons."

"I told you I was going to Budapest to see if I can get my source to release me from my promise not to pass along to anyone what he gave me. When I got here, I learned that an attempt to kidnap him had been made. I want to keep him alive. I can't do that without a weapon."

"You can protect him yourself, you think?"

"I've already started getting help. Local help."

"How long is this going to take? Getting your source to release you—or refuse to release you—from your promise?"

"Several days, probably."

"You want me to tell Mr. Franklin to help you protect this chap?"

"I think that would draw attention I'd rather not have to my source. But thank you."

"If you change your mind, let me know."

"Yes, sir, I will. Thank you."

"Tell me about explosive suitcases in Pennsylvania."

"I told Major Miller to tell you about that. Didn't he?"

"He didn't seem to think that a possible nuclear device in a briefcase was very important."

"Sir, he didn't think it was credible. Neither did the chief of counterterrorism of the Philadelphia Police Department. That's not the same thing as saying they don't think the threat of a small nuclear device is important."

"You sent people up there to look into it," Montvale challenged.

"The reason I sent them up there was to see where the AALs got the money to buy a farm . . ."

"The what?"

"AALs. That's what the Philly cops call the Muslim brothers of the Aari-Teg mosque. It stands for 'African American Lunatics.' "

"Not only is that politically incorrect but, as I recall, those lunatics were involved in the theft of the 727."

"Yes, sir, they were, and that's why the Philly cops and the Secret Service—the Secret Service at my request—are keeping an eye on them. I'd like to find out what their connection with the people who stole the 727 was—*is*."

"And you think you can investigate this matter better than the FBI?"

"I think the Secret Service agent I sent up there—he was an undercover cop in the mosque for several years—can. Yes, sir. I think that all FBI involvement would do is tip them off that we're watching them. I hope you don't feel compelled to bring the FBI in."

"You realize what a spot that puts me in, Castillo? If it turns out there's something to this, and I heard there was, and didn't tell the FBI what I'd heard . . ."

"This is what I was afraid of when we struck our deal, sir. If we hadn't, then I wouldn't have told you and the problem wouldn't have come up."

There was a perceptible pause before Montvale replied.

"On the other hand, Charley, if we hadn't come to an accommodation you'd have had to take the train to Budapest, not gotten to fly that airplane, and you wouldn't have the weapons Whatshisname is about to give you, right?"

"Yes, sir. I can't argue with that."

"Okay. Let me think about it. I won't get the FBI involved . . ."

"Thank you. All they would do right now is get in the way . . ."

" . . . *at this time*. If I do decide they have to know, I'll tell you before I tell them."

"Yes, sir. Thank you."

"And I want to talk to the cop who was undercover in the mosque as soon as that can be arranged. Is that going to be a problem?"

"No, sir. Just as soon as he gets back to Washington, I'll have Miller set up a meeting."

"Good enough. Good luck with your source. Keep me posted."

Charley said, "Yes, sir," but suspected that Montvale had hung up before he had spoken the two words.

"White House. Are you through?"

"See if you can get Major Miller at Homeland Secur—at my office, please. On a secure line."

"Colonel Castillo's secure line," Miller said a moment later.

"Is it smart to say 'Colonel'?" Castillo greeted him.

"I don't know about smart, but, frankly, I find it a little humiliating. Anyway, it's hardly a secret. All kinds of people have called obviously hoping to hear you getting promoted was just a ridiculous rumor."

"Shit."

"What can I do for you, Colonel?"

"I just told Montvale that I would have you set up a meeting with Jack Britton the minute he got back to Washington. Therefore, get in touch with Jack and tell him he is to stay away from Washington until I get back."

"Got it. And when will that be?"

"The day after tomorrow—presuming Jake arrives tomorrow morning with the Gulfstream—I'm going to Buenos Aires. Get on the horn to Alex Darby at the embassy and tell him I will need a safe house—the one we used would be fine, but anything will do—to house an important witness. A safe house and people to keep it that way. I'll also need a black car. Actually, a couple of them."

"This important witness have a name?"

"Let me sit on that awhile. And tell Darby to find Yung and have him at the safe house."

"Yung tried to call you here."

"What did he want?"

"To tell you the ambassador in Montevideo thinks Lorimer was a drug dealer."

"Isn't that interesting?"

"Yeah. And not only that, the ambassador in Uruguay wants Yung to pass this on to the secretary of state. In confidence. What do I tell him about that?"

"Tell him it will hold until I see him there."

"Got it. Anything else?"

"As soon as I get things organized in Buenos Aires—maybe two days, tops—I'll come home."

"That's it?"

"Can't think of anything. How's the leg?"

"Improved. It only hurts now ninety percent of the time. Watch your back, buddy."

VIII

There is an average of twenty burials every day at Arlington. There is a prescribed routine for enlisted men, one for warrant officers and officers, and one for general or flag officers.

Enlisted men being interred are provided with a casket team (pallbearers), a firing party to fire the traditional three-round salute, and a bugler to sound taps.

In addition to the basics, warrant and commissioned officers may be provided with an escort platoon, its size varying according to the rank of the deceased, and a military band.

Officers are entitled to the use of a horse-drawn artillery caisson to move the casket to the grave site. Army and Marine Corps colonels and above are entitled to have a caparisoned, riderless horse. General officers are also entitled to a cannon salute—seventeen guns for a four-star general, fifteen for a three-star, thirteen for a two-star, eleven for a one-star.

There is almost never a deviation from the prescribed rites and the late Sergeant First Class Seymour Kranz was entitled to the least of these prerogatives.

But from the moment the hearse bearing his casket arrived near the grave site, Sergeant Kranz's internment did not follow the standard protocol.

As the immaculately turned-out officer in charge reached for the door handle at the rear of the hearse, an immaculately turned-out Special Forces sergeant major stepped up and spoke to him.

"With your permission, sir, we'll take it from here," Sergeant Major John K. Davidson said.

"Excuse me?" the OIC, a first lieutenant, said.

It was the first time anyone had ever interrupted his procedure.

"The sergeant major said we'll take it from here," another voice said. "Do you have a problem with that, Lieutenant?"

The lieutenant turned and found himself facing another Green Beret, this one with three silver stars glistening on each of his epaulets.

"Sir . . ." the lieutenant began to protest.

"Good. I didn't think there would be a problem," Lieutenant General Bruce J. McNab said. "Carry on, Sergeant Major."

"Yes, sir," Sergeant Major Davidson said, then raised his voice slightly. "Casket detail, *ten-hut*. Execute!"

Seven Green Berets of varying ranks—including one lieutenant general plus one corporal, USMC—marched up to the rear of the hearse, halted, then did an about-face without orders. When Sergeant Major Davidson pulled open the hearse door, the casket was removed and raised onto the shoulders of the casket detail.

"Escort detail, ten-hut!" Sergeant Major Davidson barked softly, and very quickly twenty-odd Special Forces soldiers, mostly sergeants of one grade or another but including one full colonel, one lieutenant colonel, two majors, a captain, and two lieutenants, formed a column of twos and snapped to attention.

"Chaplain! Detail!" Sergeant Davidson barked. "At funeral pace, forward *h-arch*!"

The chaplain from the Military District of Washington, a captain, who now found himself standing beside a Green Beret major—whose lapels carried the silver cross of a Christian chaplain and whose breast bore the Combat Infantry Badge—looked around in some confusion until his brother of the clergy took his arm and gently prodded him forward.

The casket team and escort detail marched at funeral pace toward the open grave. As the last of them passed the hearse, a Special Forces major in a wheelchair, pushed by a Special Forces sergeant, joined the detail. Then several men in civilian clothing followed the wheelchair.

The rear was brought up, after a moment's indecision, by the Arlington National Cemetery's official casket team.

As the column made its way through the sea of crosses and Stars of David to the open grave, another detail of Special Forces soldiers, eight enlisted men under a captain, relieved the eight-man cemetery firing party of their weapons and ordered them to form a single rank behind the new firing party.

When the casket team reached the grave, the casket was lowered onto the green nylon tapes of the lowering device. All but two of them came to attention.

Sergeant Major Davidson then handed the national colors to Lieutenant General Bruce J. McNab, USA, and Corporal Lester Bradley, USMC, who placed them on the casket, making sure they were stretched out level and centered over the casket.

Then they assumed the position of attention, and when Sergeant Major Davidson gave the order the entire casket team took two steps back from the grave.

The Green Beret chaplain then led the graveside ritual prescribed for members of the Lutheran faith. Then he stepped back from the casket and grave.

The captain in charge of the new firing party barked, in rapid order, "Present, h'arms. Ready, aim, fire! Ready, aim, fire! Ready, aim, fire!" And then, a moment later, "Or-duh *h'arms.*"

"Bugler, sound taps!" Sergeant Major Davidson barked.

When the bugler was done, Sergeant Major Davidson and Corporal Bradley began folding the colors. When they had finished, the flag, now folded into a crisp triangle of blue with white stars, was given to Lieutenant General McNab, who waited until the casket team had marched away from the grave and then presented it to Sergeant Kranz's sister.

General McNab spoke briefly with Sergeant Kranz's sister, then saluted her and respectfully backed away.

A middle-aged gray-haired woman—an "Arlington Lady," one of the wives of retired general officers who voluntarily appear at every funeral—then presented a card of condolence from the chief of staff of the United States Army to Sergeant Kranz's sister, offered her personal condolences, and kissed her on the cheek.

As this was going on, the Special Forces firing detail returned the rifles of the Arlington firing detail to them, then marched to the waiting line of cars on the road lined up with the escort detail. They were joined by the casket detail, but without General McNab and Corporal Bradley, who was standing beside the general. Bradley then followed the general and Sergeant Kranz's sister as the general walked with her past the lined-up Green Berets to her limousine.

When he had seen Sergeant Kranz's sister into the limousine, General McNab stepped back and Corporal Lester Bradley stepped up.

"Ma'am," he said. "I shall treasure for the remainder of my life my privilege of having been with Sergeant Kranz when he fell. Please accept again my profound condolences on your loss."

When she looked at Corporal Bradley's young—boyish—face and saw the tears in his eyes, Sergeant Kranz's sister lost control for the first time.

"Thank you," she said, barely audibly, then turned her face away.

General McNab gently pushed Corporal Bradley out of the way and closed the limousine door. The car then slowly pulled away.

At the grave, the officer in charge of the burial detail—who had waited to oversee the one soldier, "the Virgil," whose job it was to remain at the grave until it was closed—saw that the Green Berets had decided to participate in that, too.

A Green Beret sergeant first class was standing at parade rest at the head of the casket.

The officer in charge looked at the Arlington Lady, whom he had seen at many another funeral, and the two of them wordlessly agreed to walk together back to the waiting cars.

Halfway there, the lieutenant said, "Well, that was interesting, wasn't it? Different?"

"Lieutenant," the Arlington Lady said, "my husband and I spent thirty-three years on active duty. One of the few things I know for sure about the Army is that Special Forces soldiers are indeed interesting and different."

[TWO]
Office of Organizational Analysis
Department of Homeland Security
Nebraska Avenue Complex
Washington, D.C.
1745 6 August 2005

Major H. Richard Miller, Jr., his tunic unbuttoned and necktie pulled down, sat at the desk of the chief of the Office of Organizational Analysis with his leg resting on an open drawer of the ornate desk.

There was a glass dark with whiskey on the desk and a capped plastic vial of medicine issued by the pharmacy of the Walter Reed Army Medical Center.

He knew what the label on the medicine vial warned about taking alcohol after taking "one or two tablets as necessary for pain," but he picked up the vial and read it again anyway.

"When it doubt, do both," he said aloud.

He pried the lid open, shook out two white tablets, and put them in his mouth. Then he picked up the whiskey glass, raised it, and said, "Mud in your eye, Seymour, you little shit. *Vaya con Dios,* buddy."

Then he drank half of it and set the glass on the desk.

He looked at the whiskey glass for a moment, then picked it up again and drained it.

The instant he set the glass very carefully on the green blotter of the desk pad, a light flashed on one of the telephones on the desk. He looked at it, wondered if he could ignore it, then reached for it.

"Miller," he said.

"Major, there are two gentlemen to see you," Mrs. Agnes Forbison said.

"This is a really bad time. Is this important?"

"I think you'd better see them."

"Give me ninety seconds," Miller said.

He put the telephone back in its cradle, then, wincing with the pain, lifted his leg off the open drawer and carefully lowered it onto the floor. He then put the whiskey glass and the bottle of Famous Grouse into the drawer, then closed it.

Again wincing with the pain it caused, he shifted his body so that he could get the vial of painkillers into his trousers pocket. Finally, he pulled up his necktie and buttoned his uniform tunic.

Almost immediately, there was a discreet knock at the office door.

"Come!"

Sergeant Major John K. Davidson and Corporal Lester Bradley, USMC, marched into the office, stopped twelve inches from the desk, and saluted.

"Good evening, sir!" Davidson barked.

Miller—in perhaps a Pavlovian reflex—returned the salute.

"Jack, it's been a bad day and I'm not drunk enough to be amused. What's on your mind?"

"Sir, the sergeant major has come to enlist."

"What?"

"Sir, I have a permission to enlist note from my daddy," Davidson said.

He took a half step forward, laid a small sheet of paper on the desk, then stepped back and resumed the position of attention.

Miller picked up the piece of paper, saw it was general officer's notepaper, and read it.

★ ★ ★

6 August 2005

Chief
Office of Organizational Analysis
Washington

I will defer to your judgment as to where SgtMaj Davidson will be of the greatest value to the service.

McNab

Miller looked up at Davidson and saw that he and Bradley were still standing at attention.

"I told you, Jack," Miller said, "I am not in a mood to be amused."

Davidson didn't move.

"Stand at ease, goddamn it," Miller said.

Davidson relaxed.

"You want to enlist in what?" Miller asked.

"Oh, come on. I know what's going on here, Dick."

"What's going on here is classified Top Secret Presidential," Miller said.

"So Vic D'Allessando said."

"And the pride of the jarheads here? Has he also been running off at the mouth?"

"Only after Vic told him to fill me in on the details. Before that, Lester was like a clam."

"How did you get this out of General McNab?" Miller asked, waving the sheet of notepaper.

"I reminded him that Char—*Colonel Castillo*—was going to need a replacement for Kranz. And that we were going to have to find a better place to hide Lester; Mackall wasn't hacking that. The jarheads going through the Q course were already getting curious."

"That's all?"

"And that I'd been around the block with Charley a couple of times and knew when he had to have someone sit on him."

"That's all?" Miller asked again.

Miller happened to be glancing at Bradley and saw on his face that there was indeed something else.

"Well, I told McNab that I was getting so tired of Camp Mackall that I was giving serious thought to taking my retirement," Davidson admitted.

"You had the balls to threaten McNab?"

"That was more like a statement of fact, Dick," Davidson said.

Miller saw on Bradley's face that he was shocked to hear Sergeant Major Davidson address a major by his first name.

"What do you think Charley's going to say?" Davidson asked.

"Inasmuch as *Colonel Castillo* is unable to accept that there are times when he should indeed be restrained from an impulsive act and that he knows you are one of the very few people who have proved themselves willing and able to restrain him, the colonel's reaction to being informed that you want to join his merry little band is almost certainly going to be not only no but *hell* no!"

Davidson exhaled audibly.

"I could be useful, Dick, and you know it. Could you talk to him?"

"I could, but that would be what is known as pissing into the wind," Miller said, and then articulated what he had been thinking. "What we're going to do is present him with the fait accompli. When he gets to Buenos Aires, he's going to find you there. We are going to suggest, imply—anything but outright bold-faced lie—that this is another brainstorm of Lieutenant General Bruce J. McNab."

"Thanks, Dick," Davidson said, simply. "He'll accept that. It won't be the first time the general has sent me to try to keep a tight rein on him."

"How do you think we should handle Corporal Big Mouth?" Miller asked, looking at Bradley.

"Hide him in plain sight," Davidson said. "At the embassy in Buenos Aires."

"One of the reasons Castillo brought him here was because he knew the gunnery sergeant of the guard detachment there was going to want to know what he's been up to and wasn't going to back off until Bradley told him."

"I know a master gunnery sergeant named MacNamara at Eighth and Eye—Marine Corps Headquarters?"

"I know where it is," Miller said.

"He's a heavy hitter in Force Recon. Lester said if he got on the horn to the gunnery sergeant in Argentina and told him to ask no questions, he would ask no questions."

"What are you going to tell your friend about why you want him to make that call?"

"I'll tell him I can't tell him. He'll go along."

"And if he doesn't?"

"Let's not cross that bridge until we get there."

"See if you can get him on the horn now. If you can, tell him to come here. We'll dazzle him with Charley's office and my Class A uniform and see what happens."

Davidson nodded.

"You pack a suitcase?" Miller asked.

Davidson nodded again.

"Okay. If your master gunnery sergeant will go along, we'll get you both on a flight out of Miami tomorrow night."

[THREE]
Danubius Hotel Gellért
Szent Gellért tér 1
Budapest, Hungary
0125 7 August 2005

Lieutenant Colonel Castillo—half asleep—became aware that something wet and cold was pressing against his face. The first thing he thought was that he had drooled on his pillow, then rolled over onto the wet spot.

This happened to him every once in a while and he hated it. Telling himself that he couldn't be held responsible for drooling while he was asleep didn't help any more than applying the same logic to what was euphemistically known as nocturnal emissions. It was embarrassing, annoying, and even shameful. Age seemed to have dealt with the nocturnal emission problem, but drooling remained a real pain in the ass.

He put his hand out to push himself away from the wet spot—and suddenly was wide awake, his heart jumping.

There was something warm, firm, and hairy in bed with him.

In the same split instant, he became aware of a deep growl.

"Max, you sonofabitch! How did you get in bed?"

Max growled again—but not at Castillo.

He had left Max in Billy Kocian's bedroom, presuming Max would prefer sleeping in there—on a huge, fluffy dog bed on the floor next to Kocian's enormous, antique canopied bed—instead of here, in another bedroom.

Castillo had felt like an intruder, a voyeur, in Kocian's apartment, especially the bedroom. But curiosity had overwhelmed those feelings, and he and Otto Görner had spent a half hour in the huge, high-ceilinged rooms, examining the photos on the walls and furniture. There were all sorts of photographs, some of which were obviously of Kocian's family and many of what obviously had become Kocian's second family, the von und zu Gossingers.

There were several of Castillo's grandfather and Kocian together, in uniform. And more of the former Herr Oberst in shabby civilian clothing, apparently taken right after the Second World War. There were others as Castillo remembered him, elegantly tailored.

In Kocian's bedroom there had been a photograph on the bedside table of a young girl in braids and a near-adolescent boy holding Kocian's hand—

Castillo's mother and his uncle Willi. There had been others of Kocian and Otto Görner.

The walls and furniture had held framed photographs at various places of Karl Wilhelm von und zu Gossinger—aged three, five, seven, ten—holding his mother's hand. There had been several of Carlos Guillermo Castillo, as a skinny Boy Scout, as a teenager on a horse at Hacienda San Jorge wearing a far-too-large cowboy hat, as Cadet Sergeant C. G. Castillo of the Corps of Cadets of the United States Military Academy, and as Second Lieutenant Castillo with just-awarded Distinguished Flying Cross, Bronze Star, and Purple Heart medals dangling from the breast of his tunic.

And more than a dozen photographs of women, ranging from in their twenties to middle age. They had been obviously important to Kocian, if not important enough for him to have married them.

Castillo had left Kocian's bedroom feeling sad, almost to the point of tears. The old man had to be lonely. No wonder that he was bananas about Max. Max gave him the only love he had in his life.

Castillo patted Max and was surprised at how tense—actually, he was quivering—the dog's body was. And he realized the dog was still growling, softly, deep in his throat.

"Hey, pal! What's the matter?"

Max, who had been lying next to Castillo, suddenly got half to his feet and slinked off the bed.

Castillo's heart jumped again. He sat up.

There was just enough light for Castillo to be able to see Max stalking across the floor toward the door leading to the sitting room.

He's like a lion, a panther, stalking its prey!

Castillo rolled on his side far enough so that he could slide open the drawer of the bedside table. His fingers found the suppressed Ruger pistol. He quickly chambered a round, then sat up, pushing back on the bed until his back was resting against the headboard.

It's probably Otto, looking for a glass of water. Or another dog. Maybe somebody cleaning the corridor outside the apartment.

Calm down, for Christ's sake!

Max was now crouched but no longer growling.

There was a squeak.

What the hell is that?

The door swung open quickly and two men jumped into the room in crouching positions. Both held Madsen submachine guns at the ready. Max leaped at the first one, locking his massive jaws on the man's arm. The man yelped in surprise and pain. The second pointed his Madsen at Max.

Without thinking what he was doing, Castillo raised the Ruger in both hands and fired instinctively—twice, as a reflex action—at the second man. The suppressed muzzle made a soft *tut-tut* sound. Then, without waiting to see if he had hit the second man, Castillo fired at the first. *Tut-tut.* And then he looked back at the second man. He was now sliding limply down the doorframe. *Tut-tut.* Castillo's eyes and the Ruger went back to the first man, who was now sitting down. It looked as if Max was about to drag him somewhere. *Tut-tut.*

The Ruger's magazine had held ten .22 Long Rifle cartridges. Castillo had subconsciously counted as he had fired; he had two rounds left. He leaped out of the bed and ran to the dresser, where he had left the Micro Uzi. Its magazine was fully charged and he could get it much quicker than he could charge the Ruger's magazine, the extra cartridges for which he had put in the same drawer as the Uzi.

He grabbed the Uzi and dropped to the floor, pulling the action lever back and then rolling over twice before sitting up with the Uzi pointed at the door.

There was no burst of gunfire.

Max trotted over and licked Castillo's face.

Castillo felt tears welling.

"You big sonofabitch," he said. "I love you, too."

He got to his feet and went to the men in the door.

The one Max had grabbed was on his back, openmouthed, staring at the ceiling with unseeing eyes. Castillo could see no entrance wounds. The second man was sitting in the doorway. There were two small holes in his forehead and a third next to his nose.

Castillo's heart jumped again and he felt a chill.

Jesus Christ, Otto!

He ran across the living room to the second guest room, put his hand on the doorknob, then pushed it open quickly and jumped inside, holding the Micro Uzi in both hands. There was just enough light to make out the bed.

He fumbled on the wall inside the door until he found the light switch and tripped it.

For a moment, the body on the bed didn't move—*Oh, shit, not another garroting! Not Otto!*—and then Otto sat up.

"What the hell!" Görner grumbled. "What are you doing with that gun?"

"You better get up, Otto," Castillo said. "There's a problem."

"A problem? What kind of a problem?"

"You'd better get up, Otto," Castillo repeated, then went quickly through the living room to the door to the corridor.

There was a man down—one of the security people from the *Tages Zeitung*—sprawled on his back by the door to the stairway. His pistol was lying on the carpet.

Castillo ran to him, saw his bulged eyes and blue skin, then the blued-steel garrote around his neck.

He ran back into the apartment, found his Swiss Army knife in his suitcase, and ran back into the corridor.

He managed with great difficulty to trip the lever locking the garrote, but, when it was free, he decided that it had been an exercise in futility.

This guy is dead.

He looked down at the man's face. There was no sign of life.

What the hell!

He pressed with all his weight on the man's abdomen and felt the expulsion of air from the man's lungs. But there was no sign of breathing.

Castillo inhaled deeply, then bent over the man, pinched his nostrils closed, and exhaled into his mouth.

There was no reaction.

Castillo pressed on the man's abdomen again and sensed again an expulsion of air. And then there was a sucking sensation. A small, short suck. Then another, a little greater. And then, all at once, a large intake of air.

And a gasping groan.

I have absolutely no idea what to do now.

The man thrashed around, clawing at his throat.

"Just breathe, that's all. Just lie there and breathe," Castillo ordered.

It sounded as if the man was trying to say something.

Castillo sensed someone behind him and quickly reached for the Micro Uzi.

"I'll call for the police and an ambulance," Otto Görner said, softly.

"No police. No ambulance," Castillo said. "Get Sándor Tor over here."

Görner looked as if he was going to argue but then said, "My cellular's next to my bed," and went back into the apartment.

The security man tried to sit up.

Castillo pushed him back down.

"Stay there," he said. "Help is on the way."

[FOUR]
Danubius Hotel Gellért
Szent Gellért tér 1
Budapest, Hungary
0150 7 August 2005

"What did you shoot them with?" Sándor Tor asked.

He was squatting beside the second intruder, who was sitting against the doorframe.

Castillo said, "A .22 pistol."

"You are either a fool or have a lot of faith in your marksmanship," Tor said. "Where is it?"

"On the dresser in my bedroom," Castillo said and pointed.

Tor walked to the bedroom. Castillo followed him. Tor picked up the pistol.

"Okay," he said. "A *silenced* .22 pistol."

"Suppressed," Castillo corrected him without thinking.

"Very few newspaper publishers know the difference, much less how to use one of these . . . certainly not as well as you did."

"If you're waiting for me to respond to that, don't hold your breath," Castillo said.

Another burly, middle-aged Hungarian came into the bedroom. He carried a ten-liter red plastic gas can. Castillo saw that he was wearing rubber gloves.

"There's two more of these in the stairwell," the burly Hungarian announced.

Tor nodded.

"Does that suggest anything to you, Úr Gossinger?" Tor asked.

"Plan C," Castillo said. "If they couldn't snatch Úr Kocian—Plan A—or something went wrong and they had to kill him—Plan B—then they were going to torch the place in the hope that it would destroy Úr Kocian's files."

"You think they thought Úr Kocian was here?"

"Otherwise, they would have gone to the Telki Private Hospital. I think they were watching this place and saw the lights in the apartment and decided he was here. Maybe they saw Max on the balcony. When he didn't take his usual midnight stroll, they decided to come after him."

"Certainly they knew he was in the Telki Private Hospital," Tor argued. "Why would they think he was here?"

"But they didn't know how badly he was hurt. It made more sense for them to come here in case he was here than to try a snatch at the hospital where he might not be."

Tor looked at Castillo carefully for a long moment, then turned to the man holding the gas can.

"Rákosi, leave us alone for a minute, please," he said. "See if you can find anything in their pockets. See if we can tie them to a car anywhere around here."

"I saw an Uzi in the sitting room?" Rákosi questioned.

Tor looked at Castillo, who, after a moment's hesitation, nodded.

Tor waved his hand at Rákosi, ordering him out of the room. Then he walked to the door and closed it.

"Úr Gossinger, we are both very concerned about Úr Kocian's safety. I can do my job better if I am not in the dark." He paused and waited until he understood Castillo was not going to reply, then went on: "Forgive an old policeman for not believing you are who you say you are, Úr Gossinger."

Well, he had to be told sooner or later.

"I'm an American intelligence officer."

The nod Tor made automatically told Castillo he wasn't surprised.

"CIA?"

Castillo shook his head. "No."

Sándor Tor visibly didn't believe that.

"And what is your interest in Úr Kocian?"

"Right now, to keep him alive," Castillo said, and then, gesturing for Tor to follow him, added, "Come with me, please."

Castillo led him into Kocian's bedroom and pointed to the photograph of Eric Kocian holding his mother's and his uncle Willi's hands.

"That's my mother as a girl. And," he went on, pointing to the pictures of him holding his mother's hand, "that's her as a young woman and me as a boy."

Tor looked at the photographs, then at Castillo, and pointed to the photo of Castillo with the newly awarded medals on his tunic.

"And you were a soldier. So was I."

"I am a soldier. Lieutenant colonel."

"I suppose that would explain the marksmanship," Tor said. "But this raises more questions than it answers."

"When there is time, I will try to answer those questions. But for now, my government is interested in what Úr Kocian has learned about the oil-for-food scandal."

"Enough, obviously, for those involved to send these scumbags to kill him."

"First to find out how much he knows and then to kill him."

"He told me that the night they tried to kidnap him on the bridge," Tor said.

"He tell you anything else?"

"He said he had files here in the apartment."

"Did he say where?"

Tor shook his head. "He said he didn't want me to know."

"Well, he can tell us in the morning."

"And how are we going to protect him after that?"

"In my business, there are times when you have to trust your gut feeling about somebody," Castillo said. "And tell him things that just might come around and bite you on the ass."

"I know," Tor said, simply. "And what is your gut feeling about me?"

"In a couple of hours, an airplane will land at Ferihegy Airport. After we get Úr Kocian out of the hospital here, and he has his files, I'm going to take him to Argentina in it."

"Argentina is halfway around the world," Tor said. "It must be quite an airplane."

"A Gulfstream III," Castillo furnished.

Tor nodded his recognition of the airplane.

"Why not to the United States?"

"Two reasons. One, that Úr Kocian doesn't want to go to the States, and, two, I think we're going to find what we're looking for in southern South America. And maybe three, I think I can protect him better there than I could in the States."

"That doesn't seem reasonable."

"I think I may be able to get word to whoever is trying to get to Úr Kocian that it no longer makes sense to try to get his information or kill him because the information is now in my hands."

"I will ensure that Úr Kocian gets safely from the hospital to here and then to the airport."

Castillo said, "What would it take to get you to come to Argentina with us?"

Tor met Castillo's eyes.

"You would not have to ask permission to do something like that?" Tor said.

Castillo shook his head. "Will you come with us?"

"Of course."

"What are we going to do about the police?" Castillo said.

"Nothing. If my people can find their car—and I think they will be able to—we will put the bodies in it, take it into the woods, and burn the car with them in it."

"And that'll be the end of it?"

"We will hope so."

[FIVE]
Danubius Hotel Gellért
Szent Gellért tér 1
Budapest, Hungary
0550 7 August 2005

"Why does finding you awake and dressed at oh-dark-hundred and with an Uzi on the coffee table make me uncomfortable, Charley?" Colonel Jake Torine asked as he and Fernando Lopez walked into the living room. And then, as Max trotted in, showing his teeth, he exclaimed, "Jesus Christ!"

"They're good guys, Max," Castillo said, in Hungarian. "Down."

Max walked to where Castillo was sitting and lay down at his feet.

"What is that, a Hungarian Great Dane?" Torine asked. "Where did he come from?"

"He's Billy Kocian's."

"What happened to his head?"

"We have problems, Jake. We have to go wheels-up as soon as possible."

"Charley, we just flew here from Baltimore, with only a piss stop at Frankfurt."

"What kind of problems, Gringo?" Fernando Lopez asked.

"The bad guys tried to kidnap Billy Kocian. Max grabbed the arm of one of them and the bad guy clobbered him with his pistol, whereupon another bad guy shot Billy. Twice. Luckily, not bad. We're getting him out of the hospital right about now. As soon as he shows me where his files are, we're going back to the airport."

"Why the hurry?"

"Getting him out of here is the best way I can think of to keep him alive."

"He wouldn't be safe here?" Fernando asked. "At least for eight hours, so we can get some sleep? Christ, there were half a dozen of what I presume are Hungarian rent-a-cops in the lobby and four more when we got off the elevator."

"You can sleep as long as you want to and then catch a plane home," Castillo said. "Jake and I have to get Billy out of Budapest."

"You really think they'll try something again?" Torine asked.

"They already did," Castillo said. "Two of them came in here at half past one."

"And?" Fernando asked.

"Max woke me up. I took them out."

You took them out? "Torine repeated.

Castillo nodded.

"Jesus Christ!" Torine said.

"I didn't have any choice, Jake."

"And are there going to be complications from that? The local cops, for example?"

"I don't think so."

"Are you all right, Gringo?" Fernando asked.

"I'm fine," Castillo said and turned to Torine. "If you get the Gulfstream in the air, Jake, I can steer while you take a nap."

Torine's face showed he was less than enthusiastic about that idea.

"I wouldn't ask you to do this unless I thought it was really necessary," Castillo said.

Torine shrugged.

"I penciled in a flight plan to Buenos Aires on the way over," he said. "Budapest, Dakar, and across the drink to Recife, Brazil. Then down to Buenos Aires. It's about six hours from here to Dakar. Figuring two fuel stops at an hour each and fifteen hours in the air, give or take. If we leave here at, say, eight, we should be in Buenos Aires—there's a four-time-zone difference—we should be in BA before midnight."

"That'll work," Fernando said. "We can take turns sleeping. One of us on one of the couches, the other in the right seat."

"You're not going," Castillo said. "You're going home, commercial."

"I'll go home commercial from Buenos Aires," Fernando said. "Not open for discussion."

"Who all's going," Torine asked, "besides Kocian?"

"Billy, me, a guy named Sándor Tor, and Max."

"And Sándor Tor is?" Torine asked.

"Billy's bodyguard, and a good one."

"He knows what's going on?"

Castillo nodded.

"The dog is going?" Fernando asked.

"Absolutely," Castillo said.

"I'll call for the weather," Torine said. "Somebody order up some breakfast. And—can we do this, Charley?—some in-flight rations."

[SIX]
Danubius Hotel Gellért
Szent Gellért tér 1
Budapest, Hungary
0720 7 August 2005

Eric Kocian, visibly in a foul mood, was rolled into his apartment in a wheel-chair by Sándor Tor. He was accompanied by three security guards and Dr. Czerny. Czerny, the reason for Kocian's foul mood, had made his personal approval of where Kocian would be resting in bed a condition to discharge the old man from the hospital.

Castillo wondered if Czerny's concern was based on friendship for the old man or was a manifestation of his professional concern for Kocian's health, and when the doctor came out of Kocian's bedroom Castillo took him aside and told him that he planned to leave Budapest immediately if Kocian's physical condition would make that possible.

"Ordinarily, I'd say no," Czerny replied, "but I know—Tor told me—not only what happened on the bridge but what happened here earlier this morning. So with my priority being keeping my patient alive, I prescribe getting him as far away from Budapest as possible as quickly as possible."

"That's what I'm thinking," Castillo said. "I think it'll be a day or two before these people realize he's gone. And there will be no record—no airline tickets, no rail tickets, etcetera—to give them an idea where he might be. I'm hoping they think Vienna or Fulda."

Dr. Czerny nodded his agreement.

Czerny said, "I just wish those bedlike seats on airplanes were really beds. What he should be doing is lying down."

"There *are* real beds—actually, couches—on the airplane where he could lie down and be strapped in. That is, *if* I can get him to lie down, much less get him to allow me to strap him down."

Dr. Czerny reached in his pocket and came out with a plastic vial.

"Give him one of these air-sickness pills. In ten minutes, he'll get drowsy."

"And if he won't take one?"

"Break open the capsule and mix the powder with anything he'll drink."

Three minutes after Dr. Czerny had checked Kocian a final time—to make sure he was in bed in his pajamas—and had given Castillo a package of bandages and medicines and then left the apartment, and as Castillo was wondering how soon he could get Kocian to dress, Kocian appeared in the sitting room, awkwardly trying to button the sleeves of his shirt. Castillo went to help him.

"What time's the plane?" Kocian demanded, casually.

"Just as soon as we can get your files and to the airport."

"Have you thought about Argentine regulations about taking a dog into their country?" Kocian asked, and, when he saw the look on Castillo's face, added: "I didn't think you would have, Karlchen. *I* have looked into the matter. What we have to do is go to Dr. Kincs—Max's veterinarian—and get a certificate of health and a copy of his inoculations record."

"Can we send Tor?"

"I'll call and find out," Kocian said.

Five minutes later, Tor was on his way to the veterinarian's office.

"What about your files, Eric?" Castillo asked after Tor had left.

"Oh, yes, those," Kocian replied and walked over to a bookcase.

He took a book from the shelf and handed it to Castillo.

Castillo had read the book title—*Ot Pervovo Litsa* (*First Person*)—a collection of interviews with Russian president Vladimir Putin that Putin authorized to be published as a sort-of autobiography.

Castillo looked quesioningly at Kocian.

"You can't judge a book by its cover, Karlchen."

Castillo opened the book. It had been carefully hollowed out enough to hold a black leather-and-chrome object a half inch thick, three inches wide, and nine inches long. Castillo knew what it was: a state-of-the-art external hard drive for a computer.

"Eighty gigabytes," Kocian said. "Those Japanese are really clever, aren't they, Karlchen?"

"The Japanese are good at making things, but this technology came out of Las Vegas, Nevada," Castillo said, "not Japan."

"And how do you know that?"

"Because Aloysius Francis Casey of the AFC Corporation, who came up with the technology, sent me a prototype. I've got it in my briefcase. One hundred twenty gigs. Would you like to see it?"

"That won't be necessary."

"Everything's in here?"

"Just about. I have a few tidbits between my ears."

"Is it encrypted?"

Kocian nodded.

"Microsoft encryption?"

Kocian nodded again.

"Well, see if you can remember the key while I go get my hard drive."

"You want to see this now?" Kocian asked, surprised.

"I want to copy it to my hard drive and then encrypt it with another little gift from Mr. Casey. There are a lot of people, many of them unfriendly, who know how to get around Mr. Gates's encryption technology. So far as I know, nobody's ever been able to crack the AFC encryption logarithm."

"You're serious, aren't you, Karl?"

Castillo picked up on that: *I'm not Karlchen right now. The old man is impressed.*

"Absolutely," Castillo said. "Have you got another hard drive?"

"A spare, you mean?"

Castillo nodded.

"Why?"

"Because what I really would like to do just as soon as I get this data off your drive and properly reencrypted is put it on another drive and send that in the diplomatic pouch to the United States. In case something happens to our copies."

Kocian considered that and nodded.

"There's a store across the river which sells them," he said. "They're expensive."

"Can we send somebody to buy one?"

Kocian nodded again. "Shall I have it put on my *Tages Zeitung* American Express card? Or are you going to pay for it?"

"Better yet, we'll have the Lorimer Charitable and Benevolent Fund pay for it," Castillo said. "Will this store take dollars?"

"Probably, at a very bad rate of exchange."

"Get one of the security guys in here. You tell him what store and I'll tell him to get a receipt," Castillo said and took a wad of currency from his pocket.

"You going to tell me what that fund—'the Lorimer Charitable and Whatever Fund'—is all about?"

"On the way to Buenos Aires. There's no time now."

Castillo carefully pried the portable hard drive from the pages of *Ot Pervovo Litsa,* then connected it to his laptop computer.

"Okay, Eric, it's hooked up. Let me have the password."

"You trust that machine?"

"I won't erase your data until I'm sure it's in here," Castillo said. "But, yeah, I trust it."

"I put a lot of time and effort into what's in there," Kocian said. "I'd hate to lose it."

"Not as much as I would," Castillo said, "and therefore I am going to be very careful. Let's have the password."

Kocian gave it to him, then added: "Never in my worst nightmares did I see myself as a lackey of the CIA."

Castillo entered the password, decrypted the data on Kocian's hard drive, then transfered it to his.

When he saw that was working, he said, "I don't work for the CIA, Eric."

"So you say. But if you did, you wouldn't say you did, would you?"

"Probably not," Castillo said.

Kocian elected to change the subject.

"I really hate to destroy any book," he said. "But I had seen all the spy movies on the TV and hiding the hard drive in a book seemed like a good idea. And *Ot Pervovo Litsa* was a garbage book." He paused, then added, "Full of bullshit, like the dispatches from Washington you send all the time."

Is he trying to piss me off?

Or do my paraphrases from The American Conservative *really offend his sense of journalistic integrity?*

Castillo said, "You don't think Mr. Putin told the truth, the whole truth, and nothing but the truth to those reporters?"

"You read it?"

Castillo nodded.

"In Russian or the translation?"

"In Russian."

"Then you will recall he told one journalist that practically right out of university, he went in the KGB and learned his craft by suppressing 'dissident activities' in Leningrad. That, I believe. I also believe that his father was a cook, first to the czars—where he cooked for Rasputin—and then to the Bolsheviks, most significantly Lenin himself, and then in one of Stalin's dachas outside Moscow, as he told other Russian journalists. He also said that his father served with the Red Army during the Great Patriotic War. He was a little vague about what his poppa did in uniform."

Castillo nodded.

He dropped his eyes to his laptop and saw that the transfer of files procedure was just about finished.

He held up his hand to signal Kocian that he needed a moment and then typed in the encryption code.

Kocian waited until Castillo raised his eyes to him and then went on: "Do you think that Putin's father spent that time boiling beets for the Red Army in some field mess? Or is it more likely that Putin's father—whom the regime trusted enough to let him cook for Stalin—served as a political officer, making sure no officer strayed from the path of righteousness?"

"Good point."

"Whatever he did, it made Poppa an important apparatchik. Important enough to get his son into law school at Leningrad State University and then into the KGB, where he promptly began to suppress the local dissidents. Then, he told another so-called journalist, he was next assigned to East Germany, to a minor administrative position."

"I wondered about that," Castillo said.

"Do you think, having learned how to suppress Russian dissidents, that the KGB might have had him doing the same thing in East Germany?"

"Which, of course, he would like to keep quiet," Castillo said. "In the interests of friendship between the Russian president and a now-reunited Germany."

"Think about it, Karl. After serving in a 'minor administrative position' in the KGB in East Germany, he went back to Leningrad State University, if we are to believe what he told these reporters, where he worked in the International Affairs section of the university, reporting to the vice rector. Do you suppose he got that job because he was such a good student the first time he was there? Or because—having been all the way to East Germany—he was an expert in international affairs? Or maybe because the KGB wanted somebody with experience in suppressing dissidence suppressing dissidence at the university?"

"Where are you going with this, Eric?" Castillo asked, softly,

Kocian held up a hand, signaling him to wait, and then went on: "After a year of that—in 1991, if memory serves, and it usually does—Putin was put in charge of the International Committee of the Leningrad Kommandatura— excuse me, Lenin no longer being an official saint of Russia, Leningrad was Saint Petersburg once again.

"That made it the International Committee of *Saint Petersburg* Kommandatura. Where he handled international relations and foreign investments. To show that he had put all the evil of the Soviets behind him, Mr. Putin resigned from the KGB two months after getting that job. Correct me if you think I'm wrong, but if he resigned from the KGB in 1991 wouldn't that suggest he was *in* the KGB until 1991? I mean, how can you resign from something you don't belong to?"

Castillo chuckled but didn't reply.

"Would you be cynical enough to think, Karl, that the man in charge of foreign investments in *Saint Petersburg* would be in a position to skim a little off the top and spread it around among what in the former regime had been deserving apparatchiks?"

"That evil thought might occur to me," Castillo said. "Okay, what else?"

"Well, he did such a good job building foreign goodwill and attracting foreign investment that Putin suddenly found himself first deputy chairman of the whole city of Saint Petersburg, and, soon after that, he was summoned to Moscow, where he served in what he told the reporters who interviewed him were various positions under Boris Yeltsin. What they were was not mentioned. A cynical man might suspect this was because he might have been involved again with the Komitet Gosudarstvennoy Bezopasnosti, otherwise known . . ."

"As the KGB," Castillo said and laughed.

"Or the Federalnaya Sluzhba Bezopasnosti . . ."

"FSB," Castillo said, still chuckling.

". . . The Federal Security Service of the Russian Federation," Kocian finished, nodding, "which replaced the evil KGB, and of which Putin became head, and remained head, until he assumed his present role as an international statesman."

"You think he was personally involved in the oil-for-food scam, Eric?"

"Up to his skinny little ass," Kocian said, bitterly. "Both as a source of money for the FSB and personally."

"Can you prove it?"

Kocian shook his head.

"But I'm working on it. I think I may be getting close to getting something I can print."

"You think he knows that?"

"We have more spies per square meter in Budapest than Vienna and Berlin did in their heyday. Of course he knows."

"And the people who tried to whack you? They were Spetsnaz sent by the FSB?"

"Whack meaning 'kidnap'? Or 'assassinate'?"

"Assassinate. Kidnap is 'grab' or simply 'kidnap.' "

Kocian nodded.

"Maybe, but I don't think so. They weren't Russian. They were German, which makes me think they were sent by the KSB. The KSB is too smart to send Spetsnaz. They might be identified and Putin wouldn't like that. More than likely, as we were discussing yesterday, former East German Stasi. What about the people who—what was that word you used, 'whacked'? I like it—*whacked* Mr. Lorimer?"

"They were professionals," Castillo said. "No identification on them. They had Swedish Madsen submachine guns. The CIA guys in Montevideo and Buenos Aires are trying to identify them. I don't think we're going to get lucky. They could be Stasi, or not."

"If you're really not CIA, Karl, how do you know what the CIA is doing? Or, for that matter, that they'd tell you the truth about what they're doing or have found out?"

Castillo didn't immediately reply, then he said, "I work for the President, Eric."

"Directly?"

Castillo nodded.

"And he's ordered the agency—and everybody else in the intelligence community—to tell me anything I want to know and give me whatever I ask for."

Kocian met his eyes for a moment, then nodded, then pointed at Castillo's laptop.

"Either your encryption process is awfully slow or your machine is not working."

"It's a little slow but very good." He looked at the screen. "Ninety-one percent encrypted."

"Well, while we're waiting I'll get packed. It's winter in Argentina now, right?"

"Yeah, but don't put on long underwear. We have to go to Equatorial Africa before we go to South America."

It was a little after twelve before all the errands had been run and they made their way to Ferihegy International Airport.

Castillo didn't think it would be likely that anyone would be looking for Billy Kocian at the airport or keeping the Gulfstream under observation, but he decided nevertheless that the smart way to get the old man on the airplane was to take him there in an unmarked van from the *Tages Zeitung*. With a little bit of luck, he and Sándor Tor could rush Kocian up the steps and get him and Max aboard unnoticed while the luggage and in-flight rations were being loaded.

Just before they went to the airport, Castillo had Kocian's Mercedes brought to the loading dock in the basement of the Gellért. With one of the *Tages Zeitung* security men at the wheel and another behind the darkened windows in the backseat, the car took off for Vienna.

There was no way of telling, of course, if the bastards who had tried to

whack Kocian were surveilling the Gellért, but if they were they just might follow the Mercedes. They might also try something with the car once it was
on the highway. Castillo almost hoped they would: He had given the security
men the Madsens the Stasi—or whoever the hell the bastards were—had brought
to the hotel to use on Kocian. And he hadn't had to show them how to use them.

As the Mercedes pulled away from the loading dock, they had shaken hands
with Otto Görner, who was going to stay in Budapest for at least a day before
returning to Fulda, and then gotten in the van.

Billy Kocian, surprising Castillo, had not objected to traveling in the van,
and surprised him again once they were aboard the Gulfstream by taking without question the air-sick pill Dr. Czerny had provided. Deceiving the old man
had made Castillo feel a little ashamed.

Jake Torine and Fernando Lopez, who had ridden to the airport in a taxi,
came up the stair door two minutes after the van had driven off.

"Everything okay, Charley?" Torine asked.

"If you've filed the flight plan and remembered to get the weather, it is."

"There is one small problem," Fernando said.

"Which is?"

"I know American Express boasts that there's no spending limit," Fernando
said. "But what happens if they err on the side of caution and call the office
and ask if I really filled the tanks on this thing in Baltimore, Frankfurt, and then
here? They're used to charges for fueling the Lear, not a Gulfstream, and not in
Europe. And not nearly as much fuel. They're liable to suspect that somebody's
using my Amex numbers."

"Shit!" Castillo said. "Good point. Well, the damage is done. From here on,
we'll use my card and then when we get to Buenos Aires I'll call Dick and have
him write a check on the Lorimer Charitable and Benevolent Fund to your account at American Express."

"I think we ought to do something," Fernando said.

"Agreed," Castillo said. "Jake, do you want me to sit in the right seat now
and take over once we're wheels-up?"

"I want you to sit in the left seat now," Torine said. "Preliminary flight in-
struction will begin immediately."

"Ferihegy Departure Control clears Gulfstream Three-Seven-Niner for takeoff.
Climb to flight level thirty-one thousand on a course of two-three-five degrees.
Contact Zagreb Area Control on two-three-three-point-five when passing
through twenty thousand."

"Three-Seven-Niner understands number one to go," Torine replied. "Climb to thirty-one thousand on two-three-five. Report to Zagreb Area Control on two-three-three-point-five when passing through twenty thousand."

"Affirmative."

Castillo pushed the throttles forward.

"Three-Seven-Niner rolling," Torine reported. "Thank you."

Then he switched to intercom. "Presuming you can steer it down the runway," Torine's voice came over Castillo's earphones, "I'll tell you when to rotate. And then when to get the gear up."

[SEVEN]
Yoff International Airport
Dakar, Senegal
1835 7 August 2005

Max stood beside Castillo as he opened the stair door and, the moment it had extended, pushed Castillo aside and bounded down the stairs, startling more than a little the Senegalese airport authorities who had come to meet the Gulfstream.

Max took a quick look around, then headed for the nose gear, where he raised his leg and voided his bladder. It was an impressive performance, in terms of both volume and duration.

Then he looked around again, saw where the setting sun had cast a shadow to one side of the aircraft, trotted to it, and vacated his bowels in another impressive performance. Then he returned to the stair door and looked up at it, his posture suggesting, *Well, I'm finished. What are you waiting for?*

Billy Kocian came down the stairs both regally and carefully. He was wearing his wide-brimmed panama hat and a white linen suit. The jacket was draped rakishly over his shoulder and the arm he carried in a sling. His free hand held his cane like a swagger stick.

He looked at the airport authorities, nodded, and said, in Hungarian, "Good God, it's hot! How long do we have to stand here in the sun in whatever obscure developing country we find ourselves?"

Castillo thought: *Well, there's now no question in the minds of the customs guys who owns this airplane.*

"We're in Dakar, Senegal," Castillo replied, in Hungarian. "Unless I'm mistaken, that bus will take us to the transient lounge."

He pointed to a Peugeot van.

"Do you suppose it has air-conditioning or is that too much to expect?" Kocian asked and walked to the bus.

Sándor Tor came down the stairs and followed Kocian. Max trotted after them.

Jake Torine came down the stairs, carrying the aircraft's documents, and then Fernando Lopez exited.

"I hate to tell you this, Gringo," Lopez said, "but that landing was a greaser."

"A *greaser?* For my very first touchdown, it was *magnificent!*"

"You and I will fly across the drink, Fernando," Torine said. "There is nothing more dangerous in the sky than a pilot who thinks he really knows how to fly."

[EIGHT]
Carrasco International Airport
Montevideo, República Oriental del Uruguay
2030 7 August 2005

"Legal Attaché" David W. Yung, Jr., was in a strange, good—almost euphoric—mood as the Policía Federal helicopter carrying him, "Cultural Attaché" Robert Howell, "Assistant Legal Attaché" Julio Artigas, and Chief Inspector José Ordóñez came in for a landing at the military side of the airport.

It was an almost complete turnaround of feelings from when he'd gotten on the same ancient and battered Huey at eight that morning for the flight to Estancia Shangri-La in Tacuarembó Province.

Then he had been very worried. He had just about convinced himself that the whole thing was going to blow up in his face and God only knew what that would mean, either to the mission ordered by the Presidential Finding or to David W. Yung, Jr., personally. And he hadn't been the only one worrying that he was about to fuck up spectacularly. He could tell that Howell and Artigas were watching him almost as closely as was Ordóñez.

That hadn't happened. He hadn't done anything stupid, even though on the flight to the estancia he had wallowed in the discomfiting thought that while he had conducted a great many interrogations himself, this was the first time he had been on—and all day would continue to be on—the receiving end of an interrogation conducted by an interrogator as skilled—perhaps, better skilled—in that art as he was.

And since he was lying through his teeth—and had very little experience doing that—the odds were that he had already said something, had revealed something, that he shouldn't have. And, if he hadn't, that would happen before the day was over.

That hadn't happened, either.

There had been three police vehicles—two cars and a small van—parked in front of the estancia and, as the helicopter approached, a half dozen policemen came out from under the shielded veranda of the house to watch the helo land.

And there was another man, a burly, middle-aged Uruguayan wearing a suit jacket and tie and gaucho pants stuffed into red rubber boots. He knew that had to be Ricardo Montez, the manager of the estancia.

Early in the assault, Montez had been tied, blindfolded, and "tranquilized" by one of Castillo's Green Berets, but there was still a very good chance that he would somehow recognize Yung, or at least eye him suspiciously, which, of course, would immediately be picked up by Ordóñez.

That hadn't happened. When Ordóñez introduced them to Montez and the police as "representatives of the U.S. embassy" and said they had come to have a look at the crime site and to begin the process of protecting the late Señor Lorimer's property, there had been not even a glimmer of recognition.

Ordóñez gave them a guided tour of the crime scene, beginning by showing the Americans the chalk body outlines indicating where two of what everyone was now calling the Ninja had fallen on the veranda.

Next, Ordóñez showed them the chalk body outline of the Ninja who had fallen just inside the front door. Yung had been more than a little surprised at his reaction to that one—virtually none—although he'd killed that Ninja himself, taking him down with two quick shots as he had been trained to do at the FBI school at Quantico. It was the first time since he'd been in the FBI that he'd ever taken his pistol from its holster with any prospect at all of having to use it.

What the hell is wrong with me? Am I a cold-blooded killer?

Remembering suddenly that he was still carrying his pistol had caused another moment of anxiety.

I haven't even cleaned it. Not smart, Yung!

Christ, if Ordóñez gets his hands on my pistol they can match it to the slugs in the Ninja I took down. Proof that not only was I involved in this but that I killed that man!

The anxiety hadn't lasted long: *Calm down! You have diplomatic immunity. Ordóñez can't even ask for the pistol.*

Next came the chalk body outline in Lorimer's office, showing where Lorimer had fallen.

That produced virtually no reaction, either, although it did trigger a sharp and very unpleasant memory of Lorimer's body in the morgue refrigerator in the British Hospital in Montevideo the previous afternoon.

A Uruguayan pathologist who spoke English like the queen had pulled Lorimer's naked body from its shelf in the cooler and unceremoniously pulled the sheet from it.

"Just going through the motions, you know," the pathologist had said, conversationally. "Either of the bullets in the poor chap's brain would have killed him instantly. But the chief inspector said he wanted a full autopsy, so I did one."

He had gestured at the corpse. A full autopsy had apparently required that a large incision—sort of a flap—be made in the body from the upper chest to the groin. It had been sewn shut, somewhat crudely. So had the incisions made in Lorimer's face and skull. The bullets in his head had made large exit wounds and the skull was deformed.

Ordóñez next showed them where the other three Ninja had fallen outside the house. Two of them, Ordóñez said, to bursts of 5.56mm rifle fire, probably from an M-16 firing on full automatic close up. One of the bodies had five wounds; the other, three. The third had died of a 9mm bullet to the forehead. That body, Ordóñez said, also had stab wounds, suggesting there had been hand-to-hand combat before he was killed by a bullet.

Yung, who had searched all the bodies and then photographed and fingerprinted them right after the firefight, could only hope he was making the right facial expressions and asking the right kind of questions as he "learned this for the first time."

By the time Ordóñez—watching all of them closely to see their reactions—had finished his guided tour of the main house and the grounds immediately outside and the field where he'd found the skid marks of the Bell Ranger, Yung felt a good deal less nervous. He felt that he'd handled himself well.

A four-hour search of the house had turned up nothing useful, which was not surprising, since immediately after the firefight Castillo had quickly gathered up everything he thought might be useful—including the entire contents of the safe—and loaded it on the Ranger.

That material, including an encrypted address book, was now being evaluated in Washington.

And, of course, Ordóñez's men had conducted their own search of the house. If they had found anything interesting, Ordóñez wasn't saying.

Most of the search was spent going through Lorimer's rather large library one book at a time to see if he had hidden something in the books. Or in the bookcase.

And going through his closets and bureaus, all that turned up was proof that Lorimer had spent a lot of money on luxury clothing.

On an impulse, thinking of the crudely sewn corpse in the British Hospital, Yung took a Louis Vuitton suitcase from a shelf and put in it a nearly black custom-made Italian suit, handmade Hungarian shoes, and a shirt, socks, and underwear, all silk and all bearing labels: SULKA, RUE DE CASTIGLIONE, PARIS.

"What the hell are you doing?" Howell asked, softly.

"Taking this stuff to the undertaker's in Montevideo."

"Why?"

"The last time I saw Lorimer—we saw him—he was naked."

"So what? There's not going to be an open-casket viewing. Who'll know?"

"I will."

"Yung, you're something!" Howell said. He said it with admiration.

Yung had thought of the admiration in Howell's voice on the flight back to Montevideo.

And of other things:

Artigas no longer thinks of me as a jerk, either. I told myself I didn't give a damn what the other FBI guys thought of me before all this happened. I was doing my job and doing it well, even if I couldn't let them know.

But I guess the truth is, I did mind.

And now, after I'm gone, instead of remembering me as the little Chink who was a flaming pain in the ass they'll wonder.

Artigas won't tell them what he suspects happened at the estancia, but they will all conclude that I was somehow involved in something important that they don't know about.

And Castillo, too. He didn't make much of a secret that he thought I was some sort of FBI goody-goody. The only reason he sent me back down here is that I was the only one who could hide the tracks of that sixteen million he made off with.

But he was right about that, too. I can never go back to the FBI. They gave me sort of a pass on being close to Howard Kennedy before he changed sides, sending me to Uruguay for the State Department.

But they won't give me another pass after this. They're going to want to know everything I know about Castillo, and since I won't—couldn't even if I wanted to— tell them anything about a Presidential Finding mission that'll be it. I really would, like Castillo said, wind up investigating parking meter fraud in Kansas for the rest of my career.

Working for Castillo—the Office of Organizational Analysis—now that I think about it, won't be as bad as I originally thought.

It would seem, really, that I have a talent for that sort of thing. I would have given odds that I would have broken out in a cold sweat when I saw where I dropped that Ninja. I didn't.

The sonofabitch had a submachine gun he would have used on me if I hadn't blown him away. Why should I feel guilty about taking him down?

Castillo may not be thrilled about having me. Okay. But he's stuck with me. All I'll have to do is play my cards right and eventually he'll accept me. I can do a lot for OOA. They need somebody like me. And they know when something goes down, I can hold my own. I proved it.

Fuck the FBI!

"You want to get a drink somewhere?" Artigas asked as they walked from the helicopter to their cars.

All of their cars were parked nose up against the Policía Federal hangar. Howell had picked up Artigas that morning and driven him to the airport. Both lived in apartments not far from the embassy on the Rambla. Ordóñez had met them at the airport. Yung had driven to the airport in his own car from his apartment in Carrasco.

"My ass is dragging," Yung replied. "I'm going to get in a shower and then go to bed. I'll see you at the embassy about nine, okay?"

"Your call. Goodnight, Dave," Artigas said, touched Yung's shoulder, and opened the passenger's door of Howell's car.

"Thanks for everything, Ordóñez," Yung said. "I really appreciate all you've done."

"Di nada, mi amigo," Ordóñez said. "I'll probably see you tomorrow."

"Absolutely."

And you won't learn anything more tomorrow than you did today.

Yung put the Louis Vuitton suitcase in the backseat of his Chevy Blazer and got behind the wheel.

It was a ten-minute drive from the airport to Yung's apartment.

He lived in a three-story building, two apartments to a floor, on Avenida Bernardo Barran. All the apartments had balconies overlooking the beach. He thought his—the right-hand apartment on the third floor—had the best view, and he thought that he would probably miss the apartment when he was back living in D.C., where the rents were astronomical and he couldn't afford anything this nice.

Well, fuck it. Maybe working for Castillo, I won't be spending all that much time in Washington.

The garage was in the basement of the building. There was a clicker-activated solenoid that opened the steel-mesh door most of the time when you pushed the button after you pulled off the street and into the steeply slanted driveway.

If the clicker didn't work, you had to get out of the car and open the door with a key.

The clicker didn't work.

Shit!

He turned the ignition off, took the keys from the ignition, and opened the Blazer's door.

As he squeezed past the front fender, he noticed two things. First, the flood-light that went on when you pushed the clicker—even if the goddamned door didn't open—hadn't come on.

What the hell!

And then he noticed that a bag, a cloth—something—was covering the clicker receiver.

What the hell!

And then in the same split second, he saw that a man was coming quickly down the driveway and that a car was entering the drive.

Backward! What the hell?

He pushed his jacket aside and took out his pistol.

There was a sudden burst of light, from a large handheld floodlight.

"Policía!" a voice shouted.

The car—he saw now that it was a small Fiat van—started up the driveway, its tires squealing.

The man coming down the driveway shielded his eyes from the floodlight. Then he put his other hand to his eyes. That hand held a pistol.

"Don't shoot him!" Yung screamed, in Spanish.

There came three shots—booms rather than cracks, telling Yung they were from a shotgun and not a pistol—and the man who had been shielding his eyes looked as if something had shoved him hard against the concrete driveway wall. He slid down it.

Yung dropped his pistol and raised his hands over his head. He started screaming, *"Policía! Policía! Policía!"*

Something warm dripped onto his face.

In a moment, he realized that he was bleeding.

A Uruguayan policeman, a sergeant with his pistol drawn, came down the driveway.

"Are you all right, Señor Yung?"

How the hell did he know my name?

"May I put my hands down?"

"Of course, Señor," the sergeant said, then added, "You've been hit, Señor Yung!"

Yung looked at his left hand. It looked as if someone had gouged a two-inch-long, quarter-inch-deep channel across it. It was starting to bleed profusely.

Yung thought: *There are usually twelve pellets, with a total weight of 1.5 ounces, in a 00-Buckshot cartridge. Each pellet has roughly the knockdown power of a .32 ACP bullet.*

Wyatt Earp fired three times. That translated to thirty-six pellets, each with roughly the knockdown power of a .32 ACP slug bouncing around in the OK Corral here. I guess I'm lucky I got only one of them.

He leaned against the wall and took out his handkerchief.

When he applied the handkerchief as a pressure bandage to his hand, he saw there were at least a half dozen holes in the glass and metal of the Blazer.

IX

[ONE]
Aeropuerto Internacional Jorge Newbery
Buenos Aires, Argentina
0720 8 August 2005

Castillo had flown in the right seat on the last leg from Recife, Brazil, with Torine in the left seat. But as they had approached Jorge Newbery, Torine had said, "If you have your ego under control, First Officer, you may land the aircraft."

And then, when they had shut down the Gulfstream on the tarmac in front of the JetAire hangar, Torine had two more comments.

"You came in a little long, Charley."

"I know."

"The less the gross weight, the harder these are to get on the ground."

"I'll remember."

Torine handed him the plastic envelope holding the aircraft documents.

"Dealing with the local authorities is beneath the dignity of the captain," Torine said.

"Yes, sir," Castillo said.

When he came down the stair door, Castillo saw that in addition to the Argentine customs and immigration authorities a Mercedes Traffik van also was there to meet the Gulfstream.

The driver was leaning against the van. Castillo recognized him. He was a CIA agent named Paul Sieno. He had met him the morning they had found J. Winslow Masterson's body. And when he looked closer at the van, he saw another man he recognized, Ricardo Solez, of the Drug Enforcement Administration.

Jesus, I hope Fernando doesn't take one look at him, get carried away, and pick Ricardo up in a bear hug!

Sieno walked over and in heavily accented English said, "We are from the estancia, señor, when you have finished with these officers."

"Thank you," Castillo said and turned to the Argentine officials. "Where would you like us to put our luggage for exam—"

Max came bounding down—more accurately, over—the steps in the stair door and headed for the nose gear, where he raised his leg.

The Argentine customs officer smiled.

"That won't be necessary, sir. If we can go aboard, we'll deal with the passports."

"You are very kind," Castillo said.

He went quickly back into the fuselage.

"Passports, please, everybody," he called. "And then please board the van, which will take us to the estancia."

Eric Kocian's bushy white eyebrow rose at that, but he said nothing. He handed the immigration officer his passport as if it identified him as the personal representative of, if not God, then at least the pope.

"Welcome to Argentina, señor," the immigration officer said.

Five minutes later, everyone was in the van and had left the airport.

"Where's this estancia we're going?" Castillo asked Sieno when it seemed to him the van was not headed for any of the highways leading to the countryside.

"In Belgrano," Sieno replied, chuckling. "Fifteen-sixty-eight Arribeños."

Belgrano was one of Buenos Aires's upscale neighborhoods.

"What's there?"

"My apartment, Major," Sieno said. "Sixteenth floor."

"Your apartment?"

"The Cuban embassy is on the next corner. We use the apartment to take pictures of people going into the embassy and to grab their radio transmissions. Not exactly a safe house, but there's a steel door and TV monitors, and Alex Darby figured it will do until you decide what you really need."

"He's a colonel now," Solez called from the backseat, and added for Castillo, "Doña Alicia sent me an e-mail."

"You and Doña Alicia have big mouths," Castillo said and then asked Sieno, "Where is Alex Darby?"

"I'm hoping he'll be at the apartment when we get there."

"And Tony Santini?"

"Your Major Miller called Darby, Maj—*Colonel*—and asked him to have somebody meet the seven twenty-five American Airlines flight from Miami. Tony said he'd do it. I overheard enough of the conversation to think that the corporal—from the Marine guard detachment at the embassy—you took to the States and some other military type, a replacement for the guy you lost, will be on it."

I wonder what the hell that's all about? Castillo thought, and then said it: "What's that about?"

"I don't have any idea, but Alex should be at the apartment when we get there and he'll know."

"Paul, can you get out of the habit of calling me Colonel? My name is Charley."

"Sure."

"And you, Ricardo, get in the habit of keeping your mouth shut."

"You going to tell Abuela that, *Colonel* Gringo?" Fernando asked, coming to Ricardo's aid.

Castillo ignored him and asked, "Where's Sergeant Kensington?"

"All alone—except for his radio, of course—in that luxury suite of yours in the Four Seasons," Solez said.

"Darby decided keeping him there, and the radio linkup, was more important than worrying about what that's costing," Sieno said. "At least until he heard from you."

"I am often known as the last of the big spenders," Castillo said.

He had a sudden flash of memory: Betty Schneider in his arms in the enormous bed in the master bedroom of the El Presidente de la Rua suite at the Four Seasons Hotel.

And then these bastards shot her.

And I didn't—as promised—go to see her before I started this round of the Grand Tour of Europe and South America.

I'm either a dedicated professional who allows nothing to get in the way of carrying out the mission or a four-star, world-class prick.

And if Betty believes the latter, who can blame her?

Well, I'll get on my knees, apologize, and beg for forgiveness when I see her.

[TWO]

The apartment building at 1568 Avenida Arribeños was on the corner of Avenida José Hernandez, a block off Avenida Libertador. The lobby, behind walls of plate glass, was brightly lit, and Castillo wondered if the Cubans—tit for tat—might be keeping it under surveillance.

Rule 17: Always give the bad guys more credit for smarts than they probably deserve. If Darby is working on their embassy, they almost certainly know it. They may not be able to do anything to stop the snooping, but they certainly can take pictures of everybody going into the apartment building and pass them around.

He felt a sense of relief when the Traffik turned off Avenida Arribeños, crossed the sidewalk, and almost immediately disappeared from sight down a steep ramp into a basement garage.

Castillo spotted surveillance cameras in the garage and another in the elevator, and still another when the elevator opened onto a foyer on the sixteenth floor. He had just decided that the cameras in the basement and elevator were connected with the apartment building's security system but that the one in the foyer might not be when he spotted a third lens hidden in the tack of a prancing-stallion wall decoration.

That one goes to a monitor inside the apartment.

The door from the foyer was steel. Sieno unlocked it by punching in a series of numbers on a small numerical keyboard. When Sieno pulled the door open, Castillo was surprised to see another steel door behind it, and even more surprised when that door opened inward, revealing a trim, pale, freckled redhead in a white blouse and blue jeans who smiled and said, "Welcome!"

Everyone filed inside.

"Gentlemen, this is my wife, Susanna," Sieno said, and then, pointing, "Susanna, this is Mr. Smith, Mr. Smith, Mr. Smith, Mr. Smith, Mr. Smith, and, of course, you know Ricardo."

"I'm very pleased to meet you all," she said. "How are you, Ricardo?"

Sieno smiled and said, "I was hoping the boss would be here before we got here, so he could make the introductions."

"I'm a little surprised that your wife is here," Castillo said, not very pleasantly.

"Well, she both lives here and works here," Sieno said. "Another reason I was hoping the boss would get here before we did, so he could explain that."

"Why don't I get us all some coffee while we're waiting?" Mrs. Sieno said.

"Paul, why would I not be surprised to learn your charming wife has a security clearance—clearances—not normally given to diplomats' wives?" Castillo said.

"Actually, she has several. Some with names."

"Issued here? Or?"

"In Virginia, as a matter of fact," Mrs. Sieno said.

"I've heard of husband-and-wife teams," Castillo said. "But this is the first one I've ever actually met."

"We're double-dippers," Susanna Sieno said. "The rule is that both can get paid only if both were field officers *before* they marched down the aisle."

Castillo smiled at her and then said, "Okay. Let me make if official. Anything that you hear here or see here, Mrs. Sieno, is classified Top Secret Presidential."

"I understand."

Castillo thought: *Only a Langley chairwarmer who's never been in the field would be naïve enough to think that Sieno hasn't told her—she's not only his wife but a working spook—everything that's happened from the moment Mrs. Masterson was grabbed.*

Including that a hotshot named Castillo showed up down here and started giving everybody, including the station chief, orders.

That's why she told me she was a double-dipper, a spook herself, not just married to one.

"That being understood between us, I'm Charley Castillo. This is Colonel Jake Torine, my cousin Fernando Lopez, Sándor Tor, and Eric Kocian."

"And that is Max," Billy Kocian said in English as he walked to her and— somewhat startling her—took and kissed the hand she extended to him. "It is my great pleasure, madam."

There was the sound of door chimes playing a melody as if one chime didn't work.

"That's probably the boss," Susanna Sieno said. "The chimes go off when somebody pushes the clicker for the garage door."

She turned and opened what looked like a closet door. Behind the door was a bank of monitors. One showed a Jeep Cherokee waiting for the door to the basement garage to open. Others showed the garage, the elevator, the foyer outside, the lobby, the sidewalks outside, and several antennae on the roof.

Eric Kocian's eyebrows rose but he said nothing.

One of the monitors showed the Jeep Cherokee pulling into a slot in the garage. Alex Darby got out. A monitor showed him unloading a large duffel bag that looked like it contained heavy metal objects—like guns—and walking toward the elevator.

Mrs. Sieno opened the door to the foyer before the elevator got there. Darby walked into the apartment, set the heavy bag down, and put out his hand to Castillo.

Castillo took it and said, "Good to see you, Alex."

Darby had just put out his hand to Torine when the chimes with one missing note sounded again. Everyone looked at the monitors. There was now a Volkswagen Passat station wagon waiting for the door to completely open.

Other monitors showed the Passat parking and Tony Santini, a Secret Service agent, getting out and going to the back of the vehicle and raising the rear hatch. Sergeant Major Jack Davidson, USA, and Corporal Lester Bradley, USMC, both in civilian clothing, got out and joined Santini at the back of the station wagon.

Castillo grinned slightly.

Davidson! I don't know how you got down here, Jack, but am I glad to see you!

When the monitor showed them inside the elevator, it also showed Davidson looking around for—and then spotting—the monitor camera lens.

Castillo looked at Torine and saw in his raised eyebrow that he had recognized Davidson, too. Torine saw that Castillo was watching him and raised his eyebrow even higher but didn't say anything.

Susanna Sieno opened the door for them.

Davidson, smiling, put his suitcase down and saluted Castillo.

"Good morning, Colonel," he said. "May the sergeant major offer his congratulations on your promotion?"

"The sergeant major may. But the colonel is surprised that the sergeant major doesn't know you're not supposed to salute when not in uniform," Castillo said.

"The sergeant major begs the colonel's pardon for his breach of military custom."

They looked at each other, then chuckled.

Castillo said, "I don't know what you're doing here, Jack, but—and I know I shouldn't tell you this—I'm damned glad you are."

"Oh, goody!" Davidson said and spread his arms wide as he approached Castillo, then wrapped him in a bear hug, crying, "It's good to see you, Charley!"

When he freed himself, Castillo turned to Bradley.

"I'm not so sure about you, Lester," he said. "I thought you were safely on ice at Mackall."

"That was not one of your brightest ideas," Davidson said. "Deadeye Dick stood out in Mackall like a whor—"

Davidson saw Susanna Sieno.

"Like a lady of dubious virtue in a place of worship?" she furnished, smiling.

"Yes, ma'am."

"Mrs. Sieno, Sergeant Major Jack Davidson," Castillo said.

"You can call me Susanna," she said.

"Good to see you, Jack," Jake Torine said to Davidson. They shook hands. The other introductions were made.

Alex Darby said, "Before this goes any further, I need a private word with you and Tony, Charley."

Castillo nodded.

"Okay if we go in there, Susanna?" Darby asked, gesturing toward a door.

"Of course," she replied.

[THREE]

Darby led them into a large marble-walled bathroom. The bathtub and the separate shower were stacked high with electronic equipment and there was more on a long, twin-basin washstand. The water closet was still functional, but there were racks of electronics rising almost to the ceiling on either side of it.

"We're watching the Cubans," Darby explained. "Not so much them as the people who go in and out of their embassy. And, of course, their communications. Sometimes, that's very interesting."

"Sieno told me."

Darby turned to face him.

"You've got me on a spot again, Charley," he said. "Ambassador Montvale called me and said I was to call him immediately—him personally, not through the agency—if you showed up here."

Castillo nodded and then asked, "*If* I showed up here, or *when?*"

"If," Darby said. "So what I've done—or didn't do—was not call him to let him know you had called from Recife. But now that you're here . . . you tell me what you want me to do."

"Call him and tell him I'm here. Better yet, call him and tell him I called you to tell you to call him and tell him I'm here and will call him as soon as I have a chance."

Darby considered that a moment.

Then he turned and picked up a heavily corded telephone sitting on top of the water reservoir of the toilet, then looked at Castillo.

"It's half past six in the morning in Washington," he said, making it a question.

"The ambassador said immediately, didn't he?"

Darby shrugged and put the telephone to his ear.

"This is Darby. Get me a secure line to the Langley switchboard," he ordered.

"Oh, the miracle of modern communications!" Castillo said.

"How did the ambassador react to having his sleep disturbed?" Santini asked.

"He asked what else Charley had had to say."

"And when you told him I had had nothing else to say?" Castillo asked.

"And when I told him that, he said when you called to tell you to call him immediately."

"Okay. Give me until noon and then call him and tell him you have relayed his message to me."

Darby nodded again.

"What's the problem with you and Montvale, Charley?" Santini asked.

"He has a tendency to try to tell me what to do," Castillo said. "As in, '*Tell* Castillo to call me immediately.' "

"Well, he *is* the director of National Intelligence," Santini said. "Maybe he feels that entitles him to order a lowly lieutenant colonel around."

"You heard about that, huh?"

"You got promoted, Charley?" Darby asked.

Castillo nodded.

"From both the director of National Intelligence and Corporal Bradley," Santini said. "Congratulations, Charley."

"Thank you. After what happened in Afghanistan, I was beginning to think I'd never get promoted."

"Based on my personal knowledge of what happened in Afghanistan," Darby said, "that was a reasonable conclusion to draw."

"The bottom line," Castillo said, "is that I made a deal with Montvale. In theory, I tell him what I'm doing and plan to do and he leaves me alone and helps me."

"Helps you how?"

"For example, getting to use the agency's air taxi services."

"Then why are you dodging him?"

"I told you, because he's still trying to tell me what to do. Tit for tat, I don't tell him any more about what I'm going to do than I have to."

Darby shook his head.

"Which leaves Tony and me between a rock and a hard place," Darby said. "Okay, so who's the old guy?"

"His name is Eric Kocian. He runs the Budapest *Tages Zeitung.* He's been looking into the oil-for-food scandal."

"That could be dangerous. How much has he found out?"

"Enough so there have been two attempts to kidnap him to see how much. The other Hungarian—his name is Sándor Tor—is an ex-cop who before that did a hitch in the French Foreign Legion. He kept the first attempt to kidnap/ whack Kocian from coming off. One of those guys—there were three; two got away—told the cops he was a vacationing housepainter from Dresden and had the papers to prove it."

"You don't think he was?" Santini asked, and then, when Castillo shook his head, asked, "So who were they?"

"I'm guessing ex-Stasi. But I don't know that. And I have no idea who they're working for. The second time they tried to kidnap and/or whack Kocian, there were two guys. They had Madsens and no identification. Like the people at the estancia."

"What's their story?" Santini asked.

"I had to take them down. So I don't know more than I told you."

"You had to take them down?" Darby asked, and then, after Castillo nodded, he shook his head and asked, "And how many waves did that make?"

"I hope none. Sándor took them away in their car."

Darby shook his head again.

"You can't keeping walking through the raindrops forever, Charley."

"That thought has occurred to me. I didn't have any choice, Alex."

"If they're ex-Stasi, who are they working for now?" Santini asked.

Castillo shrugged.

"That's what I'm hoping to find out. Kocian gave me everything he had. So did Ed Delchamps in Paris."

"Ed's a good man," Darby said. "So you put him on the spot with Montvale, too?"

"I suppose it's very unprofessional of Delchamps getting emotionally involved, but I have the feeling he's as pissed off at these people as I am. Or maybe with the agency for doing nothing with what he's been sending them."

"I guess that makes me unprofessional, too. Jack Masterson was a friend of mine," Darby said. "I'd really like to nail these bastards."

"What does that make, counting me?" Santini asked. "Four amateurs?"

"And I think Yung may have something in his files . . . and may not know it," Castillo said. "Speaking of him, where is he?"

"Odd that you should ask," Darby said. "I was just about to say, 'Speaking of coincidences.' "

"What are you talking about?"

"Guess who got shot in Montevideo last night by parties unknown?"

"Yung?" Castillo asked, incredulously.

"They were waiting for him at his apartment when he came back from the estancia. They probably would have got him—by which I mean grabbed him— if the Uruguayan cops hadn't been sitting on him."

"How bad is he hurt?"

"The Uruguayan cops got one of the guys going after him with three shots of double-aught buckshot. The others, probably two, got away. Yung took one pellet in his left hand. Just gouged it. No bone damage, just a canal. Yung's like you, Charley: he walks through raindrops. He was standing right next to the bad guy when the cops took him out."

"And the guy the cops shot?"

"No identification. But he did have a hypo full of ketamine—a strong tranquilizer—that I think he wanted to stick in Yung."

"Jesus Christ!" Castillo exclaimed.

"You got the word that Ambassador McGrory thinks Lorimer was a drug dealer?"

Castillo nodded.

"Well, he's been told that the people who shot Yung were carjackers."

"The Uruguayan cops went along with that?"

Darby nodded.

"For reasons of their own, they suggested that story to Yung. I can't imagine why."

"Neither can I."

"Well, if McGrory believes Lorimer was a drug dealer, he'll probably conclude that the Uruguayan cops know Yung was shot by another drug dealer and don't want to admit. I sure hope so. If McGrory finds out what really happened at that estancia, the shit will really hit the fan. And some of it will splatter on Ambassador Silvio and I don't like that."

"Can you contact Yung? Is he in the hospital?"

"He wouldn't stay. He's in his apartment. Bob Howell is sitting on him, Howell and another FBI agent who was at the estancia, and—bad news— according to Howell has figured out what really happened at the estancia."

"Well, let's get him over here. I don't want him grabbed in Montevideo. How soon can you get him here?"

"Two hours from the time I call him," Darby said, nodding at the telephone.

"That raises the question of a safe house," Castillo said. "I don't think this place is going to work. Too many people for one thing. Can we use the place we used before?"

"Mayerling? No and, maybe, yes."

"Come on, Alex."

"The place we used before is not available," Darby said. "But there's a place for rent out there that would really be better."

"Rent it," Castillo said. "How quickly can you do that?"

"The problem there is the rent. Four thousand a month. First and last month due on signing, plus another two months up front for a security deposit. That's sixteen thousand. I have just about that much in my black account. If I ask for more, Langley's going to want to know what for."

"Money's not a problem," Castillo said. "We now have the Lorimer Charitable and Benevolent Fund to draw on."

"The what?"

"Lorimer had almost sixteen million in three banks in Montevideo. Most of it is now in the Liechtensteinische Landesbank in the Cayman Islands."

"In your account?" Darby asked.

Castillo nodded.

"How'd you manage that?"

"You don't want to know," Castillo said. "I spent seven million five of it to buy an airplane. A Gulfstream."

"You bought a *Gulfstream* with Lorimer's money?" Santini asked, incredulously.

Castillo, smiling, nodded.

"A G-III. It's really nice, Tony, to be able to avoid all that frisking and baggage searching and standing in line at airports. You really ought to get one for yourself."

"Jesus Christ, Charley! You're insane!" Darby said. "What's Montvale going to do when he hears you stole Lorimer's money and then bought a Gulfstream with it?"

"Actually, taking the money was Montvale's idea. I think he saw it as a source of unaccountable funds for him. Which, of course, it would be if I didn't control it. And I haven't gotten around to telling him about the airplane yet."

"And when he finds out?"

"All he can do is go to the President and tell him—as he predicted—that I have acted impulsively and unwisely and the airplane is the proof. On the other hand, he may decide it's a good idea. If he can get the Office of Organizational Analysis under him—which is his announced intention—the airplane would come with it."

"And what's the President going to do when he finds out about the money?" Santini asked.

"He knows about the money," Castillo said. "Which brings us back to that. How do I get the rent money to you, Alex?"

Darby thought that over a moment before replying.

"The black account is in the Banco Galicia. The agency wires money into it from a Swiss account. I suppose you could do the same thing."

"How long would it take to wire it from the Riggs Bank? Before you could get at the money?"

"I don't know. Twenty-four hours, I'd guess."

"You give me the numbers and the routing and I'll call Dick Miller and have him wire a hundred thousand down here. There's going to be other expenses, and I'm going to have to give Davidson some walking-around money, too."

"Is Davidson who I think he is?" Darby asked.

"That would depend on who you think he is."

"If I'm not mistaken, the last time I saw him was in Kabul. You were both wearing robes and beards. That was when you were in charge of babysitting the eager young men Langley sent over there to win that war in two weeks."

"Yeah, that was Jack. And he never lost one of those starry-eyed young men, either. I was really glad to see him get out of your car."

"You didn't know he was coming?" Santini asked.

Castillo shook his head, then asked, "While we're waiting for the money to get here, can you rent this house right away—today, maybe—with the money you have?"

"I can," Darby said. "You sure you don't want to stash the old man here?"

"His name is Eric Kocian," Castillo said. "He's both a very old friend and a good guy. I would love to stash him here but I don't think he'd stay. A house in Mayerling might be just what he's looking for. He thinks—because of the name—that there might be a connection with Austrians or Hungarians involved in the oil-for-food business."

"I don't understand," Darby confessed.

"You don't know the story? Shame on you, Alex."

"What story?" Santini asked.

"Mayerling was the Imperial Hunting Lodge of Franz Joséf. It was in May-erling that Crown Prince Rudolph, after his father told him he had to get rid of some sixteen-year-old baroness he was banging, that he whacked the baroness and then shot himself. That's one version. The one I got from my Hungarian aunt—the version Kocian believes—is that Franz Joséf had the crown prince whacked after he learned the kid was talking to the Hungarians about becom-ing king of Hungary. Kocian thinks maybe Mayerling, the country club, was built with oil-for-food money and named Mayerling to be clever."

"That sounds pretty far-fetched, Charley," Santini said.

"So does six guys dressed like Ninja characters in a comic strip going to Estancia Shangri-La to whack Lorimer. I'm not saying I believe Kocian, but, on the other hand, he's one hell of a journalist. Whoever's trying to whack him thinks he knows more than he should. Anyway, if I can get him out there and keep him alive for a couple of days, maybe I can get the bad guys to back off."

"How are you going to do that?" Darby asked.

"You don't want to know, Alex."

Darby shrugged.

"What I need now," Castillo said, "is the boxes I sent to the embassy under diplomatic seal and a black car."

"Ambassador Silvio turned them over to me and didn't even ask what was in them. He's a good guy, Charley. I really don't want him to get burned in this."

"I'll do my best to see that doesn't happen," Castillo said. "Where are the boxes now?"

"In the backseat of the Cherokee," Darby said, and added, "which is regis-tered to a guy in Mar del Plata." He tossed Castillo a set of keys. "Registration's in the glove compartment."

"Thanks," Castillo said. "Now, let me get on the horn to Dick Miller and get some money down here."

Darby nodded.

"Do you—either of you—have to rush back to the embassy?" Castillo asked. "Or would you have time to look at some of Kocian's files and see if anything rings a bell? At least until I get back?"

"Back from where?"

"Where I'm going, Alex," Castillo said, smiling.

"Curiosity underwhelms me. I'll make time," Darby said, smiling back.

"Me, too," Santini said.

As he picked up the heavily corded telephone, Darby asked, "White House, right?"

"Right."

"Darby again," Darby said into the telephone. "Get me a secure line to the White House switchboard."

[FOUR]
Pilar, Buenos Aires Province, Argentina
1025 8 August 2005

Castillo was glad when he saw the sign indicating the exit from Route 8 to the Pilar Sheraton Hotel. He hadn't been certain that he was on the right road to the Buena Vista Country Club or, for that matter, even on the right road to Pilar.

He hadn't been able to ask directions from Santini or Darby; that would have given them more than a hint of where he was going. He had had trouble getting on the Panamericana, the toll highway that led to Pilar, but he'd finally—after ten minutes—found it.

And then he had trouble with the tollbooth. He had sat there for Christ only knew how long, holding a ten-peso note out the window with angry horns bleating behind him, until the horns finally woke him up to the fact that not only was there no attendant in the booth but that the barrier pole was up.

As he pulled away, he saw an electronic gadget mounted inside the windshield, under the rearview mirror. The gadget had triggered the barrier-raising mechanism as he approached. He hadn't noticed it.

From the tollbooth to the sign pointing to the Sheraton Hotel exit, he had wondered about a number of things, including how he was going to get past the gate of the Buena Vista Country Club once he got there—if he got there. And what he was going to do if Aleksandr Pevsner wasn't there. Or was there and didn't want to see him.

And how he was going to protect Eric Kocian if he couldn't get through to Pevsner, presuming he could get past the Buena Vista Country Club gate to get in to see him.

He knew that he wasn't functioning well and the reason for it.

In the past forty-eight hours—give or take; having crossed through so many time zones, he didn't know how long it had been in real time—he had flown across the North Atlantic, then, at the controls of an airplane he'd never flown before, across the Mediterranean. And then, while Jake and Fernando were flying across the South Atlantic, instead of crashing on one of the Gulfstream's comfortable couches he'd consumed at least a gallon of coffee so he could stay awake while trying to make some sense of Eric Kocian's notes, much of which had been written in abbreviations known only to Kocian. And then he'd made his second takeoff and landing in the Gulfstream, coming down from Recife.

And while he had been making a whirlwind tour of Paris, Fulda, and Budapest, there had been an attempt on his life, which had forced him to kill two people. Killing people always bothered him even when it was necessary.

He knew that he was exhausted and that what he should be doing—especially if he was going to have to deal with Aleksandr Pevsner, where he would really need all his faculties, presuming he was going to be able to see Aleksandr Pevsner—was to crash for at least twenty-four hours.

The problem there was, he didn't think he had twenty-four hours.

He approached the Pilar exit from Route 8.

If memory serves—and please, God, let it serve—I get off here, make a sharp left onto the highway overpass, drive past the Jumbo supermarket on the left and the Mercedes showroom on the right, take the next right and then the next left, a nd then drive past the hospital, and, four clicks later, maybe a little less, turn right into the Buena Vista Country Club, where I probably won't be able to get in. Or Pevsner won't be there.

There was a red traffic light when he reached the intersection where he was to turn right.

For the first time, he looked at the instrument panel. A warning light was flashing. The fuel gauge needle was resting on EMPTY.

"Oh, fuck! You've done it again, Inspector Clouseau!"

There was a Shell gas station to his immediate left. But there also was a steady line of oncoming traffic that kept him from turning into it. And when the light turned green, he realized that his first idea—waiting for a chance to make the turn—was impractical. There was a symphony of automobile horns blasting angrily behind him.

He made the right turn and then the left, and there was an ESSO station right in front of him.

He pulled in.

"Thank God!"

Two attendants appeared.

"Fill it up," Castillo ordered.

He took his wallet from his pocket to get his credit card.

He dropped it.

It bounced under the car and he and one of the attendants got on their hands and knees to retrieve it.

He stood up.

A tall, dark-haired, well-dressed man who appeared to be in his late thirties was walking purposefully toward the service station's restroom.

Jesus Christ, I'm hallucinating. That guy looks just like Pevsner!

He looked around the pumps. There was a black Mercedes-Benz S600 at the next row of pumps. A burly man was speaking to the attendant. Another burly man walked to the hood of the car and leaned against the fender and watched the door to the men's room.

Castillo walked to the men's room, pushed the door open, and walked to the urinal next to the man, who didn't turn to look at him.

"I just love these service station pissoirs," Castillo announced, in Russian. "You never know who you'll bump into in one of them."

Aleksandr Pevsner's head snapped to look at him.

The hairs on the back of Castillo's neck rose.

His eyes are like ice.

And then Pevsner smiled.

The door of the men's room opened and the burly man who had been leaning on the Mercedes came in. He had his hand inside his suit jacket.

"If he takes out a gun, Alek, I'll have to kill him," Castillo said.

"It's all right, János," Pevsner said, in Hungarian. "The gentleman and I are old friends." Then he switched to English. "How nice to see you, Charley. And quite a surprise. I somehow had the idea you were in the United States."

"Well, I get around a lot."

"And what brings you to this service station pissoir?"

"Aside from having to take a leak, you mean?"

"Uh-huh," Pevsner said, chuckling.

"Actually, bearing a small gift, I was on my way to see you."

"What is it they say? 'A small world'? Or is it 'truth is stranger than fiction'?"

"Some people say both," Castillo said.

Pevsner turned from the urinal and walked to the washbasins. Castillo heard water running, then the sound of the hot-air blower of the hand dryer.

"I hate these things," Pevsner announced.

Castillo finished and turned around. The burly Hungarian was gone. Castillo washed his hands, put them under the dryer, and said, "Me, too."

Then he offered his hand to Pevsner, who took it and then wrapped his arm around Castillo's shoulder and hugged him.

Then he turned him loose, put his hands on Castillo's arms, and looked into his eyes.

"You are a man of many surprises, Charley."

"I guess I should have called and told you I was coming."

"That would have been a good idea. Am I supposed to believe you just walked in here and were surprised to see me?"

"No, I knew you were in here," Castillo said. "I had just told the attendant to fill my tank—I was running on fumes when I pulled in—when I saw you headed for the men's room."

Pevsner smiled at him but didn't say anything.

"If you doubt me, Alek, check the pump to see how much they've pumped into it."

"Oh, I trust you, Charley. Why would you lie to me?"

"Thank you. I would never lie to you unless it was necessary."

Pevsner smiled.

"Well, let's go out to the house and have what the Viennese call a *kleines Frühstück.*"

"Thank you."

Pevsner waved him ahead of him out of the men's room. When they were outside, he walked directly to the pump beside the Cherokee and examined the dial.

"You were really out of petrol, weren't you?"

"You have a suspicious soul, Alek."

"In my line of business, I have to," Pevsner said. "Why don't we have János drive your Cherokee? If you wouldn't mind? That would get us past the guards at the gate to Buena Vista easier."

"The keys are in it," Castillo said. "Just let me pay the bill."

"János," Pevsner ordered in Hungarian, "settle my friend's bill, then drive his car to the house."

"You are too generous, Alek."

As the Mercedes approached the redbrick, red-tile-roofed guardhouse at the entrance to the Buena Vista Country Club, the yellow-and-black-striped barrier pole across the road went up. They rolled past the two uniformed guards standing outside the guardhouse. Castillo saw two more inside, standing before a rack of what looked like Ithaca pump riot shotguns.

The Mercedes rolled slowly—neat signs proclaimed a 30-kph speed limit and speed bumps reinforced it—down a curving road, past long rows of upscale houses set on well-manicured half-hectare lots. They passed several polo fields lined with large houses, then the clubhouse of a well-maintained golf course. There were thirty or so cars in the parking lot.

They came next to an area of larger houses on much larger lots, most of them ringed with shrubbery tall enough so that only the upper floors of the houses were visible. Castillo saw that the shrubbery also concealed fences.

"This is really a very nice place, Alek," Castillo said.

"And it never snows," Pevsner said.

The car slowed, then turned right through a still-opening sliding steel door the same shade of green as the double rows of closely planted pines cropped at about twelve feet. There was a fence of the same height between the rows.

Inside, Castillo saw Pevsner's Bell Ranger helicopter parked, its rotors tied down, on what looked like a putting green. A man in white coveralls was polishing the Plexiglas.

Then the house, an English-looking near mansion of red brick with casement windows, came into view. Another burly man in a suit was standing outside waiting for them.

"Come on in," Pevsner said, opening the door before the burly man could reach it. "I'm looking forward to my *kleines Frühstück*. All I had before I took Aleksandr and Sergei into Buenos Aires was a cup of tea."

He waited until Castillo had slid across the seat and gotten out and then went on: "They were late—again—getting to Saint Agnes's, which meant they missed the bus to Buenos Aires, which meant that I had to take them."

"What are they going to do in Buenos Aires?"

"Tour the Colon Opera House. You know, backstage. Did you know, Charley, the Colon is larger than the Vienna Opera House?"

"And Paris's, too," Castillo said. "The design criteria was make it larger than both. That, of course, was when Argentina had money."

"You know something about everything, don't you?" Pevsner said as he led Castillo up a shallow flight of stairs and into the house.

A middle-aged maid was waiting in the foyer, her hands folded on her small, crisply starched white apron.

Pevsner said, in Russian, "Be so good as to ask madam if she is free to join Mr. . . ."

He hesitated and looked at Castillo.

"Castillo," Charley furnished.

". . . *Castillo* and I in the breakfast room."

When the maid bobbed her head, Pevsner switched to Hungarian and added, "I hope that since Herr Gossinger is not here, that means Señor Castillo is not working."

"You're out of luck," Castillo said. "And actually, Alek, I know everything about everything. Like you."

A glass-topped table in the French-windowed breakfast room was set with linen and silver for two. Pevsner waved Charley into one of the chairs and a moment later a maid—a different one, this one young and, Castillo suspected, Argentine—came in, pulled a third chair to the table, and set a third place.

"Bring tea for me, please," Pevsner ordered, "and coffee for Señor Castillo."

She had just finished when János appeared in the door, dangling the keys to the Cherokee delicately in sausagelike fingers.

Castillo put his hand out for them, then said, "I would ask János to bring in your present, but it's not for the house and he'd only have to carry it out again."

"Where should it go?"

"Who maintains the avionics in your Ranger?" Castillo asked.

When he saw the confusion on Pevsner's face, he added: "What I've done is get you some decent avionics for your helicopter."

"What's wrong with the avionics in it?"

"On a scale of one to ten, they're maybe one-point-five."

"I was assured they were the best available."

"Write this down, Alek. Never trust someone selling used cars or aircraft."

"You're saying I was cheated?"

His eyes are cold again.

"Of course not," Castillo said, chuckling. "Everyone knows you can't cheat an honest man. All I'm saying is that you don't have the best available and, as a small token of my gratitude for past courtesies, now you do."

Pevsner looked at him and smiled.

"What is it they say down here? Beware of Americans bearing gifts?"

A tall, trim woman with her hair done up in a long pigtail came into the room.

"What a pleasant surprise, Charley!" she exclaimed, in Russian.

Castillo stood and kissed her cheek.

"It's nice to see you, Anna," he said. "Alek saw me on the street, saw that I was starving, and offered me breakfast."

"Actually, he accosted me in the men's room of the ESSO service station just past the hospital," Pevsner said.

She looked at her husband, then at Castillo.

"I never know when he's teasing," she said.

"Neither do I," Castillo said.

"Regardless of where you met, I'm glad you're here," she said. "And so far as breakfast is concerned, how about American pancakes with tree syrup?"

"Maple syrup, maybe?"

"Maple syrup," she confirmed. "They bleed trees to make it?"

"Indeed they do."

"There's an American boy—actually, there's several—in Aleksandr's class at Saint Agnes's. They sometimes spend the night together, at the boy's house or here. They served Aleksandr pancakes with *maple* syrup for breakfast. He couldn't get enough. So that's what they gave him for his birthday present. A bag of the flour"—she demonstrated the size of a five-pound bag with her hands—"and a liter can of the syrup."

"How nice for Aleksandr."

"And, of course, Alek's curiosity got the best of him and . . ."

"Tell me about bleeding the tree," Pevsner said.

"Actually, they tap it. Maple trees. In the winter, when it's cold. They drive a sort of funnel into the tree, the sap drips out into a cup below the funnel, they collect it and boil it until it's thick. That's all there is to it."

"Extraordinary," Pevsner said.

"We Americans are an extraordinary people, Alek. I thought you knew that."

The older maid appeared with the tea and coffee and Anna ordered pancakes with sausage. The maid, looking uncomfortable, reported she wasn't sure there was enough flour left to make pancakes for everybody.

"Then just forget it," Castillo said. "I don't want to steal Alek Junior's breakfast."

"Nonsense," Pevsner announced. "Make what you have, and I'll see about getting more of the flour."

"I'm sure they sell it in the embassy store," Castillo said. "I'll get you some before I go."

"Go where?"

"To the States."

"And when will that be?"

"Tomorrow maybe. More likely, the day after tomorrow."

"Oh, Charley," Anna Pevsner said, laying her hand on his, "could you really? I've tried every store in Buenos Aires and they just look at me as if I'm crazy."

"Consider it done."

And if that store in the embassy doesn't have any, the chief of the Office of Organizational Analysis will make sure there's five—ten—pounds of the best pancake flour available in the next diplomatic pouch.

Pleasing Madam Pevsner and Alek Junior is sure to please Alek Senior. Probably more than the fifty thousand—maybe more—dollars' worth of avionics in the Cherokee.

"How would you get it out here?" Pevsner asked.

The translation of that is, "Without anybody learning A. Pevsner, prominent Russian mafioso and international arms dealer, resides in the Buena Vista Country Club?"

"If I can't bring it myself, maybe you could have János meet me someplace."

"You just say when and where, Charley," Pevsner said, "and János will be there. Alek is really crazy for pancakes."

"Both of them are," Anna said.

"Or maybe Howard Kennedy can meet me," Castillo said. "He's in the Four Seasons, right? Where I'm staying?"

"Howard's not here right now," Pevsner said.

"Well, then, maybe Colonel Munz?"

"Didn't he tell you, Charley?" Anna said.

"Tell me what?"

"You're not going to believe this," she said, "and I know I shouldn't be smiling, but he is or was a policeman for all those years before he came to work for Alek. What he did, Charley, was shoot himself in the shoulder while he was cleaning his pistol."

"Is he all right?" Castillo asked, looking at Pevsner.

"He's fine," Pevsner said.

"And terribly embarrassed," Anna said.

"Well, give him my best regards," Castillo said. "Don't mention that you told me what happened. I can understand—sympathize with—his embarrassment."

[FIVE]

"If you'll excuse us, darling," Pevsner said over their second cups of tea and coffee, "Charley and I are going to have a look at the helicopter."

"And then I'll have to be getting back to Buenos Aires," Castillo said. "So thank you for the breakfast. You saved my life."

He stood up and Anna gave him her cheek to kiss.

Pevsner stood up, opened one of the French doors, and signaled for Charley to go ahead of him.

When they were halfway across the lawn toward where the helicopter was parked, Pevsner said, "When do you want to talk about what you're really out here for? Before you show me how that bastard cheated me on the avionics when I bought that helicopter? Or after?"

"After," Charley said, and then, after considering it, added: "Alek, I didn't say he cheated you. I just said you don't have the best equipment available. There's a difference."

"No there's not. I told him I wanted the best and I didn't get it. That's cheating."

"Cheating would be if he charged you for better avionics than you got. If he charged you fairly for what he sold you, that's not cheating."

Pevsner didn't argue but his face showed he had not accepted Charley's argument.

Christ, is he thinking of whacking the salesman?

"Alek, an aircraft salesman with a beauty mark in the center of his forehead would make people ask questions. You want as few questions raised as possible."

Pevsner nodded, not happily, but the nod was enough to make Castillo think: *That argument may have gotten home.*

"So that's it, Alek," Castillo said after pointing out to Pevsner where the new avionics would go on the instrument panel and in the avionics compartment. "Installation is no big deal. The new stuff will fit right in where they'll take the old stuff out. Just make sure . . . just make sure your pilot watches the calibration."

"I'll be sure to do that," Pevsner said. "Thank you very much, Charley."

"Like I said, a small token of my appreciation for your courtesy."

"In anticipation of asking for another favor?"

"Not right now anyway."

"Looking the gift horse in the mouth, how much is that equipment worth?"

"Do you really care?"

"I care about who paid for it," Pevsner said.

"If you're really asking is there some kind of locator device—or something else clever in there—the answer is no. If your avionics guy is any good at all, he can check that for you."

"So who's paying for it?"

"Let's just say that your friend Charley recently came into a considerable sum of money and wanted to share his good fortune."

"So I understand."

"Excuse me?"

"I heard you came into a lot of money. Nearly sixteen million dollars."

"You do keep your ear to the ground, don't you?" Castillo asked, and then went on before Pevsner had a chance to reply: "So we are now in part two of our little chat, is that it?"

"You tell me, Charley."

"Let's talk about Budapest," Castillo said. "You're a Hungarian, right? Or at least have a Hungarian passport?"

Pevsner didn't reply.

"Well, as someone who knows Budapest and keeps his ear to the ground, I guess you know who Eric Kocian is."

"I've heard the name."

"He's a fine old gentleman," Castillo said. "More important, he's almost kin."

"Meaning?"

"Well, he was a friend of my grandfather and my mother."

"Oh, yes. The Gossinger connection," Pevsner said. "I forgot that."

"And Uncle Billy bounced me on his knee, so to speak, when I was a little boy." He paused. "So you will understand how upset I was when some unpleasant people tried to kidnap him on the Szabadság híd and, when that failed, tried to kill him."

"Charley, sometimes people who put their noses in places they shouldn't be . . ."

"And how upset I was just the other day when the same people—I admit they were probably looking for my uncle Billy—came into my room in the Gellért and pointed Madsens at me. That so upset me that I actually lost control of myself."

"I'm really surprised to hear that," Pevsner said.

"I didn't think," Castillo said. "I just took them down. Which, of course, means I couldn't ask who sent them."

"You don't know who sent them?"

"No. But I strongly suspect the people who made me lose my temper were either Stasi or Allamvedelmi Hatosag."

"But there is no Stasi anymore. Or Allamvedelmi Hatosag."

"In the United States, the Marines say, 'Once a Marine, always a Marine.' And who else do you know who uses the garrote to take people out?"

"I don't know anyone who uses the garrote," Pevsner said. "And I can't imagine why you're telling me this."

"I'm about to tell you, Alek. You're right. My uncle Billy does have the unfortunate habit of putting his nose in places other people don't think he should. Like under rocks to see what slime the rock conceals. So I have this theory that whoever tried to kidnap my uncle Billy did so to see how many names he could assign to the maggots and other slimy creatures he's found under the rocks. Sound reasonable to you?"

"It could well be something like that, I suppose."

"The sad thing about all this is, these people were trying to close the barn door long after the cow got away."

"I'm not sure I know what you mean," Pevsner said.

"I mean that I know everything that Kocian learned and by now his files are in Washington. These people can't put the cow back in the barn, in a manner of speaking. The only thing that any further kidnappings or murders are going to accomplish is to draw even more attention to them and I don't think they want that. And if any further attempt is made to kill Kocian, or kidnap him, I will take that personally."

"As I said, I can't imagine why you're telling me this."

"Because I want you to get to these people and tell them what I just told you."

"What makes you think I even know who they are? Or if I did that I would go to them?"

"Oh, you know who they are, Alek. They're the people who told you about the sixteen million and . . ."

"Has it occurred to you that Munz may have told me?"

"He couldn't have, Alek. He didn't know about it," Castillo said. "And on the way down here, I read Kocian's files. Long lists of names. Some of them had data after their names. Some names, like Respin, Vasily, for example, and Pevsner, Aleksandr, had question marks after their names. Which meant they had come to Kocian's attention and, when he got around to it, he was going to see what he could come up with."

Pevsner, his eyes again icy, met Castillo's eyes but he said nothing.

"Your name—*names*—were also on a list that I got from the CIA station chief in Paris," Castillo said. "I didn't have a chance to ask the CIA in Budapest what they have on you. But I wouldn't be at all surprised if they have a file on you, would you?"

"I wouldn't be surprised if they did, but they don't have anything tying me to the oil-for-food business because I wasn't involved in that."

"So you keep telling me," Castillo said. "Right now, Alek, you don't have to worry about what the CIA has or doesn't have on you. Right now, we're friends, and the President has called off the CIA and FBI investigations of you.

What you have to worry about is your other friends going after Kocian again. If that happens, the deal is off. Not only will I give Kocian's files to every American intelligence agency, I'll spread them around to anyone and everyone who might be the slightest bit interested."

"I thought you said Kocian's files were already in Washington."

Castillo nodded. "They are. But I haven't shared them with anybody. Yet."

Pevsner looked into his eyes again and again said nothing.

Castillo stared him down and then asked, "Did I mention, Alek, that if there is another attempt to get at Kocian, I will take that personally?"

"You did. But I wonder if you really understand who these people are. Don't take offense, Charley, but you're only a major. Could it be that your understandable affection for this man Kocian has clouded your judgment to the point where you think you're more important than you really are? Can do things you really can't do?"

"Actually, I'm a lieutenant colonel now," Castillo said.

"All right, a lieutenant colonel," Pevsner said, impatiently. "You take my point."

"Don't underestimate lieutenant colonels. That's all that Mr. Putin was in the KGB. Putin's name, incidentally, is in Kocian's files, too, and there are no question marks after it."

"You're not actually thinking of going after Putin, are you?"

"I'm just a simple soldier, Alek, who will do his best to follow his orders, wherever that leads me."

" 'Simple soldier'?" Pevsner parroted and chuckled. "And what exactly are your orders, *Colonel* Castillo?"

"To locate and render harmless the people responsible for the murder of Masterson."

" 'Render harmless'?"

"The way the *ex*-Stasi, or *ex*–Allamvedelmi Hatosag in Budapest, whichever they were, were rendered harmless."

"You're not suggesting, are you, that if these people lose interest in your uncle Billy, you'll lose interest in them?"

"Absolutely not. I just want you to tell them there's no longer a reason to kill Eric Kocian."

"From all you've been telling me about these people, they are not very nice people, Charley. They may well decide that *rendering harmless* someone who has been too interested in what they've been doing might discourage others from looking under other rocks."

"In your own interests, Alek, I'd try very hard to convince them that would not be wise."

"And they may well come after you."

"They already have," Castillo said. "And nothing would give me greater pleasure than if they tried it again. The next time, I'll take prisoners. I know some people who are very good in teaching people how to sing."

"And, of course, this is all hypothetical. I have no idea who you're talking about."

Castillo laughed.

"Alek, you're one of a kind!" he said. "You said that with an absolutely straight face."

"There aren't very many people, my friend Charley, who would be so brave, or stupid, to mock me," Pevsner said and tried to stare Castillo down again and failed again.

"I wasn't mocking you, Alek. I said that with admiration. You would be one hell of a poker player."

Pevsner smiled. "Actually, I'm a rather good poker player. We must find the time to play sometime."

"I'd like that," Castillo said.

"Well, Charley," Pevsner said. "This has been an interesting conversation, and it's always a pleasure to see you, but I have a golf date . . ."

"Thank you for the *kleines Frühstück*," Castillo said.

On the way back to Buenos Aires, Castillo—who looked carefully—couldn't find anyone following him. Nevertheless, he twice left the Autopista and drove around crowded neighborhood streets before getting back on the Autopista.

If anybody can trail me though all that, he's a genius.

Which is not the same as saying no one has.

[SIX]
The Restaurant Kansas
Avenida Libertador
San Isidro
Buenos Aires Province, Argentina
1305 8 August 2005

When he pulled into the parking lot, Castillo saw that despite the somewhat chilly weather there were a few people sitting under umbrellas in the patio outside the bar and he went there and took a table.

A strikingly good-looking waitress almost immediately appeared and he ordered a Warsteiner beer and a club sandwich, although after the pancakes he'd had at Pevsner's house he wasn't very hungry.

He took a cellular phone from his briefcase and tried to turn it on. The panel didn't light up.

Dammit! The battery's dead!

What did you expect, Inspector Clouseau? That you could just throw the phone—with a probably mostly exhausted battery—into your briefcase and then expect it to work when you want to use it a week later?

And what's going to happen if I find someplace that has a charger that will fit? When the battery is completely dead, does that wipe out the memory?

I have no damned idea at all where I can get Munz's cellular number—or, for that matter, Darby's or Santini's or anyone else's—if I can't get them off this cellular!

There was a pleasant chirp from the cellular. The cellular's panel lit up. A smiling cartoon face appeared, as did the greeting, ¡HOLA!

It works!

Castillo said, aloud, *"¡Hola, hola, hola!"* and then punched an autodial number.

El Coronel Alfredo Munz answered on the second ring.

"Munz."

"How's your arm?" Castillo asked, in German.

There was a just-perceptible hesitation before Munz asked, "Same cellular number?"

"Yes."

"I'll call you," Munz said and the connection was broken.

Castillo took the phone from his ear and pushed the CALL END button. Something was really bothering Munz. It showed in his voice and what he said. If he was unwilling to speak on his cellular, that meant he suspected someone was listening to his calls.

Well, I'll find out what it is.

He pushed another autodial button and Darby answered on the second ring.

"¿Hola?"

"Do they sell pancake flour in that embassy store?" Castillo asked.

There was a moment's hesitation and then Darby replied, "Yeah, I know they do."

"Send Ricardo Solez to get me five pounds of it," Castillo ordered. "And have him get me a charger for my cellular. It's a Motorola, model number . . ."

"I know what it is; it belongs to me."

"I'll explain later," Castillo said. "Is there another black car available?"

"Yes, there is."

"Maybe he could pick that up at the same time."

"You're not going to tell me what's going on?"

"When I see you. I'm expecting another call, Alex. Have to break this off."

The cellular buzzed just as the beer and club sandwich were delivered.

"*¿Hola?*"

"Where are you?" Munz asked.

"Kansas, in San Isidro."

"Are you alone? Driving?"

"I'm alone. I've got a Cherokee registered in Mar del Plata."

"Do you know where Unicenter is, on the Panamericana?"

Unicenter is the largest shopping mall in South America.

"Yeah."

"You approach it from the Panamericana and it's on your left, and when you turn in there are two garages, one for Jumbo, the other for Unicenter. Go into the Jumbo garage and park nose out close to the exit. Make sure your doors aren't locked. Fifteen minutes."

The cellular went dead.

What the hell is going on?

Castillo got up from the table, found the good-looking waitress, and handed her money.

"That was my wife," he said with a smile. "I was supposed to pick her up fifteen minutes ago."

There was a good deal of traffic and Castillo had a little trouble finding Unicenter. It was twenty minutes before he pulled into the huge Jumbo Supermercado's parking lot.

He drove slowly through it, looking for Munz. When he couldn't find him, he backed the Cherokee into a slot as close to the exit as he could find, then turned off the ignition and checked to see the doors were unlocked.

Not quite a minute later, he heard the rear door opening.

"Don't turn around," Munz said. "Just get out of here. Turn left when you do. If there is no traffic at the next left, take that and get back onto the Panamericana. If there is traffic, don't make the left. Check to see if anyone's following."

There was a long line of cars and trucks inching along the street to the left, so Castillo continued straight. He looked into the outside mirrors to get a make on the cars immediately behind him and then adjusted the interior rearview mirror to see the backseat. He couldn't see Munz.

Which means he's lying on the floor.

"There's a green Peugeot, a Volkswagen bug, and Fiat Uno behind us."

"Try to lose them," Munz ordered.

Castillo made an abrupt right turn and accelerated. Fifty yards later, he hit a speed bump.

He heard Munz groan.

Jesus, he must be lying on his wounded shoulder. That must have really hurt.

"Sorry, Alfredo," Castillo called.

"Anybody behind you?"

"No."

"Then slow down a little and keep weaving through the streets. You might as well head for Libertador."

"Who's following us?"

"I wish to hell I knew," Munz said. "When you get to Libertador, turn toward the city. Look for a COTO supermarket on the left. Pull into the parking lot behind it."

As Castillo parked the Cherokee, he saw that the only people in the parking lot were women loading plastic bags of groceries into their cars.

"Nobody followed us," Castillo said. "And there's nobody close in the parking lot. You want to come up front?"

Castillo heard Munz sigh, then the sound of the rear door opening. A moment later, he slipped into the front seat.

"So how are you, Alfredo?" Castillo asked, in German.

"Until you got that speed bump, Karl, I was feeling all right."

"I'm sorry about that."

Munz made a deprecating gesture.

"Who are we running from?" Castillo asked. "And why?"

"People are watching me," Munz said, seriously, and then, when he heard himself, chuckled and added, " 'They probably want to beam me up to their spaceship and extract my sperm,' said the paranoid."

Castillo chuckled. "Who?"

"I don't know. What I do know is the morning after you went to the States—I slept all of the day you left and right through the night, thanks to those little yellow pills Sergeant Kensington gave me—when I went onto my balcony, there was a car, a Citroën, with two men in it, parked across the street. There was a pair of binoculars on the dashboard. And there have been other cars, other people, ever since."

"But you don't know who?"

"No, and I wasn't—still am not—in any condition to ask people questions."

"Did you tell Pevsner?"

Munz shook his head.

"Why not?"

Castillo sensed that Munz was making up his mind whether to reply at all.

"Now that I'm no longer the head of SIDE, I'm not as much use to Señor Pevsner as I was," he said, finally. "Perhaps he's decided I'm now a liability. If I wasn't around, there are all sorts of questions that I would not be able to answer about him."

Castillo considered his own reply carefully before making it. "Unfortunately, Alfredo, that's a real possibility."

Munz nodded.

"I didn't ask about your shoulder," Castillo said.

"And I didn't ask what you're doing back here in Argentina."

"Why didn't you?"

"Because I wasn't at all sure you would tell me. The truth, that is. So why bother?"

"Write this down, Alfredo. I'm one of the good guys."

"You very well may be," Munz said. "But I don't *know* that, do I?"

"Tell me about your shoulder."

"Two days ago—my wife insisted—I went to Dr. Rommine's apartment. You remember him?"

"From the German Hospital?"

Munz nodded. "He's a friend. He owes me a couple of favors. He didn't believe me when I told him I'd had an accident cleaning my pistol."

"Why not?"

"He said, 'Well, whatever physician removed the bullet did a first-class job. He must be a foreigner or you weren't in Argentina when you shot yourself. Those degradable sutures aren't available here.' "

"You didn't tell him what happened?"

Munz shook his head.

"He knows better than to ask. He really doesn't want to know."

"I'm sorry you took that bullet, Alfredo."

"I was hoping by now you would have learned who those bastards were," Munz said, "and would be willing to tell me."

"I've got some suspicions, but I just don't know."

"If I have to say this, I can take care of myself. It's my family I'm worried about."

And that's a bona fide worry, after what these bastards did with Mrs. Masterson.

"How much can you tell me about the money?" Munz asked.

"What money?"

"Howard Kennedy said there was a lot of money in Lorimer's safe," Munz said.

"He asked you about the money?" Castillo asked, incredulously.

Munz nodded.

"I realize, Karl, that there are things you can't tell me," Munz said.

"Did Kennedy say how much money?"

"No. But I had the feeling there was a lot. What did you do, find it after I was hit?"

When Castillo didn't immediately reply, Munz said, "I just finished saying I understand there are things you can't tell me. But I'm desperate, Karl. This now involves my family."

"I'll tell you what I can do, Alfredo. I can take you and your family to the States, where you'll all be safe, until I find out who these bastards are and deal with them."

"That's a nice thought, but I don't have the money for airplane tickets, much less to support my family in the States."

"The Lorimer Charitable and Benevolent Fund will take care of that," Castillo said.

"The what?"

"There was a lot of money—in sort-of cashier's checks—in Lorimer's safe, Alfredo. Almost sixteen million dollars. I'd like to know how Kennedy knew about it. Anyway, we took it. It's out of the country. I control it. I call it the Lorimer Charitable and Benevolent Fund. You and your family will have all the money you need in the States for as long as you need it."

"Can you do that? Why would you?"

"You took a bullet for us. We owe you."

"I knew what I was doing when I went with you."

"We owe you," Castillo said, flatly. "You've got your passports?"

Munz nodded. "But not visas. Could you arrange visas?"

"Not a problem."

I'll get you visas if I have to go to the President.

"I'm not going," Munz said.

"Don't be a fool, Alfredo."

"I accept, with profound gratitude, Karl, your offer for my wife and daughters. But I'm not going to let these bastards chase me out of Argentina."

Castillo looked at him but said nothing.

"Maybe I can be of some small use to you, Karl," Munz said, "in finding these people."

"You can be of a lot of use to me, if you're willing. And understand what you're getting into."

"Whatever you ask of me," Munz said.

Castillo reached for the ignition key and started the engine.

"Where are we going?" Munz asked.

"To an apartment in Belgrano," Castillo said. "In the U.S. Army, *mi coronel*, this is known as getting the fucking circus off its ass and onto the road."

Before he left the parking lot, when he was still waiting for a break in the traffic on Avenida Libertador, Castillo had second thoughts.

Jesus, what am I going to do with Munz at that apartment?

There's already too many people there and more are coming.

You're not thinking clearly, Carlos.

That your ass is dragging, for understandable reasons, is an explanation, not an excuse.

He looked out the back window of the Cherokee, then shifted into reverse and quickly backed the truck into an open space.

"Was ist los, Karl?" Munz asked, concerned.

"I need to think a minute, Alfredo," Castillo said. "Believe it or not, there are people who think I don't do nearly enough of that."

He shut off the ignition, took out a cigar, carefully lit it, and for the next three minutes appeared to be doing nothing more than puffing on the cigar and staring in rapt fascination at the glowing tip.

Then he exhaled audibly, took out his cellular phone, and punched an autodial button.

Alex Darby answered on the second ring.

"Have you been keeping Santini up to speed?"

Darby didn't seem surprised or offended at the lack of opening courtesy.

"I thought that was the thing to do," he said.

"I want to meet with your boss," Castillo said, "as soon as possible."

"I think that's a good idea. You want me there?"

"That's why I asked about Santini. I'd rather you did the real estate."

"Okay."

"Could you take Sergeant Kensington and his radio out there with you? I'd like to get that set up as soon as possible."

"Not a problem."

"Where's Yung?"

"Howell just called. Yung should be at Jorge Newbery in thirty minutes."

"Can you have somebody—Solez, maybe, or Sieno—meet him and sit on him anywhere but where you are for a couple of hours?"

"We are a little crowded here, aren't we?" Darby replied. "Solez, I think. I'd rather have Sieno here."

"Okay."

"You want me to call our friend and tell him you're coming? Hell, I don't even know if he's there."

"I don't want to go to his office."

"Any reason?"

"I don't want the Argentine rent-a-cops to recognize who I have with me."

"Let me call him and see what he suggests. I'll call you back."

"Tell Tor and Davidson that Kocian is not to leave the apartment or make any telephone calls under any circumstances."

"Okay. I'll get right back to you, one way or the other."

"¿Hola?"

"How long will it take you to make it to our friend's house on Libertador?" Darby asked.

"Give me thirty minutes."

"He'll be waiting for you on the sidewalk. Drive past his office on the way."

"You mention the rent-a-cops to him?"

"He understands."

"I'll be in touch," Castillo said, broke the connection, and turned to look at Munz.

"I'll get in the back again," Munz said. "When we get close, pull onto a side road."

"You understood about the rent-a-cops?"

Munz nodded.

"So they do work for SIDE?"

"Some of them do," Munz said. "I didn't know you brought Yung back with you."

"I sent him back here," Castillo said. "And last night he was shot by a

Uruguayan cop who killed the guy—no identification on the body—who was trying to stick a needle full of ketamine in him."

"They wanted to question him about the money? What else happened at the estancia?"

"He's not badly injured, Alfredo, just a flesh wound to the hand. Thank you for asking."

"If he was badly hurt, you would have said something," Munz said, reasonably.

Castillo shook his head, started the engine, and drove to Libertador. This time, there was a break in the traffic and he headed for Buenos Aires.

[ONE]
Residence of the United States Ambassador
Avenida Libertador y Calle John F. Kennedy
Palermo, Buenos Aires, Argentina
1505 8 August 2005

The ambassador's residence is a stately century-old mansion two blocks across a park from the rather ugly "modern" building of the embassy. By following Darby's orders to "drive past his office on the way"—which meant approaching the ambassador's office in the embassy from the Place d'Italia—Castillo, with Munz again on the back floor of the Cherokee, came up to the residence on Calle John F. Kennedy, a quiet street, instead of Avenida Libertador, which is eight lanes wide and heavy with traffic.

There was more reason, too, to Darby's orders. Castillo saw Ambassador Juan Manuel Silvio standing on the sidewalk, smoking a cigar, and apparently having a pleasant chat with members of both the Policía Federal and the embassy-hired Argentine rent-a-cops.

When the Cherokee's turn signals indicated Castillo's intention to enter the driveway of the residence, two of the rent-a-cops quickly moved to see who he was.

"*¡Hola, Carlos!*" Ambassador Silvio cried, cheerfully.

He moved quickly to the Cherokee, gesturing for Castillo to put the window down. Then he called for one of the Policía Federal to open the gate.

"I've been waiting for you, Carlos," Silvio said through the window opened barely more than a crack. "As soon as they get the gate open, drive right in and around the corner of the building."

No rent-a-cop was going to push the ambassador himself aside to inspect the interior of a vehicle.

The gate opened and Castillo drove into the drive, past the ornate front door, and around the corner of the building. As he did, a service door of some kind opened and a man Castillo recognized as Ken Lowery, the embassy's security officer, appeared and came up to the car.

"Where's your passenger, Colonel?" he asked.

"In the backseat," Castillo said, then raised his voice. "You going to need some help to get out, Alfredo?"

"Just open the door," Munz said.

Lowery opened it, then stood to the side, blocking the view of anyone who might have come around the corner of the building.

Munz, his head ducked, went quickly into the building.

Castillo followed him inside. Lowery then came in, closing the door after him. Castillo saw that they were in a corridor outside of what looked like an unused kitchen.

"Good to see you again, Colonel Munz," Lowery said, in Spanish, and put out his hand. When Munz winced as he shook it, Lowery asked, "What's wrong? Hurt your shoulder?"

"I don't think you want to know, Ken," Castillo said, quickly.

Obviously, Silvio hasn't told him much, if anything.

How much am I going to tell him?

"Sorry!" Lowery said and held up both hands, palms out.

Ambassador Silvio appeared.

"I think we better use the service elevator," he said without further preliminaries and signaled them into the kitchen.

The elevator was small and somewhat battered.

"In the grand old days, this was used to carry food to the apartment," Silvio volunteered. "About the only use it gets now is when there's a reception. But you can't see who gets on it by peering in the front door."

"Tony Santini's on the way?" Castillo asked.

"He should be here any minute," Silvio said as he pulled open the elevator door and gestured for the others to get off.

"Thank you for seeing me on such short notice, sir," Castillo said.

"I was really hoping you would come to see me . . . Colonel."

"That news got around quick, didn't it?"

"From a very high source," Silvio said. "She also said that the President was very pleased with the way you've been handling things." He paused, smiled wryly, and added: "In diplomacy, that's known as imparting information circuitously."

Castillo smiled at him.

"Congratulations, Colonel," Silvio said. "In my judgment, it's well deserved."

"I can only hope, sir, that you will feel the same way when we've had our conversation," Castillo said.

Silvio led them into the living room of his apartment and waved them into a couch and armchairs.

"Sir, I'd like a moment alone with you, please," Castillo said.

"Why don't we step into my kitchen?" the ambassador said, nodding toward a swinging door.

"Ken," Castillo said, turning to look at Lowery, "years ago, when I was an aide-de-camp to a general officer known for his piquant speech, he told me that telling someone—a good guy—that he did not have the Need to Know of certain information was like telling him that his male member had been measured and judged not to be large enough for the task at hand."

Lowery smiled, but his face showed that he anticipated what he was sure was coming next.

Silvio smiled and shook his head.

"In your case," Castillo went on, "I'm going to tell you that I am operating under the authority of a Presidential Finding and anything you might learn here today is classified Top Secret Presidential. And I'm going to evade my responsibility in this matter by dumping it on the ambassador."

He turned to look at Silvio.

"You, sir, are authorized to tell Mr. Lowery anything you think he should know."

"I understand," the ambassador said, simply.

"And I still need a moment alone with you, sir."

Silvio waved toward the swinging door.

"Thank you for that, Charley," Silvio said when they were in the far corner of the kitchen. "Lowery is a good man." He smiled, and added: "He would be hurt to be told his male member had been measured and found wanting."

"I'm not sure it was the right thing to do," Castillo said. "But I'm not think-ing too clearly."

"You look exhausted," Silvio said.

"I am, and that's dangerous. That's why I'm grateful you could see me . . ."

"Secretary Cohen made it clear—if obliquely—that you are calling all the shots."

". . . because I need your advice."

"Anything I can do to help, Charley."

"I want to say this before we get started. I don't want to drag you down with me if this whole thing blows up in my face . . ."

Silvio made a deprecating gesture.

". . . which seems more likely every minute," Castillo finished. "So I give you my word that I will swear on a stack of Bibles that I told you little—virtually nothing—about what's happened and what I'm doing or try-ing to do."

"I very much appreciate that, but why don't we cross that bridge when we get to it? And why do you think it's going to blow up in your face? Everyone else, including me, seems to have a good deal of confidence in you."

"I've got too many balls in the air and I'm not that good a juggler," Castillo said. "So what I'm going to do—with my word that I will deny having ever told you—is tell you what they are and ask for your suggestions."

"Before we get into that, may I ask about Mrs. Masterson and the children? Where are they? How are they?"

"They're fine. They're with Mr. Masterson's family on their plantation in Mississippi. Until now, they've had some Delta Force shooters protecting them. Today, or maybe tomorrow, the shooters will be replaced by some retired Spe-cial Forces types who are pretty good. I think—and, God, I hope I'm right—that the threat to them has been drastically reduced by Lorimer's death. They no longer need Mrs. Masterson to point them to Lorimer."

"That makes sense," Silvio said. "And Special Agent Schneider? How is she?"

"She's in a hospital in Philadelphia with her jaws wired shut. Almost cer-tainly wondering why I haven't been to see her as promised."

Silvio shook his head sympathetically.

"I'm sure she'll understand," he said.

"I hope you're right, sir," Castillo said.

After a long moment, Silvio said, "Tell me what you think I should know, Charley, please."

Castillo took a moment to organize his thoughts and then began, "Just be-fore I came down here the first time to see what I could find out about Mrs.

Masterson's kidnapping, I called Otto Görner, the general director of the *Tages Zeitung* newspapers in Germany, to tell him I was coming down here . . ."

He saw the question on Silvio's face, stopped, then explained, "I have an alter ego as Karl Gossinger, the Washington correspondent of the *Tages Zeitung* newspapers. I decided the best way to come down here as the President's fly on the wall was to come as Karl Gossinger."

Castillo stopped again when he saw more unspoken questions on Silvio's face.

"The *Tages Zeitung* newspapers are owned by Gossinger Beteiligungsgesellschaft, G.m.b.H. My mother's maiden name was Gossinger."

Silvio's eyebrows rose but he didn't respond directly. Instead, he asked, "And this man knows what you really do for a living?"

"Then, he suspected. Now he knows," Castillo said. "Anyway, I asked him—primarily, so I would have an excuse for being here as Gossinger—if there was anything I should look into for him while I was here. He told me a rich man from Hamburg is planning to raise the *Graf Spee* from Montevideo harbor . . ."

Silvio's eyebrows rose again and he said, "That's the first I've heard of that."

"And then, reluctantly, he told me that the newspapers were working on a story that some Germans were sending Iraqi oil-for-food money down here, to hide it, the way the Nazis did in World War Two. Then he said he was sorry that he'd brought the subject up, that people looking into it had been killed, and that I was to leave it alone.

"And then I came down here and things started happening and I forgot what Görner had said about oil-for-food money while I was getting the Mastersons out of Argentina. And then the President issued the Finding.

"I had absolutely no idea where to start looking for the people who murdered Masterson except that there very probably was a connection between Masterson and his brother-in-law, the missing UN diplomat, so I started there."

Silvio nodded his understanding.

"So I went to Paris. A source told me that Lorimer was the bagman for the oil-for-food—"

"A source?" Silvio interrupted.

"Howard Kennedy, a former FBI hotshot who changed sides and now works for Alek Pevsner."

"I know *that* name," Silvio said. "Why would Pevsner tell you? I presume Kennedy wouldn't have done that without Pevsner's permission, or, more likely, at Pevsner's orders?"

"Wouldn't you prefer to know as little about Pevsner and/or Kennedy as possible?"

"I presume your offer to deny telling me anything is still open?"

"It is. It will stay open," Castillo said. "Okay. Pevsner has struck a deal with the President. He makes himself useful—I found the missing 727 with his help and I don't think I could have otherwise—and the President orders the FBI, so long as Pevsner doesn't violate any U.S. laws, to stop looking for him—and for Kennedy—and orders the CIA to stop trying to arrange Pevsner's arrest by any other government."

"That's very interesting," Silvio said. "Who else knows about that?"

"Secretary Hall, Secretary Cohen, and Ambassador Montvale know about the deal. The director of the FBI and the DCI know they've been ordered to lay off Pevsner. I don't know how much, if anything, they know about the deal."

Silvio nodded thoughtfully.

Castillo went on: "What Kennedy told me about Lorimer was confirmed by the CIA station chief in Paris, who told me he was sure that Lorimer was now in little pieces in the Seine or the Danube. From Paris, I went to Fulda—to Görner at the *Tages Zeitung*—and told him that I needed to have all the information he had about the oil-for-food payoffs. He gave me what he had, on condition I not make it available to the CIA or the FBI or anyone else, and told me that Eric Kocian, the publisher of the *Budapester Tages Zeitung,* had more information.

"So I went to Budapest and Kocian reluctantly, and with the same caveat that I couldn't share anything with the FBI or the CIA, gave me what he had. Kocian also believed that Lorimer had already been eliminated.

"Then I came back here—actually, to Montevideo—to see what Yung might have in his files about any of it. He had a file on Jean-Paul Bertrand, a Lebanese national and a dealer in antiquities—who was, of course, Lorimer, and who was alive on his estancia. So I set up the operation to grab Lorimer/Bertrand and repatriate him.

"And you know what happened at the estancia. We were bushwhacked. Lorimer and one of my men were killed and Colonel Munz wounded."

"Doesn't 'bushwhacked' imply you walked into a trap?" Silvio asked.

"I've thought about that. It's possible, but I think it was more likely just a coincidence. The people Lorimer was running from—and they're good—found him, and they got to the estancia right after we did."

"There's no one who could have told them about your operation? Where did you get the helicopter?"

"I got the chopper from Pevsner."

"Pevsner's here?" Silvio asked, surprised. "In Argentina?"

"If I don't answer that question, you can swear both that you don't know where Pevsner is and that I refused to tell you where he is."

Silvio nodded. "Consider the question withdrawn."

"I had to threaten Pevsner with the withdrawal of his presidential protection to get the chopper. He doesn't want to lose that. The CIA really would like some other—any other—government to catch him, and either bury him in a prison for the rest of his life or take him out."

"Why?" Silvio asked.

"The CIA used him to move things around, bought weapons from him. They'd like that buried. No, Alek Pevsner didn't set us up. It would not be in his best interests and he never puts anything above his best interests."

Castillo started to say something, then stopped and took out his cigar case. He offered it to Silvio, who nodded his thanks, and they both carefully lit up. It was obvious that both were thinking.

"We took the contents of Lorimer's safe with us," Castillo said, finally. "Among them were sort of cashier's checks for nearly sixteen million dollars that he had in three Uruguayan banks."

"Can I say something?" Silvio asked.

"Please."

"Ambassador McGrory knows about that money. It's the basis of his theory that Lorimer was a drug dealer. You're saying you have it?"

Castillo nodded.

He puffed his cigar, exhaled, then said, "I *will* deny telling you this: Ambassador Montvale suggested, and the President went along with him, that we should take the money and use it to fund the Office of Organizational Analysis. Most of it is in a bank in the Cayman Islands. I call it the 'Lorimer Charitable and Benevolent Fund.' "

Silvio smiled and shook his head.

"That's why I sent Yung back down here, to cover our tracks," Castillo said.

"You've heard he's been shot?"

Castillo nodded.

"First, I flew to Paris, for a look at Lorimer's apartment," Castillo said. "It had been previously searched by the Deuxième Bureau, the UN, and our CIA guy. Nothing there. Then I went to Fulda, and cleared things up with Otto Görner. I told him what I was doing—and on whose authority—and that I wanted to be released from my promise not to share his files with the FBI and the CIA. He agreed and gave me all his files. Then I went to Budapest to get Eric Kocian to release me from my promise.

"He was perfectly willing to do so, primarily because parties unknown had tried to stick a needle in him on the Franz Joséf Bridge and, when that failed, shot him twice . . ."

"My God!"

". . . at one o'clock the next morning . . ." Castillo's voice trailed off, then he exclaimed, "My God, that was yesterday morning!"

"You were in Budapest yesterday morning?" Silvio asked in surprise, if not disbelief.

Castillo nodded.

"And at one o'clock *yesterday morning,* these people—this time, two bad guys—made another attempt to murder Kocian and to burn his apartment and whatever files he might have there."

"You said 'attempt'?" Silvio questioned.

"Eric was still in the hospital," Castillo explained. "I was sleeping in the guest bedroom in his apartment. Eric's dog woke me up. Instead of Kocian, they got me and a suppressed .22 that I had the foresight to get from the CIA armory at our embassy. Neither body had any identification on it, but the garrote they used on one of Kocian's security men was a twin of the garrote used on Sergeant Kranz at the estancia. So it seems pretty evident we're dealing with the same people."

"Who are?"

"I'm beginning to think they're either ex–East German Stasi or ex–Hungarian Allamvedelmi Hatosag—AVH—but I'm not sure of that and have no idea who they're working for."

"So Mr. Kocian and his files are all right? In your possession?"

"One copy of the files, sent in the diplomatic pouch from Budapest, should be in Washington by now. I've got another copy here. Eric Kocian is in the apartment on Avenida Arribeños."

"You brought him with you? How did you get here so quickly?"

"Him and his dog and his bodyguard, an ex–Hungarian cop who did a tour in the French Foreign Legion." Castillo chuckled. "I guess I didn't get around to telling you that the Lorimer Trust was burning a hole in my pocket, so I bought a Gulfstream III with seven and a half million of it. Colonel Torine and my cousin Fernando flew it from Washington, spent about six hours in Budapest and then we flew here. Which may explain why I do feel a tinge of fatigue."

"I'm surprised you're able to walk around," Silvio said.

"But not surprised I'm not making much sense?"

"You're doing fine, Charley. So what are your plans here?"

"Alex Darby is right now renting a house for us at Mayerling in Pilar. The Lorimer Trust will reimburse him. Kocian thinks there's a connection with Mayerling and German—or, more likely, Austrian and Hungarian—oil-for-food money. I don't know, but Eric is right more often than he's wrong.

"The idea was that I would put Kocian in the house and have Yung and him compare notes. They sent me a replacement for Sergeant Kranz—a friend of mine, Sergeant Major Jack Davidson—who has a lot of experience protecting people. We served in Afghanistan together.

"He brought with him Corporal Lester Bradley and I don't know what the hell to do with him. Just put him out there with Davidson, I suppose. Darby will move Sergeant Kensington and his radio out to Mayerling as soon as he can. Somebody will have to sit on that around the clock. Lester can help with that."

"And Colonel Munz?" Silvio said. "He'll work with Yung and Mr. Kocian?"

"Now that he's been shot, I don't think Yung will want to be out there. And that brings up Colonel Munz." He paused. "You beginning to understand why this inept juggler is worried about all the balls he has in the air?"

"So far, so good, Charley. You haven't dropped any yet."

"Stick around. It won't be long," Castillo said. "They call that the 'Law of Inevitability.' "

"Tell me about Colonel Munz," Silvio said, smiling.

"Well, he thinks people are following him around. He doesn't know who they are, but he's worried about his family—a wife and two daughters—and I don't think he's paranoid.

"He suspects—but doesn't know—that the people following him, or at least some of them, may work for Pevsner. And he knows enough about Pevsner to know that Pevsner's policy for people who know too much about him is to give them a beauty mark in the forehead."

It took a moment for Silvio to understand. Then he grimaced.

"Since Munz took a bullet for us," Castillo said, "I told him I would take him and his family to the States until we find out who these people are and stop them. They'll need visas."

"Not a problem," Silvio said. "The bureaucrats in Foggy Bottom keep whittling away at an ambassador's authority, but I'm still the man with the last word on who gets a visa."

"That'll have to be done today and I haven't quite figured out how to do it."

"It can be done."

"Munz doesn't want to go. He wants to stay here and help find out who these bastards are."

"How badly is he hurt?"

"His shoulder. I don't know if he can use a weapon or not."

"Why does it have to be today?" Silvio asked.

"Because (a) I have still more balls to juggle in the States and (b) I need to talk to Ambassador Montvale as soon as I can."

"He said the same about you. There's a secure line here, if you want to use it."

"Thank you. A little later," Castillo said, and then asked: "Do you think Santini's out there by now?"

"I'd be surprised if he's not."

"Thank you very much, sir."

"For what?"

"This is probably one more manifestation of exhaustion, but I really feel a hell of a lot better than when we walked in here. Almost euphoric."

"I'm glad," Silvio said. "But I strongly recommend that, as soon as we're finished with Lowery and Santini, you get some rest. A lot of rest."

"I just don't have the time right now. Maybe I can get some sleep in the Gulfstream on the way to the States."

Silvio looked at him thoughtfully for a moment, then said, "You said you wanted my advice. Still want it?"

"Yes, sir."

"You've been talking about juggling balls and being an inept juggler."

Castillo nodded.

"I think you're a very good juggler, Charley. If you start dropping balls, it will be because you're exhausted, not because you're inept. Stop pushing yourself. You have limits, even if you don't like to admit it."

"I readily admit it. Physical limits, mental limits, and half a dozen other kinds."

"Once everyone is set up in the safe house in Mayerling and you get Colonel Munz's family to the States, I can see no reason why you can't take forty-eight hours off. Can you?"

"I have to go see Ambassador Montvale as soon as I get to the States and I don't think I can put that off for forty-eight hours."

"There's my proof that you're exhausted and need rest. Even I can think of a way to get around that."

"How?"

"Don't let him know you're going to the States tomorrow. Tell him you're going the day after tomorrow. Better yet, the day after that."

"You mean stay here another forty-eight hours? I can't do that. I want to get Munz's family out of here as quickly as possible."

"I didn't suggest that you stay here for another forty-eight hours," Silvio said. Castillo met his eyes.

"You are a friend, aren't you?" Castillo said after a moment.

"My advice is to go to Philadelphia and see Special Agent Schneider. From what I've seen of you two, she's the only person in the world who can get your mind off this and that's what you really have to do. Get your mind off everything about this for forty-eight hours so that when you go back to work you'll be running on all eight cylinders."

"It would be very nice to be running on all eight cylinders when I go to see Montvale. And almost suicidal not to be." He paused, then met Silvio's eyes again. "Thank you very much."

Silvio nodded and waved at the swinging door leading to his living room.

[TWO]

Tony Santini was standing by the large picture window of the simply but richly appointed living room of the ambassador's residence when Castillo and Silvio entered.

"Before we get into this, Charley," Santini said, evenly, "where do you want Solez to sit on Yung? You were a little vague about that."

"Where are they now?"

"He called two minutes ago. They're riding around in the park near the waterworks," Santini said, gesturing toward the river Plate.

The Buenos Aires potable-water plant was near the river not far from the Jorge Newbery airfield, five minutes or so from the ambassador's residence.

When Castillo didn't immediately reply, Santini added, "Yung's anxious to see you. And he's got another FBI agent with him."

"What's that about?" Castillo wondered aloud, then went on immediately, "Is he in a black car?"

Santini shook his head. "An embassy BMW. We don't have much of a fleet of black cars, Charley."

"Mr. Ambassador, can I bring them here?" Castillo asked.

Silvio nodded and picked up a telephone from a side table and punched a button.

"This is Ambassador Silvio," he said into the handset. "Mr. Solez and two others will be at the gate in a few minutes. Please see they are sent to my apartment."

Castillo wondered aloud: "I hope his having somebody with him doesn't mean that he's hurt worse than we've heard."

No one replied.

Santini was already on his cellular.

"Ricardo, come to the residence. You're expected," he said without any preliminaries, then broke the connection.

Yung, Solez, and "Legal Attaché" Julio Artigas came into Silvio's living room ten minutes later.

They made their manners to Ambassador Silvio, Santini, and Lowery, then Yung walked to Castillo.

Artigas was surprised at seeing Castillo: *Jesus Christ, he's not any older than I am. And he's calling all the shots?*

"You all right, Dave?" Castillo asked.

"I'm in much better shape than my Blazer, Major," Yung said. "It has at least a half dozen double-aught buckshot holes in it."

Castillo picked up on Yung's attitude.

He's not sullen.

I was afraid he would be. He didn't want to come down here and, when he did, he got shot.

I thought I would really be on his shit list.

But he's almost cheerful. Is he a little high on painkillers?

"And this is?" Castillo asked, indicating Artigas.

"Julio Artigas, Major," Artigas answered. "I'm a legal attaché in Montevideo."

Castillo took the offered hand.

"And what brings you to Buenos Aires, Mr. Artigas?"

Their eyes met, causing Artigas to conclude, *This is one tough, intelligent character.*

"I asked him to come, Major," Yung said.

Castillo looked questioningly at him.

"Artigas has pretty well figured out what's going on, Major," Yung said.

"Figured out what that's going on?" Castillo asked.

"Colonel . . ." Ambassador Silvio began.

Castillo saw that Yung had picked up on the rank.

". . . Mr. Artigas was taken to the estancia by the Uruguayan National Police," Silvio continued. "He's . . . been around . . . this situation practically from the beginning."

"And he was with Chief Inspector Ordóñez when Ordóñez took Lowery and me to the estancia," Yung said.

"And how much did you—and/or Lowery—tell him?"

"Nothing he hadn't already pretty well figured out for himself, Maj . . . did the ambassador call you 'Colonel'?"

"Yes, I did," Silvio said.

"Well, congratulations," Yung said. "Well deserved."

He is high, Castillo thought. *There's no other explanation for that. He seems genuinely pleased.*

"Thank you," Castillo said as Yung enthusiastically pumped his hand.

"What did they give you for the pain, Dave?" Castillo asked.

"Nothing. I took a couple of aspirin."

I'll be damned!

"Artigas, you're a problem I didn't expect," Castillo said. "Mr. Ambassador, may I use your secure line?"

"Of course," Silvio said. "It's in a small closet euphemistically referred to as my office."

[THREE]

"Sir," Castillo told Silvio, "if you'll get a secure line to the White House switchboard no one in the embassy will know I'm here."

"I'll have to go through the State Department switchboard."

"They'll switch you over."

Silvio picked up the heavily corded handset.

"This is Silvio. Would you get me a secure line to the department switchboard, please?" That took about twenty seconds and then the ambassador said, "This is Ambassador Silvio. Please get me a secure connection to the White House switchboard."

He handed off the handset to Castillo and said, "I'll leave you alone."

"Please stay," Castillo said.

Silvio nodded.

"White House."

"Colonel Castillo. I need Ambassador Montvale on a secure line."

"Ambassador Montvale's secure line," a familiar voice said.

"This is Colonel Castillo, Mr. Ellsworth. Put the ambassador on, please."

Ten seconds passed before Montvale came on the telephone.

"Hello, Charley," he said, cordially. "I've been hoping to hear from you. How's things going?"

"A lot has happened, Mr. Ambassador. Can I give you a quick rundown, then fill you in completely when I'm in Washington?"

"When do you think that will be, Charley?"

Castillo met Silvio's eyes.

"I hope to get out of here late in the afternoon the day after tomorrow. It may be twenty-four hours after that."

"You must be very busy."

"I've been pretty busy," Castillo said. "An attempt to kidnap my source in Budapest was made. When the kidnapping didn't go off, they tried to kill him. They wounded him twice. The next morning, they tried again, this time to assassinate him in his apartment, then burn the apartment and whatever information he might have had in it. That attempt also failed."

"He's all right, I hope?"

"He's all right. And his files are either en route to Washington or already there."

"And when am I going to get to see them?"

"As soon as they get there, if you like. But I'm afraid in the form they're in that I'm going to have to translate them. And I can't do that, obviously, until I'm in Washington."

"And that will not be for several days, right?"

"Just as soon as I can get there, Mr. Ambassador."

"Is your source safe in Budapest?"

"I brought him to Argentina with me."

"Personal jets are really nice things to have, aren't they?"

"Oh, you heard about that, did you?"

"I hear things, Charley, as you know. That one I heard from Major Miller. I had to remind him you had given me your word that I would be in the loop. He did not, however, tell me where you had gone from Budapest. I had to learn that myself."

"Learn it? Or make a guess?"

"I made a guess and then sought confirmation. Have you by any chance been in touch with Ambassador Silvio? Or Mr. Darby?"

"I'm calling from the residence, sir. Ambassador Silvio is with me. Mr. Darby is just outside."

"And how is Mr. Yung? Was he able to accomplish what you sent him down there to do before that horrifying carjacking incident?"

"You heard about that, did you?"

"Secretary Cohen was good enough to call and tell me what Ambassador McGrory had called to tell her. Crime seems almost out of control down there, doesn't it?"

"Yung's here with me, too. He wasn't badly hurt. I presume he did what I sent him to do or otherwise he would have said something. I'm probably going to bring him to the States with me."

"To do what?"

"To see what sense he can make of all the files we now have to work with."

"Are you also going to bring your source?"

"What I'm going to do is put my source in a safe house here that the Lorimer Charitable Fund has rented and he will work with his files, Yung's files, and whatever else I can get him."

"The Lorimer Charitable Fund? I rather like that," Montvale said. "I don't want to appear to be looking for praise, Charley, but you do remember my contribution to setting up the fund, don't you?"

"And I shall be forever grateful to you, sir."

"Is there anything else I can do for you, Charley?"

"Now that you mention it, there's an FBI agent, a 'legal attaché,' in the Montevideo embassy, one Julio Artigas, who I think would be of far more use to Ambassador Silvio than he is to Ambassador McGrory. Could you arrange his transfer?"

"What's that all about?"

"He's come up—on his own—with answers to questions Ambassador McGrory may ask him."

"Is anyone else liable to do that?"

"I hope not. I don't think so."

"I'll have a word with Director Schmidt the first chance I have."

"Today would be nice, sir. As soon as we get off the phone would be even better."

"That important, eh? Consider it done. Will you spell that name for me, please?"

Castillo did so.

"Got it," Montvale said.

"That's all I have, sir, until I can get to Washington and brief you fully."

"The sooner you can do that, the better."

"Yes, sir. I understand."

"We still have the matter of exploding briefcases to deal with, you know. I find that quite worrisome."

"Yes, sir. So do I. And I'll get on that as soon as I can."

"Good to hear from you, Charley."

"Always a pleasure to talk to you, sir," Castillo said and clicked the phone. When the operator came on, he told her, "Break it down," then hung up.

He looked at Ambassador Silvio.

"Ambassador Montvale gave me everything I asked for," Castillo said. "And no static. Why does that make me very nervous?"

Ambassador Silvio smiled but didn't reply directly.

"They're waiting for us in the living room," he said.

[FOUR]

Artigas, Solez, Munz, Santini, and Yung, talking quietly among themselves while cooling their heels on two of the couches, got to their feet as Castillo and Ambassador Silva came into the room. The look on Artigas's face reminded Castillo of what he'd said about him being "an unexpected problem" just before getting on the secure line to Montvale.

He knows I was talking to someone about him. But the look on his face is concern, not fear. He is concerned about what the great and all-powerful Colonel Castillo has had to say about him—but not afraid.

He knows he's done nothing wrong, so why should he be afraid?

I think I like this guy. Let's see how smart he is.

"Okay, Artigas," Castillo said, "why don't you tell me what you think you have figured out about what may have happened down here?"

Artigas was visibly unhappy about being ordered to do that.

"It's all right, Mr. Artigas," Ambassador Silvio said. "What you say will get no further than this room, and it's important to Colonel Castillo and myself to know how much highly classified information may have been deduced or intuited by you."

"Yes, sir," Artigas said and proceeded to clearly outline his suspicions and the conclusions he had drawn from them and why.

Castillo was very impressed with how much Artigas had "deduced or intuited."

This guy is very smart. He's figured out just about everything that went down— except, of course, who the Ninjas were or where they came from. And nobody knows that.

The downside of that, of course, is that if he's figured this out, some of the other FBI agents have probably done the same thing.

"How much of this have you discussed with anyone else?" Castillo asked. "With other FBI agents? Or anyone else?"

"No one, sir."

"You're sure?" Castillo pursued.

"Yes, sir."

"Artigas, you're being transferred from the Montevideo embassy to the embassy here," Castillo said.

What? Jesus Christ! Artigas thought, then asked: "When's that going to happen?"

Castillo thought: *Not "I am?" Or "Why?" Or "Don't I have anything to say about that?" Or even "Says who?"*

Just "When?"

"It's happening now," Castillo said. "Ambassador McGrory will be told only that you're being transferred. If anyone asks you, you will say you have no idea why that's happening."

"That's easy," Artigas said, "because I don't have any idea why that's happening."

"Did Yung or Howell mention anything about a Presidential Finding?" Castillo asked.

"Yeah," Artigas said and smiled and shook his head. "But only 'hypothetically,' Colonel. And then they said they would deny ever discussing even a hypothetical Presidential Finding with me."

Castillo chuckled. Ambassador Silvio smiled.

"Everyone take your seat," Castillo said. "Get comfortable."

When they had, Castillo went on: "Okay, this is not hypothetical, Artigas. From now on, anything I—or anybody connected in any way with this operation—tells you is classified Top Secret Presidential."

"Yes, sir."

"There has been a Presidential Finding. It established the Office of Organizational Analysis, a covert and clandestine unit within the Department of Homeland Security. I am the chief. The mission is to . . ."

Ten minutes later, Castillo ended his uninterrupted lecture: ". . . until you hear otherwise from me—*me*, not from anyone else—you are on detached duty with OOA." He smiled, and added, "This is the point where the lecturer invariably says, 'Are there any questions?' I'm not going to do that."

I've got several hundred questions, Artigas thought, then said: "Not even one question?"

"One," Castillo said.

"What am I going to do?"

"Good question. The answer is, until I figure that out, you are going to contribute whatever you can from your vast fund of professional knowledge to the solving of a number of little problems OOA faces."

"Like what?" Artigas said, smiling.

"You got one question. You spent it," Castillo said, meeting Artigas's eyes.

Castillo then looked at the others and went on, "The priority problem is how to get Colonel Munz's family out of here as safely, as quickly, and as secretly as possible." He paused. "Mr. Ambassador, may I respectfully suggest that this would be a splendid time for you to find something else to do?"

"I think not, Colonel," Silvio said. "I really decided a while back that this is one of those 'in for a penny, in for a pound' situations. Maybe I can be helpful."

"You're sure, sir?"

Silvio nodded.

Castillo shrugged.

"Tony, did Alfredo tell you about the people surveilling him?" Castillo asked.

"Uh-huh."

"Okay, then let's do this the military way, by seniority. I think you're senior, Tony, so tell us how we're going to do that."

"I need all the facts, Charley, and I don't think I have them," Santini said.

"What are you missing?"

"That friend of yours who speaks Russian," Santini said. "What's his role in this?"

"And a half dozen other languages," Castillo offered. "Alek Pevsner."

"The Russian arms dealer, mafioso?" Ken Lowery asked. "Jesus, I saw a new Interpol warrant for him—smuggling, I think—just a couple of days ago. He's involved in this?"

I saw that Interpol warrant, too, Artigas thought. *And a dozen others on him. That guy's a real badass. And he's Castillo's friend?*

Castillo nodded. "The question is, how is he involved?"

"He's here? In Argentina?" Yung asked.

"I am going to say as little about Pevsner as I can," Castillo said. "As a matter of fact, from this moment on he is code-named 'Putin' and all references to him will be by his code name. Clear?"

There were nods and yessirs.

"What about Putin's friend, Colonel?" Yung asked. "My ex-friend? Do we need a code name for him?"

"I think we do," Castillo said. "How does 'Schmidt' strike you?"

Artigas's eyebrows rose at hearing the name of the director of the Federal Bureau of Investigation.

"Now that I've burned my bureau bridges," Yung said, "that's fine with me."

Artigas wondered: *Now, what the hell does that mean?*

"Okay. Kennedy is now Schmidt," Castillo said.

There's an FBI back-channel locate-report-but-do-not-detain out on a former agent named Howard Kennedy, Artigas thought, then said so aloud, adding, "Did you know that?"

"I suspected it," Castillo said.

"Same guy?"

Castillo nodded.

"You used to work with him, right, Yung?" Artigas asked.

Yung nodded uncomfortably.

"Dave, when did you decide your bureau bridges were burned?" Castillo asked.

"Couple of days ago," Yung said. "I'm still not sure if I burned them or you burned them for me, but when I looked they were gloriously aflame."

"How do you feel about that?"

"The question is, how do you feel about it?"

"I'm glad to have you, if that's what you're asking."

"Then I feel fine about it, Colonel," Yung said.

If he's not high on painkillers, or anything else, what the hell happened to make him change his mind?

Castillo gave him a double thumbs-up gesture.

"Okay," Santini said. "Alfredo thinks it's likely that some of the people after him are Putin's guys. I think we have to accept that. I think we have to presume that the Ninjas are on him, too. And he thinks SIDE may also be on him."

"Let's talk about that," Castillo said. "Why do you think SIDE is surveilling you, Alfredo?"

"What the Argentine government wants to do is forget—have everyone forget—what happened to Mr. Masterson," Munz replied. "And they've heard what happened in Uruguay and don't want to be surprised by any developments in the matter. They don't know what my relationship with Ale . . . *Putin* really was or *is*. Officially, I was keeping an eye on Putin for SIDE."

"They know he's here, Colonel?" Ambassador Silvio said.

"I found him," Munz said, simply.

"Then why didn't they act on one or more of the Interpol warrants out on him? Do you know?"

Munz answered that with the gesture of rubbing the thumb and index finger of his right hand together.

"All I was told was to keep him under surveillance," he said. "And that a decision about what to do with him would come later."

"Is there a chance he will be arrested?" Silvio asked.

Munz shook his head and said, "If he has been as generous as I suspect he has, if the decision to act on one or more of the Interpol warrants is made, he'll be given sufficient warning before the order to go arrest him is given." He paused and looked at Castillo. "But to answer your question, Karl, they're watching me so they won't be surprised by anything that might happen."

"Okay. Makes sense," Castillo said, thought a long moment, then asked, "If somebody tried to grab you or whack you—or your family—and SIDE was watching, what would happen?"

"That's what worries me, Karl," Munz said. "I'd like to think that SIDE was told to protect me—us—and that I left enough friends behind in SIDE, many of whom know my family, so they would protect us, orders or not. But that may not be the case. That's why I'm so grateful for your offer to get them out of here."

"With that—and SIDE—in mind, Charley," Santini said, "SIDE runs a computer scan of people passing through immigration."

"How hard would it be to smuggle them into Uruguay?" Castillo asked. "If that's possible, we could pick them up at Carrasco with the Gulfstream. I don't think SIDE is scanning Uruguayan immigration, are they, Alfredo?"

Artigas thought: *Gulfstream? Jesus Christ, has he got his own airplane?*

"We have . . . excuse me, *SIDE* has," Munz corrected himself, as he no longer was chief of SIDE, "an arrangement where Uruguayan immigration checks a list of names SIDE gives them against people coming in or out and lets SIDE know if anybody shows up. I don't think my name is on that list."

"I don't know if it's smuggling or not, Colonel," Artigas said, "but they wouldn't have to go through immigration to get to Uruguay. All they need is their National Identity Card to get on an airplane or the Buquebus ferry. They don't take names."

"He's right, Charley," Santini said.

"The Buquebus would be better," Munz said.

"Okay, we'll do that," Castillo said. "First we get their passports stamped, very quietly, with a . . ."

". . . five-year, multivisit visa," Ambassador Silvio furnished. "You get me the passports, Colonel Munz, and I'll take care of that."

"Thank you," Munz said.

"First we get them visas and then on the Buquebus," Castillo said. "Then what?"

"I've got to go back to Uruguay," Yung said. "And so, come to think of it, does Artigas, so he can look very surprised when McGrory tells him he's been transferred over here. One or both of us could go on the Buquebus with them."

"Why do you have to go back to Uruguay?" Castillo asked.

"I've got to get Lorimer and his casket from the undertakers and out to the airport."

"Jesus, I forgot all about him," Castillo said, then heard what he had said and smiled and shook his head. "Mr. Ambassador, there's another example that I'm playing with far fewer than fifty-two cards in my deck."

Silvio said, "That's only proof, Colonel, that you forgot the details of the repatriation of Mr. Lorimer's remains."

Castillo raised an eyebrow, then turned to Yung. "Tell me about those, Dave," he said.

"The casket will go on American Airlines flight 6002 at five after nine tomorrow night. It could have gone tonight, but the body wasn't ready."

" 'The body wasn't ready'?" Castillo parroted.

"I was afraid the bastard's father might insist on opening the casket. When I saw the body in the English hospital, it looked awful. So I took some clothes from the estancia and told the undertaker to dress him, and to do a better job of sewing him up than the hospital did after the autopsy."

"That was a very nice thing for you to do, Mr. Yung," Ambassador Silvio said.

"And it would have been even nicer if you hadn't called the deceased 'the bastard,' " Castillo said.

Yung looked at him, ignored the comment, and continued: "The airplane stops at Ezeiza, then goes to Miami. Then the casket'll be transferred to an American Airlines flight . . . I've got the number somewhere if that detail's important . . . to New Orleans."

"And you have to go with it," Castillo said.

"I wanted to talk to you about that," Yung said. "I'd much rather stay here."

Jesus Christ, Castillo thought, *he's really done a one-eighty!*

"If you're not on that airplane with the body," Castillo said, "Ambassador McGrory—and others—are going to suspect you didn't come down here to repatriate the remains. So you will be on it."

"Yes, sir."

He's really disappointed.

"And you will stay through the funeral. There's no telling who might show up for that." He paused, then looked at Santini. "Tony, could we get the Secret Service to make the plates of the cars at that funeral? Maybe the people themselves?"

"Not a problem. Who are we looking for?" Santini said.

"Names and addresses—and photographs, if that can be done discreetly—to feed to our database," Castillo said. "Anything. Right now all we have is the database."

"I'll get on the horn," Santini said.

"After that, Dave," Castillo said, "if you still want to come back here, we'll see what can be worked out."

He saw that Yung was pleased with that.

Congratulations, Second Lieutenant Castillo. You remembered that from Leadership 101: "If at all possible, do not discourage enthusiasm."

"Okay, so where does that leave us?" Santini said. "The passports and what else?"

"The pancake flour and maple syrup," Castillo said.

Artigas thought, *The what?*

"I got it," Santini said. "What's that all about?"

"Where is it right now?" Castillo asked.

"In the trunk of the embassy BMW," Solez said.

"It's for Putin," Castillo said. "I promised it to him."

Artigas thought, incredulously: *He promised pancake flour and maple syrup to Aleksandr Pevsner, international thug?*

"I'd love to know what that's all about, Charley," Santini said.

"Alfredo," Castillo said, "is there any way you can communicate with your wife without using your home phone?"

Munz nodded. "I can call her and give her a message, something innocuous, that tells her to go to the phone in the kiosk around the corner from the house."

"How is she about taking orders without question?"

"Ordinarily, not good at all," Munz said, smiling. "But under these circumstances . . ." He paused. "She knows I didn't shoot myself cleaning my pistol. And she's seen the cars."

"What about your daughters?"

"They'll do what their mother tells them to do."

"How do you think this would work?" Castillo began. "You get her on the kiosk phone and tell her to pick up your daughters and their passports—and nothing else, that's important—and take a taxi to Unicenter. Is there a place you could meet her there?"

"In the food court," Munz said. "Or, for that matter, the garage."

"The food court would probably be better," Castillo said. "I'll drive you back there and we'll sneak you in the way we sneaked you out. You will meet them in the food court. I'll follow you up there and so will Ricardo, Yung, and Artigas. You will point us all out to them so they understand we're the good guys. You get the passports . . ."

Munz held up his hand and Castillo stopped.

Munz thought for a long moment, then said, "Okay so far, Karl. Go on."

"You tell them to go shopping," Castillo continued. "Underwear, maybe dresses, whatever else they'll need for two, three days. No luggage. Shopping bags only."

"They won't be going back to the apartment?" Munz asked.

"No. They'll take a cab to the Buquebus terminal, arriving no more than ten minutes before they have to . . ."

"There's a ferry leaving at nine-thirty," Munz said. "It gets to Montevideo about one in the morning. Which means they would have to be there at nine-fifteen. Considering the traffic, they'd have to leave Unicenter no later than eight-thirty." He looked at his watch. "It's now ten to six. It'll be tight but that much can be done. What's the rest?"

"Artigas will have taken a cab to Buquebus right after you point out him and Yung to your family. That's (a) so he can buy the tickets and (b) in case Yung, who will stay in Unicenter with your family—and follow them in another taxi to Buquebus—somehow gets separated from them. In other words, Artigas'll be at the terminal with their tickets and passports when your family gets there. That should reassure them a little. And they'll stay with them as long as they're in Uruguay."

"I'm not going to drive them?" Ricardo Solez asked.

"You're going to take the passports, bring them here, have them stamped, and then take them to Artigas at the Buquebus terminal."

"Got it."

Castillo went on: "Alfredo is going to get in his car—he left it in the Unicenter parking lot—and take Putin the pancake flour and maple syrup . . ."

Artigas decided, *Pancake flour and maple syrup have to be code names for something—something they don't want me to know about. But what?*

". . . And he's going to tell Putin that I called him, had him meet me at Unicenter, and gave him the flour and syrup, then asked him to take it to him. He will also cleverly drop into their conversation that I told him I was going to the States either tonight or tomorrow."

Munz nodded.

"I'm going to follow him out there—and I think I better have a weapon—Tony?"

"I just happen to have a spare Glock in my briefcase," Santini said.

"I'm going to wait for Alfredo in the supermarket parking lot near where Putin's holed up. You know where I mean, Alfredo?"

Munz nodded.

"When Munz comes back from delivering the flour and syrup to Putin, he will drive to his apartment with me following him. There he will put his car in the garage, go to his apartment, and turn on the lights, then turn them off again and go out of the apartment and to the kiosk around the corner. Somehow, during this time, he will get into the backseat of the Cherokee without being noticed and I'll take him to the apartment on Arribeños."

"What's that?" Munz asked.

"It's where you'll spend tonight," Castillo said. "Tomorrow, presuming nothing went wrong with renting it, you—and Eric Kocian, Max, and Kocian's bodyguard—will as quietly as possible be moved to a safe house in the Mayerling Country Club in Pilar."

"Who are those people?" Munz asked.

"One is a man named Eric Kocian. He's a journalist. He's got a lot of material I want you to go through to see if we can make a connection."

"I don't like journalists much myself," Munz said. "But he needs a bodyguard?"

Castillo nodded. "They tried to kill him twice in the last week. They also tried to stick a needle full of phenothiazine in him. You'll like the bodyguard. He used to be an inspector in the Budapest police department, and, before that, a hitch in the French Foreign Legion."

"They speak Spanish?"

"German and Hungarian."

"And the third one? Max Something, you said?"

"Max Bouvier," Castillo said. "He doesn't talk much."

"Another bodyguard, Karl?"

"Oh, yes," Castillo said.

"Jesus Christ, Charley!" Santini said, shaking his head. "Alfredo, he's pulling your leg. Max is a dog. An enormous dog."

Munz looked at Castillo.

"True," Castillo said. "Which just made me think of something. I was planning to move Kocian to the master bedroom in the suite in the Four Seasons. He's in his eighties, has two 9mm holes in him, and just flew from Budapest. But I can't do that, obviously, with Max. He's going to have to stay in that apartment. And won't like it."

"Leave the dog in the apartment," Solez said.

"Not an option. Where Kocian goes, so does Max. He even had him in his hospital room in Budapest."

"Which just made me think of something," Santini said. "What do we do with *Familia* Munz in Montevideo until you can pick them up with the Gulfstream?"

"Alfredo took me to a first-rate hotel in Carrasco . . ." Castillo began.

"I sent you there," Ambassador Silvio said. "The Belmont House. I'll call over, and get them a suite."

"No," Castillo said. "That would involve you personally. I don't want that. I'll call. We'll have to get them to hold the room anyway if that boat doesn't get over there until one o'clock in the morning."

"And where is *Familia* Munz going in the States?" Santini asked. "Washington?"

Jesus, I didn't even think about that! Castillo thought.

He then said, "Not at first. At first, we need something in the boonies."

"Carlos," Solez said. "The ranch?"

"My first thought just now was to take them to the plantation—there's people already there sitting on the Masterson family—but obviously that wasn't one of my brighter ideas."

"When Doña Alicia sent me the e-mail about you getting promoted, she said she had just been up to the ranch and it was so hot she wasn't going back until November."

Castillo chuckled. "It does get a bit warm in Midland in August, doesn't it? Okay, I'll give Abuela a call and ask her to stay away until further notice. Tony, can we get some Secret Service people to go to Midland until I can make better arrangements for Alfredo's family?"

"*You* can, Charley," Santini said and pointed in the general direction of the secure telephone.

Artigas thought: *The Ranch? The Plantation? Doña Alicia? Abuela?*

For Christ's sake, abuela *is Spanish for "grandmother."*

Does everything these people do come with a code name?

And how I am supposed to figure out what they mean?

"Okay," Castillo said, "I'll do that. I'll call Doña Alicia and Miller right now. And while I'm doing that, make sure everybody has everybody else's number on their cellulars. And when you use them, remember to use the code names. Which reminds me, we'll need one for *Familia* Munz. How about 'Mother'?"

"That's easy to remember," Santini said, drily. "Give me your cellular, Charley, and I'll make sure you have all the numbers."

Castillo handed it to him, then looked at Ambassador Silvio, wordlessly asking permission to use the secure telephone.

Silvio nodded and said, "Of course."

"That was a hell of a lot easier than I thought it would be," Castillo announced when he came back into the room several minutes later.

He looked at Santini and went on: "Joel was there. He said no problem, and gave me a number to call when we know when we'll be at the ranch and they'll be waiting for us. He said to tell you hello."

Santini nodded.

Castillo turned to Solez. "Doña Alicia sends you a kiss. She made me promise to get a little rest while I'm having 'our meeting' at the ranch."

Solez nodded.

Castillo turned to Munz.

"The ranch is outside Midland, Texas, Alfredo. It's been in my family for a very long time. It's pretty large, even by Argentine standards. The reason for that is here you wonder how many head you can graze on one hectare. Out there, we wonder how many hectares it will take to feed one steer enough so that we can move him to a feeding pen. There's a nice house; your family will be comfortable. Most important, it'll be absolutely safe. There's an airstrip which can't be seen from the nearest road. No one will know who's there. And you heard what I said to Joel about the Secret Service?"

Munz nodded. "Thank you, Karl."

"Is that about it? Are we ready to move? Have we forgotten anything?"

"You can bet on that," Santini said. "But, yeah, we better get moving."

[FIVE]
Unicenter
Panamericana Highway
Buenos Aires, Argentina
1830 8 August 2005

David W. Yung, Jr., was more than a little embarrassed at the emotions he was feeling as he sat drinking a cup of hot chocolate with Julio Artigas at a small table in the food court, a collection of fast-food vendors on the top floor of the vast, multilevel shopping center.

He was sad and angry, emotions he knew were inappropriate for a special agent of the FBI, and especially for one who had just been assigned to the OOA and really wanted to stay there, which meant that he was going to have to prove he had the ability to be really calm and professional under pressure—not sad and really pissed-off.

He had just watched Colonel Alfredo Munz casually get up from another small round table forty feet away—one with a woman and two teenage girls sitting at it—and walk to the men's room.

Except going to take a leak and wash his hands wasn't what Munz was really doing.

What Munz was doing was carrying his family's passports to Solez, who was waiting for him in the men's room. What that in effect meant was that Munz was saying good-bye to his family for God only knew how long, turning them over to the protection of people—including a Chinese man with a bandaged hand—whom they had never seen before.

This showed on the girls' faces. They were young and pretty, Yung thought. One was about sixteen years old, the other a little older—on the cusp of young womanhood—and they were clearly frightened.

They should not be involved in something like this.

Goddamn these bastards!

The younger girl glanced at their table. Yung caught her eye and smiled at her, hoping it helped in some way tell her, *It's going to be okay.*

She looked startled for a moment, then looked away.

I shouldn't have done that. Someone may have seen it.

But, dammit, I wanted to give her some sign of encouragement.

As choreographed, Solez came out of the men's room, fumbled through his pockets, and just perceptibly nodded at Yung and Artigas. He took a package of cigarettes from his pocket and, taking his time about it, lit one with a Zippo lighter.

Munz, also as planned, came out a moment later, took a pack of cigarettes from his pocket, put one to his lips, then looked unsuccessfully for a lighter or match. He looked at Solez, then asked for a light. Solez produced his Zippo and lit Munz's cigarette.

Munz looked very quickly at his wife and daughters, then headed for the escalator. Solez walked in the other direction, toward the elevator. This, too, was according to plan.

Castillo now appeared from the direction of the escalator. He feigned pleasant surprise when he noticed Yung and Artigas and walked to their table. They shook hands, patted backs, and made kissing gestures in the Argentine manner.

Now Señora Munz and the girls had seen all the players.

Castillo walked toward the elevator.

Artigas murmured, "See you at the terminal," and got up and walked toward the escalator.

Señora Munz waited until Munz had disappeared into the crowd that was waiting to get on the escalator, then collected her purse and stood, motioning for the girls to get up, too.

Yung fished a bill from his pocket and laid it on the table as a tip for the busboy. He stood up and felt the weight of his semiautomatic pistol as it shifted slightly.

Jesus Christ, he suddenly remembered. *I don't have a round in the chamber!*

It'll take forever to work the action with this goddamned bandaged hand!

He walked quickly into the men's room, into a stall, locked it, took out the pistol and worked the action by pressing the slide against the toilet paper holder. Then he put the pistol back in his shoulder holster, unlocked the stall door, and hurried out of the men's room.

There was a moment's panic when he couldn't immediately locate *Familia* Munz. Then he saw them in the knot of people waiting to get on the escalator.

The younger girl saw him walking toward them, looked a little relieved, and smiled.

He smiled at her again, then made his way to the escalator.

XI

[ONE]
Piso 16, 1568 Avenida Arribeños
Belgrano, Buenos Aires, Argentina
1940 8 August 2005

When Paul Sieno opened the steel apartment door for Castillo and *El Coronel* Alfredo Munz, SIDE, retired, Castillo saw that the living room of the apartment was crowded. Eric Kocian was sitting in a dark brown leather armchair, his elegantly shod feet resting, crossed, on a leather ottoman. He had a wineglass in one hand and a cigar in the other.

Holding court, Castillo thought, smiling.

A table holding platters of cheese and cold cuts, bottles of wine and ginger ale, and glasses was between two matching couches. Sándor Tor sat beside Susanna Sieno on one of them. Sergeant Major Jack Davidson and Colonel Jake Torine sat on the other, with Corporal Lester Bradley squeezed in between them. Fernando Lopez sat in an armchair obviously dragged from someplace else.

Everyone looked at Castillo and Munz.

Castillo thought, *Davidson's wondering who the hell Munz is and what he's doing here.*

Mrs. Sieno very probably knows who he is, so she's really curious about what he's doing here.

And everybody—including Jack, Mrs. Sieno, even Eric Kocian—is looking at me because they have the mistaken notion that James Bond just walked in with the answers to all their questions.

The truth is, once I get everybody settled in the safe house in Mayerling, and Munz's family safely through Uruguay and onto the Gulfstream, I don't have any idea what I'm going to do.

Since I don't know who the bad guys are, or even who they're working for, how the hell can I find the bastards?

I'm an Army officer, not Sherlock Holmes.

"Looks like we're going to need some more chairs, doesn't it?" Paul Sieno observed and went in search of them.

Max, who had been lying beside Kocian's chair, got to his feet, and, with his stub of a tail rotating like a helo rotor, walked quickly to Castillo, obviously delighted to see him.

Castillo squatted and rubbed Max's ears.

"Until he started to behave like that to Colonel Castillo," Kocian announced, "I thought Max to be an excellent judge of character."

The remark earned the chuckles and laughs Kocian expected it to.

"Eric," Castillo said, in Hungarian, "say hello, politely, to Oberst Munz."

Kocian replied, in German, "Since I don't speak a word of Spanish, how am I going to do that?"

Mrs. Sieno smiled. She was obviously taken with the old man.

"Try German," Castillo said.

"Guten Abend, Herr Oberst," Kocian said.

"Guten Abend, Herr Kocian," Munz replied.

"You're a Hessian," Kocian said, still in German. It was an accusation.

"I'm an Argentine," Munz said, switching to English. "My parents were Hessian."

"Karl, why didn't you tell me the Herr Oberst speaks English?" Kocian demanded.

"You didn't ask," Castillo said, then, switching to English, went on: "Jack, this is Colonel Alfredo Munz. Kensington took a bullet out of his shoulder after the estancia operation."

Davenport nodded.

"Alfredo, Jack and I have been many places together . . ."

Castillo felt a tug on his trouser leg. He looked down to see that Max had it in his mouth. Max let loose, then sat and offered Castillo his paw.

"I think your friend is telling you that nature calls, Charley," Torine said, cheerfully.

"What?"

"Obviously, he's been waiting for you," Torine said. "He made it . . . uh . . . *toothfully* clear that he wasn't going walking with any of us."

"I would have been happy to take him, Karl," Kocian said. "But you made that impossible."

"What?"

"Had I known I was going to be held prisoner, Karlchen," Kocian said, "I would never have left Budapest."

"Forgive me for trying to keep you alive, Eric," Castillo replied somewhat unpleasantly, in German.

Max was now at the door, looking back at Castillo.

Castillo looked at Sándor Tor and asked, in Hungarian, "You have a leash?"

Tor reached into a well-worn leather briefcase by the side of his chair and took out a chain leash.

Why do I suspect that briefcase also holds an Uzi?

"Okay, Max," Castillo said as he took the leash, "I'm coming."

"You want some company, Colonel?" Davidson asked.

"I can handle walking a dog, Jack," Castillo snapped.

After an awkward moment's silence, Sieno offered: "When you leave the building, turn right, Colonel. There's a park a block away."

"Thanks, Paul," Castillo said. "And sorry I snapped at you, Jack. My ass is dragging." He heard what he had just said and added: "Pardon the language, Mrs. Sieno. Same excuse."

"Don't be silly," she said. "And I've asked you to please call me Susanna."

"I'll be right back," Castillo said.

"Max willing, of course," Kocian said.

Max dragged Castillo through the lobby and out onto the street and headed for the first tree, which was to the left, away from the park Sieno had spoken of.

"Your call, Max," Castillo muttered. "As if I have a choice."

It became quickly obvious that Max did indeed have a massive need to meet the urinary call of nature.

"Can we go to the park now?" Castillo asked, in Hungarian, when he had finally finished.

Max looked at Castillo, considered the question, then dragged Castillo farther away from the park.

The apartment building next to 1568 Arribeños was brightly lit. But beyond it, the street quickly became dark, as there were no brightly lit buildings and the streetlights were not functioning.

Max sniffed every tree, came to an intersection, dragged Castillo across it, then across Arribeños, where he began nasally inspecting the trees there. When he had stopped at the third tree, there was a *click* and the sidewalk was brilliantly illuminated by floodlights mounted on an old mansion.

They were turned on by motion sensors.

Well, why not? That's cheaper than burning floodlights all night.

Then he noticed the bronze sign mounted on the wall of the old building. It read EMBASSY OF THE DEMOCRATIC REPUBLIC OF CUBA.

"Oh, shit!"

I am not really conversant with the security practices of the Cuban diplomatic service but it seems reasonable to assume that if they have gone to the trouble of installing motion-activated floodlights so they can see who is loitering in front of their embassy, said motion sensors more than likely also activate one or more surveillance cameras.

He looked at Max, who apparently had taken Castillo's exclamation as a command and now was evacuating his bowels.

Max isn't going to go anywhere until he finishes!

Our likenesses are now recorded and filed under Item 405 on the Suspicious Activity Log of the embassy security officer.

Congratulations, Inspector Clouseau, you've just done it again!

Aw, fuck it!

Lieutenant Colonel C. G. Castillo, USA, turned to face the Cuban embassy, put his right hand on his abdomen, bowed deeply, and said, "Up yours, Fidel!"

[TWO]

"Have a nice long walk, did you?" Eric Kocian asked as Castillo and Max came back into the Sieno living room.

Max trotted over to Kocian, gave him his paw, allowed his head to be patted, then lay down by the footstool.

"The Cubans now have a floodlighted recording of Max making an enormous deposit on their sidewalk while I cheered him on."

"What?" Kocian asked.

"That's why, Colonel," Sieno said, masterfully keeping a straight face, "I suggested you go to the park."

"Max had other ideas," Castillo said, then asked, "Can they make me?"

Sieno thought it over before replying.

"Anybody follow you here?"

"I don't think so. I came back by . . ." He stopped. "From the embassy, I went down the hill, turned left, and came back that way. I didn't see anybody following me."

"Then I don't see how. Let's hope they think you were a wine-filled Argentine."

"Yeah," Castillo said. "Let's hope."

He looked around the room.

"Anything happen while we were talking our walk?"

"Ambassador Silvio called," Torine said. "He said to tell you that Ambassador McGrory called him to tell him that Artigas has been transferred to Buenos Aires. Who's Artigas?"

"An FBI agent—one of those in Montevideo looking for laundered money. He's clever. He pretty much figured out what happened at Lorimer's estancia, so I figured the best way to make sure he kept his mouth shut was to have him assigned to OOA."

Torine nodded.

"We haven't heard from Alex Darby?" Castillo asked. "Or anyone else?"

"Alex Darby three or four times," Sieno said. "The last bulletin was half an hour ago. He expected then to finally have the owner, the *escribiano*, and the lawyer all in one place in the next few minutes."

"Explain that, please," Castillo said.

"One of the interesting requirements of Argentine law is that when you sign a contract—like a lease on a house in Mayerling—all parties have to be present at a meeting at which the *escribiano*, who is sort of a super notary public, reads the whole thing, line by line, aloud. The lawyer's function is to explain any questions about the contract."

"They do about the same thing in Mexico, Gringo," Fernando Lopez said.

"Mr. Darby said that Kensington has the radio set up, and it shouldn't take more than an hour or so to finish signing the lease—presuming all parties did, in fact, show up—and wants you to call him and tell him whether you want to move in out there tonight."

"Are there sheets and blankets, etcetera?" Castillo asked. "Food?"

"I don't know about the sheets and blankets," Sieno said. "But I don't think there will be food. And the Argentines have another interesting custom. When they move out of someplace, they take the lightbulbs with them."

"Great!" Castillo said.

"There's a Jumbo supermarket in Pilar that would have everything we need," Susanna Sieno said.

"If you were to go out there and shop, who would watch the Cuban embassy?"

"Most of that's automated," she said. "And Paul will be here. Won't he?"

"He will. Can I ask you to do that?"

"Certainly."

"Lester will go with you," Castillo said. "Go to Pilar, please, and buy what you need in the Jumbo, but don't go to Mayerling until we hear from Darby that it's a done deal and the owner and the others have left."

"You want me to use our car?" she asked.

"There's CD plates on it?"

"We have one of each," she said.

"Take the one with regular plates," Castillo said.

She nodded.

"Can we get Lester a weapon?" Castillo asked.

The faces of both Sieno and his wife showed their surprise at the request. Davidson chuckled.

"There are those who refer to Corporal Bradley as Deadeye Dick," he said. "He's one hell of a shot."

Corporal Bradley, who had stood up and was standing almost at attention, blushed.

"Mr. Darby," Sieno began, pointing to the large duffel bag that Castillo had seen him take out of the Cherokee when he'd first come to the apartment, "he didn't know what you would want, so I brought two M-16s, a riot gun, a couple of Glocks, and a couple of 1911A1 .45s."

"Your call, Corporal Bradley," Castillo said.

"Considering the circumstances as I understand them, sir," Bradley said, "and the superior ballistics of the .45 ACP round over the 9mm, if I may I'd like one of the M-16s and a 1911A1."

"So ordered," Castillo said.

Sieno smiled. "You're one of those, are you, Corporal, who doesn't think much of the 9mm?"

"Yes, sir. Actually, it's been proven conclusively that it's inferior to the .45 ACP," Bradley proclaimed, professionally. "And as a result of that determination, the formerly obsolescent Model 1911A1 has been declared optional standard by the Marine Corps and, if I'm not mistaken, by Special Operations."

"So it has, Deadeye," Davidson said, smiling at Sieno. "Any other weapons questions for the corporal, Paul?"

"I think I'd better wrap the M-16 in a blanket or something," Susanna said, not completely able to restrain a smile, and walked out of the living room.

There was a clatter of metal.

Castillo saw that Bradley was now sitting on the floor by the duffel bag that held the weapons. He had already begun fieldstripping one of the 1911A1 pistols, had dropped a part—and was already snatching it from the floor.

Christ, that was fast!

"I have twenty bucks that says Deadeye can fieldstrip that weapon faster than anyone in this room," Jack Davidson said, admiringly. "Including, with all respect, Colonel, sir, the senior special operator among us."

"No bet," Castillo said.

Corporal Lester Bradley made no move or sound to show that he had heard any of that exchange, but the usually pink skin of his neck and cheeks, now a dark rose color, suggested that he had.

Davidson pointed at him and shook his head admiringly.

Ninety seconds after Mrs. Susanna Sieno and Corporal Lester Bradley had left the apartment, Castillo's cellular vibrated.

And I still haven't charged this thing!

"¿Hola?"

"Carlos?"

"Sí."

"Our friends Ricardo and Antonio have just left here for the bus terminal with those papers Alfredo was interested in."

Castillo recognized the voice of Ambassador Silvio. It took him a moment to understand Antonio was Tony Santini.

"If they miss the bus, Antonio said he'd call both of us."

"Well, let's hope they don't miss it. Thanks for the call."

"We'll be in touch."

Castillo broke the connection and looked at Munz.

"That was Ambassador Silvio. The passports, with visas, are now on their way from the residence to the Buquebus terminal. Charge the cellular."

Munz nodded but said nothing.

" 'The passports, with visas, are now on their way from the residence to the Buquebus terminal. Charge the cellular,' " Jake Torine parroted. "Am I cleared for an explanation of that?"

"Absolutely. The battery in this is almost dead," Castillo said. "I didn't want to forget to charge it before I delivered the briefing, so I said it out loud."

Torine smiled and shook his head.

"There's a charger in the bathroom," Sieno said. "That's one of Mr. Darby's phones, right?"

Castillo nodded and said, "Thanks."

"I was wondering, Gringo, when you were going to get around to telling us what's going on," Fernando said. "But I was too polite to ask."

"Good," Castillo said.

Fernando gave him the finger.

Sieno returned with a cellular charger and, after some shifting of chairs, managed to get it plugged in and the cellular plugged into it.

"Okay," Castillo said. "What's going on now is that Colonel Munz's family—his wife and two teenage daughters—are going to the States. He is concerned, with good cause, for their safety. Ambassador Silvio has given them the necessary visas. He called to tell me that Solez has just picked up their passports at the embassy and is taking them to Artigas, who is waiting for them at the terminal. They are now at Unicenter, where Yung is sitting on them. They will go to the terminal just before the ferry sails for Montevideo. Artigas will have their tickets, and they will leave the country using their National Identity Cards, not their passports. Yung and Artigas will sit on them during the boat ride, get them into the Belmont House Hotel, in Carrasco, not far from the airport, and sit on them there.

"As soon as we're set up in the safe house in Mayerling tomorrow, we'll take the Gulfstream to Montevideo. While Colonel Torine is getting the weather and filing the flight plan, Yung and Artigas will bring them to the airport, give them their passports, they'll pass through Uruguayan customs, and we'll head for the States."

"Where in the States?" Torine asked.

"First, San Antonio," Castillo said. "To drop off Fernando."

"We can't make that nonstop," Torine said. "It's forty-five, forty-six hundred miles from here or Montevideo. Where do you want to refuel?"

"How about Quito, Ecuador?" Castillo replied.

"That'll work. It's about twenty-five hundred miles from here to Quito, and another twenty-one hundred from Quito to San Antone."

"Once we're gone, Artigas will come here and go out to the safe house. Yung will accompany Lorimer's body on an American Airlines flight to Miami—nine-something tomorrow night—and then on to New Orleans."

"Where are you headed, finally, in the States?" Fernando asked. "Washington? I mean, you could drop me in Miami. You don't have to make a special stop at San Antonio for me."

Castillo looked at his cousin. *Well, I knew this was coming.*

"San Antonio's on our way," Castillo explained. "Colonel Munz's family will be staying at the ranch in Midland."

Castillo saw the look of surprise on Fernando's face was quickly replaced with one of anger.

Or maybe contempt.

"I presume, Carlos, that you factored Abuela into your reasoning?"

Contempt. No question about it. He only calls me "Carlos" when he's really angry, or disgusted, with me.

"I spoke with her an hour or so ago. I told her I had to hold a meeting there and asked her to stay away."

Fernando didn't reply.

"You can't see the runway from the highway," Castillo said. "No one will know anyone unusual's there. And there will be Secret Service agents waiting for us."

Fernando glowered at him but said nothing.

"And one of the things you're going to do in San Antonio is make sure no one goes to the ranch."

"For how long?" Fernando asked, icily.

"For as long as it takes," Castillo said. "Fernando, we don't know who these people are, but we have to presume they have access to credit card databases, hotel registries, all of that sort of thing. Christ, Howard Kennedy even knew where I was when I used my cell phone! The minute Munz's family used a credit card, checked into a hotel, these bastards would know it. At the ranch, they won't use credit cards. And when they talk to Colonel Munz, they'll do it over the Secret Service communications system or a Delta Force radio. No one's going to locate them because they'll be invisible. If you can think of a better place I can put them, tell me."

Fernando, shaking his head, threw up both hands in a gesture of resignation.

"I don't like it, Carlos."

Castillo looked at his wristwatch.

"It's now eleven minutes after eight," he said. "If all goes the way we hope, the following things are going to happen: In the next couple of minutes, we'll hear from Solez, reporting that he met Artigas at the Buquebus terminal. Next—I'm guessing about eight-thirty—we'll hear from Yung that Señora Munz and the girls are in a taxi at Unicenter and headed for the terminal. Forty-five minutes or so after that—at 2115—we should hear from Artigas that they arrived all right and are in the process of getting on the boat. Fifteen minutes after that, we should hear that the boat has sailed. And three and a half hours—give or take—after that, we should hear from Yung and Artigas that they're in Montevideo and on their way to the Belmont House Hotel in Carrasco. When that happens, we can go to bed."

"Where, Charley?" Torine asked.

"You, me, and Fernando in the Four Seasons. There's no way we can get Max in there, Billy, which means you and Sándor will stay here."

"There's only one guest room," Sieno said. "But it has two double beds."

"Max has been in the best hotels in Europe," Kocian said. It was a challenge.

"And I bet a lot of people talked about that, didn't they?" Castillo said, evenly. "The subject is not open for debate."

"And what am I to be fed?" Kocian asked.

"I was just thinking about that," Castillo said. "Obviously, we can't go to a restaurant. What about takeout? What's the name of that steak place by the embassy?"

"The Rio Alba," Sieno furnished.

"What about calling them after Santini checks in and get them to make half a dozen large *lomos* and a salad to match, plus *papas Provençal,* and then have Santini and Solez pick it up on their way here? It's almost on their way."

"Good idea," Torine said.

"Lomo?" Kocian asked, dubiously. Then, in Hungarian, added, "Some native dish, presumably? And what in God's name are *papas* whatever you said?"

"And ask for some bones for Max," Castillo said, ignoring him. "And a couple of bottles of wine."

"Is the wine drinkable in this country?" Kocian asked.

"I think you will find it entirely satisfactory, Úr Kocian," Sieno said, in Hungarian. "And the beef is the best in the world. A *lomo* is filet mignon. The ones from Rio Alba weigh half a kilo. *Papas Provençal* are *pommes frites* with parsley, etcetera."

"Why didn't you tell me you speak Hungarian?" Kocian demanded.

"I thought everybody did," Sieno said, straight-faced. "I know the colonel does."

Kocian saw the smile on Sándor Tor's face.

"You find this amusing, do you, Sándor?" Kocian demanded.

"I think everybody does, Úr Kocian," Tor replied.

Castillo's cellular vibrated.

"¿Hola?"

"I just gave those papers to Artigas," Tony Santini announced without preliminaries. "Want us to stick around until the bus leaves?"

"I don't think so, Tony," Castillo replied after a moment. "I'm afraid you might be recognized. And when Yung gets there, he's obviously not an Argentine. Solez and Artigas can pass. So tell Solez to stick around and then take a cab here."

"I was thinking of giving Artigas my car," Santini said. "That'd give them wheels when they get there. And it's an embassy car with a radio and CD plates, so no trouble getting it . . ."

"Good idea."

"Anything else you want me to do?"

"Take a cab to Rio Alba and pick up our supper," Castillo said. "Paul's about to order it."

"That's one of your better ideas, Charley."

"According to Napoleon, an army moves on its stomach. I'm surprised you didn't know that."

Santini chuckled.

"Tell Paul to order me a large *bife chorizo*," Santini said and broke the connection.

Sieno got the Rio Alba on the telephone and placed the order.

"So now all we have to do is wait, right?" Torine asked when he saw Sieno hang up.

"So that nobody falls asleep while we're waiting," Castillo said, "I thought we'd talk about briefcase-sized nuclear bombs."

Torine looked at him with a puzzled look on his face.

"Why do I have this odd feeling that you're serious?" he asked.

"I am," Castillo said.

"What's that about?"

"Jack Britton heard from an undercover counterterrorism cop that the same people who were involved in stealing the 727 have bought a hundred-odd-acre farm outside Philadelphia. On the farm are some old iron mines. They are stocking them with food and intend to use them as shelters when someone sets off a briefcase-sized nuke in Philadelphia."

"How reliable is Britton's source?" Torine asked, incredulously. "That sounds awfully far-fetched, Charley."

"I know. But it can't be ignored."

"Britton believes this?" Fernando asked.

"Britton thinks it can't be ignored," Castillo said. "He's up there now with some Secret Service guys and some state cops he knows, looking around. I'm going there from Midland, on my way to Washington. So let's talk about nukes. You went to nuke school, right, Jake?"

"In my youth, I flew B-29s," Torine said. "I don't know how many nuke schools I've been to. But no nuke I ever heard about would fit in a briefcase."

"Briefcase, no," Sieno said, matter-of-factly. "Suitcase, yes. There are some people in the agency who believe an agent named Sunev—"

"Who?" Castillo asked.

"Sunev," Sieno repeated. "A Russian defector. I forget his first name, if I ever knew it."

"*KGB Colonel Pyotr* Sunev, by chance?" Kocian asked, politely.

"Yeah, that's him," Sieno said.

"You know about this guy, Billy?" Castillo asked.

"His name came up several times. He's a friend of your good friend Mr. Pevsner."

"I'll want to hear about that, Billy, but first I want to know what the agency believes about what this guy said."

"Sunev testified before a congressional committee—I saw the tapes a half dozen times; he wore a black bag over his head so he couldn't be recognized—five, six years ago. He said that during the Cold War, he'd been assigned—he was a spook at the Soviet mission to the UN—to find drops across the country for weapons, including SADMs and the communications equipment necessary to make them go off. He was a little vague about whether he'd actually set up the drops or where they were."

"And the agency believes this guy?" Torine said.

"What's a SADM?" Fernando Lopez interrupted.

"Nuclear suitcase," Sieno said. "The Russians call them 'Special Atomic Demolition Munitions.' "

"Okay, let's go to basics," Castillo said. "What does a SADM look like?"

"The Pu-239 looks like a suitcase," Sieno said. "It's about two feet wide, sixteen inches high, and eight inches deep. A small suitcase, but larger than a briefcase." He demonstrated with his hands, then went on: "There's another one—I forget the nomenclature—that comes in two pieces, each about the size of a footlocker. It produces a ten- to twenty-kiloton explosion. The little one probably has a three- to five-kiloton bang."

"And the agency believes this guy hid these weapons in the States?" Torine asked.

"He didn't say he hid them, Colonel," Sieno said. "He's a slippery bastard. He said he'd, quote, been assigned to find drops for them, unquote. Some people in the agency believe that."

"Does anybody at the agency believe that nukes are hidden in the States?" Castillo asked.

"Some do," Sieno said.

"Where is this guy now?" Castillo asked. "I think I'd like to talk to him."

"Probably in Moscow," Sieno said. "The agency went through the whole business of getting him a new identity—he became a Latvian, teaching Eastern European history at Grinnell—then, one bright early spring day in 2000, he and his family disappeared."

"Disappeared?" Castillo asked. "Weren't they sitting on him?"

"Not tight enough, apparently," Sieno said.

"Perhaps," Kocian said, "on hearing that his dear friend Vladimir was about to become president of Russia, he was overcome with nostalgia for Mother Russia and simply had to go home."

"He knew Putin?" Castillo asked.

Kocian nodded. "They were stationed in Dresden in the KGB together. And Putin was sworn in on 7 May 2000."

"What else do you know about this guy, Billy?" Castillo asked.

"*Know?* I don't *know* enough to print anything. But I do know that Colonel Sunev—not under that name, of course—was in Paris, Vienna, Budapest, and Baghdad, and some other places, starting right after Mr. Sieno tells us he disappeared, and as recently as six months ago. And that he knew Mr. Lorimer of the UN, which I find fascinating. And is a good friend—I told you—of Pevsner."

"What was he doing in the States, testifying before a congressional committee?"

"I'm only a simple journalist, not an intelligence officer," Kocian said, "but I think they call that 'disinformation.' "

"To what end, Billy?" Castillo asked.

"You will recall, Karlchen, that at that time there was a great deal of concern about Soviet nuclear weapons falling into the wrong hands? That they would be stolen from depots because there was no more money to pay the guards?"

"I remember that," Torine said. "It scared me."

"Nothing personal, of course, Colonel, but if it wasn't so dangerous, I would be amused by American naïveté," Kocian said.

"Watch it, Billy!" Castillo snapped.

Kocian shook his head and went on: "This loss of ex-Soviet, now Russian Federation, nuclear weapons could be prevented if the United States came up with the money—this is a simplification, of course—to bring the guards back on the payroll. I think you actually gave them several billions of dollars to do just that.

"To convince your Congress of the danger, Russian 'defectors'—Sunev was one of maybe two dozen—'escaped' to the United States and 'told all.' Russia was no longer the enemy. Russia was now a friend. The Muslims were the enemy. They were liable to detonate nuclear weapons stolen—"

"Or bought with drug money," Sieno said, sarcastically.

"Right," Kocian said.

"What?" Castillo asked.

Sieno said, "There were stories—widely circulated—that the Russian Mafia bought a bunch of nukes from former KGB guys in Chechnya. Or at least bought KGB connivance, depending on which story you were listening to, so the Mafia could steal them themselves and then sold them to bin Laden for thirty million U.S., cash, and two tons of high-grade heroin from his laboratories in Afghanistan . . . worth seven hundred million on the street."

"Did you believe this story, Mr. Sieno?" Kocian asked.

"I had a lot of trouble with it," Sieno said, carefully, after a moment.

"Why?" Kocian asked.

Sieno almost visibly formed his thoughts before he replied, "You know that George Tenet said that the purge of the KGB when the Soviet Union came apart was, quote, pure window dressing, unquote?"

"I didn't know that," Kocian said. "Well, I suppose the former head of your CIA had to be right about something."

Castillo glared at him. Sieno ignored him.

"All they did was change the name from Komitet Gosudarstvennoy Bezopasnosti to Federalnaya Sluzhba Bezopasnosti," Sieno said, bitterly.

Castillo thought, *His Russian pronunciation of that was perfect.*

"And put Mr. Putin in charge?" Kocian asked, innocently. "So things could go on as before?"

In Russian, Castillo asked, "How good is your Russian, Paul?"

"Not quite as good as yours, Colonel, but not bad," Sieno replied, in Russian.

"And what is a nice Italian boy like you who speaks Russian like a Muscovite doing eavesdropping on the Cubans in Argentina?"

"Counting the days until I get my pension," Sieno said.

"You were a bad boy in Moscow?" Castillo asked.

Sieno hesitated for a moment before he answered.

"Not exactly a bad boy," he said. "But I was one of the major reasons Tenet said what he did. And there were a lot of people between me and the DCI who didn't want him to hear any more of that from me. So they brought me back to Langley from Moscow and told me—I should say, implied with credible deniability—that I had two choices. Option one, I could go to Buenos Aires as deputy station chief and they would arrange for Susanna to be here and we could double-dip and, as long as I kept my mouth shut, I could look forward to saving a lot of money for my retirement. Or, option two, I could stay in Washington and leak what I knew and they would guarantee that I'd be fired for cause. And, of course, lose my pension *and* my reputation."

"Jesus!" Torine said.

"And being the moral coward that I am, I took option one," Sieno said.

"So why are you telling us this now?"

"You won't like the answer," Sieno said.

"Try me," Castillo said.

"You shamed me, Colonel," Sieno said. He pointed at Munz. "And so did you, *mi Coronel.*"

"What do you mean 'shamed'?" Castillo asked.

"When this whole thing started—the night Masterson got away from Munz and me . . ."

"You're losing me, Paul," Torine said. "Masterson 'got away from you'?"

"When these bastards snatched Mrs. Masterson, Alex Darby assigned me to sit on him and the kids at their house. So Alfredo and I did just that. We sat in a car outside his house. And Masterson went over the fence in the backyard, walked to the train station, took a train downtown to meet the bad guys, and they blew him away. He's dead because I fucked up, in other words . . ."

"I don't believe that, Paul, and neither does the ambassador or Alex Darby," Castillo said.

"Let me finish, please, Colonel," Sieno said. "Bottom line is, if I'd done my job right Masterson would not have climbed the fence and gotten on that train. I took this personally. I was going to find out who did it and get back at them. Then you showed up, Colonel, and you were in charge and I didn't like that at all. At one time, I'd been a pretty good clandestine service field officer and Alex Darby knew that, and here is some Army major with friends in high places about to call all the shots. It wouldn't have been the first time I'd seen that happen.

"So I went to Darby—who is one of the really good guys—and asked him what the hell was going on. He told me that you were the best special operator he'd ever known, that he'd seen you operate in Iraq and Afghanistan and knew what you had done about getting that stolen 727 back. And that since my ego was involved, and this was very important, he was going to keep me out of whatever you were going to do. He didn't want me getting in your way."

He took a breath, then went on: "I wouldn't have taken that from anybody but Alex Darby. But I've seen him operate. So I went along. And sure enough, he was right. You found that bastard Lorimer when nobody else could. You set up and pulled off that snatch operation in Uruguay in less time than I could believe, and—"

"That was not a complete success," Castillo said. "Lorimer and one of my guys died. Alfredo took a bullet . . ."

"And you took out a Spetsnaz assault team to the last man. That doesn't happen often. They're good."

"You're sure they were Spetsnaz?" Castillo asked.

"Either Spetsnaz or Stasi or somebody else, maybe even Cubans, trained by—more important, controlled and financed by—the Federalnaya Sluzhba Bezopasnosti. Who else but the FSB, Colonel? It's time you started calling a spade a spade. You can't talk about missing or stolen Russian nukes and leave them out of the discussion."

"You said I shamed you. That Alfredo and I shamed you. What's that all about?"

"Colonel, you did what you thought was the right thing to do—and so did you, Alfredo—without thinking of the consequences to yourself. I used to be that way before the bastards at Langley finally ground me down. That was shaming. So I decided to get off the sidelines."

"Well," Kocian said, "that makes it two of us in this room who know the KSB is behind all of this. It's nice not to be alone anymore."

"Three of us, Úr Kocian," Sándor Tor said.

When Castillo looked at Tor, he went on: "I suspected after the incident on the Szabadság híd that your assailants were ex-Stasi—"

"What incident on the Szabadság híd?" Sieno asked.

"You've been to Budapest, too, Paul?" Castillo asked. "You do get around, don't you? These bastards tried to snatch Billy on the Freedom Bridge—"

"*Franz Joséf Byücke, Karlchen,*" Kocian interrupted.

". . . And when Sándor interrupted that, they shot Billy," Castillo finished. He then said, "Please go on, Sándor."

"I suspected ex-Stasi made the attack on Úr Kocian. The one Max bit and allowed us to catch said that he was from Dresden. That attack was professional. The proof came with the attack on you."

"What proof?"

"We took fingerprints from the bodies of the men you shot," Tor said. "They did not match the fingerprints of former members of the AVH or AVO. And both of the men you had to deal with had garrotes. Only three services used the garrote—the Hungarian Allamvedelmi Osztaly and Allamvedelmi Hatosag and the Ministry for State Security of the German Democratic Republic. Since they weren't ex-AVO or ex-AVH, only ex-Stasi is left. And who is running all three? The KSB."

Castillo started to say something but stopped when the door chimes went off.

Sieno got up and walked to a wall-mounted telephone by the door.

He said, *"Sí, por favor,"* hung the phone up, and turned to the others in the room.

"There's another nice Italian boy in the lobby. He says he has our supper. I told the doorman to send him up."

[THREE]

Everyone was seated around the table in the Sieno dining room, ready for their meal from Rio Alba. When Jack Davidson—who was slicing individual portions from the enormous *bife lomo* with what looked like a huge dagger—sensed Sieno's eyes on him, he looked up and said, "Nice knife, Paul."

"It's a gaucho knife," Sieno said. "I bought it to hang on the wall of my vine-covered retirement cottage by the side of the road. Then I started to use it."

"You Jewish, Davidson?" Santini asked.

Davidson looked at him curiously. "Yeah. Why?"

"Then you will be fascinated to learn that there are forty thousand Jewish cowboys—*gauchos*—here."

He stopped slicing. "You're kidding!"

"Absolutely not. Mostly East Europeans. When they got off the boat in the 1890s, what Argentina needed was cowboys, so off to the pampas they got shipped. They wear the boots and the baggy pants, and stick knives like that under their belts in the back, but when they take off their cowboy hats there's the yarmulke."

"I have to see that."

"Keep slicing, Jack," Castillo ordered. "Some of us are hungry."

Davidson made a mock bow. "I humbly beg the colonel's pardon, sir."

Castillo's cellular vibrated.

"¿Hola?"

"Congratulations," Alex Darby announced, "you are now the proud lessee of a ten-room villa in Mayerling. They finally left, just now."

"Susanna Sieno and Bradley are in the shopping center in Pilar, buying sheets, blankets, and food."

"And lightbulbs," Sieno said. "Don't forget the lightbulbs."

"And lightbulbs," Castillo said.

"I told my maid to bring lightbulbs and food. I didn't think about sheets and blankets."

"You're bringing your maid out there?"

"And her daughter," Darby said. "This place will not run itself."

Castillo, remembering who Darby was, stopped himself just in time from asking if that was smart. Instead, he asked, "Can you call her cellular and tell her she can bring the stuff to the house?"

"Yeah. I'll do it, and I'll call the gate and tell the guards to let them in. It might be a good idea if she spent the night here, Charley, to get things organized. Or would you rather that I stayed?"

"No. I want you here, to pick your brain. If you hurry, there just may be a little steak from Rio Alba left over."

"Remind Paul that a hungry boss is a difficult superior," Darby said and the connection went dead.

Before he could lay the cellular down by the charger again, it vibrated.

"¿Hola?"

"They're on their way to the bus terminal," Yung reported. "I'm sure they didn't meet anyone they knew here."

"Good. They're expected. Let me know when you get there."

"Got it," Yung said and broke the connection.

Castillo reported the exchange to Munz, who nodded but didn't say anything.

"Paul, Susanna will spend the night out there," Castillo said.

Sieno nodded.

"I was going to recommend that," he said.

Davidson handed Castillo a plate. It held thick, pink-in-the-middle slices of filet mignon, slices of vine-ripened tomato, and a stack of *papas Provençal.*

"This isn't the haute cuisine we got used to in Afghanistan, Charley, but maybe you can wash it down with enough wine to make it edible."

As a monitor showed Alex Darby parking his car in the basement garage, Yung called to report that everyone was safely at the terminal, had their tickets, and would soon be able to get on the bus.

"Let me know when that happens," Castillo ordered. "And when the bus leaves the parking lot."

"Got it," Yung said and the connection went dead.

"Alex," Castillo said as Darby helped himself to slices of steak, "what we're going to do now is I'm going to recap what we've been talking about and then you're going to tell us what you think."

"Shoot," Darby replied.

Castillo had not quite finished when his cellular vibrated.

"*¿Hola?*"

"Christopher Columbus, Confucius, and the pilgrims have sailed for the New World," Yung reported.

"Give me a call when you get to Plymouth Rock."

He put the cellular in his pocket and gave Alfredo Munz a thumbs-up.

Munz nodded and silently mouthed, "*Mucho gracias.*"

"Two things, Charley," Alex Darby began. "One, it's a reasonable scenario. My gut feeling is that if you're not right on the money, you're not far off. Two, if number one *is* on the money then you're in trouble. For one thing, you're going up against the conventional wisdom at the agency and you know how popular you are in Langley. And for another . . ."

Alex Darby gently shook Castillo's shoulder.

"Charley, why don't you go to the Four Seasons and get some sleep?"

"Jesus, what did I do, fall asleep?"

"You were asleep with your eyes open for the last five minutes and then a minute ago you closed them."

"You're right. All I'm doing here is spinning my wheels." He tried to stifle a yawn. "Can we pick up where I dropped off in the morning? In Mayerling?"

"I'll pick you up at nine?"

"Fine. How do Jake, Fernando, and I get to the hotel?"

"The Cubans may be watching this building. If they are, they know our cars. So, instead, if you walked down the hill to Libertador and caught a cab, all they would learn—even if they followed it—was that three people left the building . . ."

"Including the one whose dog took a dump on their sidewalk," Castillo interrupted.

". . . and went to the Four Seasons," Darby finished.

"Let's do it," Castillo said and pushed himself away from the table.

[FOUR]
The Buquebus Terminal
Montevideo, Uruguay
0115 9 August 2006

The *Juan Patricio,* one of the Buquebus ferries that ply the river Plate between downtown Buenos Aires and downtown Montevideo, is an enormous Australian-built aluminum catamaran with space on the lower deck for about one hundred automobiles and light trucks. The main deck can seat, in comfortable airliner-type seating, about two hundred fifty passengers. There also is a duty-free shop and a snack bar. The first-class deck, up an interior stairway from the tourist deck, offers larger seats and its own snack bar.

There are bulkhead-mounted television sets in both classes that play motion picture DVDs. But on the late-night voyages, few people watch them, preferring to doze in their seats and wake up on arrival.

The only communication between the Munz family and either Yung or Artigas on the *Juan Patricio*'s voyage to Montevideo—aside from Yung's half-dozen smiles that he hoped would be reassuring—had been a fifteen-second encounter between Artigas and Señora Munz when the lights of Montevideo appeared.

Standing at the snack bar, Artigas had caught Señora Munz's eye and nodded toward the port leading to the ladies' restrooms. She had joined him there a moment later.

"When people start going to their cars, take the girls and go down the stairs to the car deck. Señor Yung will be waiting for you there, to take you to our car. It's a dark blue BMW with diplomatic license plates."

Señora Munz had nodded her understanding, then gone into the ladies' room. Artigas saw Yung get out of his chair and walk to the stairwell. Then Artigas returned to his seat.

As Yung had discreetly followed the Munz family as they walked onto the ferry, Artigas had driven the embassy BMW onto the ferry's car deck. But then Artigas had forgotten to tell Yung where he had parked it. Luckily, Yung had had only a little trouble finding it halfway back on the starboard side.

To explain his early presence on the car deck, once he had found the BMW and unlocked it, Yung popped the hood and looked intently at the engine, as if expecting some sign of some impending mechanical difficulty.

Only when he had been standing there for ninety seconds did it occur to him that it was possible—if unlikely—someone had been watching them all along, and, as soon as Artigas had left the car deck, that someone had hooked up a primer and a couple pounds of plastic explosive to the BMW's ignition.

Unlikely but not impossible.

The bastards are capable of anything—including using C-4.

The first few drivers who came down to the car deck to claim their vehicles looked wonderingly at the nicely dressed Chinese man flat on his back, studying the undercarriage of the BMW that had Corps Diplomatique license plates.

Yung finished in time to be standing at the foot of the stairway when the Munz family came down.

He had ushered them into the car and was in the front seat by the time Artigas walked up.

By then, the ferry was nudging into the pier.

Cars began driving off the ferry a minute or two later. Immigration formalities had been accomplished in Buenos Aires. At one counter in the terminal there, Argentine officials had run passports and National Identity Cards through a computer reader, then handed them to Uruguayan immigration officers sitting at the next counter. The passports and National Identity Cards were then run through a Uruguayan computer reader, then handed back to the travelers, who, even though physically in Buenos Aires, were now legally inside the borders of the República Oriental del Uruguay.

Uruguayan customs officials, however, were waiting for the cars streaming off the ferry.

Artigas rolled down the window and extended his diplomat's carnet, a plastic card not unlike a driver's license.

The customs officer looked at it a moment, peered into the car, and said, "Welcome back to Uruguay, Señor Artigas."

"Thank you," Artigas said.

"Diplomaticos Norteamericanos," the customs officer called to uniformed officers a few feet away. They saluted as the BMW rolled past.

"Welcome to Uruguay, *señora y senoritas,"* Yung said.

"Gracias," Señora Munz said, emotionally.

Artigas turned right on leaving the port gate and headed for Carrasco on the Rambla.

Yung took out his cellular and punched Castillo's autodial number.

After the first ring, Yung heard, *"¿Hola?"*

"The pilgrims just stepped off Plymouth Rock," Yung announced.

"What?" a voice asked, in English.

"Who is this?" Yung demanded.

"Yung?" the voice said.

"Yes."

"Torine. What's up?"

"Where's the boss?"

"Crashed. He fell asleep right after dinner. Everything go all right or do I have to wake him?"

"As smooth as glass. We're on our way to the airport to pick up Artigas's car, then to the Belmont House. We'll take turns sitting on the nest."

"How's the battery in your cellular?"

"I'll make sure it's charged"—he corrected himself—*"they're* charged."

"We'll be in touch," Torine said and broke the connection.

Artigas stopped the BMW outside the parking lot at the Carrasco airfield and got out. Yung stepped out of the passenger's door, walked around the BMW, and slid in behind the steering wheel.

When Artigas, now at the wheel of his Chrysler PT Cruiser, came out of the parking lot two minutes later, he waited until Yung had backed the BMW away from the parking lot, then followed him at a discreet distance into Carrasco.

[FIVE]
The Belmont House Hotel
Avenida Rivera 7512
Carrasco, Montevideo, Uruguay
0225 9 August 2006

Yung's apartment on Avenida Bernardo Barrán in Carrasco was two blocks away from the small, five-star luxury hotel and their route took them past it.

That naturally triggered in Yung's mind the memory of the sound of the cop's riot shotgun going off and of the double-aught buckshot pellets that riddled Yung's Chevy Blazer.

When I go to the States with Lorimer's casket, what happens to the Blazer?

I won't be coming back here, certainly not permanently. Which means I'll have to get rid of the Blazer.

How the hell can I sell it with a dozen holes in it?

How am I going to get it fixed from long distance?

Jesus, what's the matter with me? I'm supposed to be concentrating on the Munzes, not worrying about my damned Blazer!

At the Belmont House Hotel, after Yung drove the BMW into the circular drive in front of the hotel, Artigas pulled to the curb and shut off his headlights.

A doorman and a bellman immediately appeared at the BMW. Señora Munz and her daughters, all appearing very sleepy, got of the car and walked into the hotel.

Yung checked to see where Artigas was.

If the cops see him parked there, they'll be curious, but with the CD plates on the car they can't ask him what he's doing.

What they'll probably decide is that he's waiting for a pal who is inside the hotel and not yet ready to leave the arms of love.

Yung walked into the hotel as Señora Munz was registering. The desk clerk obviously knew her.

That's convenient. Their appearance this late after midnight will not raise questions.

"If there's nothing else I can do for you, ladies, I'll leave you and see you in the morning. You know how to reach me."

"Thank you very much," Señora Munz said. "You are very gracious."

Yung smiled at the girls again, then walked out of the hotel. He got in the BMW and drove to his apartment.

I don't have the clicker to open the goddamned garage door. I'll have to leave the car on the street.

He pulled to the curb and started to get out of the car, but changed his mind as he took the keys from the ignition. Instead, he took out his cellular.

Jake Torine answered on the second ring.

"They're in the nest. And Julio is sitting outside," Yung announced.

"Don't forget to make sure your phones work," Torine replied. "We don't want to have to send out a search party for you tomorrow . . . I mean, later today."

"I told you I'd do it," Yung said, somewhat snappishly, and broke the connection.

He immediately realized, *Dammit! He's right. That's an important little detail, and the truth is, I didn't think about a dead cellular battery.*

There're two chargers in the apartment, one that fits into a cigarette lighter. I'll get it and walk down the street and give it to Artigas. Then I'll charge mine.

He opened the door of the BMW somewhat awkwardly with his left hand, got out, then started to lock the car.

"*Buenos noches, Señor Yung,*" a voice said behind him. "I guess it's really *buenos dias,* isn't it?"

Yung felt a chill.

Jesus, the hair on my neck actually curled. I thought that was just a figure of speech.

"You scared hell out of me, Ordóñez!" Yung said.

"Sorry," Chief Inspector José Ordóñez said. His smile revealed he was more amused than regretful.

Yung glared at him.

"You're not going to ask me what I'm doing walking the streets of Carrasco at this hour?" Ordóñez said.

"I really don't give a damn," Yung said.

"We have to talk, Señor Yung."

"Some other time, perhaps. I've had a busy day and want to go to bed."

"I really think it's necessary," Ordóñez insisted.

"Am I going to have to hide behind the shield of diplomatic immunity to get some sleep?"

"That's one of the reasons I think we really have to talk. If at all possible, I'd like to keep our little problem from getting involved with the often sticky business of diplomatic immunity."

Oh, shit! Now what?

"Let me rephrase my request," Ordóñez said. "I would really like to talk to you. Unofficially, on my word. All you have to do is listen. You don't have to say anything, unless, of course, you want to."

Yung looked at him but didn't reply.

"What have you got to lose, Señor Yung?" Ordóñez pursued. "A few minutes of your time? And perhaps a small glass of whiskey?"

"Okay," Yung said. "Come on in my apartment. With the understanding that the next time I suggest you go home so I can get my sleep, you accept it."

"You are *muy* amiable, Señor Yung."

"Charming apartment," Ordóñez said as Yung snapped on the lights in his living room.

"Thank you. What kind of small glass of whiskey would you like?"

"Scotch, if that would be convenient," Ordóñez said. "But before we get into that, may I help you with your bandage?"

Yung looked at his bandaged hand. Blood had soaked the gauze and the gauze was dirty.

What the hell? It looked all right the last time I looked at it.

I must have fucked it up crawling under the BMW on the ferry.

"If you'll forgive my saying so, it appears to need attention," Ordóñez said.

"I've got some stuff in the bathroom," Yung said, and belatedly added, "Thank you."

Ordóñez skillfully and tenderly removed the bandage, then examined the cracked, crusted blood over the gouge.

"You were lucky," he said. "Another few millimeters and there would have been serious damage."

"I'll send a box of chocolates to your guy with the shotgun," Yung said.

Ordóñez chuckled.

"I've already had a word with him. And if I may say so, his intentions were noble. He was trying to save your life."

Ordóñez was now swabbing the wound with antiseptic and Yung was trying not to grimace at the burning sensation.

Yung said, "You don't happen to know a good body shop, do you? My Blazer looks like it was in a war."

Why the hell did I say that?

"Well, it was, wasn't it?" Ordóñez said. "And, as a matter of fact, I do. I'll leave you the address and I'll also call him and tell him you're a friend of mine."

"Thank you."

"That should do it," Ordóñez said three minutes later as he let loose of Yung's freshly bandaged hand. "And can we now have the whiskey you have so kindly offered?"

"Thank you, Chief Inspector Ordóñez."

"It was my pleasure to be of assistance. And please call me José."

Yung smiled and gestured for him to precede him out of the bathroom.

"What would you like?" Yung asked, indicating the bottles on his bar.

"The Famous Grouse, please."

When Yung handed him a glass and wordlessly asked if he would like ice, Ordóñez nodded, said "Please," then went on: "I used to drink Johnnie Walker

Black. But then the Johnnie Walker people took the distributorship away from a friend of mine—it had been in his family for four generations—and I stopped drinking Johnnie Walker and started drinking Famous Grouse, which my friend now distributes."

"How interesting," Yung said.

He handed the glass of Famous Grouse to Ordóñez, then poured one for himself.

"We Latins—you must have been here long enough to know this—are like that," Ordóñez said. "We reward our friends, punish our enemies, and hold grudges for a long time."

"Is that so?" Yung said.

"Are the Chinese like that, Señor Yung? May I call you David?"

"We Chinese are inscrutable," Yung said.

"Like FBI agents?"

"Like some FBI agents. There are some FBI agents, I must admit, who talk too much. I don't happen to be one of them. I tell you that as a friend. And, yes, you may call me David."

Ordóñez chuckled.

"Thank you," he said, then went on, "Speaking of friends, do you happen to know an Argentine by the name of Alfredo Munz?"

Oh, shit!

When it was obvious that Yung wasn't going to reply, Ordóñez continued.

"Until recently, he was head of SIDE. You know what that is?"

"I know what SIDE is," Yung said.

"*El Coronel* Munz was recently retired," Ordóñez said. "The word went around that he was retired because of his inability to quickly apprehend whoever it was who first kidnapped Mrs. Masterson and then murdered her husband before her eyes."

Yung said nothing. He took a sip of his scotch.

"The Argentines, unfortunately, are like that," Ordóñez said. "They always like to divert blame from themselves. What's the English phrase, 'Find a scapegoat'?"

"Something like that."

"The Argentine government can now say, 'Why should we be embarrassed that a U.S. diplomat's wife was kidnapped and the diplomat himself murdered on our soil? We have sent the man who should have prevented that from happening into disgraceful retirement for incompetence.' "

"That wasn't very nice of them, was it?" Yung said.

"No. But that's the way it is. And when the word got around that *El Coronel* Munz had shot himself while cleaning his pistol, many people thought that he had somehow missed while attempting to take his own life because of the shame his incompetence had brought down on his head."

"Shot himself cleaning his pistol, did he?"

"You're sure you don't know at least who I'm talking about?"

Yung didn't respond.

"How do I translate your silence and the inscrutable look on your face, David? That you do know Alfredo Munz—or at least who he is—or that you don't?"

"Try, that's one of the questions Yung doesn't have to answer unless he wants to," Yung said.

Ordóñez made a thin smile.

"Well, David, I was not one of those who believed that Munz was either incompetent or had shot himself while attempting suicide or cleaning his pistol."

"You didn't?"

"Not for a second. You see, David, Alfredo Munz is a close friend of mine—one might even say a dear friend."

"Is that so?"

"We met because we were, so to speak, counterparts. He ran SIDE on his side of the river Plate and I ran *run* the Interior Police Division of the Uruguayan Policía Nacional on this side. Despite the innocuous name, my unit does for Uruguay what SIDE does for Argentina."

"I didn't know that, of course," Yung said.

"Of course you didn't," Ordóñez said. "After all, you were just one of a dozen or so FBI agents in your embassy involved in nothing more than the investigating of money laundering, right?"

"If you say so."

"Well, shortly after Alfredo and I started to work together, we learned—I'm sure to our mutual surprise—that we were both honest cops. Unfortunately, there aren't that many of us in either Argentina or Uruguay."

"I'm sorry to hear that."

"Well, over the years, as Alfredo and I worked together on projects of mutual interest—for example, dignitary protection . . ."

" 'Dignitary protection'?"

"That involves the protection of our own officials, diplomats, and visiting dignitaries, such as heads of foreign states. Fidel Castro, for example. Did you know that when Fidel Castro visits Uruguay, he and the more important members of his entourage always stay at the Belmont House Hotel right down the street from here?"

"I think I heard that," Yung said.

"Well, for example, when Castro visited Argentina, where he was under Munz's protection, and then came here, where I was responsible for his protection, Alfredo and I naturally worked together."

"I can understand why that would happen."

"Well, when I heard that my friend Alfredo had had—how do I put this?—*some difficulty involving a firearm,* the first thing I wanted to do was help. I couldn't rush across the river to Buenos Aires, of course, because I was deeply involved in the investigation of the massacre at Estancia Shangri-La. And when I tried to telephone him, using a very private line to his very private line in his apartment, there was never an answer. There were several possible reasons for this, the most likely being that he saw, on caller identification, that I was calling and didn't think it wise—for his sake or mine—that we talk."

Ordóñez raised his glass.

"May I impose on your hospitality for another of these, my friend David?" He smiled. "This glass seems to have a hole in it."

"Of course."

While Yung put ice then Famous Grouse into Ordóñez's glass, he thought, *I really should not have another of these. I'm out of my depth with Ordóñez and I have no idea where this is leading*—but then poured another two inches of scotch into his own glass.

"Here you go, José," Yung said, handing him the drink.

"Thank you. Now, where was I? Oh, yes. As I said, it was impossible for me—because of the massacre investigation—to personally go to Buenos Aires to see what I could do to help Alfredo, or even to get him on the phone, so I did the only thing I could think of to help: I put a watch on the immigration computers."

"Excuse me?"

"I instructed our immigration service to notify me personally and immediately should the Munz name appear. I already had issued such a watch for two U.S. diplomats, Julio Artigas and David W. Yung, Jr."

"How interesting."

"Aren't you at all curious why I am curious about the movements out of and into Uruguay of you and my cousin Julio?"

"I figure if you want me to know, you'll tell me."

"Actually, there have been two interesting developments in the Shangri-La massacre that I wanted to ask you both about," Ordóñez said. "We know—or at least are reasonably sure—where the helicopter out there came from, and we have positively identified one of the men who died out there from a 7.62mm rifle bullet in his head."

Oh, shit! I don't think that's a bluff!

"You going to tell me about that?"

"In due time," Ordóñez said. "Well, tonight, shortly after the parties for whom I'd issued a watch passed through immigration at the Buquebus terminal in Buenos Aires, immigration called me at my home to tell me that not only were the two American diplomats on the ferry, but so were Señora Munz and her two daughters."

Shit!

"And here I owe both you, David, and my cousin Julio an apology. I have to confess that I suspected an unpleasant connection between you two and the family of my dear friend Alfredo. I should have known better and I'm more than a little ashamed.

What the hell is this?

"So what I did was call my man on the Buquebus—as you can imagine, it's handy to have your men on the ferry. In civilian clothing, of course. We normally have two, one with a charming Labrador that has a fantastic nose."

He smiled, took a healthy swallow of scotch, then continued.

"Anyway, I called him, and told him to take the Munz family under their protection, and to be especially watchful of the two American diplomats.

"He called back in half an hour to report that all parties were on the first-class deck, sitting separated from each other. He also said that the Chinese American diplomat had smiled at one of the Munz girls as he watched and that rather than being frightened—or even offended—she smiled back.

"That, of course, confused me. As did the next call from the ferry, shortly before it docked. The Chinese American diplomat was on his back on the car deck, as if looking for drugs—or, less likely, an explosive device—hidden under the car. That's probably where you soiled your bandage, David."

Yung did not reply.

"The final call from the ferry," Ordóñez went on, "reported that the Munz family had willingly gotten into the BMW bearing diplomatic plates with the two American diplomats and were about to drive off the ferry.

"You didn't see me in the port, but I saw you, and I saw how Señora Munz and the girls smiled at you in the Belmont House. So, here I am, David, looking for an explanation."

"Of what?"

"Who are you protecting the Munz family from? And why? And what are they doing here? And what's your connection with *El Coronel* Munz, whom you say you don't know."

"I didn't say I didn't know him; I said that was a question I didn't choose to answer."

"Are you going to tell me now?"

"Are you going to tell me about the interesting developments about the Shangri-La massacre?"

Ordóñez took a long moment before he replied.

"Do the names Vasily Respin and Aleksandr Pevsner ring a bell with you, David?"

"It's one man," Yung said. "I'm not sure which is his real name, and there are other aliases. There's a dozen, maybe more, Interpol warrants out for him. For all sorts of things."

"He's in Argentina, using the name Pevsner," Ordóñez said.

"How do you know that?"

"Alfredo Munz told me."

"Why hasn't he been arrested?"

Ordóñez shrugged. "Obviously, it is not in the best interests of the Argentine government to arrest him."

"He's paid somebody off?"

Ordóñez shrugged. "That could be. He has all kinds of money. Enough, for example, to own a Bell Ranger helicopter."

Jesus Christ! Is that where Castillo got the Ranger? From an international mafioso?

"It's not like fingerprints, of course, but the skids of helicopters make skid-marks in mud—like the mud near Estancia Shangri-La—that are identifiable. I mean, it's not too hard to determine what type of helicopter made the marks in the mud. The helicopter at Estancia Shangri-La was a Bell Ranger."

"You think it was Pevsner's?"

"I don't know. I do know there aren't very many of them around Buenos Aires. I do know that after being at Jorge Newbery airport, early on the night of the Shangri-La massacre, Pevsner's Bell Ranger took off, visual flight rules, for Pilar. It closed out its flight plan over Pilar. Since there is no airport in Pilar, there is no record of it landing there. Very early in the morning on the day of the massacre, Pevsner's helicopter returned to Jorge Newbery, again flying under visual flight rules from Pilar. And again, since it had not landed at an airport, there is no record of it having taken off from one. It stayed there until late in the day, when it again returned to Pilar under visual flight rules.

"There is enough time between Pevsner's Bell Ranger closing out its flight plan over Pilar the night of the massacre and its return to Jorge Newbery early the next morning for it to have been flown to Tacuarembó Province and back. By flying very low, it would not have appeared on radar either here or in Argentina."

"You think Pevsner was involved in the business at the estancia?"

"I don't know, David. But Pevsner is not one of those people I dismiss from suspicion because of his lily-white reputation. Now I will tell you what else I have learned, with the caveat that when I finish you will tell me what you know about any of this."

"If that was the offer of a deal, it wasn't accepted."

"That's an admission, you realize, that you know something."

"No, it isn't. I had no idea, for example, until just now that this Russian mafioso was in South America or that he owns a helicopter. I said 'No deal' because, after you tell me what else you know and ask me what I know and I tell you nothing, you can't say I'm breaking our deal."

Ordóñez looked at Yung intensely for a moment but did not respond directly. Instead, he said, "You remember me telling you that, among other things we did together, we worked on the protection of foreign dignitaries, such as Fidel Castro?"

Yung nodded.

"And that one of the things that really puzzled me about the massacre was that two of the Ninjas were shot with a special rifle bullet issued only to your competitive marksmen and Special Forces soldiers?"

"I remember."

"An additional puzzling factor here was the reaction of Ambassador McGrory when Deputy Foreign Minister Alvarez very circuitously asked him if there was any possibility that your Special Forces were in any way involved. I was watching his face. His surprise was genuine, as was his anger at the question. If your Special Forces were involved, Ambassador McGrory didn't know about it. That leaves two possibilities—that they were not involved or that they were on a mission of such secrecy that the American ambassador was not told."

Christ, he's got us!

"José, there's a very strict rule that nothing surreptitious—especially using Special Forces—can take place in a country without the ambassador's knowledge and approval."

"Yes, I know," Ordóñez said. "But let me go on. All of these questions were in my mind when I went to the English hospital during the autopsy procedures on Mr. Lorimer and the Ninjas. And then, looking at the Ninja who had been shot in the head, I had the strangest feeling that I had seen him before."

"Had you?"

"It took me thirty-six hours to remember when and where," Ordóñez said. "And then I took out my photo album—and there it was. A photograph of Fidel

Castro standing in front of the Belmont House Hotel with three familiar faces in the background. *El Coronel* Alfredo Munz, me, and Major Alejandro Vincenzo of the Cuban Dirección General de Inteligencia."

"Jesus H. Christ!" Yung blurted. "Are you sure?"

Ordóñez nodded slowly. "We generally make a practice of getting fingerprints of people like that who visit our country. We have yours, for example. I checked the prints. Major Vincenzo of the Cuban DGI, who came here as Castro's security chief, was one of the Ninjas who died at Estancia Shangri-La of a Special Forces bullet in his brain."

"They were Cubans?"

"We could not match the prints of any of the others, but there is no question about Vincenzo." Ordóñez stood up. "If I may, friend David, I will have another Famous Grouse while you decide what help you can offer me."

"What the hell was a Cuban doing at the estancia?" Yung blurted.

Ordóñez laughed.

"You will forgive me if I say that your reaction is as transparent as was Ambassador McGrory's? You were genuinely surprised to hear that, weren't you, Señor Inscrutable?"

"Yeah, I was," Yung said.

"May I start asking questions?"

"I'll tell you what I can," Yung said.

He thought, *Now I really wish I was Castillo. I'm in way over my head here.*

"Let's start with the most important thing to me," Ordóñez said from the bar. "Why are you protecting the Munz family? And from whom?"

"Munz is concerned for their safety."

"What concern of that is yours?"

"We owe him."

"Why?"

"I can't answer that."

"You will forgive me if I suspect it has something to do with his wound," Ordóñez said. "Which poses more questions, including the original one: from whom?"

"We don't know. The people who murdered Masterson, probably."

"They would be the same people who sent the Ninjas to the estancia, do you think?"

"That sounds reasonable, but we don't know."

"And from the Russian mafioso, Pevsner?"

"Possibly, maybe even probably."

"Let me be honest with you, David. I am very relieved to find that Munz trusts you with the lives of his family. That means you can be counted among the good guys."

"I think we really are the good guys," Yung said.

"What are your plans to protect Señora Munz and the girls? Perhaps I can help."

"They're going to the States," Yung said. "Tomorrow."

"Alfredo will join them there?"

"No. He wouldn't go."

"If I didn't believe you were the good guys, I might suspect that his family were hostages to his good behavior."

"That's absolutely untrue," Yung snapped. "He's staying here to help us find out who these bastards are."

"Well, as step one, I will ensure that the Munz family is safe until they get on the plane with you and Lorimer's casket."

Oh, shit! And I have to tell him!

"They're not going with me," Yung said. "A private plane will come here sometime tomorrow. They'll go on that."

"A Learjet?"

He'll find out anyway.

"No. A Gulfstream."

"I thought Señor—or is it Major?—Castillo had a Learjet."

"*Lieutenant Colonel* Castillo has many airplanes."

"And you work for Lieutenant Colonel Castillo, do you, David?"

Why deny that? It's self-evident.

"I do now."

"And my cousin Julio?"

Yung nodded. "As of yesterday."

"And who does Lieutenant Colonel Castillo work for? The CIA?"

"No. He doesn't work for the CIA."

"Then whom?"

"That's another question I can't answer."

"When you worked here as an FBI agent, were you really working for the CIA?"

"No."

"What was—what *is*—your interest in Señor Lorimer?"

"Money laundering."

"That's all?"

"I thought he was a Lebanese named Bertrand and I was trying to find out where he got all those American dollars."

"Nearly sixteen million of them," Ordóñez said. "And did you find out?" Yung nodded.

"Are you going to tell me?"

"It's money from that Iraqi oil-for-food scheme. Lorimer was involved in that."

"You know, I never even thought about that? That answers some questions, doesn't it? And poses at least as many more. I'll have to give this a good deal of thought."

"I'm sure you will."

"And do you know where that money is now?"

"Next question."

Ordóñez smiled. "You did a very good job of concealing tracks at the banks when you came back down here, David, but not a perfect one. I have learned that the receipts—or whatever they're called—for the money in Lorimer's accounts here were negotiated through the Riggs Bank in Washington. That makes me think they were in Lorimer's safe at the estancia and somehow taken to Washington. I would have been prone to think Señor Pevsner had something to do with that. But if that were so, why did *you* try to conceal the tracks?"

"That was a rhetorical question, right? You didn't expect an answer?"

"Right."

"Boy Scout's honor, José, I have never knowingly done anything that would in any way help Aleksandr Pevsner. From everything I know about the son-ofabitch, he deserves to be behind bars. Or dead. I don't know—can't prove—that he's after the Munzes, but I believe it."

"So do I. The question is why? Can you put me in touch with Alfredo?"

"When I get to the States—that'll be tomorrow—I'll get word to Munz that you want to talk to him. And that you helped us get his family to the States."

"I would appreciate that. That leaves only two things for me to do."

"And what are they?"

"I'll make sure that no one gets close to the Belmont House tonight who shouldn't be there. And then you and I will walk down there and say hello to my cousin Julio and you will tell him that you and I are agreed that we are the good guys."

"Okay. I've got to give him a charger for his cellular, anyway."

"And one more thing," Ordóñez said. He wrote something in a small notebook, tore out the page and handed it to Yung.

"What's this?"

"The address of a good auto-body repairman. I told you I'd give it to you."

"Thank you," Yung said.

"And one last thing, David. I really wish you wouldn't get on the phone and tell Colonel Castillo about our conversation."

"I'm going to have to tell him, José."

"Oh, I know. But if you call him tonight, your phones are tapped—cellular and regular—and I would rather not have a record of our conversation floating around. We both said, and are doing things, that we really shouldn't be doing. Let's keep that between us."

After a moment, Yung nodded.

Ordóñez went on: "You'll have a few minutes to speak with Colonel Castillo—or someone close to him—at the airport tomorrow. Maybe if he knows what I've told you, he will tell me something he knows that may help me sort all this out."

Yung didn't reply.

"Can Castillo get the Munzes into the United States if their passports do not have exit stamps from Uruguay?"

Castillo could get them into the States if they arrived without passports.

"I'm sure he can."

"Then we will have to get them on the Gulfstream tomorrow without them going through the normal immigration procedures. We have to presume that— I like your description, David—*these bastards* may have access to our immigration computers. If there is no record of the Munzes leaving the country, perhaps they will waste a little time looking for them here."

XII

[ONE]
El Presidente de la Rua Suite
The Four Seasons Hotel
Cerrito 1433
Buenos Aires, Argentina
0815 9 August 2006

Colonel Jacob Torine, USAF, went into the master bedroom and gently shook the shoulder of Lieutenant Colonel C. G. Castillo, USA, who was asleep, lying spread-eagle in his underwear on the enormous bed.

When that didn't work, Torine grabbed Castillo's left foot, raised it three feet off the bed, then let it go.

That worked. Castillo sat up abruptly, his eyes wide-open at first, then glaring at Torine.

"I just ordered breakfast, Charley. It's quarter after eight," Torine said.

"Thanks," Castillo said, without much enthusiasm, fell back on the bed, and then, grunting with the effort, sat up again and swung his feet out of the bed.

He took fresh underwear from his bag and walked stiff-leggedly into the huge marble bath. He turned on the cold-water faucet in the glass-walled shower, took off his underwear, and stepped under the flowing water. He stood under the cold water for a full minute before, shivering with cold, deciding that he now was sufficiently awake and could adjust the temperature.

Five minutes later, shaved and in trousers and shirt, Castillo went into the sitting room. Two waiters were arranging plates topped with chrome domes on a table.

Castillo nodded at Torine and Fernando Lopez, then walked to the enormous windows overlooking the tracks of the Retiro Railroad Station, the docks beyond that, and the river Plate.

"Nice view," he thought aloud.

"I'm glad my wife doesn't know about this," Torine said. "She doesn't mind me freezing my ass on some snow-covered runway in the middle of Alaska, but this would make her jealous."

Castillo turned and smiled at him.

"I guess Yung called?" he said.

"Yeah. He said he was on his way to the Carrasco airport to pick up Artigas's car, then would take the Munzes to the Belmont House. They'll take turns guarding them. I didn't want to wake you."

"You were really wiped out, Gringo," Fernando Lopez said.

"Understatement of the day," Castillo said as he stretched his neck. He then added, "I've been thinking."

"That's always dangerous," Lopez said.

Castillo walked to the table, sat down, and lifted one of the chrome-domed plate covers. The plate held an enormous pile of scrambled eggs. He spooned some eggs onto his plate, then found ham steaks under another dome and put one of them next to his eggs, meanwhile thinking: *What I really have been thinking about is the time I spent in that bedroom with Betty Schneider. I thought about her just before I passed out. And I thought of her this morning, just as soon as I stopped being pissed at Jake for that leg-dropping wake-up call.*

But that's personal.

This is business.

"When we came in here last night, they called me Gossinger," Castillo said. "And I remembered that I rented this place as Gossinger of the *Tages Zeitung* and they're getting the bill. And that Otto Görner sent the German embassy here a wire—maybe an e-mail, maybe he even called—asking that I be given every courtesy."

"So?"

"Hiding Billy Kocian is going to be as easy as hiding a giraffe on the White House lawn."

"True," Torine said. "The old guy is spectacular. I love his hat."

He mimed Kocian's up on one side and down on the other hat brim.

"You're going to move him in here," Lopez asked, "after all that business about renting the safe house *right now*?"

"No. But I'm going to keep this apartment and tell the hotel that Mr. Eric Kocian of the *Tages Zeitung* newspapers will be staying here—*when he is not staying in a Pilar country house that the newspaper has rented for him*—and to continue to send the bills to the newspaper. And when I get out to the safe house and can get a secure line to the White House switchboard, I'm going to call Otto and tell him to call the German ambassador to tell him who Eric is and that he's here—and why—and to . . ."

"Why is he here?" Torine asked.

"He's working on three stories," Castillo said. "One, some character from Hamburg is going to try to raise the *Graf Spee* from its watery grave off Montevideo. Two, he's going to do a piece on the German sailors from the *Graf Spee* who stayed here. And, three, he's naturally interested in the story of the murdered American diplomat, which is of great interest in Germany."

"What are you trying to do, Gringo, make him a really visible target?" Lopez asked.

"Exactly. One so visible that SIDE will decide it's in the national interests of Argentina to see that nothing happens to him. The Argentine government doesn't want any more headlines about foreigners being murdered here. And a foreign journalist? If anything happened to Billy, it would be on front pages all over the world."

"You're devious, Colonel Castillo," Torine said.

"I like to think so," Castillo said. "Thank you, sir."

"They whacked the sergeant and almost whacked your girlfriend when they were riding around in an embassy car," Lopez said. "Not to mention Masterson."

"They weren't expecting trouble," Castillo said. "Billy will have at least Jack

Davidson and Sándor Tor with him all the time and they know what they're doing. And there will be others, too."

"What's Eric Kocian going to think of this brainstorm of yours?" Lopez asked.

"I won't know that until I ask him," Castillo said. "So this is what's going to happen. Darby's going to pick me up here at nine. I'll get Billy Kocian settled in Mayerling and make the phone calls. You go to Jorge Newbery and get the plane ready."

"I think it would be better to have three flight plans," Torine said. "One from here to Carrasco, a second from Carrasco to Quito, and a third from Quito to San Antonio, rather than one with legs."

"Fine," Castillo said.

"It's only about thirty minutes from Jorge Newbery to Carrasco," Torine went on. "We won't have to take on fuel, but it would be better if we did. It's almost six hours to Quito from Montevideo."

"Let's err on the side of caution," Lopez said.

"Agreed," Castillo said.

"It's another five and a half hours from Quito to San Antonio," Torine said. "Figure an hour on the ground at Quito, that makes twelve and a half, call it thirteen, from wheels-up in Montevideo until touchdown in San Antonio."

Castillo nodded and said, "We'll need food and something to drink."

Torine nodded. "It would be better if we got that in Montevideo."

"I'll call when I'm leaving Mayerling. Then you call Yung and tell him to pack a picnic lunch but not have the hotel do it."

He looked down at his plate and saw that he had eaten everything he'd put there.

"I better get dressed."

"Gringo, I'm still not happy about taking the Munzes to Midland," Lopez said.

"Right now, I don't see another option. But when I get on the radio, I'll call Abuela and make sure she stays in San Antonio."

Castillo went into the master bedroom to finish dressing.

He had just finished tying his necktie when the doorman called to say his car was waiting for him.

[TWO]
Mayerling Country Club
Pilar, Buenos Aires Province, Argentina
1020 9 August 2006

The entrance to the Mayerling Country Club was very much like the entrance to the Buena Vista Country Club, four miles or so away on the other side of Route 8, where Aleksandr Pevsner lived. There was a guardhouse, with armed guards controlling a barrier pole. And, like Buena Vista, there was a shrubbery-shrouded, twelve-foot-high chain-link fence topped with razor wire, behind which the roofs of only a few houses were visible from the road.

There was immediate proof that the security was good when the guards refused to pass Alex Darby's BMW until they called the house and got permission from someone—they later learned it was Mrs. Sieno—to pass.

"Would they have passed us if you had CD plates on this?" Castillo asked as they drove slowly along the curving country club road at the prescribed thirty-kilometer-per-hour speed limit announced every one hundred meters by neatly lettered signs and reinforced by speed bumps every two hundred meters.

"No. And I didn't put my name on the frequent visitor list, either," Darby said. "The image I want to give is that the house is rented by the Sienos, a nice young Argentine couple of means from Mendoza."

"Is her—their—Spanish good enough to make that credible?"

"Yeah. She did almost a year, clandestine, in Havana. She's good, Charley. They're both good. They had bright futures until he caught a bad case of *career suicidus.*"

"Of what?"

"An uncontrollable urge to tell Langley things Langley doesn't want to hear. I had a pretty bad case of it myself."

"You mean you're here for the same reason?"

Darby nodded.

"You never said anything, Alex."

"You didn't ask, *Colonel.* It's sort of a two-sided coin. Life is a lot nicer here than other places you and I have been to. And the people who work for me are really first-class. I wonder sometimes, however, how much useful information comes out of the good boys and girls in the unpleasant places who tell Langley what it wants to hear."

"Tell me about Edgar Delchamps," Castillo said.

"How'd you get along with ol' Ed, Charley?"

"Very well, I think."

"He's one of the good guys. I thought you two probably would get along."

"How did he avoid getting a dose of *career suicidus*?"

"He had it. I would say he had a nearly fatal case of it."

"Then what's he doing in Paris? Don't tell me that's the agency's version of Siberia."

"Maybe not Siberia, but it's one of those places where the good boys and girls don't want to go because you can't help but learn all sorts of things the Francophiles in Virginia don't want to read about while they're humming 'April in Paris.' And Ed knows where a lot of the bodies are buried. When they yanked him out of Germany, he said that's where he wanted to go and they backed down. They have sort of an understanding. He writes what he wants to and they don't read it."

Castillo grinned but shook his head in disgust.

He said, "How much do you think Delchamps would know about Colonel Pyotr Sunev of the KGB?"

"Probably a lot more than Langley wishes he does," Darby said. "They got more than a little egg on their face when the defector they marched before Congress turned out to be quite the opposite. One of the reasons they're annoyed with Ed is that he warned them the guy was bad news. Nobody likes 'I told you so.' "

"That means he knows something about Russian suitcase nukes?"

"As much as anybody, Charley," Darby said, then pointed out the window. *"Chez nous, mon colonel,"* he went on. "And a bargain at four grand a month, especially since Monsieur Jean-Paul Lorimer-Bertrand is paying for it."

Castillo saw a sprawling brick house with a red tile roof sitting fifty feet off the road on a manicured lawn.

"Surrounded by nice shrubbery concealing more razor wire and motion detectors," Darby added. "It has a pool, a croquet field, and a very nice *quincho,* in which Sergeant Kensington has set up shop."

The house also had a three-car garage. As Darby's BMW entered the cobblestone drive, the door to one of the garages opened and he drove inside.

Susanna Sieno was waiting for them at an interior door, which led from the garage into the house.

When they were in a spacious, nicely furnished living room with plateglass walls offering a view of the garden, she pointed.

"The Grand Duke seems to be satisfied with our humble offering," she said.

Eric Kocian, elegant in an entirely white outfit, from hat to shoes, was sitting in a white-leather-upholstered stainless steel recliner beside the swimming pool. He was drinking a cup of coffee and smoking a cigar. A matching table held an ashtray, a coffee service, and a copy of the *Buenos Aires Herald.*

To the right of the swimming pool was a small cottage built in the style of the main house, obviously the *quincho* that Darby had mentioned. There was a DirecTV satellite dish antenna mounted on the roof. Castillo looked but could not see the antenna that he knew Kensington had put up for the AFC Delta Force radio.

Kensington knows what he's doing. The radio is set up somewhere.

And there are two of them. I've never heard that any of them ever went down, but redundancy is always nice.

"I've got to talk to Billy and right now," Castillo said.

"Privately?" Darby asked.

"No. I want both of you in on it," Castillo said.

"You took your time coming, Karlchen," the old man greeted him poolside. "And as you can see, Max has found a new friend. He probably won't even notice you're here."

He gestured to the other side of the swimming pool, where Max was chasing after a soccer ball that Corporal Lester Bradley had kicked into the distance.

Castillo saw the grip of a Model 1911A1 Colt pistol sticking out of Bradley's waistband, under his jacket.

I can't let Billy get away with that crack, Castillo decided. He whistled shrilly.

Max, who had just picked up the soccer ball in his mouth with no more difficulty than a lesser canine would have had with a tennis ball, stopped, looked, then came happily running over to him.

Castillo looked at Kocian, smiled smugly, then looked back at Max and said, "I can't believe he got that in his mouth."

"It no longer holds air," Kocian said. "Max was annoyed the first time he bit into it and it hissed at him. So he gave it a good bite to make it behave."

Max dropped the limp soccer ball at Castillo's feet. Castillo rubbed his ears, then kicked the ball as hard as he could so that it would sail over the swimming pool. He failed. The ball landed in the pool. Max ran up to the four-foot-tall fence that surrounded the pool, looked at the barrier, then, with no apparent effort, jumped over it. He then leaped into the pool, grabbed the ball, paddled around a moment until he figured the best way to get out of the pool was via the steps on the shallow end, swam there, got out, jumped back over the fence, and trotted over to them.

"That was a mistake, Karlchen," Kocian said. "What he will do now is drop the ball at our feet and shake himself."

Max did precisely that.

"Max, you sonofabitch!" Castillo said, laughing.

"You would find that amusing!" Kocian said. "Look at my trousers!"

"That isn't the only mistake I've made. Does that surprise you?"

"Not at all, frankly," Kocian said. "But we all make them. The last time for me was in January. Or was it December? I misspelled a word. Are you going to tell me what yours was?"

Colonel Alfredo Munz walked up.

"Am I intruding?" he said.

"Of course not," Castillo said. "Your family is in the Belmont House Hotel. Everything went perfectly."

"Am I going to get a chance to talk to them?"

"Can you wait until we get to Quito, Ecuador?"

"Of course."

"The Herr Oberstleutnant, Herr Oberst," Kocian said, "is about to tell us all of a mistake he made. I'm breathless with anticipation."

"My mistake was in thinking we could hide Herr Kocian here," Castillo said. "But now I realize that would be about as difficult as concealing a giraffe on the White House lawn."

Munz, Susanna Sieno, and Darby could not resist smiling at the image.

Kocian glared at them.

"So what do you suggest?" Kocian asked, rather icily.

"The opposite," Castillo replied. "He's an important journalist, publisher of the *Budapester Tages Zeitung,* vice chairman of the board of directors of Gossinger Beteiligungsgesellschaft, G.m.b.H. . . ."

Castillo saw the sour look on the old man's face and had a hard time restraining a smile. *You didn't mind me mentioning that, did you, Uncle Billy?*

". . . and I don't think the Argentine government would be happy if anything happened to him."

"I see where you're going," Munz said.

"I don't," Kocian said.

"They would want SIDE to keep an eye on you, Herr Kocian," Munz said. "They would not want anything to happen to an important man such as yourself."

"You think it's a good idea, Alfredo?" Kocian said.

"I think it's a very good idea," Munz said.

"All I am is a simple journalist plying his trade," Kocian said.

"*We* know that, but the Argentine government doesn't," Castillo said. "We'll get Otto to exaggerate when he calls the German ambassador here."

Kocian glared at him.

"Okay, so that's what we'll do," Castillo said. "I'll get on the horn right now."

When they walked to the *quincho,* Corporal Lester Bradley came to attention as they approached him.

"Lester, try not to do that," Castillo said. "You're in civilian clothing."

"Yes, sir," Bradley said and lost perhaps ten percent of his rigid posture.

Sergeant Kensington was inside the *quincho,* on a twin of Kocian's recliner, reading the *Herald.* There was a Car-4 leaning against the recliner. Kensington lowered the newspaper but did not get up.

"How soon can you get the radio up, Bob?" Castillo asked.

"We're up and all green, sir," Kensington said. "I just talked to Major Miller."

"Where's the antenna?"

"On the roof, sir. It says DirecTV on it."

"Oh, you are a clever fellow, Robert."

"My mother always told me that, sir."

"Here's what I want to do, Bob. You tell me if I can do it and, if so, how."

"Yes, sir?"

"I want a secure line wherever possible. I have to make calls to Ambassador Montvale, to a civilian number in Germany, to a civilian number in San Antonio, and another one to a local number here in Argentina—either cellular or a regular phone—and I *really* don't want that party to know where it's coming from."

"Yes, sir. The ambassador's no problem at all. We get Miller at the Nebraska Complex on the horn. That'll be encrypted with our—AFC's—logarithms. Miller can decrypt and patch you into the White House switchboard and you'll have a secure line . . ."

"Instantaneous?"

"Yes, sir," Kensington said, then reached to the floor beside him and extended a telephone handset to Castillo. "Just like a telephone."

"And the others? How do I do that?"

"A couple of problems there," Kensington said. "You'll be secure as far as the White House switchboard for Germany and San Antonio, but not beyond, and, as far as here goes, the White House can get you secure as far as the embassy here, but I don't know if they can patch you into the local phone company."

"No problem," Susanna said. "But unless we block it, if the person you're calling has caller ID, they'll know where it's coming from, and, if they're any good at all, they could trace it to the embassy. Override the block, I mean."

"That's no problem," Castillo said. "Let him think I'm calling from the embassy. I mean, we'll put the caller ID block in, but there's no real harm if they get around it."

Kensington finally rose from the recliner. He walked to what looked like a kitchen cabinet, opened the door, squatted to examine the AFC radio, then turned and said, "All green, sir. You want the Nebraska Complex now?"

"Please. Put it on speakerphone."

"You're up."

"And how else may I be of assistance to you, Sergeant Kensington?" Major H. Richard Miller's voice—having been encrypted in Washington, D.C., then sent twenty-seven thousand miles into space to a satellite, then bounced back another twenty-seven thousand miles to earth and decrypted in the dining room of a *quincho* thirty-odd miles outside Buenos Aires—inquired cheerfully and with such clarity that amazement was on everybody's face except that of Sergeant Kensington.

"You can first get your bum leg off my desk," Castillo said, "and then we'll talk."

"Oh, good morning, Colonel. I've been wondering when we were going to hear from you. Ambassador Montvale is, in his words, 'quite anxious to chat' with you."

"Oddly enough, that's why I called. Patch me into the White House switchboard and eavesdrop, please."

"You got it, Charley."

Twenty seconds later, a pleasant voice announced, "White House. This line is secure, Colonel Castillo. Sir, Ambassador Montvale has been trying to reach you."

"Will you get him for me, please?"

"Hold one, please."

"Ambassador Montvale's secure line," the now very familiar voice of Truman Ellsworth announced.

The sonofabitch really won't answer his own phone.

"Lieutenant Colonel Castillo for the ambassador, please," Castillo said.

"Hello, Charley!" Ambassador Montvale said cheerily a moment later. "And how are you, wherever you are?"

"I'm in Buenos Aires, sir. In three or four hours, I'm leaving for the States."

"Nice not having to worry about airline schedules, isn't it?" Montvale said, and, without waiting for an answer, went on: "So I'll see you in what—twelve hours or so?"

"It'll probably be a little longer than that, sir. I'm going first to Texas and then to Pennsylvania . . ."

"That's one of the things I'm quite anxious to chat with you about, Charley: briefcases in Pennsylvania. The man you said was going to report to me has never shown up. No matter the hour, call me when you get to Washington. And bring him with you."

"If that's possible, sir, I will. But I will see him before I come to Washington."

"May I inquire why you're going to Texas?"

"What I consider to be a bona fide threat has been made against the family of one of my primary sources. I'm bringing them to the States for their protection."

"Why do you consider it to be a bona fide threat? Source and family? Or just family? And where are you taking them?"

"Among other reasons, an attempt was made—there is good reason to believe by the same parties who were at the estancia—to kidnap Special Agent Yung. He was wounded in the process."

"What's the good reason?"

"Absolutely no identification on the body we have, and he had a hypodermic full of a tranquilizer with him. Same modus operandi as the attempted kidnapping—both attempts—of my source in Budapest. And, of course, the kidnapping of Mrs. Masterson."

Montvale grunted.

"You still have no idea who these people are, Charley?"

"I've got a couple of theories. I'll tell you about them when I see you."

"How's Yung? He's going to be all right?"

At long last, he asks about Yung.

"He has a gouge from a double-aught buckshot pellet in his hand. He was lucky."

"Now they're using shotguns?"

"Yung took a hit when the Uruguayan police took down the bad guy."

"And what do the Uruguayan police think about all this?"

"That's something else I want to talk to you about," Castillo replied, and thought: *Although right now I have no idea what I'll say.*

"We do have a lot to talk about, don't we?"

"Sir, I apologize, but I've forgotten your other questions?"

Montvale took a moment to remember what they were.

"Oh, yes. Are you bringing your source and family? Or just the family?"

"Just the family, sir. His wife and two daughters."

"And where are you taking them in Texas?"

"To the Double-Bar-C. It's a ranch my family has in Midland. It's isolated."

"And floating over a sea of sweet crude oil in the Midland Basin, right?"

Jesus Christ, he knows about that, too?

"That proved very useful only yesterday," Montvale said. "I'll tell you all about it when I see you."

Castillo didn't respond. *What the hell is he talking about?*

Montvale went on, "Presumably, you've thought about security on the ranch?"

"Yes, sir. I've arranged for the Secret Service to be there by the time we get there."

"I didn't hear about that," Montvale said, making it an accusation. "I wonder why?"

Castillo again didn't reply.

"Is there anything I can do to help you, Charley? Anything you need?"

"How difficult would it be to have Edgar Delchamps brought home from Paris until we get this sorted out? He's the CIA station chief . . ."

"I know who he is," Montvale interrupted. "If you think it's necessary, I'll have him here as soon as he can get on a plane."

"I think it's important, sir."

"Then he'll be on the next plane. He'll probably be here before you get here. Is there anything he should be told?"

"No, sir."

"But you will tell me, right, why you need him when we have our chat?"

"Yes, sir. Of course."

"At the risk of repeating myself, let's have that chat as soon as possible."

"Yes, sir."

"Anything else, Charley?"

"No, sir."

"Nice to talk to you," Montvale said and hung up.

"White House."

"I need to speak with Mr. Otto Görner in Fulda, Germany," Castillo said. "The number is . . ."

"Otto Görner," Görner's voice came over the phone.

"This is the White House calling, Herr Görner," the operator said, in German. "Will you hold please for Colonel Castillo?"

"Colonel, this line is not, repeat, not secure."

"I understand. Thank you," Castillo said. *"Wie gehts, Otto?"*

Otto Görner was not at all happy to be reminded that Kocian needed protection at all and that Castillo wanted to get at least part of it from the Argentine SIDE.

"You know what happened in Budapest, Otto," Castillo said. "Even without involving the Argentines, he's safer here than he would be there."

"And you trust the Argentines?"

"I trust them to act in their best interests. Keeping Eric safe is in their best interests. And I'll have people—good people—on him as well."

It was a moment before Görner responded. "I'll call as soon as we hang up."

"I'll keep you posted," Castillo said.

"Yes, of course you will," Görner said and hung up.

Castillo turned to Alex Darby.

"The next call is the local one," he said. "Will you call the embassy switchboard and get the operator to block the caller ID?"

Darby nodded, took out his cellular, and punched an autodial button.

"This is Darby," he announced. "In the next thirty seconds or so, there will be a secure call from Colonel Castillo from the White House. He will give you a local number to call. Block the embassy's caller ID." He paused. "Yes, I understand that from our switchboard the call here will not be secure."

He broke the connection and looked at Castillo. "Done."

"Go kick the ball for Max, Alex, and take Susanna with you, please." He looked at Kensington. "You stay, Bob, but go deaf."

"Yes, sir."

Darby and Susanna walked out of the *quincho.*

"Okay, Bob," Castillo ordered, motioning with the handset, "get me the embassy on here."

"¿Hola?"

The male voice answering Pevsner's home telephone did so in Spanish, but the thick Russian accent was apparent in the pronunciation of the one word.

Castillo thought it was probably the gorilla who had followed Pevsner into the men's room at the service station.

"Let me speak to Mr. Pevsner, please," Castillo said, politely, in Russian.

"There is no one here by that name."

"Tell him Herr Gossinger is calling and get him on the line," Castillo ordered, nastily.

There was no reply, but twenty seconds later Aleksandr Pevsner came on the line.

"Guten Morgen, Herr Gossinger," he said.

"Did Alfredo get the pancake flour and maple syrup to you all right, Alek?"

"Yes, he did, and thank you very much. But why do I suspect that isn't the purpose of this call?"

"Paranoia?" Castillo asked, innocently.

It was a moment before Pevsner replied, a chuckle in his voice. "Do you know how many people dare to mock me, friend Charley?"

"Only your friends. And I don't suppose there are many of those, are there?"

"Or insult me?" Pevsner asked.

"Probably about the same number," Castillo said, solemnly.

"When was the last time you saw Alfredo?"

"When I gave him the syrup and flour. Paranoia makes me wonder if that question implies more than idle curiosity?"

"He seems to have disappeared," Pevsner said. "I'm concerned."

That sounded sincere.

"Have you asked Howard Kennedy?"

"Kennedy's the one who told me. He can't find him. Or his wife and daughters."

I am going to have to resist a strong temptation to trust him—and not tell him not to worry.

"Jesus H. Christ!" Castillo said, hoping he sounded concerned and angry. "What the hell would your friends want with Munz?"

"What friends would those be, Charley?"

"You know goddamned well what friends. The ones who tried to whack me in Budapest and tried to kidnap and/or whack one of my men in Montevideo."

"If my friends had tried to whack you, Charley, we wouldn't be talking," Pevsner said, matter-of-factly. "Other people—not my friends—might be interested in what Munz knows about that missing money in Uruguay."

"Why don't you have Howard tell the other people that I have it?"

"That presumes Howard—and, for that matter, me—know who the other people are."

"Yes, it does. I hope Howard has relayed my message that anything done to Eric Kocian I will take personally."

Pevsner didn't reply.

"Since you brought it up, Alek," Castillo pursued, "that's the real reason I called. Has Howard relayed it?"

There was a brief hesitation as Pevsner carefully framed his reply. "I believe Howard has spoken to some people who may know some other people."

"Well, tell him to speak to them again and this time tell them I'll take anything that happens to Alfredo or his family just as personally as I would anything that happens to Kocian."

"Why are you so concerned about Munz? Does he know something you don't want other people to know?"

"You sonofabitch! I'm concerned because he's a friend of mine. For Christ's sake, he took a bullet for me! We apparently define the word 'friend' differently!"

" 'Sonofabitch'?" Pevsner parroted, coolly. "It's a good thing you're a soldier, friend Colonel Charley. Soldiers swear. Otherwise, I would really take offense at that."

"Would it break your heart to hear that I hope you did?"

"No," Pevsner said, chuckling. "Not at all. Would you be surprised if I told you you're wrong? That I think we both define 'friend' the same way?"

"Yeah, it would."

"Alfredo Munz is a good man. He has become almost as close a friend of mine as Howard is. I trust him as I do Howard. He worked well for me. I try very hard to take care of my friends. As you do, Charley." He paused, then went on: "If anything happens to my friend Munz or his family, then I would take it personally."

I'll be a sonofabitch if I don't believe him!

"Maybe you better tell Howard to tell some friends who may know some other friends that you feel that way, Alek."

"I have," Pevsner said, simply.

"I'm on my way to the States," Castillo said. "If you hear anything, let me know. Howard always seems to be able to find me."

"Is your friend Kocian going with you?"

"So long, Alek. Always nice to talk to you."

Because of the complex connection, there was no easy way to hang up. All Castillo could do was cover the receiver with his hand and hope that Pevsner would become impatient and hang up before the White House or embassy switchboard operators came on the line.

He was lucky. He first heard Pevsner swear, then the sound of Pevsner slamming his handset into its cradle three seconds before the White House switch-board operator asked, "Are you through, Colonel?"

"Mrs. Alicia Castillo, please. The White House is calling."

"This is Alicia Castillo."

"One moment, please . . .

"Colonel Castillo, this line is not secure. Your party is on the line."

"Thank you, I understand," Castillo said, then asked, "Abuela?"

"I'm very impressed, Carlos. Or should I call you 'Colonel'? It's been a long time since I had a call from the White House."

"Don't be."

"Are you all right? Is Fernando with you?"

"We're both fine. He's getting the airplane ready. We're about to leave Buenos Aires for home."

"By home you mean San Antonio?"

"Yes, ma'am."

"How long can you stay?"

"Just long enough to drop Fernando off. Then, via Midland, I'm headed for Washington."

"And you can't—or won't—tell me about Midland?"

"The same people who murdered Mr. Masterson have threatened the family of a man who works with me. An Argentine. We're bringing them with us to protect them until we get this mess straightened out. That's why I don't want you anywhere near the Double-Bar-C."

"They'll be in danger at the ranch?"

"They'll be protected at the ranch by the Secret Service until I can make other arrangements for them. I'm sorry I have to use the ranch, but I just didn't have any other options."

"You can do whatever you please with the Double-Bar-C, Carlos. You own it."

"That was an inheritance tax thing and you know it. It's your ranch, Abuela."

"Whose ever it once was, the Double-Bar-C is now yours. Your grandfather left Hacienda San Jorge to Fernando and the Double-Bar-C to you. He thought you both should have a ranch for your families."

"Yes, ma'am, I know."

"How many people are you taking there?"

"My friend's wife and two daughters. Young women."

"When will you be going there?"

"We should leave in two or three hours. It's about a thirteen-hour flight."

"It's ten after nine here. If you leave there in three hours, that should put you in here about one in the morning, right?"

"And don't even think what I know you're thinking about," Castillo said. "Fernando can take a cab from the airport. And please don't tell Maria he's coming."

"I hadn't planned to say anything to Maria. Your plans have a way of changing."

"We'll only be on the ground long enough to clear customs and take on fuel, Abuela," he said, reasonably, "so don't think of coming to the airport."

"Won't you be tired after a long flight like that? Too tired to fly on to Midland and then all the way to Washington?"

"I plan to sleep all the way to San Antone," Castillo said. "Fernando may be a little tired. But that's not a problem."

"Well, I suppose you know what you're doing," she said.

"Fernando will tell you all that's happened," Castillo said. "I don't want to do that over the telephone."

"I understand," she said.

"I'll see you soon, Abuela," Castillo said. "I promise."

"Yes, I'm sure you will," Doña Alicia said. *"Via con Dios, mi amor."*

"You can break it down, Bob," Castillo said to Sergeant Kensington.

"Yes, sir."

Castillo looked out the plateglass window of the *quincho* and saw that Corporal Lester Bradley, USMC, was again playing with Max.

"Keep an eye on Lester, will you, Bob?"

"The kid's going to be all right, Colonel," Kensington said.

" 'You don't need to be all muscle to be a good special operator'—is that what you mean?"

"Yeah, that, too, Colonel. Kranz was even smaller than Lester, and he was a one hell of a soldier until these bastards got him . . ."

"Operative words, Bob: 'until these bastards got him.' Keep an eye on Bradley."

". . . but that's not what I meant."

Castillo looked at him, then made a *Well, let me know what you* do *mean* gesture.

"He knows how to handle tough situations."

"Well, he certainly performed at the estancia, didn't he?"

"I was talking about Mackall. No orders, except from you and Vic D'Allessando not to say one word about what went down here and what he was doing there. A—what?—hundred-and-thirty-pound Marine? A corporal and everybody else is a sergeant or better. You do know what happened there?"

Castillo shook his head.

Kensington grinned. "Jack Davidson told me. He thought some jarhead sergeant major was pulling his chain, that Lester was sent there as a joke. So he asked Lester how come he got sent to the Q course. When Davidson asks somebody something, he usually gets an answer. What Lester told him was, he didn't know. Davidson asked him where he came from and Lester told him he'd been sort of the clerk typist for the Marine guard detachment at the embassy here. So Davidson told him he'd better forget about taking the course, nothing personal, he just didn't have what it takes. He hadn't even been to jump school, for one thing. But since he was a clerk typist, until Davidson could straighten things out, that's what he would do. Punch keys on a computer keyboard. Lester didn't even tell him he'd done a tour in Iraq.

"So that's what he did, until General McNab and Vic showed up at Mackall to take him to Kranz's funeral and McNab thanked him for saving your ass with those two head shots in the Ninjas."

Castillo chuckled. "I would like to have seen Sergeant Major Davidson's face when McNab told him that. But Jack is formidable . . ."

"Yes, he is."

". . . and maybe Lester was just afraid to say anything."

"Oh, no. I asked him why he hadn't said anything, and what he said was that he knew you and Vic didn't want him to make waves, so he didn't. He said he knew everything would come out sooner or later. That's my point. He's a smart little sonofabitch and I like him."

"Yeah, me, too."

"You still have some clout with McNab, Colonel?"

"Nobody has clout with McNab."

"I was hoping maybe you could get Lester a waiver—probably, waivers—and let him take the Q course. He really wants to."

"He *wants* to take the Q course?" Castillo asked, dubiously.

"He wants in Special Ops. Bad. And as far as I'm concerned, he's welcome."

"Well, we know he performs, don't we? When this is over, if that's what he wants I'll see what I can do. I owe him."

"Speaking of that, Colonel, when you finally locate these bastards and start taking them out I'd like to be in on the operation."

"If it can be arranged, sure."

"Are you getting close?"

"I wish I could tell you I was. A lot depends on what Eric Kocian, Yung, and Munz come up with. So keep your other eye on them. They already tried to whack Yung."

"Will do, Colonel. Have a nice flight."

Although he wasn't in uniform and therefore was not supposed to salute, Sergeant First Class Kensington saluted crisply.

Lieutenant Colonel Castillo, who was also in civilian clothing, returned it just as crisply.

"Try hard to keep your dick—and Lester's—out of the wringer, Sergeant," Castillo said and walked out of the *quincho*.

[THREE]
Aeropuerto Internacional de Carraso General Cesáreo L. Berisso
Carrasco, Montevideo
República Oriental del Uruguay
1305 9 August 2006

"It looks like Yung got carried away again, Charley," Jake Torine said, pointing out the cockpit window of the Gulfstream as they taxied up to the business aircraft tarmac of the airport. "What I told him to do was get a picnic lunch."

Castillo, who was kneeling in the aisle just behind the pilot's seat, looked where Torine pointed and saw they were being met by ground handlers, customs and immigration officials, and a large, white van, on the body of which was lettered AIRPORT GOURMET.

"Isn't 'airport gourmet' something like 'military intelligence'?" Fernando Lopez, in the copilot's seat, inquired innocently.

Castillo was less amused.

"The idea was not to attract attention," he said.

He pushed himself upright and walked into the cabin, sat on one of the couches, and looked out the window.

The ground handlers guided the Gulfstream to a place to park and Torine shut down the engines.

Castillo lowered the stair door and looked out.

The customs and immigration officers walked up to the airplane.

"Welcome to Uruguay, señor," one of them said, in English. "May we come aboard?"

"Certainly," Castillo replied and stepped out of the way.

"We understand that you are discharging no passengers or cargo?"

"That's correct."

But how the hell did you know that?

"In that case, señor, there will be no customs or immigration formalities. The crew may go to Base Operations to check the weather and file a flight plan."

"Thank you."

"Will you require fuel or any other service?"

"We just need to top off the tanks. And we'd like to take some food for the flight."

The officer gestured at the van.

"The food has been arranged for," the officer said.

"Thank you," Castillo said.

By that goddamned overefficient Yung!

"And we can have a fuel truck sent out quickly," the officer said. "Please come again and stay longer," he added, smiling, then went down the door stairs with the other official following.

Castillo went to the cockpit.

"Jake, no formalities. Just file a flight plan."

"Where the hell are our passengers?" Torine wondered aloud.

"I don't know. First things first: file the flight plan."

By the time Torine reached the doorway, the Airport Gourmet truck had backed up to it, so close that when the doors in the rear swung open they almost touched the fuselage.

Dammit! Torine thought. *Careful near the aircraft!*

A man in a business suit leaped nimbly from the truck into the Gulfstream.

"*¡Buenos tardes!*" he said, cheerfully, then looked at the distance between the truck and where he stood, shook his head in disappointment, and went down the stairs. He stood at the rear of the truck and held up his hands, as if to catch someone.

A young girl jumped down. She kissed the man on the cheek, then looked at Castillo, as if asking for permission to climb the stair door steps.

Castillo thought, *That has to be Alfredo's youngest daughter.*

He smiled and waved her onto the plane.

In short order, another young woman and then an older one jumped from the truck, kissed the man in the suit, and came onto the airplane. The man then climbed the stairs, looked around the cabin, and went in.

"Just to be careful, I think we'd better close these," he said and pulled down the curtains over the windows beside the couches.

FBI Special Agent William D. Yung, Jr., jumped from the truck into the airplane.

"You are going to tell me what's going on, right?" Castillo asked Yung.

"Colonel Castillo, this is Chief Inspector Ordóñez," Yung said, gesturing to the man in the suit.

Jesus Christ, what the hell's the matter with Yung introducing me by name? And by rank?

Ordóñez smiled at Castillo, put out his hand, and said, "Let me express my gratitude to you, Colonel, for doing what you are doing for the family of our mutual friend, Alfredo."

Castillo shook the hand but didn't reply.

Ordóñez turned to Torine.

"You're the pilot?"

Torine nodded.

"Operations is right over there," Ordóñez said, pointing. "I suggest that you file to Porto Alegre, Brazil. That will attract far less attention than a destination farther north."

Torine shrugged, then looked at Castillo, his facing asking, *Why not?*

Castillo nodded.

"And I further suggest that the sooner you get off the ground, the better," Ordóñez said.

Torine went down the stairs and, passing a fuel truck that had just pulled up alongside the portside wing, walked quickly to the Base Operations building.

Ordóñez turned to Yung. "You will help me with the picnic lunch, David?"

Yung nodded.

Ordóñez looked at the women, who were now all sitting on the couch.

"You are in good hands. I will look after Alfredo. *¡Via con Dios!*"

Then he went down the stairs and started to climb onto the truck.

Yung handed Castillo a folded sheet of typewriter paper.

"Everything I know is on here," he said and went down the stairs.

Castillo started to unfold the sheet of paper, but before he had finished he heard Yung call his name. He went to the door. Yung was extending an insulated container to him. Castillo went halfway down the stairs and took it from him. He somewhat awkwardly turned and set the container on the floor of the passenger compartment.

When he turned again, Yung was holding another identical container. By the time he got that into the airplane and turned again, he saw that Ordóñez was hauling Yung into the Airport Gourmet truck.

"Call the office and leave a number where I can reach you!" Castillo called out.

Yung nodded as the truck doors swung closed. A moment later, the truck pulled away.

Castillo smiled.

"Call the office and leave a number where I can reach you," said the aluminum-siding sales manager to one of his problematic sales counselors.

Jesus H. Christ!

He sensed the eyes of the women on him. He walked into the cabin.

"I'm Carlos Castillo, a friend of your father," he said to the youngest daughter.

She smiled shyly at him.

"You speak Spanish very well for a *Norteamericano*," the girl said.

"Thank you very much," Castillo said.

"Here comes Jake!" Lopez called from the cockpit.

Five minutes later, after Torine dealt with the fuel crew and did his walk-around inspection of the aircraft, he came up the stairs and pulled the door shut behind him.

"Wind it up, Fernando," he called and turned to Castillo.

"We can take off local and change to Porto Alegre in the air," he said.

Torine looked at the women and addressed the youngest girl.

"Do you speak English?"

"*Sí, señor.* A little."

Torine smiled. "I'm the pilot. If the flight attendant here doesn't give you everything you want, you just let me know. I have to tell you, he's one of our worst."

She smiled at him and then at Castillo.

There came the whine of an engine starting.

Sixty seconds later, the Gulfstream started to move.

Castillo had unfolded the sheet of typewriter paper and was reading it before they reached the threshold of the active runway.

```
Colonel--

I wasn't sure if we would have time to talk.

This is written before we go to the airport, of course,
where we all may be led off in handcuffs.
```

Ordóñez is one smart cop. Luckily for us, he's a good
friend of Munz.

He knows a lot--too much, but not everything--about
the estancia.

He knows the Russian mafiosa's helicopter was there. He
suspects his involvement.

He knows what happened has nothing to do with Lorimer
being a drug dealer.

He knows it has to do with the oil-for-food business.
I'm afraid I may have confirmed this for him.

He knows that we grabbed the money. No proof, but he
knows, and I know he's good at finding proof of what
he suspects.

He has positively identified (by fingerprints) one of
the Ninjas as Major Alejandro Vincenzo of the Cuban
Dirección General de Inteligencia, who he met when
Castro was in Montevideo and Vincenzo was in charge of
his security.

I think as soon as we can get on a secure line we
should talk.

If I have screwed things up, I'm really sorry.

Yung

Castillo read the note twice, then folded it and put it in his shirt pocket.

When the Gulfstream was at altitude, he went to the cockpit and showed it to Torine and Lopez.

[FOUR]
San Antonio International Airport
San Antonio, Texas
0350 10 August 2006

Castillo woke up when Lopez shook his shoulder. He had been sleeping uncomfortably most of the way from Quito in one of the chairs next to the forward bulkhead of the passenger compartment, his feet on the facing chair.

The younger Munz girl was in the chair across the aisle. Señora Munz and the older girl had taken the two couches. When he opened his eyes, Castillo saw that they were now sitting up, and that the eyes of the younger girl, now sitting tensely in her chair, showed concern, maybe even fear.

And then he saw why.

There were four other people in the passenger compartment. One of them was nattily dressed in the uniform of a lieutenant of the U.S. Citizenship and Immigration Services. The other three were heavily armed and dressed in black jumpsuits, on the breasts of which were badges of officers of the U.S. Customs and Border Protection service.

One of the Customs officers, an enormous, swarthy man, held an Uzi in the position that caused Castillo to speak rudely to him.

"Point that goddamned muzzle at the floor!" Castillo barked, in English.

"Gringo," Lopez said, cautiously.

The officer moved the Uzi toward Castillo.

"You don't speak English?" Castillo snapped, in Spanish. "Don't point that thing at me!"

"Take it easy, sir," the Citizenship and Immigration Services lieutenant said.

The lieutenant looked at the big guy holding the Uzi and ordered, "Lower that muzzle."

"Better . . ." Castillo said, still furious.

"Carlos," Lopez said, "these gentlemen wish to search the aircraft and our luggage. Torine thought you might wish to discuss that with them."

"We *are* going to search the aircraft, understand that!" the enormous swarthy man announced, not at all pleasantly.

Castillo locked eyes with him. "Then might I, sir, with all respect and humility, suggest that you begin your thorough inspection of our luggage with my briefcase?" he asked, sarcastically. "It's right there on the floor."

"What's in the briefcase?" the enormous man asked.

"My credentials," Castillo said. "I'm Supervisory Special Agent Castillo of the Secret Service."

The swarthy man considered that a moment, then said, "Get it."

"That's what he is all right," the swarthy man said, visibly cowed by the credentials. But that didn't last long. "We are still going to search your luggage and the aircraft. That's regulations!"

"Search away," Castillo said. "I simply wanted to identify myself before you saw the weapons we have aboard." He turned to the immigration lieutenant. "How do we get through immigration?"

"There's a van outside that'll carry you to the commercial side of the airport."

"And bring us back?"

The lieutenant nodded.

"Ladies," Castillo said, "leave everything on board but your purses. We have to go through the immigration process. On behalf of the United States of America, I apologize for this rude reception."

"Thanks for everything, Fernando," Castillo said when they were back at the Gulfstream. "When you get home, blame everything on me."

"Maria will do that anyway," Lopez said.

He picked Castillo off the ground in a bear hug.

"If you need me for anything, forget it," Lopez said.

"You got it."

"I didn't mean that, Gringo, and you know it."

"What I want you to do is make sure Abuela doesn't go anywhere near Midland."

"I will. Believe me."

"I'll find someplace else for the Munzes just as soon as I can."

Lopez nodded, shook hands with Torine, kissed the cheeks of the Munz women, then turned and climbed back in the van.

As the others went aboard the Gulfstream, Castillo watched it drive away until it was out of sight, and then, not remembering if he had seen Torine do it or not, did the walk-around inspection of the plane, then went up the stairs into it.

He smiled at the younger Munz girl.

"Colonel Torine has said I can ride up in front if I promise not to touch anything."

She smiled back at him.

When he stepped into the cockpit, he saw that Jake Torine was strapping himself into the copilot's seat.

"I'm pleased to see that you remembered it's the pilot in command's duty to do the walk-around," Torine said. "Has anything important fallen off?"

[FIVE]
Double-Bar-C Ranch
Near Midland, Texas
0555 10 August 2006

As Castillo applied the thrust reversers, he saw that there were two black GMC Yukon XLs parked next to the hangar. And a silver Jaguar.

Well, the Secret Service is here.

And the Jaguar, which is almost certainly Abuela's, is here because so was she when the heat got to her. She had the Lear pick her up.

When he had taxied the Gulfstream back to the hangar from the end of the runway and stopped, Torine said, "I'll shut it down, Charley. You tend to our passengers."

Castillo unstrapped himself and went to the passenger compartment, where he tripped the DOOR OPEN switch. The door began to move and a dry heat started to blow in. It had a familiar feel and smell.

Señora Munz and the younger girl, smiling, were on their feet and looking down at the older sister, who was sound asleep on one of the couches.

Well, they say a perfect landing is one that (a) you can walk away from and (b) doesn't wake the passengers.

He smiled at the younger girl.

"I'll get some ice water," he said. "You can pour it in her ear. That'll wake her up."

"Carlos, that's an awful thing to say!" a familiar voice said from the open doorway behind him, in English.

Then the voice switched to Spanish.

"I'm Alicia Castillo. This terrible young man is my grandson. Welcome to our home!"

Castillo turned. As his grandmother pushed past him to get at the Munz family, he saw a heavyset man, obviously a Secret Service agent, standing just inside the door.

The heavyset man shrugged and held up both hands.

The meaning was clear: *I didn't know how to stop her.*

XIII

[ONE]
Lehigh Valley International Airport
Allentown, Pennsylvania
1035 10 August 2006

As he taxied the Gulfstream to the Lehigh Valley Aviation Services' tarmac, Castillo saw United States Secret Service Special Agent John M. Britton— brightly attired in a pink seersucker jacket, a yellow polo shirt, light blue trousers, and highly polished tassel loafers—leaning against the front fender of one of two black Yukons whose darkened windows identified them to Castillo as almost certainly Secret Service vehicles.

With Britton were three men—more sedately dressed—who Castillo thought were probably the local Secret Service.

Castillo parked the aircraft.

"You go deal with the welcoming committee," Torine said. "I'll do the paperwork and get us some fuel. Speaking of which, you want to give me your credit card?"

Castillo unstrapped himself, worked his way out of the pilot's seat, gave Torine an American Express card, then went into the empty passenger compartment and opened the door and went down the stairs.

"Nice airplane," Britton greeted him. "This is the first time I've seen it."

"How are you, Jack?" Castillo said as they shook hands.

Britton made the introductions: "These are special agents Harry Larsen and Bob Davis, and their boss, Supervisory Special Agent Fred Swanson. They're out of Philadelphia."

"I'm an old pal of Isaacson and McGuire," Swanson said as they shook hands.

"Then I guess you heard that my Secret Service credentials are a little questionable?"

"Yeah, and I also heard getting them for you was Joel's idea," Swanson said. "So you're among friends, Colonel."

"Call me Charley," Castillo said. "I made light colonel so recently that when someone says it, I look around to see who they're talking to."

Swanson chuckled.

"And you know that Jack can hardly be called a grizzled veteran of the Secret Service?" Castillo went on.

"He told me. He also told me Joel recruited him, which makes him okay in my book—I know what Jack did in Philly, too. Isaacson told me that just when he was going to see if he would fit in the protection detail you grabbed him for whatever it is you do."

"What did he—or anybody—tell you about that?"

"Joel was pretty vague. Britton has been a clam. And when I asked McGuire, he said you were the only guy who could decide we had the Need to Know."

Castillo considered that, then nodded. "Okay. You do. The classification is Top Secret Presidential. But let's wait until we're out of here."

"Where are we headed? The farm? There's not much to see," Britton said.

"I better see what there is," Castillo said. "But first, Jake and I need a shower and a shave. And then breakfast. It's been a long flight."

"Where'd you come from?" Swanson asked.

"Buenos Aires and that's classified."

Swanson's eyebrows went up, but he didn't say anything.

"We're in the Hotel Bethlehem in Bethlehem," Britton said. "It's not the Four Seasons—no marble walls in the bathrooms—but there's plenty of hot water and towels, and a nice restaurant, and it's near where we're going."

"Fine."

"I suppose this is also classified," Britton said. "Yung called Miller from Washington, and Miller called me. Yung was in Miami about to load Lorimer's body on a plane to New Orleans. He's really anxious to talk to you."

"And vice versa," Castillo said.

" 'Lorimer's body'?" Swanson parroted. "Can I ask who Yung is?"

"David Yung is an FBI agent who now works for me," Castillo said. "Jean-Paul Lorimer—an American, a UN diplomat, up to his eyeballs in the Iraq oil-for-food scam—was whacked by parties unknown at his estancia in Uruguay."

"This is starting to get interesting," Swanson said.

"The Secret Service is involved," Castillo said. "I asked Tom McGuire to send people to watch the Lorimer family, the funeral home, the funeral, etcetera, to see if they can make any of the mourners. And to keep an eye on Yung. These bastards have already tried to kidnap and/or whack him."

"Really interesting," Swanson said. "Neither Tom or Joel mentioned anything about that, either."

"I told you they couldn't," Castillo said. "And what I said just now about parties unknown wasn't entirely accurate." He looked at Britton. "Jack, we now know who one of the Ninjas was. He was positively identified—fingerprints— by a Uruguayan cop as Major Alejandro Vincenzo of the Cuban Dirección General de Inteligencia."

"No shit?" Britton said, in great surprise.

"I suppose you realize, Colonel, that you're really whetting my curiosity?" Swanson said.

"Let's get in one of the Yukons," Castillo said. "We can start clueing you in while Torine's dealing with the airplane. I don't think we can finish, but we can start."

Fifteen minutes later, Jake Torine handed Castillo's American Express card to the Lehigh Aviation Services' fuel truck driver, who took it without question, ran it through his machine, then handed it back with the sales slip for his sig- nature. Torine signed the slip—using his own signature, but it would have taken the expert eye of a forensic document examiner to determine that the scribble read "Torine" and not "Castillo"—then walked across the blazing-hot tarmac to the black Yukon that Castillo and the others had climbed in.

Special Agent Bob Davis of the Secret Service had to get out of the truck, fold down the middle-row seat he had been occupying, and get in the back, third row of seats so Torine could get in.

"If you weren't such a paragon of virtue and honesty, Charley," Torine said, after the introductions were made and as he handed Castillo his credit card, "you probably wouldn't have to pay for the fuel and the landing fee. I signed the bill 'Abraham Lincoln.' "

When Torine didn't get the laugh he expected, he added: "Somehow I sense I'm interrupting something."

"I have been regaling these gentlemen with the plot of the mystery," Castillo said.

"How far did you get?"

"Dropping the Munzes at the ranch in Midland," Castillo said. "I told them everything, Jake. We need all the help we can get."

"Any of this make any sense to you, Mr. Swanson?" Torine asked.

"No, Colonel, it doesn't. And I am about to be overwhelmed with curios- ity as to how these Rambo operations of yours are connected with these home- grown Muslims we're watching 'as a highest priority.' "

"Tell them, Jack," Castillo ordered.

"Okay," Britton said, and took a moment to form his thoughts. "You know,

Fred, that when I was on the Philly cops, I was undercover for a long time in the Aari-Teg mosque."

"That must have been fun," Special Agent Davis commented from the backseat. "How long did you get away with that before they made you?"

"Three and a half years—and they never made me."

"I'm impressed," Davis said in genuine admiration.

"Yeah, me, too," Castillo said.

"Right after we came back from Uruguay," Britton said, "I heard that another undercover cop in the Aari-Teg mosque, a pal of mine named Sy Fillmore, had gone over the edge—the cops found him wandering around babbling in North Philly. Once they learned, several days later, he was a fellow cop, they had him put in the loony tunes ward in Friends Hospital. So I went to see him.

"And he told me that AALs had bought a hundred-twenty-acre farm in Bucks County on which—or *in* which—were some pre–Revolutionary War iron mines that they were stocking with food and water, and in which they are going to take cover when a briefcase-sized nuclear bomb is detonated in Philly."

"Jesus Christ!" Special Agent Davis exclaimed.

"And you're taking this seriously?" Swanson asked, his tone serious. "It sounds incredible."

"Yes, it does," Britton said. "And that's what Chief Inspector Dutch Kramer decided when he heard it. First of all, it came from Fillmore, who slides back and forth between making sense and babbling, and is indeed incredible on its face value. Kramer didn't even tell the FBI. But when I told Charley, both he and McGuire, and I suppose Isaacson, too, decided I should look into it. That's when you got involved."

"You mean Joel knew this and didn't tell me?" Swanson asked, indignantly. "All I got was some bullshit about starting a 'highest priority round-the-clock surveillance' of these lunatics, the reason for which I would learn in due time."

"You weren't cleared for that information," Castillo said, reasonably.

"I've got a couple of security clearances," Swanson said. "Three or four of them with names. And Joel knows that."

"Joel couldn't tell you," Castillo said. "Only two people can decide who has the Need to Know."

The reply didn't seem to surprise Swanson. He nodded and asked, "The director of National Intelligence and the secretary of Homeland Security?"

Castillo shook his head. "The President and me."

"Only you and the President? That's impressive, Colonel," Swanson said. "Can I interpret that to mean somebody really high up thinks this threat is credible?"

"Ambassador Montvale thinks it's credible. And as soon as I have a look at this place, Jack, we're going to Washington. He wants to see you personally."

"Oh, shit," Britton said.

"Which reminds me," Castillo said. He pointed to a radio mounted under the Yukon's dashboard. "Is that tied into the Secret Service's communications system? I mean in Washington?"

Swanson nodded.

"I'd like to get word to Montvale that I'm here, and that I'm coming to Washington—with Britton—as soon as we're through here. ETA to come later."

Swanson nodded and pressed his finger to his lapel.

"Cheesesteak here," he said. "Is this thing working?"

The response came immediately: "Loud and clear."

"Get word to Big Eye that Don Juan is with me and will be coming to see him—with English—later today. ETA to follow. Acknowledge delivery."

"Got it. Will do."

Swanson turned to Castillo and said, "Done."

"Thanks," Castillo said. "Although I feel like I've just made an appointment with my dentist."

Swanson smiled, then asked, "You think this threat is credible, Colonel?"

"No," Castillo said. "I've been talking to some people who know about bombs like this and know about the Russians and they don't think so, and if I had to bet, I'd go with them."

"Why?" Swanson asked, simply. "There's supposed to be a hundred of these briefcase-sized nukes hidden around the country. There was even some KGB defector who testified before Congress that he'd scouted places to hide them."

"The defector's name was Colonel Pyotr Sunev," Castillo said. "And after the CIA set up a new identity for him as a professor at Grinnell College, he disappeared one day, then turned up in Europe, once again in the KGB."

"Disinformation?" Swanson asked.

Castillo nodded.

"And a lot of egg on the CIA's face?"

Castillo nodded again.

"And from everything I've learned about these bombs," Castillo said, "which I admit isn't much, they're the size of a suitcase, not a briefcase. And the firing mechanisms are coded. I can't imagine the Russians giving a bomb, much less that code, to a bunch of lunatics."

"What about our friends in the Muslim world?"

"I think if they had a bomb, and the code to detonate it, they would have already used it. The Russians have their own trouble with the Muslims. I just can't see them handing a nuke to any of them; they'd be liable to set it off in Moscow."

"So what's going on with these nuts in Durham?"

"I wish I knew. The first thing I'd like to know is where they got the money to buy the farm in the first place. Jack tells me the Aari-Teg mosque had trouble paying their rent."

"They paid for it with a cashier's check for $1,550,000 drawn against the account of the Aari-Teg mosque, Clyde J. Matthews, Financial Officer, in the Merchants National Bank of Easton, Colonel," Special Agent Harry Larsen said.

"Clyde, aka Abdul Khatami, is one great big mean sonofabitch," Britton added. "He's the head mullah of the Aari-Teg mosque. Before he found Muhammad, ol' Clyde was in and out of the slam from the time he was fifteen. Mostly drugs, but some heavier stuff, too—armed robbery, attempted murder, etcetera. He was doing five-to-ten in a federal slam—for cashing Social Security checks that weren't his—when he was converted to Islam."

"Mr. Matthews's account was opened six weeks before with six hundred in cash," Larsen went on. "It was essentially dormant—two small checks to pay for gas, signed by Matthews, but the payee—same one, a gas station in Riegelsville—amounts and dates filled in by somebody else . . ."

"I think one might describe Mr. Matthews as being somewhat literacy handicapped," Britton interrupted, in an effeminate voice, causing the others to chuckle.

". . . until two days before the cashier's check for the farm was drawn," Larsen went on. "There had been a wire deposit of $1,950,000 from a numbered account in the Caledonian Bank and Trust Limited in the Cayman Islands." He paused and looked at Castillo. "I don't know if you know this or not, Colonel, but the Cayman Islands have stricter banking secrecy laws than Switzerland."

"I did. Not because I'm smart, but because Special Agent Yung told me. He's our resident expert in foreign banking and dirty money."

"Our *reluctant* expert," Britton said.

"He's seen the light, Jack," Castillo said.

"Did he see it before or after they popped him?"

"So," Larsen went on, a touch of impatience in his voice, "our chances of finding out who owns that account are practically nonexistent. On the day the check to pay for the farm was issued, there was a second cashier's check, for $59,805.42, payable to Fred Beans Cadillac Buick Pontiac GMC. Inc., 835 North Easton Road in Doylestown, as payment in full for a Cadillac Escalade, a white one."

"Well, I've always said," Britton said, in his effeminate voice, "if you don't want to attract attention, get a *white* Cadillac Escalade."

Even Larsen laughed.

"Is this guy *intellectually challenged*, Jack?" Larsen asked.

"He's street smart, with a five-year postgraduate course in crime at Lewisburg behind him. He's ignorant but not stupid. Dangerous."

"And Matthews withdrew ten thousand dollars in cash," Larsen said.

"I don't know anything about this sort of thing," Castillo said. "Doesn't the IRS get involved in this somehow?"

"Believe it or not, Colonel, there are a few nice IRS agents. I got most of what I have from one of them who's a friend of mine."

"Can he keep his mouth shut?" Castillo asked.

Larsen nodded. "They get notified whenever there's a cash transaction of ten thousand or better. When Matthews took the ten thousand in cash, that gave my guy the in to go into the bank records.

"When I asked him if I suddenly had a deposit of nearly two million from an offshore bank, wouldn't I have to answer some questions? He said *I* would. But I'm not a mosque. The Aari-Teg mosque, so far as the IRS is concerned, is a religious institution. Religious institutions do not have to identify their members or their donors. Or pay taxes."

"Shit," Castillo said.

"I'd say this whole suitcase nuke thing is absurd," Larsen said. "Except for all that money . . ."

"And except for the fact that Abdul Khatami and his loyal Muslims helped the Holy Legion of Muhammad steal that 727," Britton said. He turned to Larsen. "You know that story?"

"Joel told me," Larsen said, smiled, and pointed at Torine and Castillo. "And that these two stole it back. You think this money came from terrorists, Colonel?"

"I have no goddamned idea where it came from," Castillo said, bitterly, "but the terrorists are not stupid. Would they hand this clown two million dollars just because they like him or maybe to pull our chain when we heard about it? I don't think so. But I don't know."

Swanson said, "Follow the money, I say, based on my wealth of experience and not having a clue how you'd actually do that. Larsen's right about bank secrecy in the Cayman Islands."

"What we have is a coded list of what we think are names and addresses we took from Lorimer's safe," Castillo said. "By now, the whiz kids at Fort Meade should have that decoded. And I have all of Eric Kocian's notes about European involvement in the oil-for-food scam. There's a CIA guy in Paris who knows a lot about these SADMs—"

"These what?" Larsen interrupted.

"Nuclear suitcases," Castillo said. "The Russians call them 'Special Atomic Demolition Munitions.' This guy is already on his way to Washington. He may already be there. There're two other CIA types in Buenos Aires who know something about them. We know now that one of the Ninjas was a senior Cuban spook." He paused. "In all, a lot of disconnected information. All we can do is try to put it together." He exhaled audibly. "Can we go get some breakfast?"

[TWO]
State Route 212
Near Durham, Bucks County, Pennsylvania
1155 10 August 2006

The Secret Service radio went off in the black Yukon XL as they were going down a winding road through the countryside.

"Cheesecake?"

"Go."

"Big Eye asks for Don Juan's present location, destination, and ETA as soon as possible. He will send a taxi."

Swanson looked at Castillo.

"Don't tell him where we are," Castillo said. "Jake, we're going into Baltimore, right?"

"Baltimore/Washington International Thurgood Marshall Airport," Torine corrected.

"And ETA will be furnished when available," Castillo said.

"Don Juan going to BWI. ETA will be furnished when available," Swanson said into his lapel microphone. "Cheesecake off."

Castillo saw the questions in Swanson's eyes.

"I don't care if he knows where I am," Castillo said. "But I don't want to talk to him right now."

Swanson nodded.

"The entrance to the farm is about half a mile on the right," Swanson said five minutes later. "You can't see much—nothing but an unpaved road—from the highway. I've got some people, really good at what they do, in a house directly across the highway taking pictures of everyone going into and out of the farm road. We told the guy who owns the house that we're investigating a drug operation."

"So far, I've recognized all of them," Britton said. "They're all from the Aari-Teg mosque."

"And we've got a Cessna 172 that flies over the farm every couple of hours taking pictures," Swanson said. "All that's produced is that they've got three house trailers parked near the farmhouse . . ."

"New ones," Britton interrupted, "which makes me wonder where they got the money for them."

". . . and a Ford pickup, one of those with two rows of seats, also new, registered to the mosque in Philadelphia."

"Same question about how did they pay for that," Britton said.

"Okay," Swanson said, pointing out his deeply tinted passenger's window. "Here we are. The road winds around that hill to the farm. The iron mines are in that hill. On the back side."

Castillo saw the steep, tree-covered hill, but almost missed the road as the Yukon rolled past it.

"Not much to see, is there?" Britton said.

Castillo didn't reply directly.

"Maybe you better get me a set of those pictures," he said.

"I'm way ahead of you, Colonel," Britton said. "The ones taken from the house are on their way—ain't e-mail and digital photography wonderful?—to Dutch Kramer and Tom McGuire five minutes after they're taken. The aerials go the same way ten minutes after the Cessna lands at Allentown. So far nobody we don't know."

"Is that about all there is to see here?" Castillo said.

"Yep," Swanson said, then asked, "Where do you want to go now? To the hotel?"

"Christ, we forgot to eat!" Torine said.

"Is there some place, a McDonald's or something—better yet, a Wendy's— on the way to the airport?" Castillo asked.

"I suppose a shave and a shower is out of the question?" Torine said, drily.

"I want to get to Washington and a secure telephone as quickly as I can, Jake," Castillo said. "I need to talk to Yung and see what's going on before Jack and I go see the dragon."

"The last thing I had to eat was a stringy, cold Ecuadorian chicken leg somewhere over the Pacific Ocean," Torine said. "And that was so long ago, I forget when."

"Well, that's the Air Force for you," Castillo said. "Unless they're being fed a steak by some long-legged blond stewardess with a dazzling smile, they think they're suffering."

"The Air Force teaches that an officer should never be rude to an officer junior to them in rank," Torine said. "In your case, I'm going to make an exception: Fuck you, Colonel. I want more for breakfast than a goddamned hamburger."

Castillo laughed.

"You're right, Jake," he said. "So do I. And since Montvale is sending a taxi for us, we'd better have that shave and a shower."

"My sole remaining clean shirt and fresh undies are on the airplane," Torine said.

"We can change on the way to Baltimore," Castillo said.

"If you have to talk to your guy, Yung, in New Orleans," Swanson said, "and we're sitting on him there, then once we get to the hotel I can get the number of a pay phone to our guys and Yung can call you on it. It won't be a secure line, but that's how the bad guys communicate and it works for them."

"You're a good man, Mr. Swanson."

"So they tell me," Swanson said.

[THREE]
Baltimore/Washington International Thurgood
Marshall Airport
Baltimore, Maryland
1350 10 August 2006

There was a Secret Service Yukon XL waiting for them at the Signature Flight Support building.

True to the traditions of the Secret Service, there was no change of expression on the agent's face when he came onto the Gulfstream and saw Castillo on his knees in the passenger compartment removing an Uzi, a Micro Uzi, and a suppressed Ruger .22 caliber pistol from the compartment under one of the couches and then carefully handing them one at a time to Torine and Britton.

When Castillo climbed into the front seat of the truck, beside the agent, he was just about to ask "Where are we headed?" when the Secret Service agent spoke into his lapel microphone.

"Leaving Thurgood for the OEOB," he said, "with Don Juan, Lindbergh, and English aboard. Advise Big Eye ETA 1515."

"Charley," Torine said, "why do I think there is something derisive in your code name but that English really fits Britton and Lindbergh is absolutely appropriate for me?"

"Because you are modesty-impaired, Jake. I understand that's fairly common in the Air Force."

"What do you want me to do when you and Jack are with Montvale?"

"Pay close attention, you might learn something."

"I have to be there?"

"You have to be there," Castillo said.

[FOUR]
The Office of the Director of National Intelligence
The Old Executive Office Building
Washington, D.C.
1515 10 August 2006

Ambassador Charles W. Montvale's office in the OEOB was not very impressive for the very powerful man the press had dubbed the "New Intelligence Czar." It consisted of two small, sparsely furnished rooms and the first thing Castillo thought when he saw it was that it was even smaller than the OEOB offices of Secretary of Homeland Security Matthew Hall.

There was a reason for this. Both Montvale and Hall had far larger and more ornately furnished offices elsewhere. The primary purpose of their OEOB offices was to provide them with a place to wait and take calls until time was found for them in the President's schedule.

Cabinet members such as himself, Secretary Hall had once only half jokingly told Castillo, could not afford to be seen sitting twiddling their thumbs on chairs outside the Oval Office, like schoolboys having been sent to the principal's office for disciplining. It was bad for their public image.

Castillo was surprised when Montvale didn't keep them waiting. His secretary—or executive assistant, whatever she was—went directly to Montvale's door and opened it the moment she saw them walking into the outer office.

"Colonel Castillo and two other gentlemen are here," the secretary said.

Castillo didn't hear a reply, but a moment later, the secretary said, "Go right in, please, gentlemen."

Castillo went in first, aware that a Pavlovian reflex had kicked in, trying—and almost succeeding—to make him march in, salute, stand at attention, and bark: *"Lieutenant Colonel Castillo reporting as ordered, sir!"*

"Good afternoon, Mr. Ambassador," Castillo said.

"Hello, Charley," Montvale said.

He acknowledged Torine by saying, "Colonel," then looked at Britton.

"I like that," Montvale announced with a smile. "Pink and yellow and blue go well together. But you don't bring up what usually comes to mind when someone says, 'Secret Service.'"

"I try to put the emphasis on the 'secret' in Secret Service, Mr. Ambassador," Britton said.

"On a scale of one to ten, Britton," Montvale said, his tone suddenly serious, "what's your take on the chances of a nuclear weapon being detonated in Philadelphia anytime soon?"

"Point-zero-zero-one, Mr. Ambassador," Britton responded immediately.

"That answer sounded rehearsed."

"Your question was expected, Mr. Ambassador."

"Colonel Castillo told you to expect it?"

"No. But I didn't think you were calling me down here to discuss my wardrobe."

"Now I know why Colonel Castillo likes you," Montvale said. "You're about as much of a self-confident wiseass as he is. Now you and Colonel Torine please step out for a moment—actually, it's probably going to be a bit longer than that—while I have a private word with the colonel. Tell Jo-Anne no calls except from the President personally, and to get you some coffee."

"Yes, sir," Britton said. "Thank you."

"Thank you, Mr. Ambassador," Torine said and turned and followed Britton out.

Montvale waited until the door had closed.

"You understand, I hope, Charley, how much rides on Britton's—and thus your—assessment of the threat that there is a SADM somewhere around Philadelphia?"

"I've talked to some other people, sir. It—"

Montvale shut him off by raising his hand like a traffic cop.

"Hold that until the briefing," he said.

"I thought this was the briefing," Castillo said. It was more of a question.

"Right now we have to talk about your eleven-hundred-dollar-a-day love nest in the Mayflower Hotel," Montvale said.

"Sir?"

"That's how Pulitzer Prize–winning reporter C. Harry Whelan, Jr., of *The Washington Post* described it. No. What Harry actually said when he called Secretary Hall and told him he intended to make certain allegations in a story and wanted, in fairness, to get his version before it was published, he was in 'Motel Monica Lewinsky.' " He paused, then added with a thin smile, "He has a flair for colorful phrases."

"What sort of allegations?"

"That an Army officer by the name of Castillo who is an agent of the Defense Intelligence Agency is whooping it up on the taxpayer's dollar in the Mayflower and elsewhere all over the world."

Oh, shit!

"Where'd that come from? I never was assigned to the DIA."

"Think about it a moment," Montvale ordered, "and tell me the first name that comes to mind."

Three seconds later, Castillo said, "Mrs. Patricia Davies Wilson."

Montvale nodded.

"Goddamn her!"

"Hell hath no fury like the female scorned, I understand. You might want to write that down to think about the next time you experience the sinful lusts of the flesh and are about to throw caution to the winds and, with it, your career, the mission you've been given by the President, and the many—all unpleasant to contemplate—manifestations of that."

"The next time? What next time? I'm blown. The problem now is how to keep the Finding operation from being blown with me. I'm blown, that's it. The most I can hope for is that I will be allowed to resign for the good of the service and go hide somewhere before this reporter can find me. Once I'm out of the service, I don't have to even talk to this guy—*if* he could find me—and I don't think he'll be able to do that. All the Army has to do is say they're way ahead of the reporter, and the guy with the love nest has already been allowed to resign and they have no idea where former Lieutenant Colonel Castillo is. And, by the way, he was never assigned to the DIA." He paused. "Does General Naylor know about this?"

Montvale nodded.

"He won't like it, but between him and Schoomaker I can be out of the Army and out of Washington by noon tomorrow."

Montvale just looked at him.

"Is Edgar Delchamps here yet?" Castillo said.

Montvale nodded.

"Then what I suggest, sir, is that you keep him under wraps until you can recommend to the President that he turn the Finding operation over to him."

"Why would I want to do that, Colonel?" Montvale asked, softly.

"It's the only way I can think of to keep the Finding operation from being blown. He's privy to just about everything, but there's no way that he can be tied to me, the Finding operation, or anybody else I've been working with. Once I'm gone and he's got the Finding operation, I can meet him someplace and give him everything he doesn't already have. The Finding operation doesn't have to go down the toilet with me."

"And why in the world," Montvale asked, "knowing what's happened, would Mr. Delchamps take on that responsibility? If I were he, I'd think I was being set up as the fall guy. He would reason that Mr. Whelan is not going to let this story go just because he can't find you."

"He's a pro, Mr. Ambassador. He knows the risks of doing something that has to be done. He's been doing it a long time. He'll take the job. And more than likely do a better job with it than I've been doing."

"Let me get this straight, Castillo. What you are saying you want to do is quietly fold your tent and steal away into anonymity. Pay for your carnal sins with, so to speak, professional suicide?"

"I wouldn't put it quite that way, Mr. Ambassador, but, yes, I suppose. I disappear and the Finding operation goes on. I don't have any better ideas."

"Fortunately, I do."

"Sir?"

"Fortunately, I do," Montvale repeated. "More precisely, *did*."

"Whatever you want me to do, sir," Castillo said.

"Let me tell you what I did, Colonel. When Secretary Hall called me to tell me C. Harry Whelan, Jr., wanted to talk about your eleven-hundred-dollar-a-day love nest, I suggested that he invite Mr. Whelan to luncheon with both of us the next day in his private dining room at the Nebraska Avenue Complex."

What?

"Sir?"

"Telling him that I would tell him everything there. I further suggested that he put Major Miller back into his uniform and wheelchair—the last time Miller came here to tell me what you were up to, he was wearing civilian clothing and using canes—two of them—which naturally aroused one's sympathy, but not as much as a fully uniformed wounded hero in a wheelchair would—and that he advise Major Miller of the situation and invite him to take lunch with us.

"I told Secretary Hall that Mr. Whelan was known to be fond of oysters, grilled Colorado trout *avec beurre noir*, and an obscure California Chardonnay—Judge's Peak. I told Secretary Hall that if he could handle the oysters and the trout, I would send over a case of the Judge's Peak.

"When I sent the wine, I also sent a team of specialists from NSA to install microphones discreetly around the dining room, and to instruct Miller in their use."

My God, he's telling me he bugged Hall's private dining room!
What the hell for?

"Miller, at my orders, was waiting in your office for me when I arrived at the Nebraska Avenue Complex. Mr. Whelan was already in the dining room with Secretary Hall. I shall long remember Miller's response to my question, 'What would you say Mr. Whelan's frame of mind is?'

"Miller said, 'Mr. Ambassador, his face looks like he's happily looking forward to nailing all our nuts to the floor.'

"I then wheeled Miller, his knee again wrapped in far more white elastic gauze than was necessary, into the dining room. Whelan's eyes lit up. They lit up even more when I introduced Miller as your roommate in the Motel Monica Lewinsky.

"Mr. Whelan said, 'I'd like to hear about that. What happened to your knee, Major?'

" 'In good time, Harry,' I said. 'I'll tell you everything. But first I'd like, and I'm sure Major Miller would like, one of those.'

"Mr. Whelan was drinking a vodka martini. A *large* one . . ."

I don't know where he's going with this, Castillo thought, *but he loves telling the tale.*

"   made with Polish hundred twenty proof spirits. The waiter promptly poured martinis for Miller and myself. Ours were one hundred percent ice water with a twist of lemon and two speared cocktail onions."

"You were trying to get him drunk?"

"Not drunk. Happy. One never knows what a drunk is liable to do," Montvale said.

"And did you get him happy?"

"Oh, yes. First, I complimented him on his piece about Senator Davis in yesterday's *Post*. The senator has been using an airplane just like yours, belonging to a corporation just awarded an enormous interstate highway construction contract, as if it were his own. That put Harry in a good mood.

"As did the first of what turned out to be three bottles of the Judge's Peak, consumed along with some Chilean oysters.

"And then we had our lunch, the grilled trout with *beurre noir*, washed down with more of the Chardonnay. By then, Mr. Whelan was telling us of his journalistic career, how he'd started out on a weekly and worked his way up through *The Louisville Courier-Journal* to the *Post*. It was a long story, and, fascinated with this tale of journalistic skill and prowess, I naturally kept asking him for amplification.

"Meanwhile, the wine was flowing, and there had not been a mention of Lieutenant Colonel C. G. Castillo."

"And this reporter didn't sense what was going on?"

"Eventually, he suspected he was being manipulated. Or he realized that he had been doing all the talking. In any event, he asked Miller, 'I asked before what happened to your leg and never got an answer.'

"To which I quickly responded, 'Major Miller suffered grievous wounds—he will shortly be retired—in Afghanistan. His helicopter was shot down.'

"Whelan jumped on that. 'So what's he doing here in this Office of Organizational Analysis? And, by the way, what is that? What does it do and for whom?' Etcetera. One question after another.

"I asked him if he had ever heard of the West Point Protective Association," Montvale went on. "To which he replied, 'Of course I have. What about it? What's Miller being protected from? And by whom?'

"At that point, I began to suspect I had him," Montvale said. "I told him that actually Miller was doing the protecting. That was why he was sharing the apartment at the Mayflower.

"To which Whelan replied something to the effect that we were now getting down to the nitty-gritty. What was Miller protecting you from?

" 'From himself, I've very sorry to have to tell you,' I replied, and went on. 'Major Miller is assigned, pending his retirement, to the Detachment of Patients at Walter Reed. Now he goes there daily on an outpatient basis for treatment of his knee and his other wounds. When Miller heard that Major—now Lieutenant Colonel—Castillo was in trouble, he asked—unofficially, of course—if he could try to help him. They were classmates at West Point as well as comrades-in-arms in bitter combat. Permission was granted—unofficially, of course.' "

"You told this guy Miller is protecting me?" Castillo asked, incredulously. "From what?"

Montvale ignored the question.

"This announcement caused Whelan to quiver like a pointer on a quail," Montvale said. "He just knew he was onto something.

" 'How is this Castillo in trouble?' Whelan asked. 'Something to do with his eleven-hundred-dollar-a-day love nest in the Motel Monica?'

"To which I replied," Montvale went on, "that I wasn't at all surprised that a veteran journalist like himself had found out about your suite in the Mayflower and that I therefore presumed he knew about your Gulfstream."

He told this reporter about the Gulfstream?

Where the hell is he going with this?

"Whelan said that he had heard something about it," Montvale continued, "although the look on his face more than strongly suggested this was news to me.

"I then told him I would fill him in on what few details he didn't know and told him that you had paid seven and a half million dollars for what I was very afraid he would be soon calling your flying love nest. And then I told him the last anyone heard from you, you had flown it to Budapest.

"I thought carefully about telling him about Budapest, but I decided that if I was wrong, and didn't have him in my pocket, and since you acquired it so recently he might find out about the flight there and ask questions. This way, I nipped those questions in the bud."

"I don't know what the hell to say," Castillo said.

"I'll tell you when I want a response from you, Colonel," Montvale said, evenly. "Right now, just listen. We don't have much time."

Much time? For what?

"Sorry, sir."

"So, predictably, Whelan says something to the effect that he hopes I am going to tell him where an Army officer was getting the money to live in the Mayflower and buy a Gulfstream.

"To which I replied something to the effect that I was going to tell him everything, not only because I knew he'd find out anyway, but also because I knew him well enough to trust his judgment, his decency, and his patriotism.

"At that moment, for a moment, I thought perhaps I had gone a bit too far. He was more than halfway into his cups, but, on the other hand, he didn't get where he is by being an utter fool.

"And sure enough, the next words out of his mouth are, 'Why do I think I'm being smoozed?'

"I didn't reply. Instead, I took your service-record jacket from my briefcase and laid it before him . . ."

My jacket? Where the hell did he get my jacket? They're supposed to be in the safe at Special Operations Command in Tampa where nobody gets to see them.

Montvale saw the look on Castillo's face, knew what it meant, and decided to explain.

"You asked a while back if General Naylor knew of the situation you'd gotten yourself in. He knew, of course, how you'd met Mrs. Wilson in Angola and even of your unwise dalliance with her. Still, it required a good deal of persuasion on my part to bring him on board to agree this was the only possible way to deal with this situation and to authorize flying your records up here.

"But that, too, was a fortunate happenstance, because once I'd brought him on board he provided me with a number of very touching details of your life that proved to be quite valuable."

Very touching details? Oh, shit! What does that mean?

"To go on: After first reminding Mr. Whelan that the Freedom of Information Act did not entitle him or anyone else to peruse your personal history data, I told him I was going to tell him everything about your distinguished record, which he could verify by checking the records I had just put into his hands."

"You let him see my jacket? There's a lot of classified material in there. Missions I was on that are still classified. They keep the goddamned thing in a safe in Tampa!"

"Your entire file is classified Top Secret. That impressed Mr. Whelan in no small way. I began with going through your decorations—and, I must say, even *I* was impressed, Colonel—starting with your first DFC and Purple Heart, which I pointed out you had earned when you were a mere boy just months out of West Point, and ending with your last Purple Heart, in Afghanistan.

"When that was over, I knew I had Whelan hooked because he put on his tough, no-nonsense journalist's face and tone of voice and said, 'Okay. Very impressive. But let's get back to the love nests, both of them. And I think you should know that I know all about this Karl Gossinger character.'

"I asked, 'You know *everything* about Karl Wilhelm Gossinger?' and he replied, 'The eleven-hundred-dollar-a-day love nest in Motel Monica Lewinsky is registered to him. He's supposed to be the Washington correspondent for the *Tages Zeitung* newspapers. Nobody I know ever heard of him and I haven't been able to find him yet. But I will.'

"I told him that he already had, that you and Gossinger were one and the same . . ."

"Jesus Christ!"

". . . and that you were born out of wedlock and never knew your father. That your mother was a teenage German girl whose name was Gossinger."

"You had no right to get into that!" Castillo flared. "That's my personal business."

"I had, of course, considered your personal business, before I decided I had to deal with Whelan, and concluded that protecting the president of the United States, certain members of his cabinet, and finding out who the people who murdered Masterson are and dealing with them was the most important thing and far outweighed any momentary embarrassment you might feel. You get the picture, Colonel? If you had kept your male member behind its zipper when you should have, you and I would not be sitting here, would we?"

Goddamn him . . . he's right!

"No, sir. We would not. I apologize for the outburst."

"Fuck the outburst, Castillo. Apologize for *not* thinking!"

"Yes, sir. No excuse, sir."

Montvale looked coldly at Castillo for a moment, then went on, conversationally, the anger gone from his voice.

"So I told Mr. Whelan that your father was a teenage American helicopter pilot who died for our country in Vietnam without ever knowing he had a son. And, of course, that Warrant Officer Junior Grade Jorge Alejandro Castillo was a true hero, a legend in Army Aviation, in the Army.

"I could tell from the look on his face that while he was impressed, he thought I was laying it on a little thick. Of course I wasn't through.

"I asked him if he knew General Naylor and of course he said he did. And then I told him how General Allan Naylor becomes involved in the saga of Lieutenant Colonel Castillo."

"I really don't want to know what else you told this man, but I realize I should know."

"Yes, you should," Montvale said. "I told Mr. Whelan that when you were twelve, your mother, the sole heiress to the Gossinger fortune—I told him I was sure he knew that the *Tages Zeitung* newspaper chain was owned by Gossinger Beteiligungsgesellschaft G.m.b.H.; he nodded, although I'll bet he was hearing that for the first time—was diagnosed with a terminal illness. I told him your mother went to the U.S. Army—specifically, to then-Major Allan Naylor, who was stationed nearby—and asked for help to find her son's father in the United States and told him why.

"I told him that Allan Naylor told me he promised somewhat reluctantly to see what he could do, as he had no respect for an officer who would leave a love child behind him, and was concerned about what would happen when a man of such low character came into the fortune the boy would inherit.

"And, of course, that when he did look into it, he learned that your father was a posthumous recipient of the Medal of Honor, and, not only that, but the only son of a distinguished and equally wealthy family in San Antonio. The question then became would the Castillos, who traced their Texas lineage back to two men who fell beside Davy Crockett and the other heroes of the Alamo, accept their son's illegitimate German son?"

Castillo's anger began to build again. "Why the hell did you tell him all this? I don't want any pity."

"Well, then you're not going to like the rest of this," Montvale said. "By the time I was through, I was nearly in tears myself about poor Charley Castillo."

"Oh, shit!" Castillo said, softly.

"I told him that that hadn't turned out to be a problem. That your grandmother took one look at the picture of you that Naylor had shown her and said, 'He has my Jorge's eyes,' and was on a plane to Germany that night.

"I then painted a touching picture of this poor, illegitimate, parentless boy being suddenly thrust into an alien culture with nothing to hang on to but memories of his late mother and the legend of his heroic father, of his going to West Point and then to war, determined to be worthy of his hero father. I went over your list of decorations . . ."

"Mr. Ambassador," Castillo interrupted, "I don't think that'll keep this guy from writing just about what he started to write in the first place. In fact, it would appear that he now has a bigger story . . ."

"If you'll indulge me, Colonel," Montvale said, icily, "I'll tell you how I did just that."

"Sorry."

"I ended your touching life story by telling him that you stole a helicopter in Afghanistan to save Miller's crew at great risk not only to your career but your life itself."

"Oh, boy!"

"Hearing that, Mr. Whelan really fixed the hook in himself. 'Mr. Ambassador,' he asked, 'forgive me, but wasn't that a crazy thing to do?'

"Whereupon I looked at him sadly and said, 'Precisely. It was an insane, irrational act. Major Castillo had gone to the well of his resources once too often and found it dry. Everybody has a breaking point and Castillo had reached his.' "

"In other words, you told him I'm crazy?"

"In effect. I didn't use those words. I told him you were sent home from Afghanistan for some well-deserved rest. I implied that on the plane from Afghanistan you had decided your number was about up and, that being the case, you were going to have some fun before you met the grim reaper. Fun that you were going to pay for with your personal wealth, something you had never done before. Another indication of an overstressed mind.

"And I told him that it was at this point that the West Point Protective Association came into play, in the person of General Allan Naylor. I told him that Naylor didn't know what to do with you. He could not give you, in your current state of mind, the command of a battalion to which you were entitled. The way you were drinking and chasing wild, wild women, you would soon be relieved of any command you were given . . ."

"Jesus! Is that part true?"

". . . and he was reluctant to have you hospitalized for psychological problems because that on your records would keep you from ever becoming a general."

Montvale paused when he saw the look on Castillo's face, then added: "That was an original thought of mine. Getting you psychiatric help never occurred to General Naylor.

"What I told Whelan was that Naylor went to Secretary Hall, who had been decorated for valor and wounds while serving under Naylor in Vietnam and was thus a fellow warrior who knew how even the best of men sometimes reach their limits . . ."

"Oh, my God!"

". . . and asked him if he could find something for you to do until you got some rest. Which Hall, of course, agreed to do. And Naylor also arranged for Miller, whose life you had saved, to be placed on outpatient status at Walter Reed so that he could look after you."

Castillo, shaking his head in disbelief, said nothing.

"So far, you're still stressed . . ."

"You mean crazy," Castillo said, bitterly.

". . . but you seem to be improving. General Naylor hopes that soon you will be able to return to normal duty in the Army. The Army has done what it could to help a distinguished warrior, the son of an even more distinguished warrior."

"And Whelan swallowed this yarn?"

"He had no trouble at all accepting that there were good reasons—touching reasons—for your having gone over the edge," Montvale said.

Castillo gave him an exasperated look.

"But what's important comes next," Montvale said. "Two things. First, Whelan said, 'I've written a lot of stories that people tell me have ruined people's lives and I've done it with a clear conscience and I'll do it again. But I'm not going to ruin this young man's life simply because some bitch comes to me with a half-cocked story and an agenda.'

"Whereupon I asked him, in surprise, 'A woman gave you this story?'

" 'I knew damned well she had an agenda beyond getting on the right side of me,' Whelan said. 'I knew it.'

" 'Has this lady a name?'

" 'She's in the agency,' Whelan said. 'She and her husband both work for the agency. Her name is Wilson. I forget his first name, but hers is Patricia. Patricia Davies Wilson. That's to go no further than this room.'

" 'Of course not,' I readily agreed. 'You think . . . what was her name?'

"He obligingly furnished it again: 'Wilson, Mrs. Patricia Davies Wilson.'

"I asked, 'You think Mrs. Patricia Davies Wilson had an agenda?'

" 'She did,' Mr. Whelan replied. 'I have no idea what it was, but it was more

than just cozying up to me. She's fed me stuff before. A lot of—most of it—
was useful. I thought of her as my private mole in Langley.'

"Whereupon I sought clarification: 'You say you thought of Mrs. Patricia
Davies Wilson as your private mole in the Central Intelligence Agency?'

"He took a healthy swallow of wine—in fact, drained at least the last third
of a glass—and said, 'Yes, I did. I've gotten a half dozen good stories out of her.
There's a lot of things going on at Langley that the public has the right to
know. Stories that don't help our enemies. But a story about somebody who's
been burned out doing his duty and is teetering on the edge is not a good
story. I write hard news, not human interest. Damn her!' "

"So what happens now?"

"I don't know what Whelan's going to do to her, but I know what I did,"
Montvale said. "I had my technicians erase all but the last minute or so of that
recording—anything that could identify you—and then personally took it over
to Langley and played it for John Powell."

"And the DCI didn't ask you who Whelan's story was supposed to be about
or how you just happened to record their conversation?" Castillo asked.

"I'm sure he would have liked to," Montvale said. "But he was torn between
humiliation that I had personally brought him credible evidence that Mr. Whelan had a mole in the agency and anger with himself that he hadn't done more
to the lady after I personally had sent Truman Ellsworth over there to subtly
warn them—after our conversation at the Army-Navy Club—that they had a
problem with Mrs. Wilson."

"You're sure this guy is not going to write about me?"

"I'm sure he's not. He told me so."

"Because he feels sorry for the overstressed lunatic?"

"That's part of it, certainly. And part of it is that Whelan thinks of himself
as a loyal American. Patriotism is also a factor."

"Isn't patriotism supposed to be the last refuge of a scoundrel?" Castillo
asked, bitterly.

"You're the one who needed the refuge, Colonel. If the scoundrel shoe fits,
put it on."

"It fits," Castillo said. "I guess I'm supposed to thank you, Mr. Ambassador . . ."

"You're welcome, but don't let it go to your head. I was protecting the President, not you."

"Yes, sir. I understand."

Montvale looked at his watch.

"I'd really hoped—so I would have no surprises when you brief the
President . . ."

Brief the President? Where the hell did that come from?

". . . and the others . . ."

What others?

". . . that you and Britton would be able to bring me up to speed about these people in Bucks County, on everything, but we don't seem to have the time. We're due to be over there in ten minutes and I need to visit the gentlemen's rest facility before we go."

"Yes, sir."

"If I have to say this, Colonel, not a word vis-à-vis Mr. Whelan."

"Yes, sir."

"I wonder what the President's going to think about the stylish Mr. Britton," Montvale said, then rose from behind his desk and waved for Castillo to precede him out of the office.

XIV

[ONE]
The Oval Office
The White House
1600 Pennsylvania Avenue NW
Washington, D.C.
1555 10 August 2006

The Secret Service agent standing just outside of the Oval Office—a very large man attired in a dark gray suit carefully tailored to hide the bulk of the Mini Uzi he carried under his arm—stepped in front of Charles W. Montvale, blocking his way.

"Excuse me, Director Montvale," he said, politely. He nodded once, indicating Jack Britton, who still was wearing his pink seersucker jacket, yellow polo shirt, light blue trousers, and highly polished tassel loafers. "I don't know this gentleman."

"Show him your Secret Service credentials, Agent Britton," Montvale ordered. "Quickly. We don't want to keep the President waiting."

Britton exchanged a glance with Charley Castillo, then unfolded a thin leather wallet.

The Secret Service Agent failed to uphold the traditions of his service. Surprise, even disbelief, was written all over his face as he stepped out of the way.

The President was not in the Oval Office. Secretary of State Natalie Cohen and Secretary of Homeland Security Matthew Hall were. They were seated side by side on one of the pair of matching couches that faced each other across a coffee table.

Hall got to his feet and offered his hand to them each in turn.

Then he asked Britton, "I don't believe you know Secretary Cohen, do you, Jack?"

"No, sir," Britton said.

The secretary of state stood up and offered her hand to Britton.

"Secretary Hall has been telling me what you did before joining the Secret Service," she said. "I'm very pleased to meet you."

"It's an honor to meet you, Madam Secretary," Britton said.

She walked to Castillo, kissed his cheek, and said, "Hello, Charley. How are we doing with the repatriation of Mr. Lorimer's remains?"

"They're in a funeral home in New Orleans, Madam Secretary," Castillo said. "Special Agent Yung accompanied them from Uruguay. I spoke with him a couple of hours ago." He paused, then went on, "He's got an out-of-channels message for you from Ambassador McGrory. He's supposed to deliver it personally . . ."

"That's odd, Charley," she said. "Do you know what it is?"

"Yes, ma'am."

"Let's have it."

"Ambassador McGrory believes Mr. Lorimer was a drug dealer—in his alter ego as Jean-Paul Bertrand, antiquities dealer—and that a drug deal went bad at his estancia and he was murdered and the sixteen million dollars stolen."

"My God, where did he get that?" she exclaimed.

"He apparently figured that out all by himself. He confided his theory in Ambassador Silvio."

She shook her head in disbelief.

"Unfortunately," Castillo went on, "there's a clever Uruguayan cop, Chief Inspector Ordóñez of the Policía Nacional, who's pretty close to figuring out what really happened."

That got everyone's attention.

Castillo continued, "And he's also positively identified one of the Ninjas we killed as Major Alejandro Vincenzo of the Cuban Dirección General de Inteligencia—"

"One of the *what,* Charley?" the President of the United States asked as he came into the room. "Did you say 'Ninjas'?"

"Sir, that's what we're calling the people who bushwhacked us at Estancia Shangri-La."

The President looked at him strangely.

"Sir, they were wearing balaclava masks and black coveralls," Castillo added, somewhat lamely. "Ninjas—that's what they looked like."

"Well, I want to hear about that, of course," the President said. "But first things first."

He walked to Britton and offered him his hand.

"You're Special Agent Britton, right?"

"Yes, sir, Mr. President."

"I like your jacket," the President said. "What's your assessment of the possibility of a nuclear device being detonated in Philadelphia anytime soon? On a scale of one to ten?"

"When he briefed me, Mr. President," Montvale said, "Britton said, 'Point-zero-zero-one.' "

God, you're clever, Montvale, Castillo thought. *By answering for Britton, you've painted yourself as really being on top of everything.*

"Is that right?" the President asked Britton. "You think the threat is that negligible?"

"Yes, sir."

"Well, I'm relieved. I'll want to hear why you think so, of course. But that will wait until I get things organized in my mind." He looked at Castillo. "That means I want to hear everything, Charley, starting from the moment you left the White House, what was it, a week ago?"

"Six days, Mr. President. It seems like a lot longer, but it was only six days ago."

"Charley," the President said, "I want to hear everything you think has affected—or might affect—execution of the Finding. I'll decide what's important."

"Yes, sir," Castillo said and immediately decided to leave out the first thing that had happened after he left the White House that had indeed had a bearing on the Finding—his somewhat-strained conversation with Montvale at the Army-Navy Club.

"Sir, I went to Paris . . ." he began as he thought he saw a look of relief on Montvale's face.

"My God, you really got around, didn't you?" the President said fifteen minutes later when Castillo had finished. "You must be exhausted."

"I am kind of beat, sir."

"Sum it up for me, Charley. Where are we?"

"We know a lot more, Mr. President, than we knew when I left here—that a Cuban was involved, for example, and that there's probably a connection with the KGB—but I don't know what any of it really means."

The President turned to the secretary of state.

"What do you make of the Cuban, Natalie?"

"If there wasn't a positive identification, Mr. President, I'd have trouble believing it. I just don't know."

"Can we tweak Castro's nose with that? Now or later?"

"If the Cubans sent him to Uruguay—and we don't know, or least have no proof of, that—by now they know he's dead," the secretary of state said. "So far as embarrassing the Cubans, I don't think so, sir. If we laid this man's body on Kofi Annan's desk in the Security Council chamber, the Cubans would deny any knowledge of him and the delegate from Venezuela would introduce a resolution condemning us for blaspheming the dignity of the UN."

The President's face showed what he thought of the secretary-general of the United Nations and of the organization itself.

"They've washed their hands of Lorimer, right?" he asked.

"Yes, sir," Secretary Cohen said. "One of Annan's underlings issued a brief statement regretting the death of Mr. Lorimer, but—we invited them—they're not even sending someone to his funeral."

"So what are you going to do next, Charley?" the President asked.

"Well, tomorrow morning, sir, I'm going to assemble what information we have—all the disconnected facts we have, both here and in Buenos Aires—and start to try to make some sense of it."

"Need any help?" the President asked. "Anything you need to do that?"

Before Castillo could reply, Ambassador Montvale said, "In that connection, Mr. President, I'm going to call DCI Powell personally and tell him that he is to provide to Mr. Delchamps everything that Colonel Castillo asks for."

"That's the CIA man from Paris?"

"Yes, Mr. President."

"Why are you calling Powell personally? I've already ordered that the CIA—that everybody—give Charley whatever he asks for. And now Delchamps works for Charley, right?"

"Mr. Delchamps is about as popular in Langley as is Colonel Castillo, Mr. President. And then there's the matter of our not having informed the CIA—or, for that matter, others, including the FBI—of your Finding. I thought my personal call would be useful."

The President looked thoughtfully at Montvale, then at Castillo.

"And Charley's not likely to win any popularity contest in the J. Edgar Hoover Building, either, is he?" the President said, then paused in thought. "Let me make some contribution to this."

The President walked to his desk, punched several buttons on his telephone without lifting the handset, then sat and leaned back in his high-backed leather chair.

"Yes, Mr. President?" the White House switchboard operator's voice came over the speakerphone.

"Get me Mark Schmidt, please," the President said.

Less than twenty seconds later, the voice of the director of the Federal Bureau of Investigation came over the speakerphone.

"Good afternoon, Mr. President."

The President wasted no time on the social amenities.

"Mark, what I need is a good, senior FBI agent," he said.

"There's no shortage of them around here, Mr. President. May I ask why?"

"Someone who knows his way into the dark corners over there, Mark. Someone who's really good at putting disassociated facts together. Someone, now that I think about it, who probably works pretty closely with you and will be able to get you on the phone if he needs some help."

"Inspector Jack Doherty of my staff meets those criteria, Mr. President. It would help, sir, if I knew exactly what you need."

"I told you, Mark. I need some help in putting a jigsaw puzzle together. This is very important to me, so if this is inconvenient for you I'm sorry. But I want this man to be in Ambassador Montvale's office by nine tomorrow morning. He'll be working for him for an indefinite period—until the puzzle is assembled. And Montvale is going to tell him that he is not to share with anyone—*anyone*—anything about the puzzle. I think it would be a good idea if you told him about that before you send him to the ambassador."

"That sounds as if I'm being kept in the dark about whatever your problem is, Mr. President."

"It's a question of Need to Know, Mark. And right now . . ."

"I understand, Mr. President."

"Thanks, Mark. We'll be talking."

The President reached forward and punched a button, breaking the connection.

"When Inspector Doherty shows up at your office, Charles," the President said, "you tell him about the Finding and then send him over to Castillo."

"Mr. President, I can't do that," Montvale replied.

The President was known for not liking to have his orders questioned.

"Why not?" he asked, sharply.

"Sir, only you and Colonel Castillo are authorized to grant security clearances vis-à-vis the Finding."

The President stared at him a moment, then said, "You're right. I'd forgotten that. Okay. So when Inspector Whatshisname shows up tomorrow, you relay to him my personal order that he is not to relate to Director Schmidt or anyone else in the FBI anything he learns while working for Castillo. Then send him to Castillo, who can tell him about the Finding."

"Very well, sir, if that's the way you wish for me to handle it."

"That's the way," the President said.

Well, Castillo thought, suppressing a smirk, *that ends your hope of being able to clear people for the Finding, doesn't it, Mr. Ambassador?*

Wait. What the hell are you being so smug about, hotshot?

Montvale just saved your ass.

"Come to think about it," the President said, thoughtfully, making Castillo wonder if he was about to change his mind, "that's a good way to handle the whole expert question. If Castillo decides he needs an expert from somewhere else—the NSA, for example, or State, or Homeland Security—we'll run them past you or the appropriate secretary, who will relay my order to them that nothing goes back where they came from, and then run them over to Castillo. He may be able to get what he wants out of them without having to tell them why and thus about the Finding. And he's the only one who can make that decision."

"That'll work," Matt Hall said. It was the first time he had said anything.

"I'll handle the intelligence community personally, Mr. President," Montvale said.

The President looked at him and nodded but didn't respond directly.

"Anyone else got anything?" the President asked.

There was a chorus of "No, sir"s.

"Get some rest, Charley," the President said, finally. "Get to bed early. I can't afford to have you burn out. And I think you're going to have a busy day tomorrow."

"Yes, sir."

The President thought he saw something on Castillo's face and asked, smiling naughtily, "What makes me think you have other plans for the evening, Don Juan?"

"Sir . . ."

"What's her name?"

"Actually, sir, I thought I would go by my office, pick up Major Miller, and go to the Army-Navy Club to . . ." At the last moment, Castillo had enough presence of mind to change the next words from *drink our supper* to "have our supper."

"Yeah," the President said, unconvinced. "Good hunting, Colonel."

The President got up and walked out of the Oval Office through the doorway leading to his private working office. He was gone before any of the others could rise to their feet.

Sure, she has a name. Elizabeth Schneider.

And I still haven't called her. Or, worse, even thought of calling her.

What the hell is the matter with me?

[TWO]

Lieutenant Colonel C. G. Castillo and Major H. Richard Miller, Jr., did not go to the Army-Navy Club as Castillo had announced to the President of the United States that they would do.

Instead—with Colonel Jacob Torine, USAF, and Special Agent Jack Britton in tow—they went right around the corner from the White House, to 15th Street NW. There, at the Old Ebbitt Grill (est. 1856), they sat at the massive dark mahogany bar and dined on hot roast beef sandwiches *au jus* with steak fries (Miller and Torine) and linguini with white clam sauce (Castillo) and red clam sauce (Britton), washing it all down with Heineken beer from the tap.

By ten o'clock, all four were in beds—alone and asleep—in Herr Karl Gossinger's suite in the Motel Monica Lewinsky, the management having obligingly made up one of the couches in the sitting room into a bed for Special Agent Britton.

Although the thought that he should telephone Miss Elizabeth Schneider had occurred to Charley Castillo, he had not made an attempt to do so, having reasoned that it was too late—particularly for him. He was about to crash, and crash hard, and thus in absolutely no condition to participate in a long apologetic and explanatory conversation.

I'll call tomorrow, he had thought, then buried his head in his pillow.

If I don't get distracted and forget again.

He had then groped in the dark for his cellular on the bedside table, found it, dialed its own number, and after the mechanized female voice answered that he was being transferred into voice mail he left the message, "Call Betty, you heartless bastard."

Then he pushed the END button, returned the phone to the table, and finally crashed.

[THREE]
Office of Organizational Analysis
Department of Homeland Security
Nebraska Avenue Complex
Washington, D.C.
0825 11 August 2005

"Welcome home, Chief," Mrs. Agnes Forbison, deputy chief for administration of the Office of Organizational Analysis, greeted Castillo as he led Torine, Miller, and Britton off of the elevator. "Or would you prefer that I now call you 'Colonel'?"

"I'd prefer that you call me Charley, Agnes."

She walked to him and kissed his cheek.

"We've been over that," she said, evenly. "You are now too important to be addressed by your nickname. So, which do you prefer?"

"I give up," Castillo said. "You choose."

" 'Chief' has a nicer ring to it," she said. "This town is too full of colonels. No offense, Colonel Torine."

"None taken," Torine said.

She looked at Britton. "I like your jacket, Jack."

"Thank you," Britton said. "It's all I've got to wear. I hadn't planned to come to Washington."

"What's first, Agnes?" Castillo asked.

"Well, there's already someone in my office waiting to see you," she said as she led the way to the door of Castillo's office—marked PRIVATE NO ADMITTANCE— slid what looked like an all-white credit card through the reader mounted by the lock, then pushed the door open and handed the card to Castillo.

They all followed her through the open door.

"First is getting me back to Pennsylvania," Britton said.

"First is credit cards," Agnes corrected him. "You wouldn't want to leave home without your American Express card, would you, Jack?"

"I've got an American Express card," Britton said.

"Not one of these, you don't," Agnes said. "They came in yesterday."

She went to Castillo's desk, opened a drawer, and collected what looked like half a dozen Platinum American Express cards. She handed one card to Britton and others to Castillo and Torine and put the rest back in the drawer.

"Miller's already got one and so do I," she said.

Britton examined his.

"What the hell is Gossinger Consultants, Inc.?" he asked.

"Well, I needed a name of a nongovernmental organization to spend Lorimer's money," she said. "And that seemed reasonably appropriate. The cards are coded so no questions will be asked in case somebody wants to buy a lot of airplane gas."

"That's *aviation fuel*, Agnes," Castillo said, smiling. "You're amazing."

"I told you I was going to be useful," she said. "And the Riggs Bank is going to get us checks on the Gossinger Consultants account as soon as they can. Which may mean today but probably means in three or four days. You all have to sign signature cards and I have to get them back to the bank before you can write checks."

She turned to Torine.

"Gossinger Consultants is now the official owner of the Gulfstream," she said. "And Signature Flight Support at BWI is going to direct bill the corporation for hangar space, maintenance, *aviation fuel*, and so forth."

"Yesterday, I had to give them Charley's credit card," Torine said.

"It probably hasn't worked its way through the bureaucracy," she said. "I'll give them a call and switch over the charge."

"We have a corporation?" Castillo asked.

"A Delaware corporation, and a post office box," Agnes replied.

She looked at Britton again.

"Where in Pennsylvania?"

"Bethlehem."

"How far is that, do you know?"

"I'd guess a hundred and fifty miles, maybe a little more."

"You want to take the Amtrak to Philadelphia and have the Secret Service pick you up there? Or have a Yukon take you from here? I think that would probably be a little quicker."

"And there's already three Yukons from the Philadelphia office in Bethlehem," Britton said. "Is getting one here going to be any trouble?"

"None at all. Just as soon as you sign the signature thing, I'll call."

"Thank you," Britton said.

"Charley," Torine said, "would you have any problem after I make sure the paperwork on the Gulfstream is all done and things are set up with Signature if I went home for a couple of days?"

"No. I don't think I'll be going anywhere for seventy-two hours anyway. But I never know."

"Yeah, I know you never know," Torine said. "If you need me, I'll have someone fly me back here."

"Go ahead," Castillo said. "The both of you. And thank you, the both of you."

"What now, Agnes?" Castillo asked after Torine and Britton had left.

"Why don't you sit down, Chief, and we'll have a cup of coffee while I tell you what else is going on?"

"You want some coffee, Dick?" Castillo asked.

"I'm coffee'd out."

"Why don't you get on the horn and see if anything's new in Buenos Aires?"

"It's half past seven down there," Miller replied. "Is anybody going to be awake?"

"Why don't you sit down, kill a half hour with a cup of coffee, then get on the horn?"

Miller shrugged. "Why not?"

Agnes pushed a button on one of the telephones on Castillo's desk and ordered coffee.

Then she said, "There's a man named Delchamps out there, Chief. He would like to see you at your earliest convenience but he wouldn't tell me why."

"Great!" Castillo said. "Ask him to come in, and order another cup of coffee for him."

Agnes did so.

Edgar Delchamps and the coffee came through the door at about the same time. The latter was borne by a very tall, very attractive African American woman in her early thirties.

Castillo said, "Good morning, Edgar. I'm really glad to see you!"

Delchamps nodded but said nothing.

"Juliet," Agnes said to the attractive woman, "this is the boss, Colonel Castillo. Colonel, Miss Knowles handles our classified files. She has a master's in political science from Georgetown. She's got several Top Secret clearances, but you're going to have to think about clearing her for . . ."

"Let me get to that later," Castillo said. "It's nice to meet you, Miss Knowles . . ."

"Please call me Juliet," she said.

"And I'll need to talk with you later, but right now I have to speak with Mr. Delchamps."

"I understand, sir. It's nice to meet you, too."

As soon as the door closed behind her, Castillo asked, "If she's in charge of classified files and has a master's degree from Georgetown, why is she running coffee?"

"Well, Chief, it's not in her job description," Agnes said, "and she has her own office and her own administrative assistant, but, for some reason, every time Gimpy here asks for coffee Juliet seems to have time to bring it."

"If it was anybody but Gimpy," Castillo said, "I'd say she was attracted to him. But what it probably is is morbid curiosity."

Miller gave him the finger.

"Edgar, say hello to Mrs. Agnes Forbison, who's really the boss around here, and Gimpy, otherwise known as Major Dick Miller."

Delchamps nodded at both but said nothing to them.

"I'd really like to see you alone, Colonel," Delchamps said.

He's pissed about something, Castillo thought.

"There's a list of people here, Edgar—Agnes and Dick are on it—and you just went on it—who know everything that everybody else knows. What's on your mind?"

"I was at Langley yesterday, Colonel. One of the chairwarmers there had told me Ambassador Montvale had something for me to do and I was to report to him. So I went to see him. He was too busy to deal with someone unimportant like me, of course, but his flunky, Truman Ellsworth, who I've met before, told me to report to you for an extended period of temporary duty and that you would explain everything to me."

"And explain I will. Welcome aboard, Ed."

"Before you waste your breath on that, let me finish."

Castillo raised an eyebrow. "Okay, finish."

"I wanted you to be the first to know, Colonel, that later today I'm going over to Langley and sign my application for retirement, which is being typed up as we speak. They told me it takes about three weeks to complete the process and be officially retired. But I have a bucketful of accrued leave, so I'm going to be on leave until my retirement comes through."

Castillo took a moment to reply.

"If I didn't know better, I'd think that maybe you're a little annoyed about something."

Delchamps made a thin smile. "I told you in Paris, Ace, that I would let you know if I was interested in employment—I think you said 'reasonably honest employment'—in Washington. That was not a yes. I don't want to work here and I won't."

"I need you, Ed," Castillo said, simply. "I'm sorry if Montvale summarily ordered you to get on a plane . . ."

"It wasn't even Montvale," Delchamps interrupted, disgustedly. "It wasn't even his flunky, Ellsworth. It was some goddamned chairwarmer at Langley."

". . . but yesterday—I was in Argentina—I realized how much I needed you and asked Montvale to bring you home."

Delchamps shook his head. "I realize that once you've been infected with Washington, Ace, the temptation to build an empire is nearly irresistible. But you know goddamned well I've given you—and would have continued to give you—everything I know or find out about these oil-for-food maggots . . ."

"I'm not trying to build an empire!"

"Look at this goddamned office. It's a bureaucrat's throne room!"

"Blame the office on Agnes. She said it was important. I don't know my way around Washington and she does."

Agnes said, unruffled, "Yes, I do, and I make no apologies for trying to teach Charley the rules of the game."

Delchamps looked at her, looked as if he was going to respond, then changed his mind and looked back at Castillo.

"Ace, what made you decide yesterday in Argentina that you needed me so badly that you were going to get me whether or not I liked it?"

Agnes answered for him. "It probably started in Budapest where these people—I like your term 'oil-for-food maggots'—tried to assassinate him."

Castillo looked at her.

How the hell did she hear about that?

I know. There's a list here and she's on it.

"They tried to whack you?" Delchamps said.

"They were trying to kidnap and/or whack my Budapest source. When their first attempt failed, they tried again. But I was in his apartment."

"And had to put down two of them," Miller added.

Delchamps looked at Castillo for confirmation.

Castillo nodded slowly.

"You're a regular James Bond, aren't you, Ace?" Delchamps said.

"Indeed he is," Miller said. "Ace even had the foresight to get a suppressed .22 from the agency guy in Budapest."

Castillo flashed Miller a dirty look.

"I'm surprised he gave you any kind of a weapon," Delchamps said. "He's a real agency asshole."

"I noticed," Castillo said. "It took Montvale personally to get him to open his weapons locker."

"How much does the asshole in Budapest know about this? Does he know about the two you took down?"

Castillo shook his head. "I didn't tell him anything."

"That was also smart of you, Ace," Delchamps said. He paused in thought, then added, "You must be getting close."

"And they tried to whack an FBI agent who was with me at Lorimer's estancia—that was in Uruguay—and they were following around, threateningly, the former head of SIDE in Argentina, who was also at the estancia. And his family."

"What happened to your Budapest source?" Delchamps asked.

"I moved him to Argentina, where two old pals of yours are sitting on him."

"What two old pals?"

"Make that three," Castillo said, and raised his eyebrows as he added: "Alex Darby and Mr. and Mrs. Sieno."

Delchamps considered that a moment, then nodded and asked, "You're sitting on the SIDE guy?"

"I moved his family here. He's still in Argentina, at a safe house with everybody else, trying to put all the pieces together. That's what I need you here for, to help with that."

"How could I help with that?"

"What if I told you Montvale told the President he was personally going to call DCI Powell to tell him you were coming over there and were to be given everything you asked for?"

Delchamps considered that a moment, then said, "When I asked for the retirement forms yesterday, they seemed pretty happy about that. I guess the word is out."

"I don't think so, Ed, not so soon," Castillo said. "Montvale told the President that late yesterday afternoon."

"Well, I guess they were just happy to get rid of me, period," Delchamps said. "Truth to tell, I was a little pissed about their eager cooperation." He paused, and asked: "Can Montvale be trusted to do what he told the President he was going to do?"

"Yeah," Castillo said. "I trust him to do what he tells the President—in front of witnesses—he's going to do."

Castillo went to his desk and picked up a telephone handset.

"We up?" he said into it, and, after there was a reply, he looked at Delchamps and said, "Listen to this, Ed."

He then pushed the speakerphone button and said, "Open it up."

A young man's voice, having made a fifty-four-thousand-mile trip through space, came over the speaker.

"Corporal Bradley speaking, sir."

"Good morning, Lester," Castillo said. "How long will it take you to get Mrs. Sieno for me?"

"She's right here, Colonel. She just brought me my breakfast. Hold one, sir."

"Good morning, Colonel," Susanna Sieno said. "You made it there, I guess?"

"Good morning, Susanna," Castillo said. "I'm in my office and so is an old friend of yours. He'd like to say hello."

He extended the handset to Delchamps.

Delchamps, shaking his head, took it. "Hey, sweetie, how are you?"

"Oh, Ed, it's good to hear your voice . . ."

Castillo pushed the button that turned off the speakerphone function.

"Pretty impressive," Delchamps said, ninety seconds later, after the connection was taken down. "What about the garbling?"

"We twenty-first-century spooks call that 'encryption,' " Castillo said. "This system uses a logarithm—ours alone—we think even NSA can't crack."

"Okay," Delchamps said. "I'll hang around long enough to see if I can do you any good. If I can't, I'm off to my vine-covered cottage by the side of the road. Deal?"

"Agnes, get Mr. Delchamps an American Express card," Castillo said. "And see that Gossinger Consultants, Inc., provides him with accommodations suitable for someone we really need."

"Why do I suspect that Gossinger Consultants, Inc., has some sort of connection with the Lorimer Benevolent and Charitable Trust you told me about?" When there was no immediate reply, Delchamps smiled, then asked, "What happens now?"

Castillo said, "The President, at the same meeting, called the director of the FBI and ordered him to send over a senior guy first thing this morning skilled in putting jigsaw puzzles like this one together. I think you'd better stick around and meet him, then get yourself settled in."

"Inspector Doherty is already here," Agnes said. "Shall I bring him in?"

"What was that name again?" Miller asked.

"Doherty," Agnes replied. "Inspector John J. Doherty."

"Oh, this should be interesting," Miller said.

"Meaning what?" Castillo asked.

"You don't remember him, Ace?" Miller asked.

Castillo shook his head.

Miller went on, "He's the guy they sent to you about the turned FBI agent—Whatshisname—*Howard Kennedy,* your Russian mafioso's pal. When he told you—somewhat peremptorily, I'll admit—that the FBI expected you to notify them immediately the moment you heard anything about either Pevsner or Kennedy or they contacted you in any way, you told him not to hold his breath."

"Christ, that's him? I forgotten his name, if I ever knew it."

"Well, there's a lot of Irishmen in the FBI," Miller said. "Maybe there's two or more inspectors named John J. Doherty, but I really don't think so."

"Show Inspector Doherty in please, Mrs. Forbison," Castillo said. "And Dick, you can stop calling me Ace."

"You want me to get out of the way?" Delchamps asked.

"No. Stick around, please," Castillo said.

Inspector Doherty, unsmiling, came through the door sixty seconds later. He was a nondescript man in his late forties, wearing a single-breasted dark gray suit. He wore frameless glasses and his graying hair was cropped short.

Castillo thought, *I didn't like this guy the first time I saw him and I don't like him now.*

"Good morning, Inspector Doherty," Castillo said. "Thank you for being so prompt, and I'm sorry to have kept you waiting."

Doherty nodded but didn't speak.

"This is Mrs. Forbison," Castillo said, "and Major Miller and Mr. Delchamps. These are the people you'll be primarily working with."

"Ambassador Montvale wasn't very clear about what I'm supposed to do," Doherty said.

"That's because you don't have the proper clearance," Castillo said. "I'm about to grant you that clearance. The classification is Top Secret Presidential. It deals with a Presidential Finding that charges me with locating and rendering harmless the people who murdered Mr. J. Winslow Masterson, of the State Department, and Sergeant Roger Markham, of the Marine Corps, and who kidnapped Mrs. Masterson and wounded a Secret Service agent."

"What does 'rendering harmless' mean?" Doherty asked.

"Since there is little chance you will be involved in that, I don't think that you need to know how I interpret that," Castillo said. "What you do need to know is that from this moment, you will communicate to no one not cleared for this information—and that, of course, includes anyone in the FBI who is not specifically cleared for it—anything you hear, learn, conclude, or intuit about this operation."

"I don't like this at all, I guess you understand," Doherty said.

"You have two options, Mr. Doherty," Castillo said. "You can go back to the J. Edgar Hoover Building and tell them you're unwilling to take this assignment. You may not tell anyone there why you don't want to do it, what I have just told you, identify me or anyone else you have met here, or of course repeat that there is a Presidential Finding."

"There's been talk of a Finding, as you probably know."

"There's a lot of talk in Washington," Castillo said, evenly.

"What's my second option?"

"You can bring to this operation all the skills Director Schmidt told the President you have. I was there when he made that call. I want you to understand clearly, however, that once you become aware of the details we think you need to help sort everything out, you can't change your mind. If that happens, I'm going to give you an office where you can sit all day, read *The Washington Post,* and drink coffee, then send people home with you at night to make sure you don't see anybody you should not or make any unmonitored telephone calls, etcetera. That will last until we're finished, however long it takes."

Doherty looked at him coldly.

"You realize, *Colonel,* that I was an FBI agent when you were a cadet at West Point and I don't like being threatened like that."

"Mr. Delchamps here was a clandestine agent of the CIA when you were a bushy-tailed cadet at the FBI Academy. He's operating under the same rules. What's important, Mr. Doherty, is not how old I am but to whom the President has given the authority to execute the Finding. That's me, and if you can't live with that feel free to walk out right now."

They locked eyes for a moment.

"What's it going to be, Inspector?" Castillo asked. "In or out?"

After a long moment, Doherty said, "In with a caveat."

"Which is?"

"I will do nothing that violates the law."

"Well, I guess that means you're out," Castillo said. "I'll do whatever I have to do to carry out my orders and I can't promise that no laws will be broken."

Doherty exhaled audibly.

"You want to know what I'm thinking, Colonel?"

"Only if you want to tell me," Castillo said.

"That if I turn you down, they'll send you somebody else, and if he turns you down, somebody else. Until the bureau finally sends you someone who'll play by your rules."

"That sounds like a reasonable scenario," Castillo agreed.

"When I joined the bureau, I did so thinking that sooner or later I would have to put my life on the line. I was 'bushy-tailed' then, to use your expression, and had in mind bank robbers with tommy guns or Russian spies with poison and knives. It never entered my mind that I would be putting my life— my career—on the line for the bureau doing something like this."

He sighed.

"But if the President thinks this is so important, who am I to argue with that? And, being important to me, who's better qualified to keep the bureau from being mud-splattered with this operation than I am?"

He met Castillo's eyes for a long moment.

"Okay, I'm in. No caveats. Your rules."

"And no mental reservations?" Castillo asked, softly.

"I said I'm in, Colonel. That means I'm in."

"Welcome aboard," Castillo said.

There were no smiles between them.

"Okay, Agnes, where are we going to set up?" Castillo asked.

"I figured the conference room," she said. "It's about as big as a basketball court, and there's already phones, etcetera. And, of course, a coffeemaker."

"Why don't you take Mr. Delchamps and Inspector Doherty in there and let them see it? I need a word with Major Miller and then we'll both have a look."

"Well?" Castillo asked the moment the door had closed after Mrs. Forbison and the others.

"I don't think Inspector Doherty likes you very much," Miller said.

"I don't give a damn whether he does or not. The question is, is he going to get on the phone the first time he has a chance? 'Hey, guys, you won't believe what this loose cannon Castillo is up to.' "

"I think I would trust him as far as you trust Yung."

"Going off at a tangent, Yung has now seen the light and is really on board."

"Did he see the light before or after these bastards tried to kill him?"

"Britton asked almost exactly the same question," Castillo said, chuckling.

"You know, great minds tread similar paths," Miller replied. "Well?"

"I heard about it after they tried to kidnap him," Castillo said. "But I have the feeling he'd made up his mind before."

"Your charismatic leadership?"

"I think it's more likely that he thought about what I said about spending the rest of his FBI career investigating parking meter fraud in South Dakota and realized that would happen anyway if he ever did get to go back the FBI. With going back then not an attractive option, working for us didn't seem so bad. I don't know. I'm not looking the gift horse in the mouth. Yung is smart and we need him."

"Before you sent him down south, you said you trusted him because he was moral," Miller said.

Castillo nodded. "And I think Doherty is moral. The difference between them is that Doherty's a heavy hitter in the bureau."

"But he knows (a) he's here because the President set it up and (b) that if anything leaks to the FBI and we hear about it, we'll know he's the leaker because he's the only FBI guy who's being clued in."

"Except Yung, of course," Castillo said. "What did you think of Edgar Delchamps?"

"I think he likes you," Miller said. "I think the reason he was really pissed—and *really* pissed he was—was because he thought his friend Castillo had stabbed him in the back."

"You think he still thinks that?"

"I think he's giving you a second chance," Miller said.

Castillo nodded. "I really like him. And a dinosaur like him is just what we need."

"I wonder how he and the inspector are going to get along?"

"Jesus, I didn't even think about that," Castillo said. "And there's one more guy coming. A heavy hitter from NSA. He won't work for us, but he will get us whatever we want from NSA."

"When's he coming?"

"He should be here now," Castillo said. "Let's go look at what Agnes has set up."

The conference room wasn't nearly as large as a basketball court, as Agnes had described it, but it was enormous. There was an oval table with more than a dozen spaces around it, each furnished with a desk pad, a telephone, a small monitor, and a leather-upholstered armchair. And there was room for more. One narrow end of the room had a roll-down projection screen and flat-screen television monitors were mounted in a grid on the walls. Two wheel-mounted "blackboards"—the writing surfaces were actually blue and they came with yellow felt-tip markers instead of chalk—were against one wall, and there was room for a half dozen more.

"This place looks as if we're going to try to land someone on the moon," Miller quipped.

Castillo and Agnes chuckled.

Delchamps and Doherty didn't even smile.

"Colonel," Doherty asked, "are you open for suggestions on how to do this?"

"Your call, Inspector."

"Okay, first the basics. If this room hasn't been swept sweep it, and sweep it daily."

"NSA is supposed to send a man here to get us what we need from NSA," Castillo replied. "I presume that means technicians. That sound okay?"

Doherty nodded, then went on, "And seal this room. Never leave it empty, and make sure nobody gets in here who shouldn't be. If it gets so we can't walk through the clutter on the floor, we'll shut down for an hour or so, turn the blackboards around, and have it cleaned."

"Not a problem, Inspector," Agnes Forbison said.

"And speaking of blackboards," Doherty said, "two's not half enough. Get another four—better, six—in here."

"When do you want them?" Agnes said.

"Now."

"The first will be here in five minutes," Agnes said. "It'll probably take a couple of hours to get another five."

"The sooner, the better," Doherty said.

"What's with all the blackboards?" Castillo asked.

"Inspector Doherty shares with me," Delchamps said, "the philosophy that if you're going to use a computer, use the best one."

"What about computers, Agnes?" Castillo asked.

"I can set up pretty quickly whatever you and the inspector tell me you need."

"We are referring, Colonel," Delchamps said, "to the computers between our ears."

"Then you've lost everybody except you and the inspector," Castillo said.

"Computers, Colonel, are only as good as the data they contain," Doherty said. "You know what GIGO means?"

Castillo nodded. "Garbage in, garbage out."

"Right. So anything we put into our computers, the kind you plug in the wall—and I'll get with you shortly, Mrs. Forbison, about what we're going to need: nothing fancy—has to be a fact, not a supposition, not a possibility. The possibilities and the suppositions and the theories go on the blackboards. With me so far?"

"I think I understand," Castillo said.

"We'll probably save time if you watch to see how it's done," Doherty said.

"Let's try that, then," Castillo said.

"Okay. Off the top of your head, Colonel, tell me the one name you think is at the center of your problem."

Castillo thought a moment, then said, "Jean-Paul Lorimer, aka Jean-Paul Bertrand . . ."

"Just one, just one," Doherty said. "How do you spell that?"

Doherty went to one of the blackboards and wrote JEAN-PAUL LORIMER in the center of it.

"This is the player's board," he said. "This guy had an alias?"

"Bertrand," Castillo said and spelled it for him.

On the board Doherty wrote AKA BERTRAND.

He said, "We know that for sure? The names?"

"Yeah."

"Okay, when we get a typist and a computer in here we can start a file called 'Lorimer' and put those facts in it in a folder called 'Lorimer.' When do we get the typist and the computer?"

"Agnes?"

"You want to clear Juliet Knowles for this, Charley?"

"Okay, but her *and* a typist. You got somebody?"

Agnes nodded.

"Go get them, Agnes. Tell them what's involved."

"And start on the other blackboards," Doherty ordered. He turned to Castillo. "So what about this Lorimer? What do we know for sure?"

"For sure, that he's dead," Castillo said. "We also believe that he was the head bagman for the maggots involved in the Iraq oil-for-food scandal."

"Facts first. He's dead. When did he die? Where? What of?"

"He died at approximately 2125 hours 31 July at Estancia Shangri-La, Tacuarembó Province, Uruguay, of two 9mm gunshot wounds from a Madsen to the head."

"Okay, those are all facts, right?"

"Facts," Castillo confirmed.

"Okay," Doherty replied, matter-of-factly, showing no reaction at all to the manner of Lorimer's death, "that gives us the first facts in two new folders. One folder is the 'Time Line,' the other 'Events.' Spell all that for me, Colonel, please."

Ninety seconds later, after writing everything on the blackboard, Doherty said, "Okay. Who shot him and why?"

"We have only theories about why he was shot," Castillo said.

"Then get to them later. Who shot him?"

"There were six guys in their assault party . . ."

"Whose assault party?"

"We don't know. We have identified one of them positively as Major Alejandro Vincenzo of the Cuban Dirección General de Inteligencia."

"Now, *that's* interesting," Doherty said. "Who's your source for those facts. How reliable is he?"

"I'm the source," Castillo said. "I was there."

"Why?"

"We were going to repatriate Lorimer."

"To where?"

"Here. He was an American who worked for the UN in Paris."

"How were you going to do that? And why?"

"We were going to snatch him, chopper him to Buenos Aires, load him on a Lear, and fly him here. To find out what we could from him about who might have murdered J. Winslow Masterson, who was his brother-in-law."

"Who's we? Who was there with you?"

Castillo hesitated for a moment, then shrugged and started to tell him. He stopped when a moment later Juliet Knowles and a pale-faced young woman who looked British came into the room, pushing a blackboard mounted on a wheeled frame. Mrs. Forbison, carrying a laptop computer, was on their heels.

"Colonel Gregory J. Kilgore of NSA is here, chief," Agnes said as she put the computer on the conference table. "What do you want me to tell him?"

"I better see him," Castillo said. "This is going to take a little while to get organized anyhow."

Colonel Kilgore was a tall, slender Signal Corps officer in a crisp uniform.

"Colonel Castillo?" he asked.

"I'm a brand-new lieutenant colonel and I don't wear my uniform around here, sir," Castillo said.

"Ambassador Montvale made it pretty clear, however, that you're the man in charge. What would you like me to call you?"

"How do you feel about first names? Mine is Charley."

"I'd be more comfortable with Mr.," Kilgore said.

"That's fine with me."

"What can NSA do for you, Mr. Castillo?"

"This is a covert and clandestine operation authorized by a Presidential Finding and the classification is Top Secret Presidential."

"Understood."

"I'm going to need some intercepts," Castillo said. "The priority is a wire transfer into the Merchants National Bank of Easton, Pennsylvania, from a numbered account in the Caledonian Bank and Trust Limited in the Cayman Islands. The amount was $1,950,000. What I need is who that Cayman account belongs to, what monies have been transferred into it, when and by whom."

"If NSA provided you with that information, it would be in violation of several sections of the United States Code, as I'm sure you're aware, and even if we gave it to you it could not be used as evidence in a court of law."

"Didn't Ambassador Montvale tell you, Colonel, that you are—NSA is— to give me whatever I asked for?"

Kilgore did not respond directly.

"Just a question to satisfy my curiosity, Mr. Castillo," he said. "If a messenger left an envelope here with only your name on it, would you get it? No matter the hour? Twenty-four/seven?"

"I would."

"And no one else?"

"No one not cleared for this operation," Castillo said.

"While of course we are both agreed that you would not ask NSA to provide intercepts of this nature if doing so would violate any part of the United States Code, and that even if you did NSA would not provide data of this nature to you under any circumstances . . ."

"I understand, Colonel."

"Speaking hypothetically, of course, if NSA happened to make an intercept of wire transfers into or out of, say, a foreign bank in Mexico, that's all it would have. The amount, the routing numbers, and the numbers of the accounts involved in both banks. There would be no way to identify the owners of the accounts by name."

You get me the numbers, Colonel Kilgore, and my man Yung will get me the names.

"Understood," Castillo said. "Speaking hypothetically, of course, how does this work?"

"I really don't know," Kilgore said, "but I've heard that what happens is that just about everything is recorded in real time and then run through a filter which identifies what someone is interested in. The more information that's available for the filter . . . bank routing numbers, the time period in which the data sought was probably being transmitted . . ."

Castillo took his laptop computer from under his desk, turned it on, and called up the data he'd gotten from Secret Service Agent Harry Larsen in Pennsylvania. He then turned the computer around so Kilgore could see it.

Kilgore studied it, nodded, and said, "Certainly I'll excuse you while you meet the call of nature, Mr. Castillo. I know how it is. When you've gotta go, you've gotta go. And while you're gone, I don't suppose there's a telephone, preferably a secure one, I could use? I'd like to check in with my secretary, let her know I'll be a little late getting to the office."

Castillo stood up.

"The red one's connected to the White House switchboard," he said and went into the private restroom off his office.

Kilgore was sitting behind Castillo's desk when three minutes later—as timed by Castillo's watch—Castillo came out of the restroom.

"That's an interesting handset," Kilgore greeted him. "The small black one. It looks like something AFC would make."

"And so it is," Castillo said.

"You know much about AFC?" Kilgore asked.

"I even know Mr. Casey."

"Interesting man, isn't he? Among my other duties, I'm the liaison officer between NSA and his research facilities in Las Vegas."

"I've even been there."

"Well, that would explain, I suppose, why some people in Fort Meade are reporting a stream of gibberish coming out of here, absolutely unbreakable."

"Who in a position to use your services would be interested in anything coming out of here?"

"I wouldn't know, of course, but the agency is one possibility," Kilgore said.

"I suppose it would be," Castillo said.

"I once asked Mr. Casey about a rumor floating around that he'd given Delta Force—and *only* Delta Force—an encryption logarithm that was really something. He used to be a Green Beret. Did you know that?"

"As a matter of fact, I do," Castillo said. "What did he say?"

"He said that when he was a Green Beret he was almost blown away several times because somebody with a big mouth had listened to things they didn't need to know and that he was trying to see that that no longer could happen. He said Special Forces was like the Marines. Once a Green Beanie, always a Green Beanie."

"I suppose that's true," Castillo said.

"You wouldn't happen to have a green beret in a closet somewhere, would you, Mr. Castillo?"

"A souvenir of happier times, Colonel," Castillo said.

Kilgore stood up.

"Well, it's been a pleasure meeting you, Mr. Castillo. I don't think we'll be seeing each other again. But on the other hand, you never know. We may bump into each other at an Association of USMA Graduates meeting and get to sing 'Army Blue' together."

"Thank you, sir," Castillo said.

"I left a number on your computer you can call if you need anything else," Kilgore said.

He shook Castillo's hand quickly but firmly and walked out of the office.

Castillo started to return to the conference room but Mrs. Forbison put her head in the door.

"One more," she said. "This one says from the Secret Service."

That has to be Tom McGuire. Or maybe Joel Isaacson.

Castillo made a *bring 'em on* wave of his hand and went behind his desk, sat down, and started to shut down his laptop.

"Hello, Charley," Special Agent Elizabeth Schneider said from the office door.

Castillo was to remember later that his first reaction was, *"Oh, shit, not now!"*

He got somewhat awkwardly to his feet and was aware of his awkwardness.

"I thought you'd still be in the hospital," he said.

"I've been out for almost a week," she said. "I'm on what they call 'limited duty.'"

He looked at her carefully and noticed that although she appeared not to be a hundred percent—he thought he heard a catch to her speech, as if it was somewhat painful to speak—she was, by all appearances, well on the mend now, nearly three weeks after the ambush in Buenos Aires.

He then recalled from his experience in the first desert war and in Afghanistan that it was not uncommon for certain people to rebound somewhat quickly from trauma, particularly ones who had a young strong body on their side.

And Betty indeed had a young strong body.

Castillo crossed the room to her, thinking she expected to be kissed.

He put his hands on her arms and moved his face close.

She didn't seem at all eager for his kiss, much less the passionate embrace he thought was likely.

That's what's known as a "chaste kiss." As between aunt and dutiful nephew.
Oh, I know.
She's pissed. And has every right to be.

"Baby, I tried to call you. I wanted to call before I went to Paris. I couldn't. There just wasn't time."

I don't want to get into a long explanation of what happened that night, my promotion ceremony and the conversation with Montvale at the Army-Navy Club.

"Not a problem, Charley," Betty said.

She smiled somewhat awkwardly.

"Congratulations on your promotion."

"Thank you. Undeserved, but deeply appreciated nonetheless."

"If it was undeserved, they wouldn't have given it to you," Betty said.

"Well, I'm glad to see you," he said. "And, oh boy, did you arrive at the right time!"

"Excuse me?"

"You can type, right? We've got a . . ."

"Charley, I'm not going to work for you. Where'd you get that idea?"

"What's wrong with that idea?"

"A lot, starting with Joel's got me a probationary spot in the protection section."

"I'm not sure what that means."

"It means if I work out and once I get a clear physical, I can be permanently assigned to the protection section. That's what I want to do."

"And you don't want to work for me?"

"Be reasonable. That wouldn't work out and you know it."

"What if I promise to keep my hands off you during business hours and to call you Agent Schneider?"

Agent Schneider visibly did not find that amusing.

She sighed. "Charley, that wouldn't work. I had a lot of time to think and . . . Well, what happened, happened. But there's no future in it for either of us."

"We can just be friends, right?" he asked, sarcastically.

"Frankly, I don't even think that, Charley. I don't trust myself. Or maybe it's you. I don't know. I'm sorry."

"Have I just been told that I've been dumped? Just because I couldn't get on the horn to tell you I was going to Paris?"

"One of the things I thought of is how often is that going to happen with you? 'Sorry, Betty, the movie's off. I have to catch a plane to Timbuktu and I don't know when I'll be back.' "

"This is what I do for a living. You know that."

"I didn't realize what it meant. Now I know I couldn't live with a situation like that."

"Can we talk about this?" Castillo asked.

"Sure, after I get settled. But there's nothing to really talk about."

"Let's give it a shot. You never know. How do I get in touch with you?"

"When I leave here, I'm going over to Crystal City—near the Pentagon—where another agent is looking for a roommate."

"What's his name?"

Betty made a thin smile. "A *female* agent. If that works out, I'll call Mrs. Forbison and give her the phone number."

Castillo nodded softly.

"Okay, Betty, you do that."

"Congratulations again on your promotion, Colonel," Betty said and offered her hand to shake.

He took it.

She shook it briefly, turned, and walked to the door.

There, she turned again and said, "Take care of yourself, Charley."

And then she was gone.

"Oh, shit," Castillo said, slowly.

He stared at the empty doorway, shook his head, then walked to the conference room.

XV

[ONE]
Conference Room
Office of the Chief of Operational Analysis
Department of Homeland Security
Nebraska Avenue Complex
Washington, D.C.
1015 11 August 2005

Castillo saw that there were now names and events and dates written all over the three blackboards, most of them marked with symbols, arrows, and question marks and connected by a maze of arrows. Juliet Knowles and the pale-faced girl whose name he didn't know were sitting with their fingers poised on the keyboards of the laptops.

Inspector John J. Doherty turned from the blackboard on which he was writing to see who had entered the conference room.

"I'm beginning to understand, Colonel," Doherty said, "what I originally thought was your overzealous desire for secrecy."

Castillo ignored the remark and looked at Dick Miller.

"I think we'll know something from NSA about where that two million dollars came from by tomorrow morning, maybe even sooner. But we're going to need Yung to make sense out of what they're going to be able to get for us. How about making sure he comes up here just as soon as he can after the funeral?"

Miller nodded and picked up one of the telephones.

"That's Special Agent Yung of the FBI you're talking about?" Doherty asked.

Castillo nodded. "He's an expert in money moving," he said.

"I know," Doherty said.

Castillo didn't like Doherty's tone of voice.

"I understand he also knows where the FBI hides their skeletons."

"That, too," Doherty said. "What two million dollars are we talking about?"

"The two million dollars somebody gave the Aari-Teg mosque in Philadelphia so they could buy a farm in Bucks County in which they are going to hide in old iron mines when someone sets off a suitcase nuke in the City of Brotherly Love," Castillo rattled off.

Doherty considered that for a long moment and then exclaimed, "Jesus Christ, is that credible?"

"Britton doesn't think so and . . ."

"Britton, the Secret Service agent?" Doherty interrupted, turning to point at Britton's name on one of the blackboards.

Castillo nodded, then said: "When he was a Philadelphia cop, he was undercover in the mosque for more than three years. He doesn't put much credence in the nuke and neither do others—including Edgar here—who know about things like that. But somebody gave these lunatics two million dollars and I'd like to know who and why. Maybe it's two separate things, terrorism and the oil-for-food scandal. And maybe they're connected. I have a gut feeling they are."

Doherty picked up his yellow felt-tip pen and said, "Spell that mosque for me," and, when Castillo had and he'd written it on the blackboard, asked: "Can you tie these people to terrorism?"

"They were involved with the theft of the 727 that terrorists were going to crash into the Liberty Bell."

"You really think they were going to do that?" Doherty asked, his tone making it clear he didn't think that was credible.

"Yeah, I really think they were going to crash it into the Liberty Bell," Castillo said. "When Jake Torine and I stole it back from them, it was about to take off for Philadelphia. The fuselage was loaded with fuel cells hidden under a layer of fresh flowers."

Doherty accepted that but he didn't apologize, not even to the extent of saying "I didn't know that."

"So you're saying these people are skilled terrorists?" Doherty asked after a moment.

"No, I'm not. I go with Britton and Chief Inspector Kramer of the Philadelphia Police, who refer to them as the AAL, which means African American Lunatics, and which means just that. They have been *used* by terrorists, and they still may be—probably are—being used. I want to know where they got the money and if there is a reason beyond giving them a place to protect themselves from a nuclear explosion, which we don't think is going to happen."

Doherty considered that a long moment and then went off on a tangent.

"We can get back to that in a minute. You used a helicopter on the estancia raid, right?"

Castillo nodded.

"Where did you get it? Delchamps says he doesn't know and Miller said he doesn't want to tell me until he talks to you."

Castillo looked at the two women, who were watching them in fascination. *This, they shouldn't hear.*

"Let's go in there for a moment," Castillo said, pointing toward the door of the larger of two small offices opening off the conference room.

Once the door had closed behind him, Miller, Delchamps, and Doherty, Castillo said, evenly, "I borrowed a Bell Ranger from Aleksandr Pevsner."

"The same Aleksandr Pevsner we've talked about before?"

"Uh-huh."

"Jesus Christ, that opens a whole new can of worms," Doherty said. "Did he know what you were going to use it for?"

Castillo had a quick mental image of Doherty writing *Pevsner* on one of the blackboards, followed by a very large question mark and then an even larger exclamation point.

"Yes, he knew," Castillo said.

"Has it occurred to you that your pal is the one who tipped the unknown parties to what you were up to? Or that he sent them himself?" Doherty asked and then didn't wait for an answer, but instead turned to Delchamps and said:

"Ed, this Russian mafioso is up to his ears in everything else criminal on both hemispheres, so is it likely he's involved in either this oil-for-food scam or terrorism?"

Castillo picked up on Doherty's use of Delchamps's first name.

So he likes him at least that much? Good!

"Terrorism, no," Delchamps said. "That's not saying his airplanes haven't flown terrorists or supplies—including money—around for the Muslim fanatics. But I say that primarily because his airplanes go to lots of interesting places. He has almost certainly been used by terrorists—who have paid him extremely well for his services—but he's not one of them.

"And, Jack, from what I know—*know*—the same thing is true of his association with the oil-for-food maggots. Pevsner's airplanes flew a lot of food and medicine—like Ferraris and blond Belgian hookers for Saddam's sons—and nice little hundred-thousand-dollar bricks of hundred-dollar bills into and out of Iraq. But a lot of the same thing—maybe not the Ferraris, but just about everything else—went into and out of Iraq on Air France and Lufthansa and a lot of other airlines. My information is that Pevsner's airplanes were used when Saddam and company really wanted to be sure the commercial carrier didn't get curious about what was really in the crates marked 'Hospital Supplies.' "

"There wasn't time for Pevsner to tip anybody off about the raid," Castillo said. "And, anyway, he didn't know where we were going. He only knew who we were after."

"Unless he already knew where Lorimer was, Charley," Delchamps argued. "He could have told someone 'You'd better take care of that problem before the American gets to him.' "

"I don't think he knew where Lorimer was, Edgar," Castillo said.

"Why?" Doherty challenged.

"I think if he knew, Lorimer would have been dead when we got there. Alek doesn't like people who know things about him walking around."

"And what do you think Lorimer knew about Pevsner?" Doherty asked.

"Change that to 'Alek doesn't like people who *might know anything the disclosure of which might even remotely inconvenience him* walking around.' "

"That include you, Ace?" Delchamps asked. "You know where he is and you're still walking around."

"Where is he, Castillo?" Doherty asked.

"The last time I saw him, he was in Argentina," Castillo said.

"Jesus Christ!" Doherty said. "And what about Howard Kennedy? Where was he the last time you saw him?"

"He was at Jorge Newbery airport when we came back from Uruguay."

"Doing what?"

"I think Pevsner sent him, to give him an early heads-up in case something had gone wrong."

"So Kennedy knows where you were and what went down?" Delchamps asked.

"Yeah, I'm sure he does."

"You told him?" Doherty asked, incredulously. "You're operating on a Presidential Finding and you told that turncoat sonofabitch all about it?"

"I didn't tell him anything. That he found out from either Pevsner—or, more likely, from Munz, who had been hit and was on happy pills—is something I couldn't control."

"That doesn't worry you?" Doherty asked.

"No. Kennedy works for Pevsner. He knows what happens to people who talk. What does worry me is Chief Inspector José Ordóñez of the Uruguayan police, who has figured out—but can't prove—that I used Pevsner's Ranger and that special operators put down the Ninjas."

"What's he going to do with that information?" Delchamps asked.

"He's a good friend of Munz, knows that I'm a good friend of Munz, and would probably prefer that the whole episode would go away. If anything, if I had to bet I'd bet he'd go along with the drug dealer theory advanced by Ambassador McGrory."

"The drug dealer theory?" Doherty asked, incredulously.

"Ambassador McGrory has developed the theory that Lorimer was, in his alter ego as Jean-Paul Bertrand, antiquities dealer, actually a big-time drug dealer and got whacked—and had his money stolen—when a deal fell through."

"I don't understand that," Doherty said. "Presumably, the ambassador in Uruguay knew about this operation. What's this drug deal nonsense? Disinformation?"

"He didn't know—doesn't know—anything about it," Castillo said.

Doherty shook his head in disbelief.

"You said something about money," Doherty said. "What money?"

"Lorimer had about sixteen million dollars in three Uruguayan banks. That's a fact. Whether he skimmed it from the oil-for-food payoffs he was making—which is what I think—or whether it was money he was going to use for more payoffs, I don't know."

"Where's the money now?"

"We have it," Castillo said.

"You stole it?"

"I like to think of it as having converted it to a good cause," Castillo said.

Delchamps and Miller chuckled.

"Does Yung know about this?"

"Yung's the one who told us how to 'convert' it," Miller said.

"I don't think I want to hear any more about this," Doherty said.

"Good, because I can see no purpose in telling you any more than that. And I wish Miller hadn't been so helpful just now."

"You realize, don't you, Castillo, that Yung's FBI career is really down the toilet?"

"I thought it was already—guilt by association with Howard Kennedy—pretty much down the toilet."

"So far as I'm concerned, and most of the senior people in the bureau are concerned, Yung couldn't be faulted for trusting Kennedy—a fellow FBI agent—too much to believe he was even capable of doing what he did. But after this, Jesus Christ!"

"What do I have to do," Castillo said, coldly, "remind you that you're not going to tell 'most of the senior people in the bureau'—for that matter, anybody in the FBI—about any of this?"

"He already knows too much," Miller said, forcing a serious tone. "We're going to have to kill him."

Doherty looked at Miller in shocked disbelief, even after he realized his chain was being pulled, and even after he saw the smiles on Castillo's and Delchamps's faces.

"It's an old company joke, Jack," Delchamps said. "The special operators stole it."

"And you think it's funny?" Doherty said.

"I guess that depends on the company," Castillo said, not very pleasantly. "Okay. I have reminded you before witnesses that you have been made privy to information you are not to disclose to anyone in the FBI. Are we clear on that, Inspector Doherty?"

"We're clear on that, Colonel," Doherty replied, stiffly.

"Now, so far as your blackboards are concerned," Castillo went on, "you will write 'Putin' on them whenever you wish to make reference to Pevsner and 'Schmidt' whenever you wish to make reference to Howard Kennedy. I don't think those young women will make the connection, and maybe it'll even sail over Agnes's head. Clear?"

"The director of the FBI is named Schmidt, as you goddamned well know," Doherty said. "And you use it to describe someone like Howard Kennedy? What is it with you, Colonel? You have some deep psychological need to really piss people off?"

"This is the truth," Castillo said. "We are already using those code names in Argentina. At the time—before I had any suspicion that we would be dealing with a very senior FBI officer—they seemed appropriate. Now I readily admit 'Schmidt' doesn't, but it's too late to change it."

"Let me say something, Jack," Delchamps said. "Nothing disrespectful in this, but I've always felt that the FBI could use a little humor. Castillo wasn't being disrespectful. Irreverent, sure. But what's so wrong with that?"

Doherty looked at Delchamps for a long moment and then, without replying, turned to Castillo.

"Are we through in here, Colonel? Or can I get back to my blackboards?"

[TWO]
Conference Room
Office of the Chief of Operational Analysis
Department of Homeland Security
Nebraska Avenue Complex
Washington, D.C.
1925 11 August 2005

Inspector John J. Doherty, visibly exhausted, suddenly turned from the blackboard on which he was working and announced, "Sorry, but my brain just went on automatic shutdown. We'll have to pick this up again in the morning. Half past seven, something like that?"

Castillo nodded. *He's right. You're only fooling yourself thinking you can push yourself when you're wiped out. And I'm wiped out. We're all wiped out.*

"Fine with me," Castillo had quickly agreed.

Juliet Knowles and the English girl—he finally had learned her name was Heather Maywood—had been wiped out when they quit at half past four, thirty minutes after normal quitting time. Since then, Castillo and Miller had been manning the laptops.

Surprising Castillo, Doherty had not wanted to talk to anyone at the safe house in the Mayerling Country Club. When he saw the look on Castillo's face, he offered a terse explanation.

"We'll start with what I get from you here. Then we'll get what they have and start looking for both confirmation and anomalies."

With no enthusiasm at all, Castillo had decided that he had no choice but to let Doherty do whatever the hell Doherty was doing the way Doherty wanted to do it.

Castillo had given Delchamps the printouts of the material Eric Kocian had given him in Budapest as soon as they had been ready. He had read them with one eye, keeping the other on the blackboards until immediately after lunch—paper cartons of allegedly Chinese food, the remnants of which filled a wastebasket—for Langley to see, as he put it, "First, if Montvale really got me in over there and, second, if he did, to see what I can find in the file-and-forget cabinets that matches this stuff."

At four o'clock, Yung had called saying he was about to get on an airplane in New Orleans and did Castillo want him to come to the office or what?

Castillo had told him there was nothing for him do right now, he didn't "have the data yet"—by which he meant the intercepts from NSA, which at that point he didn't expect until the next day—but to come to the Nebraska Complex at eight the next morning.

Delchamps had called a little after six and reported that "the door was really open, to my surprise," but that he'd had enough and was quitting for the day. He had refused Castillo's offer of supper, saying he was going to his room in the Marriott and get on the horn to some other dinosaurs to see what they remembered, and would see them in the morning.

Doherty had left immediately. Castillo and Miller had stayed until NSA technicians had swept the room and Department of Homeland Security maintenance personnel had cleaned it up. Then they had set up a security officer outside the door to the conference room from the corridor, locked the door to it from Castillo's office, and were driven to the Mayflower in a Secret Service Yukon XL.

In the SUV, they confessed to one another that they had no idea where Doherty was headed with his blackboard, but that he obviously did and maybe they could make sense of them in the morning when their heads were clear.

They went to the suite, ordered club sandwiches and beer from room service, and went to bed before ten, both of them first having fallen asleep watching television in the living room.

[THREE]
Conference Room
Office of the Chief of Operational Analysis
Department of Homeland Security
Nebraska Avenue Complex
Washington, D.C.
0555 12 August 2005

Castillo nearly didn't pick up when the red bulb flashed on the White House telephone on the conference table. For one thing he seriously doubted that the President of the United States wished to speak personally to him—especially at this hour—and he didn't want to talk to anyone else—especially Ambassador Montvale—who was authorized to use the system.

What he wanted to do—and had, in fact, ninety seconds earlier begun to do—was study the half dozen blackboards in the room to see if he could make any sense out of Doherty's symbols, arrows, and question marks.

And he knew that if he didn't pick up the red handset, Miller would.

But he picked it up anyway.

Before he could open his mouth, a male voice said, "Not bad. I understand the protocol requires a pickup in thirty seconds or less. That took you twenty-two."

"Who's this?" Castillo asked, although he had suspicions.

The reply came in a voice which would not win any amateur night contests, softly singing a song from Castillo's past: "We'll bid fare-well to Kay-det Gray, and don the Army Blue . . ."

"How can you be so cheerful at this hour?" Castillo asked.

"I've been up since three," Colonel Gregory J. Kilgore said. "That's when the fisherman called to tell me he'd hooked a whopper. And by the time I got over here, about four, he was waiting to tell me he'd hooked all kinds of things. And more have been caught in the net since then. I'm separating the shellfish from the trash fish right now."

"And you're going to tell me what?"

"I'm not going to tell you anything," Kilgore said. "I thought that was understood between us. But a fleet-footed messenger—actually, he's driving a Mini Cooper—is headed your way as we speak bearing some of the initial catch. Watch out for him."

"This is a secure line . . ." Castillo began but stopped when he realized Kilgore had broken the connection.

Twenty-five minutes later, a red-and-black Mini Cooper pulled up in the curved driveway of the building. A trim young man in a gray suit got out and walked toward the door.

There was little question in Castillo's mind that he was Kilgore's "fleet-footed messenger," but he resisted the temptation to intercept him.

Let's see what he does with the envelope.

The young man surprised Castillo by walking to him the minute he was inside the building.

"Mr. Castillo?" he asked, politely.

"How'd you know?"

"You were described to me, sir," the young man said. "May I see some identification, please?"

The only thing Castillo had to show him were his Secret Service credentials.

The young man examined them carefully, said, "Thank you, sir," and took a large white manila envelope from his jacket pocket and handed it to Castillo.

"This is for you, sir."

Castillo saw that the young man was wearing a West Point ring.

"Thank you," Castillo said. "Do you want me to sign for this?"

"That won't be necessary, sir. Good morning, sir."

The young man walked quickly out of the building, got in his little car, and drove off.

Castillo went to the elevator bank, ran his card through the reader, and rode up to his office. Only when he was in the conference room did he open the envelope.

It contained a sheaf of paper and an unmarked compact disc.

When he fed the CD to his laptop he saw that it contained a document in Microsoft Word format. He opened it.

He compared what came onto his monitor with the second page—the first page was blank—of the sheaf of papers. They appeared to be identical. He started to read what was on the screen:

```
SYNOPSIS:

IT ALMOST IMMEDIATELY BECAME APPARENT THAT A NUMBER OF
ENTITIES HAVE AN INTEREST IN CERTAIN ACTIVITIES OF THE
CALEDONIAN BANK & TRUST LIMITED. (SEE APPENDIX 3)
```

> SOME OF THE FILTER KEYS USED TO DEVELOP INFORMATION FOR
> THESE ENTITIES ARE IDENTICAL TO THOSE PROVIDED BY YOU.
> (SEE APPENDIX 4)
>
> INFORMATION DEVELOPED FROM YOUR FILTERS MAY BE FOUND IN
> APPENDIX 1, AND INFORMATION WHICH YOU MAY FIND OF
> INTEREST MAY BE FOUND IN APPENDIX 2.

Castillo picked up the sheaf of papers and found Appendix 3. Among the entities listed were the Central Intelligence Agency, the Federal Bureau of Investigation, and the Internal Revenue Service.

That was interesting. Maybe—probably—there was something in files somewhere that would be useful.

He turned back to the laptop and scrolled down to Appendix 1.

Appendix 1 was five pages of data, dates, amounts, and account numbers. It made no sense to Castillo at all.

He went into his office. Miller was behind Castillo's desk, studying his laptop computer screen, his stiff leg resting on an open drawer.

"Where's Yung?" Castillo asked.

Miller shrugged. "You told him to come in at eight."

"Where's he staying? I need him now."

Miller shrugged again.

"What have you got?" Miller asked.

Castillo handed him the sheaf of papers. Miller glanced through it, then said, "Yeah, you're right. You do need him." He paused. "He'll be here in an hour, give or take."

"You're a lot of goddamned help!"

"It is not nice to be cruel to a cripple," Miller said, piously.

Inspector Doherty came into the office at seven twenty-five.

"Good morning," he said without much enthusiasm.

"We've heard from NSA," Castillo said and handed him the sheaf of papers.

Doherty examined them.

"It's gibberish to me," he announced. "You need an expert, like Yung. I thought you sent for him." He looked at Castillo for a moment, his face suggesting he didn't like what he saw, then said, "Well, back to work," and went into the conference room.

Castillo motioned for Miller to go with him. Miller nodded, lifted his bad leg off the open drawer with both hands, and got to his feet.

Mrs. Agnes Forbison came to work at seven-forty. She knew where Yung was staying—"at the Marriott by the Press Club. He and Mr. Delchamps are both there."

"Could you call him and tell him I need him now?"

"Well, if you want me to, I will. But you told him to be here at eight and he's probably already on his way here."

"He might have overslept," Castillo said. "Call him."

Mrs. Forbison was still on the telephone when both David W. Yung, Jr., and Edgar Delchamps walked in together.

She gave Castillo a *What did I tell you?* expression, then exclaimed, "Look at your hand!"

She was making reference to the bloody damage on Yung's hand.

"Ol' Dave," Delchamps volunteered, cheerfully, "ever the gentleman, tried to hold the elevator door for me. It got him. No good deed ever goes unpunished."

"We'll have to get you to a doctor," Agnes said.

"There's no time for that," Castillo said, earning him a dirty look from Mrs. Forbison.

"I could use a fresh bandage," Yung said, "but I don't need a doctor. All the damned door did was crack the scab."

"You're sure?" Agnes asked and, when he had nodded, said, "I'll get the first-aid kit."

"I didn't know you two knew each other," Castillo said as he watched Agnes tenderly wrap Yung's hand with a sterile bandage.

"We met in the Round Robin," Yung said, referring to the ground-floor bar in the Willard Hotel, which is across the street from the Marriott.

"Whence I had gone separately for a little liquid sustenance," Delchamps said, "the Marriott bar being full of road warriors and ladies offering them solace for a price . . ."

"I thought you were going to get on the horn to the retired dinosaurs association?" Castillo interrupted.

". . . after I had conversed with several gentlemen whose advanced age has fortunately not dimmed their memories," Delchamps went on. "And there was this Asiatic gentleman, with a bandaged wing, extolling the virtues of Argentine beef to a tootsie at the bar. It could have been a coincidence, but I didn't think so. I thought I was looking at Two-Gun Yung, the wounded hero of the Battle of the River Plate, whose exploits so shocked Doherty yesterday. So what I did was borrow a sheet of paper from the bartender and sent him a note."

"You sonofabitch," Yung said. "You really got me!"

"The note read 'Colonel C thought you would probably talk too much. Leave immediately. Go to your hotel and wait for instructions,' " Delchamps went on, pleased with himself. "My reasoning being that if Confucius had never heard of Colonel C. no harm would be done. But if I was right . . . and I was . . ."

"You bastard," Yung said, good-naturedly.

"He read the note and became scrute . . ."

"Became what?" Agnes asked.

"As in 'inscrutable,' " Delchamps explained. "Nervously licking his lips, he looked frantically around the bar, searching for counterintel types, and . . ."

"He didn't make you?" Castillo said, laughing.

Delchamps shook his head. "I carry with me this often helpful aura of bemused innocence," he said. "So what Dave did was hurriedly pay his bill, say good-bye to the tootsie, and head for the door. At that point, I took pity on him and bought him a drink."

"We had a couple," Yung admitted.

"I hope your mind is clear, Dave. I've got a bunch of stuff from NSA I need you to translate and, after that, you can tell me about the funeral."

Castillo was not unaware that Delchamps's attitude had done a one-eighty from that of the previous morning.

Maybe because he's working?

Or maybe because he's working and he senses that he's not going to be ignored now after breaking his ass trying to do a good job.

"Good morning, Inspector Doherty," Yung said politely as he walked into the conference room.

"How are you, Yung?" Doherty replied.

And ice filled the room, Castillo thought. *So far as Doherty's concerned, Yung has betrayed his beloved FBI, and there's not much of a difference between him and Howard Kennedy.*

And Yung not only knows this, but probably—almost certainly—has to feel uncomfortable about that, maybe even a little ashamed of himself.

Is that going to fuck things up? Is Dave going to backslide and become a good little FBI agent again?

The answer came immediately.

"Well, aside from this," Yung said, raising his bandaged hand, "I'm fine, Inspector. How about you?"

"I heard about that," Doherty said.

"Colonel Castillo told you?"

Doherty nodded.

"I thought he would probably have to have told you—Edgar Delchamps told me what you're doing here. So I guess he also told you that you can't go back to the J. Edgar Hoover Building and tell them, 'Guess what? We were right all along about Yung. He can't be trusted any more than Howard Kennedy can. Wait till I tell you what he's been up to.' "

"Colonel Castillo has made it clear that your activities, Yung, are protected by the security classification of the Presidential Finding."

"I'm almost sorry they are. I wish I could tell the bastards in Professional Ethics that I'm not ashamed of anything I've done since I got involved in this and that I like being trusted by Castillo and the people around him. That's more than I can say for the bureau. They found me guilty by association—'We can't trust him anymore, send him to Uruguay or someplace'—with no more justification than a determination to cover their own asses."

Doherty paled and looked as if he was about to say something.

"Well," Delchamps said, breaking the silence, "now that the air is cleared and we're all pals united in a common cause, can we get back to work? I've got a lot of paleontological data for your blackboards, Jack."

"What kind of data?" Doherty asked.

"From dinosaurs," Delchamps said.

"And I have fifteen pages of mysterious numbers for you to decipher for us, Dave," Castillo said and gestured for him to sit down at the conference table.

"What NSA has come up with, Charley," Yung said fifteen minutes later, "is pretty good. It's a goddamned pity we can't use it to put some of these bastards in jail."

"For what?"

"Income tax evasion, most of them. A lot of other charges. But none of this would be admissible in court."

"Careful, you're starting to sound like an FBI agent again," Castillo said without thinking, then heard what he had said and looked to see if Doherty had heard him. His face showed that he had.

Oh, fuck you! Yung was screwed by the FBI—probably by you personally, Doherty—and you know it!

"I don't give a damn about the IRS," Castillo went on. "What use is it to us?"

"Well, we know from which account the people in Philadelphia or Easton—wherever the hell it was—got their two million."

"Didn't we already know that?"

"What we didn't know—this is in Appendix 2—was that there was a deposit, the same exact amount, $1,950,000, into the same account at the Caledonian Bank and Trust Limited from which the $1,950,000 was wired to the Merchants National Bank of Easton. I think we can reasonably surmise this was done in anticipation of sending the money to Pennsylvania."

"Who put that money in that account?" Castillo asked.

"It came from another numbered account in the Caledonian Bank and Trust Limited. And what's very interesting about that is—this is also in Appendix 2—is that that's a very substantial account, with just over forty-six million dollars in it."

"In cash?" Castillo asked, incredulously.

"Five million in cash, the rest in instruments something like the ones Lorimer used in Uruguay—not the same thing, exactly, but something like it. You want me to explain that?"

"First tell me what's 'very interesting' about this second account."

"There have been no deposits made to it since March 23, 2003. The invasion of Iraq began on March 20, 2003."

"We know that date," Miller said. "When Castillo and I were simple, honest soldiers, we were there."

"Which suggests to you what?"

"The oil-for-food scam ended with the invasion," Yung said. "That final deposit, nine-point-five million, was probably in the pipeline, so to speak, for that three-day difference."

"Who owns the account with the forty-six million in it?"

"We don't know. NSA can't get data like that," Yung replied. "But Appendix 3 says that a lot of people are snooping around the Caledonian Bank and Trust Limited, including the FBI. One of them should know."

"You hear that, Inspector?" Castillo asked.

"I heard it," Doherty said. "Would you be surprised if my first reaction was to say fuck you?"

"No," Castillo said. "But?"

"And not just because I don't like you and this operation of yours, but because if NSA says the bureau is interested in this Caledonian Bank that means there is a *legitimate,* ongoing investigation which may very well be screwed up by you nosing around."

"But?" Castillo asked again.

"If I don't do this for you, you'll go back to Montvale, he'll go back to Director Schmidt and he'll either order me to get the information or tell somebody else to do it."

"Please give Inspector Doherty the numbers of the accounts we're interested in, Dave."

Doherty hung up the phone fifteen minutes later and handed Castillo a sheet of notepaper on which was written: "Kenyon Oil Refining and Brokerage Company, Midland, Texas."

Castillo was momentarily surprised at hearing Midland, Texas, but then realized that it was because Munz's family was on the Double-Bar-C ranch there, not because the oil company was in Midland.

There's probably three or four hundred oil companies in Midland. And it's not surprising that I never heard of this one. Many of them are nothing more than a phone number and a post office box.

"That's the account with the forty-six million in it," Doherty reported. "The information the bureau has is that they're a small independent outfit, primarily involved in the business of buying and selling crude oil. They have a small refinery in Houston, but that's usually involved in refining other people's oil. There is an ongoing investigation that has so far not turned up anything they're looking for."

"What is the FBI looking for?" Castillo asked.

"They didn't tell me and I didn't ask."

"Get back on the horn, please, Inspector, and ask. And while you've got them on the phone, find out what the FBI have—anything, everything, they have—on the other numbers Yung gave you."

Doherty glowered at him and didn't move.

"Do it, Inspector," Castillo said, unpleasantly.

Doherty grabbed the telephone. Making no effort to hide it, Castillo listened and watched him carefully while he made the call.

"It'll take some time to get that information," Doherty reported when he had finished. "They'll call."

"And while we're waiting, we'll all going to take a quick course in how the scans worked," Castillo said.

"From who?" Doherty asked.

"From my Budapest source, who is now in Argentina."

"I told you, Castillo, I didn't want any data from those people until we sort out what we already have."

"Do you speak Hungarian, Inspector?"

"No, I don't speak Hungarian," Doherty responded in exasperation.

"Then you'll just have to guess what I'm saying to my source," Castillo said and picked up the Delta Force radio handset.

"Sergeant Neidermeyer," a voice came over the handset.

"Are we up?" Castillo asked.

"All green, sir."

"Data link, too?"

"All up, Colonel."

"Wake them up, Neidermeyer," Castillo ordered, then switched the radio to SPEAKERPHONE and hung up the handset.

"Davidson," a voice came over the speaker ten seconds later.

"Got you working the radio, do they, Jack?" Castillo asked, in a strange tongue Inspector Davidson had never heard before. He had no idea what it was but it wasn't Hungarian.

"That's not Hungarian!" Doherty accused.

Castillo looked at him and softly said, in English, "Actually, Inspector, it's Pashto, one of the two major languages spoken in Afghanistan, the other being Afghan Persian."

Delchamps and Miller smiled and shook their heads.

Castillo turned to the radio and, switching back to Pashto, said, "Do you know if the old man's up yet, Jack?"

The reply came in Pashto: "That's why I'm working the radios, Colonel. Kocian and Kensington are kicking the soccer ball for Max. I was, but that big sonofabitch knocked me on my ass and I quit."

"I need to talk to the old man right now."

"Hold one, Colonel."

"Tell him to speak Hungarian," Castillo ordered, looking at Doherty and smiling.

"Will do. Hold one."

"I wondered if I was ever going to hear from you, Karlchen," Eric Kocian said, in Hungarian. "And I am not surprised that you called ninety seconds before Max and I are to have our breakfast."

"Uncle Billy, did you ever see one of those books, *Windows for Dummies, Microsoft Word for Dummies?*"

"You called me on your science fiction radio and are making me late for breakfast to ask a stupid question like that?"

Delchamps laughed and said, "I think I like this guy," which caused Inspector Doherty to realize that Delchamps spoke Hungarian and caused him further discomfiture.

"It's important or I wouldn't have interfered with Max's breakfast," Castillo said. "What I need is a lecture: 'How the Oil-for-Food Scam Worked for Dummies.' " He switched to English. "And give it to me in English and slow, because we have a man here who's going to write it down—make a chart of it—on a blackboard."

"I have the strangest feeling this odd request of yours is important to you," Kocian said, in English.

"One can sense an enormous feeling of relief on the part of our FBI co-conspirator," Delchamps said, in Hungarian.

Castillo chuckled.

Doherty picked up on the "FBI" and glared at Delchamps, which caused Castillo to chuckle again.

"It's very important to us, Uncle Billy," Castillo said, in Hungarian. "I think we're getting close."

"I thought we were going to speak English," Kocian said, also in Hungarian. "Make up your mind, Karlchen!"

"I really like this guy!" Delchamps said. "Make up your mind, Ace!"

"English, please, Uncle Billy," Castillo said, in English. "We believe that an American company in Midland, Texas, a small broker, is involved. I need to know how likely that would be, who he had to pay off, and how that was done."

There was a perceptible pause as Kocian gathered his thoughts.

"Remember the first time we did this, Karl, in the bath at the Gellért? Let's try that again. It worked for the dummies the first time."

"Unsheath your Magic Marker, please, Inspector," Castillo said.

"I'm supposed to put what this guy says on my blackboards?"

"Yes, you are," Castillo said. "Go ahead, Uncle Billy."

"Draw a rough map of Iraq on the blackboard," Kocian ordered. "Down off the lower right corner, draw in the Persian Gulf. Put a dot on the Iraqi coast and label that Mahashar. That's the major Iraqi oil terminal. I'll spell that for you."

Doherty drew the map as ordered.

"Done, Uncle Billy," Castillo said.

"Very well. Now, understand that Iraq was a virtually unlimited pool of crude oil. Outside of Iraq, that oil was worth at least fifty U.S. dollars a barrel—say, a dollar a gallon. The problem Saddam had was, the UN had forbidden him to export this oil so it was worthless to him.

"I should mention that under his benevolent administration of Iraq, the oil all belonged to the government, which is to say *him*. He had absolute control of it and nobody could ask him any questions.

"The way he got around his problem was to have the UN authorize him to sell some of his oil, the proceeds from which could be used only to purchase food and medicine for the Iraqi people.

"Aside from saying that resulted in a good many aspirin pills being sold to Iraq at five dollars per pill—and similar outrages—do you want me to get into that?"

"Stick with the crude oil, please, for now," Castillo said.

"Very well. I presumed you knew at least a little about the price scams and payoffs," Kocian said. "About the crude oil. Do you know how much crude oil a tanker carries?"

"No," Castillo confessed.

"I seem to recall that when the *Exxon Valdez* went down, she dumped 1.48 million barrels of crude oil into your pristine Alaskan waters," Kocian said. "But to keep it simple for the dummies to whom you refer, let's say just one million barrels. Doesn't that space-age laptop of yours have a calculator? Can it handle multiplying fifty dollars a barrel times a million?"

Castillo could do that simple arithmetic in his head but he had his laptop open in front of him so he punched the keys anyway and reported: "Fifty million dollars, give or take."

"Very good! Now we go back to Mahashar. The UN has authorized Saddam to sell, say, twenty-five million dollars' worth of his oil to buy food and medicine for his people. It has also dispatched UN inspectors to Mahashar to make sure that's all that leaves the country.

"A tanker then arrives in Mahashar to take on the oil, which has already been sold to some fine fellow at a good price—the fellow being expected to make a small gift to Saddam, but that's yet another story.

"Twenty-five million dollars' worth of oil is about half a million barrels and that's about half of the capacity of the tanker which shows up in Mahashar to haul it away under the watchful eyes of the UN. So the tanker pumps out half of the seawater ballast it has arrived with, replaces that with crude oil, and sails away half loaded with crude and half with seawater.

"Now, no one has ever accused Saddam of being a rocket scientist, but it didn't take him long to figure out that if he could only devise some way to have future tankers pump out all of their ballast and sail away with the tanks full of crude there would be money in it for him.

"He thinks: *Eureka! All I have to do is slip the UN inspectors a little gift, they look away, and off goes the tanker with an extra twenty-five million dollars' worth of crude.*

"This poses some administrative problems. He can't just hand the UN inspector, say, fifty thousand dollars for looking the other way. That's a lot of money, even in one-hundred-dollar bills, and there's a chance, however slight, that an honest UN inspector exists and might blow the whistle on a dishonest one.

"Further, what happens to the half million barrels of oil that nobody knows about, once it's sailing down the Persian Gulf toward the oil-hungry world? Until it's sold, it's worthless.

"So they find some other government controlled by gangsters and thieves— the Russians come immediately to mind, but others were involved—who are oil producers and can legally export oil within the restrictions imposed by that other fine international body, OPEC.

"If they buy the half million barrels of oil—since it's otherwise worthless to him, Saddam can sell it for, say, ten dollars a barrel under the table—they can turn right around and sell it as their own. And not have to deplete their natural resources."

Castillo looked at Doherty, who had just about filled half of one blackboard with cryptic symbols.

"But who to sell it to? ExxonMobil and its peers, believe it or not, are fairly honest. They won't touch it unless they know it's clean. Your Congress would love nothing better than to send them all to jail. So what they had to do was find small oil refiners—there are thousands of them—and offer them a real deal—say, thirty dollars a barrel.

"But—you said a small refiner in Houston?"

"I said a small broker in Midland," Castillo said. "The one we have in mind does have a small refinery in Houston."

They heard Kocian grunt knowingly before he went on: "A small broker in Midland with a small refinery in Houston would be aware that your Internal Revenue Service would be looking at his books and might smell the Limburger when they saw he had been buying thirty-dollar-a-barrel oil.

"So what does he do? He writes a check—actually, has his bank wire—the full, fair price of the oil to, say, the Cayman Islands Oil Brokers Ltd. Now he either owns this business or has a very cozy relationship with it. They acknowledge receipt of the money, take a cut, and put the difference between what he actually paid for the oil and what he's telling IRS he paid for it into another numbered account. Getting the picture, Karl?"

"Yeah," Castillo said, although he was still trying to absorb it all.

"And here's where your friends Lorimer and Pevsner enter the picture," Kocian said. "The UN inspector has to be paid for closing his eyes, the captain of the tanker has to be paid for taking on more crude in Mahashar than he reports to ship's owner—and who is better able to do this than Dr. Jean-Paul Lorimer, a diplomat of the United Nations who's always flitting around the world doing good?"

"Where did Lorimer actually get the cash—I presume we're talking cash—to make the payoffs?" Castillo asked.

"Offshore banks simply will not take cash deposits," Kocian said. "They virtuously want to know where the money comes from."

"Okay."

"But there are virtually no restrictions on the *withdrawal* of funds committed to their care. They will happily wire your money to anyplace you designate and there are no export restrictions on cash from a Cayman Islands bank being hauled away on an airplane.

"I would suspect that Lorimer had one or more accounts in the Cayman Islands—you understand, Karl, I'm just using the Caymans as an example; banks in twenty other places offer exactly the same services—into which money was deposited by wire from some reputable bank and from which he made withdrawals either by wire or in cash.

"A lot of the cash went to Iraq. In one of the palaces of one of Saddam's sons, they found a billion—a *billion*—dollars in brand-new American one-hundred-dollar bills, still in the plastic wrappers in which they had come from the U.S. Bureau of Engraving and Printing.

"I suspect most of the money—the cash—was carried into Iraq on one of Pevsner's airplanes, although others were probably involved. But Pevsner has the reputation for being reliable in the quiet hauling of large amounts of cash."

"Is there a Russian or a Cuban connection?" Castillo asked.

"Karlchen, I already told you Putin is involved in this up to his skinny little buttocks," Kocian said. "I just don't have enough proof to print it."

"Which Putin is he talking about, Castillo?" Doherty asked. "Your mafiosi pal or the president of the Russian Federation?"

Castillo hesitated just perceptibly before replying, "He's not talking about Pevsner."

"Jesus Christ!" Doherty said.

"They're no longer useful," Edgar Delchamps said, softly and thoughtfully. "But the hook's been set so why not reel them in as necessary?"

"Excuse me?" Castillo said.

Delchamps raised his voice.

"Thank you, Úr Kocian," he said, in Hungarian. "We'll get back to you. I really want to hear more of this."

"Who is that?" Kocian demanded.

"My name is Delchamps, Úr Kocian. I'm a friend of Karlchen's."

"Well, that makes two," Kocian said. "May I presume I may now take my breakfast?"

"Bon appétit," Delchamps said, then turned to Castillo and, switching to English, said, "I really want to talk to your friend, Karlchen."

"Break it down, Neidermeyer," Castillo ordered and then turned to Delchamps. "I don't know what the hell you're talking about, Edgar."

Delchamps smiled. "I've been trying to make sense of Doherty's mystic symbols for two days and getting nowhere, and then, the moment I hear about the generous small-time Texas oilman, eureka!"

Everybody waited for him to go on.

"Why the hell would a small-time Texas oilman—presumably, a patriotic Texas oilman—suddenly donate two million dollars to a bunch of lunatic wannabe Muslims in Philadelphia? Answer: He's been converted. Unlikely. Answer: He did not do so willingly. So why would he? Because he's been turned, the hook is already set in him."

"What do you mean turned?" Miller asked.

Delchamps didn't reply directly.

"I also asked myself, What's with the suitcase nukes?" he went on. "Where did that come from?"

"I have no goddamned idea where you're going with this, Edgar," Doherty said.

Delchamps ignored him.

"According to Karlchen here . . ."

"Uncle Billy can call me that, Edgar, but you can't," Castillo said, evenly.

"My most profound apologies, Ace," Delchamps said, insincerely, "according to *Ace* here, the Ninjas he took down at the Never-Never Land hacienda—"

"Estancia Shangri-La," Castillo corrected him without thinking.

"Whatever," Delchamps went on, "in far-off Uruguay were professionals. And we have since learned that one of them was a heavy hitter Cuban spook. And Ace tells us the people who tried to snatch Uncle Billy on the Franz Joséf

Bridge in romantic Budapest also were pros. As were the two you took down in the Gellért, right, Ace?"

Castillo nodded. "And they all had garrotes."

"They all had what?" Doherty asked.

"It's a device—these were stainless steel—not unlike the plastic handcuffs the cops are now using. They put it around your neck and choke you to death," Castillo said.

"And what was that about you taking someone down in the Gellért? What's the Gellért?"

"It's a hotel, Jack, on the banks of the Danube," Delchamps said. "You should take the little woman there sometime. Very romantic."

"The man I lost in the Uruguayan operation was killed with a garrote," Castillo said, softly. "The men who attempted to snatch Eric Kocian on the bridge in Budapest had both garrotes and a hypodermic needle full of a tranquilizer. The two men who went to Kocian's hotel room in Budapest had garrotes. When Mrs. Masterson was kidnapped in Buenos Aires, she was knocked out with a shot in her buttocks . . ."

"You had to kill two people in Budapest?" Doherty persisted.

Castillo nodded and went on: "The garrote was used routinely by only the East German Stasi and the Hungarian Allamvedelmi Osztaly and Allamvedelmi Hatosag . . ."

"Which are?" Doherty asked.

"They were the Hungarian version of the Stasi. Sándor Tor, Kocian's bodyguard, told his people to find out if the two in the hotel were ex-AVO or ex-AVH. They were to call Dick here if that connection could be made. They haven't called, which strongly suggests they were not AVO or AVH, leaving only Stasi. It fits, Edgar."

"What fits?" Doherty asked.

"Off the top of your head, Jack," Delchamps asked, sarcastically, "who—besides the Israelis and Ace here's intrepid band of special operators—could mount, at just about the same time, professional snatch operations in Argentina, Uruguay, and Hungary?"

"You're saying you think the KGB is involved in this?" Doherty asked, incredulously.

"No, Jack, not the KGB," Delchamps said. "If we are to believe Mr. Putin, the bad old KGB, which he once led, is dead. It was replaced by the Federalnaya Sluzhba Bezopasnosti Rossiyskoy Federatsii, commonly called the FSB. And, yes, that thought has been running through my head."

"It fits, Edgar," Castillo repeated.

"Let's see if great minds really run down the same path, Ace," Delchamps said. "What's your scenario?"

"Putin's afraid his role in this is going to come out," Castillo began. "So get rid of the witnesses. Starting with Lorimer."

"Starting with Lorimer's number two, the guy who got whacked in Vienna," Delchamps said.

"Right," Castillo agreed. "And Lorimer, who suspected he was about to be whacked, put his Plan A into effect the moment he learned his pal was gone."

" 'Plan A'?" Miller parroted.

"Get the hell out of Dodge," Castillo said. "He already had his alter ego set up in Uruguay. And his nest egg. Plan A was to stay out of sight until they stopped looking for him."

"Okay," Miller said, agreeing.

"So when he disappeared, how to find him?" Castillo said. "Through his sister."

"You don't really think the FSB keeps dossiers on UN diplomats, do you?" Delchamps said. "Listing next of kin, things like that?"

Castillo nodded. "Why wouldn't they?"

When Delchamps didn't respond, he went on: "So they snatched his sister and told her they would kill her children if she didn't locate her brother for them and then murdered her husband to show how serious they were."

"So who is they?" Delchamps said. "The KSB? I don't think so. But just for the sake of argument, let's say that Putin, out of the goodness of his heart, found some sort of employment for a group of deserving Stasi types who had lost their jobs when the Berlin Wall came down. You never know when you're going to need a good assassin."

"And if something went wrong, no connection with these guys to the KSB," Miller said. "Clever."

"And they were probably very useful when the oil-for-food scam was running," Delchamps said. "Both in moving money around and removing witnesses to any connection with Putin and Company."

"And no paper trail," Miller said. "Whatever money they were spending was oil-for-food money."

"That, too," Delchamps agreed. "Okay, Ace, then what?"

"I got lucky," Castillo said. "Otto Görner heard that some West Germans were moving oil-for-food money to Argentina and Uruguay and told me about it. He also warned me that people who had been curious about this had died and to butt out."

"Which of course you were congenitally unable to do," Miller said, "and you went to Eric Kocian. He pointed you toward South America and then you got lucky with Confucius. He had a file on . . . what's the alter ego?"

"Bertrand," Castillo furnished, as he glanced at Yung. "Dave, you haven't said a word. Does that mean you think we're just pissing into the wind and you're too polite to say so?"

"Just before he changed sides, Kennedy was working on something with a Houston connection," Yung said. "I've been trying to remember what it was."

"Wouldn't there be a record of some sort? An interim report of some kind?" Delchamps asked.

"Kennedy took everything he had with him," Doherty said, bitterly. "I'm sure your friend Pevsner read it before it was destroyed. Why don't you ask him?"

"What were you looking for, Dave?" Castillo pursued. "Was there an oil-for-food scam connection?"

"Not as such," Yung said. "We were looking for unusual transfers—wire transfers—of large amounts of money. Money laundering, in other words. There's two facets of that—more than two, actually. One is income tax evasion. When we came across something suspicious—something, for example, that looked like someone was concealing income or assets—we turned it over to the IRS and let them deal with it. When the *source* of the money was suspicious— as if it might be drug money, for example, or in the case of politicians, purchasing agents, etcetera that looked like it might be bribes—we worked on that ourselves. The way we were working, I looked for anomalies, and when I found something suspicious Howard looked into it."

"And you remember something about Houston?" Castillo asked.

"Only just that," Yung said. "I've been trying hard to remember the specifics."

"Keep trying, Dave," Castillo said and turned to the others. "Where were we?"

"At the point where you decided to repatriate Lorimer," Miller said.

"Right," Delchamps said. "Meanwhile, the bad guys found out where Lorimer slash Bertrand was. How?"

"Well, at first they didn't know where he was," Castillo said. "Otherwise, they wouldn't have taken the risk of kidnaping Mrs. Masterson to find out. That was an act of desperation."

"So somebody had to tell them," Delchamps said. "Who knew?"

"Castillo's pal, the Russian mafioso, Pevsner," Doherty said.

"I don't think so," Castillo said.

"Why do you keep defending that slimeball, Castillo?" Doherty snapped.

"If he knew where Lorimer was and had told the Ninjas," Castillo said, "he wouldn't have let me use his helicopter. He didn't want me whacked."

"Because he likes you, right?" Doherty asked.

"Because that would kill the deal he has about keeping the FBI and the CIA off his case."

"Another possibility is that it was just a coincidence that everybody descended on Never-Never Land at the same time," Delchamps said. "How the Ninjas found out where he was doesn't really matter. They did and staged that operation to take him out."

"That's one hell of a coincidence, wouldn't you say?" Doherty challenged.

"However it happened," Delchamps said, "the Ninjas went to the hacienda and were more than a little surprised to find Ace and Company already there."

"Why do you think they were surprised?" Doherty asked.

"Otherwise, the score of that ball game would not have been six to one," Delchamps said. "They probably thought they'd come on a bunch of local bandits knocking off a hacienda. Not in their league. Not a problem. Just whack everybody, leave the bodies where they fell, and take off. Surprise, surprise, it's the U.S. Cavalry."

"Yeah," Castillo said, thoughtfully.

"So what happened when there was no phone call to the embassy of the Russian Federation saying, 'Mission accomplished'?" Delchamps said. " 'What happened? Who whacked our guys? Does it matter? Lorimer's dead. Next step, take out Kocian.' "

"After first finding out just how much he knows," Castillo said.

"Which would also apply to Special Agent Yung," Doherty said.

"Yeah, it would," Delchamps agreed. "Which means, as soon as they can find him, they're going to have another try at Kocian. I really want to talk to him, Ace, before that happens. We might not be so lucky again."

"Pevsner is probably on their hit list," Castillo said.

"Pevsner probably *wrote* their hit list," Doherty said.

"What do you want to do, Ace?" Delchamps asked.

"You never got around to telling us where you think the Kenyon Oil Refining and Brokerage Company fits into this, Edgar."

"Oh, yeah. Well, this may really be off the wall, but it's also possible. The Russians know about Kenyon's involvement with the oil-for-food scam. Maybe they were in it with him, I don't know, but it doesn't matter. The oil-for-food scam is over. So nobody needs Kenyon anymore."

He paused, visibly organizing his thoughts.

"You have to think of Putin as being KGB and with a sense of humor,"

Delchamps then went on, "or maybe he just has evil intentions. Anyway, he's got Kenyon on a hook. 'Do what I say or the FBI will find out what a naughty boy you have been.' Kenyon has all this money in the Caymans. 'How do I find out how deeply the hook is in him?' What is laughingly known as the intelligence community knows all about these lunatics in Philadelphia. They're being watched. 'The Americans swallowed the hidden nuclear suitcase bombs nonsense hook, line, and sinker once. Let's see if we can get them to swallow it again. So what I will do is tell the dummy in Midland to send the lunatics two million dollars to buy some tunnels to protect themselves from the nuclear blast in Philadelphia. Since they are being watched, this will come to the attention of the intelligence community. Net result: the American intelligence community runs around like chickens with their heads cut off looking for nuclear suitcases which have never left the warehouse in Siberia. Ha-ha!' "

He paused, let that sink in, then went on. "Probable benefit two: Putin knows about the forty-six million Kenyon has in the Cayman bank. Putin's pal, the famous Colonel Pyotr Sunev, now back at work after a teaching sabbatical at Grinnell University, can find many uses for forty-six mil. Or maybe Putin and Sunev will just split it between them.

"Kenyon probably would not be very anxious to hand it over. But that reluctance was before he sent the two million to the lunatics. Now Putin has him for not only illegally profiting from the oil-for-food scandal—and hiding the money—but also for sending two million to lunatics in Philadelphia known to have terrorist ties. Getting the picture, Ace?"

"I'm thinking about it," Castillo said. "It sounds off the wall, but . . ."

"Kenyon either gives them the money or goes to jail," Miller said. "To whom could he complain he was robbed?"

"Right," Delchamps said. "So what do you think, Ace?"

"I think we should go have a talk with Kenyon in Midland. Maybe we can get him to tell us who got him to send the money to Philadelphia."

"*Maybe?*" Miller said.

"What makes you think he'll tell you anything at all?" Doherty asked. "All you've got is a wild theory."

"Jesus, I just remembered Jake went home," Castillo said.

Miller immediately took his meaning.

"Charley, you steer and I'll work the radios," he said.

Castillo looked at him for a long moment before replying.

"You're sure?"

Miller nodded.

"Okay, get on the horn and have them roll the Gulfstream out of the hangar," Castillo said.

"You're going to Texas right now?" Doherty asked.

"*We're* going to Texas and then Buenos Aires," Castillo said. "Why don't you get on the horn to your wife and have her pack a bag and your passport?"

"Nothing was said about me going out of the country on a lunatic mission like this," Doherty said.

"I hope that was an observation rather than an indication you're going to be difficult," Castillo said.

"I'd like to go," Yung said.

"I wouldn't think of leaving home without you, David," Castillo said. He looked at Doherty. "I can make you go, Inspector, and you know it. But I don't want you along if you're going to be a pain in the ass. Your call."

Doherty met Castillo's eyes for a long moment before replying.

"How long are we going to be gone?" he asked, finally.

"Probably less than a week," Castillo said. "Thank you."

"What are we going to do about the blackboards?" Doherty asked.

"I was just thinking about that," Castillo said. "I'd like to have that data at the safe house in Buenos Aires. Is there some way we can photograph them and replicate them down there?"

"Not a problem," Doherty said.

"Okay, then. You start on that. I've got a couple of phone calls to make."

XVI

[ONE]
Office of the Chief of Operational Analysis
Department of Homeland Security
Nebraska Avenue Complex
Washington, D.C.
0935 12 August 2005

Castillo sat down in the leather-upholstered judge's chair behind his huge, ornate desk and looked uncomfortably around his luxuriously furnished office. He felt like an intruder. He shrugged and picked up the handset of what Billy Kocian had called his "science fiction radio."

"Neidermeyer," he ordered. "Put me through to Sergeant Major David-son, please."

"Hold one, Colonel."

Five seconds later, Davidson's voice came over the circuit.

"Yes, sir?"

"Jack, there's reason to believe another attempt to kidnap or take out Eric Kocian is likely to happen."

"Really?"

"What's that phrase, 'Take all necessary precautions'?"

"Consider it done, Colonel."

"There's also good reason to think that the bad guys are ex-Stasi, which means you should keep that in mind when you're taking all necessary precautions. These guys are pros."

"That's interesting."

"Make sure everybody else knows."

"Including Kocian?"

"Especially Kocian."

"Done, Colonel. You don't have a time, do you?"

"Anywhere from four to twenty-four hours after they find out where he is. And, by now, they may already know."

"Kocian wants to go into Buenos Aires for lunch."

"That's off. He is not to leave Mayerling. I'd prefer that he not go outside the house."

"Well, you and I have sat on difficult people before. I'll deal with him."

"We'll be coming down there after a stop in Midland, Texas."

"To see Colonel Munz's family?"

"No. We found out there's a connection in Midland between the oil-for-food scam and the two million dollars the Philadelphia Muslims got for their bomb shelter. We're going to see what we can find out and then come down there."

"Got an ETA?"

"When there is one, I'll get it to you."

"I think we can handle things here, Colonel. Anything else?"

"I was about to ask you to patch me through to the embassy, but I just decided it'll be better if I make a perfectly ordinary call from here. I don't want to be responsible for tipping these bastards about Mayerling."

"Understood."

"Okay, Jack. Keep your eyes open and watch your back."

"You, too, Colonel."

"Break it down, Neidermeyer."

Pevsner's phone numbers were in the cellular telephone Alex Darby had given him in Buenos Aires and Castillo had to go into his briefcase for it. When he turned it on, the screen read LOW BATTERY.

He pushed himself away from the desk and went into the outer—Mrs. Agnes Forbison's—office, where, the moment Agnes saw him with the cellular in his hand, she put her hand out for it. Then she pulled open a drawer in her desk, where—predictably—she had a box full of assorted chargers and in a moment had fitted one of them to the phone.

"There's a socket in your banker's lamp on your desk," she said.

"Thanks."

"I gather you're going somewhere?" she asked.

"Midland, Texas, and then Buenos Aires," Castillo replied. "I think we've found the link between the oil-for-food scam and the nuclear suitcase bombs."

She didn't say anything but her eyes asked for clarification.

"If I tell you this, there will be a nuclear mushroom over Philadelphia before I finish the sentence," Castillo said. "But right now, I really don't think there is a suitcase bomb any nearer than Siberia."

"Thank God!" she said.

"That whole scenario was to pull our chain," Castillo said. "Or, at least, pulling our chain was part of it."

"Can Dick tell me about it?"

"Dick's going with me. Jake is in Charleston."

"Is that going to work? Dick's leg . . ."

"He'll navigate. I'll steer," Castillo said. "It'll work."

Again her eyes asked for clarification.

"This is what Edgar Delchamps has come up with," he said. "Let me know what you think . . ."

"This may be the dumbest thing I've said all week," Agnes said when he had finished, "but it just may be the answer. I haven't heard anything that makes more sense."

"I really hope so," Castillo said.

"You really like Delchamps, don't you?" she asked.

"He's the one who should be sitting behind that desk," Castillo said, nodding toward his office. "He's the only one around here who really knows what he's doing."

"No, he's not," Agnes said. "And he doesn't enjoy the confidence of the President."

"That's because the President doesn't know him—yet."

"I wonder how Ambassador Montvale is going to take this," Agnes said and, when she saw the look on Castillo's face, added: "You weren't going to tell him, were you? Charley, you have to."

"No, I wasn't," Castillo said. "And, yeah, I do."

"Correct me if I'm wrong, Colonel," Ambassador Charles W. Montvale, the director of National Intelligence, said, "but you are suggesting I go to the President and say, in effect, 'Not to worry, Mr. President. There is no threat of a nuclear detonation in Philadelphia. All the Russian suitcase nuclear devices are still in the Soviet Union. It seems President Putin has been playing a little joke on us.' "

"I'm not suggesting you do anything, Mr. Ambassador," Castillo said.

" 'The source of this rather interesting theory is a veteran—some might even say 'burned-out'—CIA field officer by the name of Delchamps, who does not, I'm afraid, enjoy the full confidence of his superiors in Langley," Montvale went on.

"Why do I suspect the people you talked to at Langley cannot be counted among his legion of admirers?" Castillo asked. "For the record, I like him very much. You can find him in my dictionary under both 'highly competent' or 'widely experienced.' "

"Not for the record, the people I spoke with seem to feel that not only does he regret the Cold War is over, but that he is both a Francophobe and—am I coining a phrase?—a UNphobe."

"Maybe that's because he's been dealing with the French and the United Nations for a long time."

"They asked me if he might be considering retirement when his temporary duty with me is concluded."

"With all respect, Mr. Ambassador, his temporary duty is with me. And if they ask that question, tell them not to hold their breath."

"You're fond of that expression, aren't you?" Montvale said, then finished his original comment: " 'And no, Mr. President, there is no firm intelligence to confirm this fascinating theory. Colonel Castillo is going on a hunch.' "

Castillo said nothing.

"No comment, Colonel?"

"Mr. Ambassador, I told you I would keep you abreast of what I'm doing and plan to do. I've just done that."

"Does the FBI expert, Inspector Doherty, whom you told not to hold his breath when he said he expected you to tell him if you had any contact with Pevsner or former FBI agent Kennedy—"

"You knew about that, and still sent him to me?"

"You asked for their best man and that's who I sent you," Montvale replied. "Does Doherty know about this fascinating theory that Putin is playing games with us?"

"He does, and I'd say he shares your opinion of it, sir."

"Well, while you're off in Texas and Argentina would it be possible for him to come see me and tell me what he thinks of the situation?"

"I'm taking Inspector Doherty with me, sir."

"To South America?"

"I want him to work with the people and the data down there, Mr. Ambassador."

"I'd really like to have his take on the probability of there being nuclear weapons about to be detonated in this country."

"Yes, sir."

"Does that mean you're going to send him to see or not?"

"I've got two more telephone calls to make, Mr. Ambassador, and then we're going to the airport."

"In other words, you're not going to send him to see me."

"There's just not time, Mr. Ambassador."

"This is another of those times when I really wish you were working for me, Castillo."

"Yes, sir. I thought something like that might be running through your mind."

There was a long silence, then the White House operator came on the line: "Are you through, Colonel?"

Castillo realized that Montvale had broken his end of the connection.

"It looks that way. Thank you."

Castillo put the White House phone back in its cradle and picked up the handset of another.

"Lopez."

"Carlos. You weren't in your office, but they gave me your cellular number."

"I'm at the Double-Bar-C," Fernando Lopez said.

"What are you doing there?"

"Why do you think, Gringo? Abuela's here."

"So are half a dozen Secret Service agents."

"I thought I should be here, okay? What's on your mind?"

"What do you know about the Kenyon oil company, specifically the Kenyon Oil Refining and Brokerage Company? Is there a Kenyon?"

"Jesus, you really don't live here anymore, do you?" Lopez said, not very pleasantly. "Yeah, there's a Kenyon. There's a lot of them. One of them, Philip, is a classmate of mine. You don't remember him?"

"No, I don't."

"Now that I think about it, I'm really surprised. You belted him good one time when he said you had to be queer because you talked funny and rode a sissy saddle."

"Tubby?" Castillo asked as the memory came to him of a heavyset twelve-year-old trying to fight back tears after his nose had been bloodied.

"Yeah," Fernando said. "Tubby. Nobody calls him that much anymore."

"He runs Kenyon?"

"Yeah, he does. Why do I think, Gringo, that I am going to be unhappy when you explain this sudden interest in Philip J. Kenyon III?"

"You're not going to like it, Fernando," Castillo said. "Is he in Midland now, do you think?"

"He was yesterday," Fernando said. "I saw him in the Petroleum Club. He asked me if I still played poker and I had to tell him no because Maria and Abuela and the Munzes were with me. The Friday-night three-card stud games of fame and legend are still going."

"He'll be there—at the Petroleum Club—tonight?"

"You going to tell me why you want to know?"

"Not over the phone. I'll tell you when I see you."

"And when will that be?"

"As soon as I make one more telephone call, I'm headed for the airport. It's about three hours in the air. Figure another hour and a half to go wheels-up. It's now ten. Knock an hour off because of the time zones. We should be there sometime before three."

"Midland-Odessa or here?"

"Midland. We're going from there to Buenos Aires, and I can't do the customs stuff from the strip at the Double-Bar-C."

"Who's we?"

"Yung, a guy named Delchamps, a guy named Doherty—an FBI big shot—Miller, and me."

"Plus Jake Torine. It'll be a little crowded, but it'll be all right."

"Jake's not coming, and we may not be staying overnight."

"First things first. Yes, you are staying overnight. Abuela will expect you to spend the night. Jesus, you just don't give a damn about people's feelings, do you, Carlos?"

"Okay. We'll spend the night."

"If Jake's not coming, who's flying the Gulfstream?"

"Miller will work the radios," Castillo said after a just-perceptible hesitation.

"Sure. Why not? You've been flying that Gulfstream for, what, ten whole days now? And really racked up a lot of time. Maybe ten, even twelve, hours. And shot maybe six landings. You're out of your mind, you know that?"

"I can fly the Gulfstream," Castillo said.

"There are old pilots and there are bold pilots, but there are no old bold pilots. You ever hear that?"

"I can fly it. It practically flies itself."

"I was about to say it's been nice knowing you, but that wouldn't be entirely true."

"So I don't suppose you're going to meet me at Midland-Odessa?" Castillo asked, but, before Lopez had a chance to reply, went on: "No, actually have the senior Secret Service agent meet us. I have to talk to him and I'd rather do that at the airport."

"Your wish is my command, Carlos. See you sometime this afternoon."

The connection went dead.

He called me Carlos again. He called me Carlos three times. He must be really pissed at me.

And, unfortunately, with good reason.

He got another dial tone, and then, reading them from Alex Darby's cellular, carefully punched in a long series of numbers.

"*¿Hola?*"

"Hello, Alek," Castillo said, in Russian.

After a long moment, Aleksandr Pevsner replied, in Russian, "Ah, Colonel Castillo, my former friend. I am surprised that you would dare to call me ever again."

" 'Former friend,' Alek?"

"You lied to me, and about something you knew was very important to me."

"Are you going to tell what? Or are you just going to sulk like a little boy?"

"You dare to deny it? To mock me?"

"To mock you, sure. You're the mockable type. But I can't deny anything until you tell me what it is."

"Munz is what I'm talking about."

"What about him?"

"You knew where he was all the time and said you didn't."

"I didn't say I didn't know where he was," Castillo said. "I didn't tell you I didn't know. You jumped to that conclusion."

"Do you know where he is now?"

"Kennedy can't find him?"

"Or his family, Colonel Ex-Friend."

"I don't understand the question. Are you telling me that Howard can't find Alfredo and his family? Or asking if I know where Señora Munz and the girls are?"

"If you knew where the women are would you tell me? The truth?"

"I do and I would."

"Where are they?"

"Safe. In the safest place I can think of them to be right now."

"You're not going to tell me where?"

"No."

"And Alfredo?"

"He's in the second-safest place I could think of for him to be."

"I want to talk to Alfredo."

"Well, he has your number, Alek. If he wanted to talk to you, I think he would have called. That's his call. So far as Señora Munz is concerned, give me four hours or so to have her released from her cell and for the tranquilizers to wear off and I'll ask her if she wants to call you. But I have to say, I don't think she'd call unless Alfredo said it was okay, and we're right back to square one."

"You sonofabitch. When I find you, you will be sorry."

"Actually, you won't have to find me. I'll be in Argentina in twenty-four hours or less and I want to talk to you. And so do several friends of mine."

"Ha!"

"The reason I'm calling, Alek, is to try to make sure you'll still be alive when I get there."

"Meaning what?"

"I think it's entirely possible that certain people—certain of your countrymen, as a matter of fact—would like it a lot better if you had one of those Indian beauty marks you're always talking about in the center of *your* forehead."

There was a perceptible pause before Pevsner replied.

"My countrymen? What exactly is that supposed to mean?"

"One of the people who were there when Alfredo shot himself cleaning his pistol was a member of the Cuban Dirección General de Inteligencia. That being the case, isn't it reasonable that the KSB is involved?"

There was a perceptible pause before Pevser replied, in a tone of disgust, "The Cuban Dirección General de Inteligencia? Where did you get that? Why should I believe it?"

"You should believe it, friend Alek, because I'm telling you. And you should also believe that the people who tried to ask Eric Kocian questions in Budapest were ex-Stasi, because I'm telling you that, too."

When Pevsner didn't reply, Castillo went on. "Why don't you ask your friends? The Cuban was Major Alejandro Vincenzo. He was once Castro's bodyguard. I don't have the names of the ex-Stasi people yet, but I'm working on it."

There was another long pause before Pevsner asked, "What was this fellow's name?"

Castillo repeated it, then spelled it for him.

"Where did you get this, Charley?" Pevsner asked.

"Sorry."

"You don't trust me?"

"Why should I? A minute ago, you told me we're no longer pals." There was another long pause, then Castillo went on. "Alfredo knows. But since he doesn't trust you enough to even give you a call to say, 'Hi, Alek! How they hanging?' I guess you're just going to have to guess where we got it."

"Alfredo has no reason to distrust me and neither do you," Pevsner said, sharply.

"Well, truth to tell, I trust you. Up to a point. But Alfredo obviously isn't so sure. Otherwise, he would have been in touch."

"I want to talk to Alfredo, Charley."

"*Charley?* I thought I was Colonel Ex-Friend."

"I want to talk to Alfredo, Charley," Pevsner repeated.

"Well, maybe when I'm down there something can be worked out."

"I mean right now."

"Give my regards to the family, Alek. And watch your back. You don't have as many friends as you think you do."

[TWO]
Midland International Airport
Midland, Texas
1455 12 August 2005

"I've got it, Dick," Castillo said.

Miller raised both of his hands, fingers spread, to show that he was relinquishing control of the aircraft.

They had been cleared for a straight-in approach to runway 34R.

They could see the airfield clearly.

He really hated to turn it over me, Castillo thought. *At least, subconsciously. He knows it wouldn't be safe for him to land with only one good leg. Dick really loves to fly. I'm not like that, never have been. I do it because that's what I'm supposed to do and I try hard to do it well, because the alternative to doing it well is not pleasant to contemplate.*

I think I should be able to sit this thing down without any trouble. The approach is low and slow, and 34R is 9,501 feet long and 51 feet wide.

But Fernando was right. I really shouldn't be flying this by myself with only a few hours of on-the-job training.

The approach control operator's voice in his headset brought him to attention.

"Gulfstream Three-Seven-Nine," the controller said, "be advised that an Air Force F-15D has just begun his takeoff roll on 34R."

Before Castillo could open his mouth, Miller responded to the controller: "Thank you. We have him in sight."

Ahead of them, a dull-silver-painted Air Force fighter was moving with ever-increasing speed down the runway. It lifted off and almost immediately raised its nose so steeply that the entire aircraft seemed to be under them. The fuselage—just wide enough to hold the cockpit—was mounted on the leading edge of the swept-back wing between the intakes for the engines. There were two vertical stabilizers mounted on the rear of the wing.

The pilot kicked in the afterburners and the plane began to climb at an astonishing speed.

"Look at that sonofabitch go!" Miller said, softly, in awe.

"What's a *D?*" Castillo asked.

"The trainer," Miller replied. "Two seats."

"I wonder what it's doing at Midland-Odessa?" Castillo said, then added, "I think this is the time we put the wheels down."

Ten seconds later, Miller reported, "Gear down and locked."

As Castillo taxied the Gulfstream up to the parking ramp before the Avion business-aviation building, Miller pointed out the window.

"Why do I think that's why that F-15D was here?" he asked.

Colonel Jacob Torine, USAF, wearing a yellow polo shirt and khaki slacks, was walking from the building toward them.

"Go let him in, Dick," Castillo said. "I'll shut it down."

Ninety seconds later, Colonel Torine stuck his head in the cockpit.

"I don't recall giving you permission, Colonel, to play by yourself in our airplane."

"And I didn't know the Air Force let old men like you even ride in airplanes like that F-15D," Castillo said, offering Torine his hand.

"Only if they're full-bull colonels," Torine said. "You think that hard landing you just made did any serious damage?"

"That was a greaser, Jake, and you know it."

"Beginner's luck," Torine said. "Agnes called me and said you were headed out here and probably to Gaucholand. She didn't tell me why."

"We found out who sent the money to the AALs in Pennsylvania to buy their bomb shelter," Castillo said. "It turns out he went to Texas A&M with Fernando."

"Interesting," Torine said. "I guess that explains why Fernando—and the three Secret Service guys in the Avion building—are here. What happens next?"

"I spent most of the trip out here thinking about that," Castillo said. "I have an idea. It's probably not a very good idea, but it's all I could come up with."

"And are you going to share this not very good idea with me?"

Castillo finished unstrapping himself and stood up. He met Torine's eyes. "Yeah. And after—to use fighter jock terminology—I'm shot down in flames, you can tell me where I went wrong."

"I don't know," Torine replied. "Your flying skills leave something to be desired, but every once in a good while you have a reasonably good idea."

Castillo motioned that they go into the fuselage.

Miller was sitting on the edge of one of the left forward-facing leather seats near the door. Doherty was sitting across the aisle from him. Delchamps and Yung were sprawled on the couches. They made room for Torine and Castillo.

"It's getting a little toasty in here, Ace," Delchamps said.

"An air conditioner is on the way," Castillo said, then added: "You don't know Jake, do you?"

"No," Delchamps replied, "but I know he's all right. When Two-Gun Yung here saw him coming, he raised his eyes to heaven and said, 'Thank you, God!'"

Miller and Torine laughed.

"I'm about to get the others in here," Castillo said. "But before I do, Inspector Doherty, I want you to understand that what I'm going to propose is probably—hell, certainly—illegal. I don't expect you to go along with it. But I do expect you to keep your mouth shut. When I want your opinion, I'll ask. Clear?"

Doherty, tight-lipped, nodded.

Castillo nodded back, then went to the door.

A ground crew was installing both an auxiliary power unit and an air-conditioning hose.

Castillo raised his voice to be heard over the tug pulling the unit. "Make sure that's working," he ordered. "We're going to have a meeting in here that may take some time."

Then he looked at the Avion building and waved his arm. He couldn't see Lopez or the Secret Service agents, but a moment later his cousin pushed through the door, followed by three men in gray suits, and all started walking toward the Gulfstream.

When everyone was aboard, Castillo closed the stair door.

"I know it's a little crowded in here," he said, "but I'm pretty sure it's not bugged."

This earned him a dutiful laugh.

"I wish I could stand up all the way up in here," he said, earning a second polite laugh.

After a moment to collect his thoughts, he went on: "Okay, what follows is classified Top Secret Presidential, by authority of a Presidential Finding. You will never disclose anything you hear or learn in this cabin to anyone at any time without my personal permission. Everybody understand that?"

He looked at each man in turn until he got a nod of acknowledgment.

"Some of you are aware that American Muslims in the Aari-Teg mosque in Philadelphia—a group with known ties to terrorists—have purchased a farm near Philadelphia where they will seek shelter when a suitcase nuclear device, called a SADM, is detonated . . ."

". . . And," Castillo wound up his opening comments, "now that you know the manner in which I intend to deal with Mr. Kenyon would drive just about any civil libertarian up the wall, I'm going to give you ninety seconds to make up your mind whether you're in or out.

"Those who decide, for any reason, that they can't participate in this operation are free to go. No hard feelings. But with that caveat that they are not to reveal anything they have just heard or attempt to interfere in any manner with what I'm going to do.

"I hate to sound like a hard-ass, but we're really playing hardball here and anyone who runs off at the mouth will be prosecuted for unlawful disclosure of Top Secret Presidential material. That prosecution will go forward no matter what happens to me.

"And when I said you have ninety seconds to make up your mind, I meant it."

He raised his wrist and punched the SWEEP second button on his aviator's chronometer.

"The clock is running," he announced.

Ninety seconds passed in absolute silence. It felt like much longer.

"Time's up."

Castillo walked to the forward bulkhead and opened the door.

No one moved.

"Now's the time to leave," he said.

No one moved.

"You heard that, Inspector Doherty?" Castillo asked.

"I heard you clearly, Colonel," Inspector Doherty said.

"Okay, then let's get this circus on the road," Castillo ordered.

[THREE]
Avion Aviation Services Transient Aircraft Tarmac
Midland International Airport
Midland, Texas
1705 12 August 2005

"Here they come," Special Agent David W. Yung, Jr., said, gesturing out the window toward a black Mercedes-Benz S500 driving up to the Gulfstream.

"Wind it up, Jake," Castillo ordered as he walked to the switch that controlled the opening and closing of the stair door.

"Midland Ground Control," Torine said, "Gulfstream Three-Seven-Nine at Avion. Request taxi instructions for immediate departure."

Castillo stood in the passage between the cabin and the cockpit and watched as the Mercedes pulled up close to the aircraft.

The Mercedes stopped. The front passenger's door opened and Philip J.

Kenyon III—a large, stocky man wearing a white polo shirt, a linen jacket, khaki trousers, and tan western boots—got out as Fernando Lopez stepped out from behind the wheel.

Kenyon, perspiring in the Texas summer heat that baked the tarmac, looked admiringly at the Gulfstream. Then, smiling, he started walking toward the stair door as two men got out of the rear seat of the Mercedes.

Kenyon did not seem to notice as a black GMC Yukon XL approached the Mercedes and the aircraft and pulled to a stop, effectively screening the activity near the plane from any possible onlookers.

As Kenyon got close to the stair door, the man who had been riding in the left rear seat of the Mercedes took what looked very much like a black semiautomatic pistol from under his jacket, rested his elbows on the Mercedes hood, took aim, and fired.

There was no loud sound, as there would have been had the man fired a firearm, but instead there was a barely audible *pop,* as that of an air rifle firing. Kenyon made a sudden move with his hand toward his buttocks as if, for example, he had been stung by a bee. Then he fell to the ground and appeared to be suffering from convulsions.

The man who had fired what looked like a pistol tossed it to the man who had gotten out of the right rear seat of the Mercedes and then got behind the wheel.

The man who now had what looked like a pistol went to Kenyon and tugged at something apparently embedded in Kenyon's buttocks. Then Fernando Lopez bent over Kenyon and—with some effort, as the big man was still convulsing—picked him up over his shoulders in a fireman's carry and started to climb the stair door.

There was a whine as one of the G-III's engines began to turn.

Castillo came to the head of the stairs, got a firm grip on Lopez's polo shirt, and hauled him and Kenyon into the fuselage as the man who now had the pistol-like device pushed Lopez from the rear.

As soon as everyone was inside the Gulfstream, the Mercedes and then the Yukon drove off.

The stair door began to retract and the Gulfstream began to move as its other engine was started.

"Put him facedown on the couch," Castillo ordered, then had a second thought: "*after* you take his clothes off. Being in your birthday suit surrounded by half a dozen ugly men with guns usually tends to make interrogatees very cooperative."

"You're *bad,* Ace," Edgar Delchamps said.

"Oh, shit!" Yung said, then chuckled and added: "Literally. Charley, he's crapped his pants!"

"Is that what they call an unexpected development, Ace?" Delchamps asked.

"Put him in the aft crapper," Castillo ordered.

Philip J. Kenyon III returned to full consciousness to find himself sitting on the floor of a plastic-walled cubicle that smelled of feces. An Asian man—in shirtsleeves with an automatic pistol in a shoulder holster and holding what looked like another pistol in his hand—looked down at him.

"What the hell?" Kenyon said. "What happ—"

Yung put the index finger of his bandaged hand in front of his lips and said, "Sssshhh!"

"What the—"

Yung raised the pistol-like device and pointed it at Kenyon's chest.

"The next time you open your mouth, you'll get it again," he said almost conversationally. "What you are going to do now is take off your clothing and clean yourself. Put your filthy shorts in this and hand the rest of your clothes to me."

He handed Kenyon a gallon-sized plastic zipper bag.

Philip J. Kenyon III, naked, his handcuffed hands before him holding a small towel over his groin, came down the fuselage aisle.

"Lay the towel on the seat, Tubby," Castillo ordered. "And sit on it. I don't want you soiling my nice leather upholstery."

"God, he smells!" Delchamps said.

Kenyon did as he was ordered.

"Feeling a little disoriented, are you, Tubby?" Castillo asked.

"Jesus Christ!" Kenyon said.

"You have been Tazed," Castillo said. "Or is it *Tasered*? In any event, what that means is that we have caused fifty thousand volts and one hundred thirty–odd milliamperes of electricity to pass through your body. You may have noticed that this is somewhat incapacitating.

"If you show the slightest indication of being difficult, or if you refuse to answer completely and without hesitation any questions that I or any of these other gentlemen ask you, you will be Tasered again. You understand?"

Kenyon nodded.

"When you are asked a question, you will respond by saying, at the minimum, 'Yes, sir' or 'No, sir.' Understand?"

Castillo noticed more than a little anger in Kenyon's eyes. But his fear clearly was far worse.

Kenyon nodded and said, "Yes, sir."

"Do you have any questions, Tubby?"

It took Kenyon thirty seconds to respond, enough time for him to pick up a little bravado.

"I'd like to know what the hell is going on here, Castillo," he said, stiffly. "And where I am, where we're going. I was told I was just coming out to see your new airplane."

"That's three questions," Castillo said. "From now on, when I say you may ask a question, that means one question. But since you were unaware of the rule, I will answer your three questions.

"Where are we? We are at approximately twenty thousand feet in a climbing attitude on a course of approximately three hundred forty degrees. We are headed for Florence, Colorado. We'll get to what the hell is going on here in a bit. Another question?"

"Florence, Colorado? What's in Florence, Colorado?"

"That's two questions, Tubby. I'm not going to tell you again. The next time he asks two questions at once, Special Agent Yung, Taser him."

"Yes, sir," Yung said.

"But since your questions are somewhat related, I will answer them. Florence, Colorado, is home to the Federal ADMAX prison, ADMAX meaning 'Administrative Maximum Security Prison.' Are you familiar with the Florence ADMAX, Tubby?"

"No," Kenyon replied, somewhat impatiently.

Castillo held up his index finger.

"No, sir," Kenyon said, quickly.

"The Florence ADMAX confines very bad people—and I mean really confines: Prisoners are not allowed contact with any other prisoners and are released from their one-man cells for exercise for one hour per day. They are allowed one-hour family visits every other month, provided, of course, their behavior has earned them that privilege.

"And by *very bad* people, I mean, for example, Robert Hannsen, the FBI agent who was caught spying for Russians, and—of special interest to you—both Omar Abdel-Rahman and Ramzi Yousef, the Islamic terrorists who bombed the World Trade Center in 1993. They are all going to spend the rest of their lives without the possibility of parole in the Florence ADMAX. Personally, I think all traitors and terrorists, or those who help them, should be executed, but the court showed those scumbags leniency. Perhaps they will, too, in your case.

"I wouldn't bet on that, though, Tubby. You're an Aggie. You were an Army officer. You knew better than to do what you did. I really can't see a jury—especially a Texas jury—recommending clemency for you. Question?"

"I have no idea what you're talking about," Kenyon said, having mustered just a little more bravado.

"The next time he volunteers a mistruth, Yung, Taser him."

"Yes, sir."

"Tubby, you're not actually going to deny, are you, that you sent $1,950,000 from accounts you probably thought no one knew you have in the Caledonian Bank and Trust Limited in the Cayman Islands to the Aari-Teg mosque in Easton, a religious group with known connections to Muslim terrorists?"

Kenyon's skin paled. His eyes widened.

"Are you?" Castillo pursued.

Kenyon sat up abruptly and vomited on the floor.

"Jesus H. Christ!" Edgar Delchamps said, disgustedly.

"Go back to the bathroom, Tubby," Castillo ordered. "Get some paper towels from the cabinet and clean up your mess."

Kenyon raised his handcuffed wrists.

"I noticed," Castillo said, as the vile smell spread. "So what? Hurry up. You're stinking up my aircraft."

Kenyon struggled to his feet from the low couch and walked to the rear of the fuselage.

"Looks like something stung Tubby on the ass, doesn't it?" Delchamps asked.

The others laughed.

Kenyon came back down the aisle with paper towels in his hands, dropped to his knees, and started to mop up his vomitus. No one said a word.

Yung, a handkerchief over his mouth and nose, went aft and into the head, came out with an aerosol can of air freshener, then emptied it as he came forward in the cabin.

When Kenyon thought he had finished, he looked at Castillo, who shook his head.

"Clean, Tubby, means *clean*," Castillo said.

It took Kenyon three more trips to the toilet for paper towels and a lot of scrubbing before Castillo nodded and said, "Sit down."

"Okay, where were we before Tubby disgraced himself?" Castillo asked.

"I didn't know those people in Philadelphia were terrorists," Kenyon blurted.

"I didn't say you could speak," Castillo said. "The next time you speak without permission . . ."

He mimed shooting the Taser.

Kenyon recoiled as if Castillo's finger were the real thing.

"Are you going to talk to us, Tubby? Or wait for the people waiting for you at Florence?" Castillo asked.

Kenyon remained silent.

"Your choice," Castillo pursued. "What's it going to be?"

Kenyon looked off in the distance, thinking. Then he looked long and hard at Castillo.

"I'll tell you anything you want to know, but you've got to believe me, I didn't know the people in Philadelphia were terrorists."

"Well, we'll listen to what you have to say," Castillo said. "Can I have your recorder, Jack?"

Doherty handed Castillo a small tape recorder.

Castillo went to Kenyon.

"Put your knees together, Tubby," he said, and when Kenyon had complied, Castillo laid the tape recorder on Kenyon's legs. "If that falls to the floor . . ." he said and mimed shooting the Taser again.

Kenyon quickly put his hands out to hold the recorder in position on his knees.

"Now, before I switch that on," Castillo said, "there's something I want to tell you in case you're thinking that your civil rights have been violated and therefore it doesn't matter what you tell us, it would not be admissible in court.

"You're sitting in a sort of a court. We are your judges and the jury. Let me tell you who we are. You know Fernando, of course, and you remember me, and may even know I'm an Army officer. Special Agent Yung is with the FBI. That's Edgar Delchamps of the CIA. That's Inspector Doherty of the FBI. Those two are George Feller and Sam Oliver of the Secret Service. The airplane is being flown by Colonel Jake Torine of the Air Force. The copilot is an Army officer, Major Dick Miller.

"You're probably wondering why I'm telling you this. The reason is— presuming you ever get back to Midland or when your lawyer is finally admitted to Florence and you could tell him—that neither your lawyer nor anyone else is going to believe that you were kidnapped by your classmate at Texas A&M and hustled aboard a G-III piloted by an Air Force officer and an Army officer, where you were threatened and humiliated by another Army officer with whom you were once in the Boy Scouts, and then interrogated by a very senior FBI agent, two Secret Service agents, and a CIA officer.

"Think about it, Tubby. The only chance you have of not spending the rest of your life in a cell at Florence ADMAX is to come clean with us. Do we understand each other?"

"I told you I'd tell you anything you want to know. But you have to believe me when I tell you I had no idea that was a terrorist group or mosque or whatever in Philadelphia."

"So you keep saying," Castillo said. "He's all yours, Inspector."

Doherty moved from the forward-facing chairs in which he had been sitting and sat down on the couch facing Kenyon. He took out a small notebook and a ballpoint pen, then reached across the aisle and switched on the tape recorder.

"Interview of Philip J. Kenyon III," Doherty began, "begun at five-fifty p.m. central standard time, 12 August 2005, aboard an aircraft in the service of the United States somewhere above Texas en route to the Florence ADMAX, Florence, Colorado, by Inspector John J. Doherty, Office of the Director, Federal Bureau of Investigation, Washington, acting under Presidential Authority. Present are Colonel C. J. Castillo, team chief, Mr. Edgar Delchamps, Office of the Director, Central Intelligence Agency, Special Agents George Feller and Samuel Oliver of the Dallas Office, United States Secret Service, and FBI Agent David W. Yung, Jr.

"State your name and occupation, please."

Kenyon swallowed and then, as if he was having trouble finding his voice, finally announced that he was Philip J. Kenyon III, chairman of the board of the Kenyon Oil Refining and Brokerage Company of Midland, Texas.

"Mr. Kenyon," Doherty said. "It is my understanding that you are making this statement voluntarily, without either coercion of any kind or the promise of immunity from prosecution or the promise of special consideration because of your cooperation. Is that true?"

Kenyon's eyes glanced at Castillo, then looked at the floor. He exhaled audibly and said softly, "Yes."

"A little louder, please?"

"Yes, that's true."

"Let's start at the beginning," Doherty said. "How did you first become involved in illegal transactions connected with the United Nations oil-for-food program?"

Kenyon exhaled again.

"They came to me," he said, finally, "I didn't go looking for it. They came to me."

"Who came to you?"

"A man named Lionel Cassidy," Kenyon said. "He came to me and asked if I would be interested in some thirty-two-dollar-a-barrel oil."

"Do you have an address for Mr. Cassidy?"

"No. He always contacted me."

"But he was known to you?"

"I never saw him before the day he came up to me at the bar at the Petroleum Club. The one in Dallas. Not the one in Midland."

"But how did he know you?"

Kenyon shrugged helplessly.

"I don't know. But he seemed to know all about me and my business. And he said, 'I've heard you might be interested in fifty thousand barrels at thirty-two-point-five.' Hell, of course I was. That was ten dollars under market."

"You say he seemed to know all about your business?" Yung asked.

Doherty gave him a dirty look and held up his hand to silence any reply from Kenyon.

"State your name and occupation and then repeat the question," Doherty ordered.

"Special Agent David W. Yung, Jr., FBI, on assignment to the Office of Operational Analysis," Yung said. "Mr. Kenyon, you say the man, Lionel Cassidy, who came to you seemed to know all about you and your business?"

"Yes, he did."

"I'm going to show you a photograph, Mr. Kenyon, and ask if you can tell me who it is," Yung said.

Kenyon looked at the photograph.

"Yeah, that's Cassidy all right. The sonofabitch who sucked me into this mess."

"This is Inspector Doherty. Special Agent Yung showed Mr. Kenyon a five-by-seven-inch clear color photograph of a white male approximately forty-five years of age, approximately five feet eleven inches tall, and weighing approximately one hundred sixty-five pounds. Mr. Kenyon identified the man in the photograph as Lionel Cassidy. The man in the photograph is well known to me, Special Agent Yung, and Colonel Castillo by another name, which we know is his real name. That name is not germane to this interview."

"I'm telling you he told me his name was Cassidy, Lionel Cassidy," Kenyon said, plaintively. "Why should I lie to you about that?"

"No one is suggesting that you're lying, Mr. Kenyon," Doherty said. "So what did you do when Mr. Cassidy offered you fifty thousand barrels of oil at thirty-two dollars and fifty cents per barrel?"

"Well, I was suspicious at first, but . . ."

"And now we turn to the contribution you made to the Aari-Teg mosque," Doherty said, a half hour later. "Why did you do that?"

"Well, I certainly didn't want to," Kenyon said. "And I had no idea—I said this before but I'll say it again—I had no idea there was any kind of a terrorist connection whatever."

"So tell me what happened," Doherty said.

"It was in Cozumel," Kenyon said. "I took the family down there for a little sun and sea, you know. And Cassidy was there."

"Castillo," Castillo interjected. "Where in Cozumel was this, Mr. Kenyon?"

"You mean the hotel?"

Castillo nodded.

"Grand Cozumel Beach and Golf Resort," Kenyon said.

"Go on," Castillo said.

"Well, I saw Cassidy at the beach and at the bar. I know he saw me, but there was no sign of recognition so I left it there. That was fine with me."

"Did you happen to notice anyone with Cassidy?"

"Yeah. He was with a guy, about his age. Talked funny."

"A Russian accent, maybe?" Castillo asked.

"Could be, Charley."

"The interview will be suspended," Castillo said, "for a brief period while Castillo consults a file."

Doherty looked at him with mixed curiosity and annoyance.

Castillo went quickly to the net pouch behind the pilot's chair and retrieved his laptop. He turned it on, hurriedly searched through it, and then carried it to Kenyon and held it in front of him.

"Mr. Kenyon, I show you a computer image of a white male and ask you if this is the man you saw with Cassidy in Cozumel," Castillo said.

Kenyon shook his head. "No. Never saw that guy before."

Castillo held the computer up for Doherty to see it.

"Colonel Castillo has shown me the same computer image just now shown to Mr. Kenyon, that of a white male known to me from other photographs," Doherty said. "This man is not known to Mr. Kenyon. May I go on, Colonel?"

"Please," Castillo said.

"Hold it," Delchamps said, then went on: "Edgar Delchamps, CIA. The interview will be suspended until I can get a photograph to show Mr. Kenyon."

Delchamps dug into his briefcase, took a stack of five-by-seven photographs from it, hurriedly searched through them, selected two, and held them out in front of Kenyon.

"Look familiar?" he asked.

"That's the guy," Kenyon said.

"And this one?"

"Same guy."

"You're sure?"

"I'm sure. Cassidy was talking to him at the bar just before he all of a sudden recognized me, came over, and told me he needed a favor."

"Hold it a second," Doherty said. "Mr. Delchamps has shown two clear five-by-seven photographs, one color, one black-and-white, of a white male approximately forty-five years of age, approximately five feet eight, approximately one hundred ninety pounds, to Mr. Kenyon, who positively stated the photos were of the same man, and that this man was with Cassidy in the hotel. The man is apparently well known to Mr. Delchamps but not to me or Colonel Castillo."

Delchamps turned his back to Kenyon and mouthed the name Sunev.

Doherty looked momentarily confused until he made the connection. Then he smiled. Then he lost the smile.

"What do you think of your good pal now, Castillo?" he asked, almost triumphantly.

"I never said he was a good pal. I just told you I wasn't going to report on him to you," Castillo said. Then he looked at Delchamps and announced: "Bingo!"

"Bingo indeed, Ace," Delchamps said.

Doherty turned back to Kenyon.

"You say Cassidy came and spoke to you at the bar of the hotel?"

"That's right."

"Did the man in the photograph Mr. Delchamps just showed you come with him?"

"No, sir."

"You said he said he needed a favor? What kind of a favor?"

"He said he was having a little cash-flow problem and that he needed to make good on a promise he'd made to a mosque in Philadelphia."

"And he wanted you to wire them two million, more or less, from your accounts in the Caledonian Bank and Trust Limited?" Delchamps asked.

"He said it would just be temporary," Kenyon said. "I knew he was lying. But what could I do?"

"Indeed. What could you do? If you didn't oblige him, he'd tell the IRS what a bad boy you'd been? Right?"

Kenyon shrugged and nodded.

"And besides, you had forty-six million of oil-for-food money in the Caledonian Bank and Trust Limited. If the IRS got involved, you'd be liable to lose that, too. Right?"

"What do you want me to say?"

"This interview of Philip J. Kenyon III is terminated, subject to recall, at seven-fifteen p.m. central standard time, 12 August 2005. All parties present at the commencement were present throughout the interview," Doherty said, then reached over and reclaimed his tape recorder from Kenyon's knees.

"Go to the toilet, Tubby," Castillo ordered. "Close the door and sit on it."

"My clothes?"

Castillo pointed to the toilet.

Kenyon got awkwardly to his feet and walked naked down the aisle.

"What do we do with him?" Castillo asked when the toilet door had been closed.

"You're asking me, Colonel?" Doherty asked.

"Why not? You're in the criminal business, I'm in the terrorist business, and whatever else that miserable shit is I don't think he's a terrorist."

"He's a coconspirator," Doherty said. "And an accessory before and after the fact."

"If you say so. So what do you want to do with him?"

"Anybody interested in what I think?" Delchamps asked.

"Not that I know of," Castillo said, seriously.

"Fuck you, Ace," Delchamps said, good-naturedly. "Well, now that you've asked for my opinion: How about Jack coming up with some really good interrogators and finding out what else Tubby knows, with these two"—he nodded toward the Secret Service agents—"suitably briefed, sitting in on it to ask questions of their own."

"Transcripts of the interrogation, copies of everything, to OOA," Castillo said. "And they don't go near a United States Attorney until we decide they should."

"I don't like that last," Doherty said.

"I didn't think you would," Castillo said. "But what does that mean?"

"We do everything that Edgar said," Doherty said. "What's the risk of him getting on the phone and asking somebody for help?"

"I think we should tell him that his phones are going to be tapped and that he's going to have a Secret Service buddy with him day and night until we're through with him and that, if he's a bad boy, he goes straight to the Florence ADMAX and does not pass Go," Castillo said.

He looked at Doherty.

"Okay," Doherty said. "And now what? I mean, right now?"

"We go back to Midland, and tonight we have dinner with my grand-mother. And in the morning, we go to Buenos Aires."

Doherty nodded.

Castillo walked forward to the cockpit.

"How did it go?" Jake Torine asked.

"Better than I dared hope. But we have to go to Buenos Aires first thing in the morning."

"I figured as much. Not a problem."

"How long is it going to take us to get back to Midland?"

Torine pointed at the ground.

"As long as it takes this one-legged junior birdman to get us down from thirty thousand feet," Torine said. "We've been flying a nice big circle over North Texas." He looked at Miller. "Junior Birdman, commence a gentle descent at this time."

"Yes, sir, Colonel, sir. My pleasure, sir," Miller said and reached for the trim control.

XVII

[ONE]
Aeropuerto Internacional Jorge Newbery
Buenos Aires, Argentina
1840 13 August 2005

It was a clear winter night in Argentina and as they made their approach they could see the sea of lights that was Buenos Aires. They could even pick out the bright yellow snake of lights of the superhighway running from the city to Pilar.

They had left Double-Bar-C ranch at six, after an enormous breakfast Doña Alicia had insisted on getting up to prepare for them.

Dick Miller's disappointment at not being able to go with them—Castillo wanted him both to brief Ambassador Montvale on the "interview" of Philip J. Kenyon III and to be available at the Nebraska Avenue Complex to deal with anything that might come up—was more than a little tempered when Colonel Jake Torine got on the horn and arranged for another F-15D "training flight" to pick him up in Midland and carry him to Andrews Air Force Base outside Washington.

Castillo, concerned about Yung's wounded hand, had thought of trying to find some way to tactfully leave him behind in the States without killing his newfound enthusiasm for the OOA but in the end had decided that he would be needed in South America, both to lend his expertise to putting the pieces together at the safe house in the Mayerling Country Club and to deal with Chief Inspector Ordóñez in Uruguay if that became necessary.

Dinner at the Double-Bar-C had turned out to be very pleasant—even Jack Doherty seemed to be having a good time—although Fernando Lopez had nearly choked on his mouthful of wine when Doña Alicia had suddenly announced, "Oh, damn old age! Why didn't I think of this earlier? You remember Philip Kenyon, don't you, Carlos? You were in the Boy Scouts together. We ran into him at the Petroleum Club yesterday and, if I hadn't been asleep at the switch, we could have had him and his family here tonight. I know he would have loved to see you."

As everyone had loaded into one of the Secret Service Yukons, Doña Alicia had handed Castillo an aluminum-foil-wrapped package of barbecued beef ribs.

"For Ricardo, Carlos," she said, making reference to Special Agent Ricardo Solez of the Drug Enforcement Administration. "Give him my love, and tell him he can warm them on low in a microwave, but they would be better if he could find a grill of some kind."

"I'm sure we can find a grill for him, Abuela," Castillo had said.

On the way to the airport, they passed a Sam's Club. Probably because of the five-pound package of ribs in his lap, food was on Castillo's mind.

"Anyone got a Sam's card?" he asked.

Inspector Doherty confessed that he did.

"Go back to that Sam's Club, please," Castillo said. "It's already open."

A half hour later, Castillo came out of the Sam's Club carrying two ten-pound sacks of pancake flour and a gallon jug of Vermont maple syrup, followed by Colonel Torine, who carried plastic packages of shorts and T-shirts, a two-and-half-pound bag of Hershey's assorted miniature chocolate bars, and a lined denim jacket.

They had cleared customs and were off the ground at one minute past eight. Their first stop had been Quito, Ecuador, which was almost exactly midway between Midland and Buenos Aires. They landed there at 1335.

During a very pleasant grilled-chicken luncheon, and, looking very pleased with himself, Special Agent Yung of the FBI turned to Inspector Doherty of the FBI and said, "Before we get to Buenos Aires, Inspector, you'd better give me your pistol."

"Why in the world would I want to do that?"

"Because otherwise the Argentine customs will take it away from you."

"Doesn't that apply to you, too?"

"I have a diplomatic passport," Yung said, smugly. "You don't."

"Two-Gun Yung's got you, Jack," Edgar Delchamps said.

"And what about you?" Doherty challenged.

"I've already given him mine," Delchamps said. "If he's nice enough to sneak yours into Argentina, I guess we'll have to start calling him Three-Gun Yung."

They were back in the air at 1510. Five hours and thirty-two minutes later, Castillo—trying very hard to make a perfect landing—touched down much too long and somewhat hard on the runway at Jose Newbery.

"Because of the two-hour time difference," Jake Torine told Castillo, "I will put it in the log that we landed at 1845 local time. Because I am a really fine fellow who would never hurt a junior officer's delicate sensibilities, I will withhold critical comment on that absolutely awful landing."

They were met, as they had been the last time, by Paul Sieno and Ricardo Solez, who had the same unmarked Mercedes-Benz Traffik van and who again pretended to be Argentines sent to transfer American tourists to an unnamed estancia.

Once they were through the customs and immigration formalities and off the airfield, it was different. Sieno was obviously a great admirer of Edgar Delchamps and delighted to see him.

[TWO]
Nuestra Pequeña Casa
Mayerling Country Club
Pilar, Buenos Aires Province, Argentina
1925 13 August 2005

As soon as he walked into the house, Delchamps got an equally warm reception from Susanna Sieno and an only slightly less enthusiastic one from Alex Darby.

Castillo was not spared a welcome home. Max was so pleased to see him that he put his front paws on Castillo's chest, knocked him down, and then to show there were no hard feelings enthusiastically licked his face.

Castillo was still trying to regain his feet when Eric Kocian came down the stairs, paused halfway, and announced: "I see my jailer has arrived."

"Forgive me for trying to keep you alive, Uncle Billy," Castillo said.

"Any man who shamelessly steals the affection of another man's dog is beneath contempt," Kocian said.

"Eric Kocian, Jack Doherty," Castillo said. "I'm sure the two of you will become great buddies."

"This is the schoolteacher with the blackboards?" Kocian said. "I recognize the voice."

"And these two, Inspector Doherty," Castillo continued, "are in—or were in—your line of work. Sándor Tor, formerly inspector of the Budapest police, and Colonel Alfredo Munz, former chief of Argentina's SIDE, which is sort of the FBI and the CIA combined."

"I know what it is," Doherty said as they shook hands.

"Carlos, I don't suppose you saw my family?" Munz said.

"Oh, yes," Castillo said as he went into his briefcase for his laptop computer. "And I have to tell you they will probably want to stay in the States."

He turned on the computer, found what he was looking for, and held it out to Munz.

"There's a bunch of pictures," he said. "Just push this key with the arrow for the next one."

Munz looked at the first picture, then showed it to Tor. It was of his daughters, decked out in chef's whites, including enormous billowing hats, broiling steaks on a grill as Señora Munz and Doña Alicia, their arms around one another like sisters, smilingly watched.

"That's my abuela, Alfredo," Castillo said.

Munz went through the twenty-odd pictures one by one, then handed the computer back to Castillo.

"I think I want to kiss you, Carlos," Munz said, "and then kill Pevsner very slowly."

"Don't do either, please," Castillo said. "It would give Inspector Doherty the wrong idea and Pevsner may not be—probably isn't—the villain."

Yung took Doherty's and Delchamps's pistols from his briefcase and gave them back, which caused Darby to suggest that carrying them might become a problem but one that could probably be dealt with by making an effort to travel in an embassy car, the diplomatic plates of which would guarantee immunity from spot roadside searches by the Policía Federal.

Castillo—trailed by Max—took two bottles of beer from the refrigerator and went to the *quincho;* Susanna Sieno had told him Corporal Lester Bradley, USMC, was out there on radio duty.

As Castillo entered the *quincho,* Bradley leaped to his feet, popped to attention, and said, "Good evening, Colonel. I have the duty, sir."

"Stand at ease," Castillo replied, trying to stifle a strong urge to smile. It didn't work. He smiled, then handed Bradley a bottle of beer. "Have a beer, Les."

When he saw that Bradley was more than a little discomfited, Castillo went on: "You may wish to write this down, Corporal. When the senior officer in the area hands you a beer and orders you to consume same, you are then immunized against prosecution under the Uniform Code of Military Justice, 1948, for drinking on duty."

"Yes, sir. Thank you, sir."

"What do we hear from the States, Les?" Castillo asked.

"About an hour ago, sir, there was a message from Major Miller to be delivered to you on your arrival. I passed it to Sergeant Major Davidson, sir."

"Well, now that I'm here and Davidson isn't, do you think you could give it to me?"

"Yes, sir. Quote, the canary is really singing, end quote. Major Miller said you would understand what it meant, sir," Bradley said.

"Yeah, I do," Castillo said. "Les, go get—discreetly—Mrs. Sieno, Mr. Darby, Sergeant Major Davidson, Sergeant Kensington, and Mr. Solez. I'll watch the radio."

"Yes, sir," Bradley said and headed for the door. Then he stopped and carefully set his beer bottle on the floor. "I think it would be best if I left this here, sir. Sergeant Major Davidson might not understand that I have your permission to drink on duty."

"Good thinking, Corporal," Lieutenant Colonel Castillo said.

When they had all assembled, Castillo asked if anyone had seen anything that suggested an attack on the house or the waylaying of a car going to or from it.

"Nothing, Colonel," Davidson replied. "And we've looked. The only thing remotely suspicious was the driver of a laundry truck—a van, white, with 'ECO' on the panels—who seemed pretty interested in the house. The second time he drove by, Bradley and I followed him."

"The both of you?"

"Lester chased him around the country club on a bicycle and I went just outside the gate and followed him in a Beamer. Lester said all he did inside here was deliver and pick up laundry and dry cleaning. And then I followed him when he came out. He went to the ECO place—near the Sheraton Hotel—and unloaded dirty clothes. And that's it."

He looked around at the others and there was general agreement.

"Well, I've got a gut feeling that they're going to try to whack Billy Kocian," Castillo said. "And the chances of that happening will multiply exponentially after I go see a man I have to go see."

They looked at him for clarification but he offered none.

"I'll need a weapon, Susanna," he said. "Is that Micro Uzi I borrowed in Budapest still here?"

She nodded.

Davidson asked, "Where we going, Charley?"

"*We're* not going anywhere. I'm going to see a guy—Delchamps and I are."

Susanna Sieno said, "Colonel, you heard what Alex said. If you're going to take that Micro Uzi, you better take one of the embassy cars with CD plates. And somebody to drive it."

"I happen to be a very good Beamer driver, in case anyone cares," Sergeant Major Davidson said.

Castillo's eyebrow went up.

"For everyone's edification," he said, "it's *Bimmer*."

Davidson looked at him in a rare moment of confusion. "It's what?"

Castillo shrugged and said, "Not that it really matters, but a BMW motorcycle—the thingee with two wheels?—that's called a *Beamer,* or *Beemer* with two *es*. The four-wheel BMW is a *Bimmer.* Like I said, not that it matters, but that's that."

Davenport nodded and, without any conviction, replied, "Right. Tomato, tow-*maw*-toe. Got it."

Castillo smiled.

"Anyway," he went on, "I need you to hold the fort here, Jack."

Castillo turned to Bradley.

"Think you can handle a BMW, Lester?"

"Sir, I am certified to drive any wheeled or tracked vehicle including the M1A1 Abrams tank and the corresponding vehicle-retrieval vehicles as well," Corporal Bradley announced.

"The question, Corporal, was can you handle a Bimmer?"

"I am confident that I can handle a Bimmer *and* a Beamer, sir."

Castillo smiled.

"Okay, Lester. Go with Mrs. Sieno and—discreetly—get the Micro Uzi from her and put it in the backseat of the car she shows you. And there's two sacks of pancake flour and a gallon of maple syrup in the Traffik. Put that in the Bimmer, too. I'll be out in a minute with Mr. Delchamps."

"Aye, aye, sir," Corporal Bradley said. "And how many magazines, sir?"

"There's only two," Castillo replied.

"Extra boxed ammunition, sir?"

"I think the two magazines will be sufficient. Make sure they're charged."

"Aye, aye, sir."

When they were out of earshot, Davidson said, "You can't help laughing at him, but, when you do, you feel like you've just kicked a puppy."

"Yeah," Sergeant Kensington said.

"As for me, I have a very soft spot in my heart for people who have saved my ass," Castillo said.

"Curiosity overwhelms me, Charley," Alex Darby said. "What's with the pancake flour and the maple syrup?"

"Aleksandr Pevsner, Junior," Castillo said, "who is ten, has acquired a taste for pancakes and maple syrup from an American classmate. It's hard to get here in Argentina so I brought him some from the States."

"And just told Bradley to put it in the car," Darby said.

"Yes, I did."

"Can I put that together to mean you're on your way to see this pancake loving kid's daddy? He's here?"

"I hope, later today, that I'll be able to put it all together for you, Alex. But right now, Pevsner has my word that I won't tell anybody where he lives. That depends on Pevsner. Wish me luck."

"And taking Delchamps with you?" Darby asked.

"I want Edgar to tell him something I don't think he'd believe coming from me."

"I don't really know what's going on, Charley. Is that on purpose?"

"While I'm gone, Yung and Doherty can bring you—everybody—up to speed," Castillo said. "I don't think I'll be gone long."

He took what he now thought of as "the Argentine cellular" from his brief-case, pushed an autodial button, and put the phone to his ear.

"*¿Hola?*" a voice said.

"There you go in that heavily Russian-accented Spanish again," Castillo said, in Russian.

"What do you want, Castillo?"

"Call the gate, Alek, and tell them to pass me in. I'm almost there, and I'm bringing pancake flour, maple syrup—a gallon of it—and an old friend to see you," Castillo said and hung up.

Edgar Delchamps was already in the backseat of a dark blue BMW 720L with heavily darkened windows when Castillo came around the side of the house. Bradley was holding the door open for Castillo.

Castillo had forgotten that Max had been following him around until the dog decided the door was being held open for him and bounded into the backseat.

"Get this goddamned dog out of here," Delchamps said.

"You tell him, Edgar," Castillo said. "You have a forceful personality. Maybe he'll listen to you."

He gestured for Bradley to get behind the wheel, then opened the front passenger's door and got in.

"Go to that shopping center off Route 8," Castillo ordered Bradley. "The one with the Jumbo supermarket. I'll give you directions from there."

"Yes, sir."

Castillo put his arm on the back of the seat and turned to the passengers in the rear.

"Give that nice man a kiss, Max," he said, in German. "He's ugly and old and needs a little affection."

Purely by coincidence, of course, Max took that moment to take a closer look at his fellow passenger and, apparently liking what he saw, or perhaps what he smelled, leaned over and licked his face.

"I'll get you for that, Castillo," Delchamps said.

[THREE]
Buena Vista Country Club
Pilar, Buenos Aires Province, Argentina
2045 13 August 2005

"Turn in here, Lester, and put your window down," Castillo ordered. "They're determined to keep out the riffraff."

The BMW and its occupants were inspected at the guardhouse barrier not only by two well-armed members of the security staff but also by János, Pevsner's massive bodyguard, who stuck his head into the car and peered into the rear seat.

Surprise—and more than a little concern—registered on János's face when Max showed his teeth and growled menacingly.

Then surprise showed on Castillo's face when Delchamps greeted János in Hungarian: "János, my old friend, how in God's blessed name are you?"

János, his head already out of the car, nodded but didn't reply. He signaled to the security guards that they could raise the barrier pole and then waved the big BMW through.

Castillo turned to speak to Delchamps.

"Is there some reason you didn't want to tell me you knew János?" Castillo asked.

"I thought you had enough on your mind, Ace, and didn't want to confuse you further."

"What about Pevsner? You know him, too?"

Delchamps nodded.

"I meet a lot of people in my line of work," Delchamps said.

They were halfway to Pevsner's house when János caught up with them in Pevsner's black Mercedes-Benz S600, then passed them.

Aleksandr Pevsner, looking a member of the British landed gentry—he was wearing a Barbour rainproof jacket, corduroy pants, a checkered shirt, and a plaid woolen hat—stood waiting for them under the light over his front door. János stood behind him.

"Go open the door for me, Lester," Castillo said. "I want him to think you're an embassy driver."

"Yes, sir."

"Then get the pancake flour and maple syrup from the trunk."

"Yes, sir."

"*¡Hola, Alek!*" Castillo called in Spanish as he got out of the car. "Been out in the rain, have you?"

"I was at the stable," Pevsner said.

"Hey, Mr. Respin," Delchamps called cheerfully, in Russian. "I knew when I saw János that you'd probably be somewhere around. It's been a long time."

"Nine years," Pevsner replied after a long moment. "So long I forget what name you were using then."

"As a matter of fact, so do I," Delchamps replied. "Saffery, maybe?"

"I don't think that was it," Pevsner said. "What name are you using these days?"

"Delchamps. Edgar Delchamps. And what about you, Vasily?"

"Well, Mr. Delchamps, while I'm pleased to see you after all those years you're not the old friend I expected our mutual acquaintance to have with him."

"I'm sorry to have to tell you this, Alek," Castillo said, "but that old friend isn't at all sure you're really a friend of his."

"Why does ol' Charley here keep calling you Alek, Vasily?"

"Because that's my name!" Pevsner snapped.

"Where would you like me to put this stuff, sir?" Lester Bradley asked as he walked up with the maple syrup and pancake flour.

Pevsner looked at what Bradley was carrying.

"I just happened to be passing a Sam's Club," Castillo said. "And I remembered how much Sergei and Aleksandr like their pancakes and I figured, what the hell."

"Give it to János," Pevsner ordered.

"Hell, I'll carry it," Castillo said. "If János takes it, he'll have to take his hand off his pistol and I know how much he hates to do that." He took the flour and the gallon jug from Bradley. "That'll be all for now, Bradley," he said, then turned to Pevsner. "You are going to ask us in, aren't you, Alek?"

Pevsner exhaled audibly, shook his head, and turned around and held open the door to his house.

János followed everybody inside.

"I just remembered where it was the last time I saw you, Vasily—excuse me, Alek," Delchamps said.

"Where was that?" Pevsner said.

Delchamps turned to Castillo. "Remember when Laurent Kabila was trying to overthrow Mobutu Sese Seko in the Congo, Charley?"

"Yeah, vaguely. What was that? 1997? 1998?"

"Ninety-seven. Well, the good guys needed some guns, so I called Alek here—what does that stand for, 'Aleksandr'?"

"My name is Aleksandr Pevsner," Pevsner said, icily, "as if you don't already know that."

"Right," Delchamps said. "So I called *Aleksandr* here, and he not only had what the good guys needed, and at the right price, but was prepared to dropship it for me. He had just acquired his first Boeing 737. Before that he had—excuse me, *Aleksandr*, but it's the truth—a couple, maybe three, really ratty, worn-out Antonovs that I was always surprised could get off the ground."

Castillo looked at Pevsner and saw that while his face showed no emotion, Pevsner's ice-blue eyes could have burned holes in the old CIA agent.

Delchamps went on: "But he wanted cash on delivery, Aleksandr did. By then, I would have thought my credit was good. We'd done a lot of business before and he'd always gotten his money. And there wasn't all that much involved in this deal. A couple hundred Kalashnikov AK-47s, ammo, a few mortars, and I think there was even a dozen light .30 caliber Browning machine guns left over from Vietnam. Right, Aleksandr?"

"We all know you're not here to remember the past," Pevsner said. "Dare I hope this charade will soon come to an end?"

"Let me finish this for Charley, Aleksandr," Delchamps went on, casually. "So what that meant was I had to go to Kisangani—what used to be Stanleyville—with all this cash in my briefcase—"

"Goddamn it, Charley," Pevsner suddenly interrupted, having clearly lost his temper, "what have you done with Alfredo Munz and his family? I've had all of your sick humor that I can handle."

"The girls have been put to work in the prison kitchen," Castillo said. "They seem to have adjusted well to it. Would you like to see a picture?"

"If it would not be too much trouble," Pevsner said, icily. His face was still flushed, but he seemed to have his temper under control.

"Could we go into the living room? The pictures are in my computer. I need some place to put it down."

"You know the way," Pevsner said.

"The lady holding Señora Munz's shoulder is my grandmother," Castillo said, in Russian, when he'd opened the laptop and shown Pevsner how to cycle the images onscreen by using the arrow keys.

A minute later, Castillo said, "I should be very angry at you for even considering the possibility that I would be holding them hostage. But all I am is a little sorry for you."

Pevsner met his eyes for a long moment, then said, "I didn't know what to think."

"Your apology is accepted," Castillo said.

"And Alfredo?"

"He's near here."

"I want to talk to him."

"He won't come here."

"There are some questions I have to ask him, and I want to do that face-to-face and alone."

"Well, he won't come here—he doesn't trust you, Alek—and I won't take you to where he is. The telephone won't do?"

Pevsner shook his head. "I need to look in his eyes."

Castillo didn't reply.

"He trusts you, apparently," Pevsner said.

"I think so."

"Do you trust me?"

"Let me ask that first, Alek. Do you trust me?"

"With the caveat that we have different agendas, yes, I do."

"Same answer, Alek. And now let me tell you what my agenda is: I want Howard Kennedy. Let me rephrase that. I am going to have Howard Kennedy."

"Which means what?"

"That I am going to run him down and then take him to the United States. The deal we have is still on. But it no longer includes Howard Kennedy."

"Why do you want Howard Kennedy?"

"For one thing, I want to know what his relationship with Colonel Pyotr Sunev was . . . *is*."

"I don't think Howard even knows who Sunev is."

"Kennedy knows who Sunev is," Delchamps said. "We have a very reliable source who saw him and Sunev together in Cozumel. In that hotel you own there, the Grand Cozumel Beach and Golf Resort."

Pevsner considered that carefully but didn't challenge it. Instead, he asked, "And if I don't choose to give you Howard Kennedy?"

"You don't have any choice, Alek," Castillo said. "I'm going to have him."

"Before either of us says anything more that we both might later regret, let's get back to Alfredo Munz."

"You're not proposing a swap?" Castillo asked, incredulously.

"Now you owe me an apology," Pevsner said. "On several levels. I don't barter away my friends. Both Alfredo and Howard are friends of mine."

"You're going to have to convince Munz of that; he doesn't think so."

"That's one of the reasons I have to see him."

"That brings us back to step one. I told you he's not going to come here."

"I keep a suite in the Sheraton, the one here in Pilar, right off the highway, near the Jumbo," Pevsner said. He waited until Castillo nodded, indicating he knew what he was talking about, then went on: "I use it to accommodate business associates I'd rather not have in my home."

"And will I bring Alfredo to your suite in the Sheraton? Come on, Alek! He's my friend. I'm not going to set him up to be whacked!"

"Charley, I swear before God I mean Alfredo no harm!"

"I wish I could believe you," Castillo said. "But why should I?"

"Because it's the goddamned truth, that's why!"

"What exactly do you want to ask him, looking into his eyes with that penetrating stare of yours?"

"That's really none of your business."

"It is if you want me to even ask him to put his neck in the garrote," Castillo said.

"Then we have a problem, because I won't tell you. You'll have to be satisfied that I mean Alfredo no harm."

"And I am determined that he will come to no harm," Castillo said. "He has already taken a bullet for me and one is too many. So I suppose our conversation is over. I know you're going to tell Kennedy he is no longer part of the deal. I have no problem with that. I can find him. But anything else you do to protect him from me will nullify our whole deal. You understand?"

Pevsner nodded coldly.

"I really am sorry it came to this," Pevsner said. "I think, in the long run, we will both regret it."

"I need a minute alone with you, Ace," Delchamps said, "before you kiss Aleksandr good-bye for all time. You want to take a walk for a couple of minutes, Alek, or is there someplace we can go?"

"I will leave you alone," Pevsner said. "When you have finished, I'll be right outside that door."

"You really want to walk out of here, Ace?" Delchamps asked softly when the door had closed behind Pevsner.

"No. I thought he would cave and he didn't. But now I don't know what the hell to do next."

"He's one tough sonofabitch," Delchamps said. "Let me ask you this: would Munz tell you about their conversation if they had it?"

Castillo considered the question.

"You're wondering if he would tell you *all* about it?" Delchamps pursued.

"He'd tell me *all* about it," Castillo said ten seconds later.

"Well, then?" Delchamps asked.

"How do we explain our change of mind?"

"We tell him if there is to be a meeting, it has to happen right now, and the reason for that is that he wouldn't have time to set up a reception for Munz at the hotel."

"Those ex-Stasi bastards are pretty good," Castillo said.

"Thank you, sir. I will want to remember that, so I will write it down."

Castillo shrugged an apology.

"Want me to handle Pevsner?" Delchamps asked, and then, when Castillo nodded, went to the door and pulled it open. "Deal time, Alek," he said.

Pevsner came into the living room and looked between Castillo and Delchamps.

"Well?"

"Colonel Castillo will go this far," Delchamps said. "One, he will ask Colonel Munz if he is willing to meet with you. If Munz is willing, two, we will tell you where to meet us, and give you fifteen minutes to get there. Three, you will come alone, and if there is anything that even looks suspicious we'll take off."

"Agreed. But I would like János to drive me."

Delchamps considered that for ten seconds, then said, "Okay, János can drive."

Pevsner nodded.

"Let's go, Colonel," Delchamps said.

Pevsner followed them to the door.

As Castillo and Delchamps approached the car, Delchamps quietly but clearly said, "You get in the back with that damned dog, Ace."

"Charley!" Pevsner called from his doorway.

Castillo turned to look at him.

"Thank for the flour and tree syrup," Pevsner said and smiled.

"You're welcome," Castillo replied, then got in the backseat of the BMW. Max licked his face.

[FOUR]

"You open to suggestions as to how we do this, Ace?" Delchamps asked after they had left the Buena Vista Country Club.

Castillo nodded and Delchamps offered a plan.

"Great minds," Castillo intoned solemnly when he had finished, "walk the same paths."

"You're only saying that because you had absolutely no idea how this should be handled in a professional manner," Delchamps said.

Castillo took his cellular phone from his pocket and pushed an autodial button. He put the phone to his ear and, after a moment, said, "Castillo, Alex. We're on our way back there. ETA ten minutes or less. When we get there I want that Traffik ready to move with Solez at the wheel and Munz in the back. I want Davidson and Kensington, with Car-4s and handguns—and Whizbangs, if there are any—ready to get into this Bimmer the minute we get there. Delchamps and I will transfer to the Traffik. Delchamps will need something heavier than his pistol. If there's another Uzi there, fine. Put that and some Whizbangs in the Traffik. If not, a Car-4. There may be people watching who I don't want to see any of this happening. Do what you can about that. Got all that?"

"Yeah, I think so," Darby said. "What's going on?"

"And make sure that Solez has a cellular I can call from this one."

"Both that BMW and the Traffik have radios. Did you know that?"

"No, I didn't. But I don't know how to work them and there's not time to learn."

"You don't want some company on this excursion?"

"No. The rest of you go on high alert. It's possible that this excursion is being set up as a feint to cut down the people sitting on Kocian. The priority is still to keep him alive."

Alex Darby thought over what he had just been told.

"You're not going to tell me what this is all about?"

"Well, one thing is to determine whether Pevsner is one of the semigood guys or the unscrupulous murderous bastard most people think he is."

"How do you think that determination will come out?"

"We're about to find out," Castillo said, then added, "We just turned onto Route 8," and broke the connection.

When they reached the safe house in the Mayerling Country Club, Castillo saw that the Traffik was now parked on the driveway so that it blocked a view of the main door of the house from the street and that enough room had been left between it and the shallow steps up to the door for the BMW. From the street, no one would be able to see the BMW.

"Les, pull between the Traffik and the house," Castillo ordered, softly.

"Yes, sir."

The door of the house was closed and Castillo could see neither Davidson nor Kensington. But when Bradley had stopped the car and Castillo started to open the door so that he could go in the house and see where the hell they were, Delchamps touched his arm and pointed toward the Traffik.

The rear door was open and Davidson looked as if he was quickly prepared to jump into the BMW.

Castillo waved him off.

"There's more room in the van," Castillo said.

Delchamps opened his door and ran around the front of the BMW and quickly got into the Traffik.

"No, Max!" Castillo ordered sternly and reached around the dog and opened the rear door.

Max looked at both open doors, decided they had been opened for him, and that he had misunderstood Castillo—that what Castillo had really said was, "Go, Max!"

"Oh, shit!" Castillo said, then slid across the seat and followed Max into the van. He saw that Alfredo Munz was seated in the third row of seats.

"We're going to meet Aleksandr Pevsner," Castillo said. "They expect us—Delchamps, Munz, and me—to be in the Bimmer. So we'll be in this. If they hit the BMW—a real possibility—just get the hell out of the line of fire. If anybody is here, they're probably ex-Stasi and therefore good at what they do. And while I would really like to take them out, a firefight with bodies lying all over would cause all sorts of problems I don't need."

"Where do you think they're going to hit us, Colonel?" Jack Davidson asked. "On the road somewhere? The highway?"

"Let's find out," Castillo said and took out his cellular, punched an auto-dial button, and then the SPEAKERPHONE button.

"*¿Hola?*" Pevsner's voice loudly came over the phone.

"You really ought to work on getting rid of the Russian accent," Castillo said. "You really sound funny."

"Well?"

"Tell me more about this suite of yours in the Sheraton," Castillo said.

"Alfredo has agreed to meet me with me?"

"No. I'm thinking of taking a suite in the hotel myself," Castillo said, "and thought I'd have a look at yours first."

"It's on the fourth floor, 407," Pevsner said. "There is a stairway, then the elevators, and 407 is the second door on the right."

"And who would be in 407 if I decided to call?"

"No one. May I make a proposal?"

"Go ahead."

"You tell me when you can be there and I will get there ten minutes before you do. There is a basement garage . . ."

"People have been known to get whacked in basement garages."

"There is also an outside parking garage. But people going to and from it are far more visible than those using the basement garage. Your choice."

"That's your proposal?"

"I will have János check out the suite or he and I will check it out."

"And then?"

"There is a lobby bar. If you park outside, walk across the lobby and there it is. If you park in the basement, there is an elevator. Take it to the lobby floor and then turn right. János will go there and bring you to the suite."

"*You* will come to the bar," Castillo said.

"All right."

"I can leave here in five minutes and it will take me twenty minutes to get there," Castillo said.

"Thank you. And tell Alfredo I said thank you."

"Twenty-five minutes, Alek. Be there," Castillo said and broke the connection.

"It's only ten minutes from here to the Sheraton, Karl," Munz said, in German.

"I know," Castillo said. "As soon as Davidson and Kensington get in the Bimmer, we'll go to the basement parking garage in this. Jack, you wait five minutes and then you go there. Tell Bradley to drive slowly."

"I'm not sure Bradley knows where the hotel is, Carlos," Solez said, in Spanish.

"Good. In case somebody's watching, let them see him looking for it as if he doesn't know where it is," Castillo said. "When you get to the basement, park somewhere where we can get out in a hurry. Pevsner probably will be in a big black Mercedes, an S600, operative word *probably*."

"Got it," Davidson said. "I'm a little confused, Charley. Are you going to be in that bar or what?"

"Not on your life. If Pevsner shows up when he's supposed to, in the basement garage, the minute he gets out of it we'll get out and join him. And go right to his suite. That's when we'll really have to have our back covered."

"Got it," Davidson repeated.

"Okay you two. Get in the BMW."

Davidson and Kensington moved to the car. Kensington returned to hand Castillo a small package just as Solez was starting the engine.

Castillo opened it. It was the Micro Uzi and its magazines.

"Not to worry, Ace," Delchamps said. "Everybody gets a little forgetful once in a while, especially when they get older."

Castillo chose not to respond. Instead, he said, "Don't get us pinched for speeding, Ricardo, but the sooner we get there, the better."

Castillo had seen the Sheraton Pilar Hotel before and remembered where it was, but he had never paid much attention to it. Now he wanted to.

"Drive real slow when you get close to the hotel, Ricardo," he ordered.

Solez missed the turn off of Route 8. They now would have to go to the next exit, by the Jumbo shopping center, cross the highway on an overpass, and approach the hotel by a service road.

Castillo kept himself from snapping at Solez and was glad he had when he realized that it was probably a good thing Solez had missed the turn. Now they'd have a chance to look over the hotel and the approaches to it more slowly.

As they came close to the Sheraton Pilar Hotel and Convention Center, a fairly new brick-walled structure four or five stories high, Castillo saw, in a line of small businesses, a glass-fronted store with ECO LAUNDRY AND DRY CLEANING on the window. There were two white vans like the one Davidson had told him Bradley had chased around Mayerling on his bicycle.

Hell, better safe than sorry. Davidson did the right thing.

When they turned into the hotel's driveway two hundred yards later, Castillo saw that the outside parking lot Pevsner had mentioned was to the left of the main entrance to the atrium lobby. To the right was another entrance that looked deserted.

That one, Castillo decided after a moment, was obviously the convention entrance to the Hotel and Convention Center. There was a small sign with an arrow pointing to the underground garage.

There was a rather steep down ramp. When Solez took a time-stamped parking ticket from a machine at the bottom, a fragile-looking barrier pole rose, giving them access.

That barrier wouldn't keep anybody out of here, but it probably sets off an alarm if somebody goes through it.

The low-ceilinged garage was not crowded, maybe fifty, sixty vehicles. There was room for at least twice that many cars.

Strange. It's the dinner hour. It should be nearly full. Answer: This garage was designed to handle convention traffic. Obviously, there is no convention tonight.

"Circle it once, Ricardo," Castillo ordered. "And then park over there."

He pointed to a spot which would give them quick access to the exit ramp. Another frail-looking barrier pole guarded that.

Obviously, Ricardo is going to pay that ticket the machine gave him or have it stamped, or whatever, to get that barrier pole to rise.

If we have to leave here in a hurry, so long barrier pole and off goes the alarm!

There was, near one end of the garage, another white ECO laundry and dry-cleaning truck backed up to what was probably a service elevator. Large, white cloth-sided wheeled baskets were clustered around the truck.

This place is nice, but it's not the MGM Grand in Las Vegas with—what did

I hear?—some five thousand rooms? It probably makes more economic sense for the hotel to have the local laundry do the sheets and towels as necessary rather than running its own laundry.

When Solez had backed the Traffik into the spot Castillo had picked, he saw that it had been a lucky choice. It gave him a pretty good view of most of the garage. He could see the down ramp and the opening of a passageway with signs and an arrow pointing to the elevator.

"Now we wait," Delchamps said. "This is the part I love best about this job."

"You think he's going to come?" Castillo asked.

"Come, yeah," Delchamps said. "But with who and with what purpose in mind?"

"Ricardo, I don't suppose you have a leash?"

"A what?"

"For Max. I think he needs to take a leak. Walk him up the exit ramp and then, when you come back, walk him around the garage before you come back to the van. Let's see what he smells."

Solez didn't reply.

"I'd do it myself, Ricardo, but these people might know me, or at least have a description of me, and you're an unknown quantity."

"I'll have to use my belt," Solez said.

"Max, go with Ricardo," Castillo ordered.

Five minutes later, Solez and Max got back in the van.

"When we walked past the laundry truck," Solez reported, "Max got real antsy. It was all I could do to hold him."

"Maybe he doesn't like the smell of dirty laundry," Delchamps said.

"And maybe he smelled guns. He doesn't like that smell. When the Bimmer gets here, I'll give Davidson a heads-up."

"Why don't you do that now, Ace?" Delchamps said.

"Because Jack Davidson is a devout believer in the preemptive strike."

"Well, tell him to behave. You're a colonel. You can do that."

Castillo pushed an autodial button on his cellular.

"We're about two minutes out, Colonel," Davidson answered. "Lester missed the turn."

"There's an ECO laundry truck down here. It may be picking up laundry, but Max smelled something he didn't like. Just be aware it's there. No, repeat, no preemptive strike, Jack. Understood?"

"Yes, sir."

Two minutes later, the big dark blue BMW rolled off the down ramp.

Delchamps and Castillo readied their weapons. There had not been another Uzi available, so Darby had provided a Car-4.

Two of them, Castillo thought, as Solez picked one from the floor of the van and worked the action.

The BMW circled the parking garage and backed into a space across from them.

Nothing happened.

Castillo called Bradley on his cellular and hit the SPEAKERPHONE button.

"Lester," he said, quietly, "go into the hotel, take a look around the corner and see if you see Pevsner or his gorilla or anybody interesting at the bar."

"Yes, sir. Sir, if I may say so, that will also serve to suggest to the person in the cashier's office that I am notifying someone their car is available and alleviate any suspicion of my sitting here."

"Very good, Lester. You're absolutely right."

Castillo hit the cellular's END button, then chuckled and shook his head.

"Don't be smug, Ace," Delchamps said. "The kid is right."

"He usually is," Castillo said. "I didn't even think about the cashier."

Nothing happened in the next four minutes, which seemed like much longer.

"Lester's back," Solez said, pointing as Bradley walked back toward the BMW.

"And there's Pevsner and János the Gorilla," Delchamps said, nodding toward the Mercedes-Benz on the down ramp. "So he did show."

"Give them a chance to park the car and get out of it and then we'll join them," Castillo said. " 'Hey there, Alek! Small world, isn't it?' "

The big black Mercedes circled the garage. The heavily darkened windows of the BMW would permit him to see only Lester, which he would expect to do. But the same was true of the Mercedes. When it rolled past the Traffik, Castillo could see only János, not into the rear seat. János showed no interest in the Traffik.

Well, what does that mean? Maybe János is the stalking horse and Pevsner's not in the backseat?

János backed the Mercedes into a spot close to the parking garage cashier's office and the tunnel to the hotel. He got out, walked around to the right side of the car, and opened the rear door. Aleksandr Pevsner got out and started walking toward the tunnel, with János three steps behind.

There was suddenly the sound of submachine gunfire, very loud in the low-ceilinged garage. Castillo saw where it was coming from. There were orange flashes from three, maybe four muzzles beside the white ECO laundry truck.

"Oh, shit!" Castillo said as he jumped out of the Traffik.

He saw that Pevsner was down, sprawled flat on the floor, and that János was sitting down, pistol in hand, bleeding from at least one wound in his side and looking dazed.

Castillo emptied the Micro Uzi in two bursts directed in the general direction of the ECO truck and reached for a second magazine.

Then came fire from the other side of the ECO laundry van, the peculiar, familiar sound of a Car-4 being fired in short controlled bursts of three to five rounds each.

Who the hell is that? Davidson or Kensington? One of them must've got out of the car to cover the laundry truck.

Then immediately—before Alfredo Munz, carrying a pistol, could get out of the Traffik—there came the sound of more short bursts from a Car-4 in the vicinity of the BMW and then the familiar report of a 1911A1 Colt .45 semi-automatic. The .45 was being fired steadily but somewhat slowly, suggesting aimed fire from a skilled pistoleer.

"All down!" a voice that only after a moment Castillo recognized as that of Sergeant Major Jack Davidson called out. "Hold fire!"

As Castillo, his ears ringing madly, ran to see what had happened to Pevsner, he saw Davidson running—carefully—toward the ECO van with his Car-4 at the ready.

János, still sitting holding his pistol, looked at Castillo without comprehension—then fell over. Castillo dropped to his knees and felt for a pulse. There was one.

Where the hell is Pevsner?

Max answered the question. The big dog was growling deep in his throat and trying unsuccessfully to get under the Mercedes.

"Come out of there with your hands up!" a very sincere—if somewhat youthful—voice ordered from behind Castillo.

Castillo turned to see Corporal Lester Bradley holding a 1911A1 Colt .45 in both hands aimed at the underside of the Mercedes.

Well, now I know who that skilled, timed-firing pistoleer was.

"Okay, Max," Castillo ordered, in Hungarian. "Sit!"

Max, visibly reluctant to do so, sat but did not stop growling. His lips were drawn tight against a very impressive row of massive teeth.

"Come out, Alek," Castillo called.

When Max saw movement, he stood up.

"Goddamn it, Max, *sit!*"

Aleksandr Pevsner appeared.

"Hands up, goddamn it!" Bradley ordered.

Pevsner got to his knees, then to his feet, and raised both hands in the air.

There is fear on ol' Alek's face. But what's scaring him? Max? Or the boy with the .45 pointed at his forehead? So far, he's managed not to get shot . . .

"He's okay, Bradley," Castillo said, then saw the dog moving again. *"Max! Sit!"*

"Can you control that animal so I can go to János?" Pevsner asked.

"Go ahead," Castillo said, pointing a finger at Max and mouthing *Stay!*

"Is he dead?" Pevsner asked as he dropped to his knees beside János.

"Not as of thirty seconds ago," Castillo said.

Davidson came running up.

"All down, Colonel. Five of them," Davidson reported. "I knew goddamned well that goddamned ECO laundry truck was dirty. Now what?"

"Now you help me get this guy in the Traffik," Castillo ordered, "and then you get Kensington in the BMW and get the hell out of here. I'll take János to the safe house."

He looked across the garage, intending to signal Solez to get in the truck, and saw that the truck was already in motion but headed for the ECO van, not them.

"Help me get János in the car," Pevsner pleaded. "I've got to get him to a hospital. *Please.*"

"Take a look at it, Alek, the Mercedes isn't going anywhere," Castillo said. "And we can't take him to a hospital with bullet wounds."

The Mercedes was apparently only lightly armored. While the cabin was mostly intact, the headlights and hood were bullet-riddled, two tires—clearly not run-flat models—were punctured and flattened, there was the smell of gasoline, and the front windshield and left side windows were crazed.

"What's going on down there?" Davidson asked, nodding in the direction of the ECO van.

"I think Delchamps is taking pictures and collecting DNA samples and whatever else he can find that looks useful."

"Look what I found," Davidson said, holding up a blued-steel garrote.

Castillo shook his head slowly at the sight.

Alfredo Munz came up.

"I need to talk to you, Alfredo," Pevsner said.

"Doesn't this speak for itself?" Munz said. "You've been betrayed, Alek, and you know by who."

"I had my suspicions," Pevsner said. "I didn't want to accept them."

"Would you have believed me if I told you?" Munz asked, almost sadly.

"Bradley, go tell Solez I need the Traffik right here right now," Castillo ordered.

At that moment, the Traffik started toward them.

"What we are going to do is load János in the Traffik and get him and us the hell out of here," Castillo said. "I'm surprised the cops aren't here already."

"The garage is soundproofed," Munz said, professionally. "And the poor girl in the cashier's office is going to cower in her little cubicle and do nothing whatever until she is sure we are gone and the police are here. And she will tell them that she saw nothing for fear we'll be back. We have another minute, perhaps, until someone finishes dinner and comes for their car."

Sergeant Robert Kensington came running up and dropped to his knees beside János.

"What's he doing?" Pevsner asked.

"Whatever he can to keep János alive," Munz said. "He's a medical soldier."

"János needs a hospital, a surgical doctor," Pevsner pursued.

"Who will ask questions," Munz said. "Kensington can treat him, Alek. He took a bullet from my shoulder."

"Your call, Alek," Castillo said, evenly. "You can stay here and wring your hands over János and deal with the cops or you can help us get him in the van. In thirty seconds, we're out of here."

Pevsner met Castillo's eyes for a moment, then moved to János, putting him in an erect position so that it would be easier to pick him up.

Thirty seconds later, János was stretched across the rear row of seats. Sergeant Kensington was applying a pressure dressing to János's side.

"Watch your feet," Delchamps called. "I grabbed two Madsens and they're still loaded."

Ten seconds after Castillo and Max got in the front seat and closed the door, Solez drove the Traffik to the exit ramp and took out the fragile barrier as he went up. Castillo heard an alarm bell start ringing.

Fifteen seconds later, they were in the one-hundred-thirty-kilometer-per-hour lane of Route 8 headed south.

Castillo turned to look out the rear window. The BMW was following them.

He looked at Delchamps.

"What else did you find at the laundry van?"

"I'll tell you later," Delchamps said. "If, as seems highly likely, we shortly find ourselves chatting with half a dozen of Pilar's finest law enforcement officers, it will be better if you don't know."

[FIVE]
Nuestra Pequeña Casa
Mayerling Country Club
Pilar, Buenos Aires Province, Argentina
2155 13 August 2005

Castillo, Pevsner, and Delchamps leaned against the wall of one of the downstairs bedrooms, watching as U.S. Army Special Forces medic Sergeant Robert Kensington finished bandaging János. The bed had been raised three feet off the floor on concrete blocks to make a perfectly serviceable operating table.

"Bullets are like booze," Kensington observed, professionally. "The larger the body—unless, of course, the bullets hit something important—the less effect they have. And we have here a very large body."

János, feeling the effects of three of Kensington's happy pills, agreed cheerfully. "Oh, yes," he said. "I am much larger than most men."

"Perhaps not as smart but indeed larger," Pevsner said, fondly.

Castillo and Delchamps chuckled.

Pevsner's cellular buzzed. He looked at its screen to see who was calling and then pointed to the French doors leading from the room to the backyard.

"May I?" he asked.

"Sure," Castillo said.

Pevsner left the room and walked to the center of the backyard with the cellular to his ear. The floodlights which normally illuminated the backyard had been turned off but there was still enough light from the house and the *quincho* so that he could be seen clearly. Castillo and Delchamps left the bedroom and stood on the tile-paved patio.

When Pevsner took the cellular from his ear, they walked to Pevsner.

"Anna and the children are pleased that I am impulsively taking them to our place in San Carlos de Bariloche for a little skiing," Pevsner said. "Anna is concerned that they will lose a few days in school, but under the circumstances . . ."

"I understand," Castillo said.

"They are en route to the Jorge Newbery airfield by car," Pevsner went on.

"I have arranged for a Lear to fly us to Bariloche. Now, if I can further impose on your hospitality, there is something else I'd like you to do for me."

"Which is?" Castillo asked.

"I don't want Anna and the children to see János in his present condition, of course, and János—despite his present very good humor—is really not in shape to fly halfway across Argentina. There is a place not very far from here that is both safe and where he can recuperate in peace. What I would like to do is have the Ranger pick us up . . ."

"Not here," Castillo interrupted. "Sorry."

"Of course not," Pevsner said. "Please let me continue, my friend."

"Okay. Continue."

"There are eight polo fields at the Argentine Polo Association on the north of Pilar. Do you know where I mean?"

Castillo shook his head.

"Right off Route 8," Pevsner said. "I would like to rendezvous with the Ranger there on the most remote of the polo fields, take János to the place I mentioned, then have the Ranger take me to Jorge Newbery to meet my family. Would you carry us to the Polo Association?"

"When?"

"Right now, if that would be possible."

Castillo exhaled audibly.

Then he said: "Set it up, please, Edgar. Lead car, Traffik, trail car. Shooters in everything. I'll ride with Alek and János in the Traffik."

Delchamps nodded and walked toward the house.

"Thank you, friend Charley," Pevsner said. "I am greatly in your debt."

Castillo shrugged.

"Can I give him some money?" Aleksandr Pevsner asked.

Castillo looked at him and saw that he was looking toward the house where Kensington was leaning against the wall outside his "operating room," puffing on a cigar.

"You mean Sergeant Kensington?" Castillo asked.

"Your doctor. I am very grateful for what he did for János. I would like to show my appreciation."

"Giving Sergeant Kensington money—how do I put this?—would be like slipping your priest a few bucks for granting you absolution. Except that if you tried, Kensington would probably rearrange your face so you would remember not to make that particular faux pas again."

"Please tell him I consider myself in his debt and if there is anything I can ever do for him . . ."

"Tell him yourself, Alek," Castillo said. "He'll be in the Traffik with us and János." He paused, chuckled, and went on: "But as a shooter, he has pretty much given up his medical career."

"Similarly, my friend Charley, I am deeply in your debt. And not solely for saving my life."

"You can pay that debt by staying out of my way while I'm running down our great mutual friend Howard Kennedy. I want him, Alek."

"If I knew where he was, I'd tell you."

"I want him without a beauty hole in his forehead, you understand that?"

"With great difficulty," Pevsner said, nodding slowly. "There is only one suitable punishment for a man who enters your life dishonestly and gains your confidence and affection . . ."

"Got a little egg on your face, do you, Alek?"

"I beg your pardon?"

"Aleksandr Pevsner, that great judge of character, trusted the wrong guy and mistrusted the good guy. Good *guys,* plural."

"I'm not familiar with the expression."

"You know what I mean, Alek."

"I am where I am today because I . . ."

"By where you are today, I guess you mean hiding under your Mercedes from your good friends in the FSB while they tried to whack you?"

Pevsner's face tightened.

"If that was the case . . ."

"No 'if' about it, Alek. Edgar Delchamps knew one of the guys in the laundry truck. Lieutenant Colonel Yevgeny Komogorov, deputy to Colonel Pyotr Sunev, director of the FSB's Service for the Protection of the Constitutional System and the Fight Against Terrorism."

Pevsner glared at him.

"That's a mouthful, isn't it?" Castillo asked. " 'Service for the Protection of the Constitutional System and the Fight Against Terrorism'? And I guess they define 'terrorist' as anyone who might be able to identify former Lieutenant Colonel Putin of the KGB as just one more maggot in the oil-for-food scam."

"If Putin was involved in that, I don't know about it."

"Sunev and the late Colonel Komogorov must have thought you did. Otherwise, why did they try to whack you?"

Pevsner didn't reply.

"And to whack you, Sunev didn't send some second-rate Cuban—he sent Komogorov."

Pevsner stared icily at Castillo for a long moment.

"Howard Kennedy is not stupid," Pevsner said, finally. "He knew that you were sooner or later going to suspect him of ties—or find ties, as you did in fact—with the FSB, and that if you did, you would probably tell me. I think it's entirely possible that he told Sunev that we were becoming too close, exchanging information . . ."

"And after all, Kennedy had been really working for Sunev all along, hadn't he? Getting paid—better paid, obviously—to provide just that sort of information?"

"I paid Howard well, but nothing like nearly sixteen million dollars," Pevsner said. "The first suspicion I had of Howard—and, of course, I felt guilty about having it—was when he was so upset about those bank drafts you took from Lorimer's safe. He acted almost as if you had stolen the money from him."

"I really hope I did," Castillo said.

"I think he had a deal with the Cuban. The Cuban would shut Lorimer's mouth, take the bank drafts, give them to Howard, and they would split the proceeds. And you ruined this plan for him, Charley."

"I want him, Alek."

"What will happen to him after you interrogate him?"

"I've given that some thought. The first one I had was to have him sent to a really terrible prison in Colorado where the prisoners spend twenty-three hours a day in solitary cells with no contact with other prisoners. But then an FBI friend of mine said that all we could convict him of is stealing FBI investigation reports. That would put him away for five-to-ten, maybe. He'd be out in a couple of years."

"So you'll just . . ."

"I would like to, but we don't operate that way. What I think I'll try to arrange for him is to be sent to a medium-security prison where he would be in what they call 'the general population.' Unpleasant things happen to former FBI agents in the general population. There're even rumors that they get raped. Regularly."

There was a shrill whistle and they looked toward the house where Edgar Delchamps was standing in the door to the living room. He was signaling that the convoy was ready.

"One last time, Alek," Castillo said. "Don't get in my way."

"If I find him before you do, I'll tell you where he is. Somehow the notion of Howard being regularly traded as a sexual commodity seems a fitting consequence for his actions."

They started walking toward the house.

[SIX]
Nuestra Pequeña Casa
Mayerling Country Club
Pilar, Buenos Aires Province, Argentina
1005 14 August 2005

What Castillo thought of as the Philosophers, as opposed to the Shooters, were gathered in the *quincho,* the main room of which looked very much like a schoolroom complete to blackboards, a teacher, and nine overage eighth-graders raising their hands for permission to offer the teacher their deep thoughts.

The teacher was FBI Inspector Jack Doherty. The Philosophers were Special Agent Yung, Eric Kocian, Alex Darby, Colonel Alfredo Munz, and Mr. and Mrs. Paul Sieno. Also present was Colonel Jake Torine, who was included not so much for his knowledge of the situation but for his brains. Castillo and Delchamps sat in, although both regarded themselves far more as Shooters than Philosophers. And there was the class pet, who lay asleep with his head on Castillo's shoe and from time to time made strange, pleased sounds, which Castillo thought might be because he was dreaming of a shapely Bouvier des Flandres of the opposite gender.

Corporal Lester Bradley, technically a Shooter, was manning the radio with instructions to tell anyone who called from Washington that Colonel Castillo was momentarily unavailable but would get back to them as soon as possible.

There were still a lot of pieces to fit together and Castillo didn't want to interrupt that process.

The Shooters—Sergeant Major Davidson, Sergeant Kensington, Sándor Tor, and Ricardo Solez—were on perimeter guard duty, no less efficient because they were seated comfortably in strategically placed upholstered chairs.

Edgar Delchamps not only approved the perimeter guard but suggested that Castillo recruit more Shooters for it. He said that he trusted Aleksandr Pevsner about half as far as he could throw him vis-à-vis not revealing the location of the safe house and pointing out that Pevsner was now aware that just about everybody with knowledge was gathered in one place, which made it one hell of a rich target for somebody who wanted mouths shut permanently.

Delchamps also volunteered the hope that Castillo was not holding his breath waiting for Pevsner to tell him anything about the location of Howard Kennedy. The race was on—and in high goddamned gear—if Castillo wanted to get the sonofabitch before Pevsner did.

Castillo was of two minds.

Professionally, he agreed with Delchamps—and just about everybody else—that Pevsner couldn't be trusted and wouldn't hesitate to have them all killed to protect himself—or, perhaps more important, to reduce or remove a threat to his family.

Personally, Castillo trusted Pevsner, at least to a degree.

But, obviously, he had to go with his professional judgment.

When his cellular went off, he had just about decided that school was going to be in session for a week—or longer—and to tell Bradley to get Dick Miller at the Nebraska Avenue Complex on the horn and to tell Miller to call either General Bruce J. McNab or Vic D'Allessando at Bragg and tell them to get a ten-man A-Team on the next flight out of Miami—put 'em in civvies and tell 'em to make like they're soccer players—and, yeah, we have weapons here.

"*¿Hola?*" Castillo said to his phone.

"You, on the other hand, sound like a *Porteno*," his caller said.

"So how's the skiing?"

"Very nice, thank you. Our friend is in 1808 at the Conrad in Punta del Este."

"You're sure?" Castillo said, but after a moment he realized he was talking to a broken connection.

Delchamps looked at him with a question in his eyes.

"O ye of little faith!" Castillo said, and turned to Yung. "What's the Conrad in Punta del Este?"

"Fancy hotel. Fanciest. With a casino."

"Is there an airport there?"

"Yeah."

"Jake, could we take the Gulfstream from here to wherever Punta del Este is in Uruguay . . ."

"On the Atlantic, about a hundred kilometers from Montevideo," Yung furnished.

". . . and then to Quito without refueling?"

"No problem. What do you plan to do about immigration?"

"Worry about that when we get to the States," Castillo said.

He stuck out his tongue at Delchamps, made a loud humming sound, then said: "You can interpret that—it's the best I can do—as sounding 'Boots and Saddles.' Kennedy is in room 1808 of the Conrad and we're going to go get him."

"Who we?" Delchamps asked.

"You, Munz, me, and Two-Gun," Castillo said. "Alex, can you get on a secure line and tell the CIA guy in Montevideo . . . what's his name?"

"Robert Howell," Darby replied. "Bob Howell."

". . . to meet us with a car—better yet, a Yukon, or at least a van, something big—at the Punta del Este airport? And that we're leaving right now?"

"Do I tell him why?"

"No, just that it's important."

Max happily trotted after Castillo as he headed for the *quincho* door.

"Not this time, pal," Castillo said.

He could hear Max barking and whining even after he'd entered the big house and headed for the driveway.

[SEVEN]
Punta del Este Airport
Punta del Este, República Oriental del Uruguay
1335 14 August 2005

Robert Howell, the "cultural attaché" of the U.S. embassy, was waiting for them at the small but well-equipped airport with a blue Yukon displaying diplomatic tags.

Castillo introduced Delchamps to him—Howell knew who Delchamps was but had never met him—then explained what he intended to do: Grab Howard Kennedy, bring him back to the airport, and fly him to the States, with only a fuel stop in Quito.

"I'd like to have you in on this, but if it would make things awkward for you just give us the truck and come back in two hours. If we're lucky, I'll leave the key under the mat."

Howell said, "I'm in. We may need my diplomatic carnet. If there's trouble, all they can do is expel me as persona non grata."

"Thank you."

"How do we get him out of the hotel and into the truck?"

"Let's make sure he's there first, then worry about that," Delchamps said. "Our noble leader is placing a lot of faith where I'm not at all sure it belongs."

Castillo ignored him.

"How come this place looks so deserted?" Castillo asked. "There's nothing here but a couple of light twins and some Cessna 172s."

"It's winter," Howell said. "Punta del Este is just about closed in the winter. Wait till we get downtown."

Ten minutes later, Castillo could see a long line of high-rise apartment buildings overlooking a wide, nice-looking beach. When they came close to the
apartments, however, he was surprised at what he found: The blinds were drawn
behind almost all of the apartment windows, there were few cars on the street
(and even fewer in the parking lots under the high-rise buildings), and only a
very few people on the streets.

This is almost surreal, Castillo thought.

Five minutes after that, the Conrad came into view, an imposing structure
Castillo guessed was twenty stories high.

"They keep this open for the gamblers," Howell said. "But I'd say it's not
even one-quarter full."

He turned off the road and drove up the driveway.

"Well, there's activity here," Delchamps said. "Why does that make me
feel uneasy?"

The parking area in front of the main door of the resort was crowded with
vehicles. With the exception of two stretch limousines and a Volkswagen bug,
they were all police vehicles of one description or another.

"Why do I think going back to the airport would be a good idea?"
Delchamps asked.

"Oh, let's go play the slots!" Castillo said. "I feel lucky."

"Well, I suppose it's remotely possible that somebody tried to knock off the
casino and the entire Uruguayan police force has responded," Delchamps said
and opened his door.

They walked up a wide flight of marble stairs and were halfway across the
lobby when a voice called, "Alfredo!"

Everybody stopped. A man was quickly walking toward them.

"I am not as happy to see you, my friend," Chief Inspector José Ordóñez
said as he wrapped Munz in a bear hug and kissed his cheek, "as I would be if
you were alone."

He looked at the others. "And my friend David Yung and Mr. Howell,
of the culture department of the American embassy. How nice to see you
both again."

He turned to Castillo and Delchamps and put his hand out to Delchamps.

"Colonel Castillo, I'm Chief Inspector José Ordóñez of the Federal Police
and I've been looking forward to meeting you."

"My name is Smith," Delchamps said. *"No hable Español."*

Ordóñez smiled at him and shook his hand.

"I'm Castillo," Castillo said.

"Jose Ordóñez, Colonel," Ordóñez replied, offering his hand. "If I may say so, you're very young to have done all the things people say you have done."

"I try to live clean," Castillo said. "What did we do, walk in on a police convention?"

"I suppose it does look like a convention, doesn't it?" Ordóñez said. "But, sadly, no. We are all here on duty. One of your countrymen has run into some difficulty."

"You don't say?"

"I was just about to call your embassy and tell them, but since Mr. Howell and Mr. Yung are here I can dispense with that. I'll show them the problem. If it's all right with them, the rest of you may come along."

He gestured toward the elevator bank and they all got in.

The door from the corridor opened into the living room of suite 1808. One wall was mostly glass and offered a view of the Punta del Este downtown sky-line and the Atlantic Ocean.

There were two men sitting in high-backed upholstered chairs. One of them, who looked as if he had slipped down in the chair, had his mouth open. The back of the chair behind him was matted with blood and brain tissue.

The other man was Howard Kennedy.

He had been strapped into his chair with duct tape. There was something in his mouth, either a red ball or a ball of another color, now covered with blood. His eyes were wide-open.

His body seemed strangely limp and, after a moment, when he saw Kennedy's hands, Castillo understood.

"It would seem," Ordóñez said, matter-of-factly, "that Mr. Kennedy was beaten to death, not with a baseball bat or something like that but with a piece of angle iron. They started with his toes, then his feet, then his shins, and then changed to his fingers, hands, wrists, etcetera. You can tell by the blood pattern. It must have taken some time for them to finish. We believe this man to be Howard Kennedy."

"That's Howard Kennedy," Castillo said. "*Was* Howard Kennedy."

"We're not sure who the other man is," Ordóñez said.

"That's Lieutenant Colonel Viktor Zhdankov," Delchamps furnished, "of the FSB's Service for the Protection of the Constitutional System and the Fight Against Terrorism."

"That's not what his passport says, Señor *Smith,*" Ordóñez said. "It says he's a Czech businessman."

"Then I'm obviously wrong," Delchamps said.

"I really hope so," Ordóñez said. "What we have here is bad enough, an American businessman and a Czech businessman murdered during a robbery. Even if that robbery, as has been suggested, was part of a drug deal that went wrong, that would pose far fewer problems for me—and, indeed, for Uruguay—if I had to start investigating the murders of a senior KSB officer and a man known to have close ties to an international outlaw by the name of Aleksandr Pevsner. You understand?"

"I think so," Delchamps said.

"I am really sorry to have subjected you to this. I fully understand that it ruined your holiday and has caused you to feel that you have to leave Uruguay immediately and not to return until this terrible memory has had time to fade."

"The man has a point, Ace," Delchamps said.

"Chief Inspector Ordóñez," Castillo said, offering his hand, "may I ask you one question before I leave?"

"Certainly."

"I read something in the papers about some bodies—six, I recall—being found on an estancia somewhere here in Uruguay. What was that all about?"

"Our investigation concluded that was another drug deal that went wrong. Such an ugly business yet so common. The estancia owner apparently led a dual life as a drug dealer. I frankly doubt if we'll ever be able to make an arrest. The case is closed, for all practical purposes."

"Thank you very much."

"Not at all," he said, pumping Castillo's hand. "Perhaps we'll meet again under happier circumstances. Any friends of my dear friend Alfredo, so to speak, are friends of mine."

"I'd like that," Castillo said.

[EIGHT]
The Restaurant Kansas
Avenida Libertador
San Isidro
Buenos Aires Province, Argentina
2025 14 August 2005

Castillo waved the waiter over and called for the check.

"Why don't you let me take care of that?" Ambassador Juan Manuel Silvio said. "I can charge it to my representation allowance."

"Your pockets, sir, are nowhere near as deep as those of the Lorimer Charitable Trust, but thank you anyway. I'm really grateful to you for coming all the way out here to meet with us."

"This is Argentina. The only other place you could have eaten before eight would have been one of the places in the port. Or a McDonald's."

"Not to ask a rude question, but isn't this the place where they snatched Mrs. Masterson?" Delchamps asked.

"In the parking lot," Silvio said, pointing. "So in a way, this is ending where it began, I suppose."

"But it's not ended," Castillo said. "Masterson's murderers, for all I know, are still running around free."

"But some of their peers, and their superiors, are no longer with us, are they?" Silvio said. "And some have left us under circumstances, God forgive me, that I consider entirely appropriate."

Castillo's cellular buzzed.

"Now what?" he muttered.

He took the phone from his pants pocket.

"¿Hola?" he said into it.

"I'm sorry I had to go back on my word, friend Charley."

"You sonofabitch. You told me I could have him."

"He knew too much about me to have him talking to you, Charley."

"Fuck you, Alek!"

"And besides, I decided that five years of regular rape was not sufficient punishment for his betrayal of me."

"Fuck you, again."

There was a moment's silence before Pevsner went on, coolly: "Let me tell you what I've done."

"And why should I believe anything you tell me?"

"Hear what I have to say and then you can decide. I spoke with Sunev and told him that I have deposited with certain people envelopes that will be sent to the CIA in the event I even suspect he has sent anyone near me, my family, or anyone involved in the recent events we have shared."

"And what's in the envelopes?"

"Oh, I'm sure you can make a good guess, friend Charley."

"Goddamn you, Alek!"

"We'll be in touch," Pevsner said, and then the change in the background noise told Castillo that Pevsner had broken the connection.

Castillo punched his autodial button for Pevsner but got a recorded message saying that the telephone number called was no longer in service.

He put the phone back in his pocket.

"I hope you appreciate, Mr. Ambassador," Delchamps said, "that you are in the presence of the only man in the world who can tell Aleksandr Pevsner to fuck himself twice in thirty seconds and probably—operative word 'probably'—live until the morning."

Silvio laughed.

"Are we going to see more of you, Mr. Delchamps? If you're coming back to work with the others, maybe I could be of some assistance. Someplace to live, etcetera?"

"That's very kind of you, sir. But I'm going to spend the next couple of months trolling through the basement at Langley. Two-Gun here will be coming back, though."

"I'm going to take these two with me when I go face Ambassador Montvale," Castillo said. "In numbers, there is strength. But if you want to be useful, see what you can do about keeping Two-Gun here out of trouble upon his return."

"It will be my pleasure."

"Now we have to get a cab."

"Nonsense," Ambassador Silvio said. "I'll take you out to your jet."

[NINE]
Office of the Chief
Office of Organizational Analysis
Department of Homeland Security
Nebraska Avenue Complex
Washington, D.C.
1625 15 August 2005

"Well," Castillo said, "that went pretty well, I think . . ."

"Ace, you didn't say a word that the President was going to come with Montvale. That was just too much to spring on an old man."

". . . Except, of course, that he turned a deaf ear to my suggestion that it was time for me to return to being a simple soldier."

"You might as well forget that, Ace. He likes things the way they are."

"Yeah," Yung agreed. "The part I liked was when he said, 'It's a shame to leave all that oil-for-food money in that fellow Kenyon's account. It's not right that he be allowed to keep it. Isn't there some way we could add it to OOA operating funds?' "

Castillo said, "I hope you weren't just running off at the mouth when you chirped, 'Not a problem, Mr. President.' "

"No problem at all," Yung said. "You want me to go to Dallas and do that before I go back down there?"

"Absolutely. And you can catch a direct flight—American, I think—from Dallas to Buenos Aires. But before you go to Dallas there's something really important I want you to do."

"What?"

"Get on the Net and Google for a breeder of Bouvier des Flandres in the Dallas area."

"For a what?" Delchamps asked.

"Max is a Bouvier des Flandres. I thought you knew."

"And?" Yung asked.

"Buy the best breedable bitch available—cost is not a factor—make sure her papers are in order and take her with you to Pilar."

"I actually think you're serious," Delchamps said.

"I don't know how things are done in the spook world," Castillo said, "but in the Army when someone saves your ass, the least you can do for him is get him laid." He looked at Yung and added: "Tell Billy Kocian I want pick of the litter."

"I'll be goddamned," Delchamps said, smiling. "Two-Gun, tell Kocian I get second choice."

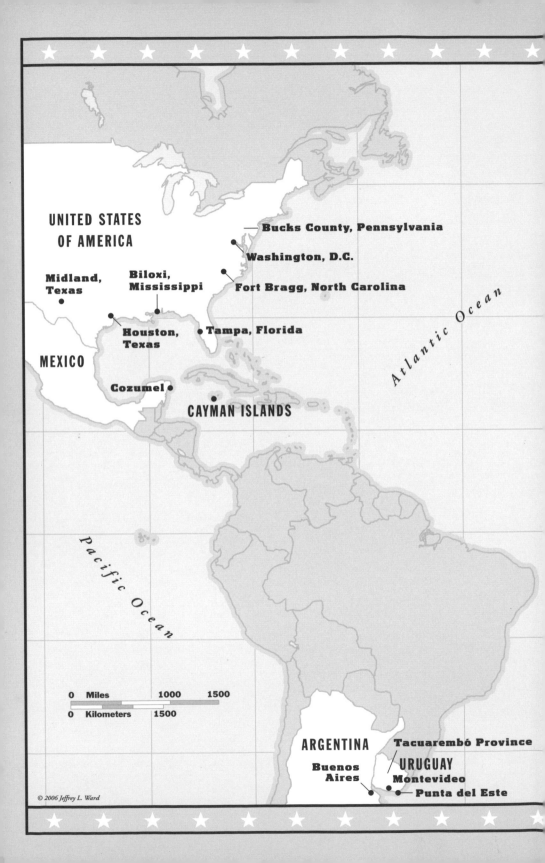

UNITED STATES
OF AMERICA

Bucks County, Pennsylvania

Washington, D.C.

Midland,
Texas

Biloxi,
Mississippi

Fort Bragg, North Carolina

Houston,
Texas

Tampa, Florida

MEXICO

Cozumel

CAYMAN ISLANDS

Atlantic Ocean

Pacific Ocean

| 0 | Miles | 1000 | 1500 |
| 0 | Kilometers | 1500 | |

ARGENTINA

Tacuarembó Province

URUGUAY

Buenos
Aires

Montevideo

Punta del Este

© 2006 Jeffrey L. Ward